THE
CHASE

CANDICE FOX

THE
CHASE

A TOM DOHERTY ASSOCIATES·BOOK

NEW YORK

THE CHASE

Copyright © 2021 by Candice Fox

A Forge Book
Published by Tom Doherty Associates
120 Broadway
New York, NY 10271

www.tor-forge.com

Forge® is a registered trademark of Macmillan Publishing Group, LLC.

The Library of Congress Cataloging-in-Publication Data is available upon request.

ISBN 978-1-250-79883-1 (hardcover)
ISBN 978-1-250-79885-5 (ebook)

Our books may be purchased in bulk for promotional, educational, or business use. Please contact your local bookseller or the Macmillan Corporate and Premium Sales Department at 1-800-221-7945, extension 5442, or by email at MacmillanSpecialMarkets@macmillan.com.

Previously published by Bantam Australia in trade paperback in March 2021

First U.S. Edition: 2022

Printed in the United States of America

0 9 8 7 6 5 4 3 2 1

For all the aspiring authors. Never give up.

THE
CHASE

CHAPTER 1

From where she sat at the back of the bus, the driver's death was a confusing spectacle to Emily Jackson.

She had a good view down the length of the vehicle from her position, leaning against a window smeared with the fingerprints of happy children. Her seat was elevated over the rear wheel axle, so as she rode she could see youngsters jumping and crashing about the interior, playing games and teasing each other across the aisle, occasionally throwing a ball or smacking a catcher's mitt into a rival's head. Half of the other parents on the bus were ignoring their children's activity, gazing out the windows at the Nevada desert, some with AirPods in their ears and wistful looks on their faces. Others were making valiant attempts to dampen the chaos and noise: confiscating water bottles, phones, and toys being used as weapons, or dragging wandering toddlers back to their seats. Forty minutes of featureless sand and scrub beyond the garish structures and swirling colors of Vegas was a lot for kids to endure. When the bus bumped over a loose rock on the narrow road to the prison, Emily saw all the other passengers bump with it, the bus and its riders synchronized parts of a unified machine.

She didn't have to nudge her son, Tyler, as they approached the point at which Pronghorn Correctional would come into view. Tyler had been coming to the annual pre-Christmas softball game at the facility since he was a kindergartener, and had only missed one year, when his father strained his back fixing the garage door and couldn't play second pitcher against the minimum security inmates as he usually did. Tyler's familiarity with the journey seemed to give him a sixth sense, and she watched as he flipped his paperback closed, shifting upward in his seat. No landmark out there in the vastness told mother and son they were approaching the last gentle curve in the road. Hard, cracked land reached plainly toward the distant mountain range. Then the pair watched through the bus's huge windshield as the collection of wide, low concrete buildings rose seemingly out of the sand.

"Who's your money on this time?" Emily asked the teen. A five-year-old in the seat in front of them started pointing and squealing at the sight of the prison up ahead. Tyler considered his mother's question, watching the boy in front of him with quiet distaste, as if he hadn't once been just the same, so excited to see Daddy at work.

"I'm betting inmates," Tyler decided, giving his mother a wry smile. "Dad says they've been practicing during yard time for months."

"Traitor." Emily smirked.

"How 'bout you?"

"Officers," she said. "If you're going for the cons, I've got to go for the correctional officers or your father won't sp—"

A thump cut off Emily's words.

It was a heavy, sonic pulse, not unlike a firework exploding; a sound Emily both heard and felt in the center of her chest. Her brain offered up a handful of ordinary explanations for the noise even as her eyes took in the visual information that accompanied it. *A blown tire,* she thought. Or a rock crunching under the bus's wheels. Some kind of spontaneous combustion in the vehicle's old, rickety engine, a piston or cylinder giving out due to the rugged terrain and the desert's usually blinding heat.

But none of those explanations aligned with what Emily saw.

The driver slumped sideways out of his seat, caught and prevented from falling into the stairwell only by the seatbelt over his shoulder. A fine pink mist seemed to shimmer in the air before dissipating as quickly as it had appeared. Emily grabbed the seat in front of her and held on as the bus swung off the road and slowed to a stop in the shrubbery.

Her eyes wandered over the scene at the front of the bus. The passengers in the first two rows were examining their hands or touching their faces as though they were damp. Hundreds of tiny cubes of glass lay over the driver, the dash, and the aisle, the side window having neatly collapsed and sprayed everywhere, exactly as it was designed to do. Emily recognized Sarah Gravelle up there, rising unsteadily from her seat and walking to the driver's side. Emily could see, even from her distant position, that half of the driver's head was gone. Sarah looked at the driver, and everybody watched her do it, as if they were waiting for her to confirm what they already knew.

Sarah stumbled back to her seat and sat down. Emily's tongue stuck to the roof of her mouth, her body suddenly covered in a thin film of sweat.

Sarah Gravelle started screaming.

And then everyone was screaming.

Grace Slanter put down her pen and pressed the speakerphone button to answer the phone that was ringing on her wide desk. Few calls came to the warden's office without first being channeled through her assistant's office in the room down the hall, so she was expecting someone familiar on the line: her husband, Joe, or the director of Nevada corrections, Sally Wakefield, a woman she spoke to almost daily. When the line connected, there was a second click she'd never heard before, and her own voice gave a ringing echo, as if it was being played back somewhere. *Robocaller,* she thought. But that was impossible. This was an unlisted line, not the kind that could appear on a database in some sweaty underground scam-mill.

"Hello, Grace Slanter."

"Pay attention," a voice commanded.

Grace felt a chill enter her spine, high, between her shoulders, as though she'd been touched by an icy finger. She looked down at the phone on the desk as though it held a malevolent presence, something she could see glowing evilly between the seams in the plastic.

"Excuse me?"

"There's a bus stopped in the desert half a mile from the prison walls," the voice said. It was a male voice. Soft, clipped. Confident. "If you go to the window behind you and look out, you'll see it sitting on the road."

Grace stood. She did not go to the window. The warden had been trained to respond to calls like this one, and though she'd never before had to put that training into action, the first thing she remembered was not to start following the directions of the caller until she had a grasp on the situation. She went to the door of her office instead, the furthest point from the window, and looked down the hall. There was not a soul to be seen.

"Are you looking at it?" the voice asked.

Grace stepped up onto the couch against the wall, to the left of the desk. She could see the bus out there, a distant white brick in the expanse of land beyond the concrete walls and razor wire of the prison. It had one wheel off the road, the vehicle tilted slightly, leaning, as though drunk.

"Okay," Grace said. "I see it. What's your name? I want to know who I'm talking to."

"On that bus are twelve women, eight men, and fourteen children," the voice said, ignoring her questions. "They're the families of guards inside the prison. Your employees. Your people."

"Jesus Christ," Grace said. The annual softball game. Inmates versus officers. The families always came to watch. It was an event designed to appease the prison staff stuck minding vicious criminals during the holiday season while their families gathered at home. The peacemaking gesture usually lifted the dismay after the rosters for Christmas Eve, Christmas Day, and New Year's were drawn up, so that officers went into those shifts with at least half a smile on their faces. After the game there was lunch and drinks for the unlucky families in the conference building outside the prison walls.

Grace staggered down from the couch and gripped the edge of the desk. Her training was forgotten, her senses blurred. She went to her chair and fell into it, relieved by the familiar feeling of her own warmth on the seat, something comforting in the chilling seconds that passed.

"The driver of the bus is dead," the voice on the phone said.

Grace tried to remember the location of the panic button on her desk, the one that would send an alarm to her colleagues inside the building, and an automatic "assistance needed" call to the nearest law enforcement agencies. All she had to do was remember where that single button was. But her mind was spinning, reeling, and for a long moment it was a struggle just to breathe.

"Are you listening, Grace?"

"I'm . . . I'm listening," she said. Grace drew in a deep breath and then let it out. She found the button under the desk by her knee and pushed it. A red light came on above the door to her office, but no sound issued. In seconds, her assistant, Derek, was there, huffing from the run up the hall, two guards right behind him. It only took one look from Grace to send them sprinting away again.

"What do you want?" she asked.

"I want you to let them out."

Grace had known the words were coming long before they were spoken. She drew in another deep breath. Across the two decades she had been in senior management at Pronghorn, she'd run over this scenario in her mind a hundred times. She knew what to do now. She was regaining control. There was a procedure for this. She grabbed her pen again and started jotting down notes about the voice and the time of the call, keeping an eye on the window as she sat twisted sideways in her chair.

"Which inmates are we talking about?" Grace asked. "Who do you want me to release?"

"All of them," the voice said.

CHAPTER 2

Celine Osbourne smelled smoke. On Pronghorn's death row, tobacco was a controlled substance. Level two contraband. Any inmate found in possession of it was punished with the same severity as if they were caught with cocaine, heroin, marijuana, or ice. She stopped in her tracks halfway down the row, outside serial killer Lionel Forber's cell, and sniffed. Forber was curled in his bed, asleep beneath a blanket, the seventy-seven-year-old predator as motionless as a snake under a rock. Celine followed the smell forward, past a serial rapist crocheting a blanket, a child killer reading a romance novel, and a cop killer watching television. The smell was not tobacco burning, she realized; it was wood. And when she found the source, a dark, worn smile crept over her lips.

"How come I knew it was you?" she asked.

John Kradle was bent over the small steel shelf bolted to the wall of his cell that acted as a desk. On the floor, at his feet, a battered silver toaster sat plugged into an extension cord that ran out of his cell and down the length of the row, where it turned a corner and disappeared from view. Kradle had a piece of smooth pine stretched across the desk, and he was using a wire that ran out of the top of the toaster as a makeshift soldering iron to burn ornate lettering into the wood's surface.

"How come you what?" Kradle grunted without looking up.

"How come I knew it was you?" Celine repeated. "I smelled smoke and I knew somebody around here was up to no good, and I immediately thought of you."

Celine examined the device in his hand. Kradle had fashioned a handle and a burning prong out of what looked like scraps of wire and wood and duct tape, elastic bands, and folded cardboard. He was just rounding the second "e" in the word "*feet*," having already spelled out "*Please wipe your*" in skillful, near-perfect cursive.

"I don't know, but if I had to guess I'd say it's because you're obsessed with me," Kradle said, flicking the iron upward gently to finish the letter with a fine line and a coil of gray smoke. "I'm never far from your mind. You smell smoke, you think: John Kradle. You smell breakfast, you think: John Kradle. You smell your boyfriend's cologne, you think: John Kradle."

The toaster at his feet popped and the piece of wire in his iron, which was glowing red, dimmed to black. He shunted the toaster handle down with the toe of his shoe and it began glowing again.

"Is that the kind of delusion that gets you through the cold, lonely nights here?" Celine asked. "Most guys turn to Catholicism, Kradle. It's more realistic."

"Uh-huh."

"Who the hell rigged this up for you?"

Kradle looked at her through the bars for the first time, a weary glance that said prisoners didn't snitch, even against guards, and that was a fact she should have learned within five minutes of arriving on her first day on the job. She sighed.

"Give me that." She beckoned for the wood.

"Nope." Kradle swiped back his gray-streaked blond hair and started on the "t" in "*feet*."

"What? 'Nope'? You don't say 'nope' to me, inmate. Ever. Give me that piece of wood. That's an order."

"I've been given an order already today. It was to create this sign here." He nodded to the wood in front of him. "I've got a few conflicting orders during my time in prison. You people holding the keys have a lot of trouble deciding what you want, sometimes. So, when that happens, I go with the one I like best. And right now, that's working on this sign."

Celine bit her tongue, turned away, and smiled. The smile held no warmth and was an automatic reaction, something burned into her from years as a correctional officer. *Never let them see your anger. If you get angry, smile. Make them think you're in control. That you expected this. That it's all going to plan and you couldn't possibly be happier about it.* But even her false smile was too good for John Kradle.

"I bet you think standing there smiling like an idiot is going to make me think you're not angry," Kradle said, behind her, as though he could read her thoughts. She turned back. He was still bent over his work, his big hands moving skillfully. "You're wrong. I know you're mad."

"You do, huh?"

"Yeah," he said. "Because you know who rigged this setup for me. You know what the sign is for. It's for the warden's office. It's a peace offering from a certain lieutenant who took the warden's directive in last month's staff notices about trudging sand into her office to heart."

The toaster popped. Kradle shoved the handle down again.

"And you're also mad because you know it's a good sign. It's pretty," he continued, gently blowing the tendrils of smoke away from his face as they rose from the wood. "It makes you mad to know that even though the warden is going to figure out an inmate made this sign, she's going to hang it outside her office anyway because it's so attractive. And for years to come, maybe decades, every time the warden calls you up for something—a promotion or a sector review or a captains' meeting or whatever the hell—you're going to have to look at this sign and know that your most loathed inmate made it and you couldn't do a damn thing to stop him."

"That's a fairly advanced narrative for a brain the size of a peanut to handle," Celine said. "You better give me that piece of wood and go lie down."

"Make me."

Celine grabbed the cord running from the toaster out through the bars and yanked it free of the extension cord. She stormed toward the control room.

She slowed as she neared Burke David Schmitz's cell. The neo-Nazi terrorist, an unrepentant mass shooter, had the highest number of confirmed victims of all the men on Celine's row. There was a kind of thickness in the air around him. A coldness. The feeling touched the cells on either side of his, which for now were empty. She peered sideways as she walked by and saw him sitting on his cot, straight-backed, looking at nothing, as he often did. The young blond man gave Celine the sense that he could see her even beyond the reach of his line of sight as she passed by.

Lieutenant James Jackson was there, as she expected him to be, slouched sideways in his swivel chair, his feet up on the control panel, clicking between the cameras on the screens before him. The coldness Schmitz had left her with was gone, and she was hot with anger again.

"Did you give John Kradle a soldering iron?" she asked. Jackson's round face was lit by the light of the camera screens, highlighting the bags beneath his eyes.

"I didn't give it to him. He built it himself."

"But you gave him the parts. You gave him the toaster," Celine said. "That's the toaster out of the break room. The old one. The broken one."

"Well, he didn't have a visitor smuggle it in up their asshole, that's all I can tell you, Captain," Jackson said. His assistant, Liz Savva, choked on her coffee.

"Help me understand." Celine leaned in the doorway, her arms folded. "I'm trying to get into your frame of mind. You let a man who shot his family to death in their home before setting the place on fire take possession of a toaster and misappropriate its mechanical parts so he could use it to burn things. Is that what you're saying?"

"Look, Captain." Jackson leaned back in his chair and stared at her. "These guys on the row? I don't sit around thinking about their crimes. If I did, I couldn't work with them. I just think of them as miserable sons of bitches who spend twenty-three hours a day locked in a cage." He pointed upward, in the direction of the warden's office. "Warden Slanter's been looking at me funny since I messed up the new carpet in her office. I was telling Kradle about it and he came up with the idea of the sign. And I think he's doing a good job. So why don't you just lay off the guy? He's helping me out."

Celine sighed.

"It'll look good for the next inspection," Jackson continued. "The inmates doing arts and crafts."

"Kradle should be bumped down to finger-painting level," Celine said. "That way, he's less likely to hurt someone."

"What's your problem with Kradle?" Savva mused, peering into her coffee mug as if the answer might lie in there. "He's one of the least confrontational inmates we have. It's like you hate him even more than the guy in six who ate all those old ladies' faces."

"I'll tell you what I hate." Celine put her hands up, ready to paint a mental picture, but a dull ringing interrupted her. At first she thought it was the phone on her hip. Then she followed the sound to the speaker hanging from the ceiling in the corner of the room. She'd never heard a phone ringing through the PA system before. There was a click, and a noise like a desk chair creaking.

"Hello, Grace Slanter."

"Pay attention."

"Excuse me?"

"What the hell is that?" Celine asked.

"It's the warden," Savva said. The gentle ex-teacher and death row rookie was slowly rising from her chair. "Sounds like her phone's being picked up by the PA."

"Oh, shit." Jackson laughed. "She's left her mic on and taken a call."

"There's a bus stopped in the desert half a mile from the prison walls. If you go to the window behind you and look out, you'll see it sitting on the road.

"Are you looking at it?"

"Somebody better get up there and tell her the whole prison can hear her," Liz said. "Before she starts—"

"Shut up," Celine said. "Listen."

There was a strange silence on the line. A silence that had flooded through the speakers and infected the entire prison. Celine stepped back through the doorway and glanced down the row. It wasn't this quiet in E Block even in the dead of night. She heard Grace Slanter huff into the phone.

"Okay. I see it. What's your name? I want to know who I'm talking to."

"On that bus are twelve women, eight men, and fourteen children," the voice said. *"They're the families of guards inside the prison. Your employees. Your people."*

"Jesus Christ."

"The driver of the bus is dead."

"Oh my god," Celine whispered.

"Hey!" an old man in the cell nearest the control room called out. Celine looked. He was holding a shaving mirror out through the bars to see her. One gray eye was scrutinizing her, its brow hanging low. Roger Hannoy, the face-eater. "What's going on out there?"

"Are you listening, Grace?"

"I'm . . . I'm listening."

Celine dashed down the corridor to the row of windows along the east side of the block. Beyond the furthest concrete wall of the prison, she could see the bus out there in the desert, stopped just off the lonely road that led to the facility. The voices on the speakers above them carried on. Jackson and Savva arrived beside her. Jackson gripped the bars.

"My family's on that bus," Jackson breathed. Celine saw all the blood rush from his face into his neck and then it was gone, leaving him gray as stone. "Tyler. Oh my god. Tyler. Tyler. Tyler."

"Who do you want me to release?"

"All of them."

"This is . . . ," Liz began, but her words fell away and her mouth simply gaped.

"Don't panic. Let's not panic," Celine said. "It's, uh . . . It's a drill." It seemed important to simply interrupt what was happening, to throw something, anything, under the wheels of the train as it came hurtling down the mountain, even though she knew it was impossible to stop it completely. The interruption didn't last long. Jackson met her eyes, and they both knew that captains were briefed on all drills. The fear on Celine's face crushed her lie the second it was out of her mouth.

"*I can't. I mean, I can't do that. That's not doable.*" Slanter's voice was bouncing off the thick walls. "*You can't just . . . What do you—*"

"*You've got four minutes to empty the prison. We're watching, and we're looking for a particular inmate. When he appears outside the prison walls, I'll call my shooter off.*"

"*Who's the inmate?*"

"*We're not going to tell you that. You'll have to release everyone.*"

Jackson's radio crackled on his belt. Celine watched him try to grip it, work it awkwardly from its holster, but he failed, his hands numb. Celine pulled it free.

"Are you guys up in E Block hearing this?" a voice on the radio asked.

It sounded like Bensley from H Block.

"Is this real?" came another voice. All call signals were abandoned. All procedures thrown into the trash. Celine knew that was one of the first signs of mass panic. People forgot their training, became scared animals working only on instinct, fighting to return to reason.

A gaggle of voices and blips came out of the device in her fingers. Calls from all over the prison, fighting for airtime.

"My husband is on that bus!"

"Can anyone tell me what the hell is going on? Is this a drill? Is this a drill?"

"This is Issei in Watchtower Eight. Somebody tell me this is a drill. Has anybody got a captain on deck?"

"Is this for real, Celine?" Jackson asked. He'd grabbed her bicep so hard his nails were biting through the fabric of her shirt. Celine tore her arm away.

"I . . . I . . . I don't know." She couldn't force the words through her lips fast enough. "Just, uh . . . just get back into the control room. Send up a code red, and—"

"*What you're asking is not possible,*" Slanter was saying. "*Okay? This is not how this works. Give me some time.*"

"*You don't have time. Meet our demands or we kill the passengers.*"

"*You're not killing anyone. If you want to negotiate, we can negotiate, but—*"

Two pops. So dim Celine couldn't tell if she imagined them, or if her brain took in the distant puffs of dust in the desert and the sight of the bus lurching sideways, and added the sounds, knowing with sickening clarity what she was seeing. The shooter had taken out both of the bus's left tires, causing the vehicle to collapse sideways and resettle, tilted, like a listing boat.

She thought she heard screams on the wind. But maybe not. Maybe they were in her mind, too.

"*Three minutes, fifty seconds. That's how long you have left, Grace. Then I instruct my shooter to fire at will.*"

"Did you guys see that?" came a voice on the radio. "He took out the tires. He took out the fucking tires!"

CHAPTER 3

Sarah Gravelle gripped her seat with her fingernails, staring at the stairwell of the bus, the mess there. It looked like cheap horror-film special effects: the blood, brain matter, and flecks and splinters of who knows what mixed in with the broken glass. The people on the bus around her were screaming in thirty-three different ways, everybody with their own distress song, toddlers squealing and men bellowing and teenagers wailing, clawing at their shirt collars, reduced suddenly to the wide-open-mouthed kids they once were. Sarah stood again and held on to the rail that separated the front passenger seat from the stairwell. Her legs were jelly as the screaming began to be punctuated by individual voices, some young, some older.

"Is it an active shooter?" a child cried. "Mom! Is it an active shooter?"

"Everything's fine! Everything's fine! Just stay down! Stay down low, honey!"

"Daddy! I want to get off! I want to get off!"

"Holy Mary, mother of God, pray for—"

Sarah gripped her way along the handrail. She told herself to keep her eyes on the prison, half a mile away, as she stepped numbly down the stairs.

"What are you doing? Sarah! Sarah? Sarah, no! There's a shooter out there!"

Sarah looked back. A woman was vomiting into the aisle. A man rambling into the phone to 911. Kids and adults were under the seats, jammed into tiny spaces, tight bundles of terrified humans.

"I've. Got to. Get off," Sarah said. Her voice was flat, ridged only with weakly hitched breaths. "We. All have to. Get off."

Two explosions. The bus lurched sideways, throwing bodies into the aisle. Sarah grabbed the door and pushed it open, let in the crisp desert air.

In Watchtower Seven, Marni Huckabee was staring down the scope of her rifle at the desert. She spent a good five or six hours a day on the tower, some of it staring through the lens at the gates, the fences, the yard, the walkways, and the cages. Once or twice a week, maybe, she lifted her scope to the desert beyond the razor wire and tracked a rabbit or coyote or tortoise out there on the plains. But she was looking now at something she had never before seen, never imagined her crosshairs trembling over as she gripped the weapon with bone-aching tension. A bus door popping open. Someone's wife or girlfriend, a woman she didn't recognize, hesitating as she stepped down from the leaning doorway like a shaken-up child exiting an amusement park house of horrors.

"Oh, god!" Marni's tower partner, Craig Fandel, gripped her arm. "They're going to run for it."

"Don't do it," Marni whispered. She could feel a droplet of sweat making the rim of the rifle scope wet beneath her eye. She swept her hat off, wiped her face with it, pushed her eye against the scope again. "Woman, please, don't do it!"

Marni and Craig watched the woman push off and sprint into the desert, running for the prison gates. Craig let go of Marni's arm.

"Give her cover! Give her cover!" he cried. Marni twisted the rifle sideways on its point, aiming into the hills, where the shooter must have been—the same side as the shot-out tires. For the first time in her career, Marni flipped off the safety and opened fire.

Warden Grace Slanter saw the flash of white gunfire from tower seven, felt the delayed booming in the pit of her stomach. A lone figure was running from the bus across the desert, the unsteady, hunched, desperate running of human prey. Puffs of dust rose and gunfire cracked. Slanter watched the woman fall and slide and tumble in the sand.

"Did you shoot her?" The words felt sharp and hard in Slanter's throat, almost unutterable. "Did . . . did you . . ."

The caller said nothing.

Slanter watched the woman struggle to her feet, turn, and run back toward the bus, throwing herself through the doorway.

"Take me," Slanter said. "I'll walk out into the hills. No one will follow me. I'll be unarmed."

"We don't want you."

"*Who do you want?*" she cried. "*You can have anyone!*"

"Two minutes, forty seconds," the caller said. "We're not playing."

Celine Osbourne watched the activity in the desert play out through the barred windows of death row. She hardly noticed when Jackson snatched his radio back from her fingers.

"This is Jackson, on the row," he said. "My son is out there. He's thirteen. My wife is also on board. Can anybody in the towers see the shooter? Can we . . . Can we take him out?"

"Nobody disarm their doors! That's a direct order!" a voice said. Celine recognized it as Mark Gravelle, from the gate. "That woman, the runner, that's my wife. We have to get through this, people. We can't empty the goddamn prison. Okay? We just can't. I don't care what's happening out there, we gotta keep these guys in. Some of these men—"

"Fuck you!" Jackson's hand was gripping the radio so tight the plastic case was creaking. "That's my family! We can recover the fucking inmates! I'm not burying my son!"

"Don't disarm!" came another shout across the airwaves.

"We've got every fucking killer in the state locked—"

"—leaving my babies out there—"

"—go to hostage protocol! All officers—"

"Look." Liz Savva's sweaty finger bashed on the window, through the bars. "Look. Look. There are guys running. They're unlocking the yard!"

Celine stared at the alarm lights mounted in the ceiling, the bell on the outer corner of the control room. Stillness. Silence. Just the stutter of gunfire from a distant watchtower. No one had announced code red. Because this wasn't a code red. This was something far, far worse.

"Celine," Jackson said. "Open the row."

"No," Celine snapped. All the hairs on her body were standing on end. She was suddenly so cold she was shivering. "No, Jacky, we're not doing this."

"I'm opening up," said a voice on the radio.

"Who is that?"

"This is Brian over in C Block. I'm doing it. You got women and children out there. My fiancée and my two girls. I'm opening the goddamn doors."

"This is Amy, in-in-in tower five. My husband just called me from the bus. This is real. Th-th-this is real. Open it up, please, everyone. Please. My baby boy is out there. Please!"

"If C is opening, we're opening, too."

"Me too."

"D Block here. We're opening up."

"No!" Celine gripped the bars on the window, stood on her toes so she could see the barred door of F Block below. She watched an inmate, someone she didn't recognize, push open the security door.

With his hands.

His own hands.

The man walked out of the door on the side of the building. He took a few steps, looked around, took a few more steps. No officers with him. No other inmates lining up behind him. Just a prisoner, on his own, where he should never be on his own. It might as well have been a zebra in a pink tutu walking out of F Block. Celine blinked but couldn't comprehend it.

She reached out for Jackson, but he was gone. So was Savva. Celine swallowed bile at the back of her throat. She sprinted back to the control room.

"No, no, no, no!" She grabbed the handle of the door just as Jackson slammed it shut in her face. "No, we're not doing this! No, no, no!"

Celine heard a sound that she had never heard before, and that was because it had never been made. It was a loud, thundering, rolling series of clanks.

It was the sound of all the death row cell doors being unlocked at once.

The monsters emerged slowly. She knew them all. It was clear in one horrifying instant how well she knew them, because as each man slid open their disarmed cell door, Celine's mind was flooded with images of their crimes. The face-eater. The strangler. The mass shooter and the slayer of innocent children. Celine watched John Kradle step out into the hall, hesitant, like a wild animal venturing into a clearing. They locked eyes. She saw the terror and excitement in his face.

"Get back inside!" she called, but her voice sounded pathetically small in all the commotion. Some men were calling out to each other, asking what they should do. Others had ducked back inside to gather a precious item. One or two had sprinted away toward the iron-barred door to the stairwell.

She turned and bashed on the door to the control room with her fists.

"Jackson, shut the doors! Shut the doors! Shut the doors!"

Men were running by her. They were going to the windows to check that the bus was really out there. That this wasn't some sort of prank or test.

Celine then did something she had only ever imagined doing. She took two steps to her office, stepped inside, ripped out the bottom drawer, and grabbed the revolver she kept strapped to the inner wall of the desk. She went back into the hall and raised the weapon.

"Get back in your cells!"

They turned, looked her over, laughed. Big Willy Henderson, who had doused his wife in gasoline and set her alight. Ainsley Sippeff, who had opened fire on his colleagues at a bowling alley and killed two teenagers and a parking lot security guy.

The men brushed past her. Celine had never been on this side of the barred doors with any of the inmates she worked with unless they were wearing cuffs. They put the cuffs on in the cells, walked the inmates out to the yard, then uncuffed them in the cages that were there under the sunshine to let them roam in a slightly bigger space for an hour a day. Big Willy's arm touched Celine's as he went by. She felt ice tumble into the pit of her bowels.

The last men ran out into the stairwell, heading for the yard. Celine went back to the windows. Men were flooding out of the prison buildings, rushing toward the gates at the front of the complex, a mass evacuation, a sea of denim flooding out into the desert. A wave of nausea hit her and she doubled over, resting her hands on her knees. The sound of the release had been deafening. Now the halls were quiet but for the words falling out of her own mouth, panicked moans.

"No, no, please," she huffed. She straightened, trying to breathe, but the nausea hit again like a punch to the gut. "Please, god, don't do this."

The monsters were gone. All of them. Out into the world. She turned away from the windows, knowing that, with each second that ticked by, the state's most dangerous men were edging closer and closer to their next victims.

She had failed. For a decade and a half, all Celine had wanted to do was keep the bad men in their cages where they belonged; away from the world, from each other, from the people they had hurt. And all of it had been for nothing.

A man turned into the hall. Celine raised her gun. It was Jackson, pausing briefly before he ran.

"It's my family." He gestured weakly, then disappeared. Liz followed him. She heard their footsteps on the gravel outside.

She went to the control room, stepped numbly into the space, which was lit dimly to accentuate the contrast on the surveillance cameras. She touched the cell discharge button and some other dials vainly, as if she would be able to reverse the last few minutes somehow if she just found the right switch. The screens in front of her showed no movement. She turned and looked at the screens by the door that gave glimpses of the yard. Remaining inmates were being hustled reluctantly toward the gates by prison staff. These were likely the elderly, infirm, or mentally ill prisoners, or some perhaps merely scared men who were close to their release dates and didn't want to step outside the prison walls and have their sentence extended for an escape attempt. Celine marveled at how seamlessly the mutiny had unfolded. Once the first call had come through announcing someone was opening up, it seemed that most of the other staff had fallen into line. When a colleague's family was in danger, you stepped up, it seemed. Even if that meant endangering everyone else out there by releasing the worst of the worst into their midst.

She decided she would go out into the yard, to see the big gates of the prison standing open. It was something she had never witnessed before. The twenty-foot-high iron gates, as thick as truck tires, usually only ever opened as far as was necessary to let vehicles into the outer enclosure. But she supposed there was no need for that now. The gates would be thrust wide, useless.

The figure that appeared at the edge of her vision was tall and slender. Her mind, still failing to comprehend the new reality of the animals running wild outside their enclosures, told her it was Jackson. But it was not.

Willy Henderson grabbed Celine by the arm and shoved her back into the control room.

CHAPTER 4

John Kradle stood in the staff parking lot of Pronghorn Correctional Facility and felt the sunshine on his face. It occurred to him that he had never in his life stood on this spot, though he was positioned a mere hundred yards or so from his cell back on the row. On the night he had been driven to the facility, the truck had come in the back way, through the rear gate, a less impressive fifteen-foot-tall iron affair on the south side of the complex. He'd hardly noticed the facility taking in the bus on which he sat, like a giant whale swallowing a fish. He'd just been sentenced to death for murdering his family. Minute by minute, he had simply been trying to resist the urge to scream.

As well as standing somewhere he had never stood before, he was also standing somewhere that he had never considered he would be able to stand. His feet on the asphalt. His hands by his sides. The sun on his cheeks. One hundred yards, give or take, into the free world.

Men were running past him, yipping and cheering as they went. Kradle was initially surprised at just how many of the inmates were able to smash the windows of the cars in the lot, get in, and get the engine running in mere seconds, but then he supposed being able to hotwire a car was among the most common skills within the populace at any prison in the world. He watched alliances forming almost wordlessly, inmates flagging down and packing into the back of cars, horns honking as the vehicles took off toward the road. In the distance he could see civilians cowering against the side of the tilted bus as cars full of criminals zipped past them, trailing dust.

Every vehicle was headed the same way: out onto the service road that led to the highway. When they reached the highway, Kradle knew, the cars could turn left toward Vegas or right toward Utah. Kradle could guess which way most would be turning.

He looked at the huge, open gates of the prison before him, standing open like welcoming arms. A cluster of staff was gathered there, gaping at the spectacle of the mass breakout with their arms folded and mildly defeated looks on their faces. Some were on their phones, pacing back and forth nervously, trying to warn loved ones of the coming tidal wave of criminality.

"Take the kids and go to my mother's place," an officer was saying into his cell phone. Kradle didn't recognize him. There were only ten staff who worked on the row, where he had lived for the past five years. "Get in the car and drive there now, Cherie. Right now. Don't stop anywhere."

"Go down to the basement and don't come out until you hear my voice." A female officer passed Kradle, on her phone, her gun out in front of her, finger on the trigger. The pistol's aim wavered over him as she moved, but her eyes didn't meet his. His was just another criminal face in the horde that was running rampant. Kradle watched her get into her car, parked at the furthest end of the lot, and shake the gun at some inmates to get them away from the driver's side door. She started the engine and sped away.

Celine hit the floor of the control room so hard that all the wind was smacked out of her lungs. The gun clattered out of her fingers and slid under the control room desk. She crawled a few paces, trying to suck in air, but Henderson snatched her ankle, dragged her back to him, started pulling weapons off her body and throwing them away. He took her baton from its sheath and smashed her a few times, the pain so sudden and all-consuming she didn't even know where she was being struck. Everything blazed with pain. *Wham-wham-wham.* There was blood in her eyes. Her vision blurred red just as her thoughts came back into focus: her brain told her she needed to be very strategic now, true with her aim, calm and cool and moving like a machine that ran on instinct and training.

She squeezed her eyes shut, and in the darkness felt him kneel on top of her. He was within swinging distance now. Celine struck out and felt her knuckles smash against the bridge of his nose.

Right on target.

She'd spent a second in offensive mode, and now reeled back into defensive mode. *Get to safety; recover; plan; strike.* She covered her face with her arms, locked her fingers protectively around her skull and waited for the barrage of rageful punches to ebb. When it did, she slammed her knee upward into Henderson's crotch. He bent double instinctively, his body folding, anticipating the pain, his sweating forehead pressed between Celine's breasts. He let out a groan, high and ear-drum rattling. She clawed at his neck and head until he rolled away. She rolled as well, gripping her way toward the door, but he was back on her before she could move more than a foot or two, and he seemed somehow stronger, as if the rage generated by the knee in the crotch had only given him power.

His arm came around her neck, thick and wet and hairy, and squeezed so hard she felt the pressure of it behind her eyes.

And then, with a crack, the pressure was gone.

He's snapped my neck, she thought.

The words in her mind were hellishly clear. She curled her toes, expecting to feel the terrifying numbness of paralysis down her body, but she found that she could move. Henderson's arm had slithered away. More cracking sounds came. Celine rolled onto her back and watched John Kradle standing over the big man who had attacked her, his arm reaching up and then swinging down, the toaster in his hand smashing into Henderson's face like Thor's hammer, shiny and dented and covered with blood.

Celine watched Kradle beat Henderson half to death, her limbs refusing to move, seized by shock. Weird thoughts drifted through her; about the blood splattering up at Kradle's face, about how he gripped the toaster with his two fingers in the slots and his thumb around the base of the machine, as if he were holding a bowling ball.

All at once her body and mind recovered, and Celine scrambled under the control desk, picked up her gun, and swung around. Henderson wasn't moving. Kradle was standing there with the toaster in one hand and her baton in the other.

"Are you—" he managed before a yelp of surprise and a look of horror. Celine fired three times. The bullets smashed into the wall behind Kradle's head, the last missing his ear by an inch or less. He cowered, the toaster and baton at his feet, forgotten.

"Sweet *Jesus!*" he howled when the firing had stopped. "I'm trying to save your ass here!"

"Get down!" Celine growled. "On your knees, inmate! Put your hands on the back of your head!"

"You're crazy." Kradle stood, backing up. "You want to shoot me, go ahead and shoot me, Celine. I only came back here for my stuff."

She didn't shoot. He turned and walked out of the control room. Celine pulled herself up to the observation window. She watched him jog back to his cell. He emerged what seemed like seconds later holding a pillowcase stuffed with items. She watched him disappear through the door at the end of the row that led out to the yard.

Celine crawled back to Henderson. She couldn't bring herself to look at his mangled face and head. The hands that cuffed him were slick with blood, her own and his. She snapped the restraints on the big man, gathered up her weapons, and limped slowly in the direction Kradle had gone.

Raymond Ackerman had been sitting listening to all the hubbub outside his cell. The phone call patched over the PA system, then the hoots and hollers of excitement from the inmates, the crash and clatter of chaos erupting beyond the bars. Two female guards stopped right in front of his cell, yammering in terror and gripping each other, and he watched them lock themselves in a storage closet only seconds before all the cell doors slid open. He was stirring a pot of noodles on his little camp stove throughout the entire affair—Picante beef ramen—the thin, lifeless packages lying discarded on the iron desk by the toilet. He thought long and hard, but couldn't remember anything like this going down during his time at Pronghorn, or in any prison he'd been at, as a matter of fact. Seventy-seven years on the planet, forty-two of them behind bars, or steel mesh, or bulletproof glass, or whatever the hell they decided to keep him in, and he'd never witnessed a mass breakout. Pretty special. He stirred his noodles and waited for it all to die down, until only the clink of his spoon against the side of the pot could be heard.

Nobody came to see if "The Axe" Ackerman had joined the breakout. People tended to forget about Old Axe. He was quiet, slow-moving, didn't want for much. When fights broke out in the chow hall he tended to back away. When his cell was shaken down he stood with his arms by his sides, face against the wall, just as he was told. He sat now, enjoying the quiet of the empty cell block, eating his noodles, thinking about how good he'd got at eating noodles with a spoon over the years. They didn't have forks in H Block—as though, without forks, guys wouldn't have anything to hurt each other with. As if without forks, everybody was safe.

Stupid.

Axe got up after a while and went to his cell door, looked out across the cluttered common area. The men had trashed the place as they fled, like they thought they'd never be back. There was toilet paper festooned around the place, hanging off the ceiling fans. Books and cups and other stuff lay about everywhere. A cell down the hall was on fire. Axe figured most of the block would be right back where they started within twenty-four hours, and the screws would make them clean up all that mess with their own toothbrushes.

Axe had no real plans about going anywhere. He saw the outside world on TV and didn't much care for it. It seemed pretty noisy and weird. People on sitcoms were rude and mean and dressed stupid, and there would be a whole bunch of things he didn't understand about how to be in society. Seemed to him that just to get a decent meal you had to order it on a phone and pay for it with a cloud, and he didn't have either of those. He figured he'd only get a hundred yards outside the gates before a flying drone would turn up and scan his face, and then he'd be turned right around and marched home to his cell. It was all too much effort for him. He was a tired sort of guy. Liked to conserve his energy. But, he thought, he'd wander out into the yard anyway, just to see the gates hanging open, and then maybe raid everybody's cells for noodles.

When he got out into the yard, there was nobody there. He went to the gates, put a hand on them, felt their warmth from the desert sun. He took a couple of steps out, just for the hell of it, and rolled a rock under his shoe. Most of the activity seemed to be clustered around a bus parked in the desert, maybe a half mile from the facility. People hugging. Kids moving about. Axe hadn't seen a kid in almost four decades. He watched the scene for a while with his hands in his pockets.

Axe hung about, not doing much, waiting for someone to notice him standing there, but nobody did. There were the unattended noodles to think of. Dozens and dozens of packets, probably. But he decided in the end that there was no sense in making the screws' jobs easy by sitting in his cell for the entirety of the breakout. He turned and started heading for a Joshua tree he could see standing all alone at the foot of a rocky hill. He figured he'd go there and check it out. Axe hadn't seen a tree up close for half his lifetime. It was something to do with himself.

CHAPTER 5

The desert sun beat on the back of John Kradle's neck. It worked its way around his ears, up into his scalp, hot fingers trying to climb around his skull. In the Nevada desert there was no winter, not until the sun went down. He kept his head down and pressed on over the cracked and dry land, one step at a time, spiky plants scraping at his pants. It wasn't long before his white rubber prison shoes were brown and rubbing at the back of his heels. They were shoes made for walking on polished concrete floors, no more than a couple of miles a day; shoes that had no hard internal structure, not so much as a shoelace eyelet that could be taken off, bent, sharpened into a tiny blade. The shoes began to squeak as sweat rolled down his calves into them. Kradle kept on, glancing back now and then to see the prison shrinking and shrinking.

A helicopter flew overhead, low enough for Kradle to feel the beat of its rotors in his chest. There were cars in the distance soaring up the service road to the facility, cars of every color and shape. It would be an all-hands call to law enforcement. Kradle figured Las Vegas Metro police and Nevada Highway Patrol would be there, and in short order SWAT, FBI, and the US Marshals would be too. Every Pronghorn staff member would be called to help out. Kradle planned to be in the mountains by the time things really ramped up. He figured he had about five miles to go before he hit shade.

It was while he was looking back, checking on the growing activity, that he spotted the man on his tail. Kradle knew he wasn't from the row. He'd seen everyone on the row, even if he didn't know their names. At home in his cell, Kradle had been able to physically call out and communicate with guys three or four cells either side of his, and one Christmas had passed a kite six cells down to negotiate the barter of two bottles of hand cream for a Snickers bar. The other guys he only saw when they were being escorted past his cell to visits with their lawyers or family in the cages.

For a while he simply hoped the guy would peel off, head into the hills another way. Maybe Kradle had picked the only sensible path from the prison to the walls of the shallow valley in which the facility lay. The shortest path. But when the man on his tail hadn't disappeared, hadn't lengthened or shortened his proximity in about twenty minutes, Kradle stopped.

The man stopped.

"Get your ass here!" Kradle called.

The man approached. The last thirty yards or so, Kradle expected him to stop growing in size, but he didn't. Somehow the outside world had added a foot and a half of height to Kradle's approximation of him, a worrying thickness to his already huge, muscular frame.

"You can't be following me," Kradle said, in a voice that was far less confident than the one he'd used already. He pointed to a fork off into the mountains. "I'm heading this way. Give me some space, okay?"

"I want to come with you." The guy smiled, showing a big gap between his front teeth that made Kradle think of a toddler. "You look like you know where you're going."

"Are you . . ." Kradle shook his head and tried to think. "Are you kidding me? I don't even know you, man."

"I'm Homer Carrington."

"Look, the smartest thing for everybody to do here is strike out on their own. And I'm heading—"

"Pretty clever." Homer ran a hand over his buzz-cut black hair. "Head for the hills. Everybody else will be going off to Vegas. Why go into the hills? It's rocky up there. Dangerous. There'll be snakes. Probably big cats. It'll take you so long to get through, everybody else will be rounded up by the time anybody even thinks to look up here."

"That's . . ." Kradle shielded his eyes from the glare of the blazing white sun. "That's exactly right. Okay? You get it. We get each other. So now that you understand my reasoning, you can split off and go your own way."

"You're a smart guy." Homer smiled again. This time he showed all his teeth. Big, white, square teeth with that sizeable gap in the middle. Kradle was at once softened by the smile and also a little creeped out. Kradle thought of a plush-toy tapeworm he saw once at a school science fair, its cute, buggy eyes and coiling, pale body.

"Thanks," Kradle said. He decided to try a different tack. "But you don't want to hang out with me. I'll be one of the top priority targets in the search."

"Oh, man." Homer stepped back a little. "You're not a serial killer or—"

"Very dangerous serial killer." Kradle nodded gravely. "John Kradle. I killed twelve women. Some of them young girls. And men. I've killed nine men. Very violently. So I'm going to be right up there on the hit list. I'm just going to try to get out of here as fast as I can."

"I guess that means I'll be high priority, too," Homer said, a little sadly. He looked off toward the rise beyond which the prison lay.

Kradle felt the hairs on the back of his neck stiffen in unison. "You're . . ." He couldn't use the words.

"Probably best if we stick together," Homer said. He walked up and passed Kradle, thumping his shoulder in a way that made Kradle even more aware of the man's dense, heavy, tree-trunk arms and the huge, skull-crushing hands hanging off them. "Two heads are better than one."

In her time as a US Marshal, Trinity Parker had seen some colossal fuck-ups. She'd once attended a near-miss mass shooting at a courthouse in Brampton, in which a guy had been able to smuggle a cache of sixty-five weapons into the building via a doughnut cart. He'd been wheeling parts of guns, knives, and boxes of ammunition right through the front doors in Krispy Kreme boxes and stashing them in a disused broom closet not twenty yards from the judges' chambers. The whole plot had only been discovered when an old lady buying a Boston cream to go with her cappuccino dropped the doughnut and spotted the barrel of an AR-15 poking out from under the cart. Another time, Trinity had seen a group of six sheriffs chase a serial rapist into a carnival, only to lose him in the mirror maze. It was like something out of a Scooby-Doo cartoon.

But as she stood surveying the scene at Pronghorn Correctional Facility, it occurred to her that she might be witnessing the greatest failure of privatized incarceration in the history of the state of Nevada, perhaps even the country.

As with all fugitive hunts, the ground zero action plan had been born on the hood of a patrol car, and had quickly grown and evolved across the facility as officers, information, and documents were added. The planning site now encompassed the prison chow hall. As Trinity commanded from the officers' watch station on a raised platform at the front of the great room, a loud, unsettled gaggle of men and women ebbed and pooled at different steel tables around her. Many of them were facility staff in tan and green uniforms, commiserating, retelling the story of the breakout from their various perspectives, gesturing wildly, some of them with bleeding noses or split brows, or with chunks of hair torn off in fights to keep inmates contained.

Among these correctional officers were newly arrived deputy sheriffs, highway patrol officers, and volunteer officers from the surrounding towns and counties, many of them listening to the tales of the breakout with incredulity. There was a special collection of people in the corner of the room: civilians in plain clothing, some of them still weeping quietly into phones or typing out long messages to family and friends. The bus people. Trinity saw toddlers bawling and traumatized teenagers madly reciting the experience to the outside world via their phone cameras.

Trinity turned and watched through the large barred windows as a couple of choppers landed outside the prison gates. SWAT, maybe, or journalists. A few leftover inmates and officers stood together, watching, at the fences, united in their bewilderment. She took the coffee that someone handed her and glanced at the slew of maps that had been placed on the table in front of her, a feast of information.

"First thing I want is for someone to stop those kids," she said, jutting her chin at the livestreaming teenagers. "Take all the phones from the bus passengers. Information about the breakout needs to be locked down. And I want the prison closed again. No press are to enter those gates."

A couple of deputies nodded and dashed away.

"Now that I'm here, we can take the fluffy-bunny initial response and give it some teeth and claws," Trinity said, looking over the maps. "The cordons—push them out by fifty miles and beef them up. I'm giving shoot-to-kill approval for any vehicles that try to rush the barricades. Most of these meatheads will be headed straight for Vegas to have a good time before they're rounded up. The really dangerous ones will go to ground, try to go on the run for the long-term. They'll be taking hostages in cars and houses, looking for supplies. Money. Clothes. Food. Licenses and papers. Put up the heat-seeking drones and send out alerts to cell phones in a five-hundred-mile radius."

People were rushing everywhere to enact her commands, phones to their ears, repeating her words. Trinity looked for a cookie to go with her coffee, but there was not a single bite of food visible in the entire chow hall.

"Someone get me something to eat, and someone drag in some partitions," she said, sipping her coffee. She waved toward the long east wall of the food hall. "I want a wall of photographs erected of the inmates we have on the loose. I want to see all their faces. I'm a visual person. Somebody categorize them by security level. The really dangerous cases up this end of the room, by me."

More people rushed away, and others took their place around her. Everyone wanted to be near Trinity. She'd experienced it before. The attraction of a calm island in a tumultuous sea. Wayward boats were drifting in, taking shelter but also wanting to witness her undertaking the plainly unfathomable task of cleaning up a mess as breathtakingly ridiculous as this.

And it was a spectacular mess. It wasn't so much the number of prisoners set free that concerned Trinity. Sure, it was the biggest mass breakout she'd ever dealt with—but the response was immediate. If she got a proper grasp on the personnel assigned to her, and they all followed her directions, there would be a huge number of inmates scooped up within the first few days simply because they were idiots who didn't know what to do when presented with sudden freedom. There would be clusters of inmates to be found in bars, brothels, and casinos all over Vegas. Trinity had worked on a mass breakout in Chicago—twenty-one prisoners escaped from a transport vehicle—and the week's delay in calling her in had meant Trinity was trying to hunt down some of the guys as far away as Venezuela.

No, it was the high-profile inmates on the loose in this particular case that filled Trinity with a sense of unease. Three of them, in fact, should never have been in Pronghorn at all.

There was Abdul Hamsi, the failed terrorist, who had wound up in a state prison rather than a federal control unit because the one death he had actually managed to chalk up was a parking-lot security guard he'd run over with his getaway car.

There was Burke David Schmitz, who should also have been a federal inmate, but who was saved from a fed stay in Louisiana, where his crimes were committed, because he also killed while on the run. Schmitz had shot two Black police officers who tried to pull him over in Nevada as he headed for California. He was not extradited back to the state where he'd conducted a massacre for fear he would be a travel security risk.

And then there was serial killer Homer Carrington, who had confirmed kills in several states, which had landed him in a federal prison in north Nevada. Until an attack on a guard had him temporarily shipped to Pronghorn for containment.

The biggest tickets on Trinity's bill should have been rapists and wife-killers. Instead she was chasing mass murderers and terrorists.

She rubbed at her temple, trying to subdue a growing headache.

A slender woman in a tan and green uniform appeared by her side, and Trinity could tell from the collapsed look of her frame and the restlessness of her hands that this was probably the warden.

"Grace Slanter." The woman gave a dead-fish handshake. "This is my disaster."

"An excellent choice of word," Trinity said. "Disaster. Congratulations, Ms. Slanter. You're about to make history as the world's worst prison warden."

"In defense of myself, and my staff"—Grace held a hand up—"we never anticipated anything like this. No one was trained in this. All our hostage protocols are designed to deal with inmates inside the facility taking control of staff. We were presented with a situation today in which—"

"Let me get this straight," Trinity said. "You put thirty-four civilians—the family members of prison staff—on a single unarmored vehicle and let them drive toward the facility without any kind of protection?"

"The annual softball game is something we've had in place at this prison for eleven years," Grace said. "There's never been an issue."

"Okay." Trinity nodded. "So not only did you wrap a bunch of children in meat and send them unguarded into shark-infested waters, you made sure you did it on the same goddamn day eleven times in a row."

"Well—"

"If I'm to understand my briefing correctly"—Trinity shifted some blueprints of the prison on the table in front of her—"on that bus you had the wife of a watchtower guard, the wife and son of a death row guard, the husband and two daughters of a gateman, and a family member of at least one guard from every single accommodation block in this institution." Trinity looked at a list of staff members with names highlighted in bright yellow ink.

"That's what I'm led to believe." Grace swallowed.

"Well." Trinity widened her eyes, shook her head in astonishment. "I don't know whether to send you home to enjoy your last few moments of professional anonymity, or to put you in a room with a couple of my investigators so that you can be questioned about any possible leads on who your inside man was."

"The inside man?"

"Yes." Trinity sipped her coffee. "Obviously."

"Marshal Parker," Grace said carefully. "Nothing is obvious to me right now. I'm still recovering from this morning's events."

"Ms. Slanter, every hostage on that bus was linked to a key staff member inside the prison," Trinity said. "That was deliberate. Somebody arranged that. Otherwise you might have had all the guards in one cell block falling over each other to meet the shooter's demands and no one else willing to do so." Trinity squinted, examining Grace's face. "Are you following me, dear?"

"I am," Grace said. "I just—"

"Go home, Ms. Slanter." Trinity gave a thin smile and patted the older woman on the shoulder. When she looked away, there was a petite woman with a bloodied, bruised face standing at her elbow. Trinity jumped, almost dropping her coffee. "Jesus!"

"You Marshal Trinity Parker?"

"The very same."

"They tell me you're heading up this operation." The woman scratched at dried blood on the collar of her uniform. "I'm Captain Celine Osbourne. Death row supervisor."

Trinity looked the woman over. Trinity was tall, which suited her, because she found herself most effective when talking down to people. But even then, the Osbourne woman was particularly short. Trinity felt the muscles in her neck tightening as she looked down at her, something she decided she didn't want to do for very long.

"So you're the one who let the worst of the worst out." Trinity turned her back on Grace Slanter, who was still hanging around for some reason. "Congratulations, you—"

"Ma'am, don't start in on me. I didn't let *anybody* out," Celine said. "My second-in-command locked me out of the control room and flipped the switch. In fact, we've got one inmate already back in his cell on the row. Willy Henderson. Wife killer."

Trinity cocked her head, reassessing the short woman with the pixie-cut blonde hair. "Uh-huh. I see. And was it Henderson who . . ." She twirled a finger around Osbourne's pummeled face.

"Yup."

"Right." Trinity beckoned a deputy with her finger. "You. Yeah. Write a statement for this woman to give in front of the cameras. Osbourne, you tell the media you single-handedly fought off one of your most violent inmates to keep him contained."

"I don't want to fuck around in front of cameras." Celine flapped a stapled sheaf of papers she had been holding by her side. "I want in on the hunt for the top fugitives. They'll all be from my row. I know these guys. Top priority needs to be a man named Kradle. I can give you the lowdown on him, and—"

"That's not the best use of your time right now." Trinity held up a hand. "We need to get out in front of this. We've got a female warden in this story. Understand? I don't care how much she actually had to do with letting the inmates out"—Trinity glanced at Grace Slanter—"but she's going to be the face of this thing. It'll be *Woman Warden Released Killers Into Public. Woman Warden Responsible for Slaying of Dozens.* This fiasco is going to decimate the progress of women in management positions in law enforcement for the next two decades unless we can change the narrative."

"I couldn't give a shit about narratives!" Celine pointed at the partitions being dragged to the side of the room, the photographs of men already being pinned up. "I want to catch those guys before they hurt anyone!"

Trinity gestured with her coffee cup, kicking an offer over to the mouthy little shrimp. "Do a five-minute bit to the press and you can be part of the lead team."

"Deal," Celine said, just as Trinity expected her to.

Trinity took the papers the woman had been waving around and started spreading them out on top of the maps and blueprints on the table before her. Thankfully, Grace Slanter took the hint and slumped away. Trinity's eyes flicked between the papers as she laid them down. She had seen plenty of prisoner profiles in her time and skipped right over the names, sorting them into piles according to body count. She flipped a couple of sheets to the corner of the desk, and Celine snatched up one of those before it could slide onto the floor.

"This is the guy who should be top of the shit pile." Celine smacked the sheet down in front of Trinity. "John Kradle. He—"

"Three victims?" Trinity cocked an eyebrow. "You kidding?"

"He came home from work one day and blew his wife and kid away. Sister-in-law, too. This guy is a cold, calculated—"

"Look." Trinity straightened. "I know you're new to this. You haven't been trained for anything like this before, blah blah blah. But I'm going to be looking for the terrorist who organized this whole clusterfuck."

She pointed to the room around them, two hundred people working like ants.

"I don't know for sure who he is, yet," Trinity said. "But he's got to have connections. We know there was a man, possibly more than one, on the inside. We know he recruited at least two people on the outside, the shooter and the caller. Probably a driver and a lookout, too. So, 'top of the shit pile,' as you so eloquently put it, is going to be someone like this." She picked up a sheet and waggled it in front of the woman's eyes, then turned it back toward herself. "Burke David Schmitz. White nationalist neo-Nazi terrorist. Mass shooter responsible for fifteen deaths and eighteen injuries." She picked up another page. The shrimp's face was slowly filling with color. "Or this guy. Abdul Ansar Hamsi. Islamic State. Killer of—"

"John Kradle is a family annihilator," Celine snapped. Trinity waited. The little woman just panted and looked aggrieved.

"You use that term like it's supposed to mean something to me," Trinity said.

"It means he slaughtered the people he loves most," Celine said. She snatched up Schmitz's paper and crushed it in her fist. "These guys? We can go after them. I get it. They're an extreme danger to the public. But they kill the people they hate. Kradle murdered his own child in cold blood while the kid was taking a shower. He gets equal weight in the hunt."

"No, he doesn't," Trinity said.

"Yes, he does, or I don't do the bit to camera."

"You do the bit to camera or I'll have you imprisoned in your home," Trinity said.

"You can't do that."

"Oh, yes I can. I'll put three agents on you. Dear, you said it yourself. These are your guys. It was your row. It's reasonable to expect that one of them might come after you, so perhaps the best thing to do is put you in protective custody for the duration of the hunt. There are a lot of inmates on the loose." Trinity widened her eyes, blew out her cheeks at the sight of the papers before her. "Might take months, a year, to round them all up."

Celine had started shaking. Trinity felt a flush of pleasure roll over her. She liked putting people exactly where they belonged. It was no different to organizing her linen closet, or stacking cans in a cupboard. She liked order.

Celine had started crawling up the shelves, and now she had been taken down and tucked away in her spot. The woman turned and stormed away, and Trinity shook her head in disbelief for the benefit of anyone who might have been watching.

1990

He found her in a newspaper.

He would always find something interesting on his trips into town. They were rare enough at that time that something special always happened. Interactions with people who weren't gator hunters or the swamp witches they married were always ripe for magic. Once, when John Kradle came onto land because the rudder on his houseboat had cracked, he found a pair of hapless Russian tourists on an unnamed back road. He'd been walking to his favorite shack bar and saw the woman sitting on a log, fanning herself in the choking heat. The guy was in the driver's seat of their RV, trying to interpret a hand-drawn map probably given to them by some gas station attendant, which had led them to this exact spot. Nowhere. A subtle little "New Iberia is not New Orleans" message the locals sometimes dished out. Kradle made his case as a trustworthy local, jumped into the vehicle, and saw the Russians back to the main road, which took him well out of his way. But they paid him a hundred bucks, which bought the supplies to fix the rudder and get a beer afterward.

He was sitting at the back of the bar, a corrugated iron and scrap-wood affair close enough to the river that it always stank of fish guts, when he saw the ad she'd placed in the classifieds section. He had been thinking he would need to do a few jobs before he could get away into the weeds again for any decent period of time, but he hadn't been looking for the kind of work she was offering. He was more of a porch-painting, bee-hive-removing, motor-oil-changing sort of guy. Most of his clients were old ladies who had deathly concerns about getting up a ladder. But he was intrigued, so he used the phone behind the bar to call her.

When he heard her voice, like a bass guitar wire thrumming, he decided he was going to do whatever he had to in order to get the job.

"What kind of camera do you have?" she asked.

"Well, here's the thing," he began. Marty, the bartender, sweat beads sticking in his arm hairs, rolled his eyes as Kradle made the play. He'd take his pay in advance, go get the camera, then do the job. Christine wasn't buying it, so he shrugged casually, as if she could see him through the phone. The shrug was really for Marty.

"I'm not trying to scam you, lady," Kradle said. "I'm going to hang up now. If you get any interested parties who already have a camera, fine. If you don't, come down to the bar on Second Street and you can see what you think of me face-to-face."

"What's the name of the bar?" she asked, but Kradle hung up, because he'd said he would, and the place didn't have a name anyway.

An hour later, she was there, wearing a flowy, leopard-print number that made Marty hang his head back and look down his nose, like he was trying to decide if he was really seeing what he was seeing. Kradle didn't know what kind of fabric it was, but he did know Southerners didn't wear it. He could see sweat rolling down her sides through the oversized armholes. He could also see her lacy pink bra. She asked Marty if he served daiquiris, and he laughed and laughed before putting a vodka Coke in front of her.

"So you didn't get ten other guys wanting to come help you catch demonic activity on film?" Kradle asked when she sat down.

"You can stop right there," Christine said, pointing a finger at his face. She pushed back her brown curls, composed herself. "I won't work with anyone who doesn't take my profession seriously."

"Wait, so you mean the demon thing is real?" Kradle said. "I was sure it was a cover."

"A cover for what?"

"Porn."

"Oh, Jesus." She shook her head. "No, honey, it's not porn."

"Well, whatever is it, I'll try to take it seriously, then." He hid his smile with difficulty.

"The couple I'm providing consultation to live over in Erath," she explained, her eyes locked on her drink, defensive. "They've had an entity threatening them for some weeks. I haven't confirmed it's demonic, because I haven't visited the residence yet. I'm just guessing. Could be we're dealing with a returner, not an outer-worlder. But I need to film all my interactions with the dwelling and its inhabitants, because the footage can sometimes prove useful in analysis of the entity's residency."

"So what happened to your last camera guy?" Kradle asked.

"He got scared off." Christine looked at him, challenging.

"Well, it would take a hell of a thing to scare me off," he said. She thought that was just the funniest thing anybody had ever said; kept saying, "Hell of a thing," and clapping. Marty gave a big, long sigh and poured himself a big, long whiskey.

It was supposed to be just a fun way to spend his afternoon. An easy four hundred dollars and a job that maybe wouldn't get him filthy with oil or covered in bee stings. But she liked to talk, and it had been a long time since he'd listened to anybody, so he sat in the bar with her all night, feeding her vodka Cokes and nodding along to her tales of ghosts and bogeys and possessed people. He learned the difference between a returner and an outer-worlder, and left pretty convinced that the previous camera guy hadn't been scared off by anything supernatural. The plan was to get a cab to a pawnshop to look at cameras, but then they figured it was too late and the place would be closed, so they ended up arriving at midnight at the little dock where he'd parked his houseboat.

When he woke up in the morning he expected her to be gone. Instead he walked out onto the back deck and found her there, sitting on the plastic chair, buck naked and dangling a handline in the water.

CHAPTER 6

Kradle was thinking about his houseboat as they hit the base of the mountains and pockets of shade began flooding over him. Long stretches out of the sun bathed him in coolness, or the illusion of coolness to a mind desperately trying not to focus on fire, burning, searing, bones cooking down to ash. The threat behind him urged him on. The man named Homer kept maybe ten yards back, his head down and his long legs crunching into the dry earth. Kradle would just get himself into the safety of his memories—of the Louisiana rain hammering down on the corrugated-iron roof of the houseboat, slapping into the surface of the river, drumming against the windows where he kept his little jars of nails and screws and hinges on the tiny kitchen windowsill—when he would hear Homer cough or sniff or mutter to himself. A zing of electric terror would erupt in his chest and he would glance around.

"Let's talk plans," Homer said eventually. Kradle waited until the big man was beside him. They had stopped in the shade of a rocky overhang.

"On the other side of these mountains is an airfield." Kradle pointed. "That's where we're headed."

"Why?"

Kradle thought about lying, but the seconds were pressing on and Homer's shockingly big hands were hanging there, and Kradle couldn't keep the words from tumbling out of his lips.

"Because I'm hopping a plane," he said.

"You've thought about this before." Homer gave a wry smile, waggled a finger at Kradle. "This is a great plan. How far to the field?"

"We'll take a break at sunset, try to catch a couple of hours' sleep," he said. His mouth was painfully dry. "Our priority has been getting out of sight and into the hills. But we don't want to stay here too long. The rocks will hold the heat of the day for a while, make it harder to track us with heat-seeking cameras. But when they cool we'll be easy to find. So by daybreak we want to be back in civilization."

Don't ask me, Kradle thought. *Don't ask me where we—*

"Where are we flying to?" Homer asked.

"*We're* not flying anywhere." Kradle straightened and looked Homer dead in the eyes. "We're going to split up."

"I don't think so." Homer gave a boy-next-door smile, dripping with sweetness. He gestured to the mountains. "This is the kind of plan that has taken awhile to think through. You've been lying in your cell, putting this together for months, maybe years. I want to be with the guy who has a plan, because I don't have a plan."

Kradle drew a long breath. "Maybe you should just come up with one of your own."

"You got a map in that bag? I bet you've got one." He pointed to the pillowcase hanging over Kradle's shoulder.

"No," Kradle said.

"But you've got water." Homer nodded to the bag. The big guy folded himself down like a tall clothes rack collapsing for storage under a bed, until he was sitting on a rock. "You were the guy who was smart enough to grab water before rushing out into the desert. I bet you there wasn't another man in E Block who grabbed water before heading out. I sure didn't."

Kradle felt another sharp prickle of energy in his chest, tight and hard. Homer was from E Block, but he wasn't from the row. There was only one other section in E Block besides death row, and that was the special housing unit. The SHU housed guys who were so violent they couldn't be moved without hand and leg irons, a shock belt, and a spit hood. Kradle had never seen the special housing unit, but he'd heard there were rarely any guys assigned to it at Pronghorn. They had more appropriate facilities for that kind of inmate on the other side of Vegas. Frankie Buchanan had gone to special housing only a week ago, after he lured an officer to the front of his cell and tried to spear him in the chest with a splinter of wood he'd broken off a chair in the visitors' center. Buchanan was gone now, shipped out to face a rape charge in Minnesota, Kradle had heard.

"Give me the water," Homer said.

Kradle handed over the water bottle. Homer sipped some and handed it back. Kradle thought he might vomit if he tried to swallow any, so he just held the bottle.

"We better stay hydrated," Homer mused.

Kradle looked at the mountains, thought about making a run for it. But he wanted to know what kind of beast he was dealing with before he annoyed that beast, and before he lost sight of it. You don't kick an alligator in the face and then leap into the water. He sank onto a rock and put the water bottle to his lips.

"I don't think I've seen you on the row," he said, forcing a sip.

"I'm new. Only a week in. Maybe that's why."

"What'd you do?"

"I ran over a cop." Homer rolled his eyes. "I wouldn't be on the row if it had just been some random dude. But I was in a car chase and they threw the road spikes out for me. I hit the cop when I swerved to try to avoid the spikes. It wasn't my fault. It was an accident."

Kradle nodded casually and crumbled a wad of dried sand in his fingers, but his mind was whirring. He'd heard that story. That was Frankie Buchanan's story. The guy had occupied the cell two down from Kradle's a few years earlier, and they'd exchanged origin stories, the way inmates did with anyone who lingered within earshot for a few months or more.

Kradle tried to tell himself that it was unlikely Homer had snatched the tale from Buchanan in the SHU and was now using it as a cover. More likely it was just a coincidence. It was a pretty common story. Kradle reminded himself that guys got into car chases. That cops threw out road spikes during those chases. That guys ran over cops. It happened. There was no reason to jump to conclusions. As long as Homer didn't say he was driving a stolen van filled with televisions, everything would be—

"See, I had all these flat-screen televisions," Homer said.

Kradle hung his head.

She walked into Kradle's cell and sat down on the rack, feeling the thin mattress compress and the steel bones of the bed dig into the backs of her thighs. Celine wondered where John Kradle was now, whether his sorry ass was riding in one of the cars stolen from the parking lot with a bunch of other scumbags, headed for Vegas, or if he was going to try to disappear into Utah or California. Celine knew the answer lay here, among his things, and she would do whatever she could to find that answer.

On the shelf by the desk, items were lined up in a single row. Envelopes organized into a cardboard shelving unit, a shaving mirror that reflected her worried, battered face, bottles of toiletries, and a stack of noodle packets a foot and a half high. Celine took the little handmade mail organizer and sat it in her lap. There were three sections labeled with marker. *Hate. Marriage. Lawyer.* She pulled out the papers in the thickest section, *Marriage,* and opened the first envelope. The writing was bulbous, juvenile, some of the ink pink and some of the i's dotted with little hearts.

> *Dear John,*
> *I read about you in the* Chicago Tribune. *I wanted to write and tell you that as soon as I saw your face in the picture, I felt a weird connection to you. My name is Debbie, and I think I can understand what you did.*

Celine's fingers gripped the paper unsteadily, as though they were numb. She skipped ahead through the letter.

> *Because if we got married, I could take care of you in there. I could send you commissary, books, whatever you want. I would understand you and come and visit you, and . . .*

Celine tore the letter to shreds and threw the pieces on the ground. She took another letter from the stack and pulled it open. A picture of a tubby woman in a lime-green bikini fell on the floor at her feet. She flicked the folded piece of notebook paper hard, so that it snapped open.

> *Have you heard that song, "I Knew I Loved You Before I Met You"? It's by Savage Garden. I've included the lyrics on the second page. John, that's how I feel about you. Please write back so we . . .*

Celine scrunched the letter into a ball and hurled it onto the floor. She shoved the organizer and the stacks of letters off her lap and onto the concrete. One letter remained on her lap, a small envelope slipped from the *Hate* folder. The paper was scrawled over with large, clumsy lettering in thick black marker.

You're a sick dirty fuck. Anyone who kills there own family has a special place in hell waitin for them. Kid killers are the worse kind of scum. Your gonna burn for eternity John Kradle. Fry fry fry. Scream scream scream.

Celine felt her heartbeat slow. She hadn't realized there were angry tears on her face until she heard a noise outside the cell and came back to herself, sitting there reading an inmate's mail. She swiped at her face and nose and went to the entrance, poked her head out.

"Hey," she called. The small, wiry man jolted at the sound of her voice. He was two cells down, looking at a notice on the wall, his hands clasped behind his back as if he were touring an art gallery. He pushed a pair of glasses up on his nose and adjusted the shirt of his uniform.

"Ma'am." He nodded.

"What are you doing here?"

"Oh, I, um . . ." He jerked a thumb behind him, but there was no one there. Celine and the man were alone on the row. Henderson had been taken to the infirmary and no other inmates under Celine's charge had been recovered yet. "Warden Slanter sent me just to, uh . . . You know. To check that everything is okay here."

Celine looked at the guy. There were prison tattoos crisscrossing his dark skin, the name *Kaylene* scrawled across his jugular. His guard's uniform had no name badge and was unbuttoned to the middle of his muscular chest. He was in his thirties, but looked slightly more worn than that. Celine sighed with exhaustion and put a hand on her baton.

"Put your hands on the wall, inmate," she said.

"Oh, damn." The guy slumped, dejected.

"You know you could get twenty-five years for impersonating a correctional officer." Celine took the cuffs off her belt as she walked toward the prisoner. "Where did you get the uniform?"

"When everybody ran out, a guard from my block left the door to the staff room open and I saw it hanging over a chair," the inmate said. "I think it's actually a lady's uniform."

"Well," Celine said, "there's going to be so much goddamn paperwork after today, and you've done such a terrible job of making like a guard anyhow, that I don't think I could bring myself to write this up."

"You're very kind, ma'am," the inmate said. He put his wrists out and Celine cuffed him.

"Who the hell are you?"

"I'm Walter Keeper. People call me ForKeeps, or just Keeps sometimes, if they're in a hurry." He brandished a tattoo on his wrist. 4KEEPZ.

"Where are you from?"

"Minimum." Keeps shrugged guiltily. "I'm scheduled for release tomorrow, so I wasn't going nowhere today. I was pretty tempted, though! I've been counting down the hours since last Wednesday. Got twenty-one hours to go. And that's not nothing."

"So to burn a few minutes you dressed up like a guard, thereby committing a felony, and came over here to death row?" Celine said. "You would have got less jail time for escaping than for—" She stopped, shook her head. Every now and then she found herself trying to explain to inmates the stupidity of their crimes, and had to remind herself it was a fruitless exercise. "Never mind."

"I just always wanted to see the row, that's all," Keeps reasoned. He looked around. "Figured it was the only chance I could get without killing somebody."

Celine smirked in spite of herself. She felt dried blood crackle at her temple.

"Well, this is it." She gestured to the corridor around her. "You had a good enough look?"

"Sure."

"Let's go, then." She took his arm. They walked down the hall, Keeps leaning forward and glancing into every cell as they went.

"Somebody pop you on the way out then, huh?" he asked.

"I got in a little tussle," Celine said. "I'm fine."

"You got all kinds of serial killers and shit up in here?"

"Not anymore."

"Man, this is some extraordinary business," Keeps said. He shook his head. "All those guys out there running around at the same time? I'm kind of glad I'm still in here where it's safe."

"The world is upside down today," Celine said.

"Inside out."

"Yeah, inside out."

"They'll be looking for an inside guy, right?"

Celine stopped walking. Keeps was peering into Henderson's cell, eyeing an unopened box of commissary sitting on the bunk.

"You know anything?"

"Nah, nah," Keeps said. "Just seems like something too big to organize from the outside, though. Too many chess pieces. You know what I'm saying?"

"Yeah." Celine nudged him on.

"Best way to catch a snoop is to send a snoop after him," Keeps said, sounding hopeful.

"Well, it won't be you. You'll be out of here legitimately in twenty hours and fifty-five minutes."

"Yeah, but I'm always looking for jail credit." Keeps shrugged. "Might be able to use the brownie points the next time I'm in."

"The next ti—Keeps, most inmates don't make plans for the next time they'll be in prison while they're packing their things to leave."

"I'm not most inmates," he said. "I'm what you call a 'forward-thinking man.'"

"Yeah, well, you provide some evidence of your usefulness to me, and I'll provide some evidence of my usefulness to you," Celine said.

"Okay, okay, okay, okay." Keeps nodded enthusiastically. "I can do that. All right, uh . . ."

They walked out into the yard while Keeps thought, chewing on his lip and staring at the ground as it passed beneath his feet.

"Oh, okay." He straightened. "Your guys on the row. They got the same kind of lighting system we got over there in minimum?"

"What do you mean?"

"In the cells," he said. "Like, on the wall. There's a long, thin, gold light behind, like, cloudy kind of Perspex?"

"Yeah."

"You might want to look into that."

"We do a check of the lights every time we shake down the cells." Celine rolled her eyes. "That's not the kind of intel I'm after."

"Maybe you ought to look *around* the lights." Keeps lifted his cuffed hands and tapped his nose. "You feel me?"

"You'll have to be more specific."

"Oh, damn, woman." He gave a huge sigh. "I'll snitch, but I'm not gonna paint you a picture and put it in a pretty frame and hang it on the wall for you."

Celine gave a little laugh.

"Those lights," Keeps continued, "they're an upgrade. Used to be, back in the day, guys had those fluorescent tubes in their cells, up in the ceiling."

"I remember those."

"Yeah. But they weren't halogen, so they cost more to run. And also they did a bunch of studies about those fluorescent lights, how they're bad for you. They hum and blink and mess with your brain. The scientists, they found out that if guys have gold light instead of white light they'll read more at night. More reading means smarter, less depressed, less angry guys. When they put the halogen strips in, they say violence went down, like, twenty-five percent or some shit."

"How do you know all this?" Celine asked.

"I read in my bunk at night. The *Times.*"

"Okay, Professor."

"So everybody's got a gold strip light above their bunk, right? But every time you add something into the prison, you weaken it. It's like if you . . . you bake a cake, and then you want to go and add something to the middle. Too bad. You got to cut the cake up. You got to bake stuff in for it to be right."

"You really like talking, huh."

"You told me to be more specific!"

"Find a middle ground," Celine said.

"Okay, okay. So when the contractors installed those lights, they were supposed to bury the wire in the concrete six inches back. That's the standard. But that's a lot of drilling, you know? Every cell in minimum, medium, maximum. That's hundreds of lights. Easier to just dig out a shallow channel, stick the wire in and smooth it over. So, take a look, and call me up if you find anything good."

"Okay," Celine said. "I'll call you up."

Celine walked Keeps back to minimum and locked him in a holding cell, then returned to the row. She went to John Kradle's cell and climbed onto his bunk again, standing and running her hands over the light set into the concrete wall.

Celine hadn't heard the light thing before, but she didn't dismiss it. Inmates had plenty of means of hiding things in their cells. They would fashion strings from strands of cotton taken from the bedding, attach them to watertight balloons made from commissary packaging, and float contraband items behind the U-bend in the toilet, retrieving the balloons on the string when they were needed. They would secret pieces of razor blades into the hems of their clothes or in the folds of their armpits and crotches, force tiny taped packages of drugs between the pages of their books, into cracks in the floor, into their anal cavities. Celine ran a hand over the wall beneath the light fixture, where she assumed the electrical wire was embedded. It was smooth, unbroken, uniform concrete.

She took a key from her belt and gouged the hard teeth across the surface of the wall. A tiny fleck of white appeared. Celine started digging around the fleck with the key. More white, fibrous material sprouted. She pulled the material away and broke it up in her fingers. Papier-mâché, probably constructed from wet toilet paper. It had been painted over with a murky gray dye, created, Celine guessed, from mop water or newspaper ink. Celine gouged out a section of the wall beneath the light until she could see the dull white plastic sheath in which the electrical cord that led to the light nestled in the concrete.

Lifting the cord carefully with her fingernail, she exposed a tiny slip of paper. She pulled it out, unfolded it, and looked at the writing.

Wagon Circle 18 m NE (7 h)
Willie McCool 16 m S (6 h)
Brandon Butte 17 m ENE (8 h)

Again, Celine thought she knew what she was looking at. She only needed to confirm it. She made to jump down from the bunk but noticed another piece of paper poking out further down the electricity wire beneath the light. Celine dug it out, leaving shreds of papier-mâché concrete to tumble onto her feet and John Kradle's bed.

This little secret package was wrapped tightly in tape. She had to walk back to the control room, rummage through the drawer full of confiscated items, and find a sliver of razor blade to open it with. With painstaking care she unrolled an oval of newspaper as big as a thumbprint. It was a picture. The images were of two faces.

A woman and a teenage boy.

CHAPTER 7

It was the first sunset Kradle had seen in five years, and it was a thick, dusty, tomato red. He was too tired to make much of it, though. He watched for a while, thinking about the sunsets over New Iberia, which were purple. In a decade he hadn't been active outside his cell for more than an hour a day, and he figured he'd walked for seven straight hours through the desert and up Sheep Peak to where he sat now. He lay down in the dark of the shallow cave and listened to Homer easing his big body down a few feet away. Keeping his back to the man was a struggle. With every sound Kradle felt as though the killer was coming for him. When Homer spoke it sent bolts of pain up through the bottom of his feet, into his bones.

"What are you thinking about?" Homer asked.

"Louisiana," Kradle said. He was so exhausted that uttering more than a word at a time seemed like a full-body effort he couldn't yet muster. He needed to conserve his energy, stay awake longer than Homer, slip away when the other man fell asleep.

"Hot there."

"Uh."

"Hot in here, too."

"Yep," Kradle sighed, and blew sand from the rocky surface by his cheek. "It'll cool down."

"If it gets real cold we'll have to share body heat."

"We're not doing that."

"You from the South? I thought I recognized the accent."

"Uh-huh."

"You going back there?"

"Yeah," Kradle said. Just saying it out loud seemed to give strength to the dreams crowding at the corners of his vision. The gentle rocking of his houseboat as tiny waves reached it across the huge, watery planes, made by distant airboats going by; gator hunters. Kradle sometimes fancied he could hear the rhythmic knocking of a reptilian spine against the hull of his vessel as the creatures rose and kissed it while gliding underneath. He heard the hammering of the rain on the windows. The wind in the swamp trees. Frog-gers calling out to each other in the dark.

"I'm going to Mexico," Homer said from a million miles away.

"Hmm?"

"Police force down there is not like it is up here."

Kradle tried to answer but there was a wire around his throat. A belt. A band. A thick, and thickening, blockage. No air in, no air out. He bucked hard, his hands flying up, grabbing at the band. It wasn't a band but Homer's hands, both of them, the thumbs locked over his windpipe, fingers gripping around the back of his neck, squeezing. Kradle's eyes were already bulging from the pressure on his jugular. He flailed wildly. Homer lowered his body and sat on Kradle's hips. Kradle's heels gouged the rocky floor of the cave.

"I'm sorry," Homer said gently. "I have to do this."

The shrimp skidded into the room like a Maltese terrier running for the open door of an old woman's house, eyes big and full of dreams of murder. Trinity barely glanced at her. She was conducting, as she had been when she first en-countered the woman, standing at the front of a room full of people, her arms held high, directing with skill and majesty. There were journalists from ten ma-jor stations, and their camera operators, filing into the small room off the chow hall. Trinity guessed it was a group meeting place for inmates. Lots of posters about alcoholism on the walls. Encouraging sentiments about taking it one day at a time, as if the morons who ended up here had enough working gray matter to delay gratification for an entire twenty-four-hour period. Addicts thought, and thereby predicted consequences, in fifteen-minute increments. Trinity knew this because she'd seen it—because she had three sisters who were all ice addicts and a brother dead in the ground, put there by Daniels, first name Jack.

"I know where he is," Celine said. "And I know where he's going."

"Who?" Trinity flapped her hand at a man who was trying to squeeze an additional mic into the huddle on the podium in front of her. "Back off, bozo. Can't you see this space is full?"

"John Kradle," Celine said.

"The wife-killer? Oh, please."

"This is a note I discovered in his cell." Celine unfolded a tiny strip of paper. "These are airfields. Walking distances and times. He's going to jump a plane back home to Mesquite. That's smart. If he flies, he'll bypass all the road blocks. And look. Look." She smoothed a fragment of what looked like gray newspaper on the papers lying on the podium.

"This is his wife and his son," Celine continued. "He hasn't let go. He's going back there to—"

"You're standing on my foot," Trinity said. She leaned in and spoke with her teeth locked. "And you're yapping in my ear while I'm trying to brief the nation on a crisis *you* took part in creating."

"But—"

Trinity brushed the fragment of whatever it was off the papers before her, snatched a sheet of paper from the stack and gave it to Celine. "You get up here when I call you, you read these lines, and then you sit back down and shut your trap."

"Listen, I want a team of—" Celine began.

"Ladies and gentlemen." Trinity smiled. All eyes and cameras in the room swung to her. Bright white lights warm on her features. She lifted her sharp chin, set her shoulders back. "We're going to begin. My name is Trinity Parker. I'm the United States Marshals Service major case director for the State of Nevada. I'll be outlining for you the current circumstances surrounding the breakout at Pronghorn Correctional Facility this morning."

Trinity stood with her hands flat on the podium, placed either side of her paperwork. Calmly and eloquently, she briefed the nation, probably the world, on the case. She made eye contact with every camera at least once. Took them through the response she had coordinated. The roadblocks, grid searches, flyovers, increased highway patrols, and doubled police manpower taking shape in Vegas.

"Volunteers are manning phones for tips and sightings," she said. "And I'm pleased to report that we have already recovered more than three dozen inmates, many of them medium and maximum security individuals hunted down by marshals and sheriffs. Inmates are *streaming* back into the facility by the minute. This situation is under control and will soon be completely neutralized."

She nodded to some nameless prison staffer standing in the corner by the projector, and a slide replaced the US Marshals' crest on the wall behind her. As she glanced around, she saw Celine Osbourne returning to the room from the chow hall.

"We have categorized our top-priority fugitives by their crimes." Trinity gestured to the four faces displayed on the slide above her. "These men, our Ace Card inmates, are all death row inmates. So, for that reason, I'm going to hand you over to Captain Celine Osbourne, supervisor of the condemned row section of this facility. Captain Osbourne?"

Trinity gestured, leveled her eyes at the woman. Celine walked up and took the podium. There was an audible ripple through the room, gasps and murmurs about her battered face.

"My name is Captain Celine Osbourne, and I am the supervisor of the condemned prisoners' row," Celine read from the pages she had been provided. "I am working with the US Marshals' department to recover inmates released from the facility this morning, having already single-handedly subdued and recontained a violent and highly dangerous inmate after he esca— Well, that's not exactly true . . ."

Celine looked up. Trinity, who had taken her place by the door, tried to communicate through her eyes all of her raw, hellcat-furious determination not to take even a teaspoon of shit from this woman in front of the world's media. It seemed to work. Celine went back to the paper. She read ahead for a moment.

Then shoved the paper aside.

"Let's get this done quickly," she said.

Trinity ground her teeth.

"This guy." Celine pointed at the wall above her, at the face of an elderly man with high, rigid cheekbones. "That's Walter John Marco. He's that kid-killer sicko from down Hackberry way. You remember that guy. Or maybe your parents remember. Anyway, the guy's eighty-one years old now. If anybody from the Marshals' office had asked me, I wouldn't have put him as Ace of Hearts. The guy can't open a can of tuna by himself and without his heart medication he'll keel over in, oh"—she glanced at her watch—"about eight hours' time."

There was a little titter of laughter throughout the room, cautious glances thrown Trinity's way. She gave a tight smile.

"These next two guys actually are pretty dangerous," Celine said, pointing. "Burke David Schmitz. The Mardi Gras Shooter. Opened up an AR-15 on crowds on the intersection of Loyola Avenue and Poydras Street in New Orleans in 2006, fled here to Nevada. Then you've got Abdul Ansar Hamsi. Failed Flamingo Hotel bomber. Plotted to blow up the casino back in 2015 when it was packed full for a World Poker Tournament. Would have killed hundreds if he'd wired the timing system on the bombs right. But terrorists aren't known for their intelligence."

Celine was working the room. The journalists were writing notes furiously, smiling all the way. Trinity couldn't believe it. She had initially been so stunned by the performance she didn't even consider putting an end to it. But she could see the shrimp was just getting started. Trinity started pushing through the crowd by the door, back toward the podium.

"Homer Carrington is the North Nevada Strangler." Celine pointed. "Now he is highly dangerous. Clever, deceptive. Comes off very friendly. He's been convicted of killing ten people, but I'd say he's got more under his belt that we don't know about." Celine glanced Trinity's way. "Homer is tricky. He made up a bunch of ruses to get his victims. Faked car trouble on the highway. Knocked on doors at night and asked to use the phone to report an accident. Pretended to have found an injured kitten in a back alley."

A cameraman stepped in front of Trinity, blocking her path. She poked him in a love handle.

"Move it. Coming through."

"Those are your Aces." Celine took a big piece of paper from her bra. She unfolded it in front of the crowd. "Now let me introduce the Joker card."

Blackness. Black creeping in from the edges of his vision, slowly consuming the red, the sweeping grip of unconsciousness taking hold over the pain. Homer's eyes were bearing down on Kradle, at once completely focused on him and distant, dreaming, surveying landscapes of pleasure as the pain shot through his victim's face. Just when John Kradle thought he was going to die, going to surrender to the blackness, Homer eased the pressure off his windpipe.

"Take a sip," the big man whispered. "That's it."

Kradle gasped a half-lungful of air, and then the band was tightened around his throat and he was kicking and clawing and struggling again, the pain somehow tenfold now that he had more air in his lungs.

"I've got to do this." Homer was speaking to him and yet at the same time not, mumbling to himself. "I'm so sorry. It's just something that I do some-times. I can't help it."

Kradle tried to focus through the screaming panic in his mind. He knew another sip of air must be coming. Homer had prolonged the strangulation three times already. Kradle couldn't hold out forever. Homer bowed his head, eased the pressure off gently. Kradle forced himself to resist the urge to draw breath, to push breath out instead, against the will of every inch of his being.

"Listen—" Kradle squeaked.

Homer squeezed. Kradle struggled. He could feel the bigger man's cock through his jeans, pressed against his thigh. It was hard. Kradle scratched helplessly at his killer's hands.

The next sip came. Kradle sucked in the air and blew it straight back out with a word.

"Money!" Kradle yelped.

Homer's head twitched. For a full second, a period of time that echoed for a thousand years in Kradle's soul, Homer kept the pressure on. Then curios-ity got the better of him, as Kradle hoped it would. The hands around his throat loosened completely.

Kradle rolled over, curled into a ball, coughed and coughed until he retched and emptied his stomach. He clung to the ground, gasping short, desperate breaths, his entire body shaking, head pulsing as blood rushed back into his brain.

"What money?" Homer said.

"I have money," Kradle managed, between long gasps for air. "Millions. I. Have. Millions."

Homer was on his knees only a foot or two away. Kradle wasn't safe yet. He was making his case. The big man would listen, and if he didn't convince him now that he was someone Homer should keep alive, Kradle knew the bone-chilling grasp of the other man's hands would come again before he could gather the strength to fight him off. He grabbed two handfuls of sand from the floor of the cave, but knew that even if Homer attacked him again and he managed to blind his attacker, he'd never outrun the guy. Not like this. Kradle had thirty seconds to come up with something. Something life-saving.

"I'm not a serial killer," Kradle said.

"Okay," Homer said slowly.

"I told you that to try to sound scary. I'm really a . . . I killed my wife and my kid."

Homer said nothing. He was watching, his hands on his knees, eyes wide.

"She found out that I . . ." Kradle sucked in air. "I was doing some work for the, uh . . . the mob. I had a stack of cash. A lot of cash. I'd walled it up in the garage at my home in Mesquite. She found out, and I killed her and the kid."

"Why did you—"

"It's a long story." Kradle held a hand up. "But the cash is still there. That's where I'm going. If you let me live, I'll give you half. You're going to need money. Think about it. Mexico. Freedom. Real freedom. How are you going to do that? You need money. You need me."

Homer was still as a stone, calculating, those big, deadly hands and long, thick fingers gripping his knees. Kradle couldn't look at them. Couldn't make eye contact while he tried to splutter a convincing stream of bullshit to his executioner as the guillotine blade inched down. Kradle couldn't tell if the story he'd grasped out of thin air, inspired by nothing more than having watched Martin Scorsese's *Goodfellas* on TV in his cell the night before, was doing the job. When Homer burst into tears, his confusion only deepened.

Kradle sat, rubbing his throat, watching the bigger man sob.

"I am so, so sorry," Homer managed.

"It's okay."

"No, it's not," Homer said. "I have this thing. I just . . . It comes over me. You could have died. I'm so sorry. There's no way I can tell you how sorry I am, buddy. Oh, man. I fucked up. Oh, man."

"Homer, it's fine. Let's forget about it."

"I've been doing it since I was a kid, hurting people like that." Homer sighed. "I knew it was wrong but I couldn't help it. I didn't know what I was doing. I blacked out. It's not my fault, really."

"I know," Kradle said carefully. "It's not your fault."

Homer dragged him into a hug. Kradle sat, rigid, his face crushed against the other man's warm chest, his stomach roiling and twisting, making audible gurgles of protest. Because he was under no illusion that Homer had been in anything other than full control throughout the strangulation. The big killer had been tasting every minute of Kradle's suffering, lapping it up. Kradle had seen it in his eyes, the way he set the pleasure aside deliberately at the mention of something possibly more gratifying: cash.

Kradle had known plenty of men like Homer in the can. Predatory pleasure-seekers. Homer was always on the lookout for something to be gained, and, luckily for Kradle, the thought of money had trumped the momentary physical pleasure of killing a stranger in a cave in the desert. Kradle got lucky. Homer was one of those very rare, very dangerous monsters who could forgo present physical satisfaction for future, less bodily satisfaction. Wait now, benefit later. Banking on Homer being a more sophisticated kind of psychopath than the average killer was the only thing that had saved John Kradle's life.

"I'm so sorry," Homer moaned. "Friends don't do that to each other!"

"Don't worry about it," Kradle managed. "Buddy."

They parted. Homer wiped his nose on his sleeve and dragged himself to his feet, grabbing the pillowcase that held all of Kradle's supplies and slinging it over his shoulder. "Guess we better go."

"Yeah." Kradle let Homer pull him up. "It's not far to the airfield."

They left the cave. Kradle saw a sliver of Homer's face in the moonlight, and noted there wasn't a single tear on his face.

CHAPTER 8

Lionel McCrabbin took the booth in the corner of the diner, his back to the wall by the bathrooms, because he'd read in novels about guys doing that so they could see any trouble approaching. He could hear the hand dryers in the restrooms, smell floor cleaner, and probably piss, if he tried. But a guy had to protect his family. His wife and daughter huddled into the bench across from him. He flagged down the waitress.

It was six hours since he'd watched the breakout on the computer monitor in his little office on Fremont Street. Night was crowding in. Outside the diner's grimy windows, in a lot jammed with cars sporting MAGA bumper stickers and dents from drunken sideswipes, his shiny Jaguar bulged with suitcases.

"How long do we have to stay here?" Deseree was watching the doors of the motel across the road, where groups of men in ball caps lingered, smoking and talking rapidly on burner phones. "This is so insane. We should have just stayed home."

"I've got thirteen former clients from Pronghorn," Lionel said, tapping the sheet of paper on the table before him with a sweaty finger. "Four of them are from maximum security. I'm talking about very, very bad guys, Des. Rapists. Murderers. I want the both of you to look at these photos. Look at the names. These are the guys we have to watch out for. If you see *any* of these men—"

"If you had only listened to me when you graduated law school, you wouldn't have rapists and murderers on your client list." Hannah took the paper and flicked it lazily, let her eyes wander over the faces there. "I wanted you to go into finance. How many embezzlers and inside traders do you see breaking out of prison and going to seek revenge on their former lawyers?"

"That's not helpful," Lionel snapped. The waitress came, and he struggled over the huge laminated menu, pointed to something. His collar was cutting into his throat. He unbuttoned it with difficulty.

"Daddy, this isn't right. Look at the place." Deseree was still focused on the motel, eyes narrowed. "We're going to get stabbed in our beds by drug dealers before any of your old clients have a chance to show up."

"I'll call the Monte Carlo." Hannah took out her cell phone. "Stanley will take care of us."

"Stanley the concierge is not taking care of you," Lionel said. "*I'm* taking care of you. We have to stay somewhere they wouldn't expect to find us." Lionel pushed down the hand holding her phone, trapping the device on the table. "I'm serious, girls. Okay? You know I always tell you not to worry. Well, now I'm saying it's time to worry. Worry hard. See this guy here? Ray Bakerfield?" Lionel tapped the paper. "I took a dive on that case, and he knew it. This guy went to prison so I could buy you that Cartier watch for our anniversary. If he finds me he's going to stick a hot poker up my ass, just like he did to his wife."

"Daddy!"

"Jesus, Lionel!"

"I'm not kidding." Lionel felt that his eyes were wide, bulging with terror, but he couldn't do anything about it. "We're in trouble here. But if we keep our heads down, play this smart, we'll be—"

He was going to say "fine." But Lionel McCrabbin had known his whole career never to say "fine," or even to plan to say it, because the second that cursed word came into his brain, the universe snuffled it out like a pig hunting around tree stumps for truffles; the slobbering, hungry, rabid, foaming universe then conspired to make life anything but. Just as his mouth went to form the word, the back door of the diner slammed open—the door just to the right of the men's room, down the short hall beside their booth—and the room was flooded with guys in prison denims. Lionel's heart sank. He watched some asshole in the booth by the front doors rise and hustle his family out in the seconds before the escapees took charge of the space.

"Nobody move! Nobody fucking move!"

One of the guys who passed Lionel and his family was carrying a huge silver revolver that still had a price tag hanging off it. He and Deseree and Hannah put their hands on the tabletop, as if they'd been robbed before, which of course they hadn't. Lionel swept the paper with the photographs onto the seat beside him with his thumb, then shifted over so that he was sitting on top of it.

"Wallets, phones, jewelry! Put 'em in the bags! Now, bitch! Now now now!"

"Oh, god." Hannah was frantically trying to work her Cartier watch off her wrist and into her bra before any of the guys came back. "Are they yours? Are any of these guys yours?"

Lionel felt his heartbeat throbbing in his ears. He looked at the men commanding the diner, crowding terrified patrons into their booths while a young, skinny guy held out a pillowcase for goods. A toddler in the next booth was red-faced and screaming. The robber by the counter was having trouble with the till, berating the waitress, slamming his gun on the top of the machine. It was all too much movement, too much noise. Lionel clutched at his throat and swiped at his sweat-matted hair.

"Uh, I-I-I don't know," he stammered. He looked again. "No. No. None of them are mine. They're too young. They're all too young. Just keep your heads down, girls. Keep your mouths shut. Do what they say."

"Yo, pig man." The skinny guy with the pillowcase was suddenly at their booth, panting behind a bandana that was tied around his nose and mouth. "Money. Now."

Lionel tossed his wallet and watch into the bag. Deseree threw in everything she had: necklace, purse, phone, even her Bishop Gorman class ring. Hannah threw in her phone and purse and looked the young man in the bandana right in the eyes.

"That's all I have," Hannah said.

Lionel shook his head. He couldn't help it. If she'd just listened to *him*, this time. If she'd just been quiet, like he said, maybe the man in the dusty, reeking prison denims wouldn't have looked over her curiously, spied the clasp of the watch poking out from between her expensive, too-widely-spaced breasts.

The guy reached for his wife's breasts. Lionel, in turn, reached for him, because he had no choice—because a guy had to protect his family. He put a hand out for the man's forearm, gripped it gently, uttered something pitiful, like "Please" or "Don't," but it was something. He did something.

There were men on him immediately, ripping him from the booth, slamming him into the stainless steel countertop, kicking him in the chest. The paper with the photographs fluttered into the fray slowly, artfully, like Forrest Gump's fucking feather, and someone snatched it up, and Lionel couldn't see for the red-hot pain clouding his vision.

"Yo, Bricks. Check this out, man."

"Oh, shit. Big Baby Ray is on here."

"You a cop, bro?"

Someone kicked Lionel in the balls. He couldn't speak.

"He's a lawyer!" Deseree was screaming. "Leave him alone! He's just a lawyer!"

Lionel felt the atmosphere change. Even the toddler had stopped screaming. He begged the universe to give him something. The sound of a siren. Commotion, trouble, at the other end of the diner. But it was all on him. He was in a silent bubble of doom, and nothing was going to get him out of it now.

"Dude . . . You Ray Bakerfield's deadbeat lawyer?" someone asked.

A spray of gunshots. Lionel curled into a ball, held his skull, braced every muscle in his body in anticipation. His teeth cracked and ground as he clenched his jaw. His eyes ached as he squeezed them shut. But when the firing stopped there was no pain. Only the thundering of footsteps.

Four of the robbers lay sprawled around him on the sticky linoleum floor of the deli. One of them had collapsed over the counter, legs death-twitching, making the tips of his rubber shoes squeak on the floor. Lionel watched as two guys, also in prison denims, marched into the diner from the parking lot, where they had opened fire through the big windows. The two new guys lowered their rifles, scooped up the guns and the bag of goodies from the bodies of their rivals, and walked out the back door into the street.

Celine held the picture of John Kradle aloft for the cameras. She flattened it against her chest, smoothed it out, held it up again, made sure everybody got a good look.

"We have reason to believe that John Kradle plans violence out there. He may be headed for Mesquite, his home town. Any information leading to the capture of this man will be greatly appreciated by law enforcement. Thanks very much."

She folded the paper and walked off the stage as the crowd erupted into questions. Celine expected Trinity Parker to follow her out into the hall, but she didn't expect the lanky, sharp-faced streak of a woman to grab her by the shoulder and shove her into the wall.

"What the hell is your problem?" Trinity was so mad she was spitting on Celine's face. "Are you mentally defective? You just completely hijacked the world's biggest manhunt."

"I'm having a busy day, aren't I?"

"Here's what you don't understand." Trinity glanced down the hall. They were alone. She took a long breath, let it out slow. Then she sucker-punched Celine in the guts.

The smaller woman went down. Trinity crouched so that they were at eye level. "I'm in charge here. You desert people are simple. I get it. So I'm going to make it as plain for you as I can, okay? Listen carefully. *I. Am. In. Charge. Here.*"

"You need me," Celine said. Her words were coming out in strained groans. "You're not going to catch these guys without me."

"Right. So I need you to get that little hick brain of yours straight on how this works." Trinity tapped Celine's head with her knuckle, hard. "I choose the priority inmates. We don't redirect the public awareness away from the terrorists to chase after your small-fry targets. You want to catch Kradle, you do it on your own time."

Celine's face was burning with shame.

"Go home," Trinity said. "Get a couple of hours' rest. Come back with your head screwed on."

Celine listened to the footfall of Trinity's heels as she walked away.

CHAPTER 9

They waited at the edge of the airfield, crouched in the darkness. The heat of the day had dissipated as they left the mountains, diminishing to a bone-chilling cold, then warming again before long. They'd walked empty streets, crossed dusty fields, presenting a mild curiosity to horses standing at rotting, sunbaked fences. Kradle saw one person, who watched them through the windows of a little brick house, a hand clutched against a curtain. He was sure the news would be flooded with coverage of the breakout, and, in their prison denims, he and Homer would be an unnerving sight as they moved by. No opportunities to steal new clothes presented themselves. Homer saw a string of washing hanging on a line, but closer inspection revealed only babies' socks and ladies' underwear.

When they reached their destination, John Kradle and Homer Carrington crouched, watching the single squat white stucco building that represented the headquarters of the Wagon Circle airfield north of Las Vegas. The parking lot was empty, tumbleweeds shivering against the rusty wire that marked its perimeter.

"What are we going to do for a pilot?"

"We don't need a pilot. I can fly," Kradle said.

"Whoa. Really?"

"I did some odd jobs when I was a kid in Louisiana." Kradle rubbed his throat. It felt like it was full of sand and splinters of glass. "Crop dusting. I used to take my boss's plane to visit a girl in Pierre Par. And the mob, too. I, uh—I would fly cash down to Mexico now and then for the bosses."

"So what are we waiting for, then? Why don't we go in now while nobody's there?"

"Because we'll need someone to open the safe," Kradle said. "The keys to all the aircraft in the hangar will be in a safe in the office. It's not like stealing a car. Not after 9/11."

"Are you going to know how to fly these things?" Homer pointed to the hangar. "You've been in the can."

"Nothing much changes in small aircraft. The basics remain the same."

Homer sat back on his haunches. "John, you must be the coolest friend I've had in ten years."

"Is that how long you were in Pronghorn?"

"No. I told you, I've only been there a week." Homer scratched his brow to hide his eyes. "I ran over a cop."

"I don't think that's true, Homer." Kradle was speaking without meaning to. The words tumbled out of him. Maybe he was concussed from the shortage of oxygen to his brain. He knew he was poking a bear, and yet couldn't put the stick down.

"Are you calling me a liar?" Homer asked.

"You said you'd been hurting people like that since you were a kid," Kradle said, for some reason. "You almost killed me back there. I get the feeling . . ." He finally managed to shut off the words.

"You get the feeling that I'm a killer," Homer finished for him. "A real killer."

Kradle looked at him. Homer chewed his lips.

"Jesus, don't cry again," Kradle said.

"I can't help it. I feel bad. I'm not like you, John. When I've killed before, it wasn't for business." Homer put a hand on his heart, rubbed his sweat-stiff shirt as if he was soothing a pain. "They were all accidents, those people. I didn't know what I was doing, and then it was too late. I think it's because I started young, you know?" He sniffed. "I got into the habit. I got addicted. Then I couldn't stop doing it."

"How young are we talking?"

"Eight maybe?"

Kradle picked grass, tried to keep his features neutral.

"She was a girl who lived up the street," Homer said. "Carol? Carly? I think it was Carly. Doesn't matter. She had this pretty blue scarf with white polka dots. I used that."

"We can stop talking about this now."

"This is what people don't understand. Being an extreme empath, as I am," Homer continued, his hand on his chest, "every kill hurts me worse than anybody else. It's like, I have to be the one to feel everyone's suffering. Not only my victim's suffering but their parents' and their friends' and everybody around them. Because I did it. I'm at the center. It was me and the victim, and now it's just me left behind to take the brunt of what I did. So I've got to hurt for everybody. You know what I mean?"

"I do."

"And that's hard, you know?"

"So hard," Kradle agreed.

"Some people would call me brave just for bearing it," Homer said. He drew a long, shuddering breath, his gray eyes fixed on the building across the plain. The two men watched a car roll into the parking lot, the sound of the tires popping on the gravel reaching them where they hid.

"So we take out this guy, get the keys, and we're gone." Homer put out a fist. Kradle reluctantly bumped it with his own.

"Sounds like a plan," Kradle said. "But, look. Why don't you let me get the guy. I know what I'm looking for. You keep a lookout from the hangar."

Homer grinned and slapped Kradle's back, rising and jogging low across the perimeter in the direction of the hangars. Kradle watched the killer go, then ran off toward the car taking its place in the lot.

The guy was old. Small. The kind of man who tucked neatly into the passenger seat of light aircraft, who walked under wings to inspect rivets in ailerons without having to double over. The kind of man whose windpipe Homer Carrington would crush like a straw in his fist.

Kradle followed the old guy from his car to the building and stood in the shadows, waiting for him to unlock the door, thinking about how birdlike the people who hung around planes could be—like dog people who ended up looking like their pets, or subconsciously chose pets who looked like them, whatever the situation was. Kradle hadn't seen a dog in five years. Nervous thoughts like this fluttered through his tired brain as the man opened the door. Kradle stepped forward, tightly focused on his task and yet fighting the urge to be distracted, to not do the terrible, terrible thing he was about to do.

"Jesus!" The old man stepped back, spying Kradle's reflection in the glass door just as he pushed it open. He gave a startled laugh. "I didn't see you, I—"

"I'm sorry." Kradle grabbed a handful of the man's shirt. He realized with horror that the words that were coming out of him were the same ones Homer had spoken to him in the cave as his fingers wound around John's throat. "I'm really sorry. I've got to do this."

The guy went rigid. Kradle had seen people do that before. Freeze up. Lock down. He'd been in jail in Mesquite before he was sentenced, and some junkie psycho had taken offense to the way another inmate was looking at him across the shower room. He'd beaten the guy to death right there on the tiles, and the officer who had been allocated to the pod hadn't been ready for it. He'd been on the job for less than a month and had just frozen up and huddled into a corner of the room, watching the beating with eyes big, howling.

Kradle marched the airfield supervisor into the cluttered office behind the reception desk and sat him in a desk chair he found there.

"I'm not going to hurt you," Kradle said, knowing that these were the wrong words—the words robbers and killers spoke in movies before they shot you—but not knowing what else to say. "I just want the keys to a plane."

"Okay," the old guy said. "Okay. Okay. Okay."

He didn't do anything. Just sat there, staring at the floor, probably figuring Kradle might not kill him if he didn't look at his face. His fists were balled, clutched against his crotch. Head down. Arms locked in. True terror. The body protecting all its vital organs. Kradle didn't even have a weapon. He didn't need one. This guy had seen the news, had probably been glued to it.

"Open the safe and get me the keys."

"Okay," the man said.

"Get up. Do it."

"Okay." The guy finally moved, stiffly, as if he was wounded. "Please don't hurt me. I have a wife. Her name's Betty. I'm Roger, and—"

"I'm not going to hurt you. I don't want to know your name. This isn't . . . You don't have to convince me."

Kradle wanted to say so much more. That he didn't hurt people. That he'd never hurt anyone. That the whole goddamn reason he was standing there scaring the life out of an innocent stranger in an airfield in the middle of no-where was *because* he'd never hurt anyone, and if he could just prove that he could go home. Not back to Mesquite, but all the way home, back to the little houseboat in the swamps, with the rain and the wild green avenues through the weeds, the huge blue skies hard as glass. Back before Christine, before Mason, before Audrey, before he stood over their bodies lying sprawled in blood on the floor of his home.

Focus, he told himself. *Focus.*

He switched on a small gray television set that sat on a desk at the side of the room as the shaking, panting old man unlocked the safe. When the screen awakened, he saw his own face. His eyes. A folded piece of paper. Celine Osbourne was showing his photograph, her mouth twisted and mean.

"We have reason to believe that John Kradle plans violence out there . . ."

"What the fuck?" Kradle breathed.

"Any information leading to the capture of this man . . ."

The old man was standing, holding a fistful of keys, looking at Kradle's image on the television set. Kradle took the keys from him and stuffed them into his pocket.

"You got a cell phone?" Kradle asked.

CHAPTER 10

Celine pushed open the door of the bar and found the timeless portal she'd been searching for. Here, it wasn't early, lightless morning. It wasn't Day Two of the worst thing that had happened in Celine's career. It was just a darkened bar, and inside she found about a dozen other Pronghorn employees taking advantage of the refuge from misery, where they could drink away their memories of the past twenty-four hours while the rest of the world headed to breakfast.

Celine took the stool next to Warden Grace Slanter and pulled it close to the bar. When the bartender brought her a glass of wine, Celine drew in a long, deep sip and felt microscopically relieved. Warden Slanter hardly acknowledged her presence. Grace's fingers were shaking as she pulled a cigarette from a cloudy brass container and stuck it between her lips. She took a matching brass lighter from her breast pocket and flipped the grinder a few times, unsuccessfully. Eventually the young bartender, a woman with a shaved skull tattooed all over with purple flowers, came and lit the warden's smoke with a match.

"I'm sixty-five," Grace said, as though they'd been talking for hours already. "That Trinity Parker woman didn't say it, but there's no denying it. That's old. But I'm not your average sixty-five-year-old. I can still put my ankles behind my head, same as I could when I was fifteen."

Celine choked on her wine. Grace didn't notice.

"But sixty-five is old in the public eye," she continued. "You get to my age, you're supposed to be raising grandchildren and pruning pimpernels."

"What?"

"It's a flower."

"I'm more of a cactus person."

"I'm old, I'm a woman, and I'm Haitian," Grace said. "So there are multiple groups of people out there relying on me to not look like the world's biggest fuck-up at the end of all this. Parker was right about one thing: it's all on me. I want to bring some of those guys home and save face, and I also want to show up Ms. Thing for underestimating me."

"All right. Good." Celine took the piece of paper she'd confiscated from Kradle's cell and smoothed it out on the bar top. "We start here. I found this in John Kradle's cell this morning. These are airfields. I think—no, I'm certain Kradle would have spent the day walking to one of these."

"Wagon Circle." Grace put a finger on the paper. "We can drive there. Forty minutes, maybe."

"No point," Celine said. "We don't know if he's headed there, or if he's at Willie McCool or Brandon. He might have been and gone already, especially if he caught a ride. I looked at the CCTV. He left by the back, walking north, but that doesn't mean anything. In any case, I know where he's going. He's going to Mesquite."

"Why?"

"These guys who kill their families, it's all about ego for them. He wants to go back to his own territory. Back to where the most meaningful thing he ever did in his whole miserable fucking life happened," Celine said. "There are plenty of targets for him there. The lawyer who represented him. His prosecutor. His in-laws. The neighbor and friends who testified in his trial. This is not over for Kradle."

"So what can we do?"

"I've called in the Mesquite cops," Celine said. "They're overrun, but they had a little time for me, being a fellow law enforcement officer. The chief said they're going to station some guys at a couple of the airfields nearby, wait for the plane to come in. I figure we go there once they've grabbed him, bring him home naked and hogtied to a pole like we're leading the village to a roast."

"Great image." Grace nodded, blew smoke across her whiskey glass and sipped it. The two women looked around the bar at tables of Pronghorn guards and other workers. Celine could feel the tension in the atmosphere. Even though there were officers in the dim, smoky room who had personally surrendered to the demands of the caller—Mike Genner from tower six playing pool by the men's room, Susan Besk tearing a coaster to shreds as she sat at the end of the bar—it was Grace who was getting the nasty sidelong glances. Grace's leg was jogging furiously, her knee knocking against the underside of the bar.

"So you're pretty sure Kradle was behind all this?" she asked Celine.

"What?" Celine looked at her boss. "No. I mean, that's obvious. It's got to be Schmitz or Hamsi, right? Only one of them would have the kind of resources to pull something like this off."

"Wait, so why the hell are we talking about this Kradle guy?" Grace gestured to the paper. "Who is he?"

"He's the family killer."

"Oh, lord no." Grace leaned back on her stool. "Celine, I'm talking about going for the organizer. The motherfucker who called me this morning. I want to get hold of him and the inmate he wanted released. I want to get them before Parker does."

"Yeah, sure. You want to go for the top dog. Undo it all. Be the redeemed hero."

"That's right." Grace slammed her empty glass down.

"So it's personal."

"It is."

"Well, if you want to work on that, we've got to work on this, too, goddamn it, or I'm out." She tapped the paper.

"Why?"

"You know why," Celine snapped.

Grace looked away. Celine saw something in her eyes, a subdued horror, that she'd witnessed in the eyes of just about everyone who had heard her story over the years. Pictures were swimming in Grace's mind. The bare imaginings possible for someone who had not experienced what Celine had.

"Because it's personal," Grace concluded.

The tattooed bartender topped up Celine's glass with a splash of dark, cheap wine. A gnat almost immediately kamikazed into the glass. Celine fished it out and flicked it away.

"Okay. We've got to wait on Kradle," Grace said. "If you're right, he's in the air or soon to be so. So let's talk Hamsi and Schmitz."

Celine put her elbows on the bar and cradled her face in her hands. Her jaw ached from grinding her molars all day and night. Her mind wanted to turn toward home, to her shower, her bed. She turned it instead to Abdul Hamsi, the quiet, neat man who occupied the cell seven down from the control room on death row. She could see the bare shelf over the little iron desk, the legal papers stacked in a box under the bunk. He was the only inmate on Celine's row who hadn't decorated his cell with any photographs or pictures of people. John Kradle had been forbidden to keep images of his victims, but he'd at least propped a Christmas card from his lawyer above his bed: a picture of Conan O'Brien in a Santa suit.

"It's not Hamsi," Celine said finally.

"Why do you say that?"

"Because the guy's a loser." She blurted out the words, working on instinct, too tired to measure what she was saying. "His own lawyer thinks so."

Grace raised an eyebrow. "It's death row. Aren't they all losers?"

"Look, I approve the visitors for these guys, right?" Celine said. "Every inmate has a lawyer. Even the serial killers. Even the guys who are flat out of appeals. An inmate might sit on the row for fourteen years, and in that time he'll probably sue the prison a dozen times for being issued a crumbled cookie, or because he got a paper cut on prison stationery. I know Hamsi's lawyer. Known him for years," Celine said. "He's a guy named May. And he's *that* kind of lawyer, the one who'll take a child killer's claim for two hundred bucks' compensation because he cut his toe on a sharp tile in the shower room. He'll work the claim so he can get his ten percent."

"Okay," Grace said. She didn't sound convinced. "So May, a clear deadbeat, thinks Hamsi's a loser. How does that help us?"

"Because if Hamsi was an important ISIS terrorist, he'd have a good lawyer," Celine said. "His associates would have paid to rush through his appeals. He'd be suing the prison at every opportunity, trying to get himself moved somewhere cushy by being a nuisance. May or someone better would be there at the prison for him every day, seeing what he needs, passing messages."

"And May's not doing that?"

"No," Celine said. "May doesn't even answer Hamsi's calls."

"So ISIS or Al-Qaeda or whoever sent Hamsi out to bomb the Flamingo Casino has abandoned him?" Grace snorted. "Tragic."

"Maybe." Celine shrugged. "Or maybe they never sent him."

"I thought ISIS claimed responsibility for it, though," Grace said. She had taken out her phone and was tapping through internet search results for Hamsi. Celine glimpsed familiar images from the time of the failed bombing. Crowds evacuating the casino. People crying in the street. Duffel bags being approached by bomb specialists in huge, puffy green suits. "They said they wanted to kill infidels in a hotbed of gambling and debauchery. I remember. I'd been at the Flamingo the week before for a girls' weekend."

"I reckon they just claim responsibility for everything," Celine said. "Even for failed attacks. Any publicity is good publicity. They want you to think they can get that close to killing hundreds, even if their guy stumbled at the finish line. No—if I had to guess, based on how lonely Hamsi is, I'd say he was just a pathetic no-hoper who watched a few recruitment videos, read *Bomb Making for Dumbasses* and thought he'd give his life some meaning. Hamsi doesn't even order commissary. He eats the prison food. Most people wouldn't feed their dog that garbage."

"Hey"—Grace looked up from her drink—"I approved the winter menu myself."

"You tasted it, or you looked at a list on a piece of paper?"

Grace said nothing.

"Sorry, boss," Celine said. "One of the C Block lieutenants got drunk and ate a chunk of nutraloaf on a dare at the Christmas party last year. He found a whole human fingernail in it."

"Oh, Jesus." Grace covered her eyes. "This is all my fault."

"Oh, come on. The food's meant to be bad. It's prison, not the Ritz."

"It's not just that. It's the whole thing," Grace said. "I don't know who's in my prison. I don't know my family killers from my terrorists. I don't know what these guys are eating. What my staff are doing. What we're trained for and what we're not."

Two guards standing at the bar smirked, obviously eavesdropping. Celine glared back at them.

"You couldn't train anyone for what happened yesterday," she said loudly.

Grace held her head in her hands. "The past five years or so it's been all about numbers on paper. Inmates in and inmates out. Safety checks, dental programs, minimum staff to inmate ratios, goddamn waste disposal and energy incentives. I've got to keep the prison population above six hundred and six inmates at all times or I lose my laundry allowance. In February, I delayed a guy's release by a day so that two hundred other guys could have clean underpants that week."

Celine didn't know what to say, so she said nothing.

"He lost a day of his life because management were beating my ass down about the budget." Grace stared at herself in the mirror behind the bar. "I've thought about that guy maybe a dozen times since. I don't even remember his name. But I remember I cost him a day of his life."

Celine's phone buzzed in her pocket. She didn't recognize the number, figured it was probably a journalist. She tucked the phone away.

"Don't let it be Schmitz who's behind this," Grace said. She shook her head sadly. "I don't know everybody on the row, but I know that guy."

Celine pictured Schmitz the last time she had really looked at him; stopped to check all was well in his cell rather than just breezing by, trying to avoid him, the way a person does when they notice a spider in their bathroom but before they are prepared to do anything about it. She'd taken the late shift last night to cover for a staff member who needed to go home to be with a sick baby. She remembered she'd cautioned Kowalski about his television being too loud. Took a towel Kradle had hung over the middle bar on his cell door and threw it at him. Ten cells up the row, she'd passed Schmitz's cell. He'd been sitting on the end of his bed, staring at the floor, hands between his knees. The mass killer's close-cropped blond hair had been sparkling in the night lights in the corridor, as if he'd just rinsed his head in the sink. There had been a shoebox on the desk.

"He packed his things," Celine said.

"Hmm?" Grace looked to be on the edge of drunkenness, her eyes lazy and unfocused.

"Schmitz. He had a box on the desk last night when I saw him. He'd packed his things because he knew he was getting out the next morning," Celine said. "It was him."

Grace Slanter put her hands on the bar mat in front of her. "I know what I'm going to do," she said.

"What?"

"I'm going to get in my truck, go home, and get my rifle," she said. "I'm going to drive through the desert, around and around, night and day, until I find one of those fuckers. I don't need to go for the top dogs. I just need someone. Anyone. I'm going to find an inmate in the desert and drag him back to Pronghorn. Nothing short of me personally escorting a dangerous inmate back through the gates of Pronghorn is going to fix how the world sees me after all this."

"Please don't do that," Celine said. "You'll get a flat out there in the middle of nowhere. You'll run out of water and the buzzards will eat you."

"I'm doing it."

"This is not the Wild West. You are not a cowboy."

"I'll be whatever I want to be, pilgrim," Grace drawled.

Celine's phone buzzed again. She picked it up this time.

"Hello?"

"It's me," John Kradle said.

There was a long moment of silence on the line. Kradle watched the old airfield attendant watching him, sitting in the desk chair as footage of the mass breakout at Pronghorn played on the news on the little television set over his shoulder, and waited for Celine to gather herself. He heard the crack and tumble of billiard balls, voices murmuring, the music of a bar. Probably a twenty-four-hour place, he guessed. Then the grind of a door, and the background of the call went quiet.

"That's what you say to me?" Celine's voice burned like acid when she eventually spoke. Kradle imagined her standing outside a bar local to the prison, probably stuffed full of officers and other prison staff hiding from the press. "*It's me?* Like you're calling your fucking mama?"

"Celine, I need you to listen," Kradle said.

"No, *you* listen," she seethed. "And it's 'ma'am,' you inmate piece of trash. You better be calling me to tell me where the hell you are, because—"

"I'm out," Kradle said.

"I know you're goddamn out."

"Right," he said. "So I'm not an inmate anymore. I'll call you Celine. I'll call you Sugar. I'll call you Queen Hellbitch. I'll call you whatever I want!" He pointed to the television set, which was displaying her image yet again, standing before the press with the photograph. "I'm calling to ask you if you're out of your goddamn mind. I'm looking at you on a television screen right now, holding a picture of me."

"How the hell did you get this number?"

"You always divert the death row control center phone to your cell when there's a crisis," he said. "I must have heard you give out the number a hundred times over the past five years. I've had nothing to do but sit in that cage and listen. There's a whole bunch of stuff I know about you, Celine. I know where you live. I know you've got a new boyfriend named Jake."

"You stupid motherfu—"

"Listen!" he snapped. "Just listen to me. I know you've got a problem with me. But you can't send the entire country after me right now."

"Why in the hell not?"

"Because I need to prove my innocence."

She laughed, hard and angry. It was an ugly, hacking sound.

"Five years, and you've never said that in my presence," she said. "Not once."

"Would there have been any point?"

"No."

"Well, at least you're honest."

"I thought *you* were honest. I thought you were the only guy on the row who owned what he did," Celine said. "Man, I've been listening to stories from inmates about how they were set up or mistaken for someone else or just plain wrongfully convicted all my career. Never heard it from you, though. Now you're out and you're suddenly innocent? Oh, honey, spare me."

"Celine, I—"

"If there's one thing I know, John Kradle, it's killers," Celine said. "They've got a way about them, and you've got that way."

"Look at you. You think you're Nancy Grace or something. You're not Nancy Grace, Celine. You're just a glorified zookeeper from Bumfuck, Georgia."

"Just shut up."

"No, you shut up," Kradle said.

"No, you—"

"*Somebody killed my son!*" Kradle roared. The words shot out of him unexpectedly, as loud and sudden as they were vicious, and for a moment there was silence on the line. The hand that gripped the phone beside his ear was shaking. The man in front of him was cowering in his seat. Kradle sucked in a long breath, then let it out slow.

"Celine, I didn't kill my wife, or my son, or my wife's sister," he continued. "I came home from work that day and I found them all dead and the house on fire."

"Uh-huh," Celine said. She didn't sound sarcastic or mean. She just sounded as though she was listening. It gave him strength.

"Now that I've got a chance to find out who did it," Kradle continued, "I'm going to use it. You don't have to help me, but you do need to back off me. There are six hundred guys on the loose, and I'm the least dangerous of all of them. It would be real good for me if the authorities were tied up chasing those other guys so I can get my job done."

"Kradle," Celine said. "I'm not going to sit here and argue with you about what kind of monster you are."

"I'm not a monster. I'm innocent."

"Tell me where you are, and I will send the police to pick you up."

"You should know that I've got a very dangerous guy with me," Kradle said. The old airfield attendant sitting close by seemed startled by the words and glanced toward the windows, out into the dark. Kradle lifted a hand, made an "It's okay" gesture. He closed his eyes and pictured Celine on the other end of the call. "I can't let this guy out of my sight. He'll hurt someone the second he gets a chance. I'm going to try to set him up for capture when the time is right. That should show you I'm on the right side of this thing."

"Who is it?" Celine asked. "Who's with you?"

"A cold-as-ice, shitballs-crazy psychopath," Kradle said. "That's who."

"Which one?"

Kradle hung up. The old man was trembling gently in his seat.

"He's out there. He won't come in," Kradle said. "But just in case, is there anywhere you can hide?"

"The bathrooms, I guess," the old man said. Kradle walked him to the men's room off the side of the office and listened while he locked himself in. Then he jogged out into the darkness, found Homer waiting at the corner of the huge hangar, the roller door pushed open and the little aircraft waiting inside, silent and black-eyed like birds in their nests.

"We've gotta go," Kradle said. He fished a key out of the pile in his fist, matching a handwritten label on a yellow plastic tag with the tail numbers of a nearby Cessna. He pointed to the plane, and Homer gave him that gap-toothed grin.

"Coolest guy in the world," the serial killer said.

1999

She pinched the tobacco between her thumb and forefinger, flicked out the rolling paper with a little more flair than she probably needed to, and laid the little caterpillar of brown fibers down in its thin, dry bed. Three boys, all cousins of hers, crowded in to watch her lick and roll the cigarette. Celine put the smoke to her lips and lit up. Their eyes were big and wild with excitement. It was a thrilling display on many levels. They were all farm kids, and lighting a match for any reason in a barn full of hay was like flipping the bird to Jesus Christ.

"This is just a regular smoke," Celine explained coolly. "But you can put other stuff in, if you want."

"Like what?" Tommy asked.

"I don't know. Rosemary. Weed."

"You don't smoke weed," Samson sneered.

"Maybe I do, maybe I don't." Celine looked at the little brat and shrugged. "How would you know, you little peckerhead?"

"You haven't even smoked that yet." Samson pointed at the cigarette blazing in her fingertips. "We haven't even seen you inhale. You're pretending."

Celine inhaled a lungful of smoke, let it trail out slowly for a while. When she got bored of that she blew a smoke ring. The boys cooed in admiration. They heard the last few steps of an adult crunching through the dry grass outside the barn and Celine did everything she could to hide the cigarette without looking panicked. The door flew open, and Grandpa Nick stood there in his gray coveralls, a big rifle hanging at his side.

Celine would wonder later whether she really saw him considering his next move as he looked over the three boys and the teenage girl huddled on the hay bales, or whether the tiny pause he gave in the doorway was something she had added to her recollection. Maybe he stood there for an eternity, his wide shoulders rimmed in red afternoon light. Or maybe he'd already decided how it would all go. Had known for months. Maybe he was already commanding her to go up to the house as his big, hard palm shoved open the door.

"Your mother wants you."

Celine grunted in derision as she slumped past him. Technically, she wasn't talking to Grandpa Nick. He'd been sour from the moment they arrived in their rickety van, her younger brothers tumbling out and running into the woods before they could be tasked with unloading any luggage. Grandpa Nick had barked at her for dragging her wheeled suitcase up the porch, letting it clunk loudly against the freshly varnished steps. When he got into his moods he trudged around snapping at people: a giant, swirling dark cloud that had terrified her as a small child and depressed her as a teenager. He was going to say something snide about everything she received for Christmas. She would have to kneel there under the tree and receive his commentary, box after box, on her pathetic obsession with technology and her narcissistic need for clothes. She was everything that he hated—a Walkman-toting, blue-haired, skimpily dressed back-talker who, if she didn't kill them all burning the barn down with a cigarette, would corrupt all the little males in the family with ideas about loose, smart-mouthed women with expensive taste. And there were a lot of little males to protect. Her two brothers, Paulie and Frankie, and Samson, Tommy, and Benjamin, her cousins.

Celine's Uncle Charlie had all the maturity of a fifteen-year-old. He was sitting on the back porch steps, reading the cartoon section of a newspaper in the sunshine, when she reached the house.

"You've gotta talk to the old man," Charlie said, without looking up.

"He's an asshole."

"Yeah, but Christmas dinner hasn't even begun yet," Charlie said. "Genny and your mother have only just started on the onions, which means we're about four hours out. Somebody will fight at dinner. You know they will."

Celine rolled her eyes and lit her cigarette again.

"So we gotta go in with a clean slate," Charlie continued. "We can't start the dinner fighting, or by the end it'll be war."

"You're just worried about yourself," Celine said. "Don't make like you're trying to look out for the family."

"Of course I'm worried about myself. I don't need any awkwardness ruining my Christmas. I wait all year for fucking Christmas, and I just want to get through it without Nanna blubbering all over me."

Celine gestured toward the barn at the end of the long, dry field. "I'm seventeen. He can't talk to me as if I'm five."

"You're still pissed about the fence." Charlie glanced at the little picket fence by Celine's hip. Three Christmases earlier, Celine had decided she would surprise Grandpa Nick by painting the fence he'd just built around the driveway. He'd come home from the store and leaped from the truck, already blasting her. She hadn't primed the wood. She was using paint she'd found in the shed, and it was interior paint, water-based, when she should have used exterior oil. The drips and lumps she was leaving everywhere were going to ruin the look of the precise miter joints he'd cut. "I might as well have nailed the thing together from driftwood!" Celine had looked up to see the whole family assembled silently on the porch, an audience to her roasting. Nanna Betty had made Grandpa apologize in front of everyone at dinner that night. He'd sulked for three days afterward, until Celine's parents decided to leave.

"I'm not pissed about the fence," Celine lied. "It was years ago."

"You've got to go easy on Grandpa. He's upset about your father."

"Dad's not gonna die," Celine said. "He told everybody so. It's a slow-moving thing. It's going to eat up his liver one bite at a time, and maybe he'll need a transplant in, like, ten years or something. But it's not that bad. It's not cancer."

"If you had a kid you'd understand," Charlie said. "Doesn't need to be cancer to get you upset." He beckoned for Celine's cigarette, glanced toward the house to make sure Aunty Genny wasn't watching.

Three gunshots. Sharp, propulsive cracks that rippled up the field and over the house like a wave. Celine and her uncle looked down toward the barn.

"They're shooting apples again."

"He's trying to run down that old rifle," Charlie agreed, drawing hard on her cigarette. "Nanna wants him to get rid of it, but it won't go for much, so he's having some fun. He's got rid of a lot of stuff the past few months. The shotguns and the musket are gone."

"Why?"

"Meh. Old people do that. They get rid of stuff."

"She better not get rid of any of her earrings," Celine said. "They're supposed to be mine."

More shots. They watched the barn, the gnats swirling in the light. The cows in the paddock by the barn were restless, trotting away from the noise, up the hill, toward the tree line.

"See, he always used to invite me to do that." Celine waved angrily at the barn. "I love shooting apples. He knows it. Fucking asshole."

Charlie shrugged, finished the cigarette. He got up and went inside. Celine was rolling another cigarette when her grandfather emerged from the distant barn door. She refused to meet his eyes as he walked toward her. She lit the cigarette and doused the match on her terrible paintwork on the picket fence.

"I want you in the house," Grandpa Nick said. He smelled of cordite and his silver hair was messed up. Celine waved her cigarette, clutched between two fingers.

"I'll finish this first," she said.

Grandpa Nick licked his dentures thoughtfully, watched the dogs in the field rushing to the barn to investigate the activity. He nodded, shouldered the rifle, a small smile on his lips. He'd made some decision.

"Suit yourself," he said, and went inside.

CHAPTER 11

John Kradle thought about killing. About whether Celine Osbourne really did know killers, whether she had spotted something in him in the half decade they'd spent together as jailer and captive that the jurors and judge had also seen. That the media had seen. That Christine's mother had seen as she stood spitting and crying with fury in the dock, reading her victim impact statement about losing two daughters and a grandson by his hand.

You've got that way, Celine had said.

Homer Carrington was asleep in the copilot seat of the Cessna as they rumbled and shook through the cold, hard sky over Nevada. The plane was a single-engine thing, tiny, designed for personal use, so small and rickety it wanted to yaw sideways through the sheets of air with Homer's substantial weight on one side. A bike with wings—something that could be brought down by an encounter with a large bird in the right circumstances. The sunrise was lighting the angles of Homer's placid, clumsily handsome face a searing orange. Kradle had made no call signs leaving Wagon Circle, no reports of his passage on the airwaves, so he had to keep his eyes locked on the unmoving brown horizon for other small aircraft approaching, unaware of his presence. But he could not stop glancing at the seatbelt buckle by Homer's hip, clicked into place, safe and secure.

Kradle had only to unbuckle the belt, reach across his passenger and unlatch the door, then tip the yoke and Homer would fall to his death.

Problem solved.

Logically, it made sense. Kradle couldn't do what he needed to do in Mesquite while dragging a serial killer along with him. Homer was distinct-looking, unpredictable, physically uncontrollable. Kradle might as well have been accompanied by a Siberian tiger. At any moment, Homer could see through the pathetic mob-money story and kill Kradle, or veer off to target an innocent bystander, and there would be little Kradle could do to stop him.

But pushing him out of the plane would mean killing him. It would mean being the executioner of another human being, bypassing the sentence that had been handed down to Homer to die by lethal injection in front of his victims' families after saying his final words to them. They wouldn't get to see justice done. He wouldn't get his last rites. And there was always the chance that Homer would fall on someone, or survive the fall somehow—or, worse, grab onto John, grip his way back into the plane and strangle him in his seat. Kradle glanced out his window at the earth passing below. Desert, cracked and ridged by sun and time and wind, the occasional town or snake of highway.

But it would be so easy, Kradle thought.

Three movements.

Buckle.

Door.

Yoke.

Kradle unbuckled Homer's seatbelt, just to see what it felt like. The killer stirred and stretched in his seat. "Are we there yet?"

"Ten minutes or so," Kradle said. "Get ready to run."

They approached the airfield from the south. Kradle saw it as a thin strip of blackness in the distance.

"How do we know they won't be waiting for us?" Homer asked. "Did you tell the guy at Wagon Circle where we were going?"

"Of course not," Kradle said. "But they'll know where I'm going. Little plane like this can only go so far without refueling, and I'll bet a good portion of inmates who go on the run head straight home. But there are a few airfields in Mesquite. They probably won't be manning every one. We'll take our chances."

"You've got this all worked out," Homer marveled. "I never spent a minute thinking about my escape plan."

Kradle had spent *every* minute thinking about it. It was all that kept him alive after the second year. That, the slow trudge of the appeals process, and trying to annoy Celine Osbourne in a new way every single day that she worked. He had tidbits of information he'd been able to gather that would aid his escape hidden all over his cell, and at night he fell asleep thinking about each one, making sure his plan was ready should the opportunity ever arise to use it. He had his lawyer smuggle tiny pieces of his plan to him once a week or so. The distances to airfields. The contact details of key people needed for his mission. Known locations for sleeping rough, where he might blend in with homeless men in Mesquite. Kradle knew the guy didn't really believe he'd ever escape. But he could see the little tidbits gave Kradle hope, and he needed a whole bunch of hope to keep filing applications, maybe for the next two and a half decades, before he ran out of appeals. Kradle built his escape plan because there was nothing else he could build on death row; because every day on the row was about being broken down so that when they took you to your death you were cowed, numb, submissive. Nobody wanted to see a grown man kicking and screaming and crying as they strapped him to the table. Not even the victims' families wanted that.

"What's wrong with you?" Homer asked. Kradle had to shake himself out of his dreams about escapes and executions.

"Huh?"

"Why'd you get into the mob?" he asked. "Like, have they done a diagnosis? Are you a 'natural born killer'?"

"Oh, uh." Kradle shifted uncomfortably in his seat. "They did a psych test on me to see if I was fit to stand trial. Didn't find anything."

"I love psych tests." Homer smiled. "They're so interesting. The last one I had, they asked, 'When you stand at the edge of a tall building or a cliff, do you think about jumping off?' I mean, what does that mean? What's the right answer?"

"Beats me," Kradle said.

Don't, Kradle told himself.

But then he did.

"What do you think's wrong with you?" Kradle asked.

"Look"—Homer shifted sideways a little, so that he was facing Kradle—"this is going to sound crazy."

"Lay it on me," Kradle sighed.

"When I was a kid I went camping with my dad a lot," Homer said. "We would go out into the desert, just him and me, get away from Mom and my sister. You know. Guy stuff. Anyway, one of these times, I woke up in the morning with this itch in my ear."

Kradle gripped the yoke in front of him, pursed his lips.

"So my dad looks in there," Homer said. "And what does he see? A black widow spider."

"Jesus."

"Yeah." Homer sat back in his seat. "I wanted him to get it out. I begged and begged him. But he said it was too dangerous. If he tried to grab it, it might turn around and bite me. I'd be dead inside of ten minutes. Plus, my dad was really good with animals. He would have wild birds, rabbits, foxes coming into our yard and eating out of his hand. So he tells me the spider in my ear canal is a good thing. He can control it. If I'm ever bad, he'll just tell it to bite me and that'll be it. Game over."

Kradle looked over at Homer. The bigger man was watching his eyes carefully.

"You serious?" Kradle asked.

"Yeah."

"And how old were you when he was telling you this?"

"I don't know. Eight? Nine? Doesn't matter. What matters is that it was true. He could control it. He had it under full control in a matter of days," Homer said. "Every time I was thinking about acting up, I'd feel this tickle in my ear, and I'd look over and my dad would be watching me. He'd tap his ear and I'd know to behave myself."

Kradle said nothing.

"Problem is, my dad *died* about five years later," Homer said. "Brain aneurism."

"So . . ." Kradle struggled.

"*So nobody's controlling the spider,*" Homer whispered.

"Haven't you had medical exams during your incarceration?" Kradle asked. "Hasn't anyone looked in your ear in all these years?"

"Oh, yeah." Homer waved dismissively. "Doctors have looked. They always say it's just dermatitis in there. They give me creams to put on it. I never do."

A shot of adrenaline hit Kradle's system as the radio in the console crackled.

"*This is Mesquite Municipal Airport, Mike-Foxtrot-Hotel. Aircraft on bearing oh-three-five call in, please.*"

"What's the plan? Are we literally just going to run?" Homer was gripping the frame of the door, watching the earth rise slowly beneath them.

"That woodland there, behind the airfield." Kradle pointed. "That's the highway just beyond it."

They aligned with the strip. Homer tugged on his seatbelt to tighten it, found it unbuckled. Kradle swallowed hard.

A dog.

A big brown-and-black creature rushed out of the grass at the edge of the woods, heading for the strip, barking at the plane. Kradle shifted upward in his seat as the flaps on the wings ground slowly down to ten degrees on either side of the fuselage. The wind roared as the drag increased. The dog got to the edge of the runway and barked soundlessly at them.

A man ran out of the woods to retrieve the animal. He was shrugging off a blue jacket with white lining, which he dropped in the grass. Kradle had seen those jackets before.

Kradle flicked the flaps off and tugged back on the yoke. The nose of the plane lifted, sinking his stomach. He held on as the g-force ripped through him. They turned away from the runway, only blue sky visible through the windshield.

"You see that?" Homer was twisted in his seat, looking back.

"The jacket." Kradle nodded. "It'll have *US Marshal* written on the back."

"Goddamn dog just saved our bacon."

"Yeah."

Kradle looked down as they turned. More marshals were walking out of the woods with dogs, the game over. He searched the land for a spot to put the aircraft down, but every street was littered with cars, the highway surprisingly busy with morning traffic.

"They might send jets after us," Homer said.

"This is not a movie," Kradle reminded him.

"Just put us in the desert," Homer said. "We need to get grounded, right now."

"We can't be out in the open," Kradle said.

He spied a field sectioned off with wire fences, surrounded by trees. Kradle turned the yoke in front of him. "Get ready."

The plane shuddered downward. The brown strip of dirt and gravel cleaved the entire garbage dump in two, like the trunk of a pale tree rimmed with branches that fed out into the piles of car bodies, broken and rusted appliances, twisted scrap metal lying like fields of thorny brambles. It was a rough landing. He consoled himself as the tires bounced twice on the earth that it had been two decades or more since he'd flown. The plane slowed, rattled violently, twisted sideways, and slammed into a pile of rubbish, the wing crumpling, the windows and windscreen blowing out. He pulled himself out of the craft as a bunch of refuse workers abandoned their truck nearby and started running toward them.

"Are you guys o—"

Kradle heard the men calling, but their voices drained away as he limped into the trash mounds, running awkwardly toward the fence line. Homer was ahead of him, leaping a washing machine like an Olympic hurdler, crashing through valleys of plastic bags, cardboard boxes, tin cans, corrugated iron sheeting. He slipped and stumbled on a flat stretch made from cardboard boxes and Kradle almost caught up to him. Something slashed at Kradle's thigh—a bent tube sticking out from the ruined body of a bicycle. Homer was halfway up the fence and waiting for him when Kradle heard the sirens on the highway in the distance.

CHAPTER 12

Celine walked into the break room, poured herself a black coffee, and stood watching the TV mounted above the staff bulletin board in the corner of the room as she drank it. Footage was playing of officers escorting inmates back into the prison through the huge gates, a symbolic gesture for the cameras, no doubt. There were few she recognized. She opened a tab on her cell phone and looked at the *New York Times* home page, which was keeping a tally of inmates escaped and inmates returned. So far there were 291 inmates returned to the facility of the 653 set free. Most had been rounded up on the roads to Vegas, Utah, or Arizona, in the desert, or in the houses most immediate to the prison—little farmhouses dotted throughout the desert wilds. With almost half of the inmates returned, Celine supposed she should be feeling pleased. But the *Times* was also reporting six common assaults, seventeen robberies, two hostage stand-offs, nine sexual assaults, and fifteen carjackings overnight. Two competing groups of criminals had engaged in a shootout in a diner in Meadows Village, leaving five escapees dead and patrons terrified. Not a single death row inmate had been recovered, unless Celine counted Willy Henderson, which she didn't, because the man had never left the building.

The *Times* had also managed to snag interviews with officers from Pronghorn about the moments after the hostage call began playing over the PA system.

I know how bad these guys are. I see what they do to each other. I know what they'll be wanting to do out there. But I also know my family was in danger, and there was nothing else I could do. I've got one daughter. You'd have done the same thing if it was you.

Everybody around me was releasing inmates. It didn't seem like my efforts would mean anything.

What if I kept the inmate back that they were looking for—the terrorists? What if he was in my cell block?

All the sources were anonymous. Celine couldn't understand that. Nobody who had willingly let inmates go from Pronghorn would be keeping their jobs. There would probably be a couple of spectacular firings, but most would be shipped out quietly over the next year or so, as officers were trained to replace them.

She checked her watch. At 6 A.M., inmates scheduled for release that day who had not participated in the breakout by leaving the general vicinity of the prison would be let out, having finished their sentences. That was unless the release schedule was delayed because of the breakout, and no one had told her. She imagined they would be driven into town and released in some inconspicuous backstreet so that the journalists waiting to interview them about their experience of the breakout would be left empty-handed.

Celine had never released an inmate in all her years on the row. This was where all hopes of walking free on the earth were abandoned.

She'd slept for an hour inside her car in the prison parking lot after leaving the bar. Dreams of her grandfather's farm and Kradle's words on the phone left her shaken and restless, the nap fitful and sweaty.

Somebody killed my son!

Kradle had said nothing about his wife or sister-in-law, Celine noted. But there were plenty of reasons for that. Family annihilators had strange ideas about their work, about the act of killing and the act of giving mercy. Maybe murdering his son had been so different an act from what Kradle did to his wife and sister-in-law that he just plain wanted to blame it on someone else. Celine didn't know. She tried not to rationalize the deeds of the men on the row. They didn't work with adult-level logic, were more like beastly children stomping on snails and then trying to talk their way out of being sent to their rooms.

"You stink," someone said.

Celine turned and looked Trinity Parker up and down. The US Marshal was immaculately dressed and smelled of perfume. Celine sipped her coffee.

"I said, you stink." Trinity wrinkled her nose. "I told you to go home, freshen up. What did you do instead?"

"I stayed here for a while," Celine said. "Checked some stuff off. Then I went driving around looking for inmates. Then I went to a bar. You want to know what I had for breakfast, too?"

"No. I want to know that you're ready to get to work."

"Is that what you call it? Work? Because being physically assaulted is something I usually do in my spare time."

"I'm hearing your poor-man's Scott Peterson tried to land a plane in Mesquite early this morning, just like you told me he would," Trinity said.

"So I was right about that." Celine shrugged. "Any chance I might be right that he's got Schmitz with him?"

Celine had called Trinity as she stood outside the bar, told her about Kradle's claims to have a dangerous psychopath in his company. Trinity had hung up on her and failed to answer her text messages.

"You're not really naive enough to believe Kradle when he says he's got an important inmate he'll help you capture, are you?" Trinity gave her a sad look. "Come on. He wants something from you, and that's his only currency."

"Where's Kradle now?" Celine asked. "Did they catch him?"

"My guys are chasing him down as we speak."

Celine felt a cold shot of exhilaration pass through her.

"Moving on to things that are actually important," Trinity said. "Your instincts about Kradle and his movements were right. Maybe you are valuable to me. I want to use whatever intel you have to find Burke David Schmitz before he shoots up another mass gathering."

"Why would I help someone who popped me in the guts less than twenty-four hours ago?" Celine asked.

"You needed a smack to wake you up," Trinity said. "I was making a kind gesture, trying to communicate with you in your own language. People from your station in life only understand high-stakes situations through pain. You're like dogs. A dog barks too much, you don't plead with it. You smack it on the nose."

"My 'station in life'?"

"Farm people."

"Oh. I see." Celine nodded. "You did some creative googling in the night, did you?"

"Sure did," Trinity said. Celine bit her tongue so she wouldn't lash out, turned away, felt that old, hard, protective smile creep onto her face. She set her features and turned back.

"It was interesting reading," Trinity continued. "You've been through some stuff. I have a little more respect for you now. But don't get excited. It's microscopic."

"You don't want to go soft on me because of what happened to me," Celine said. "Turn your back on me and I'll bite you, just like any other dog would."

"So, let's try to make this as brief a liaison as possible," Trinity said. "We snag the Nazi, maybe round up your family killer on the way, and then we're done."

"Done," Celine confirmed.

Trinity offered her hand. Celine begrudgingly shook it.

Walter Keeper was standing at the counter in the administration office near F Block when Celine and Trinity arrived at the large, secure glass doors. He was wearing a white t-shirt and dusty, baggy jeans that hung precariously on the upper curve of his butt, the pockets bulging as he stuffed them with items handed to him through the screen over the counter—keys, wallet, phone, smokes, a little black book, and a huge black watch. Celine stopped Trinity outside, in the shadow of the chow hall. The two women heard a cheer and looked through the barred windows to see someone drawing a cross through the image of an inmate's face that was pinned to one of the partitions. Slowly, the wall of faces was becoming a wall of giant red crosses.

"This will probably be touch and go," Celine said. "Let me handle it."

"Come on."

"Some dogs are so used to getting smacked they don't even feel it any-more," Celine said. She went inside and stood, waiting, while Keeps signed his release forms.

"Oh, Death Row"—Keeps nodded to her—"you look at that light?"

"Yeah, and I found something," she said. "So I want you to come and tell me where else to look."

"Nah, man." Keeps smirked, handing the clipboard back across the counter. "That's a favor done. So you owe me a favor when I get back. I'm not spending my first minutes as a free citizen hangin' out with some screws inside Pronghorn. No offense. I'm getting on the release bus and heading into town so I can grab me a big, juicy burger and an ice-cold beer."

"I'll pay you."

"Lady, you couldn't afford ten seconds of my time in here beyond what the state sentenced me."

He walked out the back doors of the administration block. Celine followed. The gravel crunched beneath their feet. A pair of guards was marching a group of twelve inmates toward the yards.

"Have fun out there, Keeps!" an inmate called. "I sure did!"

Keeps waved.

"You got someone waiting for you on the other side?" Celine asked.

"Nah. I'm freestyling it."

"No family? No girlfriend?"

"Nope."

"So, what's the plan?"

"I told you, girl. Burger. Beer. In that order."

"Let me get this straight. You're going to use what cash you have in your wallet to get a burger and a beer, and then you're on your own. No accommodation. No job. No plans."

"People like me don't need a plan." Keeps pushed his glasses up onto his nose and grinned. "We hustle. We get lucky. Don't worry, pretty lady. I've done this a thousand times."

"How about this." Celine stopped him before he could reach the caged passage to the outer perimeter and, beyond it, the bus and the back gates of Pronghorn. "First, you stop with all the *pretty lady, girl, honey pie* bullshit. Then you give me twenty minutes of your precious time over on the row in exchange for these."

She pulled a set of keys out of her pocket, jangled them. Keeps spied the car key fob and frowned.

"What?"

"My car's out on the lot," Celine said. "Blue Caprice. I'll write down my address. You go get your burger and your beer then you can head to my place. Have a shower, watch some Netflix. Eat whatever you want from the fridge. And you can stay there for . . . let's say a week. Better than a dive hotel or a crowded shelter."

"Ma'am." Keeps shook his head, laughed, flashing big white teeth. "You must be high as all fuck. You don't know me. What's say I don't go to your place and clean you out? Strip your car. Sell your stuff. What's say I don't have all my friends there waiting for you to come in the door so we can cornhole your silly ass? Oh, damn, you need to *not* be givin' the keys to your life to convicts you just met."

"I've got a feeling none of that is going to happen," Celine said. "Call me psychic."

"You just got a feeling says I'm all right? Just like that? You ain't looked at my rap sheet or nothing?"

"Nope. But I've been right before."

Keeps looked at her, at the caged path to the gate yard, at the keys in her palm. Celine got the sense that unexplained, unconditional trust wasn't something that he had seen often in his life. He took the keys reluctantly, with his thumb and forefinger, like someone gently picking up a stick of dynamite.

"Okay," he said. "The burger will keep, I guess."

CHAPTER 13

Kradle hadn't run in half a decade, but his body remembered. Somewhere deep inside him, that frantic, wild, powerful impulse to flee still lived, even though he hadn't traveled a distance of more than ten yards without chains on in all that time. There was a certain joy in it, a small flicker of happiness, his hips burning and legs reaching out and gripping the earth and pushing him forward, his lungs pumping in fresh, free air as the two men surged through the woods. But most of the experience was pure pain. The rocky earth jarred his bones. His heart struggled, hammering desperately in his chest, thrumming in his fingertips and toes. Hunger and dehydration left him wobbly, slow, his feet landing awkwardly between fallen branches or on rocks, trees appearing out of nowhere and crashing into his shoulders. Blood was pouring from the slash in his thigh. The sound of sirens pursued them for what seemed like an age, until they were both stumbling, an awkward half-jog, up an incline to a tree-lined peak.

They stopped and looked back. Maybe three miles away they could barely make out the little ridges that signified the waste piles of the landfill, the brown strip of earth they'd landed on. There were red and blue lights. Kradle thought he heard the bark of dogs on the wind.

"We've got to get a car," Kradle said. "The dogs will get here before their handlers do, and they won't just want to pin us down."

"Don't worry," Homer said. "I'll handle this."

The earth on the other side of the hill was more lush, sheltered from the Nevada sun. Kradle's once-white prison sneakers, now caked in filth, sank in the soil and leaf litter. The sound of dogs barking came again, closer this time. A road appeared through the trees and Homer was out onto it before Kradle could stop him or ascertain some sense of his plan. He watched, appalled, as the serial killer sidestepped in front of a vehicle, which veered over the center line to avoid him. Kradle glanced back into the trees, thought again of bolting. But then he would be leaving anyone Homer managed to stop at the mercy of the monster. Whoever he met, whatever happened to them, would be a direct result of Kradle helping Homer out of the mountains.

Kradle approached the road, still dry-mouthed from the cold morning air and gasping, as a small yellow Kia pulled over and Homer gripped the edge of the passenger-side window when it reluctantly lowered two inches.

"Please help us!" Homer cried. "My friend and I—we were attacked!"

"What the hell happened?"

Kradle looked into the vehicle. A woman in her forties was leaning forward over the steering wheel to get a better look at them. She was wearing a bright-pink uniform of some restaurant or bar.

"We were hunting in the woods." Homer clutched at his shirt, pointed at the tree line, swallowed hard as he tried to regain his breath. "These guys came and beat us up. Oh, god. We're so lucky they didn't kill us. They wanted our clothes. They took our guns. They—I think they were inmates from Pronghorn!"

"Oh, Jesus." The woman gripped the wheel. Kradle could see her thinking about stepping on the gas. Through the dirt, sweat, and muck, she had just noticed the inmate number embroidered on Homer's shirt. She looked at Kradle's chest, at the blood-smeared denim and the number. Her eyes met his, as though she could hear the words he was screaming in his mind.

Drive, woman.

Just drive.

"I've got to . . ." She put the car into gear, shaking her head. "I can't . . ."

"It's okay." Homer put his hands up. "It's okay. You don't have to let us in. Just. Just get your cell phone. Just call 911. Please. Please do it now. Those guys are in there somewhere and they have our weapons and our clothes. We need the police to know we're not inmates in case they shoot at us, and if those guys come back . . . We need to tell someone before they . . . before they . . ."

"I saw some cops a few miles back." The woman glanced in her rearview. "We could . . . Maybe, uh . . ."

Kradle squeezed his fists, mouthed the words even though she wasn't looking at him.

Just. Drive.

"Cops. Where? This way?" Homer pointed. He started moving and grabbed Kradle's arm. "Come on, man. We gotta get out of here before they come back. They'll kill us."

Kradle started following the big man, relief burning in his face.

His heart sank when the car reversed alongside them.

"Get in," the woman said. "I'll take you there."

Homer slid into the back seat. Kradle had no choice but to climb in beside him.

Inmates swaggered. All inmates. It was a primal thing, usually unconscious—a nervous, protective energy that made them want to present a dangerously casual facade to the predators around them. But Keeps put on a swagger as Celine led him back to Trinity that was unlike anything she had ever seen. It was that self-preservation bravado mixed with a new sense of self-importance. He was like the *Keep on Truckin'* guy on the best day of his life.

"What the hell is this?" Trinity sighed.

"This is our new inmate consultant," Celine said.

"Ex-inmate," Keeps corrected. "And, unluckily for you ladies, my services come at a premium today. It's a release-day charge of one hundred dollars per hour, starting twenty-four hours ago."

"What?" Celine blurted. "Why twenty-four hours ago?"

"That's when I started gathering intelligence on the breakout," Keeps said.

"Oh, please." Trinity started walking away.

"You're going to pay him." Celine caught up to her. "We need what he's got."

"We'll see about payment when we find out if what he's got is any more than a penchant for criminal activity and a hard-on for pretty little blonde women with big sets of keys."

Celine dropped back and walked beside Keeps.

"Your fee was the use of my place and my car, Keeps," she said.

"Ma'am, that's a US Marshal right there," Keeps said. "You got any idea what her budget for this thing would be? Between the marshals, the FBI, the sheriffs—the president is gonna be raining money on this party like a world-class pimp. And the more money I make here, the faster I'll be out of your accommodation." He poked Celine in the shoulder.

They arrived on the row. Celine led them to Burke David Schmitz's cell, which had been ransacked by agents already—tagged, photographed, and bagged possessions were arranged in piles on all surfaces. The two women stood in the hall while Keeps took in the space. He turned in a circle, noted the scratch marks on the wall under the light where Celine had searched unsuccessfully for concealed items. They watched as he checked all the places Celine usually checked during a shakedown. The hems of the bedding and uniforms, which were folded and stacked neatly in unsealed paper evidence bags. The bolts and fixtures of the bed, shelf, toilet. Keeps stuck his hand down the toilet and fished around in the U-bend, peered down the drain of the tiny sink fixed into the cistern.

"This is hardly genius-level intel I'm seeing here." Trinity was leaning against the bars. "I've had my agents sweep the place like this already."

Keeps sat on the neatly made bed, bounced a little on the mattress. He picked up a small artwork someone had peeled from the wall—an eagle perched on a twisted branch. Celine had confiscated plenty of artworks from Schmitz in the years she had supervised the quiet, bookish inmate. He wasn't permitted to have images of Hitler or swastikas in his cell, which didn't stop him from painting them now and then. She couldn't remove his artistic privileges unless he committed an act of violence, but she always made sure to let Schmitz complete the artwork, put the fine, time-consuming finishing touches on it before she took it, scrunched it, and tossed it in the trash in front of him.

"Dude got some skills." Keeps waved the picture at the women. "For a Nazi asshole."

"This is not Art Appreciation 101," Trinity barked. "It's pretty clear Schmitz pulled off this thing. He's orchestrated one of the most deadly mass shootings *and* the biggest jailbreak in American history, so it stands to reason that whatever he's cooking up next is going to be distinctly unpleasant. Time is of the essence, inmate."

"Are you having a stressful morning?" Keeps patted the bed beside him. "You want to talk about it, pretty lady?"

Trinity licked her teeth so hard she made a loud clicking sound, then turned to Celine, the veins in her neck taut with fury.

"Get him out of here."

"Wait, wait, wait, wait." Keeps held a hand up. "I got something. I got something." He slapped the picture of the eagle. "It's right here." He came to the bars and showed them the image. "See this black?"

The women looked at the picture.

"That's contraband black," Keeps said.

"What are you talking about?" Celine sighed.

"This black paint here." He tapped the paper. "You can't get that color inside Pronghorn. Not through official channels, anyway."

Celine looked at Trinity. The woman was typing out a message on her phone.

"Two things we got a lot of over in minimum—wannabe rappers and artists. There's a lot of bad music, bad pictures." He handed the paper to Celine. "All the painters on my block got the same complaint. The black you get with the commissary paint kit ain't black enough. It's a very, very dark brown. That's a problem. You don't like the blue they got? That's okay. You can mix it. Change it. Make it lighter. Make it darker. Add yellow, make it greener. But you can't make black blacker, no matter how much you try. You want real black? You've got to smuggle it in, and if you consider yourself a real artist you need black-black, not brown-black."

"Right," Celine said. She was starting to feel the first tingles of excitement in her chest. "So someone was bringing in contraband paint to Schmitz."

"How does this help us?" Trinity didn't look up from her phone. "Could have been his lawyer or girlfriend or whatever smuggling it in. All that tells me is that your visitors' center is full of holes."

"Schmitz was Grade B. Non-contact," Celine said. "He only ever interacts with outsiders from behind bulletproof glass. So it wasn't one of his visitors." Her words were gaining momentum as she thought. "It was either another inmate, or it was an officer. And Schmitz hasn't had contact with any other inmates in the past three weeks." She pointed to the cells either side of the one they stood before. "All the inmates take their yard time separately, so they don't interact in the halls, and these cells neighboring Schmitz's have been vacant. This guy on the left, he went to the infirmary a month ago. And this cell has been empty for three weeks because the sink's broken."

"So it was a guard," Trinity said. "A guard smuggled your Nazi inmate some paint."

"And if they were bringing him paint, what else were they bringing him?" Celine wondered. "And what were they taking out?"

Trinity looked at Keeps as though she was surveying an old car she wanted to buy cheap and run into the ground: a temporarily useful thing that she'd be embarrassed to be seen with. She started to walk off, talking over her shoulder as she went. "You might have been right about his usefulness," she said finally to Celine. "But don't get lost in your celebrations. They just lost your boyfriend in Mesquite."

"What?"

"He dumped the plane at a waste disposal site and disappeared." She waved her phone. "And, who knew? He did have someone with him. A big guy. Looked too tall to be Schmitz."

"I'm going," Celine said. She grabbed Keeps's arm. "You're coming with me."

Homer didn't wait to reveal himself to the woman. As soon as her foot hit the accelerator, he wound an arm around the back of her seat and hugged her throat to the headrest.

"Don't scream," he said.

Her hands came off the wheel and clawed at the arm. The pressure wasn't much, Kradle could see, not enough to completely panic her so that she ran them off the road. But enough so that it was clear. All of it. That she'd just let two escaped convicts into her car. That she was completely at their mercy. That this morning had taken a turn so bad it might end up being the very last morning of her life.

Kradle saw the terror in her eyes in the rearview mirror. He gripped the seat beneath him to stop himself from attacking Homer where he sat.

"Keep driving," Homer said gently, his cheek pressed against the side of the driver's headrest, eyes on the road. He was focused. He'd done this before. "Hands on the wheel. Foot on the accelerator. Gentle. Gentle. That's it."

"Oh my god. Please, please, please."

"Take the next turn-off. And hand your phone to my friend here. Slowly."

The woman snatched the phone from the cluttered center console. Kradle took it from her shaking fingers.

"Find 'home,' John," Homer instructed.

Kradle did as he was told. The first suggested location in Google Maps was marked "Home."

"What's your name, honey?" Homer was stroking a loose curl at the nape of the driver's neck with his free hand, twirling it around his finger.

"Uh, uh, uh, uh, uh."

"Name."

"It's Shondra."

"Just drive home, Shondra. That's all you have to do."

"Okay. Okay. Please. Oh, god, please."

"Is there going to be anyone there waiting for us?" Homer asked.

"My—my boyfriend should have—what-what-what time is it?"

"We're going to have to kill anyone we find there, so think carefully," Homer said.

"He should be gone." Shondra gagged. "He starts at seven. Oh, shit. I'm gonna throw up."

"No, you're not."

"Ease up a bit," Kradle said. He had to unlock his jaw with difficulty. Force himself to pull at Homer's arm as if he were a friend, a co-conspirator, a non-threat, and not the secret, hateful, vengeful being he really was, his whole body pulsing with the desire to launch himself at the big man sitting beside him, to gouge at his eyes and mouth, bite and kick and punch and bring him to submission.

Homer sat back, his hand extended, resting on Shondra's shoulder. Controlling.

Shondra retched a few times. Her hands were making sweat marks on the steering wheel. Kradle leaned forward.

"No one's going to hurt you," he said. Out of the corner of his eye, he saw Homer smile. "Just keep breathing. Keep it together and you'll get through this."

Off the highway, into the manicured suburbs of Mesquite. Kradle didn't recognize the place the map told him was called Bunkerville, but this might have been any of the hundreds of suburban wildernesses his wife, Christine, had been called to over the years to eradicate poltergeists, angry spirits, or demons from pastel-colored houses behind picket fences. Stone-edged garden beds nestled under shade trees, cradling succulents and little pink flowers. He had followed her, the dutiful assistant and cameraman, into family homes like this in thirty states.

Shondra's house was baby blue with white shutters. Gray slate roof, mailbox with a red flag, a wooden sign on the porch that read LIVE, LAUGH, LOVE. Homer got out swiftly and pulled Shondra, whimpering, from the driver's seat, wrapping an arm around her shoulders.

Homer instructed her simply. The experienced killer pushed through the woman's terror with single words, probably knowing it was all she could handle right now.

"Quiet. Quiet. Keys. Door. Inside. Go."

Kradle followed them into a warm, cozy house. It was messy but not dirty. Empty coffee mugs on the sink. A towel hanging off a door. Open mail scattered on the dining room table.

"You got tape?" Homer asked.

"What?" Shondra choked.

"Tape. Duct tape. Tape for your wrists."

She couldn't answer. Kradle didn't blame her. He peeled off and went to the garage, found a roll of duct tape sitting on a shelf. Homer forced Shondra to the ground. She went down easily, shaking, then limp. The trousers of her waitress's uniform were wet.

Homer left her lying, bound and gagged with tape, on the kitchen floor, and came back to where Kradle stood in the entry hall. The big man's eyes were alive, his grin so wide Kradle could see his gums hugging his molars.

"Let's think what we need," Homer said. "Clothes. Food. A phone. I need to take a shower. We'll take the car. Drive to your old place. Get the cash."

"I need a computer," Kradle said. "And listen, it's not as easy as just driving home and picking up the money. The cops will be sitting on the house. Might be that I'll have to find an old buddy of mine, send him around there instead. Maybe tonight."

"All right." Homer rubbed his palms together, making a dry sound. "You gather all that stuff. I'm taking Shondra to the bedroom."

Kradle's stomach plummeted. As Homer moved, he forced himself to put a hand out, flat, against the killer's chest.

"Whoa, whoa, whoa," Kradle said. "How about me first, man?"

Homer's face twitched, awkward.

"Do you mind?" Kradle asked. "I mean, I know some guys aren't funny about stuff like that. But I am. I don't like anybody's leftovers. No offense."

"I could go first, then we put her in the shower." Homer gestured toward the back of the house, the bedrooms beyond, as cool and calm as a man talking about arrangements to borrow a car. "Then you go."

"I like to go first."

"So do I, and I caught her."

"Yeah, but you wouldn't have caught her without me. Your ass would probably still be wandering around the desert if I hadn't led you out of there. This is my payback," Kradle said.

Homer licked his lips. Kradle forced a pleasant smile.

"Okay." Homer shrugged. "Whatever you want, buddy. Just don't tire her out."

"You might think about taking that shower," Kradle ventured. "You smell like a dead dog. It would be nicer on her."

"Watch it." Homer elbowed him, hard, in the ribs. Kradle's legs were numb as he walked into the kitchen and picked up Shondra from the tiles. The woman wriggled and screamed in his arms as he carried her to a bedroom and dropped her on the bed, slamming the door closed behind them.

CHAPTER 14

Keeps watched the desert roll by, one wrist on the top of the steering wheel, fingers resting on the dashboard. He slouched in the seat, eyelids low. Celine was gripping her jeans, sitting bolt upright, watching the mountains in the distance, which didn't seem to be getting any closer.

"Is this as fast as you can go?"

"This is as fast as I *wanna* go." Keeps glanced at her. "I ain't enthused about going any faster. I hate Mesquite. My ex-girlfriend is from Mesquite. She stole my CD player. The deal was I'd be chillin' in your hot tub, drinking your beer, while you stayed out searching for these losers, not driving you around. Do I look like Morgan Freeman to you?"

"I haven't slept in twenty-four hours. It's not safe for me to drive. And I don't have a hot tub."

"I'm pretty sure one was mentioned."

"Nope."

"Fuck my life." Keeps sighed, shook his head. "So, tell me again about this guy? He blew his wife away?"

"The wife was some kind of eccentric," Celine said. "Christine Hammond. They met while she was in Louisiana, hunting ghosts. She was a paranormal investigator, I suppose you'd say."

"You're shittin' me."

"No shit. If you heard bumps in the night, she would roll in with her bag of tricks and work out what kind of bogeyman you were hosting. Splash some snake oil around, try to kick it out of your house."

"People can make a living doing that?" Keeps asked, smiling.

"I think it was Kradle who kept them afloat. He was a handyman. Builder. Plumber. Mechanic. Jack of all trades. Her family was wealthy but I don't think they supported her. Ghost hunting wasn't really in the family line," Celine said.

"You know all this how?"

"I looked real close at the case when we took him in five years ago."

"You do that with all the row guys?"

"Only the true assholes."

"So why'd he blast her?" Keeps asked. "The wife. Money troubles?"

"I think he just snapped," Celine said. "That's what they do, these family annihilators."

"Oh jeez, they have a term for it." Keeps laughed to himself.

"There's a pattern," Celine said. "The pressure builds and builds and builds, and they just snap and kill everyone. Financial pressure will do it. Maybe a sickness in the family or a recent loss. I think they were hard up for cash, but I also I think his relationship with her family wasn't great. And she had taken off from their marriage and gone missing for fifteen years."

"Fifteen *years*?"

"She walked out the day the baby was born," Celine said. "Left the hospital. Went into hiding. You're trying to tell me she felt safe with him?"

"Maybe she just didn't want to be a mom." Keeps shrugged. "Maybe it wasn't him."

"It was him, trust me."

"So why'd she come back, if she felt so unsafe?"

"I don't know. But she was back for less than three months before he killed her, and her sister, and the kid."

Keeps's mouth twisted, and stayed twisted. Celine sat watching it, waiting for it to untwist. It didn't.

"What?"

"I don't know." Keeps shrugged one shoulder again, the way he'd been doing for the whole conversation. Celine's blood was heating up, just watching that shoulder lift up and flop down, as if what they were talking about was no big deal. "Something ain't right."

"What ain't right?"

"The guy sounds like a pretty straight-up dude," Keeps said. "He builds things. Fixes things. Makes the money while she flutters around doing her ghosty-ghosty shit. Then she drops a baby on him and bounces out of town for fifteen years? Who raised the baby?"

"He did."

"Yeah, see?" Keeps clicked his tongue. "He didn't kill her. Kind of guy who would take a bitch back after all that wouldn't turn around three months later and kill her."

"Why don't you just trust me on this, okay?" Celine patted his shoulder. "I looked at the case. They found him standing on the lawn, soaked in the blood of all three victims, covered in gunshot residue and gasoline, watching the house burn to the ground." She straightened in her seat, but for some reason couldn't find the same level of comfort she'd had only minutes earlier. "I know John Kradle. He's not a nice guy."

Kradle tried to pin her down. It didn't work. He shoved the wriggling, screaming, kicking Shondra off the bed and onto the carpet, on her stomach, held her head down, and put his lips to her ear.

"Stop!" he rasped. "Stop, stop, stop! Listen to me! You've gotta listen!"

She stopped fighting and broke into furious sobs.

"I'm going to let you go," he said. He ripped off her shirt. The cheap restaurant uniform shirt gave way easily, the buttons popping, seams cracking as the stitches burst. It became a rag in his hands with one hard yank. "You have to do exactly as I say. Understand?"

Shondra's sobs ebbed slightly. They both listened, panting, as, at the front of the house, the pipes squeaked and water hit tiles.

"You're going to get up," Kradle said, ripping the tape from her wrists and ankles. "And you're going to hit me."

He climbed off her. Shondra scrambled backward into the side of the bed, reached for the tape around her mouth, found it hopelessly wound around her skull three or four times. Her cheeks bulged as she watched Kradle tug the clock radio from its socket in the wall behind the nightstand.

"Hit me with this." He handed it to her. "Then climb out the window and run for your fucking life."

He stood. Shondra got awkwardly to her feet. Her trousers were soaked in urine. Kradle could smell it. Her left breast had snuck sideways from her bra, the strap broken and the underwire cutting into the flesh of her ribs. He tried to take a step toward her but she backed away, almost fell on the bed.

"Hit me!" He gestured to his face. "Come on. Come *on!* We don't have time. You've got to do this. I can't do it myself!"

Shondra gathered up the cord of the clock radio, wouldn't meet his eyes with her own. Her whole body was shaking, a hard, bent, uncontrollable quivering.

"For fuck's sake," Kradle snarled. "Hit—"

The movement was too fast for him to follow. There was no build-up, no swing. She lashed out with the device from her center like a basketballer making a chest pass, the clock radio crunching into his temple as he tried to twist away. His knees hit the carpet, the room tilting.

"Okay." He gripped his face. "That was—"

She was on him. Beating down savagely with the device, knocking the radio on his forearms and elbows as he raised them to defend himself; her face turned away, swift, blind, brutal downward force. A second passed in which Kradle might have blacked out. He held on to the carpet as the room spun and dipped around him, and the woman named Shondra climbed through the bedroom window and disappeared.

Homer was there suddenly. Damp but dressed, lifting Kradle up by his arms and shaking him.

"What the fuck? What the fuck, man?"

"Oh! Whoa!" Kradle was suddenly awake, snapped back into self-preservation mode. "She got me. She got me!"

"Get up." Homer wrenched him to his feet, pushed him toward the door. "Get packing."

1999

"Suit yourself."

Celine tried to grip on to those words as she hugged the cold, dry hardwood pillar in the crawlspace under the porch. She squeezed her eyes shut and tried to visualize her arms, hands, fingers folding around the two words, pulling the letters into her chest, clinging on. *Suit yourself. Suit yourself.* Because the teenager knew that if she didn't hang on to those words as if they were a rope dangling above a cavern, she would fall. The other words, the other sounds, would creep back to her. Sounds from an hour earlier, when her grandfather turned away from her and walked up the porch steps and into the house, brought his rifle down from his shoulder and aimed it.

"Jesus, Nick, what are you—"

Cha-chick. Boom.

"Oh my. Oh my. Oh my god. Oh oh oh—"

Cha-chick. Boom.

"Dad! Dad, stop! Dad!"

Cha-chick. Boom.

Cha-chick. Boom.

Celine gripped the pillar, hugged it with her knees, opened her eyes and looked across the dark space beneath the porch where she had hidden when the firing started. The dirt was lined with thin, gold pinstripes from the midday sun. She could see legs out there. Every time she opened her eyes there were more of them. Men going to the barn. Men assembling at the driveway fence. Men walking up the steps into the house.

She had seen two faces in all the time she crouched there, holding on to the porch pillar. The face of a police officer who bent and vomited into her grandmother's garden of purple petunias after returning from the barn. And the face of a paramedic who lay on his belly now, ten yards from her, his hand outstretched toward her.

"Celine," he'd been saying gently, over and over, "it's safe now. He's gone. We've got him. Okay? He's locked up. He can't hurt you. Celine, come toward me. Let me help you out of there."

Celine knew it wasn't safe. Her splintered, ticking, writhing mind knew that much. Her grandparents' neighbors were at the edge of the driveway, their dog going nuts, Michael staring at the dirt, Paula weeping madly, wringing her hair, recounting how she'd heard the shots and thought it was the boys fooling around. How she'd seen Nick's truck speeding away, the eerie feeling that gave her. How she'd gone over and seen Celine's father crawl out onto the porch and die on the steps. Celine listened as the shooting unfolded again over the telephone; a set of boots on the opposite side of the porch to the paramedic, walking back and forth, dropping a cigarette every now and then.

"He just walked into the station," the cop said, "and put the rifle on the counter in front of the sergeant and said what he'd done, plain as that. That's what they're telling me. No, sir, I'm at the house. Oh, bad. Yeah. Yeah, bad. Seven, maybe eight. And five kids. He just went through and . . . one at a time. Everybody. Fucking everybody. Just . . . There's one left. A girl. Seventeen. She's under the porch. No. Nope. No. They're gonna give her a minute or two and then go in and pull her out, I think."

"Celine," the paramedic said. Celine squeezed her eyes shut and gripped the pillar tighter. She heard him shuffling forward on his belly in the dirt, coming into a crouch, crawling toward her. He was going to pull her out, like the cop on the phone said, and a piece of her mind was screaming with fury at that. At being pulled into the reality of it all before she was ready. Because, under the porch, it wasn't real. Above her head, above the creaking wooden boards, out there in the sunlight of the Georgia day, her little cousins were still playing in the barn, and her grandfather was rattling around the house somewhere, growling at people, and her mom and nanna and aunty were making salad. It was still just a day. Christmas Day.

CHAPTER 15

Old Axe had seen *The Wizard of Oz* plenty of times during his four decades staring at tiny, convex TV screens in prison cells at night. In his experience, most correctional facilities in Nevada had pretty shitty movie collections, county jails being the worst. Any violence had to be chopped out, so anything half decent, like murder mysteries, could lose twenty minutes or more. No boobs, no butts, no kids in swimsuits, either. You didn't have to chop anything out of *The Wizard of Oz* or *The Sound of Music* or *Willy Wonka and the Chocolate Factory*. Some of the kid-heavy films tended to rattle the fiddlers, but theirs was a quiet, harmless kind of unrest. *Oz* was a safe, universal prison classic.

Axe had been thinking about Dorothy stepping out of her black-and-white world and into that magical, shiny new place as he trundled through the desert sand toward the Joshua tree. The tree itself was taller than he'd anticipated, weird bristled fingers gripping a handful of blue sky. Worth the walk. He'd decided to keep wandering north, and stopped a few times to look at almost mystically beautiful rocks, cacti, scrubby plants. He halted at the sight of a spotted lizard, and put his hands in his pockets and watched it watching him for a while. Axe the alien on a new and pristine planet. He came across a Coke can shining like a diamond, its light drawing him from about half a mile away. The air tasted different and the world seemed unfathomably big.

One of those flying drone machines did buzz over his head just before nightfall, but it didn't descend to check him out or give him any orders. He let the breeze direct him, having no real intentions, feeling jubilant for the first time in a long time. He slept under the stars, woke under them, too. His ears kept presenting him with phantom sounds, the way that solid ground must lie to sailors for a week or so after a long stint at sea, he guessed. He heard someone call out his name and turned to find only emptiness behind him. He heard the peal of the chow bell and the clatter of feet on the steel steps outside his cell.

After a while, he hit an unlined road. He saw an animal, so pancaked and sunbaked he couldn't tell which was the head or tail, or what it had once been. He turned to his left, because the wind was going that way, and kept on.

When he heard the sound of a vehicle behind him, he figured it would be a prison van or sheriff or someone coming to take him back. He stopped, and the car pulled over, too far behind him to make any sense. Axe turned to look.

An RV was sitting on the shoulder, two women in the front seats, leaning together, talking. There were more people in the back. Axe waited. Nothing happened. The RV's engine hummed. The desert gaped. In the distance, he could see something tracking across the sky—either a drone close by or a helicopter far away. Axe waited another moment or two, then turned and continued trundling. The RV came up and slowed alongside him.

He saw that the two young people in the front weren't women but long-haired men. Axe hadn't seen this kind of honey-brown suntanned faces, bleached eyelashes, and flowing, golden hair on men since the 1960s. He noticed surfboards on the top of the RV and clumps of sea grass in the wheel wells.

The vehicle stopped, and still nothing happened. He realized the kid closest to him, with his elbow hanging out the window, was listening to an argument in the cabin.

"Might be a crazy-ass serial killer or something!"

"Come on. Come on, Manny! Where's your sense of fuckin' adventure?"

"He's an old man. What's he gonna do?"

"If we leave him out here he'll probably die."

"There's only one of him and five of us."

"Dude." The sun-speckled kid in the window grinned at Axe. "Dude, hey. All this shit on the radio about a breakout. Is it true?"

Axe brushed dust off the chest of his prison denims, examined them.

"Seems like it," he said. They were the first words he'd uttered to someone outside a prison since before the man he was talking to was born.

"You, like"—the man paused to laugh at his own daring, or maybe at the absurdity of it all—"you want a ride with us?"

Axe thought about it. Sucked air down the sides of his teeth and examined the horizon. When he turned back, the window was crowded with young, apprehensive faces—curious, scared, excited, he didn't know.

"Guess so." Axe shrugged.

The young people looked at each other.

"Are you dangerous?" a girl asked from the back of the huddle.

Again, Axe thought about it. About the truth and how well it had served him in his life.

"Nope," he said.

The back door of the RV popped open. Axe went to it, climbed aboard with some difficulty. The air conditioning enveloped him, as did the scent of weed. He was standing in a cluttered kitchenette. Dirty plates. Wooden knife block on the counter, full of shiny blade handles. One of those flat-panel computers he'd seen on TV was lying on an armchair, its cover flipped open and screen blank.

"I can't believe we're doing this," someone giggled. Axe moved the computer carefully and sat down in the armchair. All the young people were grinning. The RV started up and rumbled back onto the road.

"You want a drink, old man?" a girl asked.

"Sure," Axe said.

When in Oz, he thought.

1999

He didn't believe in all the ghost stuff. But he showed up anyway. He figured that was what you did when you loved someone. You nodded and laughed and chipped in with a "She's right, you know. I've seen it!" occasionally. You held the camera steady and let her do her thing, and it wasn't as though she didn't do the same for him now and then, though it was usually a ladder she was holding, and his thing mostly ended up getting her crazy mad and covered in leaves or dirt. He sold the houseboat and made enough cash to buy a decent car, and they took her show on the road, answering emails that came through a webpage she'd been clever enough to cook up.

In Dallas, they exorcised a poltergeist from an old fishing trawler. In Long Beach, they shuffled a shadow walker out of a beachfront bar. In Chicago, they spent three days clearing an attic of a menacing presence that at first she thought was the ghost of a murdered girl, but turned out to be a demon masquerading as such while it built up its power reserves. Kradle thought Christine was taking the excitable young couple who were the owners of the attic for a ride. While Christine performed for the camera, got messages from the apparent demon in faux-Latin with her eyes rolled back in her head, he took a look at the roof joists and found some loose bolts, tightened them up on the sly. After all, he'd taken some people for rides in his life too, and these trust-fund kids seemed to get a kick out of all Christine's processes—the runes and gems she taped to the walls and the incantations she made them recite while on their knees in the middle of the living room rug. People shared the videos via the internet, and the call-outs went nuts. They spent weekends on yachts in Bermuda, talking to sea spirits, and a month in Jackson Hole, performing sage ceremonies on the log cabins of millionaires. He worked only so he could get sweaty now and then, so his hands didn't go all soft. Her money got so good they didn't know what to do with it.

So, they did with it what people usually do. They bought a house in north-west Mesquite, with a bullnose awning over a little tiled porch. They'd been in town trying to convince the ghost of an old Native American lady to cross over to the other side, and Christine liked the people and he liked the noticeboard at the supermarket covered in requests for handyman services. They spread expensive lawn all over the yard around a river-stone pool, real thick lawn that was totally impractical in the desert sun. She recruited all the neighbors as friends, because these were the kinds of people she liked to surround herself with—regulars, normies, average Joes—people who were so fascinated by her stories about ghosts and so charmed by her tasseled Miu Mius and eyeball-shaped earrings that they couldn't possibly talk about anything but her. They held backyard barbecues and she drank too much sauvignon blanc and started calling him her "rougarou," her swamp werewolf, scratching the back of his head with her nails, making the hair stick up. The way she told it, he was a backwater illiterate with yellow teeth and a beard when she found him, the Quasimodo of the bayou, a creature she alone had been clever enough to see could be taught to stand on its hind legs and wear shoes. John didn't mind her hamming up his story to make it seem as if she'd brought in a skinny street dog, tamed it, bathed it, taught it to bark on cue, and made a fine husband out of it. Christine needed people to like her, and the fact that his houseboat had been half-sunk with books when he met her wasn't as compelling a tale.

Everything was fine until that day in August. Sure, he'd caught a faraway look in her eye sometimes and knew in his heart she was dreaming of diag-nosing screams at midnight in San Francisco or vibrations in the bathroom mirror in Tennessee. But she got by on her tarot readings, her $50 copy-and-paste email consults, her newsletter membership programs. Then one after-noon she came to him in the garage, where he was taking apart a microwave, and handed him a pregnancy test with two red lines on it. He smiled, and she burst into tears.

CHAPTER 16

It was clear from the contents of their haul how panicked they had been. On a picnic table that bore cigarette burns made by workers from the nearby packaging warehouse, Kradle dumped the trash bags of things they had taken from Shondra's house. Virgin River was a blinding strip of white through the long grass. He sorted through the items while Homer broke twigs.

The most important item, a laptop Kradle had grabbed from the living room, he set aside. He devoured three slices of white bread from the half-loaf Homer had nabbed from the kitchen, his heart still hammering as he ate. They'd managed to grab a Coke, a package of sliced ham, a jar of cookies, three candy bars, and a box of raw pasta in the way of food. Other supplies included two cell phones, a kitchen knife, and three dollars in cash. A hairbrush, a sock, a label maker, and a ball of twine had also come along for the journey in the trash bags, gathered up in the sheer madness of knowing Shondra was half-naked and screaming through her gag and running god-knows-where to get help.

"How the fuck did it happen?" Homer was shaking his head, his fist full of tiny twig pieces.

"You know how it happened." Kradle pushed open the laptop and sat down. "I ripped off her tape and she grabbed the clock radio from the nightstand, smacked me in the head with it. Jumped out the window. Simple as that."

"Why did you take her tape off?"

"I needed to so I could . . ." Kradle looked at the lake. "You know. God. Man, you're making me feel like an idiot here."

"You are an idiot," Homer said. Kradle watched him. There was a meanness in his eyes for a moment that made all the air leave Kradle's lungs and the fine hairs on his arms stand on end, his primal warning system kicking in. And then it was gone. The tiger in the tall grass just a trick of the light. "Sorry. Sorry. I shouldn't have said that, buddy. That wasn't right."

Kradle nodded, tried to look chastened.

"Women have got away from me before." Homer shrugged. "It happens."

They sorted through the clothes they had managed to snatch from the floor and closet. Two of the shirts were obviously Shondra's, and two must have belonged to the boyfriend. Kradle pulled on a blue T-shirt with a logo he didn't recognize, while Homer stretched a black Nevada Wolf Pack baseball jersey over his bulky frame. Disregarding the filthy jeans and shoes, they might have been two regular people standing by the water behind a warehouse.

"What's the computer for?" Homer asked.

"I've got to get numbers for my guys. Look up their details. See if I can call in some help."

"You didn't stay in touch while you were on the inside?"

"No," Kradle said.

"Why not?" Homer asked. Kradle rubbed his neck. "I thought you mob guys got an easy ride in prison. I thought you took care of each other."

Kradle tried a new strategy: ignoring the questions, rather than trying to provide answers for things he couldn't account for. Clam up. It had made the detectives go away for a while in the seventh or eighth hour of his questioning after Christine and Mason and Audrey were murdered. Homer wandered down to the water and Kradle started to breathe freely again.

He opened the Wi-Fi app on the computer, the way he'd seen his lawyer do in the Pronghorn visitors' center, and fished around for a free internet source. He found a signal coming from the packaging warehouse, clicked it and crossed his fingers. When the icon went green he opened a window and started googling.

A search on Homer Carrington brought up hundreds of articles about the breakout at Pronghorn. Kradle shifted the parameters to exclude links that had been posted within the past twenty-four hours. All the things he didn't want to see flooded onto the screen. Naked girls lying in desolate fields, their bodies looking strangely deflated and impossibly white in the flattened grass, faces turned toward grasping, lifeless hands. There was an image of a missing person poster, the young woman grinning at the camera. Big brown eyes. A Labrador puppy cradled in her arms. Crime scene photographs of a car abandoned mid-tire-change in a shopping mall parking lot, still up on the jack, the tire lying on its side. There was an old couple lying side by side on floral carpet, the coffee table knocked over, the front door of the house ajar. The most recent news article was a week old, headed ATTACK ON GUARD: NORTH NEVADA STRANGLER REHOUSED AT PRONGHORN. Kradle clicked. A CCTV still image of Homer in a prison hallway—not Pronghorn, somewhere older. The huge serial killer had his hands around the throat of a small, plump male guard. Kradle clicked out of the article, scrolled down, reading headlines.

NN STRANGLER HOMER CARRINGTON PLEADS INSANITY

CARRINGTON SENTENCED TO DEATH

CARRINGTON VICTIMS MAY BE DOZENS, EXPERT SAYS

CARRINGTON TRIPS TO MEXICO MAY REVEAL MORE VICTIMS

TWELVE-YEAR-OLD MISSING GIRL LINKED TO NN STRANGLER

Kradle knew he didn't have much time before the cell phone and laptop both became weapons against him. When Shondra found help, she would describe him and Homer to the police, and it wouldn't be long until someone somewhere decided they sounded just similar enough to two of the top-classified fugitives that they should prioritize tracking them down. He had minutes, not hours. He punched in a name that echoed loudly into the dark halls of his past.

Patrick Frapport.

Mentions of the detective online were scarce. No social media. Images of the heavyset, bald police officer were also rare. A blurry image of him receiving a medal from some police boss. A profile shot of him sitting in a courtroom, waiting to testify, the bulge under his chin tucked uncomfortably into the collar of his shirt, red raw from being recently shaved. Kradle read quickly over an article announcing Frapport's promotion in the *Mesquite Sun*, and clicked on a picture of the man and his slender wife, her the decidedly friendlier-looking of the two, with warm, rosy cheeks and a sharp brunette bob cut.

Shelley Frapport. Kradle clicked on her Instagram page. He knew Instagram only from television shows he'd watched inside prison, couldn't navigate the site for precious minutes, trying to figure how it worked. Unlike her husband, Shelley's online activities were full of breadcrumbs leading to her location. He recognized the caramel-leather-lined booths of Eden's Diner in one of the happy selfies of the woman, and noticed a slice of a public pool with a big yellow water slide in the background of another. He knew that pool, had taken Mason there when the boy was young for the birthday party of a school friend. For a moment Kradle was swamped with memories: standing with other dads in the shade of the kiosk, Mason tugging his arm, begging for candy money, a puddle of water pooling at his feet and his black hair plastered to his fleshy forehead. The pool and the diner put Shelley Frapport in the neighborhood of Beaver Dam. When Kradle clicked on the second-most-recent image he saw Shelley Frapport sitting on a porch swing. *#afternoon #suburbanbliss #pinotgrigio*. In the bottom right-hand corner of the screen, a little brass number was affixed to the front fence of the house. Number seven. Kradle stared hard at the image, trying to determine the angle of the sun, the style of house, anything that could provide a hint as to where it lay. In the background of the image, over Shelley's shoulder and past the side of the house, he thought he could see the top of a structure in the distance. A red and green water tower.

"My seatbelt was undone," Homer said.

Kradle looked up. The serial killer was standing just near him, the big knife from Shondra's kitchen clutched in his fist, the blade glinting in the light bouncing off the lake.

"What?"

"In the plane," Homer said. "I remember buckling it. I remember shoving the buckle closed, hearing it click, pulling on it to make sure it was tight. It stuck in my head because at the time I was thinking to myself, *What if this guy is lying? What if he can't fly?* But you weren't lying about being able to fly. You were lying about being my friend."

Kradle felt all the blood rush out of his head, face, neck, as if a plug had been pulled somewhere and all the life was draining downward at a dizzying speed. For a moment he just gripped the table and stared at the man holding the knife.

"There's no money, is there?" Homer asked.

"No," Kradle said.

"Because you're not a mob guy."

"No, I'm not."

"You let that woman get away, didn't you," Homer said. It wasn't a question. "And if you'd had the chance, you were going to push me out of that plane."

Kradle didn't answer. All his focus was on his body, his limbs, his breath, keeping the blood flowing, keeping his wits about him. But for all his focus, all his planning, he was tired, dehydrated, probably concussed, and half-crazed with terror that at any moment he was going to be seized again by any one of the half a dozen government agencies that were after him. The fear that he was going to wake up back in his cell on the row, staring into the deep dark forever, was suffocating. So when Homer lunged at him, Kradle dove sideways off the bench, staggered backward. But the big man's arm seemed to have infinite reach, and he wasn't fast enough to move out of that reach before it was coming forward, enveloping him, consuming him. That big arm that had swept around so many throats, those killer hands, those knuckles misshapen and scarred and scraped by fingernails trying to claw them away, including his own only hours ago. Kradle felt the blade slash through his arm as if it was butter.

"So, let me get this straight." Celine folded her arms. "You had a grab-all set up for Kradle, and a *dog* blew your cover?"

She stood in the parking lot of the Mesquite Police Department office, which seemed to have become a kind of field command center for fugitive-related activity. In the shade of a huge navy-blue US Marshals' intelligence van, Celine addressed an audience of four men—two sheriff's deputies and two marshals, who had reluctantly turned from their maps, laptops, charts, and radios to examine the two interlopers in their midst. Keeps was trying to disappear into a nearby bush, the recently released felon standing as close to it as he possibly could while sheltering a cigarette against the breeze.

"Sorry." The biggest marshal flicked his head at Celine. "Who are you again?"

"I'm Captain Celine Osbourne, death row supervisor from Pronghorn Correctional."

"So you're not a cop, a marshal, or a fed," the guy said. Celine didn't answer. "Captain Osbourne, we appreciate your interest in this matter. But my line to you is the same as it is to all civilians. We're doing the best we can to round up any fugitives who might come into town, but—"

"What's your name?"

"Lowakowski." The guy gave a heavy sigh, looked at his colleagues. *You hearing this?*

"Lowakowski," Celine said. "Those journalists over there by the vending machine just told me you had John Kradle in your hands and you fumbled it. I want to know what you have on his current location."

"Please step back, Captain Osbourne." Lowakowski put up a fleshy palm. "You're in an operational area here."

"The guy who was with him," Celine said, scrolling through apps on her phone to find her saved photos. She held up a picture of Burke David Schmitz. "Did he look like this?"

"I can't reveal—"

"Or this?" Celine held up a picture of Homer Carrington. The marshals glanced at the sheriffs. Celine nodded, then walked over to where Keeps was trying to turn himself inside out to avoid being looked at by the swarm of authorities.

"It's bad news," Celine said.

"Oh, excellent."

"Kradle has Homer Carrington with him."

"Who?"

"The North Nevada Strangler," Celine said.

"Okay, look," Keeps said. He took Celine's car keys out of her pocket. "This is where I bounce. All I wanted was a goddamn burger and a beer, and now somehow I'm miles from where I wanna be, chauffeuring your ass around while you chase Hannibal Lecter. I'm not going to end up in a hole in the ground putting lotion on myself. I'm done."

"If you've got such a big problem with being the driver, I'll drive," Celine said. "We'll drop by a gas station and I'll grab a Red Bull and you can get a beer and then you'll be halfway to—"

"No."

"Keeps, I need—"

"You need therapy," he said. He tapped his temple with his finger. "You need your head checked out, because you ain't a cop, okay? You don't fight crime. You don't solve mysteries. You don't hunt fugitives. You're a jailer, okay? Man, I've seen some egos on screws in my life, but this takes the cake."

"Egos?" Celine scoffed.

"Yeah," Keeps said. "You're acting as if this is all your doing. Like you let them out and you've got to get them back again. This. Ain't. About. You!"

Celine couldn't speak. She stared at her boots on the asphalt and felt far from home in an upside-down world.

"All I have been doing for the past fifteen years is keeping them boxed up, away from the world. Keeping people safe from them. This is me," she said. "This is who I am."

"No, it's not." Keeps eased smoke from between his lips.

Celine held up her phone. "You happen to notice how many people are *not* calling me on this thing?" she asked. "A normal person finds herself at the center of a history-making fuck-up at work, and she has all kinds of people calling her. Friends. Family. Why aren't people calling me and asking if I'm okay? What's happening. What I'm doing about it. If I need help."

"Because you don't have any friends or family."

"Why have I got a goddamn inmate I don't know from Adam helping me out on this thing?" She gestured to him.

"Because you promised me beer."

"Death row is what I've got, Keeps, and I'm just trying to get it back."

Keeps laughed, and a puff of smoke came out of his mouth and was snatched away by the breeze. "Look, I've heard guys talk like that on the inside. They spend so much time surrounded by prison walls they start to think that's all there is. You're just as institutionalized as I am."

"It's more than that," she began. But Celine didn't know how to tell him that driving home at night to her empty, immaculate house, knowing that all the men she was responsible for were locked away safely, was the warmest feeling in the world. That she liked to think that every minute, every hour they weren't on the street causing more pain to the people whose lives they had already devastated was due in part to her. That, somewhere out there, there were men and women and children going to bed safely because she spent her days checking green lights, turning keys in locks, punching codes into alarm systems, watching shadows of humans move about on security cameras. There were men on Celine's row who had climbed into the bedrooms of little girls in the dark hours and carried them away from their warm sheets, and their bones were still unlocated, their faces remembered only in photographs. There were men on her row who had wrung the life from desperate women working the streets, who had watched from the roadside as cars with whole families in them burned, who had fired shots on panicked crowds from on high, indiscriminately cutting down souls. And there was John Kradle, who had one day decided that his family didn't deserve to go on living.

Celine's phone rang and she grabbed at it. When she heard his voice on the line, her heart twisted in her chest.

Kradle stopped by the front of the warehouse and pulled his hand away from the wound in his arm. He couldn't tell how bad it was. It looked deep, black, wet. There were people running from the office at the back of the packaging warehouse, having spotted the fray from the windows that looked out over the water. They were rushing to assist the man lying by the picnic table, bleeding his life away. If he were a religious man, Kradle would have said a prayer for the warehouse worker who had been brave enough to come and intervene as Homer swung wildly at him with the kitchen knife. But Kradle wasn't the praying type. He could only hope the guy wasn't dead.

"Celine?"

"Oh my god." He heard her muffle the phone with her hand. "It's him."

"Listen to me," Kradle said. He limped across the warehouse parking lot between cars, heading for the road. "Homer Carrington just stabbed a guy behind the . . . the Resco Industries Packaging warehouse. It's near the river. He ran off, heading north."

"Who's the guy?"

"Some warehouse worker who tried to save me from Carrington."

"Is . . . is he dead?"

"I don't know."

"Stay there."

"I can't. You know I can't."

He heard her cover the phone again, shout the story to someone. He could only assume she was surrounded by other fugitive hunters. She would be in the midst of it all, trying to undo what she could of the breakout. Celine took everything personally. He heard a car door opening and closing, an engine starting.

"Celine? Celine?"

"I'm here."

"Homer and I carjacked and robbed a woman named Shondra." Kradle headed down an alleyway at the end of a strip mall, his bloodied shirt causing a couple with a dog to scurry away to safety. "I don't, uh . . . You'll find her. She escaped from us. We stole two cell phones from her house. This is one of them. Homer might have the other one. He took everything we had—the whole bag. He might . . . I don't know if the other phone works. It looked old. But you might be able to track him by it if he turns it on."

"Stay where you are, Kradle."

The alley opened into another strip mall. He spotted a secondhand clothing store with racks of coats hanging in the sunshine. When he spoke again he heard an echo, as though the phone was on speaker.

"I have to find the man who killed my son," Kradle said.

"Oh, Jesus," Celine sighed.

"Celine, I know your story," Kradle said.

"What?"

"I know what happened to you," Kradle said. He heard sirens. "My lawyer told me. He worked with your grandfather's lawyer over in Georgia way back when. I've known for years, Celine. Are you there? Are you listening?"

"You . . ." She was having trouble breathing. He heard her gasp, her breath hitch. "You never said anything. You never—"

"Listen, I get it." Kradle stopped and wiped sweat from his face. He was leaning against the window of a nail salon. A woman doing a pedicure just inside the window had stopped her work and was staring at him, open-mouthed. "What happened with your family . . . Of course you would hate someone convicted of a crime like mine. But I need you to take the emotion out of it now. I need you to put it aside. It didn't matter if you believed me when I was on the row, but it sure as hell matters now. You can help me. I know you can."

"I wouldn't help you if you were on fire, John Kradle," Celine said.

"Take an hour," Kradle said. "One hour. Just do me that much, please. Take an hour, look at my case. Have someone look at it with you, someone who isn't weighed down by the kind of history you've got. Your boyfriend or . . . someone. It doesn't matter. You'll see it if you open your eyes."

There was no answer. John Kradle dumped the phone in a trash can and limped down another alleyway, slid through a gap in a chain-link fence, and crossed the cracked concrete of an abandoned lot, passed threads of dry, brown grass hanging like hair over an old flight of steps. He found a park with a public bathroom and walked into the cool, dark brick building to rest.

CHAPTER 17

Trinity Parker sat down across from Lieutenant Joe Brassen and took a moment to stir her coffee. She had requested many things since she'd arrived at Pronghorn to handle the breakout. The partition walls with the faces of inmates. A quiet space with a sturdy chair where she could take briefings from her section chiefs, sit and map out her forty-eight-, seventy-two-, and ninety-six-hour plans, answer the odd phone call from Washington. Somewhere with a window, where she could look out over the press camped outside the gates. Truth was, she could have done without all those things. She wasn't prissy. Trinity had squatted in broken-down houses in Detroit while hunting fugitives, shitting in a bucket and living on candy bars and bottled water, cockroaches crawling up her ankles. But what she couldn't do without was strong, good-quality coffee, and at the thirty-hour mark a proper machine had arrived and the whole catastrophe had seemed impossibly easier to handle.

She put down her spoon and glanced at Brassen as she lifted her cup. Trinity enjoyed dealing with people whose worlds were slowly crumbling. They were refreshing. Joe Brassen had to know he was on the verge of losing everything, of becoming one of the things he feared and dreaded most. An inmate. He was ripe for being taken advantage of. When someone is trapped in a grain silo, sinking desperately into the abyss with every movement, they'll take anything offered to pull them out. They'll grab at a red-hot poker. Trinity put her coffee down, smacked her lips, and flattened her hands on the table in front of her.

"Paint," she said.

"Huh?" Brassen gulped. He had been expecting a threat. A barrage of abuse. But not that word. Colors flushed through his face as he tried to find an emotion to center on. Trinity took her time.

"Black paint," Trinity said. "I know. I know. I could hardly believe it myself. But that's what will be your undoing. That's what will put you in a prison cell for the rest of your life. A three-dollar tube of acrylic paint, manufactured in China, imported to the US. 'Midnight True Black' is the shade. Number 4035."

"I don't know what you're talking about." Brassen smoothed back his thinning black hair, then pushed his glasses into place from where they had slipped down his nose on skin greased by sweat. "I want my lawyer."

"The minimum security guys were happy enough to talk about where they got their black paint," Trinity said. She sipped her coffee. "They're all snitches over in minimum. It's the same in every prison. They're in for short stints, so they don't have time to get used to bad conditions. They want to be comfortable. They all pointed to a guard named Maria Dresbone who was bringing in their contraband black paint."

"What the hell's that got to do with me?"

"Maria was harder to crack," Trinity said. "You correctional officers are somewhat more loyal to each other. Who among you hasn't snapped and slipped an elbow into an inmate's face, and relied on your colleagues to keep quiet about it? But she turned you in eventually. Maria told me that you supply her and three other guards with contraband items for inmates in minimum because you alone are able to get those items through security. Your girlfriend is the Entry B X-ray operator. She hasn't checked your backpack since you started dating six months ago."

Brassen stared at the ceiling of the office they occupied—some pencil-pusher's cluttered workspace inside the prison's administration block. There was a model truck on the edge of the desk, sitting by a framed photograph of a young girl. Trinity pushed the picture with her fingertip so that it was at a perfect forty-five-degree angle to the edge of the desk.

"The snitching inmates led me to Maria, and Maria led me to you," she said. "You work on death row. You're the only guy who could have got that paint to Schmitz. My agents found other contraband items in Schmitz's cell. His pillow isn't regulation, and there was a bottle of antibacterial nasal spray under his bed that wasn't on his list of approved meds."

"Lawyer," Brassen growled. It was the weak sound of a cornered animal, a hollow warning.

"If Burke David Schmitz kills again, and he will . . . ," Trinity began.

"I want my lawyer," Brassen said.

"You don't get a *fucking* lawyer," Trinity snarled, leaning forward in her chair. "Not here, not now, not until I decide you deserve one. I'm the person who decides everything you get from this moment onward, you gormless, knuckle-dragging sack of turds. You assisted a known neo-Nazi terrorist in escaping custody! You can sit here and tell me everything you know, or you can sit in a cell in Gitmo for the next three years while they burn out your eyeballs with strobe lights and blast the *Sesame Street* theme song until you chew your own tongue off."

Trinity leaned back in her chair and drained her coffee cup while Brassen stared at her, his eyes wide with visions crowding in of orange jumpsuits, hoods, electrodes. The images, Trinity knew, would be competing with hopeless dreams of safety, of his plywood trailer stuffed to bursting with cans of Bud and bags of Cheetos, a mixed-breed dog in there somewhere, probably something beefy, a pit bull or ridgeback with a big underbite of crooked teeth. It would sleep on his bed and be named something stupid: Blaze or Dagger or Harley. Trinity knew Brassen would choose the right path, choose the trailer and the dog over Gitmo and the orange jumpsuits and hoods. She just didn't know how long that was going to take. She put her feet up on the desk.

"I don't care about the paint and the pillows. I want to know what else you were bringing in for Schmitz."

Brassen looked at his hands on the edge of the table. The thumb of one hand was rubbing the knuckles of the other so vigorously that the skin was becoming pink and raw.

"Gun magazines," Brassen said. "Candy bars. Letters."

"Are you a neo-Nazi, Brassen?"

"No," the big man continued. "Not, like, uh . . . I mean, I don't like Black inmates. That's all. The Black inmates are worse than the white ones behavior-wise, and that's just plain old fact."

Trinity waited for Brassen to get uncomfortable and fill the silence. He did.

"Like, if you got a shank on the pod, you know it belongs to a Black inmate," Brassen said. "They get here, and it doesn't matter what crime they're coming in for. They weapon up straight away. I think it's just the violence in them. And that's my opinion." Brassen sniffed. "It's a free country, and I've got a right to my opinion."

Trinity stared at him.

"What, uh, what Schmitz did was terrible, though." Brassen cleared his throat loudly. "I mean, all those people down in New Orleans. The shooting. Nazi or not, you can't—"

"What did they offer you?" Trinity said. "And what did you bring?"

"Nothing. I don't—"

"What was in the letters you brought him?" Trinity said. "You mentioned letters. Stands to reason they would have contained communication Schmitz wanted to get past the censors. I assume you snooped."

"I didn't snoop. They told me not to."

"They told you not to, or they offered you money not to?"

Brassen wiped sweat from his neck with the collar of his shirt.

"Those letters will be gone," Trinity said. "Schmitz took a box of belongings with him when he escaped. I need something else."

Brassen gave a long, heavy sigh. "I want to make some kind of deal with you here."

"There's no deal. You give me what you have, and you hope that this time tomorrow somebody isn't waterboarding you," Trinity said. "In fact, I'll see to it that if you're waterboarded, it's a Black man who does it."

"You guys don't really do that kind of thing." Brassen ventured a small laugh.

Trinity said nothing.

"I let him use a cell phone," Brassen said.

Trinity sat forward. "Where's that phone now?"

"I was supposed to get it back from him. Yesterday morning. I never let him keep it because of the shakedowns. I'd give it to him and let him have it overnight. He must have taken it with him if it's not in his cell."

"Do you know who he was calling?"

"No."

"Do you remember where and when you bought the phone?"

"Yeah." Brassen nodded, took his own cell phone out of his pocket. "And I have the number saved, too. I put it into my phone in case I had a night off and I needed to tell Schmitz there was going to be a shakedown."

Trinity took Brassen's phone from him, sat with her feet on the desk and her elbow hanging off the side of her chair while she opened the device. On the wallpaper screen was a picture of a big, ugly dog sitting on the porch of a plywood trailer. She smiled to herself.

By the time Celine and Keeps arrived at the waterfront, the place was a swarm of people and vehicles, a concentrated hive of activity reminiscent of the chaos that had descended on Pronghorn after the breakout. It was early afternoon, the sun beginning to fall. Celine pressed forward through a group of people in gray coveralls with RESCO WAREHOUSE CREW embroidered on the breast pocket to find them clustered around a dead man lying twisted on the thin grass. She discerned from the sobbing account of a big man in a trucker cap that a couple of guys had been on their way to the picnic table from the warehouse for a smoke break, when they'd noticed two men getting into an argument. Whether Nugent, the skinny, bald man on the ground, saw that there was a knife in the fray before he ran forward to help was unclear.

"He just ran up there and the guy jammed the knife in his guts," the big man said. "Oh, Remy. Man, he's dead. He's dead."

Celine found herself being pushed back by the hands of a police officer. There were sirens on the wind, onlookers assembling in the warehouse parking lot, frowning, arms crossed, murmuring to each other the way that strangers will do when presented with a public spectacle of tragedy, sharing information, awe. Celine noticed a spot of blood in the grass at her feet. She let the cop push her back until she noticed another one, then turned and started following the dark splotches on the ground.

"Let's go, Celine." Keeps took her arm.

"He went this way." Celine pointed at the blood. "Come on. Come on."

"No, we're going."

"We can follow—"

"We're going!" Keeps barked. For an instant, Celine saw the inmate in him again. The prisoner defending himself against the other dangerous men stuffed behind the wire, bottled rage carefully pressurized and stored until it was needed. He pulled her out of the crowd and she tried to build her fury to match his, to fight him, to make him continue doing what she needed him to do. But she was so tired, and the night was not far away.

"You're exhausted." Keeps pointed at her chest, accusatory. He turned the finger on himself. "So am I. They're about to lock down this whole goddamn suburb to try to find those guys. I'm not spending my first night as a free man in Mesquite."

"We can just follow the trai—"

"What are you gonna do?" Keeps threw his hands up. "You're what—five foot nothin'? You're gonna chase down a pair of murderers and wrestle them to the ground yourself? Is that the plan? Because I sure ain't helping you. I don't like you enough to do what I'm *already* doing, let alone mess with some fugitive psychos."

"Keeps—"

"You might have been the big, tough officer with all the power over these guys while they were behind steel mesh and bulletproof glass, Celine. But right now you ain't nothin'."

Celine looked at the blood on the ground at her feet. Homer's blood, or Kradle's blood, or the blood of a murdered man, the first confirmed casualty of the men from her row. Her men. The ones she couldn't keep contained.

"Get in the car," Keeps said. "We're going home."

An hour and a half of heavy silence, the road roaring beneath them, the red sun creeping toward the rocky horizon through the windshield. When cars blasted past them, Celine saw one law enforcement vehicle after another— tan FBI vehicles and sheriffs' cruisers, the occasional border patrol car probably carrying officers who had been called in to assist. She slept thinly for a while, and switched wordlessly with Keeps at some unmarked point in their journey, the two passing each other at the back of the car in the warm, windy desert without meeting each other's eyes. He started texting someone maybe twenty minutes from home, and she wondered if he was trying to organize a a pickup. It made her a little sad, but she didn't know why, exactly. She had lied, manipulated, and bullied him into helping her for an entire day with no tangible reward, on a mission that meant nothing to him. If he could beg his way onto someone's couch, away from her and her desperate, angry, stupid need to find John Kradle, then she believed wholeheartedly that he should.

He surprised her as she pulled onto her street, sitting up in his seat to examine the narrow Spanish-style homes drifting by, their stone-and-succulent gardens and darkened windows.

"So *is* there a boyfriend?" Keeps asked.

Celine laughed with surprise. "You heard Kradle say that?"

"I heard it. You got your phone turned all the way up."

"It's loud at Pronghorn. You can barely hear yourself think." She took her phone from the center console and tapped the button on the side to turn it down.

"So?" Keeps pushed.

Celine thought carefully about her answer. "Yeah," she said. "And he'll be pissed as all hell."

"Damn, man."

"And he's not warm and cuddly at the best of times."

They parked and walked up the drive. Celine tried not to think about the fact that if Keeps had heard John Kradle talk about her boyfriend on the phone, he'd also heard Kradle say that he knew what had *happened* to her. That word had cut through the line like a razor, slicing into her ear, into her brain, neatly parting sealed wounds and making blood run. She had heard it so much in the years after the massacre. How was she coping with what *happened*? Would she ever recover from what *happened*? It was as if a thunderclap had burst in the sky and snatched up with it every family member she had. It was a faceless *happening* that had moved through the house with the rifle that day, and not a man.

She punched a code into the panel inside the front door. Keeps stood on the stoop, looking into the eye of the doorbell camera.

"High security," he said.

"It's what I'm used to," Celine said. They went inside. There was a flapping sound, and she and Keeps stood in the spacious living room and watched as a heavy, brown tabby cat made its way toward them from the kitchen, trotting, head down with determination. The animal stopped at Celine's feet, looked up, and opened its mouth to let out a long, angry wail.

"Somebody's hungry," Keeps said.

"Like I said. Pissed as all hell." Celine picked up the cat. "Come on, Jake."

Celine went into the kitchen to feed the cat. She smiled as she thought about how Kradle must have overheard and misinterpreted a conversation between her and Jackson earlier that month about the "new man" in her life; the large, mean, wild cat she had befriended on her evening walk. *I'd seen him around the neighborhood before. He turned up again last night. I think we're going to make it a regular thing.*

Keeps followed her into the kitchen, smoothed a hand over the huge, bare marble surface of the kitchen island. She knew what he was seeing. That the house was enormous, that it was immaculate and loveless and cold as a tomb, that there wasn't a single photograph in the entire place—no happy-snaps of girls' getaways in Tijuana, no portraits of nieces and nephews in elf costumes from Christmases past. There was no sign of a human boyfriend. No cutesy notes about remembering to feed the cat or bring home milk, no calendar hanging on the wall, "Date night!" on a Wednesday, dinner and a movie and home by nine. Only Celine lived here. The house was a mistake she had made as a teenager in possession of three inherited estates. She figured she'd buy a big house on the other side of the country to the *happening*, one as far as possible from the seat of her memories, a place with high ceilings and a pool and a double garage, close to somewhere big and fun and filled with people, like Los Angeles or Vegas. She would fill the house with nice things, because she could afford it, and she thought things would make her happy. She couldn't have known back then that the bigger the house, the louder it yawned with emptiness.

"I don't have any burgers," Celine said as she scooped a tin of tuna into a bowl for the wailing, mewling, tail-flicking creature pawing at her ankles. "But I have beer."

"I ordered Uber Eats," Keeps said. He held up his phone. "It'll be here in ten. I got enough for the both of us."

"I'm not hungry." Celine tossed the tuna can into the trash. "Just put mine in the fridge."

"But—"

She waved as she walked to the bathroom.

An hour later, she had climbed up from where she sat on the floor of the shower, letting the hot water run over her face and neck and back as she stared down the drain into the darkness. She had pulled on sweats and a T-shirt, and walked into the living room, where she found the former in-mate stretched out on the leather lounge, his body lit blue and green and red by flashing images on the enormous television screen. Jake was curled on Keeps's crotch, the cat's boxy head resting on the man's stomach. Celine stood examining the detritus of burger and fries wrappers on the coffee ta-ble, the empty beer bottles, letting her eyes wander briefly, indulgently, over Keeps's sleeping figure. The taut tendons in his tattooed hands and the rise and fall of his muscular chest under his singlet. Jake the cat hadn't let her pet him for two weeks, hadn't yet dared to venture onto her lap. The animal's tail was curled around Keeps's knee, twitching gently as the two rested.

"Oh, shit." Keeps jolted awake, bouncing Jake onto the floor. "Woman, how long you been standing there like that?"

"Start a timer," Celine said, tossing her laptop over the back of the couch so that it landed on Keeps's flat stomach. "One hour. That's all I'm giving him."

CHAPTER 18

He wanted to stand in the woods, so they took him there. Burke asked them to pull over maybe ten minutes into the drive through the lush, dark woods, and he got out and walked to a spot just far enough from the roadside that he couldn't see the asphalt if he looked back. He had missed the color green inside Pronghorn. Not institution green—a milky, numb, plasticky paint color that was routinely slapped over everything that stayed still long enough. Psychology green. Neutral green. But the rich, vibrant green of sunlit leaves. He sat in the undergrowth and breathed the forest air.

If he'd asked, someone would have brought him a drink. A barrel-aged whiskey was what he wanted. They would do that, his handlers, rush into town while he sat there and scrounge up anything he desired. He could have women, food, clothes, guns—these were *his* days, his first free days, and he was going to enjoy them. Because he was a someone now. The Camp had promised that to him when they found him as a teenager in Massachusetts, lurking around the Columbine forums, a nobody. Burke had been *that* kid—the quiet, shy, monosyllabic "coaster" at the back of the classroom who the teacher only called on when there was a problem with the screen projector, the one who did the assigned task in the first ten minutes of class and then spent the rest of the time discussing third-shooter theories online with other mass-shooting followers.

He'd been searching around for raw footage from the Columbine library security cameras, rumored but not confirmed to exist, when another 4channer popped up in his messages. The lurkers online who still hero-worshipped Eric and Dylan, when so many younger people had moved on to your Elliot Rodger incel types, were the real diehards. Rodger and his contemporaries, the *Call of Duty* generation of shooters, were so focused on women that the media had a party every time one of them arose. The overbearing mother was pictured weeping on the front porch. The fat, nerdy, pimply friends described him as pussy-obsessed. Eric and Dylan, on the other hand, had a real cause. So the Camp watched patiently for lurkers like Burke, who came to the forums consistently, wanting to see the diaries, the autopsy reports, the unseen footage, wanting to discuss the theories, wanting to know why.

Burke's recruiter hadn't provided anything more than a gentle nudge into the online world of neo-Nazi groups and their plans for a race war, and Burke fell in love. He liked all the serial killer angles and the calls for disruption, chaos. Black-and-white photographs of a short, angry, determined Charles Manson, his beautiful, waif-like followers, his legions of admirers. Burke followed his recruiter's links into Timothy McVeigh's work in Oklahoma, and on and on it went, until Burke was lying in bed at night staring at the laptop until his eyes ached and teared with exhaustion, watching videos, reading manifestos, making notes.

After about a month, Burke's recruiter, RauffsPlan1, invited him to call him by his real name, Ken. He wanted to invite fifteen-year-old Burke to the Camp: a five-day retreat in the woods near Pelham for young people who he thought had potential. Potential for what, he didn't say. But the Camp had a legit-looking flyer he could present to his mom, listing all the activities she figured would be good outlets for the unexplained hostility he presented at home—wilderness survival, bushcraft, teamwork, fitness training. She didn't question why a kid who lived on energy drinks and Ruffles, who spent sixteen hours a day in front of a screen, wanted to go tramping around the woods. Burke went, and found everything he had been searching for in life there in the green, green wilds. When he'd returned home with a shaved head, a pleasant attitude, and a big hug, his mother hadn't queried him on a single thing he'd learned out in the mountains.

He'd completed some small tasks for the Camp over the years. Firebombings, scare raids, the supervision of a couple of drug shipments to bring in money for the organization. Always group work. The Mardi Gras shooting had been his own idea. He'd run it past his recruiter, who had sent it up the chain. He'd been given the green light. Burke didn't think they really believed he'd do it. He'd only been a part of the Camp for five years. He wasn't even a recruiter yet. This would bypass all that. He'd be a hero the likes of which the brotherhood had never seen.

The breakout had also been his idea. Initially the senior people in the Camp hadn't wanted to do it. Too risky. Too much exposure. Didn't Burke think that remaining behind bars as a martyr to the cause was better for them in the long run? Burke was a legendary figure. He got letters from potential recruits wanting to join the cause from all over the world. But when Burke had told them why he needed to be released, that he planned to unleash an operation he liked to think of as the Ignition, they'd been on board.

Now, the twenty-eight-year-old Burke rose to his feet, taking up a twig with him, and stood there testing it, not breaking it, as he listened to the sound of a nearby creek. Burke had thought about calling his mother over the years, trying to answer some of the questions she'd had for him after the shooting. Where had it all gone wrong? What could she have done to prevent it? Was it his father's death, or her being tied up all the time caring for his disabled sister, or bullies at school that made him do what he did? No. Those were all textbook explanations, gentle placations people developed for themselves about why *their* son or daughter would not wake up in the morning and do exactly what he did—take a rifle and a backpack and head down to New Orleans, fight his way through the jolly crowds to a roost above the avenue, then open fire and rain almighty hell on a bunch of Black people like a god stretching out his fiery hand.

In truth, Burke had been too young to really have been affected by his father dying. His mother got in the way of his activities, so he was grateful to Danielle for occupying her. And the kids at school mostly treated him like a sagging house plant—something a little depressing to stare at, best ignored. What had truly caused it all was a genetic quirk that made Burke intelligent enough and self-aware enough to see that America was suffering, and only brave individuals willing to set down their rightful, constitutional pursuit of happiness would be able to aid their country. Burke knew he could be "happy" getting an IT job at the local mall, working his way up to manager, pottering around in the garage attached to his rental condo diagnosing software upgrade problems in his spare time for grannies with too much cash. But he decided to trade in that happiness for three glorious, delirious, ecstatic moments of happiness made possible by the Camp and his devotion to it.

The moment he lined up his first victim at Mardi Gras and pulled the trigger, the swell of screams that erupted from the people below.

The moment the PA system at Pronghorn clicked on and he heard the phone call with Warden Slanter blast through the row, signifying the beginning of the breakout.

And the moment that would soon come, the Ignition that would spark the glorious war.

With his lungs full of inspiration, the thin, strong twig still in his hand, he wandered back to the van, where his handlers were waiting. These were the men and women who had conducted the Pronghorn breakout, pure-blood youths from all over the country. They were foot soldiers, like he had once been, people who could follow orders and intricate designs handed down from on high, like the Pronghorn plan, but who could be disposed of easily if they failed.

Like Charles Manson, the Camp's leaders knew that survival of the group meant sending in capable hands to do the dirty work while the brains of the operation stayed safe, to cook up new ideas for dominance should a plan go south. The Pronghorn plan had been a success. The Ignition would be, too. Burke would have to go into hiding for a while then. For some years, as the race war raged on, Burke's true genius and heroism would have to remain a secret. But when the white man triumphed, the full story would be told.

As Burke approached the van, the young woman sitting on the rear bumper shot to her feet, and the heavily muscled driver snapped to attention. Burke understood it was this guy—Henry, he thought his name was—who had figured out how to hack into the prison's PA system, transmit the call he made to Warden Slanter. Henry would probably get a commendation for his work. The shooter who had taken out the bus driver was the dull but pretty girl standing at the front of the vehicle, doing her best to finish a cigarette before Burke got back. She flicked the butt away and straightened, smiled. Silvia, he thought her name was.

"Better get him out," Burke said, nodding sternly to the back of the van. He hadn't offered a single shred of praise or admiration to his handlers since the breakout. Hadn't thanked them for their service, hadn't asked their names, just picked up that information as they spoke among themselves. Praise was poison, Burke believed. "I don't want to ride in the back with the smell of his piss. Make it quick."

The kids dragged the prisoner out of the van and threw him onto the asphalt at Burke's feet. Burke knew this guy's name for certain. Anthony Reiter had spat on Burke's shoes as the two passed one another in the visitors' center, one day maybe a month after Burke had arrived. Both of them had been cuffed and were being escorted by different sets of guards. *You ain't so tough now, huh, bitch? You punk-ass bitch!* The plan originally had been to secure any Black inmate from the rush outside the prison, but as Burke had climbed into the van in the Pronghorn parking lot, he'd noticed Reiter jogging by, testing the doors of cars, trying to find one that was unlocked. Burke stood over the inmate now and smiled as he writhed in pain on the roadside.

"Who's the bitch now?" Burke asked.

Axe had got his first hint that a cruiser was coming for him when his shadow against the side of the RV sharpened. The moonlight was pretty good, but the high beams of police cruisers could blast unabated for miles across the flat desert, and by the time the car was closing up on him, Axe could see individual whiskers in his stubble outlined as he turned his head. He closed the hood of the little camp barbecue he'd been cooking on, put the knife he'd used to cut the meat into the waistband of his jeans, and turned to show his face to the officers as the rocks at the side of the road popped and sputtered under their slowing tires.

The officers got out and put their guns on the rims of their car doors, the empty black eyes of their weapons watching Axe where he stood holding a pair of tongs and wearing an Iron Maiden T-shirt.

"Show us your hands!"

Axe showed them his hands.

"Drop it, whatever it is," the officer barked.

Axe dropped the tongs on the desert dirt.

They came for him, and the bigger one shoved him into the side of the van so that he bounced off the aluminum.

"Watch it, Roxley," the smaller one said. "Not too rough."

"What are you doing out here, old boy?"

"Barbecuing." Axe had shrugged. If being a long-term inmate, a "career criminal" as the occupation was known, had taught him anything, it was that the less a person offered in the way of information to screws, jacks, PIs, judges, or cops, the better things tended to turn out. The guy named Roxley shifted and shuffled around Axe and his barbecue before tugging open the door of the RV and looking in. Axe knew what he saw in there. Nothing. Prison life had made Axe very tidy indeed. The smell of washing detergent had replaced the smell of weed, and Axe had flipped the cover of the little panel computer shut and put it away in a cupboard with the phones and electronic watches and other technological things he'd found lying about.

Roxley, the big cop, came back to Axe and stood over him again. Axe stared at the guy's boots, the way he had at the boots of hundreds of correctional officers in his time, and waited.

"You just some old coot out here in the desert, alone, cooking a barbecue?"

"Seems like it." Axe shrugged again.

"And you didn't think to get the fuck out of here when a prison not fifty miles up the road got emptied this morning?"

Axe looked up briefly, made like he didn't understand. The smaller officer, whose name badge read NAWLET, was kicking stones.

"Just leave him, man," Nawlet said. "He's minding his business."

"What are you cookin'?" Roxley asked. "Where's your phone? Who else knows you're out here?"

"I got ID in the van," Axe said, gesturing to the door. "I can get it. Don't know nothin' about a prison, though."

Roxley was almost chest to chest with Axe. The old man could smell the young officer's breath coming down on the top of his head. He felt the whoosh of it on his brow, and then the stark absence of it as the cop lost interest, like a dog snuffling at a rat hole suddenly distracted by a noise behind him.

"Sir, it's not safe for you to be out here," Nawlet said. "We strongly suggest you take your vehicle into town and camp there for the night."

"Can't," Axe said. "I ran out of fuel. Was going to hitch into town in the morning, fill 'er up."

"Then get in the cruiser, for fuck's sake," Roxley snapped, his mind already on other things, on escaped inmates out there in the desert, calling to him, begging to be rounded up. "Sit in the back and shut the hell up."

Axe turned off the barbecue, didn't think it was smart to try to grab any belongings, not under the umbrella of the angry cop Roxley's impatience. He locked the RV, went to the cruiser, and climbed in behind Nawlet. The knife in Axe's jeans slid sideways along his thigh. He hitched it so that the handle was just poking out of the top of his pocket.

The car took off, rolling its high beams over the RV, then the darkness of the desert air. Nawlet hung his hand backward over the seat, a shiny silver wrapper pinched between his thumb and forefinger.

"Gum?" he'd asked Axe.

"Sure," Axe said.

CHAPTER 19

They sat together at the eight-seater dining room table, a solid oak affair she had bought in an online auction that looked as if it was designed to host a Viking feast but had never hosted anyone but her. Keeps sucked the end of his beer and let it make a loud pop as he unsealed his lips from the bottle.

"We got one problem here," he said.

"What is it?" Celine asked.

"I don't know nothin' about investigating murders," he said.

"Well, neither do I."

"And I also don't see what this is going to achieve," he continued, opening his email account, the fingers of one hand dancing over the keys. Celine tried not to look, but she noticed he had plenty of emails from women. "I mean, what? You find out the guy is innocent and you're gonna stop chasing him?"

"I just need to know the truth about this, Keeps."

"You gonna turn around and *help* him?"

"Keeps, please."

"All right." He tore out a page of the notebook she had brought to the table and took up the pen. "We're gonna do what I always do with my lawyer. We're gonna write down some stuff in a couple of lists, *Guilty* and *Not Guilty*."

"You do this with your lawyer?"

"Yeah." He smirked. "We look at what evidence we got, then we decide how we're gonna plead."

He folded the page in half lengthways, unfolded it again, drew a line down the crease, and labeled the columns.

"You have surprisingly delicate handwriting," Celine said.

"You're probably shocked someone with my record can write at all."

"I'm not," she said. "I've been looking through inmate mail for fifteen years. I've seen the best and the worst of the written word in there. What I am surprised by is the loop on that 'y.' Look at that. That's adorable."

"Stay focused. I'm tired. And we've got fifty-eight minutes on the timer."

Celine glanced at the numbers ticking down silently on her phone, felt a desire to crack more jokes, to draw the numbers further and further down, until she ran out of time to discover that she had been wrong about John Kradle for all these years. Because if she was wrong about him, that meant not only had her grandfather's actions on that fateful day taken away everyone she had ever loved, but she had also let him take something away from another human being. A man outside the family. It meant that the destruction hadn't stopped, hadn't been contained, when the firing ended on that day. The pain and the loss had in fact, through her own stubbornness and weakness and bias, her inability to shake off what had happened, stretched into the present moment. With as much courage as she could muster, she pulled the laptop toward her and followed a path she had trodden almost a decade earlier, into the online information regarding the Kradle Family murders.

The screen lit up with images of John Kradle, his tall, broad-shouldered son, Mason, and his petite, curvy wife, Christine. Kradle's other victim, the second to be shot dead in their house in Mesquite, only appeared in some of the images. The press liked to forget about the sister-in-law. The real horror and intrigue here was the suggestion of a ticking time bomb nestled in every family—the father who snaps, who comes home from work and cleans house, either to start afresh with a mistress or to go out himself in a blaze of glory. Celine scrolled through headlines.

MESQUITE FATHER SLAYS FAMILY.

LOVING HOME BLAZES AS KILLER FATHER WATCHES.

The infamous photograph of John Kradle appeared, a picture taken by a neighbor—Kradle stood on the lawn watching smoke billow into the sky from the upper windows of his house, hands by his sides, face expressionless. It was the picture that had made national and, briefly, international headlines. A father doing nothing to remedy the most terrible of actions, the slaughter of his loved ones.

"Guilty," Celine said. She was startled by the vitriol in her tone, so cleared her throat and tried to sound expressionless. "Put it in the guilty column. This, right here. He did nothing to fight the fire raging through the house, to go back in and try to get any of the members of his family out. He just stood on the lawn and watched the place burn with them inside. Everybody in the street saw him."

"Says here"—Keeps scrolled—"that physical evidence showed Kradle had just been in the house. That he was covered in his son's blood and there was soot in his clothes."

"Right," Celine said. "He went in, shot Christine and Audrey in the kitchen. They were standing in there having a glass of white wine. Then he went upstairs and shot Mason while the boy showered. Mason fought him, even with a bullet in his skull. The police know this because the shower screen was smashed. He had to shoot the boy in the head a second time to kill him. Kradle then poured gasoline all down the stairs, lit up the place, and walked out."

Keeps made notes in the *Guilty* column. Celine looked at the blank stretch of page that said *Not Guilty* in Keeps's glorious, curly, schoolgirl handwriting. Celine scrolled Google until she found a true-crime website that had a section on the Kradle Family murders. A signed copy of Kradle's statement in his chunky, windblown lettering loaded on the screen.

"*I walked in and found my wife and sister-in-law lying dead on the floor of the kitchen,*" Keeps read. "*I went upstairs and found Mason in the shower. I tried to pick him up, but he was gone. The house was getting smokier and I was worried I was going to get caught in the fire. I tried to drag Mason down the stairs, but—*"

"See?" Celine pointed at the screen. "Look at the language. *My wife and my sister-in-law.* He doesn't say their names."

"He says Mason's name," Keeps said.

"*I* was worried *I* was going to get caught in the fire. *I* went upstairs. *I* tried to pick him up," Celine said. "He's a narcissist. I've read about psychopaths, they—"

"How about we stop trying to read what we want to read into this," Keeps said. "You're just trying to see signs of guilt, and you can see them everywhere if you try. I can do the same thing in reverse. Look. Look, uh—" He pointed to the screen. "He says he knew Mason was gone. Like, he was dead. But then he says he tried to drag him down the stairs. That's a father trying to get his son's body out of the house even though he knows there's no point."

"I guess," Celine said.

"And all this *I, I, I* stuff," Keeps snorted. "Man, the dude is a tinkerer. He messes around with cars and wood and shit all day. He's not a poet. There might be fifteen ways to write a sentence, but *I did this* and *I did that* is just the plainest."

"So find me something to put in the Not Guilty column, then," Celine said.

Keeps clicked around the website. The timer told Celine they had thirty-five minutes left.

"What are you doing?"

"I'm looking for the experts." Keeps was scrolling through a scanned document that Celine could see was seven hundred and sixty pages long. "The DNA guys. Fingerprint guys. Blood guys. Bullet guys. Whatever. That's the sort of stuff we should be looking for here. The hard facts."

"What is this?"

"It's the trial transcript."

"It'll take longer than an hour to look through this," Celine said.

"They usually bring in the experts on day three of defense witnesses in a murder trial," Keeps said. "Two days to paint the picture, tell the story, get the emotions going before you bring in all the boring old guys with their graphs."

Celine tapped the table and shifted in her seat. Keeps sucked his beer dry.

"You know a fair bit about investigating murders for someone who doesn't know anything about investigating murders," Celine ventured.

"I know about trials," Keeps said. "I'm not a killer, in case you were wondering."

"Good to know. I figured as much, though, you coming from minimum."

"But you looked at my jacket, right?"

"No."

"You googled me."

"No."

"What?" Keeps turned and gawked at her. "You serious, girl?"

"I told you that already."

"Man." He shook his head. "You're some kind of fool."

"I told you, it's all about the feeling," Celine said. She nodded at the screen. "I'm making a point here. Kradle gave me that feeling as soon as I laid eyes on him. I knew he was bad. I got the feeling you're good, Keeps. I don't need to check up on that."

They sat in silence for a while, Keeps scrolling, not focusing on the words traversing the screen before him.

"I'm a con man."

"We really don't need to get into it."

"No, we should," Keeps said. "Even if it's just so you get to know your feelings about people can be wrong sometimes. I'm a bad person. Real bad. But I seem good. I use the same skills you've seen in me, and I take them out there into the world to do my work of ripping people off. I notice details. I've got the gift of the gab. People underestimate me because of the tattoos and the baggy pants. Sometimes I wear cornrows. That's my costume. That's my in. Some con men wear suits. I wear this. Kaylene? There is no Kaylene." He gestured to the tattoo on his neck. "It's an act. I show up looking like this, but I let people know I'm smart and they think: *Here he is, my diamond in the rough. All he needs is someone to trust him and give him some responsibility, and he'll be all polished up.*"

"That's not true," Celine said, smirking. "None of that is true."

"I'm sitting in your *dining room.*" Keeps looked at her, his eyes wide. Celine glanced about them at the empty house, the gaping, dark rooms. A clock was ticking somewhere. A pipe groaned. Keeps's hand was resting gently on the keys of her laptop, where all her banking, email, and credit card details were auto-saved. Jake leaped from nowhere up into Keeps's lap, and he scratched the cat behind the ears.

"Maybe you've got a point," she said.

"Mmm-hmm."

"What kind of scams do you run?" Celine asked.

"It's not important."

"Come on. You started this. I'm curious now."

"I try to invent something new every time," he sighed, reading the screen, half paying attention to her. "I've done the traditional robocall scams and confidence games. You dig around on social media, find somebody whose kid is at summer camp. You call them up, tell them the kid's been in an accident, their insurance isn't covering the ambulance or whatever. They need to direct transfer some money to you via Western Union. Or maybe you find an old lady, an old veteran: you bug their house, bug their car, find out a bunch of stuff, worm your way in as someone from the energy company or someone from the bank. All that stuff gets very routine after a while. It's shooting fish in a barrel. You're just hanging around in nursing homes or sitting in front of a computer playing sound effects from YouTube in the background of calls. Sirens. Kids crying. People screaming."

Celine felt her stomach turning. She watched his eyes as he read, those expert fingers stroking the keys.

"Lately I've been into tools. I was in Pronghorn last year with this guy who's deep into wood. Like, real deep. He builds furniture out of crazy expensive wood from, like, Colombia or some shit. Anyway, I went to his workshop and found out he's got table saws in that place that are worth fifteen grand." Keeps smiled, remembering. "Fifteen grand! For a saw! So we knocked up this scam together. He made all these signs out of real nice wood that read DADDY'S WORKSHOP. We made a hundred of them. Advertised them on mommy'n'baby pages on Facebook. Whole bunch of wives bought them for their husbands for Father's Day. Then we looked at who bought them. Like, where do they live? What kind of space do they have on their property? What do they do for a living? That kind of thing. Once we figured out who was most likely to have expensive tools, we hit the road with the list of delivery addresses, and when—okay, look here."

He turned the laptop toward her. Celine was so lost in her thoughts she had to shake herself to remember what they were doing.

"This guy here, the expert, guy named . . ." Keeps peered down his wire-framed glasses to read the name. "Dr. Martin Stinway. He's here talking about Kradle's shirt. Says he's some kind of micro-pattern-whatever analyst."

They read quietly together, Keeps scrolling as Celine tapped the edge of the laptop to tell him she was ready to turn the page.

"Stinway says gunshot residue on Kradle's shirt indicated he fired the gun that killed all three victims," Celine said.

"Right, so that's bullshit," Keeps said.

"How so?"

"Gunshot residue is the most junk science there is," Keeps said. "The FBI don't even use it no more. I know that because my lawyer won a major defense case with it. Guy had been sentenced to twenty-five to life, hanging on gunshot residue as the major piece of evidence that locked him up."

"But Kradle had the residue on his shirt," Celine said. "There's no mistaking it. Says so right here. Look. There are photos."

"Right." Keeps shrugged. "It was there. But how did it get there? Stinway says it was because he fired the gun. But the dude had been in the house. He admitted it. You fire a gun in a house, there'll be gunshot residue all over the place. It'll be on the floor, on the ceiling, hanging around in the air. It'll be on the victims. It'll also be on the cops who come into the house to check out what happened. They will have picked some up from touching their own weapons. Man, police stations are covered in that shit. Anybody who walks into a police station will come out with gunshot residue on them. The guy who my lawyer saved from the life sentence? The police sat him in the back of a squad car. There was GSR all over that thing. They did some tests and showed it."

"But I'm looking here." Celine was typing into the laptop. "This Dr. Martin Stinway guy has been doing this for thirty years. Look at all his college degrees. He'd know the difference."

"Would he, though?" Keeps said. "I mean, maybe you should ask him."

"It's three o'clock in the morning."

"So?"

Celine tapped the keys, scrolled. She left Dr. Martin Stinway's Wikipedia page and started down a list of newspaper articles.

"Oh, no," she said.

"What?" Keeps leaned over. Celine clicked the article and the screen was dominated by a huge headline.

RENOWNED SCIENTIST DISCREDITED IN SHOCK RULING

The timer went off on Celine's phone.

CHAPTER 20

Kradle could walk. He reminded himself that this was an achievement in itself. The streets of Mesquite were dark, the streetlights blurry and molten in his vision, and the cold breeze coming off the desert felt like cactus needles slicing at his neck and hands. But he had patched the hole in his body, kneeling in a godforsaken corner of a parking lot, using the sickly green light of an exit sign to stitch himself up. He had cash in his pocket and a destination in mind, and his limbs were still cooperating with him. All was not lost.

The encampment consumed the base of the highway overpass on both sides and was surprisingly loud. Rap music thumped from a long shanty at the center of the collection of dwellings, a lopsided headquarters made from blue tarps and sheets of plywood. It was bigger than Kradle had anticipated, but he remembered a documentary he'd watched about fentanyl and knew that smaller cities like Mesquite were having trouble with it. Tiny police forces, giant wildlands of desert in which to cook and mix and bag drugs in RVs and campers.

Kradle had never technically been homeless, but he knew from the tales of other inmates that many of the guys here probably had records, were on the run from the law, or were in active pursuit of criminal enterprises. And if he knew anything about cons and ex-cons, it was that they hated strangers encroaching on their space. He decided the best course of action, then, was to try to pick off a target from the edge of the herd. He approached a man who stood at the curb, smoking, the sharp angles of his face lit red by the burning end of his hand-rolled cigarette.

"Hey man, can I—"

"Fuck off, bro."

"Right." Kradle backed up, his hands out. "Right. No problem."

He received a few more "Fuck offs" for his trouble, approaching and finding men on the outer limits of the camp from the north and west. On his fourth attempt, he found an old man sitting on a wooden crate, staring at the lit screen of a cell phone.

Kradle forwent the greeting this time.

"I have money," he said, instead. It was the same thing that had saved his life only a day before, and it saved him again now. The old man looked up. One side of his face was webbed with burn scars, which took on hideous depths in the harsh, blue light.

"Whatchu want?"

"A place to sleep. Someone to keep lookout. Some new clothes. Food, if you've got it."

"You one of those Pronghorn creeps?" the scarred man asked.

"Yep."

"Well, you better have more cash than they'll give me as a reward for turning you in."

"You're not going to turn me in," Kradle said, and they both knew he was right, because bringing the law down on the camp for any reason would have the man blacklisted for life among the homeless community of Mesquite. And, chances were, he was probably wanted himself. The old man extracted himself from his little wooden seat with difficulty, and when he rose to full height he was a foot taller than Kradle, who stood slightly bent from his injuries. Kradle pulled out his bundle of cash, money he'd taken from Shondra, and handed over a couple of hundred-dollar notes to his new friend.

"Hey now." The old guy gave a hacking, wet laugh. "Anything else I can get you, master?"

"A cell phone, maybe."

"What's wrong with you?"

"I'm just tired."

"You need painkillers?"

"That would be nice," Kradle wheezed. The old man nodded and went away, and Kradle crawled into the little canvas tent that stood near them. It was black as pitch inside, smelled of sweat and mold and alcohol. He settled onto his stomach, felt objects beneath the thin blanket spread over the ground and spent a few minutes clearing them out of his way, identifying them by feel. A steel mug. A box of tissues. A tennis ball. A glass bottle.

He didn't realize he had fallen asleep until he was shocked awake by the feel of the side of the tent shifting against his hand. Someone was entering. He turned and saw the outline of something huge and hairy against the gloomy orange streetlight. The odor of dog enveloped him, chokingly strong.

"Oh, Jesus, Jesus!" Kradle pushed at the beast. "Hey! Get out! Get out!"

Laughter outside. The big dog lay down beside him with its back to him, hitting the ground with a heavy sigh and shuffling into place on the blanket.

"What the fuck, man?"

"You said watch out for the law. Didn't say nothin' about no dogs."

"Come on! Get it out of here!" Kradle groaned. But only more laughter answered him. The big animal was impervious to shoving, nudging, yanking by the thick, long hair of its neck. In the dark it felt like a shaggy bear, a mysterious collection of angles—elbows, hips, ribs under slabs of fur. The scarred man tossed a tiny baggie through the flap and Kradle examined it in the poor light, the sad little pill in the corner of the bag impossible to identify. Foolishly, he'd imagined the old man tossing him a box of Advil or something. The pill could have been anything, from ecstasy to fentanyl. Kradle threw it away and lay down beside the dog.

In time he reached out and touched the warm fur, sank his hand into it and felt the chest of the dog. Its heart was beating in there, ticking insistently. The bones rising and falling with gentle breath.

It had been half a decade since Kradle had given or received the touch of another living creature with any kind of genuine affection. He noticed every touch. He'd been medically examined at the prison, of course. He'd seen a dentist a few times. When he was removed from his cell for yard time, lawyer time, or to be let into the shower room, a guard, sometimes Celine Osbourne, took his elbow occasionally, as though there was any reason to run off when his wrists were cuffed and several yards of brick, concrete, steel, and iron stood between him and the free world. Once, a few years earlier, there had been an outbreak of hepatitis in the prison, and as an unexpected novelty, he and five other guys had been chucked together, uncuffed, in a cell while the row was disinfected. He'd shaken a hand, and punched a guy while trying to intervene when the inevitable scuffle broke out.

Now, he stroked the dog tentatively for a while, discovered and worked a bramble from its fur and flicked it away. Then he shuffled over and wrapped an arm around the beast, hugged it to him, buried his face in its fur, breathed in the smell of it. He squeezed it, and the dog gave a little groan that might have been irritation, but generally didn't object much to the hug.

Kradle lay there spooning the dog in the tent in the homeless camp, and he laughed quietly to himself at the furious stupidity of it all until sleep took him again.

CHAPTER 21

She'd been there the night of the bombing. Well, the bombing that was not. Becky Caryett knew that technically nobody had been injured when Abdul Ansar Hamsi walked into the Las Vegas Flamingo Casino six years earlier and deposited a bag of explosives right at the edge of the blackjack area. Nobody had been blown apart. Nobody had been incinerated alive. But, to Becky, it had happened, even if only in her daydreams, and its occurrence wasn't something she had been able to brush off in the half-decade since. In her mind, sometimes, while she stood there sweeping and pushing cards across the green felt mat before her, spouting rehearsed lines and giving half-smiles to the gamblers who came and went in the chairs, the bombing had actually happened. She stood there in her ridiculous flamingo-pink waistcoat, and Abdul Ansar Hamsi walked in, just like he did that night, a dusty gray ball cap hiding his eyes, a black T-shirt and jeans hugging his petite frame, his get-up as carefully designed in its casual, forgettable nature as military camouflage. He walked right up to the blackjack area, stood for a while, pleasantly and unobtrusively, with the duffel bag hanging from one hand, playing the newly arrived tourist musing on the idea of stopping for a few hands before he headed up to his room. Trying to decide if he felt lucky.

Just like she did that night, in her fantasies Becky locked eyes with Hamsi, and he returned her phoney smile, wandered over to where she was dealing out cards to a heavy, old white couple from Idaho wearing matching I HEART VEGAS shirts. Then he sidestepped and stood by the seat at the very edge of the table. He put his bag down right next to her. *Right at her side.* Maybe only two feet away. Practically touching her. At that moment, that fateful night, the wife from the Idaho couple decided to split her hand, and Becky got distracted, and Hamsi walked away. She didn't notice he'd left the bag. Not until a pit boss came over after a few minutes and asked what it was doing there, if it was hers.

In Becky's daydreams, the bomb went off at that moment. A colossal explosion erupted that consumed her first, of all the victims, a shocking white light billowing out, vaporizing the pit boss, the couple from Idaho, the rest of the blackjack area, eating up the poker tables and roulette station, taking out the third floor of the Flamingo in a single compressive boom. It crunched through structural-support beams as if they were sticks of Styrofoam. It collapsed the fourth and part of the fifth floor, leaving the huge building hollowed out like a lava cake and dripping concrete, electrical wires, plaster, brick, twisted steel, bodies. The blast killed hundreds of people, leaving dozens of others maimed and crawling, limping, dragging themselves through gagging smoke and roiling flames to try to find safety.

Technically, all that hadn't happened. But tonight it was happening as Becky arrived at her station and set up her decks. The table was cold—empty, unlucky, not warmed up yet by the presence of smiling, cheering people winning small bets in their losing battle against the house. Becky tried to push the visions away, called out a little invite to a couple walking by, another matching-shirt duo fresh off the plane from somewhere, bags in hand. *Try your hand, sir? Madam? Feeling lucky?* As the booms and crashes and screams played out silently in her mind, Becky swept her cards expertly over the table, fanning them, gathering them, shuffling them in a wide, horizontal stream from one hand to the other. Sometimes it was the hand tricks that brought bored patrons over from the nearby poker machines, following their desire to interact with a human being, who could do more than bleep and flash and sing robotic tunes. She played with her cards and wondered, as she had a million times already, why Hamsi had chosen her that night. If it was because she was a woman. If it was because she was Black. If it was because she was a casino worker. If it was because he'd spied the crucifix hanging around her throat.

When a man sat down at the table before her, rushing in and flopping down quickly, his pulled-low ball cap made Becky's heart leap into her throat.

"Hey, Beck," Elliot said.

"Oh my god." Becky dropped cards everywhere and stepped back, fanned her face, checked the blackjack stations around her. Everyone was distracted, warm tables full of happy players. "Elli, what the hell you doing here?"

"I need help."

Becky held her head. "Urgh. I knew this would happen. I saw the news yesterday and I said to myself, 'Becky, Elli ain't gonna make a run for it. Man's got eighteen months left on his sentence. He's gonna stay put. He's for sure not gonna come right into the goddamn Flamingo goddamn Casino in front of three hundred people and ask his ex-wife, of all the people in the world, for money. He's not that stupid.' And then I said to myself, 'Yes, Becky, he is.'"

"We're still technically married," Elliot said.

"You need to get your ass out of here." Becky scooped up the cards and dealt Elliot a hand, growling the words through her teeth. "They probably have cops watching me, waiting for you to show up."

"They don't." Elliot gathered his cards with his hairy hands. "They'll be saving those guys for the big fish. There are rapists and all kinds of punks on the loose."

"I wouldn't count on it. They did a special on the breakout on NBC last night. They said cops are gonna be sittin' on friends and relatives of inmates. They said half of the guys will run away, half of the guys will run home." She smirked. "I guess you were one of the dumb ones who ran home, huh?"

"Look. Hear me out. You can tell the bosses I threatened you." Elliot glanced sideways at the pit boss at the end of the row, who was watching a game with interest. "Tell them I showed you a knife, hell, I don't care. All you have to do is go use your swipe card to unlock that door over there. After that, it's all me."

They both turned and looked at the door to the back halls, manned by a security guard in a pink blazer. Between them and the guarded door, a bachelor party of young men with big hairstyles was laughing too hard, carrying plastic cocktail glasses shaped like cowboy boots.

"And then what?" Becky snorted. "You going to march in there and rob the vault? It's six levels underground, Elliot. There are about a hundred guys between you and it, and some of them have semi-automatics. Or so I hear—all that crazy shit starts at level minus two. I've never been down there and I wouldn't know how to—"

"I still love you, Becky."

"Oh, for the sake of all that is holy." She massaged her brow, pinched the bridge of her nose.

"Just go with me. Play along." Elliot reached for her hand. "We'll tell them you're my hostage."

"It's this table," Becky sighed. She smoothed the leather armrest of the table as though she was consoling an old, devastated friend. "This is a bad luck table. I never believed in them before, but I do now. I was standing right here when he came in. Hamsi. The bomber. He put the bag right there." She pointed to the colorful carpet. "I told myself I was going to go back to my table. I wasn't going to let him change a single thing about me. I like this damned table. I can watch the basketball from here. And then your sorry ass comes in and sits here and tells me this shit."

"Becky—"

"This ain't *Ocean's Eleven*." Becky shook her head. "You're not George Clooney. You got locked up in the first place for stealing a truck full of shaving cream, Elliot. You gonna upgrade your criminal status from *shaving cream bandit* to *casino robber* and *international goddamn fugitive* just like that?"

"You're getting kind of loud." Elliot was rising to his feet.

"Do you have *any idea* how much I need this job?" Becky slammed her fist on the felt. A tiny old woman in a yellow dress, carrying a tray of casino chips in her withered hands, stopped a few feet out from Becky's table to listen. "You think I want to stand here all night on my aching feet, taking retirement funds from grandmas and grandpas who can't afford to eat in the downstairs bistro, and giving it to the assholes upstairs? You think I want to watch a guy blow his daughter's college fund on bad hands, just so I can hear he went and threw himself off the roof so he wouldn't have to call home and tell the wife? I need this job, Elliot, and you know why? Because your daughter needs pre-braces. Yeah, that's a thing. Not only do they have braces, they have *pre-braces* now, and your kid needs them because she got nasty, crooked teeth from your side of the family, and those pre-braces are even more expensive than—"

Becky stopped. Elliot was staring at her. The group of young men with cowboy-boot cocktails were all staring at her. The old woman with the chips was staring at her, and so was her pit boss, and the pit boss from the nearby roulette station, and a few patrons turned sideways in their swivel chairs at the poker machines, fingers resting on un-pressed buttons. But Becky was ignoring all of the attention she was receiving, because her own attention was focused on a man standing hesitantly at the edge of the next table.

Hamsi wasn't wearing a ball cap this time. He was dressed in a white pressed shirt, gray trousers, prison sneakers, the security tag hanging from the sleeve of the shirt telling Becky he'd probably grabbed the outfit, sans the shoes, from a mannequin somewhere and bolted. He wasn't carrying a bag. He wasn't smiling. But, aside from all that, he was as pristinely, perfectly identical to her memory of him the night that he almost killed her as if he'd opened a door and stepped right out of her nightmares. Hamsi edged toward her table, all time and sound and movement standing still around the two of them, and Becky found herself stepping toward him, too, around the back of the table.

The failed terrorist and the casino dealer he'd tried to murder came together at the edge of the blackjack section, and Hamsi spoke first.

"You're here," Hamsi said. He gave a little laugh. "I can't believe it. I can't believe it. I just came here . . . I wanted to tell you that I'm sor—"

Becky Caryett had never punched anyone before. She'd never so much as hit a punching bag, a pillow, or a wall. She didn't like violence. Couldn't even stand to watch it on TV. But she delivered an uppercut to Hamsi's jaw that was so immaculately aligned and direct and powerful, using all the force of her shoulder, her neck, her rib cage, twisting and surging upward, that the man was unconscious even before his head snapped back, before his legs buckled and he slumped to the ground. She fancied she could feel through her knuckles the man's brain sloshing backward in his head and whumping against the inner surface of his skull, too fast for his neurons to handle.

Becky stepped back from the liquified figure on the floor that, only seconds before, had been an animated, talking, moving man, and she shook her hand loose, shooting Elliot a vicious glare of parting as her ex-husband dissolved into the press of people around them.

"Anybody else feeling lucky?" Becky asked the crowd.

CHAPTER 22

It was still dark when Kradle emerged from the tent with fresh clothes clinging to his reeking body. The dog exited beside him, shaking itself, and he got his first good look at it in the light of a Budweiser truck rolling under the overpass. It was big, black, pointy-nosed, and yellow-eyed.

"Here's your fee for last night." He handed some notes to the scarred man, who hadn't moved from his wooden crate. "And I'd like to buy this dog."

"Sure," the scarred man said, his hand still out.

"Fifty bucks cover it?"

"About right."

Kradle peeled off the notes and started handing them over, then held them back at the last second.

"It's your dog, isn't it?"

"No," the scarred man said, as if it was obvious.

"Well, whose dog is it?"

"Fucked if I know, man."

"Then why am I giving you the money?"

"Because you're the kind of idiot who would pay real-ass money for a stray dog any moron could grab off the street for free." The old man rocked back on his crate and laughed. "Look around, genius." Kradle did. There were dogs everywhere, pools of fur lying outside tents, silhouettes nosing around piles of trash, trotting through the camp with a sense of purpose.

"I'm just trying to do the right thing here," Kradle said.

"Yeah? Well fuck off out of my face then, and take your stupid dog with you."

They walked for an hour, side by side, Kradle saying nothing, the hood of the jacket the scarred man had given him pulled up around his face, the dog stopping now and then to piss on trees or stare back the way they had come, examining noises or smells on the wind. Once, Kradle spied a squad car doing slow laps of the silent streets. He ducked into a driveway to crouch in the moon-etched shadow of a trailer. The dog sat beside him, waiting. He didn't understand the beast's sudden loyalty, could only put the way it had rushed into the tent to lie beside him down as a resemblance to some past owner who had treated it well. Christine would have called the appearance of the dog a sign, an omen. She'd had all kinds of knowledge about mythology, about animals that showed up in the middle of fairy tales to guide lost wanderers through dark forests or give warnings about caves they were about to pass through. Kradle didn't know about anything like that. He just felt happy to have someone by his side. It had been strangely quiet and lonely in the hours since he and the serial killer parted ways.

He waited half a block down from 7 Solitaire Street, Beaver Dam, for what he guessed was an hour, looking for the telltale signs of surveillance: men sitting in parked cars, leaning on trees, watching from the windows of neighboring houses. He sniffed the air for cigarette smoke, leather, gun oil, fried food, strong deodorant—the kinds of smells he associated with law enforcement personnel—but found nothing but cold, clean desert breeze. Then the side door of number seven opened and a figure stepped out. Kradle grabbed the dog and moved forward.

He held the animal with two hands by a hank of its neck fur and shuffled in an awkward crouch toward the boy, who was locking the door behind him, a backpack hanging on one shoulder.

"Hey, kid," Kradle said.

"Whoa, shit! You scared me."

"Sorry, sorry." Kradle pretended to struggle with the dog, who was surprisingly placid, letting itself be manhandled by its new owner on the pavement without a shred of protest. "I just caught this dog. I saw it run out of a driveway down the street. Number twenty. It bolted right here. Can you give me a hand?"

"Oh, uh, yeah. Uh." The kid turned in a circle, bewildered, thinking, the way Kradle hoped he would. Ripe for instruction.

"You got a rope or something in there?"

"Sure," the kid said, and opened up the door. Kradle dropped the dog and followed the kid into the house, let the animal in behind him and then closed the door.

It did not escape Kradle that he had just used the kind of ruse Homer Carrington employed to stun and then corner his victims; that, as he deadbolted the door and sealed himself and the young man in the little kitchen, the boy was probably experiencing the same jolt of sudden, painful clarity that men and women had felt under the North Nevada Strangler's gaze. The kid turned toward him with a *What did I just do?* look on his face, the duped, the trusting, the naive, and Kradle felt bad for making the boy realize that everything he'd ever been told about strangers in vans with candy was bullshit. The real danger could come right to your house and cook up a pathetic story about a lost dog, and have you let them inside in ten seconds flat.

"Just stay calm," Kradle said. "I'm here to talk to your dad."

The kid was as tall as Mason had been, but not as broad or muscular. He was all sinew and veins, probably half the weight of the son Kradle had lost. Mason had died at a time when all the kids were shaving weird patterns into the backs of their heads and taking chunks out of their eyebrows with a razor, to look like rappers or fighters or something. This boy was long-haired and long-lashed, with lips so red he might have been wearing lipstick. But, aside from the physical differences, the boy and Kradle's son could have been brothers in their wide-eyed, eager, curious expressions, the look that said they knew they were in the best years of their lives and now was the time to notice everything, taste everything, be awake as long as they could every day, be ready for whatever the world threw at them. Spirit. Energy. Kradle felt tired just thinking about it.

"Tom? What happened? You forget your lunch?"

Shelley Frapport appeared in the doorway to the tidy kitchen in a pink fluffy robe, with a cat tucked under her arm like a football. The cat spotted Kradle's dog, struggled out of the woman's grasp and scrammed up the hall. Shelley took in the sight of Kradle, eased a long breath out of her lungs, and let her hands fall by her sides.

"I hoped you'd come," she said.

2000

Curses. Demons. Bad omens. Mason's birth was exactly as the pregnancy had been: a long and mildly hysterical affair infused with a kind of supernatural energy. From the beginning, when she learned of the baby growing inside her, Christine had begun to hear talk about the child's existence being much more than an accident brought about by a boozy Sunday afternoon barbecue and Christine forgetting to take her pill. Fast, dirty, half-hearted sex on the couch, Christine sprawled on a blanket on the living room floor watching *The Frances Falkner Show* long into the night, Kradle dozing beside her, lifting his head now and then to read the caption at the bottom of the screen with the show's subject. *Cheating Spouses Come Clean! I Married My Xbox! My Uncle is my Boyfriend!* Dread of the coming hangover and the roof-cleaning job Kradle had booked for the next morning, in the blazing sun. Christine's typical Sunday afternoon moroseness about the demise of her medium and ghost-hunting business, the soulless commercialism of people like John Edward and Allison DuBois.

No—to Christine, her pregnancy was an act of malignant forces so powerful and terrifying she dared not even talk about aborting the baby, because she feared upsetting further whatever cursed thing had made her pregnant in the first place. She spent the pregnancy reading runes, saying prayers, rubbing oils and herbs and ash and smelly lotions into her growing belly to try to remove the curse. Kradle mostly ignored all the weirdness, dismissing it as the anxiety of an expectant mother, and buried himself in his work so that they could have a nice little cash bundle to buy all the fluffy toys and stripy suits he noticed babies around town possessed.

Then, in early March, Christine sat bolt upright in bed and vomited up the roast lamb dinner they'd had that night, and he drove her to the hospital, calling her sister, Audrey, on the way.

In a dark, hot room, Kradle sat sweating in a plastic chair in the corner while his wife was exorcised of their infant son.

Audrey arrived at a respectable 11 A.M., wearing her court suit and talking on her flip phone all the way up the busy hall. She didn't get off the phone, even when Kradle leaned in and showed her the baby in his arms, gingerly pushing a fold of the blanket away to reveal the most beautiful face he'd ever laid eyes upon. Audrey wrinkled her nose and let her eyes flick to the ceiling.

"You can try to take it to the DA if you want, Georgia, but I'm telling you now you won't get any traction without Ferlich there."

Kradle followed when Audrey jerked her thumb toward the end of the hall. She carried on the phone call all the time as she made them coffee in the little maternity ward common room. He sat and marveled at his child and thought about creation and god and destiny and the universe, and Audrey tried to negotiate to get Ferlich, whoever he was, wherever he needed to be, then snapped the phone shut partway through her own sentence, having apparently given up.

"Idiots," she said, and leaned over, glancing again at her nephew.

"What do you think?"

"He's pretty fat."

"He is." Kradle laughed and wiped the tears that clung to his aching, exhausted eyes. "He's a big, healthy fellow."

"What's the name?"

"Mason."

"Urgh." Audrey smoothed out her skirt. "How obtusely masculine. As if people aren't going to know it's a boy from that Neanderthal brow."

"Christine wanted something that communicated the idea of stone, because the grinding of a stone in Wiccan mythology is—"

"John, spare me, please." Audrey held up a hand. "She's not here. We can avoid the idiotic blather about this kid and the mythological spiritual bullshit apparently infused with his being. If people ask you, just say you're a builder and you wanted something that sounded tough."

They sat, drinking their coffee from Styrofoam cups, Kradle setting his on the center of the table between sips, far away from the baby. Now and then, nurses in sickly pink scrubs came into the room to retrieve diapers or bottles from the cupboards lining the walls. The big baby with the heavy brow slept soundly in Kradle's arms, and Audrey leaned over to look occasionally but made no move to hold him.

"It's going to get worse from now on," Audrey said.

"What is?"

"The attention-seeking. Christine. All the mystical garbage. The drama. The ghosts and demons and crap. She's been cooking up reasons why she's special since she was a kid and she realized she didn't have the analytical mind to go into law like everybody else in the family. But guess what? When you have a baby you're not special anymore. The baby is special."

They both looked at the infant.

"Suddenly you're not a medium," Audrey said. "You're not a conduit. You're not a white witch. You're somebody's mom, and there isn't anything less unique in all the world. Everybody's got a mother somewhere."

"She'll be fine," Kradle said. "I like her attention-seeking. Gives me something to focus *my* attention on."

He didn't voice the rest of the thoughts that flooded his mind. That Christine mightn't have been the needy child that grew into a needy and praise-hungry adult if someone had bothered to look at her every now and then. If her parents had glanced up from their legal pads to watch her prancing around the living room at some point during their mutual race for district attorney. If someone had only listened to her fanciful tales instead of diagnosing them or relegating her to the kiddie corner at the charity balls and college fundraisers and gallery viewings her family frequented. He'd heard tales of a ten-year-old Audrey practically glued to her father's hip, trying to chip in to conversations about tax reform, while an eight-year-old Christine drew pagan symbols with the toe of her shoe in the dirt under her chair.

Audrey's phone rang and she took the call. Kradle stroked the single lock of blond hair sticking out of the top of his new son's head. He lost himself in thoughts of how to make Christine feel special again when she woke from the thick, open-mouthed slumber he'd left her in. Then he realized a nurse was tugging on his arm.

"Mr. Kradle?"

"Yes."

"Your wife just left."

CHAPTER 23

Bernie O'Leary had seen all kinds of things in his time manning the road-house on Cortez Gold Mine Road. There were few regular reasons a person would find themselves in Lander County at all. The bulk of his clientele was gold miners, the five regulars who stopped to sink a beer at the end of their shifts before heading up to their trailer homes on Battle Mountain or out on the plains. Those guys, only two of whom had ever shared their names with Bernie in the four years they'd been coming, were the predictable type. They came in and sat at the five deflated leather barstools at the counter in the otherwise featureless room, each guy to his regular stool, so that after a few years the seats had molded to each individual ass, and swapping places for whatever reason would have just been silly. Bernie figured that down in the mines it was dark and loud, and maybe nobody had ever bothered to introduce themselves or talk over the din on the first day down the shaft. Maybe, after eight hours below the earth's surface, not talking, not shaking hands, it seemed strange to introduce themselves in the elevator going back up, and after a while the awkward silence that settled around these men became acceptable, even natural. The five came in every day, sat down, drank their beers, and none of them ever lifted their eyes from the counter to exchange so much as a joke or a comment. Bernie had seen one nod to another once, when they announced Hillary had lost to Trump on the little television in the corner of the bar. But that was it. They all left at different times. Five in. Five out.

Aside from the five miners, Bernie had served a few geologists once. He'd listened with interest as they talked about Crescent Valley quartz deposits and fossils as he nailed fresh timber veneer around the windows of the trailer that served as the bar where the sun had baked it clean off. Some film people had come through the year before, scouting locations for a spaghetti Western, their trailer full of angry pampered horses huffing in the heat. Every few months there was an Area 51 pilgrim or two who came to Bernie's bar, having bought their share of rubber aliens and novelty T-shirts, and taken all the squinting selfies they wanted to take, before deciding to keep traveling north through the middle of the state to catalog what wasn't there.

Bernie didn't know what he was dealing with when the cop arrived. The guy didn't walk like a cop, didn't check his five and seven when he came in the door the way Bernie knew became natural to cops after they'd passed through enough unfamiliar thresholds and received a punch in the back of the head for their trouble. The old man's badge said NAWLET. He dusted his hands off and put them on the counter to balance himself while he climbed up onto Number Three Miner's stool. Bernie leaned sideways and saw a police cruiser with a dent in the hood sitting at the pumps outside.

"You want a beer?" Bernie asked.

"Sure," the old guy said.

The daily silence of the miners had set Bernie up not to feel weird when a vacuum of wordlessness descended on the bar. Nevertheless, he felt weird for some reason now, handing the guy a Bud and trying to busy himself behind the counter. The old-timer's knuckles were bone-white on top from being skinned once too many times, and when Bernie rounded the counter to open a window and let some of the weirdness out, he saw the guy had one foot on the floor, as if he was ready to shift his weight onto it in the event he needed to get up suddenly.

Bernie slipped back behind the counter, just because he felt as if he should put something between the old cop and himself. He fooled with some glasses and a cloth, not really polishing them, keeping an eye on the old guy. The cop patted all his pockets, found a wallet eventually and opened it on the counter. Bernie watched as the man fumbled through it and seemed to find it empty. He extracted a credit card and examined it, tapped it on the counter a couple of times, thinking. Bernie found himself looking then at his own wallet, for some reason, which was sitting in a bowl by the register. Emu skin. A gift from his ex.

"How 'bout that breakout?" Bernie said, just to stop his ears from ringing in the quiet.

"Yeah," the old cop said. Bernie noticed he had to swallow a mouthful of beer he'd been holding in his cheeks, just swooshing it around his tongue like a fancy wine person.

"Were you there?"

"Why would I have been there?" the old guy asked.

"I thought you might have got called in, that's all," Bernie said. "Thing like that, I figure they'd call everybody in."

The old man sipped his beer again, held the liquid in his mouth while Bernie counted off seconds.

"Cruiser is shot," the old man said. He gestured to the door but didn't take his eyes off Bernie. "I hit a deer. Thought I'd come in and see if you knew your way around a vehicle. Help me figure out what's been knocked loose under the hood."

Bernie hesitated, tapped his knuckles on the bar. "I don't know nothin' about cars," he lied.

"Guess I'm stranded," the old man said.

"You could take my car," Bernie said. He put his keys on the counter.

"Then you'll be stuck here."

"I'll have a friend bring it back."

"Sounds inconvenient."

"It is." Bernie nodded. "But you're the law. You've gotta help the law."

The cop whose name badge read NAWLET took the keys and weighed them in his scarred hands.

He rose from his stool. Bernie stepped back and gripped the counter, and felt something like a cold hand release its grip from around his innards.

The old guy dressed as a cop walked to the door, stopped and turned back.

"One for the road?" he asked.

"Sure," Bernie relented, feeling a little as if he'd been unstrapped from the electric chair only to be asked if he wanted to sit back down and take a breather before he left the building. He turned and squatted and reached into the fridge, felt its soothing breeze against his sweat-damp cheeks.

When he rose again the old man was standing just near him, by the liquor cabinet, a hand's reach away.

2000

Celine had never been to a prison before, and it was prettier on the outside than she had imagined it would be. Where it stood on the hill, huge walls of smooth brick baked in the summer sun, cut by long geometric shadows made by iron gates, sheets of mesh, coils of wire. She stood in the parking lot and fingered the keys of the car that still smelled like her mother's perfume, her little brothers' farts, the occasional box of fried chicken her father used to sneak on the way home from work. They'd all been dead a year, and the smells and sounds of them lingered everywhere in her life. She heard her mother calling her name, and if she was distracted or tired she sometimes answered. She would feel the tug of a little boy's hand on her elbow, look down to find she was alone. Celine wanted there to be some stronger remnant of her lost family when she arrived outside Baldwin State Prison to visit her grandfather. But there was just the smell of them, and a familiar sense of impending doom as she prepared to face the old man, the same as it had been before the massacre.

A pretty woman in shiny black high heels met her at the admission checkpoint. Everyone Celine had dealt with since the killings had been young, pretty, cheerful—people possessed of the kind of limitless enthusiasm and delusional hope required to work with traumatized, "at risk" youths. The team who walked her through her deposition were a collection of grinning, laughing, toned and terrific types that looked as if they'd just stepped off a beach somewhere in Florida. The attorney that informed her that her grandfather had entered a guilty plea couldn't have been older than twenty-five. Celine followed the pretty blonde woman, whose name she had been too consumed with dread to grasp during the screening procedures, out of the building and down the caged walkway to the huge gates of the facility.

Passing through them, Celine felt a strange sense of calm envelop her, a bubble of numbness that wrapped around her limbs, distinctly at odds with what she was seeing. She put it down to some kind of trauma response, simi-lar to that which had stripped her completely of emotions in the first days after the killing. She glided past fenced yards of orange-jumpsuit-wearing inmates, who hooted and hollered in her direction. Passed a pair of guards changing shifts with the watchtower staff, the two men loading and check-ing their rifles at the bottom of a concrete stairway. She was buzzed through five sets of big, clanging iron doors and down a tight hallway, past rows of empty windows with battered phone receivers mounted beside them. They arrived in a room with a steel table and two chairs bolted to the floor. Celine balked in the doorway like a wild horse being led into a truck.

"He's not coming in here with me," she said.

"No, no," the woman said, laughing. "No. You'll be behind glass. I thought you'd like a second to collect yourself."

"I'm collected," Celine said. "Just show me to him."

"Celine." The woman put a hand on Celine's arm. "You don't have to be brave all the time. I'm here with you. We'll take it slow. You can just sit here a moment and—"

"If I don't do this now, I'm going to lose it, okay?" Celine said through gritted teeth. She was so exhausted by speeches from the beautiful victim-liaison people about being "there" for her and her "bravery." Nobody was with her, not in this. And her survival for the 352 days since her family had been slaughtered was more a matter of anesthesia and habit than bravery, the un-feeling ability to follow directions and eat and sleep and move from one min-ute to the next without screaming.

She was escorted to one of the glass booths with a phone receiver, and the woman who was there for her went away. Celine didn't have to wait long before he was brought before her.

While movies and novels about prisons had prepared Celine for the smell of disinfectant, the cheap paint slapped over everything, the institutional coldness of the hallways, and the general grimness of the men she passed, nothing prepared her for seeing her grandfather the way that he was. He lowered himself onto the steel stool on the other side of the glass. He was ex-actly as he had been the last time Celine saw him, maybe a couple of pounds heavier. She had expected him to be as physically ravaged as she was by what had happened. For his cheeks and eyes to be sunken, his frame withered by neglect or abuse, perhaps months of sleepless nights thinking about what he had taken from the world. But he was as tanned as he had been by the farmyard sun, and his hair was thick and silver, and when he looked at her his gaze was bright and attentive but expressionless, like someone waiting for their name to be called at the DMV.

"Well?" he said after a while.

Celine opened her mouth to speak but couldn't find the words. She lowered her eyes and stared, her face burning, at the counter between them. The seconds ticked by. In the distant halls, men shouted and doors banged, an alarm started bleeping and was soon shut off. Celine tasted a sourness on her breath that made her think of rotting meat, and when she swallowed it was as if a rock was lodged in her throat.

"Why me?" she said finally.

Her grandfather laughed, a single bark, and shook his head.

"Of course." He nodded. "Not 'why.' But 'why me.'"

Celine was shaking in her chair, her fingers sliding in her own sweat as she gripped the edge of the table between them.

"Because of the damned fence," her grandfather said. "That's why."

Celine sucked air, tried to ease it out slowly.

"I had to look at that fence every day for three years, you know that?" he said. He leaned on an elbow, the phone clutched in his chained hands. When she glanced up now and then she saw that he was skewering her with his cold, blue eyes. "I had to remember what a shitshow you made of it. Not just the job itself. But me offering you any kind of basic advice about it and you losing your stupid little mind. What a performance you put on. Wow. Yeah. Because that's you. You've never been able to accept even so much as a shred of constructive criticism. You're perfect. You're fucking perfect, Celine, and Lord help anyone who tries to suggest differently. I mean, my god, child. If you're so perfect, how come you made such a hash of painting a goddamn fence?"

Celine found some words. Not many, but some.

"The . . . fence?"

"I mean, there was even dirt in the paint." Her grandfather snorted, shook his head. "You painted all the way down to the ground and flicked up the dirt, and just kept on painting over it. It looked like that expensive goddamn cookies-and-cream ice cream you insisted Nanna buy for the pancakes on Christmas morning."

He was carrying himself away now into the rageful memories. Celine saw a vein bulging from the skin of his temple, near where the receiver rested.

"Anyway," he said after a while, "I came up from the barn after I sent the boys on their way and I told you to get inside and you refused, standing there by that fence with your cigarette. With your fucking hip dropped and that bratty little pout. So I just thought, *You know what? Fine.*" He sat back and folded his arms. "Fine," he said again. "Suit yourself."

Celine snapped. She felt it as a physical break, a crunching of shards so hard and splintered with grief and fury that they sprayed out inside her, cut the underside of her skin to shreds. Her words sliced out of her, painful to form with her lips, her eyes burning as she banged the phone receiver on the glass with both fists.

"The fucking fence?" she roared. "You left me here to live with all this because of the fucking fence?"

"You and me, baby girl." Her grandfather shrugged. "We're in this together. Don't try to tell me you didn't ask for it."

Celine hardly heard his words. She was banging on the glass with her open palms, smashing it with her forearms and elbows, trying to get at him, trying to claw her way into the room with him. But then there were arms encircling her and pulling her away, voices cautioning her and commanding her, and for all her thrashing and twisting and screaming, nothing seemed to get through the glass protecting the old man as he sat, looking slightly amused, in his seat. Celine let the big female guard who held her carry her all the way back down the hall to the room with the steel table, and she sat there crying and clawing at her hair and face, trying to pull the words out of her brain even as she knew she would never be able to.

People came to the door, but the guard just waved them away. She sat near to Celine but did not touch her, twisting a little strand of hair at the bottom of her Afro hairstyle and staring at the corner of the ceiling. And, for the first time in a long time, Celine was glad for the silence of the other woman. For the fact that she wasn't smiling. That she wasn't talking about bravery or closure or justice. Her just being there, rather than talking loudly about how she was there, was a tiny comfort.

As her sobs subsided into helpless little hiccups, Celine distracted herself from the memories burning and staining their way into her brain by looking at the guard's uniform. The name badge that said *WEBBER*, and the shiny buckles, the equipment on her belt. She tried to memorize it all. To try to drive out the sound of the old man.

"You want to go home?" Webber asked eventually.

"Yeah."

"I'll walk you out the back way." Webber nodded toward the door. Celine got up and walked shakily, a few steps behind the broad-shouldered woman, her bones aching, feeling small and cold in the huge prison. They followed a convoluted path along shaded gravel walkways and empty, caged yards, buzzing through gates and doors, until the guard stopped by the entrance to a building and seemed to consider something.

She decided, and said, "Come with me." Celine followed. They emerged into a cell block. Celine was hit with the smell of men. The barred doors revealed small spaces crowded with personal belongings—posters, books, medicine bottles, clothes. In the tiny, boxy rooms, men sat quietly, one reading a book, one lying on his bunk, apparently asleep, one watching a small television set. The cells were like messy closets, with thin bunks rammed into one corner and a toilet squeezed into another.

"See this?" the guard named Webber said.

"Yeah?"

"This is death row," she said. "Small row, ours. We've only got seven guys. Your grandfather isn't here yet. He's still in processing. But he'll end up here, next week maybe."

Celine looked. In the cell nearest to her she could see a towel with brown stains on it hanging over the corner of a bed. The man who sat there was hunched over a little desk, staring at nothing, wringing his fingers and rocking gently. In another cell, a kid's drawing hung over a bed where an inmate lay with his arms behind his head, staring at the ceiling. The silence was icy.

Webber stepped back, and Celine followed, until they stood against the furthest wall from the cells, out of earshot of the men. Celine looked at the windows high above them and saw blocks of white sky cut with steel mesh.

"Let me tell you what I'm gonna do," Webber said. She pointed to a cell at the end of the row. "I'm gonna keep your grandfather in that cell there for the rest of his life."

Celine looked at the gray, striped mattress. The low ceiling. Nicks and scratches in the paintwork of the walls, some names and clumsy pictures.

"I'm going to make sure he doesn't get out." Webber was watching her eyes carefully. "Not soon. Not ever. This here? This is the little box he's going to get stuffed into. And he's going to scramble around in that box hour after hour, day after day, year after year, maybe until they take him out of there and kill him."

"You have to be his guard?" Celine asked.

"Me, and a couple of other guys." Webber nodded. "We keep them here until their time runs out. We make sure they live the life they're supposed to live. They don't get hugs or kisses. They don't get special food. They've got a menu they can order off from commissary, but there's nothing on there that would brighten up your day. Your grandfather has drunk his last glass of wine, girl. He's had his last good night's sleep. He's seen his last sunrise and his last sunset and his last tree. I don't know if he ever saw the ocean, but if he didn't, well, he's lost his chance. It's over for him."

Celine nodded.

"But none of that matters," Webber said. "What really matters is that now he can't hurt you anymore. He's going in the box, and he'll stay there, and he won't hurt anybody ever again."

Celine threw her arms around the woman. Webber stumbled a little, said "Whoa" and laughed, but Celine held on. Some of the inmates on the row were watching them. The guard's words had filled Celine with such happy, vicious, hateful emotion that she couldn't speak, could only hold the woman and watch the inmates and curse her grandfather with all her soul. She stared at the empty cell because she wanted to remember every inch of it, the smell of it and the shape of it, the hellish box into which he would be thrown and buried alive.

She walked out of the gates that day and unlocked her car, climbed in, and drove away without looking back at the prison reflecting the sunlight on the hill.

CHAPTER 24

When Celine woke up, Keeps was gone. One side of her face was aching from resting on her hands on the tabletop, her lower back yowling with pain as she straightened, stretched, tried to determine what had happened. The laptop and sheet of paper still lay beside her, and as she came to her senses she felt a wave of relief rush over her that the *Not Guilty* column still held only the name Dr. Martin Stinway. She recalled some half-hearted argument between her and Keeps about calling the specialist then and there to question him about Kradle's case, and Keeps fishing around on the internet, trying to hunt down contact details for the man. She must have drifted off.

The doorbell rang, and Celine realized the sound must have been what woke her. She walked numbly into the foyer and unlatched it, and it swung, hard, in her hand as Trinity Parker pushed it open, walking in as if she owned the place.

"Good," she said. "You're awake. Make me some coffee, will you? Please tell me you've got something better than instant. I'll get set up. You want me to call animal control while I'm at it?"

"Wha—" Celine shook her head. "Animal control?"

"There's an inmate swimming in your pool," Trinity quipped.

Celine returned to the dining room and looked through the glass doors. Keeps was hanging over the side of the pool, his elbows splayed on the tiles, looking at the desert plants in the manicured garden. Celine could see his bare feet gently paddling just under the surface of the water.

"Oh, Keeps," Celine said. "He's helping me with some—"

"I'm too busy for bullshit." Trinity held a hand up. "You want to bang an ex-con, go ahead. It's not my role to judge you. Not everybody's standards are as high as mine."

Celine sighed.

"Don't get me wrong. I understand the appeal," Trinity said. "The tattoos. The muscles. The danger. The deep-seated psychological need to rebel against your parents' dreams of you having missionary sex with a stockbroker once a month until he's too old to get it up anymore. What's he wearing? I assume he didn't bring his swimming trunks. Should we shift this meeting to the dining room so we can work with a view? Will that get you filled with vigor and verve?"

"Please stop talking."

"In all seriousness, you might want to look more carefully at that guy. He has rather a sketchy—"

"I know," Celine said. "I know."

"So, make the coffee then, Osbourne."

She did. Trinity sat at the kitchen island and opened her laptop. When Celine came to sit beside her there was a video set to play. She was watching CCTV camera footage from what looked like a large department store. The shadowy figure of a man limped onto the screen, powering up the aisle as fast as his wounded body could take him, snatching items off the shelves.

"Guess who?" Trinity said.

"John Kradle," Celine said.

"Clever boy, your *other* criminal beau," Trinity said, tapping the screen, following Kradle around the department store from video file to video file. "Most fugitives, if they get injured and need medical care, hit a pharmacy. Some will break into a veterinary clinic. Some go so far as to hold up a doctor. Not your guy. He broke into a Joanne's."

"Joanne's?"

"Craft supplies," Trinity said. "He took needles, wire, scissors, gauze, cotton balls. He went into the paint section and took some methylated spirits. Then he hit the manager's office and stole a cash box with four hundred dollars in it. Nobody responded to the alarm going off because it was a goddamn hobby craft store, and we've briefed all the sheriff's departments to be on alert for break-ins at doctors and vets."

"I thought you weren't interested in chasing John Kradle," Celine said. She watched Kradle limp down the hardware aisle and grab a hammer off the wall, probably for the cash box. "Especially since he and Homer Carrington have split."

"That's just the thing," Trinity said. "They haven't split."

Celine watched as Trinity pulled up a video of Kradle exiting the store through the rear fire doors. He disappeared off screen, carrying a plastic shopping bag of items. After a second or two, a dark shape materialized, seemingly from the shadows themselves. A big man stepped out from where he had been standing against the wall and turned, passing under the camera in pursuit of Kradle.

"Oh, shit," Celine said. A strange impulse pushed its way to the front of her mind, a tangle of emotions, the desire both to tell John Kradle he was being pursued and not to tell him—to both watch and intervene in his death. Trinity seemed to sense her conflict.

"I was in my kitchen once, and I looked out onto my lawn and saw the neighbor's parakeet had got loose from its cage." Trinity sat back, reflecting, smiling. "It was sitting there eating grass seeds. Then I noticed another neighbor's cat stalking it from my hedge. I felt the same thing you're feeling now, I suppose. The delicious, godly power of being able to stop death. Change fate. That wonderful curiosity that pulls you back before you can do so, that wants to witness things playing out in all their beautiful savagery."

"You really are incredibly full of yourself, aren't you?" Celine said.

"Should I tell you what I did?" Trinity asked.

"No." Celine sipped her coffee. "You should tell me why you're here, why you're giving me this lead on Kradle."

"Because I want something in return," Trinity said. "It's the only reason I do anything in life."

"Sounds about right."

"I want you and your delinquent squeeze to come and lean on Joe Brassen for me. I've managed to get a little traction with him by threatening to cut off his balls. But I've hit a wall. He'll sing for me but he won't dance, and I think you two could help."

"Joe Brassen!" Celine felt her mouth fall open. "He's not—"

"Oh, yes he is."

Celine rubbed her eyes. "Urgh, Jesus," she moaned. "It makes sense. He manages the prison baseball game. Not the team itself—he's not the coach—but he runs the event."

"Yeah, we already put the coach's head in a vice," Trinity said. "First guy we went to. He's clean."

"Brassen advertises the game in the staff rooms," Celine said. "He organizes catering. He would have been able to recruit personnel from all over the prison to be on the team, or at least invite their families to come watch."

"Is he a known white supremacist?"

"What? No!" Celine said. "You think I'd have a white supremacist on my staff?"

Trinity shrugged. "I think you'd have capable, punctual, and dedicated guys who can handle the most dangerous inmates in the prison on your staff. You'd look at their work performance and ignore their personal beliefs, because that's what you're like—all work and no personal life."

"I have a personal life," Celine said.

"Really?" Trinity glanced around. Celine refused to take her eyes from the woman's face.

"Let's just get going," Celine said.

"Before we do"—Trinity turned back to the laptop—"there's something else I want to show you."

She pulled up another CCTV file, this one attached to a news story. Celine watched people milling around the card tables in a casino. A woman in a frilly shirt and vest was shuffling cards for a guy in a ball cap. Nothing looked out of the ordinary. Befuddled tourists sidestepped young men on a big night out.

Celine watched the card dealer leave the table, cross the floor, and walk up to a man in a white collared shirt, her fist already balled.

"Whoa!" Celine blurted as the punch played out. "Ho-ly cow!"

"Hell of a right arm." Trinity smiled.

"Is that—"

"Abdul Ansar Hamsi."

"Jesus. She's KO'ed him." Celine found herself smiling alongside her adversary.

"I want her," Trinity said. "I want to give her a counterterrorism job. First, I want to take her somewhere and feed her martinis and have her tell me all about her life. Then I want to give her a counterterrorism job."

"You'll have to fight talk show hosts for access to her for the next year and a half."

"Enough fun," Trinity said, slamming the computer closed. "We've got to roll."

Celine heard the glass doors slide open in the dining room, and wet footsteps on the hardwood floors.

"Yo, can I smell coffee?" Keeps yelled. "Where's mine?"

Keeps slid into the passenger seat and Celine climbed behind the wheel. They sat watching as Trinity Parker pulled away from the curb in her silver Mercedes and disappeared into the morning. Celine felt a strange, unspoken tension between her and Keeps, as though a line had been crossed, not when she recruited him as her fellow fugitive hunter but when she fell asleep in his presence. She imagined herself drifting off there beside him, and him wondering whether to disturb her, rouse her or try to move her, the self-professed conman and criminal who had talked his way into her life now completely and truly alone with all of her world laid out in front of him. How vulnerable that made her.

Keeps took the lid off the reusable coffee cup she had filled for him and sipped the brew. He gave a small snort and she followed his eyes to the house across the road.

"What?"

"That outdoor setting there," Keeps said. "In the yard." Celine looked through an open gate and could see the outline of a six-seater wooden setting under a pergola.

"What about it?"

"That's a *Jacqueline* setting," Keeps said. "Six seater, solid oak with UV and water-resistant Texteline and cotton-blend cushions."

"You're an outdoor furniture connoisseur now?" Celine frowned.

"Yeah." Keeps sipped his coffee again, staring out the window. "I got that way. Used to be when I needed a quick buck I would slip into a nice neighborhood like this, have a look around, find a house with a big ole expensive outdoor setting in the yard. I'd hop the fence, take a picture of the furniture, put it on the internet at a ridiculously low price. You'd have people turning up within a half an hour with a trailer to haul it away."

"How much would you get for a setting like that?" Celine asked.

"It retails for about three grand," Keeps said. "You'd list it for four hundred. Get people climbing over the top of each other to get to you."

"Don't even have to break into the house," Celine said. Keeps didn't seem to register her tone.

"It's a good play." Keeps shrugged. "Not the best."

"What's your best?"

He thought for a moment.

"The Burn and Return." He gave a smile, remembering. "It's simple and it's fast. You can play it anywhere, and it doesn't require a huge set-up."

"How does it work?" Celine asked.

"You buy an electrical device—say, a waffle maker—from a department store. You don't spend much. Twenty bucks. You take it somewhere, set it on fire. When it's peak hour at the store, you bring it back and get hysterical with the manager that the thing almost burned your house down. You either demand a top-of-the-range, ultra-expensive replacement, which you then go and pawn, or you demand cash for your trouble."

"And you've done that?"

"Plenty of times. When I was young and stupid." Keeps nodded. "I'd use my girlfriend sometimes, maybe, if I had one. She's there screaming that she's going to sue the franchise, she's going to call CNN. If you can rope in some-body who's got a little kid, that ups the stakes. You put a bandage on the kid's arm and tell the manager your kid got burned. The manager doesn't check with head office. You're causing a scene. The kid's crying. People are staring. He hurls money at you."

Celine sat for a while, her stomach shifting uncomfortably.

"Listen," she said eventually. "Now's the time to bounce if you want to bounce."

"I'll hang in for another day," Keeps sighed. "This game is a bit smarter than the old Burn and Return. I'm interested. And I need the cash."

"You think Trinity is really going to pay you a hundred bucks an hour for your services?"

"It's ninety now," he said. "I told you. A hundred was the release-day pre-mium rate. And yes, I do. She'll give me the money or I'll take it."

Celine felt a tremor of uncertainty in her core and reminded herself that she really didn't know this man at all. She started the car and pulled out, and Keeps flicked on the radio.

"... *dinary tale of an encounter with two of the most wanted fugitives on the loose from Pronghorn Correctional Facility. The woman—*"

"Turn it up," Celine said.

"*—Shondra Aguirre, claims that the North Nevada Strangler, Homer Car-*

rington, and family killer John Kradle abducted her when she stopped to assist them on the Route 15 highway in south Mesquite."

"That's your boy," Keeps said.

". . . of true terror and survival, with an unlikely twist: John Kradle let me go. He was going to hurt me, the big one, Carrington. The strangler. He was gonna rape me. I know it. I know it. But Kradle, he, like, set it up so I could get away. He made a show, like, 'Ahh, yeah, bro, I wanna go first,' and then he let me go out the back window of my house.'"

"You want to put this in the *Not Guilty* column?" Keeps asked. "Or should we save it for the *Character Witnesses* column?"

"I don't know where to put it." Celine gripped the wheel and tried to focus on the road. "I don't . . . I mean, we can't judge it. It's not relevant. And there's not enough information. I'm still undecided on Kradle, okay?"

Keeps took out his cell phone and began to dial.

"What are you doing?"

"Helping you decide," he said.

Celine drove. They had left the suburbs and turned onto the highway, heading toward Pronghorn, and as her speed rose so did a growing dread creeping like bile up her throat. She turned down the radio as Keeps's call connected.

"Ah, yes, hi. I'm calling to speak to Dr. Martin Stinway," Keeps said. His voice had changed. His words were clipped, thin, his jaw jutting forward as he snuggled back in his seat, eyes on the road ahead. "That's you? Excellent. Listen, this is Damien Koenig-Hadley calling. I'm an investigative journalist with the *New York Times.*"

Celine widened her eyes, reached over and slapped his chest. Keeps didn't react.

"Yes, I know that, yes. It's only a couple of quotes that I'm after, or a *no comment.* Whichever you'd prefer. I'm working on a story about John Kradle, one of the escaped fugitives from Pronghorn Correctional Facility in Nevada, and the ongoing investigation into his case. You've been watching it all on the news, I presume?"

Keeps took the phone away from his ear and put the call on speaker. Celine heard the high, sharp voice of Dr. Stinway coming through the line.

"What investigation? What are you talking about?"

"Oh, well, I'm surprised you haven't been informed. Perhaps the FBI hasn't got to you yet," Keeps said. He gestured for Celine to keep her eyes on the road.

"Son, I don't know what you're trying to tell me here," Dr. Stinway snapped.

"Let me explain," Keeps said. "My story about Kradle and the re-examination of his case has been cooking along for some time now, and with the breakout in the headlines, I've been approved for a massive feature. A source told me some months ago that agents from the Bureau were looking into the possibility that Kradle was framed for killing his family, that perhaps there had been some police involvement in that framing. Crooked cops tampering with evidence, trying to pin the murders on the husband."

Celine yanked the car to the side of the road. Keeps covered the receiver just in time to mask her growl. "This is not how—"

"Shhh!" he hissed.

"Are you still there?" Stinway said.

"Yes, I'm here. Sorry. I'm sharing my office today with another journalist who's also on a call." Keeps shot Celine a warning glare. "She's the loud, inconsiderate type but, you know, cutbacks in the media! What were you saying?"

"I was saying I don't know anything about a-a-a frame job." Stinway gave a hard, short sigh. "This is all news to me."

"So you recall the case and the evidence you gave in it?"

"Yeah," Stinway said. "I remember it well. And I'll tell you what I told John Kradle's lawyer: That I stand by any evidence I've ever given in any case of which I've ever been a part. I'm a scientist. We value truth above all things."

"You testified that a microfiber examination of Kradle's clothing definitively proved he and no one else committed the murders."

"Yes."

"That gunshot residue patterns indicated that he'd fired the weapon."

There was a pause. Celine wrung the steering wheel.

"Look, you can discount the gunshot residue stuff," Stinway said. "That doesn't hold up anymore."

"But you believed at the time that it did *hold up*, as you say?"

"It was . . ." Stinway sighed again, making the line rattle.

"The truth, above all else?"

"Yes," Stinway said. "Gunshot residue evidence was, at the time, undergoing some . . . some, uh, peer review. It was tricky. But if you did it right . . . Look, never mind. The truth has to take into account not only what I'm examining on my table but what the overall picture is. The evidence I had

before me was . . . was part of the story. The overarching story. You understand? It's all part of a picture."

"What about the blood spatter? You said patterns indicated that Kradle
had struggled with his son while the boy was still alive. That those patterns
could not have been made after the fact—when, perhaps, Kradle found the
bodies."

"Listen to me," Stinway said. "I'm a man of science."

"So you've said."

"And I'm not . . . I'm not the world's tallest man."

"The . . . world's tallest man?" Keeps frowned.

"Have you met the detective who worked on this case? Frapport? He's
a big guy. He's a big, loud, intimidating guy. Full of confidence. Full of-
of-of bluster. Okay? Imagine you're there and he comes in with a stack of
notes—a binder, a big binder with pieces of paper sticking out of it and photographs and witness statements. He tells you he just wants your piece of the
puzzle—of the picture—to match up to everything that's in this binder."
Stinway cleared his throat. "This *huge* binder. You-you-you say you're going
to look into it. And the next thing you know, he's calling you. Barking down
the phone. Wanting to know if you've checked it out yet."

Celine rolled down her window. The desert air was cool, but it gave her
no relief.

"So you're saying Detective Frapport intimidated you?" Keeps asked.

"No." Stinway gave a pause. "I mean. Some of the evidence . . . sometimes
it's the kind of thing that can go one way or the other."

"It can?" Keeps asked.

"Sometimes you've got to make a ruling. Is it inconclusive, or is it positive?
Maybe it's inconclusive on its own. We're talking about a couple of specks
of blood on a shirt. But you have to interpret the evidence. And you have to
consider what else you know about the case."

"What else did you know?"

"I knew that the father confessed."

Keeps reached over and slapped Celine's arm. She didn't move.

"The detective told you that John Kradle had confessed?" Keeps asked.

"Yes," Stinway said. "Detective Frapport said I wouldn't have to testify,
because the guy had already confessed."

Keeps was tugging on Celine's arm. She brushed him off, her eyes locked
on the horizon.

"What else did you know?" Keeps asked.

"Well, I knew there was an enormous goddamn binder full of evidence Frapport had collected which said he did it. Imagine you're there, and he's leaning on you to say the same—"

"He leaned on you?"

"No. I mean. He never said he—" Stinway made a sound, like a groan, an exhalation. Celine could almost see him leaning his forehead in his hand. "I can't have another scandal in the papers," Stinway said. "I can't have the FBI turning up on my doorstep. I mean, when it was the lawyer looking into it, I could blow it off. But I'm not . . . I can't be talking to the FBI and . . . Not now. I'm already on thin ice here."

"With your employer, you mean?" Keeps asked.

"No, with my wife." Stinway laughed sadly.

Keeps and Celine stared at the phone resting now in Keeps's lap, the green light indicating the call was on.

"It made sense that it was the husband," Stinway said. "It's always the husband. And my job is to look at the evidence and *make it make sense.*"

"I've heard enough," Celine said. Keeps ended the call and the two sat quietly, the car engine ticking as it cooled down. "How did you know that would work?" she asked.

"People always talk to journalists," Keeps said. "Sometimes not right away. But eventually. They figure the story is going to get written one way or another, and this is their chance to put the record straight."

Celine nodded.

A sheriff's cruiser breezed past them on the road, heading for Pronghorn. Keeps started to speak again, but Celine held a hand up to silence him. She started the car and pulled out onto the road.

CHAPTER 25

Kradle tugged back the hood, certain that the light of the kitchen would reveal his true identity to Shelley Frapport and that some change would come over her. That she would cower and scream, twist away, that the numb terror that had infected the woman named Shondra would envelop her too, once she fully realized the situation she was in. But none of that happened. The boy named Tom took all of the shock into his thin frame instead, stepping back hard into the countertop and gripping it with his hands.

"Oh, wh-wh-whoa," he stammered. "Whoa. *Whoa*!"

"Tom." Shelley took the boy's arm. He grabbed her in response, his fingers buried deep in the fluffy fabric of her robe.

"Mom, Mom, that's—"

"John Kradle. I know."

"You *know*?" Tom said.

"Tom, it's okay." The woman smoothed her son's head. She had an eerie calm about her, as though she had been prepared for one of the nation's most wanted men to turn up in her kitchen. "Just sit down. Sit here."

She pointed to a chair at a small dining setting in the corner of the room. The boy didn't budge. His eyes were on Kradle, huge and quick, like those of a frightened bird. Kradle went and sat instead. He felt as if he was walking in a dream, and, if this was indeed some kind of hallucination, getting into a chair seemed like a good idea in case he started floating around the ceiling. Shelley went to the cupboard and took out a loaf of bread, opened the fridge and extracted a gallon of milk, and the man and the boy watched her from their separate strongholds in the small room. The black dog treated itself to a trotting tour around the dining room and, not finding the cat or anything else that interested it, came back and sat by Kradle's chair, eyes on the bread.

"You must be starving." Shelley selected a knife from a drawer. "Let me make you something, and then we can talk."

"I . . ." Kradle found himself looking at the boy, almost for help. "This is . . . You've been . . . ?"

"Expecting you." Shelley nodded. "Well. Not exactly expecting you. I thought it was a long, long shot that you'd make it all the way here. But I told the detectives assigned to the house that we were going away to stay with my sister in Minnesota. Just in case you did show up. I said we would be back once they gave us the all clear that you'd been captured."

"Mom." Tom was shivering from head to foot, still clutching the counter-top as if floating around was also a concern to him. "What the *hell*?"

"Would you sit down, please?" Shelley pointed to the chair beside Kradle. Again, the kid didn't move.

"Is your husband here?" Kradle asked.

"He's dead."

Kradle felt a whump of pain, like a punch, to his chest. He gripped the fabric of his shirt and stared at the floor at his feet, bracing against the impact as the walls of his plan began to fall, one after the other.

"Patrick had a heart attack in the garage three years ago," Shelley continued. She put a peanut butter and jelly sandwich and a tall glass of milk down in front of Kradle. "I think he'd been trying to lift a tire. I found him. Luckily, it happened while Tom was away for the weekend. Probably the nicest thing Paddy ever did for this family."

"I'm calling 911," Tom announced.

Shelley walked over, confiscated the cell phone that the kid produced from his pocket, and pushed him toward the table where Kradle sat. Even in the chair, the boy was a half a foot taller than Kradle. The child and the fugitive sat face to face, both with their hands on the tabletop and their backs rigid, like poker-playing gunslingers about to draw over a fifth ace.

Shelley sank into the third and last chair at the table. She put Tom's cell phone down near his hand, the screen up, blank. The dog at Kradle's side started scratching its ribs with one back paw, its bony leg joint knocking rhythmically on the floor. It gave a dry kind of cough, as if it had a hairball, and then slid down into the sphinx position, and the room fell back into icy silence.

"Nobody's calling anyone," Shelley said. "Not until I explain."

Kradle stared at his sandwich. He wondered if he would be able to keep it down. His body was both raging at him to eat it and flooding his belly with nausea.

"I was going to divorce your father," Shelley said, taking her son's hand.

"What? When?" Tom shook his head sharply. His voice slowly rose to a yell. "What are you talking about? What divorce? *How is this relevant? There's a goddamn murderer in our kitchen!*"

"Don't lose your mind, Tom," Shelley cautioned.

"*I'm losing my mind!*" the kid yelled.

"He always says that." Shelley looked at Kradle knowingly. "Just listen, Tom. It'll all make sense."

The boy and Kradle locked eyes again. Kradle felt the sudden, strange urge to apologize for his smell. For the smell of the dog. His hands on the pale pine tabletop were filthy, the nails black.

"In 2015, I told Paddy I wanted a divorce," Shelley said. "Actually, I started raising the possibility about a year earlier. Paddy was working on a gangland shooting that was driving him nuts, and he was never home. You know these gang guys, they're up all night like cockroaches. Paddy started living their way, and he was always on the phone, trying to sort this guy from that guy. They all had nicknames. They all had records and pasts. He would come home for an hour to eat dinner and try to explain it all to me until I had a headache trying to figure out who Fisho was and who Nettles was and who stole whose girlfriend or corner or stash or whatever the hell. By the time Paddy was done it was as if he'd just vented and blasted steam all over me, and then he was out the door again before I could even say goodbye. I climbed into a cold bed every night for a year, and I just thought, *I don't want to do this anymore.*"

The boy burst into tears, then quickly tried to disguise the emotion behind his big, thin hands, wiping and rubbing, almost as if he was attempting to shove the emotion back into his face. Kradle kept his eyes on his sandwich.

"Maybe I should give you guys a minute," Kradle said.

"No." Shelley rubbed his arm, sending electric pulses deep into his bones. "Just listen. You need to hear this. It's maybe . . . It could be my fault you were put away."

Shelley Frapport drew a long breath and let it out slowly.

"Paddy came home for dinner, barging in like he always did, throwing his stuff on the floor in the doorway and sitting down at the table, ready to be served. And I just said it. I said, 'I want a divorce.' I told him I already had a lawyer." Shelley wrung her hands on the table, near Kradle's. "That was the day your family was killed, John."

Kradle listened to the rest, though he didn't need to. He could see it playing out in the room around him. The crying and raging and arguing, the desperately uttered promises, the young boy kneeling behind the door of his bedroom trying to make sense of all the tension in the air and how it weighed against his parents' constant reassurances that everything was normal and fine. Patrick Frapport, overweight, exhausted, mind-numbed and basically nocturnal, struggling through the daily jet lag of his previous gangland case and then being loaded with a triple homicide and a potential divorce just as he rose to come up for air. Kradle sat and imagined, perhaps in the very seat where Patrick had sat imagining, how the divorce would go. He saw the man pulling his books off the shelves in the living room, leaving hers oddly spaced among the fine dust, and loading the books into whatever would carry them, with the rest of his possessions, because getting boxes and packing tape would make it all too real. Carrying his stuff out to the car in laundry baskets and trash bags. Sniping with Shelley over who owed which utility bills, who should buy a new cutlery set. Moving into a loud, dirty motel where he could walk to work to save cash. He couldn't do it. It was undoable. The gangland trial and the Kradle Family killings and his divorce and his stomach ulcer and his alcohol problem and his untapped trauma and anger caused by too many years on the job was a mass of blackness that threatened to strangle him. So Paddy let something give. He did it to save his home life, because he knew that even if he put everything he had into his cases, they weren't going to fuck him on his birthday, stroke his hair in the middle of the night after he came back from the bathroom, tell him he didn't look like a beached whale in his swimming trunks.

And Kradle's case was the easiest thing to let give, because it was obvious. The husband did it. The husband always does it.

"Things were okay for a while. Then, just before he died, I said it again," Shelley said. "I told him I wanted the divorce. Paddy had tried. He'd really tried. He was home every night and he was listening to me and . . . I just . . . My heart wasn't in it."

"And he told you then that he'd phoned it in on my case?" Kradle asked.

"Not in so many words," Shelley said. "He just said, 'I did really bad things for you. For us.' But I knew. I'd been married to that man for twenty years. Whenever someone would bring up the case, or they'd say something about it on the TV, he would shrivel up like a prune."

Kradle was afraid to ask his next question, so he just sat there with his eyes closed and the words on his lips, hoping and praying and willing the answer to be the one that he wanted. When he finally drew a breath he could taste the terror coating his tongue like acidic wax.

"Did you keep Paddy's case files after he died?" Kradle finally asked.

"The police came and took everything," Shelley said.

Kradle covered his face with his hands. He put his elbows on the table and willed himself not to scream.

"But I have something that might help," he heard Shelley say. Her chair squeaked on the floorboards as she rose. Kradle rubbed his eyes, clawed his fingers down the stubble on his ruddy cheeks, trying to push everything back in, the way he'd seen the kid do. He heard the black dog get up. When he looked over, it was sitting at the side door of the house, the one through which Kradle had come, its ears pricked and listening to something rustling out there in the morning light.

"Helping a fugitive is a crime," Tom said.

Kradle said nothing.

"I'm not going to let them arrest my mom," the boy continued. "Not for you. Not for anybody."

"It won't come to that. I'll be long gone before the police ever knew I was here."

The boy didn't look convinced.

"My son was about your age," Kradle said. "Someone came into our family home while I was out and shot him dead. My wife and her sister, too."

"So why'd they arrest you for it?"

"Because I was there," Kradle said. "Maybe only seconds after it happened. I went in and tried to save them but I was too late."

"If they locked you up for it, you must have done it," the boy said. "I mean, they . . . they have all kinds of stuff. Evidence and trials and stuff."

"I admire your unquestioning faith in the justice system," Kradle said. "I wish it was merited."

"All this stuff Mom's saying about Dad, it can't all be true. I was there too, you know. My dad was a good guy and he wouldn't send an innocent man to jail."

Kradle thought about telling the boy that it wasn't as cut and dried as that. That sometimes good people got tired, made mistakes, looked the other way, went into denial. Good people could convince themselves of bad things, sometimes. The boy was doing a pretty good job of it right now, trying to convince himself that his father hadn't sacrificed a human life to save his marriage. Kradle wanted to tell the boy that the easiest lies people told themselves were about the dead. But he didn't want to crush that lovely, naive spirit, something he hadn't encountered in many years.

"I mean, say there is some other guy who really did do it," the kid said. "What's your plan? You're going to find him?"

"Yes," Kradle said.

"And you're going to turn him in to the police?"

Kradle didn't answer.

"Why don't you just get, like, somebody else to do that? Like, your lawyer or whatever? Or a friend?"

"My lawyer has been working on my case for five years," Kradle said. "But sometimes it takes extra-legal activities to get to the heart of the matter."

"Are you going to turn him in when you find him?" Tom asked again. Again, Kradle didn't answer. The boy snorted a derisive laugh. "See? You are a bad guy."

"I'm starting to get the feeling I can't win with you, kid," Kradle said.

Shelley Frapport came back into the room. She put a stack of papers onto the table and smoothed them out. "I dug these out of the basement yesterday," she said. "In case you came."

"I can't believe you did this." Tom shook his head, his mouth twisted and mean. "You called off protection on our house. You got these things ready. How did you know he was going to come here, trying to look for evidence? He, like, could have been on his way here to *kill* us. To get revenge on Dad."

"I have an enormous gun under the couch," Shelley said.

"You what?!"

"There's another one in the laundry." She nodded toward a door by the fridge.

"Are you freakin' kidding me?" the boy yelled.

"Your dad taught me to use them."

"What are these?" Kradle touched the papers before him.

"They're phone records," Shelley said. "Paddy and I were fighting like crazy over the bills in the months after he took your case, while I was working out if I still wanted to be with him or not. I kept these. I hoarded them up. Here."

Kradle looked at the pages, the highlighted and notated sections.

"This number." Shelley pointed to the account information panel at the top of one of the pages. "This was Paddy's work phone. I was always bugging him about getting the station to pay for the phone, the whole bill, but they wouldn't because he didn't use the phone completely for work stuff. I kept the papers because I wondered if my lawyer might want them. This is every phone call Paddy made and received in those months. Look at the date here."

She pointed. Kradle saw numbers that he'd seen a thousand times before, numbers that always made his heart seize.

"July eighth," Shelley said. "The day your family was killed. So from here down . . ." She stroked the list of figures. "Almost all of these calls will be related to your case."

They all leaned over and stared at the numbers.

"There might be leads in there." Shelley gestured wildly to the pages when Kradle didn't respond. "It . . . it has to help, right?"

Kradle folded the pages into a bundle and held them in his hands. He had traveled what seemed a million miles to this place, expecting so much. Expecting to grab the man who had put him away by the throat and wring the truth from him. Expecting to look at the files, the notebooks, the photographs and interview sheets relating to the murders of his family. Expecting to hear confessions, promises, revelations. But all he had were tales of a dead man and some phone records that sat so lightly and hopelessly in his hands.

That wasn't true. He also had a sandwich and a glass of milk.

Kradle nodded encouragingly to Shelley, ate half the sandwich, and gave the other half to the dog. Kradle was so hungry he didn't taste the sandwich, though he was aware in some deep, quiet corner of his mind that it was the first time he'd experienced peanut butter in half a decade. He stood and tucked the phone records into his back pocket.

It was then that he realized the boy's phone was no longer on the table where his mother had placed it. Kradle lifted his eyes from the empty space where it had been, lying face up, the screen blank, and saw the same cold blankness in the child's eyes.

"Sorry, dude." The boy shrugged. He took the phone out of his lap and put it back on the table.

Kradle heard the front door of the house being kicked in.

CHAPTER 26

"It was fifty thousand dollars," Brassen kept saying, hunched over the cinderblock and plywood coffee table dominating the living room in his trailer. "That's life-changing money!"

"Yeah, it's going to change your life, all right," Celine sighed. "It's going to change everything about your goddamn life."

She sat in the big, plush recliner chair opposite Brassen and held her head, just as he was doing, trying to accommodate the physical weight pounding in her brain with horror at the man's situation. Celine had hired Joe Brassen to work on death row exactly for the reasons Trinity assumed she had. Because he was punctual, efficient, methodical. Joe paid attention to detail, and detail was important, because the men they dealt with had little to no hope left in their lives. If anything slipped through, even so much as a smuggled shoelace or a single hoarded pill, it could mean an inmate was planning to take a life—either a guard's or his own.

She'd ignored Brassen's past—the unanswered questions about his firing from the Las Vegas Police Department, the written cautions from his boss over in medium security about racist remarks—because all she cared about was his ability to keep the inmates and her colleagues alive.

Now he would be lost. He would end up an inmate, the only remaining question being where. The psychologically crushing monotony of protective segregation, a hothouse of corrupt cops, pedophiles, and child killers separated and locked away from the rest of the prison; or in general population, where his past as a prison guard would have him dead within the first month by shanking or stomping in the yard.

Celine was sitting across the shitty coffee table from a dead man who was breathing his last free air.

Trinity stood by the flyscreen door, refusing to touch anything in the cluttered trailer. Celine could see Keeps's silhouette on the porch, sitting and stroking Brassen's huge, hideous dog.

"Didn't it occur to you," Celine said, "that fifty grand was a hell of a lot of money just to let an inmate use a phone?"

Brassen shrugged. "You don't look a gift horse in the mouth. I figured he had a girlfriend and his Nazi pals were paying for them to talk. I didn't question it."

"You didn't question it because you're a Nazi," Trinity said distractedly, tapping away at her phone with one thumb. "You liked Schmitz. You liked what he stood for. And you liked his money."

"No," Brassen whined. "I'm not a Nazi. Celine, you can tell her. It's me, boss!" He tapped his chest. "It's *me*. Joe. You know me. I'm not into killing people."

"So long as you consider them 'people.'" Trinity smirked.

"Can you just let me do this?" Celine turned and glared at her. "What did you bring me in here for?"

Trinity shrugged and brushed invisible detritus from Brassen's trailer off her jeans. She wandered into the tiny kitchenette to ogle the filthy frying pans and takeout containers on the countertop, as if they were artifacts from a strange, forgotten civilization.

"Remember that camping trip to Big Bear?" Brassen's eyes were huge and pleading across the gloomy space, like those of a cornered deer. He gave a desperate laugh. "The team-building thing?"

"I remember you and Jackson having a grand old time getting drunk together, fishing in that creek. You remember Jackson? The guy whose wife and kid were almost taken out by a sniper because of you?"

Brassen eased a huge sigh.

"You don't need to remind me that you and I have a warm history, Brassen," Celine said. "I like you. I've always liked you. Somehow it got by me that you were a racist asshole deep down inside. I guess when people come into my life . . ."

Celine didn't continue the thought out loud. That when people came into her life that she liked or cared for, even just a little, she ignored everything unpalatable about them because she feared losing them so badly. She was too down about Brassen to think further about the string of cheating, gambling, idiotic, and emotionally abusive boyfriends her habit had brought into her life over the years. The convicted conman currently shar-ing her home.

"Tell me what happened," Celine said. "How did all this start?"

"Look," Brassen sighed, "they didn't pick me because I'm, like, some kind of KKK guy. I don't attend meetings. I don't talk to them online. I'm not *one of them*. It just started with Schmitz wanting some stuff that other inmates were getting from me. Certain candy bars. He stopped me on the row and said he heard I got some Cashew Crush Bars for Donahue, and I said, yeah, did he want some? Ten bucks each. Then I started bringing him the paint for his artworks. Then, you know, he wanted a letter brought in from the outside. Wanted it to get past the mail room."

"Where did you have the letter sent?"

"My place." Brassen massaged his brow. "It didn't seem like such a huge leap, you know?"

Celine did know. She had heard the story a thousand times, of inmates securing small favors from guards that they later parlayed into bigger favors. One day an inmate was asking you for an extra napkin with their dinner tray, and a few months later you were letting them and another inmate have sex in a storeroom once a week on your watch. Celine had taken years of hurt from her colleagues for never allowing an inmate so much as an extra packet of sugar with his morning coffee ration.

"Did you ever have contact with anyone who worked for Schmitz in per-son?" Celine asked.

"No," Brassen said. "He'd ask for stuff, and I'd have somebody send it to my place. When he wanted the cell phone I went out and bought it from Walmart."

"And what about the baseball team?" Celine said. "How did that happen?"

"Schmitz just said he wanted certain people at the baseball game that day." Brassen swallowed hard. His eyes were glistening. "I figured he was organizing something inside the prison. Like, they were going to start a riot or something. Have key personnel all tied up seeing their families after the game so they could get it off to a good start."

"You were fine with them starting a goddamn riot at Pronghorn?" Celine barked.

"It was fifty grand!"

"Jesus, Joe!"

"Our riot procedure at Pronghorn is foolproof." Brassen wiped hard at his eyes. "It was going to be a storm in a teacup. As soon as they kicked off, we would knock 'em down, same as always."

"Somebody could have been hurt!"

"I need the money, Celine!" Brassen gestured to the walls around him. "Look at this goddamn place!"

Celine looked.

"My father died last year. Left me seventy thousand bucks." Brassen's lip was trembling. "I pissed it away into the slot machines in three weeks."

"Jesus."

"I got problems."

"No shit," Celine said.

"How could I have guessed what they were really going to do, huh?" Brassen said. "How could anybody have guessed that?"

"Do you have any idea what they're going to do now?"

"No."

"Nothing?" Celine insisted. "I mean, all those phone calls you facilitated. All those letters you delivered. You never saw or heard *anything* that would give you even a hint as to what they're going to do?"

Brassen shook his head helplessly. "I . . ." He swallowed hard. "The only thing I ever saw was some drawings."

"What drawings?"

"I don't know!" He shrugged. "Sketches. I saw them in a letter."

"When?"

"Maybe two weeks ago. I was standing outside Schmitz's cell. I gave him a letter, he opened it up and unfolded it, and I saw there was a sort of sketch in there. He saw me watching him and folded the paper back up again."

"What were the sketches of?"

"Boxes. Blocks. Lines."

"You're not helping me here, Joe."

"What do you want me to say? I saw a flash of shapes. That's it. It could have been anything," Brassen groaned. "It could have been the layout of Pronghorn. It could have been a map or . . . I don't know. I'm telling you, Celine, I don't know, I swear to god! Maybe you could put me under hypnosis, see if it's in my brain somewhere."

"Hypnosis is bullshit," Trinity said from the kitchen.

"Joe," Celine said. "You have to do what Trinity's asking you to do. You have to make contact with them somehow and tell them you need their help."

"If I make contact with these guys, they're going to laugh in my face," Brassen said. "It'll be completely obvious that the marshals are pushing me to get in touch so that they can hunt them down. They probably won't even answer."

"You have to try. You have no choice."

"What am I going to say?" Brassen spread his hands wide. "That you guys found out I'm the inside man and, what, I want to become one of them now? *Grab me a pointy hood in a large size, fellas! I'm all outta friends over here!*"

Celine caught Trinity's eye and nodded toward the porch. When they went outside, Celine saw that the big, ugly dog was lying on its back in the sunshine while Keeps rubbed its taut gray belly.

"He's right," she said. "He can't just call them up."

"Not literally," Trinity said. "We tried the number of the cell phone he gave Schmitz and, as expected, it's been dumped. No activity since the breakout. But there are ways we can get their attention. The FBI have been monitoring a bunch of websites known to recruit members of the Camp."

"The Camp?" Keeps asked.

"Schmitz's particular subgroup of unhinged losers," Trinity said. "They trawl the internet looking for angry, young, white male virgins everywhere you'd expect to find them. Sites related to mass shootings, revenge porn, serial killers. Stuff like that. They message potential members with pseudonyms and start filling their heads with junk about race wars and how that's going to make them kings of a new world."

"I get that," Keeps said.

"You do?" Trinity jutted her chin at him.

"I mean, I get the strategy." Keeps stood, making the dog groan with sadness that its belly rub was over. "You want to hook someone, you make them feel special. Make them feel seen. Like, you understand them and what they've been through, and the pain they're experiencing right now, and you offer them a safe place away from that pain. Because they're the chosen one. They deserve it. They're different. These groups are just finding directionless people and giving them a direction. Same things cults do."

Celine watched Keeps's eyes, which were blank and distant with thought.

"You gotta give Brassen what he wants," Keeps said quietly. "Make him feel special. Yeah, okay, you can keep threatening him with torture and life in prison or whatever. But if you make him feel like a hero, he'll work harder for you. And you gotta give these Nazi assholes something that they want, too, or they'll ignore him, just like he said."

"So what do they want?" Trinity said. "That they don't already have?"

"They want to know their plan is safe," Celine said. "Whatever it is. But that's the thing, we don't even know there is a plan. The whole breakout was staged to get Schmitz out of prison, but that doesn't necessarily mean they wanted him out so he could stage another shooting."

"We're *betting* they're going to stage another shooting," Trinity said. "It's almost Christmas. It's a good time for shooting people. So many gatherings."

Celine felt a ball of pain gather in her throat. Trinity flicked her eyes up from her phone briefly. "Oh," she said. "Whoops."

"What?" Keeps asked.

"Nothing," Celine said.

Keeps and Celine watched Trinity. She was leaning on the porch rail, her long-lashed, dark eyes cast down to her phone screen, casual and slightly bored, the way she always was, as if preventing mass death was just part of the job.

"If we know anything about terrorists like Schmitz, it's that they like momentum," Trinity said. "Once we announced to the press that we believed Schmitz was behind the whole thing, activity in the neo-Nazi online world went ballistic. The Camp and groups like it will be swarmed with recruits, and those recruits are going to become bored quickly if there isn't a follow-up event. Schmitz can't go into hiding in some farmhouse in rural Texas now. It would be cowardly. Their new members will want another demonstration of power."

"So how do we make Schmitz feel as if all that is under threat?" Celine said.

"Easy," Keeps said, smiling. "We pull a con, of course."

The shouting was so loud and frenzied that Kradle couldn't pick out individual words, but he knew what they were. He'd heard them dozens of times before, when shake teams busted into his cell for surprise searches, when officers responded to inmates getting violent or trying to trash their cells. *Get down. Get down. Get down on the ground. Hands on your head. Don't move.* He went down, as he was told, flattening on the floor with his hands on the back of his head, fingers interlocked, the dive an almost automatic thing. His cheek hit the plastic seam between the floorboards and the dining room carpet. Kradle felt the carpet against his temple and tried to think of the last time he'd touched carpet anywhere. He focused on the tiny loops of wool near his nose so his mind wouldn't tumble downward, as it wanted so desperately to do, into the black abyss of knowing that it was over.

It was all over.

A cuff snapped on his wrist.

"Shit," a voice above him hissed. "Shit. *Shit!* Reed, come here. Look. It's John fucking Kradle."

Kradle's wrist was dragged behind his back. Shelley and Tom were out of their seats, clutching each other.

"Oh, man! We gotta call for backup."

"No way. Let's get him back to the station ourselves. We're gonna be fucking her—"

Kradle felt the second cuff loop around his free wrist, and then the floor shuddered with a concussive boom.

Another boom as Kradle twisted to see what had caused the commotion.

His face was sprayed with dirt and blood. It was the smell that told him it was buckshot. He saw the second cop, Reed, fall against the table Tom and his mother were struggling to hide underneath, squeezing into the space like frightened mice. Reed had a huge hole in her chest.

Kradle tried to get up, but the cop who had pinned him had taken the second gunshot blast in the face and collapsed onto him, headless and dead as a stone.

Homer Carrington stood in the side doorway with a sawn-off shotgun hanging from one hand, assessing the damage through the gun smoke. He turned and looked at the spray of blood and brain matter on the wall beside Kradle's head.

"Stop yelling," Homer said, and Kradle realized that Shelley Frapport was screaming so hard her throat was grinding, making the sound like a high growl. Sounds were returning to his ringing ears. The black dog was guarding the couple under the table, barking at Homer, and Tom was shouting pleas, and Homer was raising the gun to blast the dog and the boy and his mother all at once.

That's when Kradle lost it.

He rose and smacked the barrel of the gun upward just as Homer pulled the trigger. The blast took out a massive chunk of ceiling, spewing dust all over the pair as they struggled for control of the weapon. Kradle had fought Homer once before. He knew his favorite move—that huge arm that came from outside his peripheral vision, sweeping toward him like a snake, trying to hook him into a deathly hug. Kradle let go of the gun, bowed, and slammed his shoulder into Homer's rib cage, sending the huge man backward into the kitchen counter. Kradle kept on, reaching for the gun with one hand, sweeping the counter for weapons with the other, pushing his body against Homer's chest, trying to avoid that big arm with its constrictive embrace or haymaker fist always threatening, always there, a yacht boom swinging in an unpredictable tide. Homer dropped the gun just as Kradle felt the smooth, wooden handle of a chef's knife in a block brush against his knuckles. Homer grabbed his whole face in one of his big palms, and Kradle's fingers barely grasped the knife. Homer pushed with that gigantic hand, and Kradle's whole head snapped back and he fell against the floor, tucking the knife against his body just in time for Homer to fall on it.

The serial killer wrapped two hands around Kradle's throat. Kradle remembered the cave, the sick, detached look in the other man's eyes, the feel of his body above him, and all the vicarious horror the weight and smell of him brought—of young women struggling under his grip, scratching helplessly at the air, inches from his smiling face. But this time was different. Homer had a knife handle sticking out of his chest, and his hands were weak and growing weaker, and Kradle could just repress the animalistic urge to buck and jolt and twist under the crushing pressure of those hands so he could see the darkness crowding into Homer's vision.

"You were supposed to be my friend," Homer yelled, defiant, trying to load the pressure back on, his thumbs pinching down against Kradle's windpipe like a clamp.

Kradle surged upward, flipped Homer's weight, took the knife out and shoved it immediately back in.

"I was never your friend, you idiot!" he snarled. He couldn't believe the words as they came out of him, that he was having this conversation with a man as he murdered him. That it had come to this; to convincing a psychopath that he wasn't the victim, that his life was being taken not due to betrayal by a loyal companion but as a reaction to him killing two innocent police officers only seconds earlier, and as a denial of him taking further lives. It wasn't personal. It was for the greater good. Kradle let out a hard, exhausted, angry laugh, just one, and then stabbed Homer in the heart a third time.

Homer grabbed Kradle's wrists, blood-soaked and warm, and Kradle expected some further admonishment of his performance as a fugitive compadre, but only dark blood poured from the corner of Homer's mouth as he tried to speak. Kradle heard sirens in the street. Tom and Shelley Frapport were holding each other under the table, their heads tucked together, their bodies racking with frightened sobs.

Kradle was looking at them when he heard the ratcheting sound of his loose handcuff as it closed on Homer's wrist. The killer let the cuff go, smiled, and then died, chained to his betrayer.

CHAPTER 27

Reiter had got himself into some fixes in his life, but nothing like this. The trouble for him had traditionally come from women, and part of that was his fault, he was man enough to admit. He liked women who answered back. Women who fought and challenged him. He liked to go into a bar and tell a woman her shoes looked stupid with her outfit and see what her reaction was, and the woman who threw a drink in his face was usually the one he took home. It was like finding a wild horse that bucked and yanked and kicked, and grinding it down and down until it was tame, until it came trotting up for the bridle happily, as if being a kept beast was all it had ever wanted out of life. Other men liked to shower women with gifts when they were courting. Call them up. Leave them messages. Take them places and open doors for them. Reiter liked the rage he saw in a woman's eyes when he let a door slam in her face, or when he threw the dinner she'd cooked on the floor. He liked to play games. Throw gas on fire.

And then, after a while, the reactions softened and the rage subsided, and the women learned all his moves and started ducking his swings. Reiter usually got bored then and shuffled the women on. A smooth ride wasn't his desired mode of transportation. And he should have guessed that enough years messing around with wild women was going to get him kicked in the jaw some time or another.

But this. This was something else entirely.

Reiter sat against the wall in the van with his wrists chained to a bolt in the floor and wondered if what was being done to him was just. Because Reiter was under no illusion that Burke David Schmitz had brought him along for the ride simply because of the spitting incident on death row. He'd seen the raw amusement in the white boy's big, blue eyes as the spittle landed on his prison-issue white sneaker, the look that said, *Just you wait*. He saw it again after Reiter ran with the crowd out of the gates of Pronghorn, through the shadows in the back of the van, two big, blue eyes full of amusement. *You waited. Now your time has come,* they said. But Reiter believed in fate, and this wasn't supposed to be his fate. He'd ended up on the row for trying to tame the wrong woman, pushing her too hard one night after a few too many cheap tequilas and accidentally crushing her skull against a concrete step in the backyard. But to end up in the middle of a plan like this, just for spitting on the shoes of a Nazi asshole, seemed like getting slapped in the mouth for telling the truth.

And that was exactly the attitude he took to Schmitz when he was hauled out of the van and brought into the house. He tried to look around as the young men dragged him across the short distance between the van and the front door, but someone smacked the back of his skull, so he kept his eyes on the gravel, the wood, the thin, dusty carpet. When he looked up and saw Schmitz standing there, freshly showered and rubbing his short blond hair with a towel, Reiter winced as the tape was pulled off his lips, and then blurted the words the first chance he got.

"This ain't fair."

Schmitz laughed, and having heard their leader laugh, all the cronies did too.

"It ain't clever, neither," Reiter said.

"It's not?" Schmitz asked.

"It's not," Reiter said. "See, I know what the plan is here."

"Okay." Schmitz took a beer that someone handed to him and twisted the top in his fleshy palm. He took a chug and said *Ahh* in the way Reiter had always hated people doing, then said, "Enlighten me."

"You gonna do another shooting," Reiter said. "Like the New Orleans thing. Open up on a crowd of innocent people. Only this time, you're going to try the other route. You're going to kill a bunch of whites, frame a Black man for it, try to start your big, stupid race war that way."

Schmitz gave a delighted laugh, looked around the group sitting on the busted, tattered furniture or leaning in the corners of the room.

"Has somebody been chatting to this guy?" Schmitz asked.

"I had a KKK guy for a cellmate in 2011," Reiter said. "I know all your schemes. You think one of these days you're going to shoot or blow up or gas enough people that you'll kick off a big man-on-man battle and, at the end of it all, you guys will be able to establish your . . . your *new world order*, or whatever you like to call it."

"This is amazing." A skinny girl, standing in the doorway to what looked like an old kitchen, laughed. "He's taking us to school."

"I am. I am taking you to school," Reiter sneered. "So listen up, bitch. Learn something. You think you got this all worked out. That if you keep yanking and yanking on that cord, eventually the lawn mower is going to start up. You think you're going to kill somebody from one side, and the other side's going to retaliate. A shooting sparks a riot. A riot sparks a crackdown. A crackdown gets some fool killed in custody, which sparks another riot. Places get looted. People get beaten, raped, killed. It all gets filmed, and it all gets shared around. There's turmoil in other countries. Enough sparks, you got a big-ass fire."

The group nodded along.

"And then, at the end of it all, when the military and the police can't get everybody to calm down, they'll be looking for someone else to lead. And there you are. Burke David Schmitz. President of the New World Order."

Burke smiled.

"Well, here's the problem, assholes," Reiter said. "Your New Orleans thing didn't work. And this here ain't going to work either."

"Why not?" Schmitz sipped and *ahh*ed again.

"Because you got the wrong patsy," Reiter said. "I'm not a mass shooter. I'm just some small-time guy from Mesquite killed his girlfriend by accident and landed on the row for it. I didn't even graduate high school. Before I got locked up I used to deliver linen for restaurants. Nobody's going to believe I did all this."

"You're underestimating yourself," Schmitz said. "You don't have to graduate high school to know the world needs to change, and that we have the power, and the duty, to change it now. Some of the greatest men in the history of this country were everymen, just like you and me."

Schmitz drew a breath, preparing to carry on his history lesson. Then the enthusiasm for it seemed to leave him. His shoulders relaxed with the ease of someone realizing their efforts weren't worth the trouble.

"I can understand your anxiety about having a meaningful death," Schmitz said. "I had the same concern. I would have martyred myself at the scene on Dumaire Street if I had known for certain that what I had done that night would have the impact that I'd hoped it would."

Reiter looked around. All the Nazi losers were listening to their leader with fixed eyes and shallow breaths, quiet children. He felt sick.

"And I haven't failed," he said. "I—"

"No, you haven't, that's the last thing you've done," a guy behind Reiter gasped. Reiter looked over his shoulder at the paunch-bellied, red-headed guy with a lightning strike brand just visible above the collar of his shirt. Lightning Strike didn't seem game to go on. Schmitz looked torn between annoyance at being interrupted and gratitude at the encouragement.

"I have been able to inspire others," Schmitz continued cautiously. "Recruit a new generation of soldiers. But this will be bigger. And I assure you, this is going to make its mark. *Your* actions will make their mark."

Lightning Strike and a small woman standing with him high-fived.

"Your role in this won't be mistaken," Schmitz said, looking Reiter over. "We're planning on making things as convincing as we can. We think your body, left at the scene, with a self-inflicted gunshot wound to the head is going to get some people nodding along. We think a manifesto, handwritten by you, mailed to the *New York Times* on the evening of the massacre, is going to sew things up very neatly."

"You kidding me?" Reiter snorted. "How the hell you going to get me to hand-write anything? You give me a pencil and I'll stab you in the eye with it, you stupid motherfucker."

"I really doubt that," Schmitz said. He nodded at one of the men in the room, a lean, tattooed guy with jet-black hair and a goatee. The goateed guy took a pair of pliers out of his left back pocket and a pencil out of the right. Reiter gripped the chain between his wrists and looked at the faces around him, trying to find a friendly eye among them, but all he could see was the bored gazes of cats trying to think of new ways to play with their trapped mouse.

"Which is it?" Schmitz asked Reiter. "The pencil or the pliers?"

For a few seconds of sheer, electric panic, Kradle simply tugged on the chain connecting him to the dead man. He pushed his cuff against his wrist with all his might, grabbed Homer's and did the same. He got up, yanked hard, felt the impossible weight of the killer's body anchor him to the kitchen floor. The sirens in the street were getting louder. He heard people yelling.

His senses came to him in a painful whump, knocking clarity into his brain. This was his second chance. Two police officers had died trying to contain him, and he was still free. If he was captured now, all that lay ahead was the story that had been written for him; of a quiet death behind a sheet of one-way glass, maybe with Christine and Audrey's parents watching, crying, whispering abuse from the darkened viewing room. John Kradle wanted to die where he had been happiest—under a Louisiana sunset on the swamps. He leaped onto the body of the officer who had restrained him and started fishing in the pockets of his shirt and trousers, his shaking fingers pulling at pouches on his belt.

He heard a noise, looked over, and found Shelley Frapport was desperately searching the body of the officer named Reed. The black dog was dancing around madly, trying to console the boy under the table, trying to attack the fallen body of Reed, grabbing her sleeve and tugging, letting go, the animal utterly confused by the situation and which people belonged to which team. It realized its only known friend, Kradle, was searching for something and decided to help, snuffling and pawing at the pockets Kradle searched, trying to nose the man out of the way.

"There's no key!" Kradle cried.

Shelley was shaking her head madly. "It's not here either."

Kradle made a decision. He wrenched the knife out of Homer's chest. It came out slickly, soundlessly, trailing blood. Kradle wiped it on his jeans.

Shelley looked at the knife and nodded her understanding. "I'll try to hold them off. You head out the back. Take the car. The keys are hanging on the hook by the door. It's parked in the alley."

"Take the kid," Kradle said. Shelley gathered up her bug-eyed, trembling son and all but dragged him out of the room. The sirens were deafening now. Kradle took Homer's still warm hand in his, gritted his teeth, and set the blade to his unfeeling skin.

The last time Old Axe had been inside Whisky a Go Go on Sunset Boulevard, he'd been twenty-eight years old, sporting a nose ring and wearing a necktie he'd swiped from his father's dresser drawer tied around his forehead to keep his long hair back. The Whisk wasn't a place he'd tended to go—he was more of a Pandora's Box man when he wanted a crowd, but he'd followed the horde down to the rock club when he heard there was a protest kicking off. A young Axe had liked a protest, and at that time in his life there had been many, and he had known from the heat of that afternoon that this would be a goody. People jostling together, chest to back, hips to butts, yelling and spitting and rushing the police. Sweat. It had made him feel as if he were part of a living organism: a hot-blooded snake coiling and striking, and he was a guy who didn't feel part of things very often. He remembered that night the upset had been about curfews at the Whisk or something like that. All he could remember now was that he'd taken an egg from a carton a guy was carrying around, hurled it and hit a line cop right in the face, and a guy wearing pigtails, with SLUT! painted across his bare chest, had burst out laughing at the accuracy of his shot. He was thinking about that guy now as he put a shoulder into the door of the club, a heavy thing that got stuck in the heat from too many layers of black paint over the years.

It was cool inside, and nothing but the structure of the place seemed the same to Axe. There was the old scaffolding the dancers and bands had been forced to scale above the writhing masses, and the big dusty lights hanging precariously from rusty framework above that. The floor was still tacky, but where it met the bar it was littered with used electronic cigarettes and not the stubs of hand-rolled joints and peanut shells like he remembered. He didn't recognize the names of any of the bands that were going to perform there over the coming weeks, and half of the signed posters hanging in frames behind the bar were mysteries to him, too.

He put his policeman's cap on the bar and pulled himself onto a stool. Midday. The Whisk was quiet. The bartender, who was probably born about half a century after the Whisky a Go Go opened its doors, came and looked at the badge on Axe's shirt.

"Nawlet," she read.

"Yep," Axe lied.

"Should you be drinkin' in uniform, Officer Nawlet?" she asked.

"All I want is a Coke," Axe reasoned.

The girl made him the drink and put a lemon slice in it, for some reason, and a fancy coaster under it. Axe opened his emu-skin wallet and pulled a note from a thick stack, paid her. He was following this girl with his eyes while she was stacking glasses on a high shelf when the older couple walked in and set their bags on the floor.

He was tall, gray-haired, pear-shaped, and she was his short carbon-copy in chinos and sneakers. Sensible haircuts that fit nicely under sunhats. They clambered onto the stools two down from Axe, and he admired the gold-rimmed reading glasses the guy had hanging from a chain around his neck. Axe had been wearing tamper-proof plastic reading glasses at Pronghorn for some years, and his record for days between the prison issuing him a new pair and somebody chewing on them or sitting on them and snapping them in half just for the hell of it was only about two and a half weeks.

Axe felt a little tingle of energy in his bones when the couple started speaking in German. He'd taken some German classes as a young man, when he was locked up for the first time, and as he listened some ancient, creaky door of his brain popped open and began interpreting the sounds.

"All right, let's take stock for a moment. Did you give the hotel key back or did I?"

"I did."

"And where's my puffer?"

"In your pocket, there."

"I've got my passport . . ."

Axe glanced over, saw the guy slap a blood-colored booklet with gold lettering on the bar top, flip it over as though he wanted to check it wasn't a forgery, then slip it back into a kind of cash-hiding fanny pack strapped to his waist under his T-shirt. The German lady was patting the pockets of her chinos, searching the zippered pockets of a similar nervous-tourist-style cash belt.

"It's . . . ," she murmured, trailing off.

"Where is it?" the guy demanded. "Did you leave it in the room?"

"I brought it from the room. I know I did. It was the first thing I packed!"

"Well, where is it?"

"I, uh . . ." The woman's face was flushing pink.

"Jutta, don't tell me you've lost it. We—we have half an hour until we have to leave!"

The couple started attacking their bags, ripping open zippers and making Velcro flaps roar. Axe sipped his drink. It was while he was turning back to the bar that he saw the door to the Whisky a Go Go shunt open again, a guy muscling a crate of wine bottles through. He noticed a shape in the light reflecting off the shiny floor and put his drink down, turned around, and looked behind him.

"Ent . . . ," Axe said clumsily. The German couple kept searching their bags. Axe thought for a moment.

"Entschuldigung?" he said. *Excuse me?*

They looked up. Axe nodded to the doorway, the passport on the floor.

The German man strode over and snatched up the passport.

"Oh, thank god, thank god." He shoved the passport at his wife. "Thank god. Thank you, Officer."

Axe shrugged, turned back to the bar.

"No, really." The German man came over. "You have helped avoid certain disaster."

"Es ist in ordnung," Axe said. *It's okay.*

The big German smiled. Axe saw crooked teeth, a bit like his own.

The German man switched to English, clapped Axe on the shoulder. "May we buy you a drink?"

Axe thought about it.

"Sure," he said.

CHAPTER 28

Celine was sitting with her feet in the water, staring at the shards of afternoon light flickering against the sides of the pool, when she felt the soft trace of a tail running up the back of her arm. Jake the cat wandered by her, the perhaps accidental tail-flick his only acknowledgment of her presence, and took his place at the head of the pool like a swimmer warming himself up for the first plunge. She'd heard some cats simply preferred men, but the fact hadn't taken away the sting of jealousy when she and Keeps arrived home and the beast greeted him by headbutting his shin, purring heavily.

Keeps slid open the dining room doors and wandered out, barefoot, watching the screen of a phone Trinity had given him. Celine had her own new device that mirrored one given to Brassen. While the traitorous guard languished in his isolated cell at Pronghorn, he would be tasked with monitoring the chatlines connected to sites owned and run by the Camp, waiting for a response to his message about needing to talk. She, Keeps, Trinity, and Brassen were all logged in to the message boards under the same account. If any messages came through, they would all see the exchange at once.

Celine hadn't waited around at Brassen's trailer to watch the man being escorted again into custody. She thought letting him go back to his home, to taste and smell his former life while knowing that every part of it had been destroyed, was a cruel trick by Trinity. She'd let the man wander in the tomb of his past. Celine didn't envy the night that lay ahead for her former friend and colleague. He would be lying on an inmate bunk, listening to the sounds of the prison around him, familiar sounds made somehow horrifyingly new and foreign, awakened from fitful dozes now and then by Trinity asking questions. Celine guessed she wouldn't let Brassen sleep too long at any point, just for the pleasure of tormenting him.

Back at Pronghorn, Celine, Keeps, and Trinity had taken a table in the chow hall to plot their strategy with Brassen. Celine had scanned the printed faces of the inmates pinned to the petitions, a sea of scowls, many of them slashed with red marker. In the hours she sat there, only once had a woman in a sheriff's deputy uniform walked up triumphantly and crossed off a face, causing a little tired cheer from others in the room. Celine knew that, like her, the men and women who had joined in the recovery effort could be presented with an almost complete wall of red-crossed faces, but while the really dangerous ones were still out there, there would be no cause to celebrate. One rapist running free because of her inability to keep him contained was too many for Celine. One child molester. One spree killer. She wouldn't feel safe or satisfied until they had all been put back where they belonged.

She wore the unease now as she sat with her feet in the pool. "It's been hours," Celine said to Keeps. "Anything on the line?"

"Not so much as a nibble." Keeps sat down beside her and slipped his feet into the water. Celine tapped the phone next to her, which was open to the message board where Brassen had left his note. *Need to talk. Situation changed. Urgent.*

Keeps put down the phone he had been monitoring and took up his own device, flipping open the screen cover and hitting a news app.

"You seen what your boy got up to today?" he asked.

"What? No. I got distracted. Why?"

"Check this out," Keeps said.

He opened an article. The header image was of John Kradle's and Homer Carrington's mugshots superimposed over a small blue house in a narrow street that was crowded with police cars and mobs of gawkers behind a police cordon.

THREE DEAD IN POLICE SHOOT-OUT WITH TOP FUGITIVES.

Celine snatched the phone away. She felt Keeps's eyes on her.

"*The department stated that Kradle killed Carrington after the wanted serial killer murdered two as-yet-identified Mesquite Police officers at a suburban house in Beaver Dam,*" Celine read. "*Police said that body-cam footage from one of the fallen officers appears to show Kradle intervening when Carrington tried to turn his gun on two residents of the property—*"

"He's looking like a solid guy," Keeps said. "While he's on the lam, anyway. First he lets that abducted lady go. Now he's diving in front of bullets to save women and children."

Celine held up a hand. "I'm not trying to find out what kind of guy he is now. I'm trying to find out what kind of guy he was when his family was killed."

"When are you gonna tell me why you care so much?"

"Because me and this guy, we've had a . . . a thing, for the past five years," Celine said. "Just about from the first day he arrived at Pronghorn, Kradle has been . . . in my head. You know?"

"No, I don't know."

"Like . . ." Celine struggled. "Okay, so I wasn't very nice to him when he arrived. The moment he got there. I . . . I didn't give him the best greeting."

"In what way?"

Celine tapped her knees.

"I knew he was coming," she said. "I'd been following the case on the TV and I was disgusted, just like everyone was, I suppose. I was almost happy he got sent to Pronghorn. I made sure he got the worst cell. The worst mattress. I held back his dinner until it was stone cold, and I held back his commissary papers so he couldn't order so much as a razor for three weeks. All that was before he even slept the night."

She let her mind go back, just for a moment, saw him being led in on that morning. She remembered being shocked at his bruised eye, his nose still pumping blood, the limp. She didn't bother asking who had done whatever had been done to him. Child-killers either got a pummeling for their crimes in county jail or they got a rough ride between prisons from vengeful transport guards. She'd seen it many times. Celine remembered standing outside Kradle's cell while he sat numbly on the mattress, staring at nothing.

"I asked him if he needed to go to the infirmary," Celine said. "He said no. I kept needling him. Saying, like, 'If you have internal bleeding and I come down the row in the morning and find you dead, that's a problem. That's *my* problem. So do you need to go to the infirmary or not?' He kept saying no, no, no. And maybe, you know . . . Maybe I should have realized this was a bad time for him. He'd just got to the place where he was going to rot for the rest of his life. He's just been introduced to the walls. The four walls."

Keeps nodded knowingly.

"So what happened?"

"I pushed him over the edge and he snapped," Celine said. "He leaped up and hit the bars at a hundred miles an hour and tried to grab me. It was what I wanted. I stuck him in the hole for a couple of days. From then it was, like, *on*. It was on between us. He came up from the hole with this mean look in his eyes. It said *I'm going to get you*. And I gave him that look right back."

"And did he get you?" Keeps said.

"Oh, yeah," Celine said. "Not right away. Nothing big. He just watched for a while. And before long he found something. He found out I hate it when people cluck."

"When they *cluck*?"

Celine flicked her tongue off the roof of her mouth, making a hollow *cluck* sound.

"Why do you hate that?" Keeps laughed.

"Because it's annoying!"

"Okay."

"He sends a kite down the row asking inmates to do it while I'm around," Celine said. "Like, he actually gives out commissary as payment for people to do it."

"That's hilarious."

"Everywhere I go it's like, *CLUCK!*" Celine said. "I'm putting my stuff in the control room and I hear *CLUCK!* I'm going to the bathroom and someone out in the hall goes *CLUCK!* I'm doing my rounds and all the inmates are going *CLUCK! CLUCK! CLUCK!*"

"I like his game."

"He started everybody drinking from their mugs backward." Celine shook her head ruefully. "Gripping the cup with the handle turned toward you."

"So, like, the handle is under your mouth?" Keeps asked.

"Yes."

"You hate that?"

"Yes."

"Why?"

"Because it's not—that's not how you do it."

"Ha. I love it."

"It's got a handle for a reason! Use the handle!"

"I need to remember some of this stuff."

"One time," Celine said, "I was walking past his cell and he just said, 'Thirty days.' I said, 'Thirty days to what?' He just shrugged. So, next day, I'm coming past and he says, 'Twenty-nine days.'"

"A countdown," Keeps said. "Interesting."

"Yeah, interesting," Celine said. "So I really ask him what he's counting down to. I'm dead serious. He won't budge. By the time it gets to twenty-seven days, I say, 'All right, I've had enough of this.' I pull him from the cell, sit him down, do a formal questioning. I write a report for the warden. I brief all the staff. By twenty-one days, other inmates are in on it. And there are hours and minutes attached now. Like, there are nineteen days, seven hours, and forty-one minutes left."

Keeps sat laughing quietly to himself.

"So I do another formal questioning," Celine sighed. "I issue an official warning. I read him all the prison regulations about violence toward staff, breakout attempts, riots. I tried to write him up for threatening staff, get him sent to Special Handling, but the warden says it's just a countdown, it's not a threat—we don't know what he's counting down to. I'm up all night looking at calendars, astrological signs, looking at his case. When was his kid's birthday? When was his wife's birthday? What time of day did they die? The numbers keep coming down and down and down, and in the last three days I'm just . . . I'm pulling my hair out."

Keeps was laughing harder now.

"On the day the countdown was supposed to end I finally convinced the warden to put the prison into Code Orange. I organized a raid team to get all suited up and stand outside Kradle's cell. I'm standing there, too, with a fucking helmet on. I'm a mess. I look at my watch and my whole arm is shaking."

Keeps grinned. Celine glared at him.

"It was nothing," Keeps said.

"It was nothing," Celine confirmed.

"Funny motherfucker," Keeps said.

"It was about as funny as a brick to the face."

"You ever do anything back to mess with his head?" Keeps asked.

"Oh, yeah," Celine said. "Of course. I did everything I could think of. I put sand in his coffee. I sent him to the infirmary with a request for a brain scan. On the request form I wrote, 'Appears to be a moron.' I know he hates spiders, so every couple of months I hide a tarantula in his cell somewhere, or I at least give him the impression that I have."

"Where the hell do you get a tarantula?"

"It's Nevada. You can get them at any pet store." Celine kicked her feet in the water. "They're not expensive."

Keeps kicked his feet beside hers. "You know, I didn't ask you why you care so much about this Kradle guy being guilty. I said, *When are you gonna tell me why you care so much.*"

Celine froze.

"How did you . . ."

"I have my sources."

Celine looked away, shook her head. She took a long time finding the words.

"You change your name," she said. "You move to the other side of the country. You don't tell a living soul. And still, every man and his dog knows your secret."

"Any of the guards at Pronghorn know?"

"Maybe." She shrugged, the anger making her shoulders hot and tight. "Probably. Seems like all the inmates do. Warden Slanter knows, and her predecessor Wilke knew. He hired me. He had to know. But my personnel file is supposed to be confidential."

She felt tears behind her eyes, found herself putting on that hard smile to make them stop. Minutes passed in which they sat and watched the water.

"It's fucked up, man," Keeps said. "It's just about the most fucked up thing I ever heard."

"You're telling me."

"Is he still alive? Your grandfather?"

"No," Celine said. "I visited him once when he was in prison. Never again after that. He asked his lawyer to ask me to come to the execution, so I said no. I just sent a note back saying, *I'm not coming.* That was it. He killed himself three days later."

"Jesus."

They fell into silence. Celine knew more questions were coming. All her muscles were hard, bracing for blows.

"Were you not there that day, or . . . ?"

"I was there," Celine said. "Everybody was there. He spared me."

"Why? Were you the favorite?"

Celine looked away, swallowing a sob, which passed like glass down her throat. "No," she managed. "I wasn't the favorite, Keeps."

"I'm sorry. I should keep my questions to myself."

"I'm not that person," Celine insisted. "I'm not what happened to me."

"And a part of not being that person is not letting it cloud your judgment," Keeps said.

"Right." Celine looked at him. "Exactly."

Keeps touched her hand with his, just barely, the knuckle of his pinky brushing against hers, and Celine felt a rush of warmth immediately doused with a torrent of ice.

His words returned to her from outside Brassen's trailer.

You want to hook someone, you make them feel special.

Make them feel seen.

Like you understand them and what they've been through.

The phones bleeped, an unfamiliar tone, and Celine looked at hers at the same time that Keeps looked at his. A red bubble had appeared on one of the messenger apps. Celine opened it. At the top of the screen was Brassen's message.

Brass_on: Need to talk. Situation changed. Urgent.

Underneath it, a new line of text had appeared.

Addam123: Situation changed?

"Addam123," Keeps read.

"Trinity will be cross-checking people named Addam who are known members of the Camp." Celine shrugged. "But it's probably just a pseudonym."

They waited, watching their screens.

Brass_on: I want more money.

"He's going in too hard." Keeps eased air through his teeth. "This is not what we talked about at all. This is not making them feel as if he knows their plan, as if he's a threat. This isn't the script."

"Trinity must not be with him," Celine said. "She must not be there to coach him."

"Or maybe she is," Keeps said. "Woman's pretty direct."

"He's typing."

They watched the screens. Jake the cat had wandered over to Keeps's side and was trying to muscle his way onto his lap. Celine sighed.

Addam123: Fuck off, man. You got paid.

Brass_on: It wasn't enough. The marshals are grilling everybody at Pronghorn. They know there was someone inside and it's only a matter of time before they get around to me.

Addam123: So run.

Brass_on: I need money to run. 50k isn't enough. I'll need to start a whole new life.

Addam123: Your problem, not ours. You served your purpose.

Brass_on: But it IS your problem. I know more about your plan than you think I do. If they decide to snatch me up I will talk.

Addam123: What do you know?

Celine realized she was gripping the phone with all her strength when her knuckles started to throb. Her fingers were sliding on the case with sweat. This was the moment. The con. The bluff. Brassen needed to do the impossible: to convey a poker champion's confidence in his hand without the aid of face-to-face acting. The flicker of a smile, the straightening of his back, the idle shuffle of cards. Every typed word was critical. The seconds that passed while he figured out what to say. Too long a response time and he would seem uncertain. Too quick and it would all seem too rehearsed. Celine saw the words appear on the screen and reminded herself to breathe.

Brass_on: I have copies of the drawings.

"He made the play," Keeps said, his voice tight.

"This is it," Celine said. "This is all we've got."

"It isn't much," Keeps said. "But, hey, I've worked with less."

They watched for the bubble that indicated Addam123 was typing. It didn't come. After a minute or two they saw the bubble appear on Brass_on's side of the screen.

Brass_on: This is a risk-free venture for you. I'm proposing you put a bag of cash in a locker or under a tree, or goddamn anywhere, I don't care. Just drop the money and get out of there, then tell me where it is and I'll go get it. Another 50k. Pretty cheap to buy my silence.

They waited.

Addam123: We don't work with cash. You know that.

"Oh, god," Celine said. "They're calling it. They're calling the bluff."

"Just hang on."

Brass_on: Bitcoin is too risky for me right now. There's a trail. It's got to be cash.

Silence. Celine chewed her lip.

Addam123: We'll be in touch.

"You think they'll go for it?" Celine asked.

"They have to," Keeps said. "It's all we've got. They *have* to."

Jake had settled into Keeps's lap and was curled into a thick ball, vibrating with purrs, his front paws tucked beneath his bulk. The tabby's auburn mottles were flaming in the sun. Celine met eyes with the creature and the cat gave her a mean glare.

"A match made in heaven," Celine said. Keeps stroked the animal's back, running his fingers down to the tail.

"This is trust," Keeps said. "I move my legs? Splash. Boy's in the pool." He smiled. "It's all about trust," he continued. "How fast you can get it."

Celine's phone rang. She picked it up.

"Me again," Kradle said.

CHAPTER 29

John Kradle shut the driver's-side door of Shelley Frapport's car after the black dog leaped out. He knew from one of the probably hundreds of crime novels he'd read in his cell on death row that burning the vehicle wasn't a good idea. That it would only draw attention, bring looky-loos and cops, and the car would be identified pretty quickly anyway. The smartest move was to leave it in a bad neighborhood and hope it was stolen or stripped before the police located it.

He pulled his hoodie up, took out the phone he'd snatched from the Frapports' kitchen table, and dialed Celine. Kradle knew it would only be a matter of time before, in all the chaos of the scene at the Frapport residence, somebody noticed the boy's phone was missing. It felt as though, in the hours since he had left Pronghorn, a dozen tools of sanity and survival had slipped through his fingers. This would just be another of them. He had slid the knife with which he had killed Homer Carrington into his back pocket, and a pistol taken from one of the dead officers into his waistband. In the pocket of his hoodie he clutched dearly to the phone records Shelley had given him. The handcuffs were also there, one shackle still closed on his wrist, the other closed on nothing and sticky with blood. He watched the dog trotting faithfully beside him as he walked the streets north of the Riverside district and wondered whether the beast was just another comfort, a survival tool, that would eventually be tugged away from him.

Celine gave a kind of huff he couldn't interpret when she heard his voice on the line.

"You again," she confirmed.

"So, I just sawed off a dead serial killer's thumb with a kitchen knife. How was your day?"

"What? Why? Urgh. Never mind. My day was tiring," she said. "I was up all night trying to figure out the truth about you."

"You mean 'How wrong you are about me'?"

"Oh, I'm not wrong about *you*," she said. "I know you're an A-grade jerk. Everybody knows that."

Kradle found himself smiling, despite everything. There was silence on the line for a moment and the smile faded.

"But your crime," Celine said. "Maybe . . . maybe there's something there."

"A 'shadow of doubt,' even?"

"Something," Celine said. "I spoke to Dr. Martin Stinway."

"How?" Kradle rounded a corner, tucked his head low against his chin as he passed a group of teenagers. When he snuck a sideways glance he realized they were all staring at their phone screens, oblivious to him. "How did you talk to Dr. Stinway? He's been stonewalling my lawyer for years."

"We pretended to be from the *Times*."

"What?"

"People always talk to journalists. Or so I'm told."

"That's good. I might use that," Kradle said. "Who's 'we'?"

"You said to find someone impartial. Give it an hour. So I did."

"My man Jake."

"Jake is a cat, Kradle."

Kradle thought for a moment. "Oh." He laughed. "Ohhh!"

"Yeah."

"So what did you find out?"

"I found out there was a confession."

Kradle stopped walking so suddenly his sneakers skidded on the cracked concrete. "I never . . ." He could barely form words. The fury clamped down hard and fast around his throat like a manacle. He put a hand on a fence for support. "I have never, *ever*—"

"You never confessed," Celine said. "I know."

Kradle was trembling with rage. The dog stood watching him, alert, ready to fight again.

"Frapport said that?"

"Yeah, to Stinway."

Kradle couldn't speak.

"If you'd confessed, it would have come up at the trial," Celine said. "It would have been in the media. They'd have recorded it. I mean, they recorded all your interrogations. Why not that? And why not have you sign a sworn confession?"

Kradle stood and shook and said nothing.

"No mention of it," Celine continued. "Except by Stinway, on the phone to us."

"Frapport told Stinway I'd confessed so he would fall into line on the forensic stuff," Kradle finally growled.

"Maybe," Celine said.

"I've just seen Frapport's wife," Kradle said. "She thinks he phoned it in on my case. Actually, she's so certain about it she let me into the house and sat me at a table with her son. She thinks her husband played quick and dirty, pinning the murders on me so he could spend his time at home trying to save his marriage."

"Well, I don't know anything about that." Celine sounded distant, as if she was pulling the phone away from her mouth.

"But you're still in?" Kradle said.

"I'm still in," Celine said. "The Stinway stuff, it's dodgy. I'm not all the way to believing you're innocent, but I'm some of the way to believing something fishy went on with your case. And I want to know where that goes."

"Because you're personally invested." Kradle felt the corner of his mouth twitch with a dark smile.

"Personally invested?" Celine asked.

"Yeah."

"Maybe."

"You're obsessed with me."

"Oh, Jesus." The phone crackled as she huffed. "Look, I know you're not real smart, so I'm going to say this slowly. *You need to hand yourself in, before somebody shoots you.* We can get Stinway and Frapport's wife to say what they know. It might get you a new trial, at least."

"Sure. Sounds great. I'll just do another ten years on the row waiting for it to go through the courts."

"Urgh, Kradle—"

"Celine, you're wasting your breath."

"I know," she said. "I know."

"I'm going to send you pictures of some documents," he said. "Phone records. This is every number Patrick Frapport dialed in the months after my family was killed. It might help us. You start at the bottom, I'll start at the top."

Kradle pulled the phone away from his ear, looked at the numbers ticking by as the call ran on. Precious, dangerous minutes.

"I've got to dump the phone after that."

"How am I supposed to—"

"I'll call you," he said. He hung up.

Kradle stopped in the street and looked around. There were people at a nearby bus stop. An old woman, two more teenagers, a stringy guy with a ball cap pulled low. All of them were watching their phone screens, heads bowed as though in prayer. Kradle crouched and spread the sheets of paper from his pocket on the sidewalk. He photographed the pages with the phone, spent some precious moments fiddling with the message functions on the device, trying to understand how to send the images to Celine's mobile. In the seconds he paused there, swiping and tapping, she didn't attempt to call him back. Kradle told himself that didn't mean she was going to stop helping him. That she wasn't lying when she said she wanted to know the truth.

That's why he'd chosen her. Because she had to know the truth about a crime like his.

The phone made a whoosh sound as the pictures flew away to their destination. He popped the phone open with his bloody fingernails, took out the SIM card, and tossed it over a chain-link fence. The phone he dumped down a storm water drain. He glanced at the people at the bus stop as he passed, but none of them looked up.

Celine looked at the phone screen, watched it go dark in her fingers, the call ended. Keeps was standing at the fence, watching the red desert sunset. Celine imagined that, all over Nevada, criminals she knew were feeling the effects of their incarceration through their bodies, and this would be the time their institutionalized brains told them they were hungry for dinner. Even as a correctional officer, Celine reacted to sounds—the ringing of a certain type of bell, the blaring of a horn, the snap of heavy switches—and she felt tired, hungry, alert, or relaxed in response, as if chemicals had been dumped into her system, powerless to resist the prison routine. Keeps turned and walked toward her and she felt her stomach lurch, her fingers restless, remembering the touch of his hand against hers.

"He's sending pictures. Phone records," she said. She looked at the device in her hand. "He sounded tired and weird."

"Well, he just killed a dude." Keeps shrugged. "If you believe his story, he's never done that before."

"I don't know what I believe anymore," she said. Keeps's hand was just by hers again, and Celine felt as though her very skin was alive with desire, tingling and singing, sensations rushing up her arms, anticipating a touch that had not yet and might not ever happen. "Everything is inside out."

He touched her cheek, lifted her face, and he was kissing her, and Celine heard a clear voice in her mind telling her that he was taking advantage of what she had just said. That he knew her brain was spinning and now was the moment to strike. But she also didn't care. Celine grabbed his hips and dragged him to her and she felt so good with his hands around her head, cradled, kissed, wanted, that by the time the sun gave its last flicker of light she was following him back into the house with her hand in his.

The phone woke her. She jolted in the sheets, reached out, felt the hard curve of his arm. He was lying turned away from her. Something about that—about reaching to hold his hand or put her hand on his heart or to roll toward him and kiss him and instead feeling his hard shoulder blade, his cold back—made her snap into consciousness with terror.

She didn't recognize the number. Celine realized she wanted it to be John Kradle. When it wasn't his voice, she felt the air go out of her, and that made no sense at all. Nothing made sense. She went into the kitchen and gripped the bench, just to get some idea of time and space and reality.

"Ms. Osbourne?"

"Yes."

"My name is Diana Fry. I'm calling from the Bank of America anti-fraud squad in regards to some suspicious activity we have noticed on one of your accounts. Could I please confirm some details with you?"

Celine felt her mouth go dry. She worked quickly through the identity confirmation questions, staring back at the door to the hall, to the bedroom, where Keeps lay sleeping.

"What kind of activity are we talking about?" she asked.

"It's what we call a 'test payment,'" the woman said. "A small amount was transferred from your Maxi Saver account to an account located in Kuala

Lumpur. That amount is reading seven dollars and twenty-five cents in US dollars. You didn't purchase anything online for that amount recently?"

"No." Celine felt her back teeth lock together. "I didn't."

"Sometimes these scammers will push the boundaries, try to transfer a small, inconspicuous amount to see what the security is like on your accounts. If the payment is successful and you don't challenge it, that gives them the opportunity to make a bigger transfer. Then they'll go for a larger amount," the woman said. "We'll shut everything down and ask you to come in to a branch and confirm your identity as soon as possible, ma'am, so that we can reset everything. Is that okay?"

"No problem," Celine said. "I'll get it done."

She hung up and put the phone on the counter before she could be asked to complete a customer service survey. In the bedroom, she heard Keeps call her name. She rubbed her face with her hands and tried to focus on keeping her expression neutral, even in the dark.

2000

He considered himself a terrible father to an infant.

It began on the first day, as he carried the baby, squalling and mewling against his chest, from maternity ward to hospital administration, from hospital administration to the security department, from the security department back to the maternity ward, where police were waiting to ask him questions about where Christine had gone and why. On his son's first day on the earth, Kradle sat by his wife's empty hospital bed, joggling and shushing the fleshy pink bundle, trying to figure out why he kept spitting out the nib of the bottle while officers gazed upon him with their soul-destroying eyes. Half his brain wondered in terror at the spots and blushes of color in his newborn's face, at the rise and fall of his chest and the restless movement of his eyes beneath the lids, while the other half struggled to convince the officers that he didn't know why Christine had run away from him. Why she would climb out of her hospital bed, pull clothes onto her birth-ravaged body, and walk out into the sunshine of the day without saying a word to anyone, without even taking her bag with her. Kradle told himself that this was one of her dramas, her "attention-seeking episodes," and she would be back within hours or days, ready to help him figure out how the hell to get the baby to stop screaming and what he was supposed to dress the child in and whether or not he was going to accidentally—terror of all terrors—do something to cause little Mason to die in his sleep.

But she was not back within hours or days.

And she was not back within a month.

There was a flurry of help in the beginning. Friends, quiet and strangely watchful, dropped around to show him how to change a diaper and how to burp the baby and how to figure out if Mason was cold or hot or hungry. The police came, and there were interviews and updates on the search for Christine. The cab company connected to the car she hailed from the hospital parking lot knew she'd been dropped in downtown LA, and that was all. Kradle's household was a flurry of noise and activity.

Christine's parents visited the baby, and there were weighty questions delivered in deceptively casual voices as they stood in the darkness over Mason's crib. Had Christine been depressed during the pregnancy? Had he shouted at her? Had he "lost his cool"? Had either of them been seeing someone else? Kradle kept it together, because where he came from men were hard and didn't go to pieces when a woman walked out on them, or a baby shit through his diaper all over a car seat. But when the house was empty and the baby was asleep, Kradle would go out across the back porch and down into the blackness of the furthest corner of the yard and sit on the grass under the stars and cry out of sheer confusion.

The help died away. His friends couldn't figure out why, if Kradle was the guy they'd all thought he was, Christine would bail on him and go into hiding. Running off was one thing, but completely disappearing was another. Christine's parents stopped answering his calls, and the police answered every fifth or sixth. They let him know they'd inquired unsuccessfully after Christine with an encampment of artists in Detroit after hearing a rumor that she was there. They chased similar rumors of her as far as Nova Scotia.

For two years, he leaped at every phone call. When there came a knock at the door, his scalp tingled. Sometimes when he was standing in the kitchen in the blue-lit morning, stirring hot water into semolina, or scrubbing food stains out of tiny shirts in the laundry room, he thought he smelled her shampoo or saw her standing there out of the corner of his eye.

When Mason was two years old, Kradle was bent over a garden bed outside a house in East Mesquite, digging irrigation into the soil. The boy toddled across the lawn, crouched beside him, and grabbed a handful of the soil in his meaty fist. Kradle watched as the kid leaned back and threw it so that it scattered against the side of the house. Kradle laughed and the boy, cheered on by his father's amusement, laughed too. Kradle handed the child a little trowel he had tucked into his back pocket, and the boy plopped onto his butt on the dirt and started digging.

That's when Kradle realized he could not only keep the boy alive. He could also teach him things.

He taught the boy to throw his handfuls of dirt into a plastic bucket, and then to lever them in awkwardly with the trowel, and by the time the kid was three he could be set to digging in one spot so Kradle could plant flowering ground cover in commercial parks in Mesquite. Kradle taught the kid to lay mulch, to water, to weed, to prune, and by the time the boy was ready for kindergarten he could hammer a nail and paint a semi-decent undercoat. Kradle trusted him with a handsaw by the time he was seven, and a nail gun by the time he was eight, and when he was ten the kid was taking all the measurements for the porches, garden sheds, picnic tables, and Adirondack chairs Kradle found himself building for strangers who called him up from his ads in the paper. Mason and Kradle lay together on shady concrete under old cars, changing oil filters and replacing gaskets, and they crawled into steamy ceilings, gloved up and sneezing in the dust, to catch families of possums.

Mason had been big when he was born. Boxy-headed, heavy-browed, with roly-poly arms and jiggling thighs and cheeks that bobbed as he rode in the carrier in the car. And he remained big, towering over the other kids at school, busting seams in the shoulders of his shirts, wearing and then growing out of Kradle's boots before he had entered puberty. While he'd been slightly caveman-esque as an infant, his awkwardly oversized features began to make sense in grade school and then smoothed out and arranged themselves in a way that made women turn their heads in the street by the time he hit his midteens. Kradle came around the side of a house on a property maintenance job one day and found the woman who had hired him and her friend sitting on the porch, drinking iced tea and admiring his child, who was bent over, clearing the pool filter of leaves with his oven-mitt hands.

"Your buddy." The younger of the two women nodded toward Mason. "Is he single?"

"He's fourteen," Kradle replied.

The woman choked on her drink and fell silent.

It was a December morning, before sunrise, when Kradle roused the boy, like he usually did. He walked into Mason's room and tugged on the toe of the foot that the boy always hung over the side of the bed during his sleep, regardless of the weather. The boy let out a big sigh and buried his head beneath his pillow, thereby completing a father-son ritual that had been in place since the child was big enough to move from a crib to a bed.

"What is it?" the boy asked as Kradle headed for the kitchen.

"Turf."

"It's too cold to grow turf!"

"Yeah. That's what I told him."

Kradle handed the kid a mug of tea when he finally reported for duty, and then sat down to drink his own coffee in the light from the oven range-hood. Mason was a kid who wielded an axe like a lumberjack, stuck his arm fearlessly down rat and snake holes, and could carry six rolls of buffalo grass under one arm, but he liked to start his day with English breakfast tea and comic books at the kitchen table, for reasons Kradle didn't understand or question. The two sat wordlessly together for a while until Kradle decided he would go ready the truck. He opened the front door of the house just as Christine was raising her hand to knock on it.

For a full five seconds, maybe more, Kradle didn't recognize her. Her hair was streaked with white in the front and her skin was tanned coconut brown and she was dressed all in black—wispy, wavy, layered sort of stuff that she and other people who believed in fairy magic always wore, but black, which had never been her thing. He stood in the doorway, his brain telling him that something was deeply amiss here but being coy on what it was, and she took a deep breath and held it, waiting for his response to her presence. And then it all came back to his under-caffeinated brain in one compulsive blast—the baby, the blood, the lost hours being questioned by police, the crying, the dark, unsleeping hours, the pointless phone calls—and he knew that Christine had returned and was standing on his porch, and the very fact of it froze each of his limbs in place and arrested the words he'd dreamed of saying so many, many times.

She was the one to speak first.

"John," she said. "Hi."

Kradle wet his lips and tried to speak, but he felt the floor vibrate beneath his feet with Mason's heavy step, and he turned to put a hand on the boy's chest only a second or two before he could reach the door.

"Whoa. Whoa. Just back it up a bit, buddy."

"I gotta get my—"

"You've gotta get nothing." Kradle pushed the boy away. "Go away. Go to the yard. Wait there. Just do it."

Kradle had said "Just do it" plenty of times in the boy's life. Mason knew what it meant. It meant put that thing down, or hand me that tool, or stand back, or go away, and do it right now or one of us will get hurt. Kradle was already hurt, and all he knew was that he needed to stop that hurt spreading, so he said "Just do it" and watched his son walk quickly but uncertainly back down the hall. He stepped out onto the porch and pulled the door closed. He faced Christine in the growing light of day, after wondering for a decade and a half if she was even alive.

"Was that him?" Christine asked.

"Yeah," Kradle said.

She didn't say anything else. Her silence made the words, gentler words he'd planned and practiced, dissolve in his mind, so that what came out was a vicious, white-hot hiss.

"Where the fuck did you go?"

She seemed shocked. The shock, the silence, wasn't helping. He walked to the end of the porch, telling himself not to scream that she hadn't tottered off to the local mall for an hour without leaving him a note on the fridge. That she had completely missed the childhood of a young man so strong and brave and handsome and smart and funny Kradle could hardly comprehend it; not just missed that childhood but actively avoided it. Dismissed it. Discarded it. That she had made him feel like a failure and look like an abuser and act like a madman over the years, and he was so mad his eyeballs felt as though they were on fire.

"I went to Tibet," she said finally.

"Of course you did." Kradle almost laughed. He cracked his knuckles and kept his eyes on the grass. He counted his breaths. "Of course you did."

He let her speak. She said some things about needing to find her essence, to discover her spirit, to communicate with the earth and the sky, to drink mountain snow and consult ancient beings, and for once Kradle didn't give her his attention. He listened instead for sounds of the boy in the house, creeping up to the door to eavesdrop, of which there were none. Then he straightened his cap and put a hand on the doorknob, and she took a step forward as if he was going to invite her in, and he almost laughed again at the idea that she thought she deserved that. When he didn't budge she stepped back again.

"I want to see him," she said.

"Well, if you want to do that, you'll have to do a lot more talking," Kradle said. "And not here, either. I'll meet you tomorrow at the diner. Eight. I've gotta go. We've got a job."

He went inside, into the empty hall, and shut the door.

CHAPTER 30

It was the neon blue that pulled him in. Kradle saw the tech store from the end of the street, a glowing artificial sapphire wedged in a tiara of white-lit stores. On the right of it sat a pet supply store, on the left a massage parlor and a deep, narrow place that sold socks for fifty cents a pair and big novelty sunglasses inset with plastic rhinestones. He stood for a while on the sidewalk, looking through the windows of the tech store at shelves crammed with devices he didn't recognize in white boxes and shrink-wrapped plastic. Everything seemed to come with some sort of garden-themed name. There were buds, pods, seeds, stems. When he walked inside the store with the dog, a buzzer announced their presence. It was the same kind of buzzer used at Pronghorn to indicate that the door to the shower room had been unlocked. For a moment he reeled, trying to get a grip on where he was, the young man at the counter ignoring him completely as he pushed aside lank black hair to read his phone. Kradle tugged up the hood of the sweatshirt he'd stolen from a clothesline, found it tighter around his head than the last one.

"I've got a question," Kradle said.

"Shoot," the kid said, reaching for a huge lime-green can of soda without lifting his eyes from the screen.

"Is there a way I can make phone calls from a phone without the device being traceable?"

He was expecting an upward glance. A quizzical frown. A flat-screen TV mounted on the wall was playing footage of the breakout, now and then flashing on his mugshot in the collection of carded fugitives. MOST DANGEROUS flashed on the screen as the mugshots were shown—Burke first, then himself. He remembered having that picture taken. How weird it was, the instinct to smile when it was the last thing in the world he wanted to do.

Carrington's mugshot didn't appear on the screen. Kradle guessed that his death would be public knowledge by now.

The kid flicked a hand at a rack of black phones sitting in little plastic stands.

"Buy a basic burner," the kid said. "Download an onion router to hide your IP and use an app to make the calls. Switch or Neevo or one of those. Something with end-to-end encryption."

"Man, you're speaking Greek to me," Kradle said.

"I'm not Greek, I'm Korean." The guy finally looked up. He had some kind of piercing at the corner of his eye, set into the skin. The neon blue light from the front of the store was bouncing off it, making it look like the point of a laser. Kradle saw no recognition in his face. He took some bills out of his pocket and lay them on the counter.

"Can you set up all that stuff for me? Just make it so I'm using the right programs."

"Programs." The kid smirked. He took the bills and slipped them into the cash register sitting on the glass. Kradle wandered the store while the young man unboxed a phone. He kept one eye on the store clerk and the other on the television screen. Soon he recognized the porch of Shelley Frapport's house on the late news, the lanky figure of Tom Frapport huddled in a crowd watching a stretcher being lifted down the stairs. A huge shape encased in a black body bag. Homer, or maybe the male cop, the one who had held Kradle down. He realized he'd never learned the guy's name. The scrolling text under the news anchors said something about the announcement of rewards for the capture of inmates from Pronghorn, but Kradle saw nothing about how much that reward was, or how a person qualified for it.

The kid whistled after ten minutes and Kradle went to the counter.

"Okay." The clerk leaned lazily on the glass, pointing at the phone screen. "You open this guy up. Type in the number you want to dial here. Press the green button and you're good to go."

"Thanks," Kradle said. He reached for the phone, tried to take it, but the kid held on. Kradle looked at his eyes, followed their gaze to the handcuff dangling from his wrist.

Kradle saw the nose of the revolver emerge from behind the glass. He could do nothing but watch as the kid lifted it, extended it, and pointed it right at his face with the confidence of someone who had grabbed that same gun from its holster under the counter and aimed it at three or four scumbags a month who were trying to rip him off for burner phones. Kradle looked at the gun, looked at the kid, looked at his own hand and the kid's hand both still gripping the phone. Finally, he looked at the dog, sitting by his side, watching the whole exchange with the tired skepticism of an animal who had already run for its life once in the past few hours and didn't feel particularly enthused about doing it again.

On the screen above the store clerk's head, Kradle's face was showing again. *MOST DANGEROUS.*

"You one of the big ones or the little ones?" the kid asked.

"What do you mean?"

"There's a million bucks going for each of the big fugitives," the kid said. The piercing at the corner of his eye lifted as he smiled. "And ten grand for everybody else. Please tell me you're one of the big ones."

"I'm neither," Kradle ventured. "I'm just a guy with a broken phone who thought he'd try some kinky sex games with his girlfriend and ended up losing the handcuff key down a drain. Now I've got to call a locksmith before I'm forced to turn up at work like this in the morning."

"Good story. I like it. You come up with that just now?"

"Yeah," Kradle said.

"Fast on your feet."

"Desperate times."

"So, if your story's true, what's the phone got to be untraceable for?"

"I don't know," Kradle said. "I'll come up with something soon as you take this big-ass gun out of my face."

The kid pulled back the hammer on the gun. Kradle watched the cylinder rotate, loading the bullet into the chamber about eight inches from his nose.

"Let's talk about this," Kradle said.

"What makes you think I want to talk?" the guy asked. Didn't wait for an answer. "Let go of the phone and put your hands on your head."

"You haven't hit the button yet," Kradle said.

"What?"

"The panic button under the counter. The one that calls the police. You haven't hit it. So I assume you want to talk."

"I haven't hit the button yet because I've got one hand on this gun and one hand on the phone. Let go of the phone and I'll hit the buzzer."

"You're not delaying the arrival of the cops because you want to hold on to a twenty-dollar piece-of-shit burner phone," Kradle said. "I'm guessing you're doing it because there are things in the store you don't necessarily want the cops looking at."

"Okay, fine," the kid said. "You got me." He let go of the phone. Kradle pocketed it. "Here's the plan. You're going to get down on the floor, nice and slow. I'm going to cuff you all the way up and we're going to walk down to our sister store on the next block."

"Who's going to lock up this store while you're taking me to the next store?" Kradle asked. The guy's face twitched. Kradle felt a surge of hope and leaped at it. "Police!" he yelled.

"Shh!" the kid snarled. "Shut your fucking—"

"Police!" Kradle yelled again. "Everybody get on the ground! This is a raid! Come out with your hands up!"

The dog at Kradle's side caught the fever of the game and started barking loudly, the noise ear-splitting in the tiny store.

"Daeshim?" An elderly lady's voice came from upstairs. The kid yelled a string of words in Korean. Kradle assumed he was telling the old woman to stay where she was, that it was not the police, that everything was fine, but Kradle could hear boards creaking over his head, a thump like a book hitting the floor.

"Police! Put the gun down! Put the gun down!" Kradle bellowed.

"Shut up!" Daeshim yelled.

"Go ahead," Kradle said to him. "Shoot me. Shoot me. Blow my brains out in front of your grandma just as she gets to the bottom of the stairs."

Don't shoot me, Kradle thought. *Please don't shoot me.*

"Daeshim? What's happening down there?"

"Go back upstairs!" Daeshim yelled. The gun was shaking in the kid's hand, wavering between Kradle's nose and his left eye. Kradle was waiting for it, watching for it, and as the footsteps down the creaky stairs on the other side of the wall behind the counter became louder, it came. Daeshim turned his head to look for the arrival of the woman. Kradle grabbed the gun with one hand, pushed it sideways, twisted it out of the kid's grip. He used the other hand to shove the kid so that he fell into a rack of buds and stems and pods or whatever the hell they were against the back wall of the store.

Kradle caught a glimpse of the old woman peering timidly out from the doorway, reflected in the glass doors, as he burst out into the street.

Kenny Mystical was overconfident. His momma had been saying it since he was a child. She'd drive him to the local hospital with a broken forearm or a twisted ankle or a fractured skull and tell the nurse behind the counter, who she knew by name, that he'd got overconfident again. That little Kenny had decided, without a shred of credible evidence, that he had the engineering know-how to construct workable wings out of PVC piping and cardboard, and had tried to fly from the roof of the garage to a tree in their backyard, only to land spectacularly on a stack of wrought-iron yard furniture. In high school he had got overconfident about the looks he was receiving from Gretchen Cubby across the science lab and challenged her boyfriend Herb Mirouse to a fight for her devotion, only to have the much larger boy put his head through the glass doors of a cabinet full of frog skeletons. An excess of confidence kept Kenny warm on the streets of Los Angeles for twenty-six years while he pursued Hollywood stardom, until a casting agent told him he was too old and his paunch too prominent for him to be hired anymore as one of the henchmen, security guards, butlers, angry villagers, and Egyptian slaves he was accustomed to portraying on screen.

It took confidence for Kenny to pick himself up from that, brush himself off and pack his car for the long and humiliating drive back to Texas to begin again in his hometown of Rockwall. He only got as far as Vegas before he had an idea.

The new girl was staring at Kenny's framed pictures of his Hollywood days as he locked the register and put the day's takings into his briefcase. It had been a three-wedding day, which was about standard for the end of the year, but Kenny was beat. He took off the shiny, jet-black Elvis wig he'd been wearing all day and slipped it onto a Styrofoam head behind the counter just as the new girl got to the picture of him, midtwenties and oiled and shirtless for his role as a dead gladiator being consumed by a lion.

"Is that a real lion?" she asked, as he crossed the shop toward her. Kenny had a new girl in the shop about every three months, and every single one of them asked if the lion in the picture was real. His endless renditions of "Love Me Tender" for awkwardly giggling tourists, up to eight pairs of them in a single day, would drive the girl away before long. The itchy wigs, the leering drunks, the crushing monotony of the ceremonies would get to her, and the chapel that had probably seemed kitschy and cute when she arrived looking for casual work would become a hellish place of creaky floorboards, thin carpet, dusty plastic flowers, and chipping candy-pink paint before long. But, for now, she was under his spell, and Kenny was confident that he'd bed her before her first week was through, with the help of his wall of silver-screen memories.

"It's real," he said. "Friendly beast, actually. I've worked with lions a few times, and they can be a bit unpredictable."

"Wow."

"Did you see this one? This is me in *Cleopatra*."

"Whoa, with Elizabeth Taylor?"

"No! How old do you think I am? It was an independent remake."

"Oh."

"And look at this. This is me auditioning for *Mission Impossible*."

"Amazing!" She clapped, bouncing her platinum-blonde Marilyn wig. "What part did you play? Did you meet Tom Cruise?"

"Uh, we better lock up." Kenny flipped one of her synthetic curls and turned away. "And remember not to wear the wig home this time." She giggled and took it off, set it on the wig stand beside his behind the counter. She paused, smoothing the bangs on the inky-black Morticia Addams wig beside it.

"You going to be okay?"

Kenny laughed.

"I'm fine." He waved her off. Gave her his best Johnny Depp "*Fugged-aboudit!*"

The door shut behind her. He was alone.

The girl's words were a worrying reminder. Kenny had indeed forgotten about Ira Kingsley and the breakout, the reason he had shut the store before sunset the past couple of nights and walked out either with the new girl at his side or his phone in his hand, 911 already dialed. The day's events—the happy Australian couple who slow-danced to "Can't Help Falling in Love," and the stonkingly drunk ladies who'd signed their marriage certificate while he crooned "Always on My Mind"—had taken his mind off the danger. Love, even when it was $500 a pop, gimmicky, plastic-wrapped love under fluorescent lights, shot for novelty cardboard frames that would only go in a box somewhere back home, was distracting. Now Kenny faced walking to his car in the dark of the Nevada night, knowing Ira Kingsley, the man who had tried to murder him, was out there somewhere.

Kenny drew a deep breath, held it, and pushed open the door.

He didn't even get one foot out onto the concrete.

Ira was there in the dark. He pushed a woman wearing a stretchy yellow tracksuit into the shop in front of him. It was all so perfectly in keeping with Kenny's nightmares that he stood dumbly in the hall, watching with his hands by his sides while Ira shoved the woman to the floor and locked the door, the knife poking from his hand, long and silver and cleaner than the one he'd used to stab Kenny ten years earlier. Kenny stared in wonderment as his night-time imaginings played out right in front of him, and asked himself why, if he'd known so plainly that Ira would come back for him, he'd allowed himself to be cornered alone and defenseless like this.

The answer was simple. Overconfidence.

"You," Kenny managed to say.

"Yeah." Ira grinned, showing those little, beady teeth under his mustache that Kenny remembered like it was only yesterday he'd seen them for the first time. "You remember me, don't you, Kenny?"

The woman on the ground was sobbing. Kenny could see as she rolled onto her side, struggling to sit with her hands tied with wire behind her back, that her belly was swollen with pregnancy.

"Oh, god," Kenny said.

"You don't even look surprised," Ira said.

"I'm not."

"Then you should know why I'm here," Ira said triumphantly, lifting his skinny arms, the knife glinting in the light of the studio lamps. "We're gonna do this, finally. We're gonna do it right."

"Please, help me," the woman moaned. "Please don't let him hurt my baby."

"Who is this?" Kenny asked.

"Don't you recognize her?" Ira said. He crouched on the threadbare carpet and yanked the lady's hair, showed Ira a face he didn't remember. "It's Marissa. Look. It's Marissa. You remember her, right? She married some asshole who designs playgrounds and preschools and let him knock her up. But it's her, and she's here, right back where it all started. And you're gonna marry us, Kenny, like you should have done the first time. Get your fucking wig on. We don't have a lot of time."

Kenny didn't remember Marissa. He remembered Ira, the stupid mustache, the playful mood he'd been in on the day he and the woman now bound on the floor had come in to be wed in the chapel. He remembered ribbing Ira about the French tickler, getting a shark-eyed glare at the counter, deciding that was going to be his thing for this couple. It was supposed to be funny. Supposed to be a gag. He was going to incorporate it throughout the ceremony, hopefully get snickers of delight, the way he did when he sang "*Oh let me be, your cream eclair*" to French couples, or "*Don't you, step on my veal ragu*" to Italians. But he was only three jokes in, and the couple hadn't yet decided if they wanted Hawaiian Elvis or Rhinestone Elvis, when Ira shoved the butterfly knife into his belly and Kenny knew he'd stepped over the mark with this one.

Kenny pulled his wig off the Styrofoam head, held it like a hairy hat in his hands, and went to Marissa, whom Ira was trying to heft into a folding chair.

"It's okay, honey," Kenny said. "We're going to be okay."

"All you had to do was sing a couple of fucking songs," Ira said. "Get away from her. Get away. Stand over there on the stage. Over there. Behind the microphone. Yeah, look at you. Kenny Mystical. Master showman. A couple of songs, some vows, a certificate. That's all you had to do. And you go running your goddamn mouth. Trying to be funny. You ruined everything, you fat piece of shit, and I've waited ten fucking years to come back and put everything right."

"Tell me what you want me to do," Kenny said.

"You know what to do!" Ira snapped. "You do this every day! Sing two songs. Do the ceremony. Sing another song. I paid my money ten years ago, and I want what I goddamn paid for. You're gonna marry Marissa and me, right here, and I get the twenty-four-photograph package with the bonus DVD. Then you're gonna die, you motherless fuck."

"Okay. Okay. Okay. We can do this. You, uh . . . you just gotta pick the songs," Kenny said. "That's part of the deal. There's a list, there, on the wall."

Ira stood looking at the laminated list, clutching Marissa's arm as she hunched in the seat. The man's eyes lingered over the traditional favorites. "Love Me Tender," the well-used favorite, sat at number one. Kenny let his eyes drift down the list, his brain seeking a distraction from the terror in his gut, and when he landed at number thirty-one his lips twitched with electric anticipation.

He told himself not to. Then he found he couldn't resist.

"Can I make a suggestion?" he ventured.

Ira looked at him.

"'Jailhouse Rock'?" Kenny shrugged.

Ira launched himself at the stage.

CHAPTER 31

Celine put her feet up on the dashboard of her car and leaned back in the passenger seat, resting her morning coffee on her stomach. Outside, her garage was unlit, but she could make out the edges of boxes that had stood against the wall since she moved in, taped and labeled in handwriting she didn't recognize. One of the social workers, she guessed. There were ten boxes of her family's belongings from her grandfather's house, all that was left after the massacre. The rest had been destroyed on her request—anything that belonged to Nick, and anything that was even slightly damaged in the event. A single speck of someone's blood or a fresh nick in the paintwork that could conceivably have come from a bullet, and Celine instructed that the item be incinerated. In the decades since, she had not regretted her decision or ventured into the boxes.

With the phone against her ear, waiting for the line to connect, she wondered if she ever would.

"Hello?"

"Hello," Celine said. "My name is Anita Fulton. I'm calling from the features desk at the *LA Times*."

"The *LA Times*!" the voice said. "Jeez!"

"We're running a story on the Kradle Family murders, in connection with John Kradle, the escaped inmate from Pronghorn Correctional Facility," Celine said. "I wonder if I could speak to you for a few moments."

"Well, I don't know why you'd want to talk to us," the man said. She heard shuffling on the other end of the line. "We don't know anything."

"Perhaps." Celine chewed her lip. "Could I just confirm the spelling of your name, sir? Is it with an 'e'?"

"It's Aaron Scott," the man said. "There's no 'e' in it at all."

Celine cleared her throat. "Oh, uh, you never know." She wrote the name next to the phone number on the sheet of paper beside her. She had made five calls already that morning, working up the list Kradle had given her. "So you remember the murders, Mr. Scott?"

"How could I forget? I'm one of the guys who called 911. I smelled the smoke from my backyard."

"Right, because you lived next door," Celine said.

"Across the street. John Kradle built the deck around my pool. It's still here. Sturdy as anything. If you want pictures for the article, I can send them to you."

Celine heard the man's voice drop to a whisper. "*It's the* LA Times*!*"

"I'm just trying to confirm what you told the police back when the crimes were committed," Celine said. "I've got your statement here." She shuffled the pages of phone records.

"I never made a formal statement," Aaron said.

"I mean, uh, the police report. The report the detective wrote that, uh, detailed what you said."

"Well, it can't say much. That detective guy never even came to the house. He just called. Must have been two minutes he was on the line."

Celine glanced at the pages. "Three minutes thirty," she said.

"What?"

"The report says some"—Celine squeezed her eyes shut, struggled—"interesting things. Would you mind retelling me what you told the detective? Just so I can see if you remember anything new that isn't already here."

"Well, all I told the guy is that John Kradle was innocent," Aaron said. "I believed it then and I believe it now."

"You do?"

"Yeah. We would go around there for barbecues sometimes. Great guy. One time my car wouldn't start—me and my wife were supposed to fly to Florida—he drove us all the way to the airport, and when we got home two weeks later he'd fixed the car. Didn't even charge us! Cracked radiator head, it was. Oh, crap. *Hang on a sec. Hang on!* Oh, god. Look, my wife wants to speak to you. She wan—"

"Hello," a new voice said. "This is Lydia Scott. Wife of Aaron Scott. Former neighbor of John Kradle and the Kradle family."

"Okay." Celine eased a sigh.

"We believe John Kradle is innocent."

"I know, Mrs. Scott. Your husband was just saying so," Celine said.

"I'd like to make it known officially, in an official sense, that if John Kradle turned up here in the middle of the night looking for shelter from the police, I would give it to him. And I don't care who knows it."

"That's really nice, Mrs. Scott, but I'm looking for details," Celine said. "For the article."

"What kind of details?"

"Something that tells me Kradle is innocent. Something a bit more substantial than the fact that he drove you to the airport once and the guy grilled a mean steak."

"Well, that's all we know," Lydia huffed.

"The murder weapon was found at the scene of the crime," Celine said. "It was too badly burned to be identifiable. Did you ever see guns at the Kradle house?"

"Certainly not."

"What about that day?" Celine said. "He's supposed to have returned from a job only minutes after the gunshots were heard. If that story is correct, he must have missed being killed himself by only seconds. Did you see him driving around the neighborhood that afternoon?"

"No."

"Ever see him fight with Christine? Or his son?"

"That man was as gentle as a lamb," Lydia said. "And very tolerant. We knew the family well, even before Christine did her disappearing act. She was what you'd call an eccentric. But not a genuine one, either. The kind who wants to be *thought of* as eccentric. She would get drunk at the barbecues and start talking about spirits and auras and all kinds of junk. Reading people's heads. It was embarrassing."

"Kradle didn't mind all the theatrics?"

"He laughed it off. He was a plain kind of guy. Real. Reliable. Solid. Like a house brick," Lydia said. "Some people are fairy princesses, and some people are just house bricks. And two of the same in a relationship gets a bit tiresome, I think."

"Okay," Celine said. "What about after Christine left?"

"Oh, he handled that with so much dignity," Lydia sighed. "He raised that boy really well. I'd see them at the local hardware store together sometimes, buying supplies. I'm ashamed to say I hid once or twice so as not to run into them. The whole thing was just so strange. I didn't know what to say about her running off on him like that. I mean, what do you say?"

"I don't know," Celine admitted.

"Whatever happened in that house that day, it's got to do with her," Lydia said. "I can tell you that much. Christine was trouble. She was always talking about evil, and what happened was evil. I say she brought it home with her. That's my take on it all."

"Okay," Celine said. "Look, Mrs. Scott, I have to go."

"Will you use that quote, about the fairies and the bricks?" Lydia asked. "I think it's quite clever. I just came up with it."

Celine hung up and crossed the Scotts off her list. The car door popped open and Keeps, wearing only boxer shorts, slipped into the driver's seat, slung a wrist over the steering wheel.

"The king is dead," Keeps said.

"What's that mean?"

"It means somebody stabbed Elvis Presley dead last night in Vegas," Keeps said. "He's left the building."

"That'll have them crying in the chapel."

"You ever hear of an inmate named Ira Kingsley?"

"I have, actually." Celine's eyes widened as she realized. "I knew Ira back when I worked over in medium. Oh, no. He—"

"He did it." Keeps nodded. "He always said if he ever got out he was gonna go back there and make the guy perform the whole thing again. The Elvis wedding. Make him apologize about the mustache thing."

"It was a pretty stupid mustache," Celine said. "I'm with Elvis. That was too much mustache for just one face."

"Yeah, well, now Ira's dead too."

"Elvis kill him?"

"No. The woman broke her binds and ran away, got help. Police came and shot Ira."

Celine sighed. She hadn't had enough coffee to deal with everything she was being exposed to this morning: death, evil, innocent incarcerated men, celebrity impersonations. When Keeps reached over and stroked her knee she closed her eyes and tried to access the warmth and anticipation she'd felt only hours earlier. But all she felt was dread.

"What are you doing sitting here in the car?" he asked.

"I didn't want to wake you. I've been making calls from Kradle's list." She opened her eyes and showed him the pages. "I've spoken to two sets of neighbors, the owner of a gun shop, and a couple who had Christine clear their shed of a malevolent spirit about a month before the murders."

"And what did they say?"

"The neighbors and the couple said Christine was a weirdo and Kradle was the long-suffering but gentle husband." Celine heard the exhaustion in her own voice. "The gun shop owner says he never sold a gun to John Kradle. And he said Detective Frapport never asked about anybody else. It was just, 'Did you sell this guy a gun?' and showing a picture of Kradle."

"So Frapport had his tunnel vision on."

"Yes."

"Let me have a look at the other gun stores around," Keeps said, and took her phone from the dashboard. Celine felt her hands stiffen in her lap.

"Huh. A passcode," Keeps said.

"Oh, yeah." She took the phone and typed in the numbers as casually as she could, then offered the device back. Keeps didn't take it.

"There wasn't a passcode on your phone last night," Keeps said. Celine didn't answer. He continued, his face unreadable. "I know, because I used it to order dinner."

"My phone prompted me to add one," Celine lied. "I thought it was probably good practice."

"Your phone just randomly prompted you to add one?" Keeps asked.

"Yeah."

"Did you add one to your laptop, too?"

"No."

"So if I go in there and try to use your laptop right now, it won't ask me for a password." Keeps pointed to the door ahead of them through the windshield. Celine felt her neck burning, threatening sweat. They sat in silence for a while.

"What the hell happened?" Keeps turned to her.

"I was scammed."

"What?"

"The bank called me last night to tell me I'd been scammed. A test payment to Kuala Lumpur."

"And you . . ." Keeps struggled to form the words. A tight, unfriendly smile played about his lips. He touched his chest. "Whoa. Whoa, now. You think *I'm* the one—"

"No, no, no."

"Oh, this is amazing." He laughed, slumped back in his seat. "This is *amazing*."

Celine stared at the dashboard, chewing her lip. That old, protective smile wanted to rise to her lips, but she forbade it. She felt angry, and she deserved the anger, and she wanted to feel it transform her face into an ugly mask.

"Is it really *that* amazing?" she asked suddenly. "You're in my life for what, two days? And suddenly I get scammed? I've never been scammed before. Why should it happen now? You scam people *for a living*, Keeps. It's *what you do*."

Jake the cat wandered alongside the car, from the rear to the front. Celine spotted his tail in the side mirror. The animal leaped soundlessly onto the hood, sat and watched them through the glass, seemingly aware of the tension and curious at its source.

"You know," Keeps said carefully, "I think this is just about this Kradle guy."

"Oh, come on."

"You're starting to believe he might be all right," Keeps said. "And if he's all right, that means you don't know your bad eggs from your good ones. And maybe you never have."

Celine listened. She knew the words were true. That she was starting to believe that John Kradle might have been a good man all along, and that the same cursed blindness that had prevented her from seeing her grandfather as a potential killer had blinded her to his goodness. Was she still blind? Was the same man who had held her and stroked her and gasped in her ear in the dark the night before—who had led her to break every rule she'd ever made about men who she'd kept behind bars—a man who wanted to hurt her?

Keeps opened the driver's-side door and slipped out. He scratched Jake's ear briefly as he headed back into the house. Celine didn't leave the car until she heard the front door of the house slam behind him.

CHAPTER 32

Trinity Parker was walking out of the small office outside the front gates of Pronghorn as Celine arrived in her car. The US Marshal had a tactical vest strapped to her chest, black jeans and black combat gloves pulled on, a black cap securing her dark hair. Celine saw for the first time the Trinity Parker she must have known was underneath the managerial facade the whole time, the one who went out into the wilds and hunted men for a living. She opened the door and made to get out of her car, but Trinity waved her back into the vehicle and came around to the passenger side. Celine noticed that, in the corner of the parking lot, a crew of maybe twenty men in the same tactical gear as Trinity were assembling near two big black vans.

"I'll ride with you," Trinity said as she slipped into the vehicle. "I don't like to head out to a mission with the men. Gives them the idea you're one of them. And there's always someone who starts nervously farting."

"We're going on a mission?"

"We have the pick-up details for Brassen's money," Trinity said. "What did you think, I was calling you in so we could head to a salon and get our nails done?"

"The message just said *Come to Pronghorn*," Celine said. "You know, part of effective personnel management is telling everyone what's going on."

"Here's what's going on. We got a message this morning, at five, from someone on the other side. They've left a duffel bag of cash for Brassen at the Rancho Salvaje Wildlife Park outside Coyote Springs."

"A wildlife park?" Celine pulled out of the parking lot, heading into the desert.

"Makes sense. We've scoped out the venue. Great place for a sniper to set up shop. The park is in a valley. Lots of rocky hills around, just like Pronghorn.

And by this time of day the place will be flooded with early visitors, trying to beat the Christmas rush. Children, families, park workers."

"Well, we have to shut the place down," Celine said.

"Not a chance," Trinity said.

"You can't carry out an operation like this with hundreds of innocent by-standers in the crosshairs," Celine said.

"Are you telling me how to do my job?" Trinity smirked. "Please, carry on. I didn't know you'd brought down extremely dangerous terrorist organizations before."

Celine sighed.

"The park has to run as normal," Trinity said. "If we shut it down, the first thing that will happen is that angry families will take to social media to complain, and the gig will be up that we're helping Brassen. We're going to fill the area around the lockers where the bag is with agents dressed as civilians, and we'll siphon any real civilians who come through the gates away from the danger zone. There won't be park visitors or staff within five hundred yards of the drop point. That's the best we can do."

"Sounds terrible," Celine said. "Go on."

"We need the contact from the Camp to believe Brassen is on his own, and scared. Best-case scenario is that the target will be lying in wait somewhere near the bag so that he can take Brassen out in close quarters. Shoot him, or stab him maybe." Trinity leaned back in her seat and put a big boot up on the dashboard. "We should be able to spot that. Anyone hanging around the danger zone who's not a part of my team will likely be involved, so we'll just grab him. The second-best-case scenario is the target from the Camp tries to pick off Brassen from afar with a sniper, like they did with the bus driver. If that happens, we'll have to try to scoop him up with the outer cordon crew. That'll be harder. It's a big area."

"What if Burke's guy really has just dropped the bag for him to pick up?" Celine asked. "And they trust Brassen to take the money and keep his mouth shut?"

"That's the worst-case scenario," Trinity said.

The two women rode in silence for a while, the flat earth stretching wide and featureless all around them.

"I just noticed that your buddy isn't here." Trinity glanced into the back seat. "Lover's tiff?"

"We're not lovers."

"That hickey on your neck tells me otherwise."

Celine grabbed the rearview mirror and turned it toward her, tugged down the collar of her T-shirt. "What hickey? There's no hickey."

"No," Trinity said. "But now I know everything I need to know."

Celine felt a rush of anger billow up inside her, a painful swelling under her ribs.

"Like I said," Trinity continued. She was tapping away at her phone. "I understand the temptation. Point is, you can get confused by criminals. Especially when they're out there blending in with everybody else like foxes among the dogs. Best thing to do is just stick to your job, Osbourne. Your job is to put them where they've been deemed to go. In a cell or in the ground. You're not a judge, or a jury, or a detective."

Celine moved as though through a dream, parking the car in a crowded lot under a big sign directing patrons toward the ticket booths. Trinity pulled a jacket over her vest and zipped it to the neck, stuffed her hands in her pockets and nodded toward the side entrance to the park. Celine didn't see the huge black vans or the rest of the team until she found herself wandering the concrete back halls of the park with Trinity and a very nervous man in a navy-blue suit. They passed one-way viewing windows that looked into lush green enclosures, the windows passing by so quickly that Celine didn't catch a glimpse of any animals. It struck her how like the prison the zoo was, with its swipe-card security doors, motion-sensor cameras, and iron gates. There was a smell here, more fetid and primal than the one at Pronghorn, but not by much.

While Trinity and the park manager walked ahead, Celine suddenly looked back and found the tactical team walking behind her, more joining the convoy from side halls as they moved along.

"I don't understand why we weren't given more notice about this," the park manager was saying. "My park is full of customers. I've got more than a hundred staff on duty today."

"Yeah, and I need those staff to keep doing what they're doing, diverting civilians away from the section I indicated on the map I sent you," Trinity said. "How's that going?"

"Well, I'm losing a lot of merchandise sales," the manager said. "If I'd had more of a briefing—"

"I don't give people notice, Mr. Eprice." Trinity stopped and put her hand on the guy's shoulder. "What I do is more like a blitzkrieg. I can't have a hundred park employees, all with cell phones, assembling in a boardroom with coffee and cookies while I lay out the plan with a PowerPoint presentation. There's no rehearsal dinner. We're at the wedding and it's time for the vows."

"What do I do?" Mr. Eprice glanced at Celine, the only other person not in tactical gear, but she could only offer him a small smile of mutual confusion.

"Go have a coffee and a cookie somewhere. We'll make sure we clean up after we're done." Trinity nodded to two of her team members, who grabbed the park manager and ushered him away. A person dressed in a huge, fluffy zebra costume stepped into the hall from what looked like a staff cafeteria, turned this way and that, surveying the scene, and then backed into the room again and closed the door.

They stopped at a small room full of computers, monitors. Celine noted there was a station of monitors for "enclosures," one for "transit," and one for "retail." Trinity went to the "retail" monitors and stood watching. Celine came up beside her.

"These are civilians," Trinity said, pointing to the screen. Celine saw a bank of turnstiles and ticket booths. She watched as a family paid for entry into the park, pushed through the turnstiles and were immediately intercepted by a man dressed as a tiger who gestured wildly to a place off screen, bouncing on his tiptoes.

"Where is he taking them?"

"He's not taking them, he's luring them." Trinity gave a small smile. "We're giving away cuddly toys, T-shirts, and ball caps. Nobody says no to a free ball cap. Once the tourists are through the giveaway area they're forced down a long path toward the elephant enclosure, which takes them to the complete opposite side of the park."

"It's working," Celine conceded, watching a couple with a baby being diverted sideways from the area immediately outside the ticket gates. "But what if some of the Camp's people try to walk through there and your staff direct them away?"

"I have a feeling they won't let themselves be lured with the promise of free gifts." Trinity smiled. "Come on. We haven't got much time," Trinity said to Celine, beckoning. Two female tactical team members followed close behind them as they took a set of stairs. They emerged into an empty building, a large, sprawling affair with boarded-up windows and display cabinets shrouded in white sheets. Trinity led them to a bare room on the second floor with a balcony that overlooked a sunny square. Celine peered down toward the intersection of wide, clean streets between the buildings.

"What is this place?" she asked.

"Used to be the reptile and insect house." Trinity was peering through a shutter at the people below. "They're turning it into a restaurant, I think."

"Where's Brassen?"

Trinity nodded. Celine came to the shutters, looked out over a large paved intersection between storefronts of gift shops and restaurants. Looking to the left of the square, she could just make out the entry turnstiles in the distance. She watched as another costumed mascot scooped up a family for free gifts, while a solitary man bypassed the crowds and made his own way down the avenue toward the square. She realized as he neared that it was Brassen, walking uncertainly, head down, hands in his pockets.

"The bag, we're told, is in locker twenty-three," Trinity said. Celine followed her gaze. Across the square, under a long green awning festooned with fake tropical plants, a wall of lockers stood. Celine could barely read the big sign displaying the rental prices. She watched a couple in T-shirts and ball caps wander past the lockers and stop by a glass-walled enclosure that held fairy penguins flapping and waddling on white sand. The woman posed by the glass as her partner snapped a picture with his phone.

"These are all your people?" Celine asked.

Trinity nodded.

Brassen stood nervously outside the gift shop windows, pretending to be fascinated by a postcard stand. Trinity lifted a radio off her belt and gave some commands to her team, checked on the assembly of the inner and outer cordons. Celine only had eyes for her former colleague. Even from a distance, Joe Brassen looked thin and wan compared to his usually plump, sunburned self. It was impossible that he had lost a substantial amount of weight in the days since he had been exposed, but something had loosened inside him, deflated, sagged. He wandered the front of the gift shop and then crossed to a cotton candy stand, watching a man in a pink hat fiddling with the dispenser.

"Teams Alpha, Bravo, and Charlie, you're all checked in," Trinity said. "Command team is good to go. Brassen, you can approach the lockers."

Celine saw Brassen jolt at the sound of his name. He wiped his nose and mouth, a clumsy cover as he spoke into what she guessed was a collar microphone.

"I . . . I can't. I can't do this. I feel sick."

"He looks like shit," Celine said. "He's a sitting duck out there and he knows it. You can't make him do this."

"You're right, I can't," Trinity said. "But he wants to be able to tell a judge he put his life on the line to redeem himself after helping Burke break out of Pronghorn. It might be the difference between a life sentence and twenty-five years."

"I can't do this," Brassen repeated.

"He wants to back out," Celine said. "You have to let him."

Trinity nodded to one of the women positioned by the window, who took a radio out of a pouch on her thigh and tossed it at Celine. "He just needs encouragement. Your time to shine, Osbourne. Do your thing."

"That's why I'm here? You want me to talk him into it?"

"You did all right the first time."

"Look, you're asking me to walk him into the danger zone," Celine scoffed. "He could have a sniper lining him up as we speak. Any of those people down there could be about to—"

"He's wearing a vest," Trinity said. "And I've got five men down there within a stone's throw of where he's standing. See there?" She pointed. "In the gift shop window? That's one of my guys. I've got two guys up there, behind that screen. One guy there at the cotton candy stand. One guy over there. If anyone attacks Brassen, they'll rush to his aid."

"What if the sniper—"

"Heel, little doggy," Trinity snarled. "Just fucking heel, and do what you're told. You remember what it felt like the last time I gave you a smack for messing me around?"

"Yes," Celine groaned.

"So, take the radio and get your friend into line before I shoot him myself."

Celine snatched the radio. Her lip twitched with the urge to cry or smile, she wasn't sure.

"Brassen, it's Celine," she said.

"Celine?"

She saw Brassen turn and look around the square.

"You're safe, Joe," Celine said. Her throat felt hoarse. "I'm here with Trinity's team. They've got everything under control. Just do what they're telling you to do."

"I don't want to die, Celine." Brassen wiped his brow. Celine bet he was drenched in sweat. "I shouldn't have . . . I know I shouldn't have done this.

But I . . . I just . . . I'll do the time in prison. I'll do it. I-I-I just don't want to die out here."

"Command, we got a possible target," a voice on the radio said.

Trinity shoved Celine aside, looked toward the ticket booths. A tall, thin man in a heavy green jacket was shaking his head in refusal at a costumed parrot trying to lure him toward the free gifts.

"This might be one of the Camp's guys," Trinity said to Celine. "We need to get Brassen to pick up the bag." She held the radio to her mouth. "Alpha team, cover the possible target. Don't let him come any further down the avenue."

Celine watched as a pair of women in colorful uniforms rushed out of a restaurant with a tray of food to intercept the thin man. He stopped and started picking from their sample tray.

"Celine?" Brassen called. "Can you tell them? I want to back off."

"It's too late for the ballad of the condemned," Trinity growled in Celine's ear. "Tell him to go to the locker and, while he's at it, stop looking around everywhere like a fucking moron. He's going to blow our cover."

"Just go to the locker, Brassen," Celine said. "You're safe. Just go."

"What if it's a bomb?" Brassen said. "We-we don't know that it's not a goddamn hand grenade tied to the inside of the locker door."

"He's got a point," Celine said. "He might open that locker and blow up the entire building. What exactly do you know about what's in that locker?"

Trinity gave a hard, rueful laugh.

"What we know, *Captain*," she sneered, "is that at seven twenty-five p.m., just before the park closed last night, someone in a cap, gloves, and jeans paid cash at the ticket booths, came in, and deposited a duffel bag in locker twenty-three. We have CCTV footage of the drop. The guy walked in, shoved the bag into the locker, slammed the door shut, and locked it at the pay station. He didn't rig it as a trap. We know that from the footage. From the length of time he spent standing in front of the locker."

"That's some pretty good footage," Celine said. "Was it very clear that he—"

Celine noticed Trinity's right hand curling into a fist.

"Okay, okay." She put a hand up, pressed the button on her radio. "Joe, we know the locker isn't rigged."

"W-what if it's remote detonated? What if the bag's rigged?" Brassen said. "For when I open it."

"You're not going to open it, genius!" Trinity shouted into her radio. "Go to the locker, get the bag, turn, and walk out of the park. That's all you have to do. Now do it!"

Brassen stood frozen. Celine put the radio to her lips.

"You're safe," she said again. "Joe, you can do this."

Celine watched as Joe Brassen turned from the cotton candy stand and started moving across the square like a man walking on a tightrope above a pit of fire. For years, it seemed, he walked. One foot in front of the other.

"I'm gonna have a heart attack," he said. Celine watched him reaching for the keypad on the front of the locker. His breath rattled on the line. "I can't breathe."

Celine looked around the square. There were three people outside the gift shop—one perusing postcards, one talking on a cell phone, one fiddling with the lid of a water bottle. The thin man seemed to be flirting with the waitresses. In the seconds that had passed, two more people had refused the free gifts blockade and were walking down the avenue, one holding a phone to her ear, stopping by the gift shop to peruse the items there, the other heading for the toilets just inside the gates.

Brassen opened the locker. Celine held her breath.

He took down the black duffel bag. Celine saw the weight of the items inside the bag shift as it came off the shelf, sliding downward beneath the thin fabric. Brassen gripped the straps of the bag, weighed it a little in his fist, then turned toward the building from which Celine watched him.

"Okay." She heard his wet, rattling breath. "Okay. I'm okay. I'm okay. I'm okay."

"Turn and walk out of the park," Trinity said. "Alpha team, move out. Delta, get ready in the parking lot."

Brassen turned toward the ticket booths at the front of the park. Celine watched him emerge from the shade of the awning that covered the wall of lockers. It seemed as if the sun hit his face like a punch. His mouth twisted, one hand rising and gripping at his chest. Brassen dropped the bag and went down on his knees, flopping on his front in the sun.

CHAPTER 33

A tearing. That's what it felt like. Pieces coming apart. Skin ripping, blood oozing, warm and delicious. She felt it all over her body. Kerry Monahan pressed the phone too hard against her ear, standing outside the Rancho Salvaje gift shop, watching the man with the bag go down. She was wild-eyed, being torn apart by competing desires: wanting to stay and watch the man die, and wanting to get out of there, to pull her focus away from what she was seeing and concentrate on what she was hearing on the phone. The voice of Burke David Schmitz. The boss. The others had told her that he would personally call to listen in on the assassination, but Kerry hadn't believed it until the phone started ringing in her pocket. She was just a kid from Michigan with big ideas about how the world should work. About self-awareness, and genetics, and peace. Now she was a killer, and the master of all killers was talking to her, of all people, telling her she was doing a good job.

She was a soldier. A warrior.

"They're rushing in to help," Kerry said. Her chest felt tight, hard, only small amounts of air getting in and out, the adrenaline zapping and tingling in her veins. "Jesus. They're everywhere. There are people coming from everywhere."

She backed up a little as men and women in tactical gear seemed to materialize from the very air, rushing in to assist the man who'd taken the bag from the locker. People she had thought were other park visitors were rushing over, too. A pair of waitresses dropped a tray and turned and ran, while the customer they'd been giving samples to stood staring at the fray.

"Do not get snatched up," Burke insisted.

"I won't. I won't."

"He's definitely down?" Burke said on the phone.

"Oh, yeah, he's down."

"Good," the boss said. "Good work. Get out of there. Call when you're clear."

The line went dead. Kerry felt herself sucked back into the present moment. The man on the ground. The woman with the black cap shaking him, yelling at him, dragging him up while others tried to push him down. They seemed like they were going to try to resuscitate him. Like they thought it was a heart attack. Kerry shifted her feet and turned to walk away, but then she saw one of the tactical squad going for the bag, the bare hand reaching for the handles, the exposed skin slipping around the fabric, and she had to stay and watch her second ever kill.

The effect of the poison on this man was almost instant. He clutched at his throat, gagged, coughed white foam onto his chest. Kerry was shivering with excitement. The first one hadn't foamed at the mouth. She wondered why the effect was different, supposed everybody took the chemical differently. The man went down. Finally, they were coming to their senses, realizing what was happening. Pushing each other away from the bag, fumbling, yelling. Kerry really had to go now. Had to force herself. She gripped her way along a railing and pushed toward the ticket booths. She treated herself to one last backward glance at the scene she had created.

That's when she locked eyes with the short blonde woman.

She was not part of the tactical team, but was dressed in jeans and a T-shirt. Kerry hadn't noticed her in the square while she waited for the man to pick up the bag. Perhaps she had burst out of a shop or emerged from one of the roads into the square at the sight of the chaos. Kerry told herself she was okay. She had time. She walked to the ticket booths and put a hand on a turnstile.

Something made her look back again. She saw the blonde woman had started to run toward her.

Celine saw it in her eyes. The excitement. She'd seen it in the eyes of inmates before, a kind of primal ferocity that was the closest thing, she was certain, to the hunter inside every human being. The thing that liked the sight of blood and gore and death. A fight would erupt in the cell block, and while the faces of some men showed shock, horror, fear, there were some whose eyes glowed with adrenaline.

She was kneeling by Brassen in the center of the square, which was crowded now with members of Trinity's team, including the marshal herself, who stood directing her personnel to secure the area, grab the three civilians who had made it down the avenue, and drag Brassen to safety. That's when Celine looked up and saw the girl by the gift shop.

Wild eyes. Her mouth taut, face hard, thoughts obviously whizzing through her brain. The eyes were recording everything, gathering up pleasurable memories of Brassen and the male agent's deaths. Then the girl looked at Celine, and knew she had been made.

She ran.

"She's there! She's there!" Celine shouted.

She got up and sprinted after the girl.

The first indication that Celine wasn't alone was a boot scraping against the back of her shoe as she ran. Celine glanced over her shoulder and saw Trinity so close behind her she could feel her body heat. Celine burst through the turnstiles after the reedy, thin teenager, who had slipped through the hands of the team members posing as ticket sellers as if she were made of smoke. She was now halfway across the parking lot. Trinity and Celine ran side by side, feet pounding on the asphalt, their breaths in unison.

They slid seamlessly into single file, sprinting between cars, a side mirror bashing against Celine's arm as she turned into an aisle, following the bobbing shape of the girl's head.

"She's going for the trees!" Celine called. Trinity surged ahead of her, shoving her out of the way. Celine skidded to a halt at the sight of the black pistol rising in Trinity's hands.

Two blasts. The girl stumbled and pressed on.

"No! Stop!" Celine grabbed at Trinity, catching her jacket briefly as she took off again. "She's a kid!"

"She's a killer," Trinity huffed. Celine felt the ground beneath her feet rise, becoming concrete, then dirt, then grass. The woods swallowed them. Trinity kneeled and lined up another shot, and Celine rushed past her, unable to slow herself. She heard the crack of the gun and watched the girl tumble onto the ground in front of her.

"Oh, god! Oh god! Oh god!" Celine scrambled to the kid's side and threw herself on her warm, writhing figure. "Don't kill her! Trinity, please!"

"Get off, idiot." Trinity grabbed Celine's shoulder and shoved her aside. The girl was flushed pink and gasping for air, blood smeared on her pale, freckled face. Celine watched as Trinity climbed on top of the girl, strad-dling her.

"What's the target?" Trinity said. "Tell me now before I put another bullet in you."

"I don't know. I don't know. I don't—"

Trinity pushed the girl's wrist against the earth, pressed her gun into the center of her palm.

"Trinity, please!" Celine begged.

"I'm not taking you into custody, little girl." Trinity grabbed the teenager by the throat to silence her cries. "I'm not spending another two days rattling around a stinking prison, bouncing threats and promises off another halfwit-ted piece of redneck trash. You tell me now what Schmitz's target is, or I'll put a hole in your hand."

"I can't!" the girl screamed. "I don't know—"

A gunshot. It was loud, thunderous, echoing. It rolled over Celine like a wave, thumping in her chest, pulsing in her eardrums. Trinity slumped side-ways off the girl and fell near Celine's legs. Celine wiped blood out of her eyes, gripped her way toward the girl as the second shot came whizzing past her, sputtering dirt and grass.

She gathered the shaking girl under her arm and dragged her to a small tree, which exploded almost instantly, shorn in half by another shot. Celine used the cover of the falling branches to run with the girl to a different tree, then another, away from where she guessed the sniper was. As the trees began to thin before them, a huge black tactical van skidded to a halt at the edge of the shade, and Celine shoved the girl through the door just as it slid open.

The firing had stopped.

She sank to the carpeted floor, gripping the girl, the two of them still screaming as the van pulled away.

2015

He'd calmed down a little by the time they met at the table in the very back corner of Ballie's Diner. It was the place they'd used to go to when they first moved to Mesquite, when they had grown tired of living on the road, chasing ghosts and cramming themselves into tiny, moldy motel showers. Kradle arrived first, looked at the menu, which still served the blueberry pancakes she used to order before she disappeared from his life to find herself in Tibet. It was about the only thing that remained the same. The new owner had painted the place, ripped out the shelves Kradle had installed above the cash register for the last owner, added a gelato freezer. Christine appeared in the doorway twenty-five minutes late and stood there for a moment, just looking at him across the restaurant, half-seeming as if she was going to step back out into the street and disappear again for another decade and a half without explanation.

When she finally slid into the booth, Kradle nodded to the waitress. He expected Christine to order coffee with room for milk, the way she always had, but she ordered chai tea instead with a side of hot water, in case it came too strong, he guessed.

He leaned back in his chair and drank his coffee, and waited for her to say sorry for running off on him. He'd run their conversation at the door of their house through his mind a hundred times during the night, and was sure she hadn't said sorry yet. She'd said hi. She'd told him she went to Tibet. She'd asked to see their son. But she didn't say sorry, and she wasn't saying sorry now, and Kradle took a long breath because he could feel the tips of his ears getting hot again, and he knew what that meant.

"He looked handsome," Christine said. "From what I could see."

"He is handsome," Kradle agreed. "And he's smart. And he's funny. He's so funny he brings me to tears sometimes."

"I bet."

"He was a funny kid. A trickster." His words were coming out angry, as if he felt he had something to prove. "He used to put things in my shoes before he left for school—buttons, paperclips, notes, a whole banana one time. He sings all the time. On the worksite. At home. In the shower. He never shuts up. We don't own a radio for work. Don't need one. The kid knows the words to every song he's ever heard, from show tunes to heavy metal. The past week it's been all Etta James. Beats me why that is. It's not my kind of stuff."

Christine laughed.

"You've missed all that," Kradle said, his face stiff.

Christine's smile disappeared slowly.

"You missed him learning to walk." Kradle lifted his cup to drink his coffee, realized his hand was shaking. He put it back down. "You missed all the hard stuff. I was terrified when he was little. There was nobody to help me. I didn't know anything about babies. One time he just stopped eating for a week and a half. All I could get into him was cheese. Just cheese. That's it."

"John—" Christine began.

"No, let me talk," he said. "When he was nine he read a magazine about UFOs and lost his goddamn mind about it. He was up screaming in the middle of the night that they were going to come abduct us and experiment on us. When he was twelve, he fell in love with his math teacher. I'm talking real love. I found a note in his room proposing marriage to her."

Christine sipped her chai.

"Right now he's all torn up about this terrorism stuff." Kradle waved at the next table, where a newspaper lay face up by an empty plate. A picture of Abdul Hamsi, the failed Flamingo Casino bomber, dominated the cover. "I can't stop him watching the news."

"What did you do about the woman?" Christine asked.

"What woman?"

"The teacher."

"Oh." Kradle put his arms on the table, looked at the holes in the wall above the register where his shelves had once been. "Uh. Well, I sat him down and told him he had the wrong idea. That he was just a little boy and she was a grown adult and they weren't going to run off together and get married."

Christine listened.

"And I started bringing women around the house," Kradle said. The flicker of emotion in Christine's eyes gave him a mean little thrill. "I figured he didn't have enough women in his life if he was getting the idea that his math teacher was in love with him because she'd had a few friendly conversations with him in the schoolyard. So, after that, when I had a girl on the go I would bring her to the house, let her meet him, hang around him a little. Show him that just because a lady's talking to you, doesn't mean she's in love with you."

"Did you have many 'girls on the go'?" Christine asked. "After I left?"

"Are you really asking me what my dating life was like after you disappeared on me and our newborn child?"

"I guess." Christine stared into her cup.

"It was clear to me after about—oh, I don't know—three *years*, that you weren't coming back. I got lonely."

"I get that," she said.

"You didn't even leave me a note," Kradle continued. "The police thought I must have abused you. People around here thought I abused you. I don't . . . Urgh. I don't even know what to say to you."

"Well, you're saying plenty."

"I thought about having you declared dead."

"Why?"

"So I could get a divorce." He shrugged. "So I could sell the house. So I could have a memorial. Some fucking closure."

"I'd have liked to have seen that. My own memorial."

"Oh, I bet you would."

"I wasn't dead," Christine said. Her smile twisted something in his chest, made him snap.

"You don't seem to understand the fact that *I didn't know that!*" he growled. The waitress looked over from behind the counter, worried. "Do you know what it's like to wonder if your wife is dead?"

"No, John, I don't. Of course I don't."

"Where the fuck did you go?"

"I told you, Tibet."

"No. I mean, that day."

She told him about the frantic moments after he'd left the room with their child, pretending to sleep while he closed the door and then slipping out of the bed and grabbing her wallet from the hospital bag. He sat and watched her face, listening to the story as it rambled on. The group of hippies she found herself with in Vegas, their rusty campervan where she slept during the journey to Los Angeles. Slumming with street people in Santa Monica. Hitchhiking to Oregon. Picking strawberries and living in a barn, deciding to travel with a group of young poets to Vietnam, then China.

"Was it me?" Kradle asked when she ran out of words.

"No," Christine said. "It was the baby."

"What about him?"

"His spirit," Christine said. "I felt it, when he was inside me. He might be all right now, but back then he was a dark spirit destined for pain and sadness."

"You can say something normal about it, you know," Kradle said. "You don't have to couch it in all that weird stuff. You can say 'I was depressed' or 'I was scared.' Maybe you never wanted a baby. Or maybe you thought you did and then changed your mind. Maybe you were ashamed of that, or terrified of telling me. Maybe me being so excited about the baby intimidated you or—"

"It was none of those things," Christine said.

"Well, what was it then?"

"It was his spirit."

Kradle put his hands on the table, stared at them, and felt a wave of relief roll over him. A part of him had known, in all the years that Christine had been missing, that she had left simply because she was broken. That even if an explanation ever came, it wouldn't be rational or healing to him. Whether Audrey had been right, and it was a flair for the dramatic and a need for attention that had driven her away, or whether it was because of any of the reasons he had just given her, Kradle knew then that the only person in the relationship who could sew up what had been ripped apart was him. She wasn't going to say sorry. She wasn't going to make it all better. He had to do that for himself. He also knew that, faced with the challenge of it, he could do it. If he could raise a boy like Mason, he could eventually be all right with what Christine had done to him.

But he had to say it. For Mason.

"There's nothing wrong with that kid," Kradle said, stabbing the table with one finger to the beat of his words. "He's a glorious child. Was then. Is now."

Christine sat in silence, her tattooed hands cupped around her chai, and Kradle thought how old she looked. How beaten down by the foreign winds that had carried her around the earth from place to place, anywhere but where he was.

"*The Frances Falkner Show* is coming to town," Christine said suddenly.

"Don't tell me you came back here just for that."

"No." Christine looked wounded. "It was time. It was just time to come home. But I also noticed, after I got back, that she's going to be here in a month's time."

Kradle nodded, knowing the discussion of her actions was over for now, but not really wanting to talk about anything else.

"So?" Christine asked.

"So what?"

"Do you want to go?"

"Are you kidding me?" Kradle's mouth ached with a tight smile. "No, Christine, I don't want to go to *The Frances Falkner Show* with you. That's your thing."

"I was thinking if you said no, I'd ask Audrey," Christine said.

"Have you spoken to Audrey at all in the past fifteen years?" Kradle asked.

"No," Christine said.

"So, you're just . . . You're just going to call her and say, 'Hello, I'm back. Do you want to go to a taping of *The Frances Falkner Show* with me?'" Kradle's smile loosened.

"Well, yes, something like that." Christine sipped her chai.

Kradle waited for more. There was none. He felt a laugh burst out of him.

"Can I listen in?" he asked.

CHAPTER 34

The dog woke him, snuffling in his ear, a cold, wet nose that jolted him out of a thin slumber. Kradle's mind reeled through snapshots of the past twenty-four hours—the Frapport house, the car, the kid with the gun in the technology store, the mad sprint into the street and away from the scene. He'd found a bike leaning against a fence and taken it, pedaled until the scenery around him changed, becoming warehouses and garages, chain-link fences and unpaved streets. The dog, which had trotted faithfully by his side when he started riding, began to hang back before long, its pink tongue foamy and wagging between loose jaws. Kradle had stopped in the shadows behind a quiet warehouse, sunk down into the dirt, and taken out the phone and list of numbers, ready to dial.

Then he'd fallen asleep. At some point he must have slipped down onto his side, worrying the beast, who nudged at his neck and chin now, trying to rouse him.

"I'm all right," he told the dog, looping an arm around its neck. "I'm okay. I'm just tired."

His charge revived, the dog wandered off to find water or food, Kradle supposed. He knew he needed some sustenance himself, but that was a concern for another time. The numbers, and then answers, were waiting. With the sun creeping toward his sneakers, splayed on the gravel, he started to dial.

"Hello?"

"Hello." Kradle cleared his throat. "This is . . . My name is, uh, John. John . . . Sky."

"What?" the voice asked.

"I'm from the *New York Times*."

"No thanks. I read the *Post*."

The line clicked. Kradle looked at the phone in his hand, blinked, and decided he would circle back to the number he had just tried. He shook his head awake and dialed the next number on the line.

"Hello?"

"This is James Mackley," Kradle said. "I'm a journalist calling from the *New York Times* with some important questions for you."

"What?" The voice was female, husky, vaguely familiar. Kradle felt the hairs rise on the back of his neck.

"I'm looking into the breakout at Pronghorn," Kradle said. "Some of the more infamous prisoners who are on the loose. We're doing a . . . a profile. I understand you were questioned about John Kradle. About those murders."

"Oh, jeez, I sure was." The woman laughed. "And I had plenty to say, all right."

"Can I just confirm who I'm talking to?"

"My name's Jasmine O'Talley."

Kradle thought. Remembered. Swallowed wrong and coughed.

"How'd you get my number?" Jasmine asked.

"We have our sources," Kradle wheezed. "You . . . uh. The detective on the Kradle case called you, didn't he? Back in 2015? You spoke for . . . seventeen and a half minutes?"

"Well, I don't know how you know all that stuff, but yeah." Jasmine sniffed. "I can't remember how long we talked. But he called me. Asked me if John Kradle was a nice guy or not."

"And what did you say?" Kradle's face burned.

"I said he was a real piece of shit," Jasmine said.

"Oh. Wow."

"I said he probably murdered his wife, for sure," Jasmine sneered. "He was a cold, callous jerk and probably a psycho-maniac. And the guy snored like a train. Not that it's relevant, I guess."

"It's not."

"Like sleeping beside a goddamn chainsaw factory."

"Jasmine, I think that's all I have for you," Kradle said. "Thank you for answering my questions."

"I hope the police catch his ass and put him back in jail where he belongs," Jasmine said.

"Is . . ." Kradle licked his teeth. Decided he couldn't help himself. "Is it possible your low opinion of the man may be just because he never called you back?" Kradle said.

"What?"

"You went on three dates. He took you to that nice steakhouse. And then he never called you again. You ran into him at the grocery store that time and it was weird."

"How do you . . ." The line was silent for a moment. "*John?*"

Kradle hung up quickly. The dog was back, sitting upright at his side, staring at him with its big brown eyes, judging.

"Sometimes you just . . . ," he began. "Never mind. You're a dog."

Kradle dialed. He spoke to three neighbors, two gun store owners, the owner of a hardware store he had frequented at the time of the murders. He looked at the list of numbers and saw that most of the calls were outgoing. Then he noticed an incoming call that was very short, fifteen seconds. A short call back, forty-five seconds. Another short call incoming. The caller and Frapport were playing phone tag. When they finally connected, they spoke for only three minutes. Kradle called the number.

"In Focus Studios."

Kradle opened his mouth to speak, then paused, thinking.

"Hello?"

"Yes, hello," Kradle said. "Sorry, who is this?"

"This is In Focus Studios."

"What's In Focus Studios?" Kradle asked.

"We're a production company. How may I direct your call?"

"I don't know," Kradle answered. He struggled to his feet, feeling weirdly lightheaded. It was exhaustion, hunger, low blood sugar, burnout. But also something else. A sense that he had just taken some kind of important step toward his goal, without any basis for knowing why or how. "I'm, um. I'm calling from the *New York Times*."

"Oh . . . kaaay?" the woman said. She sounded young, bored. Kradle could hear something tapping rapidly, a pen on a table, maybe. "So what can I do for you today, sir?"

"Let me level with you here," Kradle said. "I've got a list of numbers that I'm dialing. They're connected to a murder I'm writing a story about."

"A murder?" the girl snorted. "Whoa. Well, this just got a bit more interesting. And creepy."

"Yeah, it is creepy," Kradle said. "It's a creepy story. Guy murdered his whole family. I'm trying to get to the bottom of what happened."

"Is this a joke?"

"No."

"What did you say your name was?"

"John . . ." He shook his head helplessly and looked around. "Uh. Dog."

"John Dog?"

"With two Gs."

"Mr. Dogg, I don't know if—"

"Look, I'm a researcher, and I've got this number. Someone at your studio called a detective connected to a murder case back in 2015, and I'm trying to find out who that person was."

"Well, what department did they call from?" the girl asked. "What extension?"

"I don't know. This number."

"This is the front desk."

"So who worked on the front desk in 2015?" Kradle asked.

"Dude, I don't know."

"Could you find out?"

"Maybe." A frustrated sigh. The novelty of the call was wearing off and becoming hard work. Kradle felt his throat tightening with desperation. "Urgh, I'd have to look it up. And I don't know if I can tell you that. It's, like, private, probably. Confidential information."

"What does your studio do?" Kradle asked.

"TV shows," the girl said. "We're the home of *NDN News*—the voice of Nevada!"

"What else?"

"*Ready, Set, Clean,*" the girl said. "*Paulie the Pawn-King, Trailer Park Wars, The Frances Falkner Show, The—*"

"*The Frances Falkner Show?*" Kradle said.

"Yeah. Look, can you hang on?"

Kradle's mind was racing. It made sense that Detective Frapport would think to speak to the producers of *The Frances Falkner Show*. Christine had attended a taping two months before she was murdered. What didn't make sense was Frapport actually doing it. Almost all the calls Kradle had made so far were to people Detective Frapport had selected because they knew

Kradle. They were his neighbors, local businesspeople who he bought from, clients he had serviced. Frapport was tunnel-visioned, bent on proving Kradle was the killer, without seeking to examine any other suspects. The *Frances Falkner* producers didn't know Kradle, and had never met him. Christine had attended the show by herself after he and Audrey refused to go with her.

And *the show* had called *Frapport*. Kradle looked at the list of numbers, checked and rechecked. Yes, the first contact made between Frapport's number and the studio was incoming, not outgoing. After they'd chased each other back and forth, the detective and whoever called from In Focus Studios had spoken for only three minutes. Whatever the issue had been, it seemed Frapport had shut it down fairly quickly. Kradle ran his finger up and down the list of numbers, trying to find any calls to or from an extension at In Focus Studios other than the number he was now on hold with.

A voice came back on the line. It was not the bored girl from the front desk but a high, male voice that was thick with disapproval. Kradle thought he noted a Southern accent, something familiar, from his corner of the world. Maybe Carolina.

"Are you there?"

"Yes," Kradle said.

"In Focus Studios has no comment to make on anything related to the Pronghorn breakout," the voice said. "And we'll ask you please not to call here again."

"Can I maybe—" Kradle started, but the line went dead. His stomach growled, half with hunger, half with a physical acknowledgment that he was getting traction, the instinct that he was on the right path.

He sat again against the wall, put a hand on his heart and found it hammering. He went to the internet app on the phone and opened it up, tapped through to YouTube, and started searching. There were weekly episodes of *The Frances Falkner Show* dating back to 1996. He scrolled them, trying to think which week Christine must have attended the show.

He closed his eyes. It had been a month after she returned. He saw the little motel room she was staying in down by the river, her backpack slumped in the corner by the bathroom, festooned with badges, patches, ribbons, and other keepsakes from her travels. He remembered going there to pick her up, to take her to a park to meet Mason for the first time. How awkward it all was—the smell of her body in the motel room, his bizarre nervousness that something intimate might happen between them, then the big green park sprawling around them, Mason sitting upright at the picnic table with his hands between his knees, the way he'd sat in countless doctors' offices as a little boy waiting for check-ups and vaccinations. It had been three weeks after that that Kradle stopped going with them to their meetings, stopped trying to explain to Mason why his mother was back, why she'd ever gone away. Maybe a week after that, Kradle had let her come around the house for the first time. Maybe another week before Audrey had come to the house to meet her, and Kradle had gone to work, leaving the three of them alone.

He remembered the boiling tension as Audrey and Christine talked on the back porch. Kradle making use of himself in the kitchen, lying on the floor fixing a leak under the sink, hearing mention of Frances Falkner through the parted back doors.

"Don't tell me you came all the way back here finally to go to that fucking show!" Audrey had screeched.

Kradle remembered smiling in the dark, surrounded by cleaning bottles and the smell of dampness, the heaviness of the wrench in his hand.

He opened his eyes now as the phone buzzed in his lap. A message. He opened it. The number was unfamiliar, not one he had dialed, not one he recognized from the list.

Will talk about Kradle murders in person only.

Kradle tried to answer, feeling sick with exhilaration. His fingers were trembling so bad he had to type the word out in full twice.

Where?

The phone buzzed. An address in Vegas. Kradle gave a sharp sigh of disappointment.

You will have to come to Mesquite, he typed.

I'll be at that address at midnight. You're not there, I don't talk.

Who is this? Kradle typed. He waited for an answer. None came. He called Celine. She didn't answer either. He called four more times. The dog sank down beside him in the gravel and put its head on his thigh. A little sunshine had leaked into the desolate, empty corner of the world where they sat, and it was picking up flashes of chocolate brown in the animal's fur. Kradle smoothed the creature's head as the phone rang and rang.

It was dark by the time Celine arrived in her driveway, which seemed to have doubled in length while she was away. Though she had checked her phone, and none of the media coverage of the incident at Rancho Salvaje Wildlife Park had mentioned her by name, her neighbors seemed to know she had danced closely with death. Across the street, she spied a couple she had never spoken to huddled in their doorway, openly watching her wave off the cab that had driven her home. As she turned to shut the front door behind her, she saw a man standing on the corner with an impatient little dog, looking toward her property. Celine had never interacted with any of her neighbors. There seemed no point. She was never home long enough to make meaningful connections with them, to share stories on front lawns, to borrow tools, to remark at kids learning to ride bikes on the sidewalk. Celine's life was at Pronghorn. It felt like years since she had walked its halls, and she yearned for the clanging of doors and sounding of alarms as she closed the door and flicked the deadbolt.

Her phone was jammed with missed call notifications and unread messages, all of which she had ignored as she sat in an isolation room at the Mesa View Regional Hospital. She had been escorted there by members of Trinity's team after being rescued from the woods. She had lain on the bed in the room, listened to the noises out in the hall—people talking, walking, rolling gurneys. Sounds of life. No one seemed to know what to do with her, uninjured yet numbed with trauma, sectioned off from the world in her little room, awaiting instructions and avoiding the press. Celine supposed she was not a high priority. There would be the teenage girl to question. Brassen's body and the body of the fallen tactical team member to deal with. Another US Marshal would need to be assigned as head of the Pronghorn inmate recovery effort. Celine didn't care. She put her head on the pillow and let her phone buzz and buzz and buzz. When someone came for her, she asked them if Trinity Parker was dead. The man, who she'd never seen before, said that was classified information. Celine gave up and went home.

On the cab ride home she learned of the death of "a second US marshal" at the Rancho Salvaje Wildlife Park. She thought about Trinity's body slumping to the ground, how the fall had made her seem like a rag doll when only seconds before she had been a powerful beast terrorizing the girl on the ground.

Celine sank now onto her couch. Jake the cat came and tried to breeze past her, offering no more than his usual tail flick against the back of her arm as consolation. She grabbed the cat by the hind legs as it reached the end of the couch and dragged it back to her, where it struggled, yowling with horror.

"I don't care." Celine hugged the animal to her. "I don't care. I need this right now. I need this."

She hugged the cat until the yowling turned to growling, her chin buried in the fur at the top of its head. When she let it go, the animal sprinted away, claws skittering for traction on the floor.

Celine opened her phone and looked at the notifications. There were sixteen calls from a number she didn't recognize, and a bunch of text messages.

Need your help. K.

Please please please answer.

It's JK. Pick up.

Have got something major and need to be in Vegas by midnight. Can't get there. Need you to go.

Trying to get out of Mesquite. Road blocks. Will keep trying.

CELINE WHERE R U?

There was only one missed call from Keeps's number. And a single message.

Talk 2 me.

Celine opened his number, let her thumb hover over the call button. Then she closed the message, went back to Kradle's messages, and dialed him.

"Oh, thank god," he said when she answered. "Listen, I—"

"No, you listen," Celine seethed. "I killed someone today."

Celine waited. Kradle didn't speak. She heard cars passing in the background of his call. Wind rattling through the line. A dog barking. The wilds of the fugitive life. She didn't realize how close to tears she was until she tried to speak again.

"I talked a guy to his death," Celine said. "He was scared. He . . . He didn't want to do it. He trusted me. And I walked him right into it. I said it was safe and I knew it wasn't. And then . . . And-and then we ran, and someone was shooting at us, and Trinity . . ."

"Celine?"

"Three people died in front of me, Kradle."

"Celine," Kradle said. "You're okay. You're okay. You're okay."

His voice was gentle. Warm. She'd never heard it that way, and it pulled her out of the long descent into misery. For most of the time she had known him, Celine had listened to John Kradle's prison voice. The voice that had to be strong, unflinching, confident, because prison was a place where the slightest waver could indicate to a nearby predator—whether staff or inmate—that a person was vulnerable. She'd heard John Kradle's mocking voice. She'd heard him challenging, taunting, raging, but she had never heard him comforting, and for a moment she had to stop and check the number she had dialed to make sure there was no mistake.

"Seriously, though," Kradle said after a time. "When you're finished feeling sorry for yourself, I need your help."

"You are such a dick!"

"I am a dick," he agreed. "But listen." He explained the call to In Focus Studios, the messages that came from the unknown number, the address in Vegas. Celine held her head and felt the weight of the day crush her spirit, and with it the very last remnants of who she was before the breakout, of the woman with the keys, the rules, the rock-solid sense of who was good and who was bad and what that meant for her.

"I can't believe I'm going to say this," she said when he was done talking.

"What?" Kradle asked.

Celine drew a deep breath, let it out slowly.

"Tell me where you are," she said. "I'm going to come and pick you up."

CHAPTER 35

For four days, Randy Derlick had been stationed at the desert roadblock closest to Las Vegas from the south: a small, slapped-together job that had been set up at short notice and never strengthened. He guessed that the brains running the Pronghorn recovery effort probably had minimum quotas in place for roadblocks and the people staffing them. Most policing, he had discovered in his nine months on the job, was about meeting certain numbers. The setup of five checkpoints was probably more about keeping to a number written in a handbook about prison breakouts somewhere, and less about the chances of actually catching an inmate. An escapee from Pronghorn would have to get through four other roadblocks to get to where the twenty-one-year-old probationary police officer stood now on the asphalt, and that's if they were coming from the south, having looped around the city for some obscure reason before deciding to head in. If they made it past Randy and his fellow officers, it would be another couple of miles before they saw the barest hint of pink neon lighting, cheap hookers, and palm trees.

So for four days, Randy had done nothing but wave cars, vans, trucks, motorcycles, and every other known type of vehicle into the bay by the side of the road and search fruitlessly for escaped prisoners. As the days wore on, his hopes of finding a real-life fugitive stowed away in someone's trunk or pretzeled into a box in the back of a cargo truck were dwindling, and his irritation with tourists from the West Coast was increasing. There was only so many times a guy could hear, "How 'bout that breakout, huh? Catch any bad guys yet?" before he wanted to blow out his own or somebody else's brains. The one highlight from his searches was the RVs full of sorority girls heading into the city of sin for Christmas fun. On day two, a blonde with big tits had run a hand up the inside of his thigh as he bent over a huge cooler searching for stowaways. While it had been a cheap thrill, all it left him with was a hankering for vodka pre-mixers on ice and a hard-on that wouldn't quit for the rest of the day.

If he enjoyed anything about standing in the desert sun, sweating into his jockey shorts and staring at the unchanging rocky horizon, it was shooting the breeze, or lack thereof, with his teammates. Somehow, the last-ditch roadblock between Pronghorn and Vegas had ended up being staffed entirely by rookies, none of whom Randy had ever met before. Vinnie from Enterprise District, Tuko from Paradise South, and Randy from Silverado Ranch bonded over their frustrated desire to find anything interesting in a car headed for the great gambling city behind them. And when Tuko nabbed a bag of weed from a car on day two and smoked it in the cruiser, and Vinnie suggested a rotation of afternoon naps in the shade on day two, Randy knew he was with a good crew.

The van appeared on the distant horizon just as Tuko's phone bleeped in his pocket. The young officer was leaning on the road partition, his arms folded, his aviator sunglasses like devil eyes, colored sunset red. The text message and the van were the first things to happen in forty minutes, so Randy felt a little buzz of excitement in his chest. He watched the speck in the distance become a watery ball, then sprout two black tire legs as the van grew closer.

"Aw, shit."

"What is it?" Randy glanced over.

"My buddy," Tuko groaned. "He's on a checkpoint in the north. They just caught an inmate."

"You serious?" Vinnie was sitting nearby in the driver's seat of the cruiser, with the window rolled down and his elbow on the sill. "God*damn* it."

"Anybody good?" Randy asked.

"Nah," Tuko sighed. "Some medium security guy. Smash'n'grab robber. Found him curled up under a blanket in the back seat."

"Criminal genius."

"This is such bullshit." Vinnie thumped the steering wheel. "I just want one inmate. I don't even care if he's minimum. He could be a tax evader. A fucking DUI dirtbag. I just want to bring *somebody* in."

"Not me," Randy said.

"Huh?"

"I don't want just anybody," Randy said. "I want someone with money.

Somebody who's gonna slide me a tasty bite so I'll let them through the roadblock."

"Oh, yeah." Tuko smiled. "Like a, like a . . . bank robber. He just hit a place in some shitty town down in Mexico, and now he's all cashed up. He wants to get to Vegas for a big score, so he slides us ten grand each to say we never saw him come through here."

"Or a rich guy." Randy lit a cigarette, his eyes on the approaching van. "He's been locked up in Pronghorn for ten years for trying to kill his wife. Now he's out and he wants to finish the job. So he transfers a million bucks each to our bank accounts." He grinned. "We take off into the sunset. Rich-ass motherfuckers."

"You two ought to write a screenplay," Vinnie yawned.

"It could happen." Tuko shrugged.

"Yeah." Randy nodded at the van. "This van right here might be full of the big four ace cards. Hamsi driving. Carrington riding shotgun. Marco taking a nap in the back . . ."

"Schmitz hanging on underneath the van like Pacino in *Cape Fear*." Tuko laughed, holding up his hands like they were claws.

"They got Hamsi already," Vinnie said. "And Carrington's dead. Marco never left Pronghorn. He's a million years old. They found him in the prison infirmary, taking a nap. Don't you guys watch the news?" He shook his head. "And it was DeNiro in *Cape Fear*, for Chrissake."

"I love that movie," Randy said. He took a few steps toward the van as it slowed for the last hundred yards, and held up a hand to halt it. Two young women in the front seats: tattoos, glasses, college types, probably. Feminists. Randy went to the driver's side and Tuko headed for the passenger side.

"Ladies," Randy said as the driver rolled down her window. Randy heard Beyoncé on the radio and smelled pomegranates. Disappointment flooded him. "What you got in the back?"

"Tampons."

"*Tampons*?" Tuko said from where he crouched at the passenger-side wheel, shining a flashlight beneath the van for signs of Max Cady–type characters.

"We're from an organization in South LA called Debbie's Dignity. You've probably heard of us. We supply care packages for homeless women in Los Angeles." The girl tossed a little pink backpack through the window at Randy. He unzipped it and glanced in. Womanly things. Bottles, packages, baggies.

"So now you're spreading the hobo-love in Vegas, are you?" Randy said.

"We've had a surplus of stock. Christmas givers. People have been very charitable."

"Uh-huh," he said. He reached through the window to hand the bag back. 'Tis the season, all right."

The passenger leaned over to take the bag from Randy. Her paisley top slid up her forearm, exposing a tattoo of a rope swirling in and out of itself as it wound around her arm.

Randy felt all the hairs on his arms rise.

"Interesting tattoo you have there," he said as she settled back in her seat. He said it just to see her reaction. The girl glanced at her sleeve, tugged it down.

"Oh, yeah. Stupid."

"What's it mean?" Randy leaned his forearms on the windowsill.

"Togetherness," the girl said. "Like, uh, loyalty. Being bound together with someone."

"Oh, really?" Randy said.

"They're all good." Tuko came to Randy's side. "Ladies, you can shoot through."

Randy stepped back. Then something pushed him forward again, an urge that seemed to come from nowhere. It made him shove a hand into the windowsill again just as the van lurched forward.

"Do you ever get any shit for it?" Randy asked.

"What?" the passenger said.

"Your partner said we could go." The driver glared at Randy.

"Just hold on. I want to know if you ever get any shit for it," Randy said. He turned to Tuko. "She's got a rope tattoo."

"So?" Tuko frowned.

"So sometimes people interpret tattoos in different ways." Randy shrugged. "My dad was a tattoo artist. He had a shop back home. In Texas. I've seen tattoos like that. The rope with the swirls going in and out."

"I have too," Tuko said. "The hipsters are getting all kinds of weird tattoos. Arrows and ropes and swallows. It's, like, symbolism and shit."

"What's going on?" Vinnie had appeared out of nowhere, his hands in his pockets. Tuko and Randy backed off from the van. As they assembled a few yards away, it seemed to Randy that night had slammed down on them like a cupped hand. The horizon was gone. Dust swirled in the air, gold and thick as smoke in the van's headlights.

"Something doesn't feel right here," he said.

"It's a fucking tattoo." Tuko rolled his eyes. "Jeez. She also has a dolphin tattoo on her neck. You see that one?"

"No."

"He was like this yesterday about the guy with the beard."

"It looked like a fake beard!" Randy said.

"It was very thick," Vinnie conceded.

"Listen"—Randy huffed an excited breath—"we're supposed to be on the lookout for skinheads, right? Skinheads love rope tattoos. I've seen dozens of them in my dad's shop. Nooses and swirly ropes. Ropes spelling out letters. It's a thing from a book that they like. The, uh . . . *The Day of the Ropes.*"

"You're thinking of *The Day of the Jackal*," Vinnie said.

"No, I'm not."

"They're not skinheads," Tuko said. "They're feminists."

"When I said something about the tattoo," Randy said, "she pulled her shirt down, not up. It's not a hipster tattoo." He waited. The guys weren't reacting. "I just—"

"You're bored, Randy," Tuko said. "If you want to strip a vehicle, let's wait for something fun. You want to get knee-deep in tampons and Vagisil? Because I don't."

"Look." Vinnie put his hands up in surrender. "Let's just go back, we'll quickly open the van and we can—"

Thumping. That's what the gunfire sounded like. Randy's mind told him an old generator had started up behind him, and the rapid thumping was its engine turning over, coughing to life. But he felt the thumping through his center, three hard knocks against his back, and the big black bowl of the Nevada sky whipped downward from above him as he arched and hit the ground. He rolled, saw another staccato blast of white light as the shooter rounded the back of the van and sprayed the three officers again. Randy felt Tuko against his legs, fallen sideways, already dead. He heard Vinnie give a wet cough from somewhere to his right. Randy reached for the gun on his hip, but the driver of the van was standing over him now, and she kicked his wrist away.

And then Randy saw a man whose face he had spent hours memorizing. Burke David Schmitz walked up and stood over him with the AR-15 still clutched in his hands, his finger on the trigger guard. The crew from the van talked, their voices barely reaching Randy as he lay dying at their feet.

"One more roadblock," Burke said. He let out a long, disappointed sigh. "We were so close."

"Sorry, Burke," the woman with the rope tattoo said. "I'll go get the shovel."

"Hurry up," Burke said. "I'm hungry."

Randy reached up, tried to say something to them all, but all he got for his efforts was them staring down at him as Burke lined up the barrel of the gun against Randy's forehead.

CHAPTER 36

Celine parked the car on a side road leading to the ballpark and looked around. There was no game, though the street seemed to tell the story of a recent celebration, the asphalt festooned with French fries and take-out containers. She sat with the phone in her lap, watching a rat inspecting the contents of a brown paper bag, the thrumming of a nearby club leaking into the brick walls around her, making it sound as though she was waiting in the artery of a great living being. She counted down ten minutes on her phone, then got out, looked up the alley toward the stadium entrance, then back the way she had come, to the main street. A night jogger passed and was gone before Celine could really focus on her. With her nerves making her scalp itch, she dropped her keys and her phone on the driver's seat and raised her hands in the air.

"Would you just get in the damned car!" she yelled. "I haven't got all night!"

John Kradle emerged from his hiding place: a stairwell above a dumpster twenty or more yards down the alley. A large black dog trotted out from behind the dumpster itself. The dog walked up and, without acknowledging Celine at all, leaped in the open driver's-side door, crossed to the front passenger seat, and sat down.

Kradle glanced nervously behind him as he approached. In the thin light Celine saw that he sported thick gray stubble. His hoodie was bloodstained and there was dirt on the knees of his jeans. A dirty hand with blackened fingernails rose and swiped nervously at his face.

"This isn't a trap," Celine said.

"If you say so."

"You look terrible. I've watched *The Fugitive* a thousand times," she said. "Great movie. Harrison Ford looks immaculate throughout, even after he jumps off the dam. Look at you. Four days in Mesquite and you're an island castaway."

Kradle seemed distracted, didn't take the bait. Celine chewed her lip. It was her nerves making her babble, the blaring alarm bells ringing in her head at the very sight of inmate number 1707, one of her men, walking and talking in the free world, wearing civilian clothes, going to the passenger side of her car. She was walking in a nightmare. She slid into the car as Kradle shooed the dog into the back seat and sat down.

"Did you bring the key?" he asked.

She opened the glove compartment and took out a handcuff key. He lifted the wrist that had the cuff connected to it. Celine looked at the swinging, empty cuff that was covered with blood.

"Oh," she said. "That's why you . . ."

"The thumb."

"Don't say it." She held her throat.

"Why I cut off Homer's thumb? He shackled himself to me."

"Are you deaf? I said don't say it."

"Harder to cut off a thumb than you might think," Kradle mused. "Lots of connecting tissue. Sinew. Veins. Tendons."

"Stop!"

Kradle laughed as he uncuffed himself, pocketed the cuffs and key. They sat in silence for a moment.

"This is weird," he said.

"Sure is."

"I've never seen you in civilian clothes."

"Likewise."

"This is your car." He ran a hand over the dashboard. "I'm in Captain Osbourne's car."

"It's my neighbor's car. I borrowed it. Mine's in the parking lot of a wildlife park. But let's not talk about that, either," Celine said. She started the engine. "The less we put into words what I'm doing, the better I'll feel about it."

"You mean, assisting a fugitive?"

"Yes. It's a felony, but I'm sure you knew that. Five years in federal prison and a hefty fine. Certainly the loss of my job, my credibility, and probably my sanity. The worst thing that can happen to a prison guard is finding yourself on the other side of the bars."

"You're doing a lot of talking for someone who says they don't want to talk," Kradle said.

"Right."

"Did you bring food?"

"At your feet," she said, and pointed. Kradle picked up the bag and pulled out a McDonald's burger, unwrapped it with shaking hands.

"Oh, god," he moaned. Celine cringed as she drove, listening to his munching and moaning. "Oh, god. Ohhhhh god. Oh god. Oh god."

"There's a loudly orgasming fugitive in my car," Celine sighed. "So what's with the dog?"

"Just someone I met on my travels who recognized how great it is to be on the John Kradle train. Like you," he said through a mouthful of burger. He handed the dog a chunk of bun.

"Don't do that."

"He's hungry."

"What kind of person spends five years in prison and four days on the lam waiting to have their first taste of takeout, and then shares that takeout with a dog?"

"This guy."

"Talk to me about this message," Celine said.

He opened his phone, looked at the message. *Will only talk about Kradle murders in person.*

"No indication who it's from?"

"No."

"But you think it's someone from In Focus Studios?"

"Yeah."

"What even is *The Frances Falkner Show*?" Celine asked.

"You've never seen it?"

"I've heard of it, but I haven't paid much attention to what it actually is."

"It's trash TV." Kradle pulled up his hood as they stopped at a traffic light. People passed on the crosswalk before them, oblivious to his presence. "It's in the *Jerry Springer, Ricki Lake, Jenny Jones* kind of category."

"Oh."

"Christine never missed it. And she would watch the reruns. Sometimes she would search for the people who had appeared in certain episodes online, try to find out what had happened in their lives after the show, how they dealt with the problems they'd presented to Frances."

"She sounds like a very serious fan," Celine said.

"She was. She liked drama. Her favorite shows were all about people yelling at each other. Devastating secrets revealed, betrayals, back-stabbings, scandals."

"And you weren't into that?"

"No." He smiled. "Christine and I were very different people. She was sort of . . . dramatic. Theatrical. You know me. I'm a bit more simple."

Celine shifted uncomfortably in her seat. His words rattled in her brain. *You know me.* She had indeed spoken to John Kradle almost every day for the past five years. She had passed his cell and seen him sleeping, eating, crying, bouncing off the walls with boredom bordering on madness. It made her uncomfortable now, how well she knew, and also didn't know, him. The very sound of him breathing in the seat beside her seemed familiar, but she couldn't say yet, one way or another, whether she believed he had killed innocent people.

"So people come on the show to reveal secrets?" she asked, trying to focus.

"Sometimes," Kradle said. "I managed to track down the episode where she attended the taping. I've watched the footage. The subject was *My Psycho Father Doesn't Know I'm Gay!*"

"Seriously?" Celine said. "In 2015?"

"They've cleaned up their act lately, but not by much." Kradle was fishing around in a box of fries, shoving some in his face and handing others over his shoulder to the dog. "On this episode, a bunch of people come out on the show to their crazy dads. There's a woman who reveals she's a lesbian to her father, who's a welder. Pretty tough dude. There's a lot of build-up to suggest he's going to lose his shit, but he doesn't. It's kind of cute. There are other less gentle reactions. Some people throw chairs."

"You watched the episode in full?"

"Yeah."

"And you saw her in the audience?"

"I did."

"Anything happen?"

"No." Kradle drew a long breath, shrugged helplessly. "She sits in the audience, claps and cheers when everybody else claps and cheers. There's an empty seat next to her. She bought two tickets but couldn't find anybody to go with her."

"Why didn't you go with her?" Celine asked.

"The show is not my thing. They basically just get people on camera and pay them to be publicly humiliated. And, aside from that, I was angry with her," Kradle said, like it was the most obvious thing in the world. The silence swelled, and enveloped the car. With no food left, the dog sank across the back seat of the car and blew out a huge sigh, smacked its lips.

"I've never denied the fact that when Christine returned, I was mad as hell," Kradle said.

"What happened that day?" Celine asked.

Kradle smoothed the knees of his jeans and watched the town rolling by, becoming suburbs stretching toward the desert.

"Christine and Mason were at the house," Kradle said. "I went on a job by myself. The plan was that I'd be home by four o'clock. Audrey was going to be there already. We were all going to have dinner together. I kept meeting Christine for meals—first in a diner, then at the house, thinking eventually it would get easier. When you're eating you don't have to talk the whole time, and you've got something to look at. Your food."

"Okay."

"Tensions were high." Kradle nestled back in the seat beside Celine, covered a yawn. "Audrey never liked me. I think she figured I was a meathead, and nothing I ever did around her challenged that theory. And all the time Christine was gone, we didn't speak. She didn't offer any help. So that was weird. What's worse is that Christine was trying to build something with Mason, but it wasn't really working. She was trying to slap a Band-Aid over a wound that was going to take a lifetime to heal, if it ever healed at all. About two o'clock that day I got a call from the kid saying Christine had bought him a bubble machine."

"A bubble machine?"

"Yeah," Kradle sighed. "It's like this: When Mason was a boy, a toddler, I bought him a bubble-making machine. It was this little box you poured dish soap into that spewed out thousands and thousands of bubbles. He went mad for it. Running all around the yard, squealing and laughing and trying to catch the bubbles."

"Okay."

"I told Christine that at one of our meetings," Kradle said. "So she goes and buys him a bubble machine. She presented it to him at the house, poured the dish soap in, and set it off in the yard. Well, it did what it was supposed to do. It spewed out all the bubbles. But the kid is fifteen now. Who buys a teenager a bubble machine? Mason found the entire thing incredibly forced."

"She was trying to re-create a magical moment," Celine said.

Kradle nodded. "Exactly."

"And it didn't work."

"No," he said. "It was wildly off target with him. He froze up and didn't know what to say. Christine got upset that Mason wasn't getting into the moment, and Mason got upset that Christine was upset. They both called me, angry. And I sided with him."

Celine said nothing.

"Imagine this. I'm underneath some old lady's house, trying to fix some creaky floorboards. I got dirt in my eyes and I'm drenched in sweat and I'm fielding calls and texts about this bubble machine." Kradle heaved a sigh. "I just snapped. I told Christine she was being a spoiled little princess. Mason rejected her and her little bubble machine performance. Rightfully so. He's fifteen, not five. And you know what? She needed to taste a little rejection. It was her getting exactly what she deserved."

Celine swallowed. She turned onto the highway.

"What?" Kradle said eventually.

"You know how all this sounds, right?" Celine said. *"I was angry. I just snapped. Christine was getting exactly what she deserved."*

"Yes, I do," Kradle said. "I know how bad it sounds, because I said all those things in my initial interviews, before I'd called in a lawyer, and then they were all played back to the entire courtroom. But I'm saying them again to you now because they're the truth. And you want the truth, right?"

"Right," Celine said, and she meant it. They fell silent, and the highway stretched ahead of them, a long, dark path that sliced the earth in half, forming two identical black slabs of desert. Celine thought about the truth—how precious it was, how she had never really received it. Because while she had sat as a teenager and listened to her grandfather tell her that he'd spared her life because of a fence, and psychologists had told her over the years that he'd murdered her family because he was a narcissistic sociopath, Celine knew she still didn't have the truth of the matter. She would never know what those moments had been like when her grandfather made the decision to kill everyone. She imagined him sitting in his chair in the den and sipping wine and watching her little brothers playing with their trucks on the carpet. Him musing about his plan and deciding that they must be included. Had it been a moment like that, months or years before the murders? An otherwise ordinary evening filled with dark thoughts? Or had something shifted on the morning of the event? Had one last domino finally fallen? Had he gone down to the barn to shoot apples with the boys and relented to a sudden urge? She imagined him taking his gun from the cabinet, checking it, loading it, heading down the hill. Passing Nanna in the kitchen. Her father in the den. She didn't know if he had said anything to anybody at the house before he left to kill the children. Whether there'd been some kind of cryptic goodbye that alerted no one to the danger that was approaching, yet satisfied some sick desire inside him to have the final word.

As her thoughts turned darker and darker, Celine glanced over and realized John Kradle was asleep with his head against the window and his hands in his lap.

If he was innocent, Celine thought, then he still had a chance to get that truth. To find whoever had done to him the worst thing a human could do, and ask him why. Celine might never have been able to understand the pain that had been such a large part of her life since she was child, the pain that had formed and deformed her as an adult. But John Kradle had a shot. And she was helping him. There was no denying it. He was in her car now, and her hands were on the wheel, and before them stretched the road that would take him to her house, to a plan, maybe to his freedom. Celine felt an aching in her chest, a joyful, shimmering kind of pain, relief and excitement at the idea of seeing the truth uncovered through the fight of another person. It wouldn't be the same as having it for herself, but it was something.

She wiped at a tear. Carefully, silently, she reached over and took Kradle's hand. It was warm and hard in hers.

And then it moved.

"Whoa." Kradle stirred. "What are you doing?"

"Nothing." Celine snatched her hand back. "Nothing."

"Were you . . . trying to hold hands with me?"

"No."

"You were."

"I was having a moment." Celine sighed. "Just . . . Just shut up."

"That was so awkward."

"Go back to sleep."

"I would, but I'm afraid you'll hug me or something."

Celine gripped the wheel, shook her head, her cheeks flaming.

"God," she said. "I hate you so much."

Celine was pulling into her garage when Kradle roused in the seat beside her, giving a full body stretch and scratching at his scalp and stubble the way she had seen him do inside Pronghorn. He snapped to attention as the walls of the garage enveloped the car, turning and watching the automatic door close behind them.

"I told you, this isn't a trap," Celine said.

They had stopped twice on the road from Mesquite, Celine talking her way through searches at roadblocks with her prison ID while Kradle lay curled in the trunk of the car. Between the roadblocks, the inmate had slept soundly with his head against the window.

They went inside, Jake the cat trotting to meet them at the door to the garage and arching into a defensive position at the sight of the dog.

"It's okay." Celine put a hand out. "It's fine, we just—"

Jake lifted wild yellow eyes with huge pupils to Celine, the glare of the betrayed, and darted away.

"Of course." Celine let her hands fall. "Because it's my fault you brought a dog."

"He'll get over it," Kradle said.

While Kradle showered, Celine went to the couch and opened her phone. Another message from Keeps sat on the screen.

I'm not a bad guy, Celine, it read. *And I like you.*

She swiped the message away, turned on her TV, and connected the phone to the big screen in front of her. She opened YouTube and searched *Frances Falkner Psycho Father Gay.*

Celine recognized Frances Falkner in the thumbnail image of the first video that came up. The petite brunette appeared on the screen wearing a turquoise pants suit and holding a microphone. Behind her stood a crowd, clapping and chanting her name, breaking into cheers as a guitar riff closed off the show's opening credits. The camera swirled in to focus on Falkner from above the stage, leaving glimpses of the studio setup—hot lights in the rafters, a security crew guarding the edges of the brick room.

"Wow! Wow!" Frances flipped her hair, adjusted the question cards pinned between her fingers and the mic. "Thanks very much. Thank you. Good crowd. Back at ya, everybody! Have a seat! Have a seat!"

Celine cringed, slipping off her shoes and putting her sock-covered feet on the coffee table.

"Today my guests are here to reveal intimate details of their private sexual lives to people they love the most." Falkner grinned at the camera over the microphone and raised a coy brow. "They say their families won't accept them for who they are in the bedroom, and they're here to tell them that ain't right!"

"That ain't right!" the crowd cheered.

"We're gonna find out what happens when deeply held prejudices clash with family loyalties." Falkner smiled. "Let's start with our first guest!"

The crowd erupted into cheers. Celine watched a young Asian woman dressed in gray work coveralls walk out onto a stage and take a seat in one of two empty, plush pink armchairs.

"Please meet Tammy," Falkner said as the camera cut back to her standing among the crowd. "Tammy says she and her father have been working together at his welding business since she was a kid. But Tammy wants her father to know it's not men who make her sparks fly. Tammy, tell us all about it!"

"Oh, Jesus." Celine slumped back on the couch.

By the time Kradle appeared at the end of the couch, Celine had watched the welder's daughter confess to her father about her girlfriend and the other women she had dated. She listened to the audience coo over their hug, and scream with delight as the next guest, a male flight attendant, revealed to his police officer brother that he was gay, only to have the brother pick up a chair and hurl it across the stage at him. Kradle's hair was wet, and he was wearing the clothes Celine had picked up from Walmart on her way to Mesquite. He was drying his ears with the corner of Celine's favorite towel.

"I haven't smelled this good in years," he said, bending to sniff his armpit.

"Did you use my toothbrush?" Celine grimaced.

"Was there something else I was supposed to use?"

Celine closed her eyes. "Note to self: Burn all belongings."

He sat and they watched a teenage boy tell his mother he was having a secret love affair with his first cousin.

"This show is terrible," he said.

"Yeah. But it's probably not the worst thing out there."

"Hmm."

"Where's Christine?" Celine asked, handing Kradle the remote. He watched the screen carefully for a while, then paused the clip. He walked to the screen and pointed to a blurry image of a plump woman sitting three rows from the back of the studio. An empty gray chair sat beside her.

"Right there."

"Okay."

They watched the show in full. At the end, while credits slid slowly across the bottom half of the screen, members of the audience stood and asked questions or made comments about the guests, who were all assembled on the stage in pink chairs.

"Does Christine make a comment?" Celine asked.

"No," Kradle said.

They watched a woman in a red dress stand and take the mic from Frances.

"I just wanna say y'all need to have your heads checked." The woman cast a finger over the people on the stage. "What you're doin' is against God's word, and—"

The audience exploded with jeers.

"And it's Adam and Eve, not Adam and—"

The camera panned over the people in pink chairs on the stage. Some of the guests were nodding. Others were calling back insults. The welder reached over and hugged his daughter into his side.

"Well, I feel stupider," Celine said as the In Focus Studios logo flashed onscreen. She looked over. Kradle was asleep with his head hanging against the back of the couch, his mouth open. As she watched, he drew a snoring breath. Celine guessed it would take some time to recover from the fugitive life. She opened her phone to disconnect it from the television and paused with her finger above the episode she had just played.

The length of the video was displayed on the thumbnail. It read 33 minutes and 3 seconds. As she glanced down the list of videos, she read the numbers indicating the length of the other episodes.

44 minutes, 19 seconds.

46 minutes, 3 seconds.

41 minutes, 20 seconds.

Celine scrolled. There were no other episodes of *The Frances Falkner Show* from season eight that were under forty minutes. She went back to her initial search, opened a collection of videos marked season five, and scrolled through the running time of the videos. As her excitement built, she reached over and slapped Kradle in the chest with the back of her hand.

"Something's been cut out," she said.

"Hmm?"

"Of the episode. A segment's been cut out."

"Trade you," Kradle murmured, turning his head away. "Five sachets of coffee."

Celine got up and pushed Kradle sideways on the couch until he lay down, then lifted his legs onto the seat.

"Don't get too comfortable," she said. "We leave in an hour."

"Hmm."

She went into the bedroom and flicked on the ensuite light, throwing light on her bed, where two figures curled side by side. Jake made a small, round ball near the pillow on the left side of the bed. The black dog made a bigger ball of fur on the right side.

CHAPTER 37

Burke David Schmitz took his blue snow cone from the food truck vendor and made his way through the crowd to the edge of the rink. On the ice, there seemed to be three types of people skating: confident zoomers, who twirled and skidded and danced around the inner circle; semi-confident skaters, who shuffled awkwardly in a wider circle around the blue-lit rink, now and then slipping and thumping dramatically onto the hard, white surface; and an outer ring of newcomers to the sport, who gripped and giggled their way around the edge of the rink, gloved hands trembling as they slid along a surface painted with colorful snowflakes. Schmitz pulled the edges of his hoodie up around his face, adjusted the fake glasses on the bridge of his nose and scanned the crowd. Mostly white faces. The following morning, Christmas morning, there would probably be a good mixture of races in attendance, but what mattered would be the colors of the targets as they lined up on the big stage at the far end of the rink. For now, the stage was empty. A sound technician was fiddling with a microphone mounted behind a podium. Burke looked at the huge Christmas tree dominating the left side of the stage, twinkling with fiber-optic stars transitioning between pink, purple, and blue.

Burke looked at the ice in front of him and thought about a mixed crowd of people, rubbing shoulders, exchanging smiles, some of them running into each other, gripping each other's arms, tumbling to the ice. He thought about the ice itself, a huge, circular slab sitting like a jewel in the middle of the desert, exactly where it didn't belong.

Beyond the rink, the Planet Hollywood Resort hugged the park in which the rink lay, at the center of a makeshift winter wonderland. The hotel was a huge black mass in a sea of buildings lit with hundreds of gold windows, strips of flashing globes, upturned golden cones of light from inground lights. Along the front of the building, painted wooden panels were hung with signs detailing the building's renovation timeline.

Burke stood licking his blue snow cone, running his eyes along the wall that sectioned off the front of the hotel. It was ten feet tall, windowless, seamless, a perfect barrier that at that moment stopped civilians interfering with the construction site that lay beyond it, but on Christmas Day would prevent panicked, screaming civilians from escaping that way.

Burke could just see the faint traces of #VegasStrong tags that had been painted on the panels back in 2017. Like the memory of Stephen Paddock's massacre, the tags had been exposed to time and had lost their strength. Rain, the searing Nevada sun, splatters of dirt and paint, and the coming in contact with the shoulders of passers-by had taken the edge off the lettering, but Burke knew that the ink would be layers deep under the surface, seeped there, immoveable.

What he would do on Christmas Day wasn't just going to deeply stain the memories of men, women, and children in Nevada. It would not be rubbed down and faded by time. What he would do would blast right through the world, splinter it, shatter it, crush some of it to dust. Because Burke was not some lunatic with no discernible motivation cutting through young lives at a concert. He was a soldier with a specific target, a strategic intent, a master plan.

On the ice, a family with two little blonde girls were shuffling haltingly along the middle circle, grinning and holding hands. Burke turned, put an elbow on the edge of the rink, and watched. The family was heading for the stage, the Christmas tree, and, beyond it, a line of trucks backed bumper to bumper containing equipment for the Christmas Day extravaganza on the ice. Burke turned again and surveyed the third wall that corralled the ice rink, a second row of wide, high trucks, these painted bright colors and hung with signs. The food trucks were giving off a mixture of enticing smells, the strongest of which was the Mexican truck, which had just put on a fresh batch of ground beef. Burke locked eyes with the woman behind the counter of the snow cone truck, who was squeezing red food coloring out of a ketchup bottle onto a dome of ice in a pointed cone. The woman raised the cone in a small salute, and Burke nodded back. From where he stood he could see the sleeve of her shirt slide back down over the rope tattoo on her forearm.

He turned back to the ice. The family with the little girls had stopped to rest against the barrier. Burke heard Christmas carols on the wind and smiled.

CHAPTER 38

An hour's solid rest on the couch, and the snippets of sleep he had snuck in the car, had filled Kradle with a disproportionate amount of energy. The shower, the fresh clothes, and the first substantial meal he'd had since the breakout had probably also helped. He sat in the passenger seat of the car, itching to get going, while Celine readied herself inside the house, now and then passing the door to the garage, a dog or cat following close behind. He honked the horn a couple of times and she leaned into the doorway and flipped him the bird before disappearing again.

By the time they were pulling out onto the street, his heart was hammering in his chest and his fingers were dancing on his knees.

"Would you chill?" Celine asked. "You're making me nervous."

"You should be nervous. You're driving a wanted man to a secret meeting with a mystery person in the middle of the night."

"Stop."

"Pretty ballsy stuff."

"Yeah, well." Celine shrugged one shoulder. "I'm a pretty ballsy chick."

"I haven't said thanks yet."

"Any time is good!"

"Thank you," Kradle said. "Although, now that I say it, it doesn't seem like enough."

"It's not."

"I appreciate it," he said. "After everything you've been through."

"Kradle, I don't want to talk about that with you. At all. Not ever."

"I'm not talking about what happened to your family. I'm talking about what I put you through at Pronghorn."

"You think you're the most problematic inmate I've ever had?" She rolled her eyes.

"I do."

"Well, you're not."

"What about the countdown?" He was smiling. "What about the Valentine's Day cards I sent you from Satan? What about Fingernail Jesus?"

"Urgh, Fingernail Jesus," Celine groaned, remembering the six-month period when Kradle had refused to shave, have a haircut, or trim his fingernails. He had ended up a taloned, Christ-like figure who preached nonsensical commandments at passing officers.

They drove toward Vegas. Through five checkpoints, Celine showed her ID, smiled and joked with the checkpoint police officers about being the angry Pronghorn correctional officer who introduced the world to the five most wanted men from the breakout. A young officer took a selfie with her at the third checkpoint. At the fifth, on the crest of a hill looking down toward the valley where the great shimmering city lay, the tone was more solemn.

"They got no word from them at all?" she heard one officer ask another.

"Nothin'," the officer responded. He was a young man, looking at his phone. "The cruiser is gone. The barricades are gone. It's as if they just bailed out. I'm calling Tuko but he won't pick up."

Celine stopped behind a Costco just inside the city limits and let Kradle out of the trunk. They followed Route 95 through a block of shopping malls north of Summerlin, the blazing white lights of Target, Walmart, and the little chain restaurants that clustered at their base making the highway seem lit almost by daylight. Kradle watched the stores pass as if he were a kid at the aquarium. They stopped at an intersection and saw a family wheeling a huge flat-screen TV across the six lanes of the highway in a shopping cart. Kradle glanced at the clock set into the dashboard.

"Must have been a sale," Celine said.

Kradle shrugged. "Hey, you want to go to Walmart at midnight? Go to Walmart at midnight. Go to a bar. Go to the beach. If you're free to do it, do it."

"I guess you'd come away from death row with that kind of attitude," Celine said.

"I used to go on little mental journeys if I woke up in the middle of the night in my cell," Kradle said. "Drive down the highway, stop at a gas station, look through the aisles. Pick up a Coke and a burrito, maybe."

Celine drove through the intersection. "You nervous?" she asked.

"A little," he said. "More . . . More excited. I've wanted an answer for so long."

"What are you going to do? When this is over?" Celine watched the road, the streetlamps crawling overhead. She couldn't deny the jealousy that was making her throat ache, that Kradle had a chance of not only learning the truth about his family's murders, but of going back to something that resembled the life he had once lived. There was no place Celine could go where she could be who she had been—the teenager, the daughter and sister and niece and cousin, the naive kid filled with hope and dreams about her future. She realized before long that she had got so caught up in imagining Kradle back in the swamps on his houseboat that she had not heard him say that was his plan. In fact, he had not said anything at all.

Celine fidgeted in her seat.

"Because, I mean, when we . . . you know," she said. "When we catch whoever did this to your family, we'll bring him to justice. You'll be found innocent and set free."

Again, Kradle didn't answer.

"That's the plan," Celine said slowly, firmly. "To find him and bring him in."

"Here it is." Kradle pointed.

They pulled alongside the parking lot of the Everpalm Motel, at the corner of an intersection. Celine felt her jaw aching with tension.

"Don't go in," Kradle said. "Pull in here and we'll watch."

Celine turned left instead of right and parked in the lot outside the Best Western across the street from the Everpalm, and the two watched from between rows of short palm trees bordering the road. There were only three cars at the Everpalm. Celine could see no one hanging around the edges of the lot, no one watching from the laundromat next door or from the Chili's restaurant on the other side of the street to the squat blue building.

"Text him," Celine said. "Tell him to come out and wave."

Kradle did. As they watched, the door to room three opened and a man stepped out, dressed in jeans and a pinstriped business shirt. He looked up and down the road, waved, and pushed the door open fully with his boot. Kradle leaned forward and squinted at the doorway.

"Recognize him?" Celine asked.

"No."

"Maybe I should go first," she said.

Kradle nodded.

Celine got out, crossed the highway, and went to the door. The man was sitting now on the edge of the faded floral coverlet on one of two single beds in the room. He swiped a hand nervously over his long nose and chin and gestured to the bathroom.

"You can check," he said. "It's just me."

Celine went in and checked. A tiny bathroom that smelled of mold. A plywood closet, empty but for laundry bags and empty hangers. Nothing under the beds but dust. She walked to the doorway and waved.

"You have a friend with you?" the man asked.

"'Friend' is a strong word," Celine said.

John Kradle walked into the room and shut the door behind him, pulling down his hood as he did so.

"Oh, *shit*!" The man got up and backed into the dresser, rattling the fingerprint-spotted mirror.

"Calm down," Celine said. "He's fine. You're safe. It's him you've been texting."

"*You* called the studio?" The man pointed at Kradle.

"I did," Kradle said. "I'm not from the *New York Times*."

"Yeah! Ha! No kiddin'!" the man said. "I agreed to meet a journalist here, not a fucking escaped prisoner. I could—I could get arrested for this!"

"Right," Celine said. "So let's get this over with quickly. The longer we all sit here wailing about what we're doing, the more likely it is that we'll get caught doing it. You're from In Focus Studios?"

"Yes."

"What's your name?" Kradle asked.

"Never mind." The man put a long-fingered hand up as though to hide his face. He sank to the edge of the bed again. "Let me just tell you what I know so I can get out of here."

Celine sat on the edge of the opposite bed, next to Kradle.

"I was . . . an employee at In Focus back in 2015," the man said. His eyes were searching the patchy carpet, his mind sifting through what he could and couldn't say. "I worked on the front desk during the day. That was my regular job. But I was also interning on *The Frances Falkner Show* two days a week. I ended up giving up the internship. It wasn't paid, and my interest in television—"

"You're babbling," Celine said.

"Okay, okay, sorry. Point is, I worked on the show, and I worked on the desk. The episode your wife attended, Mr. Kradle—I was there when they filmed that."

"*My Psycho Father Doesn't Know I'm Gay?*" Kradle said.

"Right." The man nodded. "We had guests bring a loved one on the show and come out to them. I was in charge of a lot of the arrangements for the family members. Booking flights, organizing hotel rooms, catering, that kind of thing."

The man fidgeted with the cuff of his shirt, glancing now and then at Kradle.

"The episode that aired on TV had four sets of guests," the man said. "But there were actually five."

"I knew it," Celine gasped.

"We were well ahead on filming the program," the man said. "Three or four months. So when what happened *happened*, we deleted the footage of the extra guests and your wife's comment. A shortened version of the episode went to air. And after that—"

"You're getting ahead of yourself," Kradle said. "What happened on the show? Who was the guest?"

The man rubbed his hands together as if they were cold.

"The guy's name was Mullins," he said. "Gary Mullins. Military guy. His son Brady wrote to the show after we put a call-out online. He said he was gay, and his dad didn't know, and the guy was going to blow his stack big time when he found out. It was exactly the type of letter we were looking for. Most of the time we wanted to set up the show with one guest who was probably going to react well to the secret—whatever it was—and one guest who we could guarantee was going to react badly, and a couple who could go either way. We had a pregnancy-reveal show once where all the reactions were cute and the ratings tanked. We needed at least one explosion."

"So how did Gary react to the son's news?" Celine asked.

"On camera, he was bad," the man said. "I don't mean, like, he blew his stack, as his son predicted he would. As we hoped he would. I mean he was bad for TV. He . . . he just went icy. Kind of weird. He froze, I think. I've seen it before. People get this fake, hard kind of smile. We call it the lizard smile."

"The lizard smile?"

"Yeah. They smile and they don't say much."

"You do that." Kradle turned to Celine. "When you're cornered."

"It's like a defense mechanism," she agreed.

"It was a disappointing segment," the man continued. "But that's reality TV for you. The director told Frances to cut it short and move on."

"So Christine asked the guy a question at the end of the show?" Kradle said. "When people from the audience stand up and take the mic?"

"She made a comment about Mullins."

"What did she say?" Celine asked.

"I can't even remember. I . . . I have a USB with the full episode on it with me. She just said something about fathers and sons, or sons needing love or something."

"So what the hell makes you think this Gary Mullins guy murdered my family? Because this all seems pretty thin to me," Kradle said. Celine looked over. Kradle's neck was taut, his jaw muscles flexing. "If there's nothing else—"

"Just hold on," the man said. "I'm getting there. A week after we finished taping the show, Gary Mullins called the front desk. He said he wanted to know the name of the woman with the long brown and gray hair and tattoos, who made the comment at the end of the show. He sounded mad. Not screaming mad, but, like, cold. I said I couldn't tell him. And I got this . . . this feeling."

Celine watched Kradle. His eyes were locked on the man sitting on the bed before him.

"What kind of feeling?" Kradle asked.

"As if it wasn't over."

Kradle nodded.

"Then a couple of days later, he calls again," the man said. "Only this time he's pretending it isn't him. He's pretending to be someone from ticketing. He wants the address of one of the guests, because he says she's requested a refund and he doesn't know where to send it to. He knew her name by then. Christine Kradle."

"And you knew the caller was Gary Mullins?" Celine asked.

"I knew." The man nodded. "And I knew all that stuff about the ticket refund was bullshit. I managed refunds and bookings at the front desk."

"So what did you do?" Celine asked.

"Well, I was so creeped out that I called and checked on the son, Brady. I had all his details from having organized his appearance on the show. He said he hadn't seen his father since the taping. His boyfriend had picked him up and they'd flown back to San Francisco. They hadn't spoken at all. I kind of got the feeling Brady was really just in it for the ten thousand bucks we paid him to appear."

"Did you tell the show's producers?" Kradle asked. "About the phone calls?"

"Sure did," the man said. "They blew it off. It wasn't even the weirdest thing a guest had ever done after the show. We had this one woman who came on the show to reveal to her husband that she was dating his brother, and—"

"Stay focused. What happened after the murders?" Kradle snapped.

The man shifted uncomfortably. "I went right back to the producers. I told them we needed to go to the police about this. That it might be a . . . a lead. Someone calls trying to hunt the lady down, and then she's killed? I mean, come on!"

"Yeah," Kradle said. The malice in his voice was thickening. "Come on."

"They told me to shut my mouth about it," the man said. "They cut the segment and your wife's comment. I was the only person in the studio that seemed to think it was a big deal. People were telling me I was trying to cook the Kradle Family murders up as a *Jenny Jones* thing."

"A *Jenny Jones* thing?" Celine asked.

"*The Jenny Jones Show* was a *Frances Falkner Show* predecessor back in the nineties," the man said. "A couple of weeks after a taping, one of the guests blew his friend's brains out with a shotgun in the doorway of his home for embarrassing him on the show. They canceled the show and the guy's family sued for twenty-nine million dollars."

"And your producers didn't want *The Frances Falkner Show* ending up the same way," Kradle said.

"They said I was being crazy. But, yeah"—the man shrugged—"I knew that was why they were doing it. A lawsuit like that would shut down the show and tie everyone up in court for five years."

"So that was it? You just dropped it?" Celine asked.

"No," the man said. "I went ahead and called the detective on the case on my lunch hour when the place was quiet. When he finally called me back, he told me they already had a suspect locked in for the murders and it wasn't our guy."

Kradle's lip was twitching hard. He stood so fast the man in the striped shirt cowered back from him.

"Give me the USB." Kradle put a palm out. The man grabbed a backpack that was sitting at the head of the bed and extracted a thumb drive from it. Kradle took the drive, walked stiffly to the door of the motel room, and was out of it and halfway across the parking lot before Celine could catch up to him.

"Hey." She grabbed his shoulder. They stopped beside a row of bike racks under a bright street lamp. "Let's stay calm. We're making progress. We have a lead now. Let's go back to my place. We'll call the police and tell them what we know, go from there."

"Good plan." Kradle nodded. His fury was slowly dying, his face softening. "Give me the car keys. I need to drive. I can't sit around doing nothing any longer. I'm too itchy."

Celine handed him the car keys. He took them, grabbed her wrist, and snapped a handcuff to it, yanked the other cuff to the bike rack and clicked it closed.

"What? No!" Celine grabbed at Kradle as he pulled away. "You mother-fucker!"

"Little trick someone taught me recently," Kradle said. "I'm sorry, Celine. I'm really, really sorry." He turned and threw the handcuff key with all his might toward the hotel, then jogged away, across the highway to the car parked at the Best Western. Celine roared after him, but he didn't look back.

CHAPTER 39

Both the cat and the dog were behind the door when Kradle entered the house. He ignored them, heading for the laptop on the dining room table. He opened it, flipped the machine, and looked for the USB port. There was none. Helplessly, he swiped a finger over the mousepad and the screen came to life, an empty box requesting a password.

Kradle groaned, then spied the television and went there. While he fiddled around at the back of the machine, the dog and cat assembled on the rug, watchful, curious. Kradle found a place for the drive and stood between the animals, the remote in his hand. All three of them watched as the video file opened and began to play.

Frances Falkner in her turquoise pants suit. The gawdy set with the plush pink armchairs and low-hanging spot lamps, the rock music. Kradle scrolled through the video, watched people hug, cry, writhe in the chairs. He stopped the video when a man he didn't recognize walked onto the screen: a tall, stubbled young man with an immaculate jet-black quiff. He sat in the pink chair and grinned at the crowd, tugging at the chest of a thick black knitted sweater.

"Audience, meet our next guest." The video cut back to Frances, who was wandering the aisles of the audience casually. "Brady says his dad, Gary, is an ex-Marine who doesn't approve of his career in graphic design or his ownership of a cavoodle, Sparkles. But Gary's really going to lose it when he learns his son has been keeping a deep dark secret from him since he was thirteen years old. Welcome to the show, Brady!"

The audience cheered. Brady waved and grinned.

"Thanks, Frances! I've always wanted to be on your show! I'm a huge fan!"

"Oh, stop it, you." Frances flapped a hand at the stage. "First off, tell me what the heck a cavoodle is. Sounds like a type of pasta."

The audience giggled. A picture of the Cavalier King Charles spaniel cross miniature poodle flashed on the screen above the stage, and the audience cooed as one. Brady explained the curly brown puppy's heritage.

"She's my little baby." Brady smiled.

"And your dad doesn't like her?" Frances gave a quizzical frown. "How could you not like her? Look at her! She's a peach! That ain't right!"

"*That ain't right!*" the audience cheered.

"I know, I know. He says she's a glorified cat."

"But there's a lot more about you that doesn't rub with your father's way of life, isn't there, Brady?" Frances said.

"He doesn't know . . . ," Brady paused for effect, looking at the audience with a coy grin. "I've been dating guys since I was about thirteen years old."

The audience erupted. Kradle fast-forwarded. Brady and Frances jittered and jostled as they presumably discussed Brady's childhood, his father's prejudices. Kradle hit play as Frances swept an arm toward the side of the stage.

". . . bring him out!"

A taller, thicker version of Brady walked stiffly onto the stage. Gary Mullins was suntanned and heavy-jawed, with the kind of ropy forearms and wide knuckles reserved for men who had never hired another man to fix or clean or kill or carry anything for them in their entire lives. He took a seat next to Brady and gave the boy a kind of smile that was laden with hidden meaning. With dark, uncertain meaning.

Kradle had to remind himself to breathe.

"Welcome to the show, Gary." Frances beamed.

"Thank you."

"Or, should I say, Sergeant Major Mullins?"

"Gary is fine."

"Your son Brady invited you to the show a couple of weeks ago, didn't he? He told you the studio put a call out for veterans and their children to come on the show to celebrate Memorial Day."

"Right." Gary nodded. Kradle watched the older, bigger Mullins gripping his knees, his eyes locked on his son, the younger man twitching and shifting in his seat, leaning as far away from his father as the seat would allow. Frances left space for Gary to elaborate on his journey toward coming on the show, on the delicious misapprehension he had about the show's purpose and subject. He did not. A couple of awkward beats passed in which Kradle could hear individual voices in the crowd calling out taunts or encouragements, he couldn't tell.

"So, uh"—Frances shuffled her question cards—"so, why don't you tell us about your son, Gary?"

"He's a good kid." Gary gave an exaggerated nod. His head was turned toward his son, eyes locked on his face, which was turned toward the audience. "Yep. Never had a problem with him."

The audience tittered, gave a rumble of anticipation.

"Why don't you look up here, Gary?" Frances said.

"Oh, sorry."

"Over here."

"Right. I got you."

"Is there anything your son could ever do that would make you—"

Kradle hit the fast-forward button. His stomach was roiling with vicarious terror and humiliation. Brady did his big reveal and his father's smile stiffened even further, so that Kradle could see the molars at the corners of his mouth and the veins in his temples. Then the big man hunched forward in his chair, his elbows on his knees, his face turned toward his son, and the grimace was hidden from the camera, which Kradle knew was exactly what the show's directors didn't want. They wanted to see and smell and taste the humiliation. Before he knew it, the segment was over. Kradle kept rolling through the tape until he got to the audience questions at the end and, his skin tingling with excitement, he watched his murdered wife rise from her chair as Frances approached her with the microphone.

"Frances, oh." Christine clasped her hands around the mic as soon as the host was within reach, her hands around Frances's hands, the two of them gripping the device like it was a torch. "I'm just so in love with you and this show. I've been a diehard Frances Falkner fan forever."

"Thank you, thank you." Frances winced. "Do you have a question for our guests?"

"Look." Christine turned to the stage. "I just want to say, you guys all need to get back to the love. It's all about love, people. These are your kids. I'm a parent to a beautiful, beautiful boy, and I've always tried to raise him to believe in—"

Kradle felt his mouth twist. He gripped the remote in his fist.

"—people being who they are. I'm just so proud of him."

The audience cheered. The camera panned across the guests, resting on Brady and Gary Mullins at the very edge of the stage. Brady was staring at his fingernails. Gary was expressionless, rigid. Kradle thought Christine's time with the mic must be over, and felt a chill rush through him as the camera turned back to her.

"I happen to be a medium," Christine continued.

"A medium?" Frances was trying to extract her hands from Christine's. "Really?"

"Yes, and I'm feeling an incredible pull toward you, on the end of the row. Mr. Mullins."

The camera cut to Mullins and his son. The father's mouth was a toothy grimace.

"There are dark energies clustered around you." The camera cut to Christine as she waved an illustrative hand. "Spirits that have passed and have been disturbed from their slumber, brought back to wakefulness, by your refusal to accept your son."

"Jesus, Christine," Kradle breathed.

"Is your mother still with us, Mr. Mullins?" Christine asked.

"I think we better move on," Frances said. The crowd was beginning to jeer again, sensing Christine's intent to hog the mic for as long as Frances would allow it. As the camera panned away, following Frances as she left Christine's side, Kradle saw his murdered wife yell out toward the stage.

"She wants you to love him!" Christine called.

Kradle ran through the rest of the tape but saw nothing he wanted to examine further. He stepped around the television and extracted the USB, then pulled his phone out of his pocket and searched for Brady Mullins, San Francisco.

With his heart pumping, throbbing in his fingers, he tapped open a stylish website advertising "corporate asset design," whatever the hell that was. He scrolled until he found a phone number, then dialed.

"He—hello?"

"Brady Mullins?"

"Jesus, who is this? Wha—what time is it?"

"Is this Brady Mullins?" Kradle insisted.

"Yes, yes, yes, wha—"

"My name is . . . Terry Sellers. I'm a paramedic."

Kradle heard blankets rustling. A muffled voice in the background of the line.

"What's going on?" Brady asked.

"Your father has just been in a car accident."

"Oh . . . whoa. Whoa. Where? Is . . . Is he okay?"

"He's okay," Kradle said. "He's going to be fine. But he's in and out of consciousness. Took a bit of a knock to the head. He's saying he has some . . . some medication at home that he needs. Do you know anything about that?"

"Um." Brady heaved a sigh. "Oh, god. We, uh. To be honest with you, we don't really talk."

"Okay." Kradle squeezed his eyes shut.

"I mean, he had high blood pressure. Back when . . . He's always had high blood pressure."

"We need to know exactly what medications he's on," Kradle said. "Could you give us his address? We'll send someone out to his home to see what's there."

"Isn't his address in his wallet?" Brady asked.

Kradle's stomach sank. He took the phone away from his ear, hovered his thumb over the red button to end the call.

"The wallet is . . . uh, it's not here. I'm not seeing it. It's probably back at the crash site."

"Seventeen Cloudrock Court, MacDonald Ranch," Brady said.

Kradle's heart swelled in his chest.

"Just outside Vegas . . . ," Kradle said.

"Yeah," Brady said. "Let me get a pen. Which hosp—"

Kradle hung up. He went to the front door and opened it. The dog and cat watched him go.

Kradle paused before he swung the door closed. He looked at the dog, at its huge, earnest eyes, and when he spoke he heard that his voice had lost all warmth and humanity, all soul. It was almost robotic.

It was the voice of a man with only one purpose.

"I won't be back," he told the dog, and shut the door.

CHAPTER 40

Celine watched the black Lexus pull into the lot, driving diagonally across the empty parking spaces toward her at a leisurely pace. When Keeps finally pulled to a stop, the headlights of the car were pointedly directly at Celine, illuminating her like a hog with its hoof snared in a trap. He had a delicious smile on his lips as he popped open the door, rounded the hood, and sat on it, folding his arms.

"Okay, okay," Celine said. "Drink it in."

Keeps looked at the motel nearby, cold and quiet, the red neon sign painting the sidewalk pink. The door to number three was closed. Celine had considered calling out to the man she and Kradle had met in the room after Kradle chained her to the bike rack, but sheer embarrassment had caused her to stand in front of her cuffed wrist and wave with her other hand as he too fled the scene. Calling the police was out of the question. The last thing Celine wanted to do was answer queries from authorities about how she had found herself attached by a bloody handcuff to a bike rack in the parking lot of a dingy hotel at one o'clock in the morning. She knew what an incident like that meant. It meant police reports. Interviews. Waiting rooms. A glance at her personal records. A raised eyebrow. Whispers.

Keeps lit a cigarette and blew the smoke over his shoulder, looking her up and down.

"You arrived fast," Celine said.

"I happened to be nearby."

"I'd ask how a man who had nothing to his name a couple of days ago is now driving a Lexus," Celine said. "But you're the guy who can turn a twenty-dollar waffle maker into five hundred bucks, so . . ."

Keeps didn't answer. Didn't smile.

"He threw the key that way." Celine pointed at the motel. "I heard it bounce."

"I didn't come here to let you out." Keeps smirked.

"What?"

"I came here to see you chained up. Not every day you get to see that. Pronghorn guard locked down like an inmate, stuck in one place, watching the world tick by. This is a real hoot."

Celine felt her mouth fall open. Every limb seemed to be growing numb, one after the other, so that she felt she wanted to slip awkwardly to the ground.

"I was always going to scam you, Celine," Keeps said.

"*What?*"

"Come on." Keeps lifted his hands. "It's what I do. I *told* you that's what I do. I *showed* you it's what I do!"

Celine bent in two and stared at the concrete at her feet.

"I am going to *murder* you," she growled.

"I don't know why you're so angry. This is you. This is all you." Keeps gestured to her with his cigarette. "You let me into your house. You let me into your bed. You opened your world to me. We both know you were trying to test the limits, see if your radar was working. Whether you knew good from bad. Well, you were wrong about me, Celine. I had it in for you from the very beginning. So, now you have what you wanted. You know at least some of your instincts aren't good."

"You sent that payment from my account," Celine said.

"Actually, no." Keeps shook his head. "No. That's stupid. That's the short game. I didn't have to go to your house to access your bank account. Come on. And why the hell would I send the money to Kuala Lumpur? You ever *been* to Kuala Lumpur?"

"No."

"Don't. Stay home. Save yourself the trouble."

"You wanted me for the long game," Celine concluded.

"The long game." Keeps nodded. "The big payday. I was going to make you love me. I was going to see how long it would take for you to give me the house, the car, the jewelry, the bank account. Didn't take you long to give me your body. I figured by the end of the month I could ha—"

He had stood and wandered within striking distance. Celine lunged, got the edge of his sleeve and nothing else.

"Shhh, shhh," Keeps said. "You're making a scene."

Celine gave a hard smile that cracked into a vicious laugh.

"What's so funny?"

"I'm just thinking," she said. "About the next time you wind up in Prong-horn. Having John Kradle on my row was just training. I'm going to have myself put on whatever cell block you're assigned to and I'm going to make your life a nightmare. You will *beg* to be put in the hole, you slimy son of a bitch."

"Not this time." Keeps tapped his temple. "I told you. It's the big payday. And when you get one of those you move on, somewhere far, far away, where nobody knows your tricks yet."

Celine exhaled hard. "Kradle."

"Yup. The million-dollar man," Keeps said. "You brought him to my at-tention."

"I won't tell you where he's going," Celine said. "Not in a lifetime."

"I don't need you to," Keeps said, and Celine realized why he had come for her so fast after she sent the message asking for help. Because he had been nearby, just like he said, following the tracker he'd probably placed on her phone, probably the first time she brought him into her house. The bug he'd told her he used to scam old people, to decipher key parts of their lives he could use to convince them he was trustworthy.

"I told you I was a bad man, Celine," Keeps said.

"Yeah, well." Celine gave a miserable sigh. "I guess I should have trusted myself. At least that time, anyway."

He reached for her, and she took advantage of the slip, grabbed his wrist and yanked him toward her. But with her other wrist chained, there wasn't much she could do. Keeps laughed and pushed her off. He was gone into the night before she could get her phone out of her pocket.

He could see Gary Mullins. For five years, John Kradle had lay on his bunk in his cell at Pronghorn and stared at the scratches in the paintwork on the ceiling and imagined a faceless figure murdering his family. But now that figure had a shape. He had a name. Kradle gripped the steering wheel and watched the white lines passing on the road in front of him while, in his mind, Gary Mullins walked down the side of the house in Mesquite where he and his son had lived.

Kradle watched him round the corner of the yard, stepping over the bike

Mason always dumped on its side at the end of the porch, sliding open the unlocked glass door to the living room. He saw Gary stop as he heard Christine and Audrey arguing in the kitchen. Audrey pouring wine and admonishing Christine for trying to make her fourth phone call to Kradle about the bubble-machine fiasco. Audrey telling her sister she would have to suck it up, stop being a spoiled brat, accept the fact that she had fucked off on her family and they hadn't thrown a parade when she returned like she'd expected. Kradle saw Gary Mullins walking in from the living room with the rifle raised. Cutting the two women down where they stood. He saw Mullins lift his head as Mason called out from the upstairs bathroom, wanting to know what the noise was, the water still running. Mullins standing there, trying to decide if he was going to leave a witness or not.

Kradle saw his son murdered where he stood in the shower, the glass door pulled open, the blast, the shattered tiles. Kradle didn't know if he'd uttered a single word. Sometimes, in his musings, Mason did cry out. Sometimes it was all so fast there was only the sound of the gunshot. He saw Mullins pouring gasoline in a straight line from the garage, where he found it, to the glass back doors. The fire licking the walls. Kradle saw a stronger, healthier, more fresh-faced version of himself opening the front door and stopping dead at the sight of the strip of fire working its way up the living room walls, already billowing against the ceiling in the kitchen. He saw his body snap out of shock and into action as he heard a groan from upstairs. Running past the flames, feeling their mighty heat against his cheek as he swung around the banister, finding Mason half in, half out of the shower. He saw himself gathering his dying son up in his arms.

The rage had been something Kradle kept tightly leashed at Pronghorn. Whenever he felt it burbling up his throat or pulsing behind his eyeballs he'd always talked it down, strapped it in tight, a twisting and groaning and snarling thing that was always waiting for an opportunity to burst free. Waiting for a weak moment. The right provocation. Eventually, the rage had exhausted itself and fallen asleep. As he'd walked through the desert, run through the forest, then walked the streets as an escaped man, the rage had started to stir. It had begun to break its binds in the motel room when, for the first time, he heard the name of the man who had ruined his life.

And now the rage was free.

It was wielding Kradle's body like a precise weapon, every muscle zinging with tension, every movement sharp, silent, fast.

The phone on the seat next to him buzzed. He looked over and saw Celine's name on the screen. Ignored it.

His intention had been to blast through any roadblock that he encountered on the way out of Vegas city proper, but all he found were abandoned wooden barriers standing like restful horses by the side of the road, flashing orange lamps making geometric shadows on the sand. It occurred to him for the first time that he hadn't seen any roadblocks on the way from the motel back to Celine's house. They had all fallen, disappeared into nothing.

The unexpected ease with which he headed toward his fate continued. Christine would have called it that. Fate. Destiny. He drove through empty streets off the highway, past a gas station with a big blue Bud Light bottle resting on the awning above the pumps. A police cruiser sitting behind a billboard advertising home insurance took no notice of him. It was as if he had frozen time. He turned into a sprawling estate of manicured houses. Wide lawns without fences, plastic Christmas reindeer grazing over rock gardens full of cactuses. Before sunrise, Christmas morning—a time that had been filled with joyful anticipation back in the days when Kradle had a child and the boy was small and excitable. The memories seemed too distant, and yet at the same time perfectly reachable. He could hear socks on the stairs. Whispers, giggles. Time ticking down. Kradle's jaw was grinding as he turned onto Cloudrock Court and stopped the car outside number seventeen.

The house was unremarkable. A modern Spanish-style villa identical to two others Kradle had noticed in the street. Beyond the property, a shallow valley stretched toward a ridge of rocky hills. Kradle supposed that Gary Mullins could probably sit on the back porch at sunset with a Coors and watch coyotes emerging from their dens to hunt jackrabbits.

He crossed the driveway, past the sensible Buick with the yellow-and-red VETERAN bumper sticker, and found the side gate of the house unlocked, bags of potting mix stacked by a rack of garden tools. He was walking in Gary Mullins's footsteps now. The killer trembling with dark anticipation, sliding open the unlocked glass door, walking into the house. His senses were alive, sucking in the smell of hand soap in a dispenser shaped like a chicken on the edge of the spotless sink. The big kitchen windows looked out over the porch, the desert beyond, framed by curtains with bright yellow lemons on them. Kradle could see the sharp outlines of a framed cross-stitch hanging on the wall of the living room. BLESS THIS MESS. He turned and walked past a portrait of Gary Mullins in uniform, turned three-quarters to the camera, a classic textured gray backdrop.

Kradle pushed open the bedroom door. One lump in the bed, turned away from him, buzz-cut gray hair on a white pillow. A full glass of water on the nightstand. On the other nightstand, an empty glass. Kradle walked to the head of the bed and lifted his pistol, nudged Gary Mullins in the back of the skull with it.

The man rolled over fast and looked up at him in the dark.

"Get up," Kradle said.

CHAPTER 41

"Settle a bet for me," the officer said. The handcuff key looked comically small in his huge fingers as he took Celine's wrist in his hand. He jerked his head toward a troop of officers standing around a nearby cruiser, drinking coffee from the local Dunkies. "You that Pronghorn guard who was on TV?"

"No," Celine said.

"You sure look like—"

"Can we just do this, please?"

The car smelled like every police cruiser Celine had ever been in. Of fried food and sweat. She slumped against the greasy window while the officers said long goodbyes to the others, and then watched the parking lot slide out of view, the words catching in her chest as she spoke them.

"Please take me to your captain," she said.

"Why?" the officer riding shotgun asked.

"Because I have to make a report," Celine said. "About a possible murder that's about to happen. That may already have happened."

"*How* possible is the murder?" The driver wiped his nose on the back of his hand. "Because we're pretty overrun as it is, lady."

"Just take me there, please," Celine groaned.

"I'm afraid we can't. We got instructions to drop you off on the corner of Beatie and Ellett," the cop said. "Probably be somebody there who can take your report."

"Huh?"

"The call was from on high," the driver said. "That's all I know."

Celine was too exhausted, too furious, to play further guessing games with the officers. She waited, and, in time, the cruiser pulled up at an intersection outside a game fishing supply store. Celine walked to the silver Mercedes that was pointed out to her and opened the passenger-side door.

"Whoooooa!" she moaned as she slid into the passenger seat.

"Whoa what?" Trinity asked.

"I thought you were dead!" Celine's voice was higher, more hysterical, than she intended. "That's what!"

"Oh, please." Trinity rolled her eyes. "It'll take more than a gunshot to the neck to kill me. My people are indestructible. After the nuclear apocalypse it'll be cockroaches and a bunch of Parkers who crawl out of the rubble."

Celine sat staring at the other woman as she pulled the car onto the road and drove. Her entire neck and left shoulder were strapped tightly in gauze that was speckled in parts with blood. She had two black eyes, exposed stitches in her chin, and dried blood in the hair that was visible under her black cap.

"You got shot in the neck in the forest!" Celine screeched. "What the hell are you doing here?"

"Please adjust your volume," Trinity said. "You're at a nine. I need you at a two. And it was shrapnel. The bullet must have hit a tree and shattered, and I got a piece of it in my neck. What's more bothersome is the rock I must have smashed into when my head hit the ground. Raging headache. Bad, bad. So there it is! I'm disgruntled but alive. Get over it. I am."

Celine sat back in her seat.

"And, alas, while I'm still kicking in bodily form, my term as director of the Pronghorn breakout is officially over," Trinity continued. "As soon as someone prescribes you Vicodin, you become operationally ineffective, apparently, whether you actually take the drug or not. It's an inconvenience we will have to overcome, and quickly, before word of my usurping spreads. At the moment I'm hoping we can still get in to see Kerry Monahan at the Mesa View Regional Hospital."

"Who?"

"The girl you saved." Trinity glanced over. "The little red-haired redneck who killed your friend Brassen."

"I can't get into that right now," Celine said. "I've got to stop Kradle."

"Stop him from doing what?"

"From killing the man who killed his family," Celine said. "We know the guy's name. Or, at least, we have a very good suspect. Kradle is on his way to—"

"Save it." Trinity held up a hand.

"No, I can't *save it*," Celine yelled. "It would take you five minutes to get someone out to this guy's address to watch for Kradle. It's a human life we're talking about here."

"Take my phone," Trinity said. She tapped the enclosed compartment in the center console between them. "Text whatever information you have to a number saved as GS in the contacts list."

"Who's GS?" Celine asked.

"Just send the text." Trinity waved, bored. "I guarantee you, the Kradle thing will be met with the swiftest possible response."

Celine grabbed the phone and typed out a text about Gary Mullins, John Kradle, and the revenge mission she believed he was on. She didn't know where Mullins lived, how Kradle planned to get to him, or whether she was already too late to save the killer's life. When it was done she gripped her seatbelt and watched the horizon beginning to glow with approaching dawn.

"Why me?" Celine asked.

"Why you?"

"Yeah," Celine said. "You wake up in hospital, discharge yourself, find out you've lost your job, decide you're going to keep going after Schmitz anyway—"

"You don't decide a thing like that, Osbourne." Trinity smiled to herself. "It's either in you or it isn't."

"Your remarkable self-sacrifice and humility aside"—Celine rolled her eyes—"the next move is to come and find me, of all people?"

"I like you, Osbourne," Trinity said. "Is that what you want me to say? It isn't true. But I'll say it if it means you'll be quiet."

"How did you know I was there?"

"I happened to be trying to recruit the chief of police to help me continue my crusade to find Schmitz," Trinity said, "when I heard a very interesting report on his radio. A short-ass white woman was handcuffed to a bike rack outside a crappy hotel on the outskirts of Vegas. A bystander witnessed an African American man pull up in a black Lexus, and, while the bystander thought the guy was there to rescue her, he seemed to taunt her and leave her there."

Celine waited, feeling tired.

"Seemed like a familiar scenario to me." Trinity smiled. "I thought—could it possibly be?"

"You knew Keeps was bad," Celine said. "You tried to warn me."

"You thought you were dealing with a cute little conman," Trinity said. "But that guy's got missing people all around him. Ladies with deep pockets who went out on yachts and never came back."

"He's not . . . ," Celine said. "He's not a killer . . . ?"

"Like I said. Nothing confirmed. There are just unanswered questions. Blank spaces." Trinity shrugged. "That's what you get with confidence men. Part of the picture. Never all of it."

Celine looked at her hands sitting folded in her lap.

"What are we going to do to Kerry Monahan that hasn't been done to her already?" Celine asked. "You threatened to shoot the girl in the hand, Trinity, and she gave up nothing."

"She'll talk for us," Trinity said. "Don't worry."

"Why?"

"Because we're going to pull a con." Trinity smiled, exposing a chipped front tooth. "Of course."

CHAPTER 42

Mistakes happened in war, Silvia reminded herself. Battles were full of failures, overestimations, accidents. It was human nature, especially in the face of a prolonged engagement—that exhaustion caused by nervousness and eagerness for triumph made soldiers, even highly trained soldiers, stumble. She leaned on the counter of the snow cone food truck and watched the first tendrils of Christmas morning light creeping along the windows of the empty Planet Hollywood hotel across the ice rink.

For a few hours, the radio at her elbow by the syrup pumps had been playing reports of the discovery of the bodies of the three police officers they had murdered at the last roadblock into Vegas. The cleanup after the shooting had been a real rush job. There hadn't been time to bury the bodies. The earth was too hard, too dry. She and Clara and Willis and Burke had driven the bodies and the two cruisers out onto the plains, found a crevice, and rolled the cars in. But the second cruiser had hit a rock shelf and wedged itself half in, half out of the hole, the rear bumper visible for miles around. Burke had taken it all pretty well. He was focused on the plan, on the steps ahead, on getting back on track. But Silvia felt terrible. It had been her slip-up with the rope tattoo that had caused the whole detour. She'd almost sunk what would be the most glorious event in the struggle of the Camp and the Aryan nation it served.

It had been a fluke, just getting on the team in the first place. She learned, after Burke recruited her, that he'd already had a sniper lined up for Day One of the plan, an ex-military guy from Hawaii who had written to Burke in prison. When he'd backed out, Silvia was called in by her team leader at the Camp to talk in confidence about a mission to further the cause of the brotherhood. Silvia had been teaching sharp-shooting and hunting skills at the Camp to new recruits for only three months. Her leader wanted to know if she could hit a moving target at more than eight hundred yards. Whether she'd be willing to kill for their cause. Silvia knew there were better shooters than her, even in the intake she had been instructing at the time. But Burke was looking for someone who could live up to their word. Who could keep a secret. Who could follow orders. Someone who would show eagerness. Her team leader suggested to Silvia that some of her more visible white power tattoos might have to go if she was going to be a part of the plan. She'd made a booking and had her first laser treatment for the removal of the lightning bolt tattoo from her shoulder that afternoon.

She'd had eight tattoos removed in total. She figured the rope tattoo was far enough up her forearm, and obscure enough, that she could keep it.

"Idiot," she whispered aloud. The sound of her voice stirred Reiter from a sickly slumber on the food truck floor. The prisoner lay out of view of the serving window with his arms twisted behind his back, secured with cable ties, and his knees and ankles duct-taped together. The duct tape across his mouth was folded in the middle where he had been sucking it between his lips, probably trying to dampen the glue. The fentanyl in his system would make him drool like crazy, Silvia had heard. She wrinkled her nose at the smell of him, but counseled herself that the alternative was worse. She and Willis had been in charge of toileting the captive from the moment he was picked up at Pronghorn, through the journey to the safehouse, from the safehouse to Vegas. Now that they were at their destination, there was no need to bother anymore. Reiter was never going to leave the truck. He would die here, inside the tin walls, in a spectacular fireball created by the gas tanks that lined the cabin around him.

Silvia leaned on the counter again and looked at the ice rink. The first morning skaters were arriving, some of them wearing what looked like brand-new skates probably freshly opened that morning from under Christmas trees. People were assembling around the ice, smiling, rosy-cheeked. Soon the stage would fill with pretty carollers from the Saint Agnes Catholic Girls' School. Those little girls would just be opening their mouths to sing the first chorus of something merry and beautiful, Silvia dreamed, when Burke burst out of the truck and mowed them down. While his primary target was the girls, the painfully adorable angels in their fluffy costumes strung with silver bells, he was going to rake the panicked crowd with as many bullets as he could before heading back toward the truck. The smoke from the explosion would mask him slipping into the car that Clara and Willis would pull up nearby when the shooting began. The police would find Reiter's charred remains in the driver's seat of the truck and, if all went to plan, the rest of the world was going to wake to find their Christmas morning cartoons interrupted with a special news bulletin containing photographs of twelve murdered white babies and a Black man's mugshot right next to them.

And then, Silvia thought, *the war. The beautiful war.*

Burke the commander of the new world. Silvia in his inner circle.

Burke opened the back doors of the truck and slipped in. Silvia backed away from the counter, straightened her spine, awaiting commands.

"It's time to get him dressed," Burke said.

Silvia nodded. She pulled the serving window of the truck closed and went to a backpack sitting behind the driver's seat. She pulled a black ski mask and a pair of black tinted tactical goggles out. As Burke pulled on his own black ski mask, rolling it into a beanie on top of his head, Silvia pulled her mask onto a struggling, groaning Anthony Reiter.

"Urgh," she groaned. "His head's sweaty."

"I saw some of the little girls arriving," Burke said as he worked. "White satin dresses. I thought they might wear red, like in last year's calendar."

"It's going to be so beautiful," Silvia said. "All of it."

"As long as there are no more fuck-ups." Burke shot her a warning glance.

"There won't be."

They crouched together in the small gap between the gas bottles and the stainless-steel cupboards that lined the food truck's interior, surveying Reiter's get-up, his black T-shirt, jeans, boots. An exact match to what Burke was wearing.

Silvia counted silently to three, then said it.

"Burke," Silvia said. "When history looks back on this moment, when it's finally revealed after the war that it was you and me here, preparing like this, I . . ."

The words came in a flurry, then abruptly ran out. Burke was watching her, his eyes hard and his lips taut.

"I just hope they understand how honored I feel," she said.

Burke rose to his feet, flipped the serving window of the truck open again. "Just focus," he said. "Don't get distracted by grand dreams."

"Of course. I won't. I won't."

"You know what you're doing?"

"Yes. Yes."

"Let me hear it."

"When you start shooting, I let him loose," Silvia said. "I get him into the driver's seat, and then I get clear. I wait until you come back toward the truck and give me the signal, then I set off the bomb so you can escape."

"Good," Burke said. "Just memorize that. Go over it again and again. We can't have any more problems."

She nodded.

"I'm going to go take another lap." He pulled up the hood of his sweatshirt and slipped out the doors, slamming them behind him.

Silvia held her head.

"Idiot," she scolded herself.

The bump came as Silvia was securing the serving window open again. Burke was walking around the opposite side of the rink, near the hotel. She was watching him, and a jolt shuddered through the truck that was so hard it almost knocked her off her feet. She stumbled over Reiter, went to the back door of the truck and tried to open it. It was stuck. In bewilderment, she tried again, and the door smacked open against the front bumper of another food truck.

Silvia squeezed out and jumped down from the truck, slamming the door behind her and marching to the driver's-side door of the truck that had rammed her tailgate. The driver was a huge Black man in a blazing yellow T-shirt that matched the truck. On his chest, a little smiley-face button gave his name as Rick.

"What the *actual fuck*, dude?" Silvia mashed her palm on the window.

"Sorry, honey!" The driver wound down the window. "We've all got to move up. They're trying to make room for a churro truck down the back there."

"You hit my truck!"

"Yeah, sorry! Sorry!" He held his hands up, palms out. "It's not bad. Looks like I dented your numberplate. Let me just get set up here and I'll pull it off and pop the dent out."

"I don't want you to do that."

"It's no big deal. It'll pop right out, baby."

"I said I don't want you to do that!" Silvia snarled. Rick the driver reeled in his seat. "Open your big flappy fucking ears!"

"Open my *what*?"

"You heard me, *boy*," Silvia said. "Open your ears. I'm not moving my truck. I booked this spot three months ago. And if you touch my number-plate I'll call the fucking cops on your ass."

Silvia left Rick with his mouth hanging open and headed back to her truck. She opened the back door as hard as she could, smashing the edge into his bumper, and then slammed it shut behind her.

CHAPTER 43

Kradle grabbed Gary Mullins by the front of his nightshirt and dragged him out of bed, kicking him to the ground. The shockwave rippling up through his foot, ankle, knee, hip, from the kick to the man's side made his heart warm. He stood on Mullins's neck, pinning his face to the rug, and pressed the barrel of the pistol to the back of his ear.

"Where's the woman?"

"Ma-Marie, Marie, Marie's," Mullins babbled. "Marie's in Denver w-with her sister."

"Get up," Kradle said again. He didn't give the man a chance to comply. He yanked him up, threw him into the side of the door, bounced him into the hall. While every breath was hot and heavy and filled with the sweet, dark pleasure of revenge, something else was growing in Kradle as he shoved the man through his dimly lit house toward the porch doors. It was disquiet. A kind of empty rattling, the sense of something amiss, a screw loosened or a fixture pulled from its housing. Because, while his fantasy was playing out exactly as it had ten thousand times in his mind since his family died, something about what was happening felt hollow. His punches weren't landing hard enough. Mullins's cries of terror and pain weren't loud enough. Mullins wasn't fighting back. Kradle pushed him out onto the porch. The older man's shoes slipped on the stairs as Kradle forced him out into the yard.

"You know who I am?" Kradle snarled.

"I know. I know. You're John Kradle."

"You murdered my family." His voice sounded thin to him, an impossible instrument for communicating the agony inside. "My son Mason was fifteen years old."

"Listen to me." Mullins tried to turn around. Kradle slammed the butt of the pistol into his face, knocking him down. He followed as the man crawled toward the edge of the yard. Kradle picked him up and pushed him out the small wooden gate in the back fence.

Before them, the hard, unforgiving desert gaped. A featureless slab of cracked clay and sand, bowing and rising toward razor-sharp ridges being lit by morning glow. *This is the place,* Kradle thought. He couldn't replicate the coldness and loneliness and hardness of the bathroom tiles on which his son had breathed his last breath, but he could try. Mullins shuffled along weakly until Kradle told him to stop.

"You're going to die here," Kradle said. "You're going to die in terror and pain, just the way my family did."

"Listen," Mullins said again, his hands up, showing the lines of his palms etched with blood from a split lip. "Listen. What I did was the greatest act of evil a man can do. I know you've suffered. Your son suffered."

"Don't talk about my son!" Kradle barked.

"I was . . ." Mullins shook his head. There were tears running down his cheeks. "I want to try to explain this to you. Please. Please. I want to explain. I was over the edge, okay? I'd been in combat, and I—I was living in a place of darkness. My own son had revealed something to me, and I was confused and traumatized. I was in the valley of darkness, and I hadn't felt God's love—"

"*God's love?*" Kradle said.

"I hadn't heard his word. I'm in a good place now," Mullins wheezed. He rubbed his side, where Kradle had kicked him. "I can, I can look back and see, through the wisdom I have gained, what made me do those things. Those sinful things. I'm—I'm asking for your mercy."

"Where was mercy for my son?" Kradle bellowed. "For my wife? For her sister? Where was—" He couldn't talk. The words felt strangled. "Oh, god. God. This isn't the way it was supposed to be. You weren't supposed to beg me. How dare you fucking *beg me!*"

"I-I-I." Mullins gripped the ground, struggled to explain, his eyes restless, focused on everything but Kradle's eyes. "I needed someone to blame. And it became your wife. After the show, after what happened to me, I needed to direct that anger to someone. My son had just revealed to me that he wasn't . . . He wasn't the person I knew. He was someone else. It was as if he—"

Kradle felt his whole body brace for it. For Mullins to say it was like his son *had died*. Mullins saw the white-hot rage in Kradle's eyes and stammered over it.

"What Christine said to me that day—it hurt. It hurt me. I was a sick man, and I lashed out in a sick way. But almost immediately after I left your house, as I was walking away, I heard the voice of God."

Kradle forced himself to breathe.

"God's word said—"

"What did he say, Mullins?" Kradle asked. "He say anything about coming forward? He say anything about leaving me to *rot* on death row?"

"Listen," Mullins said. "Please listen."

Kradle could hardly focus. The gun was shaking in his hand. He could do nothing but listen, let the useless words wash over him, because what he had wanted was dissolving right before his eyes. He'd wanted to fight his son's killer. He'd wanted to conquer and punish him, to see a flash of the evil that had driven him that fateful day and meet it, quench it, with his own. But all he had before him was an old man simpering and crying and bleeding in the desert, a man who could do no more than die at his hands like a miserable hound.

Kradle had come to the house on Cloudrock Court to be a force of hatred and violence, and now all he felt was disappointment and disgust. He lowered the gun from Mullins's chest, let it hang, impossibly heavy, by his side.

"I can't kill you," Kradle said. "I can't do it. Not like this."

He sucked in a long breath and tried to tell himself that he would find some satisfaction in seeing Mullins behind bars, living in the stale, maddening purgatory he had experienced himself over the past five years.

"If you—"

"No, shut up," Kradle said. "Get on your feet. We're leaving. I'm taking you in."

"You have nothing," Mullins said carefully. "Okay? Think about it. You have nothing left. I took that from you, and I'm so, so sorry. But I have a wife. I have a son. I have people from my parish and my community who love me and need me. So I can't do what you want me to do. I can't go to jail."

"Wha—" Kradle shook his head. "What makes you think—"

"Please say you forgive me. Forgive me now before they take you away."

Kradle felt his mouth twist with confusion.

He took a step back and, as he did, felt two things. He felt his eyes widen as they fell on the shoes on Mullins's feet, as the realization materialized that he'd been wearing them in bed when Kradle woke him and yanked him free of his sheets. Kradle also felt the barrel of a gun against the back of his neck.

"Drop it," a deep voice said.

Kradle felt the man behind him gather a hand around his own. Kradle released the pistol and let the man take it away.

"On your knees."

Kradle did as he was told. He sank to the desert sand. The man side-stepped so that Kradle could see him. He didn't recognize the lone figure nudging glasses back onto his nose, pointing his own gun at him as he pocketed the one he'd pushed against the back of Kradle's neck. Kradle dropped his eyes to the man's wrist and noticed a tattoo that read 4KEEPZ.

"Where's everyone else?" Mullins was shivering from head to toe now, his bloodstream being flooded with chemicals as his terror morphed into relief. "You said there'd be a whole team."

"Yeah. I lied," Keeps said. He shrugged. "It's kind of my thing."

He shot Mullins in the forehead.

CHAPTER 44

Kerry Monahan was lying on her side when Celine entered the hospital room. She was bigger than Celine remembered. Fragments of the hellish moments running with the girl through the forest outside the Rancho Salvaje Wildlife Park lingered in Celine's mind, and from them she had a sense that the girl was small and narrow, like a frightened bird. But one broad shoulder slid from under the sheet as Kerry pushed herself into a sitting position, and her long legs stretched toward the end of the bed, rattling the chain around her ankle that connected to the bed frame. Celine sat down in the only chair in the room.

"Don't even bother," Kerry said before Celine could open her mouth, holding up her good hand. "I know exactly what you're going to say."

"You do, huh?" Celine asked.

"Yeah." Kerry smoothed back her hair, which was still clotted with dirt at the end of her ponytail. "There's been about three versions of you in here already through the night. Good cops trying to tell me they understand me, they feel sorry for me, they want to help me. Problem is, none of you can. It's too late now."

"First of all, I'm not a cop," Celine said. "And second of all, it's not too late. Whatever Burke's plan is, there's still time for you to tell us what it is and save lives, Kerry."

"I've killed," Kerry said. The teenager picked at a bandage around her finger. "That guy from the wildlife park? The one who picked up the bag from the locker? That was me. I killed that guy. I wasn't keeping lookout. I painted the straps of the bag with the stuff that they gave me. The poison, whatever it was. All the good cops who have come in here, the lawyers, they've all tried to tell me they can go easy and charge me with just being a lookout, someone Burke put in position to make sure the target went down. But I'm admitting it. I did it." The girl tapped her chest with one finger. "I want to be a part of the story when it's told."

"Tell me what the story is," Celine said. "Tell me how it ends."

"Forget it." Kerry smiled. "You'll know in less than an hour."

Celine shook her head, overwhelmed with sadness suddenly. The girl in the bed just stared at her impassively, unable to fathom the depth of what Celine was feeling.

"Don't take it personally," the girl said. "You tried to protect me in the forest. I remember it was you. And I'm grateful. I'm not doing this because of you. I'm doing this because I'm trying to make the world a better place."

"The Camp," Celine said. "It was their sniper who shot at you. Do you understand that? They knew Trinity and I were going to chase you down, and they wanted to make sure you were taken out so you couldn't reveal—"

The girl held up a hand, closed her eyes.

"These people aren't your friends. They have no loyalty to you."

"We're all loyal to the cause," Kerry said. "That's what matters."

Celine's phone buzzed in her pocket. She picked it up and stared at the screen. Then she covered her mouth with a trembling hand.

"What?"

"Oh, god," Celine said.

"What? What is it?"

Celine stood, her eyes locked to her phone.

"He did it," she said. Her words came in fitful starts, rushing out of her with horror. "He . . . He did it. Oh, Jesus, no."

"Let me see." Kerry reached for the phone with her good hand.

"Two massive explosions," Celine read. "One inside, one outside the Saint Joan of Arc Church. Emergency response teams estimating several dozen killed."

Kerry's face was a mask of confusion. She reached again for the phone.

"That . . . That wasn't the plan," she murmured. Celine let the phone go. "The plan was the kids at the rink."

Kerry looked at the phone, the lit screen, the small green bar showing the alarm Celine had set to go off only seconds earlier, now counting off a snooze timer. Kerry's mouth turned downward and her small, mean eyes flicked toward Celine.

"What rink?" Celine asked.

Kradle dropped onto the sand, crawled to Mullins, and grabbed his head, his body working of its own accord while his mind tried to catch up to what had just happened. The first gold beams of morning light made the blood on the sand look purple. Keeps was watching him, his finger still on the trigger, his head cocked slightly and his eyes searching the scene before him as if he was trying to preserve every detail of this moment for future reflection, the gallery viewer assessing a painting: Kradle Over Fallen Man.

"Take a few more seconds," Keeps said. "Then we gotta go."

"Who . . . ," Kradle managed. His hands were soaked in the blood of the murdered man. "Who . . ."

"I'm Walter Keeper. Friend of Celine's. Well, I was." Keeps shrugged. "I'm the kind of guy whose identity changes quickly. Like a chameleon, I guess. Right now I'm prepping to become Mister Millionaire."

Kradle was hardly hearing the words. Fury was unfolding inside him, the ache of knowing that his last chance of proving his innocence was leaking away before his eyes, while the chance to have his vengeance was already gone.

"Second ago I was a killer," Keeps continued, almost to himself. "It's not the first time. Usually I don't mind it, but I wanted to avoid it this time if I could. But I couldn't have this guy going on about the phone call I made to him, pretending to be the police, telling him to get into the bed, that you were coming, that we needed to set a trap for you. Too complicated. And the police don't like to be impersonated, in my experience."

Kradle's hands were balling into fists.

"Look, man, I did you a favor," Keeps said. "I know what the guy did to your family, and that's fucked up. We both know you weren't going to kill him. Now you can go back to Pronghorn and know everything got tied up neatly, even if you didn't do it."

Kradle rose to his feet. He turned in the sand. Keeps raised the gun and pointed it at his chest.

"Don't be stupid," Keeps said. "Don't be stupid! Don't be stupid!"

Kradle kept coming. Keeps shot him in the upper chest. He kept coming. "No, no, no, no!" Keeps wailed.

Kradle seized him by the throat with one hand and knocked the gun out of his fist with the other. He smashed his body down into the sand, making his head bounce, squeezing hard, the smaller man gripping desperately at Kradle's hands and neck. His nails tore and bit into Kradle's skin, but no pain registered. There was only a deep, heavy silence pressing down on him, making it impossible to break the force of his hands, his arms, his weight coming down on Keeps. The smaller man kicked and flailed, got traction in the sand, somehow, twisted around, elbowed Kradle in the face and scrabbled away. Kradle walked while the other man crawled, gasping for air, toward the house. He didn't get far. Kradle slammed his boot down on the man's back, flattening him against the dirt, then kneeled by his head as Keeps coughed and gasped for air.

"This was the wrong fight to get involved in," Kradle said.

"Yeah. Yeah. I see that now," Keeps rasped. He spat blood on the sand. "Please, please, man. Please just—"

Kradle punched him in the back of the head. Keeps went limp against the dirt, his unconscious breath shallow and rattling.

Keeps was a dead weight as Kradle lifted him and slung him over his shoulder. He walked back through the gate into Mullins's yard, up the porch stairs to the sliding door. He pushed it open and went inside, moving without direction, knowing only that he had to do something with the man he carried, the only man who could testify to his not having murdered Gary Mullins out in there in the desert. Because while losing his opportunity to punish Mullins for his family's deaths, either with murder or with jail time, was cruel enough, Kradle knew serving time for the act would only be worse. He couldn't bear it. Not the sight of Pronghorn on the horizon, nor the feel of its walls enveloping him again, the sound of its clanging gate and buzzing alarms. He fancied he could smell now, in his despair, the other men on the row. His brothers awaiting death. Kradle had no plan. He simply walked across the living room toward the hall with Keeps hanging over his shoulder.

"Reach for the sky, inmate," a voice said.

Kradle turned toward the kitchen, the big windows and the curtains patterned with cheerful lemons.

Warden Grace Slanter was standing there with a bolt-action rifle in her hands, the long black nose of the weapon steady as a rock and pointed right at Kradle's head. The warden was wearing dusty jeans and a flannel shirt, boots caked in desert sand.

"John Kradle," the warden said. "You look awful."

"People keep telling me that," he said. "How'd you know I was here?"

"I got a text," Slanter said.

"Okay," Kradle said. He didn't understand. But it didn't seem to matter. None of it mattered. His shirt was slowly darkening with blood, and his shoulder hurt. He rubbed the hole just under his collarbone and knew there was bad pain, but not death, on the horizon.

"I saw what happened." Grace Slanter took her aim off Kradle for a second, flicked the gun toward the windows. "All of it. Saw you decide not to kill that man out there. Saw that guy you're carrying do it instead."

Kradle gripped the back of Keeps's legs, hefting him higher on his good shoulder.

"If you could maybe memorize that," Kradle said, "say it again when you're asked, I'd be very grateful."

"No problem."

"Anything I can do in return?" Kradle asked.

"Yeah," Grace said. With one hand holding the rifle on Kradle, she took a pair of handcuffs from the back of her belt and tossed them at Kradle's feet. "Put those on him and carry him out to the truck. When we get there, I'll give you your very own set."

CHAPTER 45

Burke stood before the stage, watching the little girls being led on stage and arranged on the platforms. There were twelve of them, mostly blondes, each wearing a satin baby-doll-style dress trimmed in white faux fur. Frilly socks and halos made from wire and white feathers. Around him, people were gathering slowly, some of them clearly the parents of the girls, waving and blowing kisses and giving thumbs-ups. Willis had studied the Christmas morning carolling event that had played out on this exact spot a year earlier, taking segments from the local news and what footage he could acquire online to give a timeline that was as precise as possible. It was 8:42 A.M. With all the jostling and arranging and cajoling necessary to get the girls in position on the stage, the announcer had come out to introduce them and get the first song underway by about 9:03 A.M. Burke wanted the ice rink and the standing area for the audience to be at maximum capacity before he started firing.

He walked back to the truck and, before getting in, glanced down the street to where Willis and Clara would be waiting with the getaway car. He could just see a slice of the front left headlight of the white van, the faithful old vehicle that had seen them from Pronghorn to Vegas, and which would take the whole team safely out of the vicinity of the massacre once it was time to flee. He wondered if the vehicle would end up in a museum someday, along with the rifle, debris from the snow cone truck.

A little girl in the front row of the carolling ensemble was looking at Burke. He raised a hand and waved, and she giggled and hid her face.

"I'm sorry," he mouthed. Because he was sorry for what he was about to do, genuinely miserable, aching in his very bones about it. That it had come to this was not personally his fault—it was a product of hundreds of years of weakness, of the white man laying down his weapons when he should have taken up arms, of listening and bending when he should have remained steadfast, of denying plain realities that were present for all to see. That these little girls should have to be sacrificed so that the world could evolve into a new order was a tragedy, but some futures had to be born out of blood. Innocent blood. The most innocent of all innocent, and purest of all pure. It wasn't going to be easy. But it had to be done.

Burke walked back to the food truck and opened the rear doors, slipped inside, and found Silvia waiting there. He picked up the rifle bag and unzipped it, glancing again at his watch.

"Almost time," he said.

Celine gripped the handle above the window and the edge of the center console of Trinity's car, jamming her feet against the sides of the footwell as Trinity smashed the vehicle over a speed bump at the exit to the parking lot of the Mesa View hospital.

"What if it's not the Planet Hollywood ice rink?" Celine groaned as the car skidded sideways, zooming blindly through an intersection packed with cars. "What if it's a rollerskating rink? What if it's some other—"

"It needs to be this one," Trinity said. "We need to be right about this."

"Because she said kids," Celine said.

"Yes," Trinity said. "If we're wrong—"

"We're not wrong," Celine insisted.

The two women sat rigid in their seats as they turned onto the highway. Trinity slammed on the brakes as a wall of traffic rose before them.

Burke flicked the safety selector on the rifle to fire, put a hand on the handle of the rear door of the food truck and looked back one last time at Silvia, who was standing with her fingernails clawing the edge of the serving counter, her jaw flexed tight.

On the wind, he heard the announcer introducing the choir of little girls. He waited until he could hear the first bars of a carol, smiled as he recognized the tune. "White Christmas." Perfect.

"Here we go." Burke smiled.

Silvia could only give a hard nod.

Burke pushed the handle and shoved against the door.

It didn't open.

He heard a vehicle pull alongside the truck on the opposite side to the serving counter, and the sickening sound of metal grinding metal as another food truck scraped against the counter side, wedging itself tightly against the vehicle so that both serving windows were aligned. Burke stepped back and saw that the kitchen area of a bright yellow truck was now perfectly matched and mirrored with their own, a Black man in a bright yellow shirt standing there with his arms folded. Through the windscreen, Burke saw the truck ahead of them backing up. They were sandwiched between four food trucks, boxed in on all sides.

"Bitch!" The man in the yellow shirt leaned on his counter and pointed at Silvia, standing behind hers. "Me and a few of my friends got together. We thought we'd come over here and encourage you to apologize for what you said to me and—"

Burke stepped up beside Silvia, raised the rifle, and sprayed gunfire through the serving window. The man in the yellow shirt ducked faster than Burke's eyes could follow. He put a foot on the shelf under the serving counter, grabbed the edge of the window, and hauled himself up. Outside the truck, he could already hear screams, shouts of confusion at the sound of gunfire. He could only hope the little girls weren't shuffled off the stage before he could get a few of them.

He tucked his rifle under his arm, pulled down his mask, and raised the goggles over his eyes. He was ready. Game on.

Burke pushed up through the gap between the trucks and placed the rifle on the roof of the truck. He climbed onto the roof of the yellow truck, stepped to its edge, and looked out over the scene before him.

It was just as he'd imagined it. Men and women running for their lives, the flow of people bottlenecking at the natural barriers made by the line of tightly parked trucks and washing up against the wooden partitions that marked out the edge of the Planet Hollywood hotel—human waves of panic. People were trying to find shelter in and around the stage. The inner cordon made by the ice rink was causing terrified families to cower at the edges, no idea where the shooting was coming from, a couple still skittering and stumbling out on the white plain, ripe to be picked off. While some little girls were being dragged off the platform on the stage, a good handful were still standing there, frozen in confusion, their feathered halos bobbing on wires above their heads.

Burke lifted his rifle and aimed at the stage.

His finger had not yet come off the trigger guard and onto the trigger it-self when he heard a voice cutting through the screaming, and looked down to see a woman with a bandaged neck dropping to one knee on the grass before the ice rink.

Trinity fired. Burke felt the bullet smash into his thigh. The bullet that blasted through his cheekbone and into his skull was like a punch, a whump that knocked his head back, made the truck beneath his feet feel as if it were a boat rocking on a turbulent sea.

He fell off the truck and landed on the road. The truck that had boxed in his truck from behind had fled when the firing started, leaving the back door free. Burke saw Silvia's shoes as she dropped onto the ground, turned, and tried to sprint away. A second pair of shoes appeared, blocking her.

"Not so fast, bitch!"

Burke looked up in time to see Celine Osbourne punch Silvia in the face so hard she hit the ground and bounced onto her side. But that couldn't have been right. His jailer from Pronghorn could not be here now, cutting off the escape of his comrade. All that must have been fantasy.

So too, he assumed, the distant vision of the white van doing a three-point turn in the street, almost mowing down a mother running with one of the lit-tle angel-girls in her arms, as it roared away into the morning. Burke knew his teammates would not abandon them. It must have been the lies of his slowly failing mind, the last desperate pictures of a brain with a bullet lodged in it.

Burke gripped at the asphalt, felt darkness closing out the sounds of peo-ple running, crying, screaming.

They were nice sounds to die to.

CHAPTER 46

From the prison van that had driven John Kradle to Pronghorn Correctional Facility for the very first time, he had been able to see exactly zero percent of its exterior. Chained to a ringbolt on a steel bench, he had stared at the floor for the entire trip, resisting the attempts at conversation made by the correctional officer lumped with the responsibility of riding in the back with him.

From where he sat now, in Grace Slanter's truck, Kradle watched as the small hill fell away and the road to the facility opened before them. It was the same road traveled by the bus full of family members of guards only days earlier. He shuffled a little in his seat, his palms flat against the backrest, the chain between his cuffs stretched taut. Grace Slanter had wrapped his shoulder tightly with tea towels she found in the Mullins house before they left for Pronghorn, but the wound felt warm and Kradle knew that the adrenaline that was keeping the pain away was almost used up.

He watched the prison slowly growing, the minimum, medium, and maximum security sections at first appearing as one gray mass against the huge walls, then dividing like cells. In the back of the truck, Keeps still lolled, unconscious, bleeding from the nose onto a seat that was covered in desert dust. Slanter, who had done little in the way of talking on their journey back to the prison, pulled the truck over and stopped it a few miles out from the facility.

"I'm going to make a phone call," she said, and took out her cell phone. As the device came out of her pocket, Kradle watched a thin stream of sand trail onto the bench seat between them. Grace noticed him looking and shrugged.

"I've been out in the wilds for a day or two," she said.

"Okay." Kradle nodded. He watched the prison in the distance, the little cars and vans and helicopters assembled beyond the parking lot, and listened to Grace make a call to the press, telling them she was bringing a prisoner in and to get their cameras ready for her arrival. When she hung up the phone, Kradle met her eyes, and the old warden gave an embarrassed kind of smile.

"I really need this," she said.

"I bet," Kradle answered.

"I'm going to pull up the truck outside the gates and walk you in," she said. "Try to look . . . you know. Defeated."

"Shouldn't be hard," Kradle said.

The warden smiled. Kradle smiled back. She started the engine and pulled back onto the road.

The gold-rimmed glasses with the chain were just exactly Axe's prescription. Lucky thing, he thought. He put them on so he could read a little plaque set into a sandstone block at the edge of the marina. Marina del Rey, it told him, was the largest man-made small-craft harbor in North America. Axe didn't think that was a very impressive claim, but as he straightened and scanned the harbor he guessed there were probably a thousand or so boats in view of where he was standing, which wasn't bad. He picked up his bag, pushing down a Velcro flap that was hanging loose and slapping in the sea breeze, and walked down the harbor, reading boat names as he went. *The Adventurer. Explorer. Distant Sunsets. Flying Free.* The people on the boats didn't much look like they'd ever not been free, Axe thought. He passed a forty-footer that was crowded on the back deck with people in white shorts and long socks drinking orange juice from wine glasses and picking at platters of sliced ham. On another boat, a pair of kids were hanging upside down from a rail, trailing their fingertips in the water, as a bronze-tanned woman in a long yellow dress rushed down from the upper cabin to scold them, reel them in. Axe was heading nowhere in particular, thinking he might stop at the end of one of the piers and look through the bag, when he passed a guy hauling one of those waterproof trunks with the flip-latches on the sides down a short gangway toward the deck of a big white yacht. Axe watched him reach the bottom of the gangway and curse himself, try to shift the heavy trunk up onto his knee so that he could unclip a small chain at waist height that secured the deck. The guy flipped a lank fringe out of his eyes, glanced around, and saw Axe standing there.

"Hey, fella!" the guy said, and threw Axe the smile of a dumbass who should have thought ahead before he started on the path to loading the boat. "Lend us a hand?"

"Sure," Axe said.

Axe made sure his German passport was zippered up in his little under-shirt bag, thinking to himself that if it fell into the water it would be a real disaster. He waited for the guy holding the trunk to back up, then went down the gangplank and unlatched the chain. There was nowhere for Axe to go but onto the boat itself to let the guy through. He stood there, holding his bag and feeling mildly pleased with his usefulness, as the guy heaved the trunk onto a table and gave a huge sigh of relief.

"Thanks, buddy," the guy said. "You're a real champ. Stupid me. I put the chain across again, not thinking."

"You headin' out today?" Axe asked.

"Yeah." The guy brushed sea salt that had rubbed off the trunk from his polo shirt. He proudly put a hand on top of the trunk. "Koh Samui, baby. Should take me a couple of weeks. This is the last box of supplies right here. Now I'm all set to go."

Axe smiled and set his bag down on the deck.

CHAPTER 47

Celine Osbourne heard the shunting sound of the toaster lever being kicked down as she rounded the corner of the row. The woodsmoke traveling down from cell eleven was thinner this time. John Kradle was putting the finishing touches on the "t" in "*feet*" when she arrived at his cell. She rested her forearms on the crossbar, her hands hanging near his face as he bent over the slab of wood on his little desk.

She watched him blow gently on the seared letter, then sit back to appreciate his work.

"*Please wipe your feet,*" she read.

"There's room for a punctuation mark," Kradle noted, pointing with the makeshift soldering iron at the end of the piece of wood. "A period, maybe."

"Seems a bit final, doesn't it?" Celine asked.

"What?" Kradle said. "Like you might want to add more?"

"Please wipe your feet before entering."

"Who's going to wipe their feet *after* entering?" Kradle asked.

"Urgh." Celine massaged her brow. "Why do I do this? Why do I talk to you?"

She knew the answer. In the six weeks since John Kradle had returned from the outside world, Celine had done a lot of talking to him. Part of it was wanting to reassure him on his journey to being released.

It had taken a week for police to take Walter Keeper's statement over in county jail, where he admitted to killing Gary Mullins before being apprehended by Kradle. Another day for them to come to Pronghorn and confirm Grace Slanter's story, that she had witnessed Walter Keeper murder the man in the desert while Kradle stood helplessly by. It had taken two weeks for

Celine to get an appointment to enter into the official record all that she knew about the Kradle Family murders, about Gary Mullins and what she had learned from the unnamed man in the motel room. While Kradle's lawyer worked tirelessly, another week had passed before Dr. Martin Stinway was quizzed by police about his forensic evidence on the Kradle case and Shelley Frapport had given her statement in full about her late husband and his actions around the time of the murders.

While the case had been assembled, and a time arranged to present the findings to an appellate judge, Kradle and Celine had existed as they had before the breakout: him behind the bars and her walking the halls, now and then stopping to reprimand him about his towel hanging on the rail or him drinking backward from his coffee mug. But there was no heat, no hatred, in the banter. Celine took a chair from the breakroom and positioned it in front of the bars, and every night, long into the night, the two talked, Kradle sitting on his bunk with his back against the wall and Celine resting her boots up on the bars. Death row was half as full as it had been, and while three cells on either side of Kradle's still stood empty, their whispering and laughing drew complaints from inmates further down the hall who were trying to get some sleep. Particularly vocal about their noise was Anthony Reiter, who took some time to recover from his treatment at the hands of Burke and his crew. The killer had needed to recover physically from the ordeal, but emotionally as well, from the disappointment that his victimhood at the hands of Burke's crew had not afforded him some kind of pardon from the killing of his girlfriend in the backyard of their home.

Some of what caused Celine and Kradle amusement long into those evening talks was Celine's updates on the public life of US Marshal Trinity Parker. Footage of her stooping to one knee, raising her gun, and shooting Burke David Schmitz before he could open fire on another crowd of innocent civilians had swept the world, as had the news that Parker was less than twenty-four hours into her recovery from being shot in the neck by one of Burke's snipers at the time. Celine noted that nowhere in Trinity's many interviews with journalists did she mention that the wound to her neck had been caused by shrapnel, not a bullet.

Celine watched Kradle working now, drawing out the last moments he would remain as she had always known him, as she had always been comfortable with him. A man behind bars.

Then she closed her eyes, drew a deep breath, and slipped her key into the lock.

Kradle looked up from the sign he had made. Celine smiled and nodded. "It's through?" he asked.

"Yeah," she said. "Just got the call a minute ago. They've stamped the vacation of your charge. You're free to go."

Kradle put the sign down, lay the soldering iron beside it. He stood and picked up the box of items he had packed and set on the end of the bed. As he walked through the doorway, something changed in his face, and he turned back and grabbed a stack of envelopes sitting, bound with an elastic band, on the shelf.

"I'll be needing these," he said, showing Celine the label marked MAR- RIAGE.

"Those women are sickos," Celine said, smacking the envelopes out of his hand. "And they won't want you, now that they know you're innocent."

The envelopes landed on the floor of the cell. Kradle left them there, and she took his arm and led him, uncuffed, up the hall.

She dropped him at the administration building to sign his papers. With the front of the building crowded with press, cameras clicking and people yelling, she was certain he hardly heard her goodbyes, and she barely caught his. There wasn't time for hugging, and he wouldn't have liked it, with all the people watching, she supposed. But just before she turned to leave, he took her hand and gave it a squeeze, and something about the hard fingers she had felt in the car on the way to Vegas told her everything she needed to know. She watched him walk into the fray and march straight over to where the black dog sat uncertainly in the huddle of humans. Kradle's lawyer held the leash, grinning, as the ex-con crouched and ruffled the fur of the dog's head and neck, saying nothing to the journalists that barked all around him.

It was a long, quiet walk back to the row, her swipe card bleeping through gate after gate, until Celine Osbourne was again where she belonged. The smell of smoke still lingered in the air, but the first man she had ever released from death row was long gone, and Celine knew she would probably never see him again.

Past Kradle's empty cell, she saw a hand poking out from one cell, wrist resting idly on the crossbar. Celine wondered if there were more men here who had been deemed guilty by judges and juries, whom she had made it her life's work to keep from the world, who deserved instead to be out there, walking free.

She decided then that she had a new mission.

She was going to find out.

ACKNOWLEDGMENTS

The publication of this novel will mark my millionth word in print. I have no idea which one it was. I hope it was something meaningful and not ordinary (or profane!). Something like "tenacity" or "determination" would have been good, or indeed, "hope."

My career has been buoyed by a ridiculous amount of hope. I hoped, with every waking moment, to be published. That hope was obsessive, exhausting, soul destroying. It flew in the face of so much discouragement in my life, in the media, from other authors, and from my inner critic. When that hope was finally realized, rather than dissipating, it grew. I hoped from one book to another, from one publication territory to another, and my hope ignited hope in other people. I could never have hoped to have a million words in print when I first decided I wanted to be an author. But here I am, deciding what to hope for next.

I have dedicated this book to all the aspiring authors. It's not an easy road. Waiting. Trying. Daydreaming. Being rejected. Having your hopes destroyed and trying to rebuild them. It's lonely, frustrating, and tedious. But whatever you do, my advice is never to let it become hopeless. Only you have control over that.

When it came to research for this book, I am forever indebted to Michael Duffy and Governor Faith Slatcher, who organized a tour for me of Lithgow Correctional Centre, a maximum security institution in New South Wales. Thank you to all of the staff who answered my questions there, and to the inmates, who, for the most part, behaved themselves. I also consulted extensively with Detective B. Adam Richardson of the Writer's Detective Bureau, who was so generous with his time and knowledge.

I am represented in Australia by Gaby Naher, in the US by Lisa Gallagher. My publishers are Bev Cousins, Justin Ractliffe, Linda Quinton, Kristin Sevick, Thomas Wörtche, and a whole host of others across the globe. My main editor is the wonderful Kathryn Knight. I will never be able to repay the kindness, patience, and encouragement these people have provided me.

Never will I reach a point in my successes at which I forget that my ability to write was shaped and developed by my academic studies at the University of the Sunshine Coast and the University of Queensland.

Thank you, Tim, for loving, supporting, and caring for me. Thank you, Violet, for being the most beautiful thing in my world. Thank you, Noggy, for the cuddles.

ABOUT THE AUTHOR

CANDICE FOX is the award-winning author of *Crimson Lake, Redemption Point*, and *Gone by Midnight*. She is also the cowriter with James Patterson of *New York Times* bestsellers *Never Never, Fifty Fifty, Liar Liar, Hush*, and *The Inn*. She lives in Sydney.

candicefox.org

Facebook: candicefoxauthor

Twitter: @candicefoxbooks

Decisions and Organizations

James G. March

Basil Blackwell

British Library Cataloguing in Publication Data

March, James G.
    Decisions and organizations.
    1. Decision-making 2. Organization
    I. Title
    658.4'03   HD30.23

    ISBN 0-631-15812-X

Library of Congress Cataloging-in-Publication Data

March, James G.
    Decisions and organizations/James G. March.
        p.   cm.
    Collection of previously published essays.
    ISBN 0-631-15812-X: $49.95
    1. Decision-making. 2. Organization.   I. Title.
HD30.23.M366 1988   87-29362
658.4'03--dc 19   CIP

Typeset in 10 on 12pt Times by Dobbie Typesetting Service, Plymouth, Devon
Printed in Great Britain by T. J. Press Ltd, Padstow, Cornwall

Contents

iv   Contents

Acknowledgements

The papers reprinted here are products of drinking wine with friends and corrupting them into conversation. Their specific contributions are recorded to some extent by references in the papers and by the fact that many of the papers are co-authored. I am grateful for the collaboration of my co-authors Vicki Baier, Michael Cohen, Richard Cyert, Edward Feigenbaum, Martha Feldman, Richard Harrison, Scott Herriott, Daniel Levinthal, Curtis Manns, James C. March, Johan Olsen, Harald Sætren, Guje Sevón, and Zur Shapira; and for the cooperation of the journals in which the papers first appeared. The financial support of various foundations and institutions on particular projects is acknowledged in the individual pieces, but I should like to emphasize the importance of the support given by the Spencer Foundation. Blame for the present volume lies with Tony Sweeney, who conceived the idea, and Carol Busia, who put it all together.

The contributions of others accumulate, however, and these papers cover a span of more than thirty years. Consequently, I should like to take this opportunity to acknowledge my debts to four groups of associates. The first group is a group of colleagues whom I have long known, admired and read with particular profit: Kenneth Arrow, Robert Dahl, Jon Elster, Alexander George, Albert Hirschman, Harold Leavitt, Charles Lindblom, Martin Lipset, Robert Merton, John Meyer, Charles Perrow, Jeffrey Pfeffer, Richard Scott, Herbert Simon, Arthur Stinchcombe, Amos Tversky, Karl Weick, Harrison White and Sidney Winter.

The second group is a group of Scandinavians who have contributed greatly, not only to extending my appreciation of organizations but also to making my life richer: Flemming Agersnap, Torben Agersnap, Lennart Arvedsen, Torben Beck-Jørgensen, Ingmar Björkman, Finn Borum, Berit Bratbak, Nils Brunsson, Søren Christensen, Morten Egeberg, Harald Enderud, Lars Engwall, Arent Greve, Chris Gudnason, Ingemund Hägg, Bo Hedberg, Gudmund Hernes, Helga Hernes, Gull-May Holst, Knut Jacobsen, Bengt Jacobsson, Finn Junge-Jensen, Birgitte Knudsen, Kristian Kreiner,

Per Lægreid, Janne Larsen, Helge Larsen, Johan Olsen, Dick Ramstrom, Torger Reve, Kåre Rommetveit, Jens Ove Riis, Paul Roness, Kjell-Arne Røvik, Harald Sætren, Majken Schulz, Janne Seeman, Guje Sevón, Jesper Sørensen, Per Stava, Jesper Strandgaard, Risto Tainio and Bengt-Arne Vedin.

The third group is a group of former doctoral and post-doctoral students of mine. I cannot claim them, but they can claim me. They include Svein Andersen, David Anderson, Jonathan Aronson, Elaine Backman, Vicki Eaton Baier, James Barr, Jerry Beasley, Charles Bonini, Anthony Bower, Ross Boylan, David Brereton, Warren Brown, Alan Campbell, Hanoria Casey, Ellen Chaffee, Geoffrey Clarkson, Carol Clawson, Kalman Cohen, Michael Cohen, Rey Contreras, Dwight Crane, Patrick Crecine, James Crotty, John Cumpsty, Larry Cuban, John Curry, Bryan Delaney, William Dill, Julia Dilova, Elaine Draper, Carla Edlefson, George Ekker, Omar El Sawy, Carson Eoyang, Suzanne Estler, Edward Feigenbaum, John Feilders, Julian Feldman, Martha Feldman, Tammy Feldman, Fernando García-León, Mary Garrett, Donald Gerwin, James Glenn, Jane Hannaway, Elisabeth Hansot, Peter Harris, Richard Harrison, Scott Herriott, Dean Hubbard, Herschel Kanter, Alice Kaplan, David Klahr, Kenneth Knight, Lena Kolarska, Thomas Kosnik, Theresa Lant, Daniel Levinthal, Barbara Levitt, Raymond Levitt, Ferdinand Levy, Arie Lewin, Pertti Lounamaa, Mary Ann Maguire, Curtis Manns, Gloria Marshall, Lynn Mather, Timothy McGuire, William McWhinney, Debra Meyerson, Stephen Mezias, Anne Miner, Brian Mittman, Chadwick Moore, Dale Mortenson, Patrick Murphy, Alan Patz, John Payne, Vance Peterson, Lawrence Pinfield, Stanley Pogrow, Louis Pondy, William Pounds, Lorraine Prinsky, Daniel Quirici, Amylou Reyes, Allyn Romanow, Jeffrey Roughgarden, J. Rounds, Stephen Rowley, Kaye Schoonhoven, Jitendra Singh, Sim Sitkin, Peggy Smith, Peer Soelberg, Lee Sproull, William Starbuck, Nelly Stromquist, Charles Sullivan, Stephen Swerdlick, Michal Tamuz, Theodore Van Wormer, Dale Weigel, Stephen Weiner, Andrew Whinston, Gail Whitacre, Matthew Willard, Oliver Williamson, David Wolf, Wayne Wormley, Jo Zettler and Stanley Ziontz.

The fourth group is a group of secretaries who have given intelligence, sanity, and imagination to the ordinary life of academe: Evelyn Adams, Julia Ball, Barbara Beuche, Ethel Blank, Donna Dill, Jackie Fry, Marsha Mavis, Carolyn Nattress and Mary Tomkinson.

If despite this impressive array of teachers I have failed to extract a good idea or two, the fault lies with me – or perhaps with the wine.

James G. March
Stanford, California

Introduction:
A Chronicle of Speculations About Decision-Making in Organizations

James G. March

A Prologue

This is a story of several decades of speculations about organizational decision-making, a chronology of sorts. The story is fiction in at least two respects. First, it is organized around one person's work, and life is not. Second, it does not describe how the speculations actually evolved, but rather how they might be imagined to have evolved in a more orderly world. Unlike the former, the latter fiction may be defensible. A record of research can be written better as an interpretation of an incomplete tapestry of ideas than as a description of the curious chaos of its weaving.

  The background is a simple set of ideas that had become the received doctrine about decision-making by 1950. Although they have been modified substantially as a result of research since that time, these ideas continue to shape the questions asked in empirical and theoretical studies of individual and organizational choice. They portray decision-making as intentional, consequential, and optimizing. That is, they assume that decisions are based on preferences (e.g., wants, needs, values, goals, interests, subjective utilities) and expectations about outcomes associated with different alternative

This chapter is based on a paper originally prepared for presentation at the Exxon lecture series on decision-making, Northwestern University, 24 October, 1986. The research has been supported by grants from the Spencer Foundation, the Mellon Foundation, and the Stanford Graduate School of Business. It has benefited from a large number of collaborators, some of whom, but not all, are listed in the references. I should acknowledge particularly my debt to Johan P. Olsen.

actions. And they assume that the best possible alternative (in terms of its consequences for a decision-maker's preferences) is chosen.

These canons of choice, found most purely in statistical decision theory and microeconomic theory, and often somewhat sullied to deal with specific cases, underlie a substantial share of the descriptive theories of modern social science. Everyday and cataclysmic events are interpreted as happening because decision-makers with the resources to make them happen expect them to lead to better consequences (as measured by the decision-maker's preferences) than will other alternatives. The ideas also are the basis for modern prescriptions for intelligent choice. A good choice from this perspective is one that considers alternatives in terms of their outcomes, normally in the form of a probability distribution over the possible consequences, conditional on a particular choice, and chooses that alternative that has the highest expected utility. Improving the quality of decision-making, in these terms, involves inducing decision-makers to follow such precepts and providing analytical aids to assist them in their calculations.

Such a theory of choice has a strong claim on scientific enthusiasm: It has been used to predict important elements of aggregate human behavior and to improve the performance of individuals and organizations; it has an axiomatic base and theoretical structure of elegance and grace; and it celebrates a view of human capacities that reinforces and extends dominant Western ideologies glorifying the role of reason in human affairs. Although decision theory has some widely-recognized problems, it has become a modern classic of truth, beauty, and justice. And although there are contending religions, it is the established church of social science.

Students of organizational decision-making are members of a deviant sect within the same church. Their challenges to dominant doctrines are in some respects fundamental, but there is a persistent symbiosis between their ideas and more doctrinaire conceptions of choice. Even while rejecting important features of the theory, behavioral speculations about decision-making in organizations, for the most part, treat the basic framework of decision theory as compelling. And although organizational theorists are outcasts from the church, ideas consistent with many of their criticisms have found their way into established dogma. As a result, the recent history of the relation between the bishops of choice theory and the heretics of organization theory is a story of disagreements that have, for the most part, not led to a decisive schism but rather to a record of tension and accommodation (March, 1965; 1982; March and Sevón, 1987).

This chapter examines a semi-chronology of some of these heresies. The discussion is organized around four broad challenges to classical decision theory: First, a set of ideas emphasizing the importance of attention to decision-making. Second, an approach to conflicting interests in organizations that focuses on attention buffers to conflict. Third, a conception of organizational action as involving the following of rules that adapt to experience, rather than anticipatory choice. Fourth, a concern with the implications for decision-making of ambiguity about preferences, technology, and history. The ordering of the ideas is not entirely arbitrary. Some ideas mostly preceded other ideas. The ordering is not a strict chronology, however, and a more proper history would examine the ways in which the ideas evade conceptions of sequential development.

The Allocation of Attention

One of the oldest behavioral speculations about decision-making in organizations is that time and attention are scarce resources. Neither all alternatives nor all the consequences of any one of them can be known (March and Simon, 1958). Nor can organizations attend to all of their goals simultaneously (Cyert and March, 1963). Awareness of limitations on attention has led to concern for making the costs of obtaining information an explicit part of the structure of decision problems, and to the development of various forms of information and transaction cost economics that comprise a large part of contemporary microeconomic theory. Students of organizations, however, have generally been less interested in treating observed anomalies in organizational behavior in terms of information costs than in developing a behavioral theory of attention allocation. That interest leads them to see the organization of attention as a central process out of which decisions arise, rather than simply one aspect of the cost structure (March and Simon, 1958; March and Olsen, 1976). Since only a few alternatives, consequences, and goals can be considered simultaneously, actions are determined less by choices among alternatives than by decisions with respect to search.

Behavioral theories of organizational search are built on two little ideas that have proven remarkably durable. The first idea is that success is less a variable than a state (March and Simon, 1958; Cyert and March, 1963). That is, organizations distinguish rather sharply between meeting a target (success) and not meeting it (failure). They do not distinguish nearly so sharply between various levels of success or failure. In a sense, this suggests a step-function utility; and the idea of satisficing as reflecting a simplification utilities or a decision-rule was common in initial treatments (March and Simon, 1958). However, in theories of organizational decision-making, a target, or aspiration level, is not so much a step-function preference as it is a trigger for search. Organizations devote more attention to activities that are failing to meet targets than they do to activities that are meeting targets (March and Simon, 1958; Cyert and March, 1963). This squeaky wheel conception of attention is the second little idea in organizational theories of search. In periods and domains of success, search is reduced. In periods and domains of failure, search is increased. If an existing alternative is not good enough, search is undertaken for another one. An organization begins with a target and searches until it finds an alternative that meets that target. Search for new alternatives continues until a satisfactory alternative is discovered or created (Cyert and March, 1956). Thus, alternatives are not compared with each other so much as they are reviewed sequentially and accepted or rejected on the basis of target aspirations for their consequences (March and Simon, 1958; Cyert, Dill and March, 1958; Cyert and March, 1963).

This simple theory of search has been used to illuminate two broad kinds of phenomena in organizational decision-making. The first is the way in which an organization directs energies among its various activities and goals. Organizations vary their search efforts in response to patterns of success and failure in their performances or expectations (Cyert, Feigenbaum and March, 1959; Cyert, March and Moore, 1962; Manns and March, 1978). For example, when faced with risky alternatives, managers do not simply assess risk as part of a package of exogenously determined attributes, but actively seek to redefine alternatives, looking for options that retain the opportunities but eliminate the dangers (March and Shapira, 1987). Such behavior fits naturally into a theory that sees choice as driven by attention allocation, less naturally into a theory that sees choice as driven by explicit optimization.

The second set of phenomena illuminated by such a theory of search involves organizational slack, i.e., resources and effort directed toward activities that cannot be justified easily in terms of their immediate contribution to organizational objectives. Slack increases during periods of success and declines during periods of failure (March and Simon, 1958; Cyert, Feigenbaum and March, 1959; Cyert and March, 1963). Early theories of slack saw it primarily as a form of waste or as an incompletely rationalized reallocation of resources to subunits or individuals (March and Simon, 1958). But it was also pictured as an emergency reservoir of unused performance capabilities. By providing an inventory of unexploited efficiencies, slack serves to smooth performance in the face of a variable environment, a property not entirely lacking in organizational intelligence (March, 1981b). Subsequently, it has been observed that slack is also associated with changes in patterns of control in organizations and that activities stimulated by slack can be interpreted as forms of search. Slack search proceeds without the explicit organizational targets that distinguish problem-oriented search (Cyert and March, 1963; March, 1981b). Thus, it is less likely to solve immediate problems, more likely to be directed to subunit or individual objectives, and more likely to discover distinctively new alternatives. The distinction between slack search and problem-oriented search is at the base of several efforts to understand innovation in organizations and to explore the conditions under which different kinds of innovation are associated with failure or success (March, 1981b; Levinthal and March, 1981).

Limiting a theory of organizational search to search that is stimulated either by problems (problemistic search) or by the relaxation of organizational controls (slack search), however, underestimates the contribution of the market in alternatives and information to attention allocation. Although problems search for solutions, solutions also search for problems for which they might be imagined to be the solution (Cyert and March, 1963; March and Olsen, 1976; March, 1981b). Organizational discoveries, thus, are related not only to an organization's performance and aspirations, but also to the successes and failures of solution mongers in meeting their own targets. In such a conception, solutions for one organization are generated by the existence of problems in another; and a theory of organizational attention and search becomes a theory of a system of interacting organizations, rather than a single organization responding to an inert environment.

Conflict in Organizations

Some early treatments of organizational decision-making, particularly in economics, viewed organizations as actors possessing attributes commonly assigned to single individuals, particularly a coherent, well-defined set of preferences. But for the most part, decision-making in organizations has been seen as involving multiple actors with inconsistent preferences, thus a political system (Cyert and March, 1959; March, 1962a, 1962b). On the one hand this leads to some classical issues in evaluating alternative institutions for decision-making in the absence of agreement on objectives. Contemporary work on comparative institutions, both in economics and in political science, tends to focus on solving the problems of aggregation, the merging of prior individual preferences into the collective choice having favorable properties (e.g., with respect to reflecting Pareto-preferred solutions). The classical political institution for such a task is a system of elected representatives making bargains in the context of a representation function (Levitan and March, 1957; March 1958). The classical economic instrument for solving such problems is a contract and its associated incentives for inducing mutually beneficial behavior. Recent treatments, in economics as well as other social sciences, are substantially more sensitive to the problems of conflict than were some previous discussions of the employment contract, recognizing the difficulty of designing incentive schemes for strategic agents that lead them to behave in ways compatible with the wishes of principals, particularly where information is not completely shared. Students of organizations, like classical political philosophers, are inclined to augment this focus on representative systems and bilateral contracts between self-interested actors with an emphasis on institutions of integration that use processes of choice to develop shared preferences or senses of civic and bureaucratic virtue (March and Olsen, 1984; 1987), or to manage the salience of potential conflicts (March and Simon, 1958).

This search for appropriate institutions from a prescriptive point of view has been paralleled by a search for descriptive models of decision-making in conflict systems. Initially, these models emphasized the familiar mechanisms of classical theories of collective choice: power and exchange. Problems in the measurement of power in an organizational or social setting have been examined at some length (March, 1956a; 1957), and have been recognized to involve not only difficulties in measurement but also more profound inadequacies in model specification (March, 1966). Power has proven to be a disappointing concept. It tends to become a tautological label for the unexplained variance in a decision situation, or as a somewhat more political way of refering to differences in resources (endowments) in a system or bargaining and exchange (March, 1970).

The idea that individuals and groups within an organization use their resources, including their control over information, as leverage for pursuing their own interests has proven more useful as a way of framing organizational problems of conflict of interest. It has led to an interest in the ways in which the interests of different organizational participants fit together (March, 1954; 1955; 1980), and in the role of misrepresentation of information (lying) in organizations (March, 1978b; 1981a). Although it is by no means clear that organizational participants always lie when it would be in their immediate self-interest to do so; self-interested manipulation of information is a palpable feature of organizational life. The lack of innocence in organizational information is potentially important. For example, most standard procedures for statistical estimation implicitly assume innocent data, and it has been suggested that one reason experienced organizational participants do not follow such procedures is that they recognize the inadequacies of standard sampling theory in dealing with information provided by strategic actors (March, 1987a).

If strategic behavior is not only common but commonly anticipated, an adequate theory of information in organizations must deal with both the reality of lying (and other strategic action) and the likelihood of its anticipation. This concern for the equilibria of systems of anticipated reactions has made game theory an attractive vehicle for examining the interplay of known liars. In a more behavioral tradition, one early experiment of a very simple estimation problem under partial conflict of interest showed that counter-biases tended to correct for biases (Cyert, March and Starbuck, 1961), a result that has secured some support in more recent studies. But a more general treatment of the problem involves concepts such as trust and reputation that are familiar to behavioral students of organizations and have become a significant concern to modern game-theoretic treatments of strategic information (March, 1981a).

Students of conflict of interest in organizations, however, have also highlighted a somewhat different way in which organizations make decisions in the face of disparate individual and sub-unit goals. A conspicuous feature of standard theories of conflict is the assumption that all competing interests, desires, goals, and preferences in an organization are evoked at the same time and in the same place. Empirical observations of organizations, on the other hand, indicate that attention buffers in organizations limit the simultaneous salience of conflicting demands and the responsiveness of organizations to apparent power (March and Romelaer, 1976). Those buffers are the consequences of three standard features of organizational life. The first is departmentalization and the division of labor (March, 1953; March and Olsen, 1976). Hierarchical organizational structures narrow the audience for any particular decision process, and thereby restrict the realizations of potential conflict across divisions.

The second buffer arises from the limitations on attention imposed by scarcities of time and energy (Cyert and March, 1963; March and Olsen, 1976). Not everything can be attended by everyone. Attention is focused on current problems (currently evoked goals). Action taken to solve current problems produces new problems with respect to other (conflicting) goals, which are then activated. But by then, the individuals or groups who share the first set of concerns are likely to be no longer active. Thus, competing objectives can be addressed sequentially, and conflicts that would threaten a coalition if they were simultaneously salient are buffered from each other.

The third buffer that shields an organization from having to make latent conflict manifest is organizational slack. Excess resources reduce the likelihood that inconsistent demands will be triggered by simultaneous failures to meet targets (Cohen and March, 1974; 1986; March and Olsen, 1976). They reduce the need for joint decision-making (March and Simon, 1958). Large in-process inventories limit the occasions for conflict between producing and consuming units. Large uncommitted resources reduce the risk of facing multiple budget demands that are, in total, impossible to meet (Cyert and March, 1963).

The buffers that make attention to conflicting pressures sequential rather than simultaneous result in organizational phenomena that are often viewed as perverse or inefficient. Organizations solve problems in one part of their domain by creating problems in another, which in turn are solved by creating problems in the first (or another) domain (Cyert and March, 1963). They set policies that they do not subsequently implement (March and Olsen, 1976; Baier, March and Sætren, 1986). They are tolerant of substantial inconsistencies among the actions of different subunits, and they allow the elaboration of multiple duplicative resources and activities (Cohen and March, 1974; 1986; March and Olsen, 1976). These apparently peculiar processes, however, cannot be trivially eliminated. Despite conventional modern ideologies advocating the confrontation and resolution of conflict, organizational experience with conflict indicates that institutions that would otherwise be seriously threatened by internal inconsistencies are able to sustain themselves for long periods by buffering inconsistent demands from each other. And this is possible, primarily because a fundamental feature of organizations is that not everything can be attended at once.

Adaptive Rules

Much organizational behavior, including choice behavior, involves rule-following more than calculation of consequences (March and Simon, 1958; Cyert and March, 1960; Cyert, March and Moore, 1962; Cyert and March, 1963). The logic of rule-following is one of appropriate, rather than optimal, behavior (March, 1981a). Organizations have standard operating procedures, some formally specified and less formal but nonetheless observed. Organizations use employees who are members of professions or who have learned crafts that specify proper procedures. Even where strong elements of consequential decision-making are observed, there are symptoms that the procedures are followed because they have been learned as appropriate in a particular situation or as part of a particular role, rather than because they reflect a deeper commitment to rational choice as a basis for action (March, 1978a; March and Olsen, 1983).

Recognition that rule-following characterizes much of the behavior in organizations directs attention to the processes by which rules are created and changed (March, 1981b; Levitt and March, 1988). The central presumption of most students of organizations is that rules encode experience, that they reflect but normally do not record the lessons of history (March, 1981b, March and Olsen, 1984). To see decisions as driven by rules, and rules as reflecting history, is to argue that a theory of anticipatory, consequential choice will be inadequate to describe many decision situations in organizations. In contrast to the way consequential decision processes look forward in terms of expectations about the future (Cyert and March, 1955), history dependent processes look backward to experience.

Consequential processes of decision-making match contemporaneous desires and actions; history dependent processes are independent of subjective preferences (at least at the time of action).

Most treatments of history dependent processes in the study of organizational decision-making involve either models of variation and selection, as found in population ecology, or models of direct and vicarious experiential learning, as found in theories of organizational learning and imitation (March and Olsen, 1975; March, 1981b; Levinthal and March, 1981; Herriott, Levinthal and March, 1985; Lounamaa and March, 1987). As instruments of intelligence, such processes have the advantage of summarizing the implications of irretrievable past events experienced by many different individuals and groups. As a result, it has occasionally been argued that history-dependent processes of selection and learning assure that surviving rules and organizational forms will have properties of optimality, that inferior rules will be eliminated or transformed, leaving the remaining rules as implicit solutions to optimization problems that are not explicitly solved nor solvable by current rule-followers. Such arguments have been used both to support theories of rational choice in the face of the observation that they posit unrealistic capabilities on the part of decision-makers and to sustain the proposition that effective organizations will be those that learn relatively quickly and relatively precisely.

More careful work on history-dependent processes suggests that they do not reliably lead either to a unique equilibrium or to optimal decisions (March and Olsen, 1975; 1984; March, 1987a). They have the disadvantage of assuming, but not assuring, a fit between the situation in which a rule is applied and the situation in which it has developed, thus of being insensitive to changes in either the environment or the preferences of rule followers (March, 1981b; March and Olsen, 1984). The processes often have multiple equilibria, often seem to be relatively slow compared with the rate of change in the environment, and under some characteristic circumstances trap an adaptive system in behavior rather far from the best (Levinthal and March, 1981; Herriott, Levinthal and March, 1985; Lounamaa and March, 1987).

The work can be illustrated by models of experiential learning in organizations. Several analyses of learning in organizations suggest that experiential learning often leads to intelligent actions, but that it is not guaranteed to do so (March and Olsen, 1975; Herriott, Levinthal and March, 1985). For example, organizations can be described as learning along two dimensions: First, they learn what allocations, strategies, or technologies to use. They come to pursue allocations, strategies, and technologies that have led to success in the past, tend to avoid those that have led to failure (Cyert and March, 1963; Lave and March, 1975).

Second, they learn competence. They become better at things they do often, lose competence at things they do infrequently (Levinthal and March, 1981; Herriott, Levinthal and March, 1985). Within such a framework, it has been shown that learning organizations can rather easily become fixated on sub-optimal allocations, strategies, or technologies. These models show how false learning can lead to actions that compound an error rather than correct it (Lave and March, 1975; Levinthal and March, 1981; Herriott, Levinthal and March, 1985). They indicate that even in a single organization operating within an exogenous environment, rapid learning is frequently a poor learning strategy. Rapid learning tends to overreact to noise and to foreclose the experimentation necessary for discovering good alternatives (Levinthal and March, 1981; Herriott, Levinthal and March, 1985; Lounamaa and March, 1987). When the analysis is extended to an environment of learning organizations, the complications of learning become more profound and the intelligence of rapid learning even more questionable (Herriott, Levinthal and March, 1985; Lounamaa and March, 1987).

These effects are moderated somewhat if experiential knowledge is pooled among a group of organizations through diffusion. Diffusion of experiential knowledge increases the sharing of experience, and average performance of organizations that share knowledge tends to be better than that of isolated learning organizations (Herriott, Levinthal and March, 1985). However, diffusion is a mixed blessing in the long run. As organizations become similar in their choices, their experiences tend to become similar, the information gained from the learning of one tends to become redundant with the learning gained from the learning of the others, and variation among organizations is reduced (Herriott, Levinthal and March, 1985). As a result, profiting from the experience of others appears to be a strategy that is often more sensible from the point of view of any one organization than it is from the point of view of the family of organizations (e.g., an industry or society) unless it is combined with some measures that assure continued experimentation, or foolishness (March, 1971; 1981b).

Such problems in identifying intelligent actions within complex ecologies become more obvious as we explore the development of strategies (whether learned or calculated) within competing organizations containing several levels existing over long periods of time. What is optimal in the short run is not necessarily optimal in the long run, so it is quite possible that strategies permitting an organization to thrive in its maturity make it unlikely that it will reach that stage (March, 1981b; Levinthal and March, 1981). What is optimal for a subunit is not necessarily optimal for the organization (March, 1955; 1980). What is optimal for each organization in a family of organizations may not be optimal for the family viewed as a renewable collection (March, 1956b; 1956c; 1981b; 1988). These complications have led to considerable diminution in our confidence in simple models for assessing the intelligence of alternative organizational actions.

Models of experiential learning treat success as rewarding and failure as punishing. In the tradition of earlier studies of organizations, success and failure are differentiated by a target or aspiration level. The sharpness of the distinction has consequences (Levinthal and March, 1981), but even greater consequences follow from the fact that the aspirations adapt to experience, generally rising with success and falling with failure – though not necessarily at the same rate (March and Simon, 1958; Cyert, Feigenbaum and March, 1959; Cyert and March, 1963). Aspirations also adapt to the experience of others within a reference group (Cyert and March, 1963; Herriott, Levinthal and March, 1985). These relations between aspirations and past experience have long been noted. Their importance has only gradually been recognized.

Aspirations that adapt strictly to the experience of the single organization change the original slack/search model. Slack adjustment and aspiration adaptation are, in effect, alternative mechanisms for bringing organizational goals and organizational performance together. When aspirations change in the direction of performance, parallel fluctuations in organizational slack are reduced (and vice versa) (March and Sevón, 1987). Adaptive aspirations also have consequences for risk taking in organizations. Risk taking is sensitive to the difference between performance and aspirations. A context of moderate failure leads to greater risk taking than a context of moderate success (March and Shapira, 1982; 1987; March, 1988). This variation in risk taking is usually discussed in terms of its contribution to improving the likelihood of survival (March, 1981b). Such a risk strategy protects survival; but because survivors become risk averse, the strategy limits the aggregate performance of the population of survivors. Thus, it may not be attractive to a family of organizations. However, it has been shown that variable risk taking, when combined with an appropriately adaptive aspiration, leads not only to a higher survival rate but also to higher average performance of survivors than is achieved with a fixed risk preference of the same scale (March, 1988).

Finally, adaptive aspirations have implications for understanding organizational learning. If there are modest fluctuations over time (due either to noise or to exogenous shocks) in the potential of the environment, rapid adjustment of an organization's aspirations to its own achievements tends to produce a sequence of successes and failures that is independent of the strategies chosen. Thus, it leads to high rates of experimentation but little effective learning (Levinthal and March, 1981; Herriott, Levinthal and March, 1985). On the other hand, if aspirations diffuse through a population of organizations, targets tend to become more similar across organizations than do achievements. As a result, organizations tend to have either long strings of subjective successes or long strings of subjective failures. Either kind of experience produces superstitious learning (Herriott, Levinthal and March, 1985). Organizations that are persistently successful tend to become fixated on one strategy or another, independent of their comparative values. Organizations that are persistently unsuccessful tend to keep shifting strategies (Lave and March, 1975).

Decision-making under Ambiguity

Classical models of choice and their modern derivatives ordinarily recognize two major kinds of complications in making decisions. The first is the fact that although the possible outcomes due to nature are known, it is not known which of these possibilities will be realized. Consequences can be anticipated only up to a probability distribution. This complication has led to considerable elaboration of procedures for dealing with single-person decision-making under risk. The second major complication is the fact that some consequences depend on the action of other strategic actors (who are simultaneously aware of the interdependence). This complication has led to considerable elaboration of game theory. Students of organizational decision-making have profited from, and contributed to, speculations about the consequences of these two classical problems in choice, but they have added several others that have come collectively to be called the problem of ambiguity.

The first ambiguity is an *ambiguity about preferences*. Within decision theory, preferences are treated as important but unproblematic. A decision-maker is assumed to have preferences that are consistent, stable, and exogenous to the choice process. Observations of organizations suggest that preferences are often far from consistent, stable, or exogenous (Feigenbaum and March, 1960; Cohen and March, 1974; 1986; March, 1978b). Indeed, organizations are frequently criticized for their inabilities to exhibit such preferences. The criticism is sometimes articulated in terms of implementation problems, although some of the more conspicuous studies of implementation failures seem to exaggerate the probable clarity of policy maker intentions (Baier, March and Sætren, 1986). More generally, organizational preferences change, partly as a result of exogenous pressures but also partly as a result of the actions they control. Aspiration levels adapt to experience, and the dimensions of desires are transformed through the experience of deciding among actions, implementing them, and observing their consequences (March, 1978b).

The second ambiguity is an *ambiguity about relevance.* In classical discussions of decision-making in organizations, a logic of causality connects policies to activities, means to ends, solutions to problems, and actions in one part of an organization to actions in another part. All of these linkages are seen as driven by a logic of causal connection. Actual events in organizations appear to be much less tightly coupled (March 1978a). Often there appear to be deep ambiguities in the causal linkages among the various activities of an organization, between problems and their 'solutions', and between how managers act and how they talk (Cohen and March, 1974; 1986; March and Olsen, 1976; March, 1984a). The garbage can model of organizational decision-making is one effort to define an alternative order in terms of which processes might be understood (Cohen, March and Olsen, 1972; March and Olsen, 1976). In a garbage can model, problems, solutions, and decision-makers are connected less by their causal relevance than by their simultaneity (March and Olsen, 1986). It is not a system of disorder, but it appears disorderly when considered within a standard means-end frame.

The third ambiguity is an *ambiguity about history.* Particularly within experiential learning models, but also in anticipatory models in so far as they use history as a basis for expectations about the future, the clarity of history is vital. Yet, history is clearly and notoriously ambiguous (Cohen and March, 1974; 1986; March and Olsen, 1975; 1976). For example, ambiguities about historical causality lie at the heart of difficulties with the concept of power in studies of social institutions (March, 1956a; 1957; 1966). Students of organizations have been particularly interested in the possibilities for, and consequences of, misunderstanding ambiguous experience (March and Cangelosi, 1966; March, 1974a; 1987a). One reflection of this interest is found in discussions of incomplete learning cycles. A complete learning cycle is one in which individual cognitions and preferences affect individual actions, which affect organizational choices, which affect environmental responses, which affect individual cognitions and preferences (March and Olsen, 1975). Although the ambiguities of history compromise the linkages, organizations continue to 'learn' as though the cycle were complete. As a result, a theory of organizational learning has to comprehend both the ways in which ambiguity affects the cycle and the dynamics of learning under such conditions (Cyert and March, 1963; March and Olsen, 1975; Herriott, Levinthal and March, 1985).

Recent interest in the confusions of history in organizations has focused especially on the ways in which well-known human biases in inference and attribution are observed, and facilitated, by the structure of organizations and the ways in which they make decisions (March and Shapira, 1982). Organizational arrangements confound the interpretation of history most clearly through systems of hierarchical promotion, with their powerful potential for superstitious learning on the part of successful managers and their biographers (Cohen and March, 1974; 1986; March, 1978a; 1987b). Although it is not always easy to distinguish observed patterns of mobility from those that would be observed if there were only modest differences among managers (March and March, 1977; 1978; March, 1978a), a system of hierarchical promotion yields top managers who are relatively confident of their own control over their destinies (Cohen and March, 1974; 1986; March and Shapira, 1987) and the appropriateness of their positions and rewards (March, 1984b).

The fourth ambiguity is an *ambiguity about interpretation*. Thinking about life in terms of choice introduces systematic bias into interpretations of decision processes (March, 1973). The fundamental presumption of virtually all theories of decision-making is that decision processes are organized around the making of decisions and understandable in terms of decision outcomes (March and Olsen, 1976; March, 1981a). Thus, information is seen as clarifying decision outcomes; participants in the process are seen as primarily concerned with influencing substantive decisions; the activities surrounding the making of decisions are interpreted in terms of the decisions that are made. Observations of organizations suggest that these presumptions may be misleading. Although information is used in making decisions, the gathering and citing of information is often better understood as symbolic action (Feldman and March, 1981; March and Sevón, 1984). Although participants care about outcomes, they also often care about the symbolic meaning of the process and the outcome (March, 1956d; March and Olsen, 1976; 1983). Although participants come and go partly as a function of the importance of the issues involved, they also enter the decision arena and leave it as a function of the rest of their lives within which any particular organizational decision often is relatively unimportant (March and Olsen, 1976; March and Romelaer, 1976). In short, decision-making is a highly contextual, sacred activity, surrounded by myth and ritual, and as much concerned with the interpretative order as with the specifics of particular choices (March and Olsen, 1983; 1984; March and Sevón, 1984).

Understanding these ambiguities is necessary not only for understanding and predicting organizational choice behavior, but also for improving it (Cohen and March, 1974; 1986; March 1978a; 1978b; 1984a). On the one hand, intelligent tactics within ambiguous worlds require an understanding of ambiguity even by a decision-maker who is endowed with unambiguous goals and a clear comprehension of history. Successful tactics for the Machiavellian actor in an ambiguous world call for the exploitation of garbage cans and incomplete learning cycles in the name of rationality (Cohen and March, 1974; 1986). They recognize the implications of superstitious learning for managerial motivation and education (March and March, 1977; March, 1978a; 1984a; 1987b). They include procedures for dealing with decision disappointment and biases in inference (March and Shapira, 1982; Harrison and March, 1984). They involve developing a culture of interpretation that organizes the actions of others and provides cultural support for desired actions (March and Olsen, 1983; 1987).

Such strategies are characteristically ways in which clever people can exploit ambiguity for unambiguous ends. Prescriptive discussions of ambiguity go beyond such tactics, however. It is argued that ambiguity is not only a fact of life, thus a necessary context for action by rational actors, but also often a normatively attractive state. The argument is that ambiguity about preferences allows goals to develop through experience (March, 1971; 1978b; Cohen and March, 1974; 1986). Ambiguity about relevance allows relevance to be explored (March and Olsen, 1976; 1986). Ambiguity about history facilitates motivation to cope with it (March, 1974b; 1975; 1987b). Ambiguity about interpretation allows communication to evoke more than a communicator knows (March and Sevón, 1984; March, 1987a). At a more general level, it is argued that the development of meaning through myth, ritual, and the elaboration of cultural symbols is a major part of modern organizational life. Interpretation, not choice, is what is distinctively human (March and Olsen, 1983; 1984; March and Sevón, 1984; March, 1987a).

An Epilogue

If scientific progress is measured by simplification, this is a story of retrogression. From a simple perspective of anticipatory, consequential, rational choice, we have gone first to a recognition of the limitations on rationality, then to concern for internal conflict, then to history dependent conceptions of human action, and finally to an awareness of the profound ambiguities surrounding action in organizations. Although decision-making as it occurs in organizations can probably be better understood and improved through these speculations, the speculations force us to less simple formulations. Life has proven to be more complicated than our earlier mythologies of it.

The research has been on organizational decision-making, and the speculations are about that domain; but they highlight a few issues that transcend the study of organizations or decision-making. These issues are particularly significant for understanding research on behavior that might be interpreted as being intentional or functional, thus as being understandable in terms of its consequences. Studies of decision-making in organizations are natural contexts for examining the limitations of consequential logics as bases for the interpretation of human action. The meta-theoretical issues that differentiate speculations about decisions in organizations from more classical ideas about choice are broad ones that permeate the social and behavioral sciences; and it is possible that some of the speculations that have arisen within the relatively limited context of modern hierarchical organizations as they make decisions may have implications for other speculative endeavors.

1. The question of *historical efficiency*. Many theories in a consequential tradition treat outcomes as a functionally necessary consequence of environmental conditions (at equilibrium). They assume that the processes of history are efficient in driving organizations to unique equilibria relatively quickly. As a result, such theories are relatively uninterested in time paths to equilibria or in the details of historical development. They are substantially indifferent to understanding the processes or mechanisms that translate environmental imperatives into action. The traditions of organizational decision research, on the other hand, are traditions of understanding the mechanisms by which outcomes are realized, even when correct predictions can be made without such understanding. And those traditions embrace the proposition that history is often inefficient in the sense that it has multiple equilibria and moves toward those equilibria relatively slowly.

2. The question of *ecological complexity*. Many theories of strategic action assume that strategies of decision-making that are intelligent for a single actor in an ecologically simple world will also prove to be intelligent in a complex ecology involving many actors making choices simultaneously. In effect, a complex world of intelligent action is assumed to be decomposable into numerous simple worlds whose interactions can be ignored. In a structure of nested interactive learning institutions, such a decomposition assumption is likely to be implausible. The problems include, but go beyond the interactions considered within n-person game theory. Studies of organizational decision-making suggest that the environmental context of human behavior is relatively complex, thus that determining intelligent action in a particular case is difficult, and many apparently attractive strategies will prove to be less attractive with deeper analysis or longer experience.

3. The question of *preferences*. Many contemporary theories of human behavior and human institutions assume that preferences are important to action, that choice is driven by human desires, wants, interests, values, goals, or subjective utilities; and that intelligence requires such a linkage. At the same time, the creation and modification of those preferences are typically treated as being incomprehensibly subjective, thus beyond the realm of either descriptive or prescriptive theories. In effect, we have

theories of willful and intentional action without a theory of will or intention. Theories of organizational decision-making are different in two respects. On the one hand, many elements of a theory of organizational decision-making are devoid of explicit preferences. Choices are made by following rules and roles and criteria of appropriateness, rather than by a calculation of expected consequences. On the other hand, decision-making is seen as a primary arena for the molding of preferences as well as acting on them. As a result, preferences become endogenous to a theory of choice.

4. The question of *coherence*. The idea of coherence is central to modern thinking about human existence. Individuals are seen as seeking and securing coherence in attitudes and between attitudes and action; institutions are seen as coherent assemblages of tasks and activities; intra-individual and inter-individual conflict is seen as moving toward resolution; health in individuals and institutions is associated with internal integration. Observations in organizations, on the other hand, suggest enduring incoherence. Although there are pressures and processes leading to coherence in organizations and action in organizations are in some ways impressively coordinated, the apparent coherence is produced less by resolving inconsistencies than by obscuring them. By limiting attention at any one time to a relatively small number of problems, values, participants, and constraints, organizations maintain an ideology of consistency within a reality of contradictions and dualities among actions and beliefs.

5. The question of *meaning*. Theories of intentional action generally build on ideas of comprehension mediated by language. These comprehensions are treated as substantially self-evident. The terms of reference of choice are taken as given and imposed on decision makers by the logic of the choice situation. Within the tradition of organizational decision research, on the other hand, all human behaviors, including the making of choices and learning from experience, are seen as embedded in interpretive systems to which they contribute and from which they draw meaning. It is through understanding these contributions to the interpretive order that the institutions of society can be understood.

At the outset, organization theorists were described as a deviant sect in the church of rational choice. Like many deviants, they simultaneously treasure their heretical status and labor to convert the faithful. In the latter mode, they cannot avoid noting the substantial extent to which the speculative heresies of students of organizational decision-making have achieved respectability in the catechism of the mother church. In the former mode, they observe, with an unreconciled mixture of dismay and gratification, the extent to which the bishops continue to sustain and reproduce their orthodoxies, leaving to the deviants the gratifications of savoring and elaborating their heresies.

References

Baier, V. E., March, J. G., and Sætren, H. (1986) Implementation and Ambiguity, *Scandinavian Journal of Management Studies*, 2: 197–212.

Cohen, M. D., and March, J. G. (1974) *Leadership and Ambiguity: The American College President.* New York, NY: McGraw-Hill.

Cohen, M. D., and March, J. G. (1986) *Leadership and Ambiguity*, 2nd ed. Boston, MA: Harvard Business School Press.

Cohen, M. D., March, J. G., and Olsen, J. P. (1972) A Garbage Can Model of Organizational Choice, *Administrative Science Quarterly*, 17: 1–25.

Cyert, R. M., Dill, W. R., and March, J. G. (1958) The Role of Expectations in Business Decision-Making, *Administrative Science Quarterly*, 3: 309–40.

Cyert, R. M., Feigenbaum, E. A., and March, J. G. (1959) Models in a Behavioral Theory of the Firm, *Behavioral Science*, 4: 81–95.

Cyert, R. M., and March, J. G. (1955) Organizational Structure and Pricing Behavior in an Oligopolistic Market, *American Economic Review*, 45: 129–39.

Cyert, R. M., and March, J. G., (1956) Organizational Factors in the Theory of Oligopoly, *Quarterly Journal of Economics*, 70: 44–64.

Cyert, R. M., and March, J. G., (1959) A Behavioral Theory of Organizational Objectives, in M. Haire (ed.), *Modern Organization Theory*. New York, NY: Wiley, pp. 76–90.

Cyert, R. M., and March, J. G., (1960) Business Operating Procedures, in B. von Haller Gilmer (ed.), *Industrial Psychology*. New York, NY: McGraw-Hill, pp. 67–87.

Cyert, R. M., and March, J. G., (1963) *A Behavioral Theory of the Firm.* Englewood Cliffs, NJ: Prentice-Hall.

Cyert, R. M., March, J. G., and Moore, C. G. (1962) A Model of Retail Ordering and Pricing Behavior by a Department Store, in R. Frank, A. A. Kuehn, W. Massy (eds), *Quantitative Techniques in Marketing Analysis*. Homewood, IL: Irwin, pp. 502–22.

Cyert, R. M., March, J. G., and Starbuck, W. H. (1961) Two Experiments on Organizational Estimation under Conflict of Interest, *Management Science*, 7: 254–64.

Feigenbaum, E. A., and March, J. G. (1960) Latent Motives, Group Discussion, and the 'Quality' of Group Decisions in a Non-objective Decision Problem, *Sociometry*, 23: 50–6.

Feldman, M. S., and March, J. G. (1981) Information in Organizations as Signal and Symbol, *Administrative Science Quarterly*, 26: 171–86.

Harrison, J. R., and March, J. G. (1984) Decision Making and Post-Decision Surprises, *Administrative Science Quarterly*, 29: 26–42.

Herriott, S. R., Levinthal, D., and March, J. G. (1985) Learning from Experience in Organizations, *American Economic Review*, 75: 298–302.

Lave, C. A., and March, J. G. (1975) *An introduction to Models in the Social Sciences.* Philadelphia: Harper and Row.

Levinthal, D., and March, J. G. (1981) A Model of Adaptive Organizational Search, *Journal of Economic Behavior and Organization*, 2: 307–33.

Levitan, R. E., and March, J. G. (1957) A Set of Necessary, Sufficient, and Independent Conditions for Proportional Representation (abstract), and *Econometrica*, 25: 361-2.

Levitt, B., and March, J. G. (1988) Organizational Learning, *Annual Review of Sociology*, 14: forthcoming.

Lounamaa, P. H., and March, J. G. (1987) Adaptive Coordination of a Learning Team, *Management Science*, 33: 107-23.

Manns, C. L., and March, J. G. (1978) Financial Adversity, Internal Competition, and Curricular Change in a University, *Administrative Science Quarterly*, 23: 541-52.

March, J. C., and March, J. G. (1977) Almost Random Careers: The Wisconsin School Superintendency, 1940-1972, *Administrative Science Quarterly*, 22: 307-409.

March, J. C., and March, J. G. (1978) Performance Sampling in Social Matches, *Administrative Science Quarterly*, 23: 434-53.

March, J. G. (1953) Husband-Wife Interaction over Political Issues, *Public Opinion Quarterly*, 17: 461-70.

March, J. G. (1954) Group Norms and the Active Minority, *American Sociological Review*, 19: 733-41.

March, J. G. (1955) Group Autonomy and Internal Group Control, *Social Forces*, 33: 322-6.

March, J. G. (1956a) An Introduction to the Theory and Measurement of Influence, *American Political Science Review*, 49: 431-51.

March, J. G. (1956b) Sociological Jurisprudence Revisited, *Stanford Law Review*, 8: 499-534.

March, J. G. (1956c) Reply, *Stanford Law Review*, 8: 772-3.

March, J. G. (1956d) Influence Measurement in Experimental and Semi-Experimental Groups, *Sociometry*, 19: 260-71.

March, J. G. (1957) Measurement Concepts in the Theory of Influence, *Journal of Politics*, 19: 202-26.

March, J. G. (1958) Party Legislative Representation as a Function of Election Results, *Public Opinion Quarterly*, 21: 521-42.

March, J. G. (1962a) Some Observations on Political Theory, in L. K. Caldwell (ed.), *New Viewpoints on Politics and Public Affairs*. Bloomington, IN: University of Indiana Press, pp. 121-39.

March, J. G. (1962b) The Business Firm as a Political Coalition, *Journal of Politics*, 24: 662-78.

March, J. G., (ed.) (1965) *Handbook of Organizations*. Chicago, IL: Rand McNally.

March, J. G. (1966) The Power of Power, in D. Easton (ed.), *Varieties of Political Theory*. Englewood Cliffs, NJ: Prentice-Hall, pp. 39-70.

March, J. G. (1970) Politics and the City, in W. Gorham (ed.), *Urban Processes as Viewed by the Social Sciences*. Washington, DC: The Urban Institute, pp. 21-37.

March, J. G. (1971) The Technology of Foolishness, *Civiløkonomen* (Copenhagen), 18(4): 4-12.

March, J. G. (1973) Model Bias in Social Action, *Review of Educational Research* 42: 413-29.

March, J. G. (1974a) Analytical Skills and the University Training of Educational Administrators, *Journal of Educational Administration,* 7: 17–44.

March, J. G. (1974b) Competence and Commitment in Educational Administration, in L. B. Mayhew (ed.), *Educational Leadership and Declining Enrollments.* Berkeley, CA: McCutchan, pp. 131–41.

March, J. G. (1975) Education and the Pursuit of Optimism, *Texas Tech Journal of Education,* 2: 5–16.

March, J. G. (1978a) American Public School Administration: A Short Analysis, *School Review,* 82: 217–50.

March, J. G. (1978b) Bounded Rationality, Ambiguity, and the Engineering of Choice, *Bell Journal of Economics,* 9: 587–608.

March, J. G. (1980) *Autonomy as a Factor in Group Organization: A Study in Politics.* New York, NY: Arno Press.

March, J. G. (1981a) Decisions in Organizations and Theories of Choice, in A. Van de Ven and W. Joyce (eds), *Assessing Organizational Design and Performance.* New York, NY: Wiley Interscience, pp. 205–44.

March, J. G. (1981b) Footnotes to Organizational Change, *Administrative Science Quarterly,* 26: 563–77.

March, J. G. (1982) Theories of Choice and Making Decisions, *Transaction/ SOCIETY,* 21: 29–39.

March, J. G. (1984a) How We Talk and How We Act: Administrative Theory and Administrative Life, in T. J. Sergiovanni and J. E. Corbally (eds), *Leadership and Organization Culture.* Urbana, IL: University of Illinois Press, pp. 18–35.

March, J. G. (1984b) Notes on Ambiguity and Executive Compensation, *Scandinavian Journal of Management Studies,* 1: 53–64.

March, J. G. (1987a) Ambiguity and Accounting: The Elusive Link between Information and Decision Making, *Accounting, Organizations, and Society,* forthcoming, 1987.

March, J. G. (1987b) Mundane Organizations and Heroic Leaders, in L. Mayhew and F. León García (eds), *Seminarios Sobre Administración Universitaria.* Mexicali, México: Centro de Enseñanza Técnica y Superiór.

March, J. G. (1988) Variable Risk Preferences and Adaptive Aspirations, *Journal of Economic Behavior and Organizations,* 9: forthcoming.

March, J. G., and Cangelosi, V. E. (1966) An Experiment in Model Building, *Behavioral Science* 11: 71–5.

March, J. G., and Olsen, J. P. (1975) The Uncertainty of the Past: Organizational Learning Under Ambiguity, *European Journal of Political Research,* 3: 147–71.

March, J. G., and Olsen, J. P. (1976) *Ambiguity and Choice in Organizations.* Bergen, Norway: Universitetsforlaget.

March, J. G., and Olsen, J. P. (1983) Organizing Political Life: What Administrative Reorganization Tells Us about Governing, *American Political Science Review,* 77: 281–96.

March, J. G., and Olsen, J. P. (1984) The New Institutionalism: Organizational Factors in Political Life, *American Political Science Review,* 78: 734–49.

March, J. G., and Olsen, J. P. (1986) Garbage Can Models of Decision Making in Organizations, in J. G. March and R. Weissinger-Baylon (eds), *Ambiguity*

and Command: Organizational Perspectives on Military Decision Making.
Cambridge, MA: Ballinger, pp. 11–35.

March, J. G., and Olsen, J. P. (1987) Popular Sovereignty and the Search for Appropriate Institutions, *Journal of Public Policy*, forthcoming.

March, J. G., and Romelaer, P. (1976) Position and Presence in the Drift of Decisions in J. G. March and J. P. Olsen, *Ambiguity and Choice in Organizations.* Bergen, Norway: Universitetsforlaget, pp. 251–275.

March, J. G., and Sevón, G. (1984) Gossip, Information, and Decision-Making, in L. S. Sproull and J. P. Crecine (eds), *Advances in Information Processing in Organizations,* Vol. I. Greenwich, CT: JAI Press, pp. 95–107.

March, J. G., and Sevón, G. (1987) Behavioral Perspectives on Theories of the Firm, in W. F. van Raaij, G. M. van Veldhoven, and K–E. Wärneryd (eds), *Handbook of Economic Psychology.* Amsterdam: North-Holland.

March, J. G., and Shapira, Z. (1982) Behavioral Decision Theory and Organizational Decision Theory, in G. Ungson and D. Braunstein (eds), *Decision Making: An Interdisciplinary Inquiry.* Boston, MA: Kent Publishing Company, pp. 92–115.

March, J. G., and Shapira, Z. (1987) Managerial Perspectives on Risk and Risk Taking, *Management Science,* forthcoming.

March, J. G., and Simon, H. A. (1958) *Organizations.* New York, NY: Wiley.

Part I
The Allocation
of Attention

1

Organizational Structure and Pricing Behavior in an Oligopolistic Market

R. M. Cyert and J. G. March

One of the most common propositions in the literature of organization theory is that a change in organizational structure results in a change in operative organization goals.[1] To the extent that this is true, it should be possible to develop a model that specifies a meaningful relationship between significant characteristics of organizational structure and some important attributes of organizational behavior.[2]

The theory of price determination in an oligopolistic market situation is generally unsatisfactory to economists.[3] Typically, neither the level of

1 See, for example, E. Dale, *Planning and Developing the Company Organization Structure*, AMA Research Report No. 20 (New York, 1952), pp. 23–38; H. A. Simon, D. W. Smithburg, V. A. Thompson, *Public Administration* (New York, 1950), pp. 136, 168–72. For a study of a specific example, see H. A. Simon, Birth of an Organization: The Economic Cooperation Administration. *Public Administration Review*, Autumn 1953, XIII, 227–36.

2 For a general discussion of the application of organizational theory to the economic theory of the firm, see A. G. Papandreou, Some Basic Problems in the Theory of the Firm, in B. F. Haley, (ed.), *A Survey of Contemporary Economics*, Vol. 2 (Homewood, Illinois, 1952). The present paper may be reviewed as an attempt to meet the comments of E. S. Mason, *ibid*, pp. 221–2, with reference to the need for specific theoretical examples of how the addition of organization theory variables contributes to the explanation of firm behavior.

3 See K. N. Rothschild, Price Theory and Oligopoly. *Economic Journal*, September 1947, LVII, 299–320.

This paper was first published in the *American Economic Review*, XLV, March 1955. It is based in part on work done under a grant made to the Carnegie Institute of Technology by the Ford Foundation for the study of organization theory. The authors, who are, respectively, assistant professor of economics and senior research fellow in administration at the Carnegie Institute of Technology, Pittsburgh, wish to express their thanks to their colleagues on the faculty of the Graduate School of Industrial Administration and to Professor James W. Fesler for their helpful comments on an earlier draft.

price nor price changes can be explained. The tendency of oligopolistic firms to change price relatively infrequently in comparison with firms in competitive markets has frequently been noted.[4] While it is not maintained here that organization theory can provide the whole, or even the major answer, it is the purpose of this paper to indicate some of the ways in which such theory can be brought to bear on the problem of the price behavior of a firm in an oligopoly market.

Since 'organizational structure' and 'price behavior' are ambiguous terms, they are defined in section I. In addition, the development of the model requires the specification of a series of functional relations between organizational features and pricing behavior. This is done in section II. In section III, an example of two ideal-type organization models, which under our hypotheses will exhibit distinctively different price behavior, is presented, and the implications of the paper are illustrated by an application to a classical problem in economic theory. Finally, in section IV, a program for empirical analysis is indicated.

Definition of Variables

The approach taken here should not be viewed as challenging the basic variables that have been treated as price determinants in economic theory. For firms operating in a perfectly competitive market, for example, nothing discussed in this paper has much relevance. The position taken is that the firm's perception of the market and the firm's perception of its capabilities for action are both affected by its own organizational structure. Given significantly different organizational structures, two firms facing the same external market and using the same set of variables in decision-making will exhibit substantial differences in price behavior.

Price behavior is defined in terms of three characteristics:

1 frequency of price change is measured as the number of changes per time unit;[5]
2 magnitude of price change is measured for any given change by the ratio of the amount of change (i.e., the absolute difference between the old and the new prices) to the old price;
3 direction of price change can be positive or negative, measured with respect to the last previous price.

---

4 P. Sweezy, Demand under Conditions of Oligopoly. *Journal Political Economy,* August 1939, XLVII, 568–73. See also, G. J. Stigler, 'The Kinky Oligopoly Demand Curve and Rigid Prices,' *Journal Political Economy,* October 1947, LV, 432–49.

5 In the present analysis, the primary interest is in the organizational effect on price behavior of firms operating in the same market. The restriction to firms operating in the same

Organization structure is defined in terms of two characteristics:

1 The communication pattern of the organization. Pricing decisions are assumed to be based upon expectations concerning future sales, costs, and competitors' behavior. One of the functions of the organization of the firm is to provide information upon which such expectations can be based, and the design of informational channels by means of which such information reaches the decision-makers comprises the communication pattern of the firm.[6]

Primary interest is in the relay points in a communication chain. A relay point is a 'message center' which receives, decodes, encodes, and then retransmits an item of information.[7] Relay points can be distinguished by the number of major variables (e.g., cost) about which they transmit information. This distinction is hypothesized to have important consequences for the amount of bias introduced at a particular relay point. Bias is defined to occur if any information is eliminated, modified, or added before a message is retransmitted. The character of control over a relay point is hypothesized to be decisive for the direction of the bias introduced, as is indicated more explicitly below.

The communication pattern of the organization is described by the nature of four different communication chains within the organization: the communication chains for demand information, for cost information, for information on competitors' behavior, and for information on firm policy. The nature of a given communication chain is determined by: (a) the number of relay points in the chain; (b) their character; and (c) their order. The number of relay points in a communication chain is represented by a nonnegative integer. The character of a relay point is determined by the type of information transmitted through it. If a relay point transmits only one type of information, it is defined to have the characteristic of that information. If information relating to more than one variable is transmitted by a relay point, the character of the relay point is determined by the relative

---

in the same market is made in order to hold constant the restraints imposed by market forces upon the frequency of price changes. Since the stringency of such restraints varies from one market to another, a comparison across markets of the organizational effect upon frequency of price change could not be made without the introduction of some concept of 'opportunities for change'.

6 Obviously, the relevant communication channels are those actually in use – not necessarily simply those specified by formal organization rules. There is no reason to believe that such insistence creates insuperable observational difficulties. See K. Davies, A Method of Studying Communication Patterns in Organizations. *Pers. Psychology*, Autumn 1953, VI, 301–12; A. H. Rubenstein, Problems in the Measurement of Interpersonal Communication in an Ongoing Situation. *Sociometry*, February 1953, XVI, 78–100.

7 See C. E. Shannon, *The Mathematical Theory of Communication* (Urbana, 1949).

frequency over time of incoming communications concerning the different variables. Thus, if most of the messages received relate to cost information, the relay point is considered to be a 'cost' relay. The ordering of relay points is specified to distinguish, for example, a communication chain for competitors' behavior in which information on competitors passes through a 'demand' relay point and subsequently through a 'cost' relay prior to reaching the decision-making unit from a similar chain in which the ordering of 'cost' and 'demand' relay points is reversed.

2 The size of the decision-making unit in the organization is measured by the number of individuals in the decision-making unit for each of whom it is correct to say that there is no more influential person in the unit. Thus, if the decision-making unit for a pricing decision is a committee of four in which two committee members are dominant over the other two but equal in power with respect to each other, the size of the decision-making unit is 2. The problem of identifying the distinguishing power differentials within the formal decision-making unit is susceptible to solution by the application of social-psychological techniques of influence measurement to the decision-making activities of the unit under investigation.[8] For example, one method for defining power relations that has been used successfully consists in an analysis of the remarks made during decision-making conferences.[9] The variable, therefore, is operationally defined although one should not expect the analysis in any given case to be simple. Under certain conditions, distinctive pricing consequences are seen as arising from critical differences in the size of the decision-making unit. These hypotheses are found below.

Functional Relations

Demand, cost, and competitors' behavior have been the standard variables of most oligopoly models since Cournot. This paper makes no attempt to deviate from that tradition. On the contrary, the goal is to augment oligopoly theory by introducing into it some fundamental propositions of the theory of organizational behavior. Two modifications of traditional oligopoly models are suggested by such theory. The first is recognition

8   For some examples of influence measures, see C. I. Hovland, I. L. Janis, H. H. Kelley, *Communication and Persuasion* (New Haven, 1953); R. Lippitt, N. Polansky, S. Rosen, The Dynamics of Power. *Human Rel.,* February 1952, V, 37–64.

9   J. G. March, Husband–Wife Interaction over Political Issues, *Public Opinion Quarterly,* Winter, 1953–4, XVII, 461–70; T. M. Mills, Power Relations in Three-Person Groups. *Am. Soc. Rev.,* Aug. 1953, XVIII, 351–57; F. L. Strodtbeck, Husband–Wife Interaction over Revealed Differences. *Am. Soc. Rev.,* August 1951, XVI, 468–73.

of the fact that the values of the relevant variables actually used within the firm for establishing price are functions both of data drawn from the real world and of the organizational structure through which those data are transmitted to the decision-making unit; the second is similar recognition of the fact that the method by which perceived information on the relevant variables is translated into pricing decisions is a function of the decision-making unit's perception of, and adherence to, official firm policy.

Official firm policy, in the sense in which it is used here, consists in a specific set of constraints placed by the holders of legitimate authority in the firm upon the pursuit of organizational goals by their subordinates. A series of hypotheses with respect to the relative dependence of a pricing decision upon official firm policy, given the size of the decision-making unit, is made. The mechanisms involved are also specified.

1   Decisions by a group will, in general, be more dependent upon firm policy than will decisions by an individual. The proposition is deduced from the theory of group norms and reference-group behavior.[10] There is a reasonable amount of evidence to support the prediction that an individual with an attitude at variance with his perception of the group's attitude will tend (according to the relevance of the group for the satisfaction of individual goals) to adjust his 'public' position to conform to the position he expects the group to take.[11] Such behavior may be exhibited even in the limiting case where all members hold a position at variance with their common perceptions of the group standard.[12] Thus, even if every member of the decision-making group is 'cost-minded', if each believes all of the others to be 'sales-minded', the decision will tend to be a sales-minded one. Since in the absence of contradictory evidence, each member of the group can be assumed to believe all other members of the group to be in agreement with firm policy, the operation of group norms serves to enforce conformity to that policy.

10   A reference group for a given individual consists in those other individuals with whom he perceives himself sharing common evaluative criteria for judging an attitudinal position. The literature on reference-group theory is fairly extensive. For example, see T. M. Newcomb, *Social Psychology* (New York, 1950), chapter 14, pp. 220–32; R. K. Merton and A. S. Kitt, Contributions to the Theory of Reference Group Behavior, in Merton and P. F. Lazarsfeld, (eds), *Continuities in Social Research, Studies in the Scope and Method of 'The American Soldier'* (Glencoe, 1950). The theory of group norms is less well developed. See S. A. Stouffer, An Analysis of Conflicting Social Norms. *Am. Soc. Rev.,* December 1949, XIV, 707–17; J. G. March, Group Norms and the Active Minority. *Am. Soc. Rev.,* December 1954, XIX, No. 6.

11   For example, see R. L. Gorden, Interaction Between Attitude and the Definition of the Situation in the Expression of Opinion. *Am. Soc. Rev.,* February 1952, XVII, 50–8; M. Sherif, A Study of Some Social Factors in Perception. *Archiv. Psychol.* (1935), No. 187.

12   On this point, see H. A. Simon, Notes on the Observation and Measurement of Political Power. *Jour. Pol.,* November 1953, XV, 500–16, especially 510–11.

From this it should be clear that when a relationship is predicted between the size of the decision-making unit and the extent to which decisions will be independent of official firm policy, the assumption is made that reference groups (e.g., Board of Directors, professional associations) other than the pricing unit itself can be ignored. Such an assumption is based on a prediction that all decision-making units, whether composed of an individual or a group, will be subject to the same outside pressures; but only the members of a group unit will have the additional pressure of internal group norms.[13]

2   If a decision contrary to firm policy is reached by a decision-making unit, it will be more stable if made by a group than if made by an individual. This follows from the premises of the preceding hypothesis. A group provides the individual with a defense against outside pressures and simultaneously exerts a pressure toward intragroup conformity upon him.[14] The group will ordinarily be less effective in enforcing a 'revolutionary' decision than in enforcing an 'ideologically sound' decision. This stems from the prediction that the latter type of decision will ordinarily create fewer cross-pressures than the former.[15]

With respect to the communication-structure variable, two hypotheses of perceptual bias are made:

1 As the length of the communication chain is increased, factors are introduced that have the effect of inhibiting change. The temporal bias introduced by the change in conditions during the interval from the original transmission of the information to its final receipt by the decision-making unit is represented as a function of the number of relay points through which the information must pass. Clearly, this is only an approximation. The significance of variations in transmission speed among the relay points (e.g., cost data travels more rapidly through cost channels than through demand channels) is neither denied nor introduced into the system, except implicitly in the statement of the second bias below.

The consequences of the temporal bias for the frequency of price adjustments stem both from the fact that one never 'catches up' with

13   Otherwise, it might be argued that where a pricing decision is made by a single individual, he will act with the originators of firm policy as a referent, and that, therefore, the test of the mechanism posited here would be vitiated by this restraint upon his 'independence'.

14   For a general introduction to the study of group pressures, see L. Festinger, S. Schachter, K. Back, *Social Pressures in Informal Groups* (New York, 1950); D. Cartwright and A. Zander, *Group Dynamics: Research and Theory* (Evanston, 1953), Part 3.

15   For discussions of the consequences of cross-pressures, see L. M. Killian, The Significance of Multiple-Group Membership in Disaster. *Am. Jour. Soc.,* January 1952, LVII, 309–14; L. Festinger, The Role of Group Belongingness in a Voting Situation. *Human Relations,* November 1947, I, 154–80; A. H. Leighton, *The Governing of Men* (Princeton, 1945).

current information and also from the attempts of members of the organization to adjust for the bias by means of forecasts (e.g., 'What will the situation be by the time this information reaches the decision-maker?'). It is hypothesized that both major consequences of the time-lag in communication serve to introduce into the premises of the pricing decision a bias against change. Note that this bias operates not only in the communication of, for example, cost information upward but also in the communication of firm-policy information downward.

2 The character of the communication chain introduces a bias into the information transmitted to the decision-making unit. The form of the bias is a tendency for a relay point to de-emphasize information inconsistent with the information with which it is primarily concerned. For example, let us make the assumption that the size of the market is consistently overestimated by sales departments and costs are consistently overestimated by accounting departments.[16] Let us further assume that overestimation of demand results in an aggressive price policy (i.e., frequent price changes, price-leadership), overestimation of cost in a passive price policy (i.e., infrequent changes, price-following). Under these assumptions, the firm's reaction to the behavior of others will be related to the number of biasing relay points through which cost data must pass relative to the number for demand data. In particular, it is predicted that the communication of demand data through a cost relay point will tend to produce a passive price policy, and the communication of cost data through a demand relay point an aggressive price policy. Similar deductions can be made with reference to communications downward regarding firm policy.

If the organization is stable, it is expected that the biasing of information will be reinforced by a learning phenomenon, resulting in a gradual lowering of the level in the communication hierarchy at which consistently suppressed information is filtered out of the communicated message. Thus, for example, if a given relay point has been transmitting information on the potential market but finds that this information is never retransmitted by the next relay point, and if there are no alternative channels of communication, the transmission of information on the potential market will tend to cease at the lower level.

Two Extreme Models

It is now possible to present two models that arise as antitheses from the propositions advanced above:[17]

16 See C. C. Saxton, *The Economics of Price Determination* (London, 1942), p. 148.
17 It should be clear that these are only two out of a large number of permutations and combinations of organizational features that might be defined.

1 A model of a firm in which price changes tend to be infrequent and reaction to competitors primarily passive might have the following organizational characteristics:

(a) Price is determined by a committee of equals.
(b) Communication chains between the decision-making unit and the primary sources of information are long (both upward and downward).
(c) The unit making the actual price decisions does not have the responsibility for establishing the criteria for price decisions (i.e., the decision-making unit is decentralized and is subject to dicta from above with respect to price policy).
(d) Demand information is channeled through a cost relay point.
(e) Firm policy information is channeled through a cost relay point.
(f) Information on competitors is channeled through a cost relay point.

2 A model of a firm in which price changes tend to be frequent and reaction to competitors tends to take the form of price-leadership might have the following organizational characteristics:

(a) Price is determined by an individual.
(b) Communication chains between the decision-making unit and the primary sources of information are short (both upward and downward).
(c) The decision-maker for specific price decisions also has the responsibility for establishing the criteria for price decision (i.e., the decision-making unit is centralized).
(d) Cost information is channeled through a demand relay point.
(e) Firm policy information is channeled through a demand relay point.[18]
(f) Information on competitors is channeled through a demand relay point.

In order to make explicit the implications found here for the analysis of the behavior of the firm, consider the predicted behavior in a classic duopoly situation of firms possessing the characteristics listed above. The Cournot duopoly model is taken for purposes of illustration.[19]

Let there be two duopolists in the market. Assume that Firm 1 has the organizational characteristics of the first model above, Firm 2 the

18   Strictly speaking, if '(c)' holds, there are no channels of firm-policy information since firm policy is made by the decision-maker; but in so far as one deals with approximations to the model, '(e)' becomes relevant.
19   See *Recherches sur les Principes Mathematiques de la Theorie des Richesses* (Paris, 1838), chapter 7. English translation: N. Bacon (trans.) *Researches into the Mathematical Principles of Wealth* (New York, 1897).

organizational characteristics of the second model above. Following Cournot, let there be no costs.

The market demand function is defined to be:

$$p = 25 - \frac{x_1 + x_2}{3}$$

where p = price
x_1 = output of Firm 1
x_2 = output of Firm 2.

It is further specified that each duopolist expects no reaction on the part of the other in response to a change in output:

$$\frac{dx_1}{dx_2} = \frac{dx_2}{dx_1} = 0 \text{ (conjectural variation terms).}$$

The Cournot market solution is reached by setting marginal revenue for each duopolist equal to zero (i.e., the point of optimal production under the assumption of no costs) and solving the resulting equations.

$$px_1 = 25x_1 - x_1 \frac{(x_1 + x_2)}{3} \tag{1}$$

$$\frac{dpx_1}{dx_1} = 25 - \frac{2x_1}{3} - \frac{x_2}{3} - \frac{x_1}{3} \frac{dx_2}{dx_1} = 0 \tag{2}$$

$$x_1 = \frac{75}{2} - \frac{x_2}{2}. \tag{3}$$

Similarly

$$x_2 = \frac{75}{2} - \frac{x_1}{2}. \tag{4}$$

And thus,

$$\begin{aligned} x_1 &= 25 \\ x_2 &= 25 \\ p &= 8.33. \end{aligned} \tag{5}$$

To explore some of the implications of this paper, assume that in the market specified above, Firm 1 and Firm 2 have reached the equilibrium point specified by the Cournot solution and are both producing 25 units. Next, assume that the market demand increases, such that

$$p = 30 - \frac{x_1 + x_2}{3}.$$

Under the assumptions previously outlined, it is predicted that Firm 1 will tend (a) to be slow in changing its perception of the market demand, (b) to underestimate demand when its perception does change, and (c) to give a positive value to the conjectural variation term. Thus, Firm 1 might have expectations with regard to the market demand function and the conjectural variation term as follows:

$$p = 25 - \frac{x_1 + x_2}{3}$$

$$\frac{dx_2}{dx_1} = 1.$$

Similarly, it is predicted that Firm 2 will tend (a) to change its perception of market demand quickly, (b) to overestimate demand, (c) to give a value of zero to the conjectural variation term. Thus Firm 2 might have the following estimates of key information:

$$p = 100 - x_1 - x_2$$

$$\frac{dx_1}{dx_2} = 0.$$

Under these conditions, the market solution deviates significantly from the standard Cournot solution.

$$x_1 = 10$$
$$x_2 = 45$$
$$p = 11.67.$$

The effect is to make Firm 2 dominant in the market.

Note that the solution above will be stable only if the new production level and the resultant profits are acceptable to the dominant control groups of the two firms. If, for example, the control groups of Firm 1 are not satisfied, they may demand a reorganization of the firm. Specifically, they may insist that its organizational structure be more like that of Firm 2. Such a reorganization would have obvious consequences for the estimation of demand, etc., with a resultant impact upon the market. In point of fact, it is possible to specify a set of values for organizational structure and the aspiration level of control groups such that a market which has, under standard economic analysis, a given equilibrium point has, with the addition of the organizational factors, either a different equilibrium point or no stable equilibrium at all.

Program for Empirical Analysis

In this paper a framework has been presented for dealing with certain variables which have not previously been formally introduced into oligopoly theory by economists but which, nevertheless, seem to be significant. That framework, and the hypotheses suggested, have been based explicitly upon a substantial body of empirical research previously reported in the literature of economics and the other social sciences. However, further refinement and testing of the hypotheses advanced here depends upon research specifically directed toward that end. While it is not the intention here to indicate in detail the types of empirical study that are being used to test the theoretical structure proposed above, some indication of the research program may be desirable.

Three stages of research are projected. On the basis of the framework outlined above, a myriad of models could be constructed by imputing values to the variables and by taking various combinations and permutations of these variables. Consequently, it seems clear that the most economical first step to be taken is a study within the theoretical framework defined in this paper of a number of firms in oligopolistic markets, with the goal of determining the patterns most commonly observed in the organizational variables specified above. Secondly, with constraints thus imposed upon the organizational variables, it will be possible to approximate more accurately the quantitative relationships existing. At this point, it is believed that the facilities of the laboratory can be exploited, since it is possible in the laboratory to study the effects of a single variable (or pair of variables, etc.) while holding others constant.[20] Such manipulation

20   In general, economists have not utilized laboratory studies to validate propositions concerning firm behavior to the same extent that students of the other social sciences have. On the basis of the experience of social psychologists in the use of the laboratory for the observation of organizational phenomena, it seems possible to utilize such techniques for the study of pricing behavior. For example, Harold Guetzkow, of the Carnegie Institute of Technology, has recently developed a laboratory design for testing certain propositions in organization theory. In his design, individual participants assume roles in sales and production departments in a firm and attempt to maximize firm profits in an experimentally standardized environment. Tests are made of the differences in profitability associated with differing organizational structures. It is anticipated that such a design can be modified, or a new design of this type developed, to provide experimental tests for the hypotheses relating pricing behavior and the organizational characteristics discussed in this paper.

is ordinarily impossible in the study of existing organizations, although under some conditions environmental circumstances may, in essence, duplicate an experimental situation by providing examples of all possible combinations of values for the variables under examination. The advantages of the laboratory stem from the opportunity to guarantee such examples. Finally, on the basis of the clarification provided by the laboratory results and the preliminary field study, a set of hypotheses appropriate to actual situations will be made. These hypotheses will be in the form of specific predictions of the dimensions of price behavior listed above and will be tested systematically against actual organizational and market data. In this fashion, the hypotheses generated will be accepted or rejected and a further refinement of oligopoly theory will be feasible.

2

Models in a Behavioral Theory of the Firm

R. M. Cyert, E. A. Feigenbaum, and J. G. March

Abstract

How do business organizations make decisions? What process do they follow in deciding how much to produce? And at what price? A behavioral theory of the firm is here explored. Using a specific type of duopoly, a model is written explicitly as a computer program to deal with the complex theory implicit in the process by which businesses make decisions. This model highlights our need for more empirical observations of organizational decision-making.

Recent attempts to develop a behavioral theory of the firm have focused particularly on the internal characteristics of a business firm as a decision-making organization. They have used the rough framework of both the theory of competitive pricing and the modern efforts to extend that theory to situations of imperfect competition such as the case of oligopoly and duopoly where only a few, or possibly only two, firms supply a given market. They have, however, gone further in introducing as an important part of the theory the process by which business organizations make decisions. Since business firms are organizations, it has seemed reasonable *a priori* to assume that a theory of business behavior ought not to treat them as individual decision-makers. (Alt, 1949; Bushaw and Clower, 1957;

This chapter was first published in *Behavioral Science*, Vol. 4, No. 2, April 1959. It is based on research supported by grants made by the Graduate School of Industrial Administration, Carnegie Institute of Technology, from the School's research funds and from funds provided by the Ford Foundation for the study of organizational behavior. The authors owe a considerable debt to a large group of colleagues and students for their comments on the general approach and specific models presented here.

Chamberlin, 1946; Cooper, 1951; Cyert and March, 1955; Cyert and March, 1956; Gordon, 1948; Papandreou, 1952; Weintraub, 1942).

Two major obstacles to the acceptance of such a theory of pricing are obvious. First, it must be shown that the theory is at least as good as other existing theories in its ability to predict firm behavior (Friedman, 1953). Convincing demonstrations on either side of this point are not available. In our judgment, a major portion of the effort in the next decade of research on pricing should be directed to answering this question (or to making it irrelevant). But we do not propose to discuss the point in detail here. Second, a way must be found to deal with the complex theory implicit in the decision-making process approach. A major problem perceived by those sympathetic to a behavioral theory has been the lack of a methodology suitable for handling the kinds of complexities that seemed to be needed (Koopmans, 1957). It is to this problem and to the development of a specific model to which we address ourselves in this paper.

We show that a relatively complex model of the firm as a decision-making organization can be developed and used to yield economically relevant and testable predictions of business behavior. The methodology involved is computer simulation. The model is one of a specific type of duopoly. As a rough test of resonableness, we compare the predictions of the model with actual data. Our hope is that the model will illustrate the promise of simulation as a technique of model building in economic theory and the behavioral sciences in general and at the same time demonstrate a general method for examining many of the concepts previously discussed in more abstract terms.

The Decision-Making Process

Recent theories of organizational behavior have emphasized several important characteristics of the decision-making process that are dealt with awkwardly in the theory of the firm. First, organizational decisions depend on information, estimates, and expectations that ordinarily differ appreciably from reality. These organizational perceptions are influenced by some characteristics of the organization and its procedures. The procedures provide concrete estimates – if not necessarily accurate ones (Cyert and March, 1955). Second, organizations consider only a limited number of decision alternatives. The set of alternatives considered depends on some features of organizational structure and on the locus of search responsibility in the organization. This dependence seems to be particularly conspicuous in such planning processes as budgeting and price–output determination (Alt, 1949). Finally, organizations vary with respect to the amount of resources they devote to organizational goals on the one hand and suborganizational and individual goals on the other. In particular, conflict and partial conflict of interests is a feature of most organizations and under some conditions organizations develop substantial internal slack susceptible to reduction under external pressure (Cyert and March, 1956).

The concept of organizational or internal slack is used to describe a situation within an organization in which individual energies potentially utilizable for the achievement of organizational goals are permitted to be diverted. The form of the slack may vary from a labor force not working at its full capability to overly large departmental budgets. The extent and regularity with which the organization meets its goals, especially the profit goal, will affect the amount of internal slack.

Our objective is to show how the general attributes of decision-making, some of which have been described above, can be introduced into a behavioral theory of the firm. Although our elaboration is an obvious abstraction of the details of procedures used in a complex organization, each of the processes specified can serve as headings for a further set of subprocesses. We have specified a decision process that involves nine distinct steps:

1 Forecast competitors' behavior. The fact that firms assume something about the reactions of their rivals is, of course, incorporated in any theory of oligopoly. Our approach is to build into the model some propositions about the ways in which organizations gain, analyze, and communicate information on competitors. The concept of organizational learning, a process by which expectations of competitors' behavior are modified on the basis of experience, is a major element in this formulation.

2 Forecast demand. We have attempted to build a model that can encompass descriptions of the process by which the demand curve (the relationship between the price of the product and the quantity which can be sold at that price) is estimated in the firm. In this manner, we are able to introduce organizational biases in estimation and allow for differences among firms in the way in which they adjust their current estimates on the basis of experience.

3 Estimate costs. We do not assume, as in the theory of the firm of economics, that the firm has achieved the optimum combination of resources and the lowest cost per unit of output for any given size plant. We believe it is necessary to introduce the factors that actually affect the firm's costs, estimated as well as achieved.

4 Specify objectives. As has been noted above, organizational 'objectives' may enter at two distinct points and perform two quite distinct functions. First, in this step they consist in goals the organization wishes to achieve and which it uses to determine whether it has at least one viable plan (see step 5). There is no requirement that the objectives be co-measurable since they enter as separate constraints all of which 'must' be satisfied. Thus, we expect to be able to include profit goals, share of the market goals, production goals, etc. (Simon, 1955). Second, the objectives may be used as decision criteria in step 9. As will become clear below, the fact that objectives serve this twin function rather than the single (decision-rule) function commonly assigned to them is of major importance to the theory.

The order of steps 1, 2, 3, and 4 is irrelevant in the present formulation. We assume that a firm performs such computations more or less simultaneously and that all are substantially completed before any further action is taken. Since the subsequent steps are all contingent, the order in which they are performed may have considerable effect on the decisions reached. This is particularly true with respect to the order of steps 6, 7, and 8. Thus, one of the structural characteristics of a specific model is the order of the steps.

5 *Evaluate plan.* On the basis of the estimates of 1, 2, and 3 alternatives are examined to see whether there is at least one alternative that satisfies the objectives defined by 4. If there is, we transfer immediately to 9 and a decision. If there is not, however, we go on to step 6. This evaluation represents a key step in the planning process that is ignored in a model that uses objectives solely as the decision-rule. Certain organizational phenomena (e.g., organizational slack) increase in importance because of the contingent consequences of this step.

6 *Re-examine costs.* We specify that the failure to find a viable plan initially results in the re-examination of estimates. Although we list the re-examination of costs first here, the order is dependent on some features of the organization and will vary from firm to firm.[1] An important feature of organizations is the extent to which a firm is able to 'discover' under the pressure of unsatisfactory preliminary plans 'cost savings' that could not be found otherwise. In fact, we believe it is only under such pressure that firms begin to approach an optimum combination of resources. With the revised estimate of costs, step 5 occurs again. If an acceptable plan is possible with the new estimates, the decision-rule is applied. Otherwise, step 7.

7 *Re-examine demand.* As in the case of cost, demand is reviewed to see whether a somewhat more favorable demand picture cannot be obtained. This might reflect simple optimism or a consideration of new methods for influencing demand (e.g., an additional advertising effort). In either case, we expect organizations to revise demand estimates under some conditions and different organizations to revise them in different ways. Evaluation 5 occurs again with the revised estimates.

---

1 Although we have identified these re-evaluations in terms of strict sequence, an alternative interpretation can be made in terms of intensity of search.

8 Re-examine objectives. Where plans are unfavorable, we expect a tendency to revise objectives downward. The rate and extent of change we can attempt to predict. As before, evaluation 5 is made with the revised objectives.

9 Select alternative. The organization requires a mechanism (a) for generating alternatives to consider and (b) for choosing among those generated. The method by which alternatives are generated is of considerable importance since it affects the order in which they are evaluated. Typically, the procedures involved place a high premium on alternatives that are 'similar' to alternatives chosen in the recent past by the firm or by other firms of which it is aware. If alternatives are generated strictly sequentially, the choice phase is quite simple: choose the first alternative that falls in the estimate space, that is the set of positions determined by the estimated demand and estimated cost curves. If more than one alternative is generated at a time, a more complicated choice process is required. For example, at this point maximization rules may be applied to select from among the evoked alternatives. In addition, this step defines a decision-rule for the situation in which there are no acceptable alternatives (even after all re-examination of estimates).

There are two important observations to be made about a theory having these general characteristics. First, as we increase the emphasis on describing in some detail the actual process by which the firm makes price and output decisions, we decrease the relevance of one of the major debates in the theory of the firm. Whether the firm maximizes, 'satisfices',[2] or just tries to survive is not the main issue (if indeed it is an issue at all). The emphasis on the process of making decisions in an organization obviates the need for the simple decision-rules and simple models implicit in much of that controversy.

The second point is a related one. Conventional mathematics is a somewhat awkward tool for developing the implications of a theory such as the one described here. It is no accident, therefore, that interest in detailed process models has grown with the development of the digital computer. Computer simulation is well suited to the complexities that are introduced when internal firm variables are utilized in the theory. The significance of simulation for business behavior has been explored vigorously in the so-called 'business games' developed as business training devices; their potential for economic theory is at least as great.

2 'The key to the simplification of the choice process in both cases is the replacement of the goal of *maximizing* with the goal of *satisficing*, of finding a course of action that is "good enough".' (Simon, 1957, pp. 204–5).

A Specific Duopoly Model

The theoretical framework we have outlined in the preceding section can be viewed as an executive program for organizational decisions. That is, we conceive of any large scale oligopolistic business organization as pursuing the steps indicated. A change in decision must (within the theory) be explained in terms of some change in one of the processes specified. As we have noted above, such a conception of the theory seems to suggest a computer-simulation model rather than treatment in mathematical form (Cyert, Simon and Trow, 1956). The rationale, of course, remains the same. We wish to explore the implications of the model.

The intention has been to construct a plausible set of estimation and decision-rules for different types of organizations, and to simulate on a computer the behavior of these firms over time. When we attempt to develop models exhibiting the process characteristics we have discussed above, it becomes clear that our knowledge of how actual firms do, in fact, estimate demand, cost, etc., is discouragingly small. We know with reasonable confidence some of the things that many firms do but at a number of points in the model we can make only educated guesses. Moreover, what knowledge we have (or think we have) tends to be qualitative in nature in situations where it would be desirable to be quantitative.

Because of these considerations, the models of firms with which we will deal here should be viewed as tentative approximations. They contain substantial elements of arbitrariness and unrealistic characterizations. For example, we believe that each of the models as it stands almost certainly exaggerates the computational precision of organizational decision-making. In general, we have not attempted to introduce all of the revisions we consider likely at this time primarily because we wish to examine whether some major revisions produce results which reasonably approximate observed phenomena.

The model is developed for a duopoly situation. The product is homogeneous and, therefore, only one price exists in the market. The major decision that each of the two firms makes is an output decision. In making this decision the firm must estimate the market price for varying outputs. When the output is sold, however, the actual selling price will be determined by the market. No discrepancy between output and sales in assumed, and thus no inventory problem exists in the model.

We assume a duopoly composed of an ex-monopolist and a firm developed by former members of the established firm. We shall call the latter, 'the splinter', and the former, 'the ex-monopolist' or, for brevity, 'monopolist'. Such a specific case is taken so that some rough assumptions can be made about appropriate functions for the various processes in the model. The assumptions are gross; but it is only through some such rough model that a start can be made. To demonstrate that the model as a whole has some reasonable empirical base, we will compare certain outcomes of the model with data from the *can industry*, where approximately the same initial conditions hold.

We can describe the specific model at several levels of detail. In table 2.1 the skeleton of the model is indicated – the 'flow diagrams' of the decision-making process. This will permit a quick comparison of the two firms. In the remainder of this section of the paper we will attempt to provide

Table 2.1 Process model for output decision of firm

(1) Forecast: Competitors' reactions	Compute conjectural variation term for period *t* as a function of actual reactions observed in the past
(2) Forecast: Demand	Keep slope of perceived demand curve constant but pass it through the last realized point in the market
(3) Estimate: Average unit costs	Cost curve for this period is the same as for last period. If profit goal has been achieved two successive times, average unit costs increase
(4) Specify objectives: Profit goal	Specify profit goal as a function of the actual profits achieved over past periods
(5) Evaluate:	Evaluate alternatives within the estimate space. If an alternative which meets goal is available, go to (9) if not, go to (6)
(6) Re-examine: Cost estimate	Search yields a cost reduction. Go to (5). If after evaluation there, decision can be made, go to (9). If not, go to (7)
(7) Re-examine: Demand estimate	Estimate of demand increased after search. Go to (5). If after evaluation, decision can be made, go to (9). If not, go to (8)
(8) Re-examine: Profit goal	Reduce profit goal to a level consistent with best alternative in the estimate space as modified after (6) and (7)
(9) Decide: Set output	Selection of alternative in original estimate space to meet original goal, in modified estimate space to meet original goal, or in modified estimate space to meet lowered goal

somewhat greater detail (and rationale) for the specific decision and estimating rules used.[3]

The decision-making process postulated by the theory begins with a 'forecast' phase (in which competitor's reaction, demand, and costs are estimated) and a goal specification phase (in which a profit goal is established). An evaluation phase follows, in which an effort is made to find the 'best' alternative given the forecasts. If this 'best' alternative is inconsistent with the profit goal, a re-examination phase ensues, in which an effort is made to revise cost and demand esimates. If re-examination fails to yield a new best alternative consistent with the profit goal, the immediate profit goal is abandoned in favor of 'doing the best possible under the circumstances'. The specific details of the models follow this framework.

Forecasting a Competitor's Behavior

The model being analyzed in the paper assumes two firms in the market (a duopoly). As a result one of the significant variables in the decision on the quantity of output to produce for each firm becomes an estimate of the rival firm's output. For example, assume the monopolist in period (t) is considering a change in output from period ($t-1$). At the same time the monopolist makes an estimate of the change the splinter will make. At the end of period t the monopolist can look back and determine the amount of change the splinter made in relation to his own change. The ratio of changes can be expressed as follows:

$$V_{m,t} = \frac{Q_{s,t} - Q_{s,t-1}}{Q_{m,t} - Q_{m,t-1}}$$

where $V_{m,t}$ = the change in the splinter's output during period t as a percentage of the monopolist's output change during period t.

$Q_{s,t} - Q_{s,t-1}$ = the actual change in the splinter's output during period t.

$Q_{m,t} - Q_{m,t-1}$ = the actual change in the monopolist's output during period t.

In the same way we have for the splinter the following:

$$V_{s,t} = \frac{Q_{m,t} - Q_{m,t-1}}{Q_{s,t} - Q_{s,t-1}} = \frac{1}{V_{m,t}}$$

The Ex-monopolist

When the monopolist in period t is planning his output, he must make an estimate of his rival's output, as noted above. In order to make this estimate

---

3   The computer program, developed in the IT language for the IBM 650 computer, can be obtained from the authors.

we assume that the monopolist first makes an estimate of the percentage change in the splinter's output in relation to his own change, that is, an estimate of $V_{m,t}$. We have assumed that the monopolist will make this estimate on the basis of the splinter's behavior over the past three time periods. More specifically we have assumed that the monopolist's estimate is based on a weighted average, as follows:

$$V'_{m,t} = V_{m,t-1} + \tfrac{1}{7}[4(V_{m,t-1} - V_{m,t-2}) + 2(V_{m,t-2} - V_{m,t-3}) + (V_{m,t-3} - V_{m,t-4})]$$

Where $V'_{m,t}$ = the monopolist's estimate of the change in the splinter's output during period t as a percentage of the monopolist's output change during period t, that is, an estimate of $V_{m,t}$.

Note that $(V'_{m,t}) \cdot (Q_{m,t} - Q_{m,t} - Q_{m,t-1})$ is the monopolist's estimate of the splinter's change in output, $Q_{s,t} - Q_{s,t-1}$.

The Splinter

We would expect the splinter firm to be more responsive to recent shifts in its competitor's behavior and less attentive to ancient history than the monopolist, both because it is more inclined to consider the monopolist a key part of its environment and because it will generally have less computational capacity as an organization to process and update the information necessary to deal with more complicated rules. Our assumption is that the splinter will simply use the information from the last two periods. Thus $V'_{s,t} = V_{s,t-1} + (V_{s,t-1} - V_{s,t-2})$.[4] In the same manner as above $(V'_{s,t}) \cdot (Q_{s,t} - Q_{s,t-1})$ is the splinter's estimate of the monopolist's change in output, $Q_{m,t} - Q_{m,t-1}$.

Forecasting Demand

We assume that the actual market demand curve is linear. That is, we assume the market price to be a linear function of the total output offered by the two firms together. We also assume that the firms forecast a linear market demand curve (quite different, perhaps, from the actual demand curve). There has been considerable discussion in the economics literature of the frequent discrepancy between the 'imagined' demand curve and the actual demand curve (Weintraub, 1942), and it is this concept that is incorporated in the model. The values of the parameters of the 'imagined'

---

4 Obviously we do not maintain that the form and parameters of these 'learning' functions are empirically validated. The functions are somewhat arbitrary but we hope not unreasonable.

demand curve are based on rough inferences from the nature of the firms involved.

The Ex-monopolist

We assume that, because of its past history of dominance and monopoly, the ex-monopolist will be over pessimistic with respect to the quantity which it can sell at lower prices, i.e., we assume the initial perception of the demand curve will have a somewhat greater slope than the actual market demand curve. On the assumption that information about actual demand is used to improve its estimate, we assume that the ex-monopolist changes its demand estimate on the basis of experience in the market. The firm assumes that its estimate of the slope of the demand curve is correct and it 'repositions' its previous estimate to pass through the observed demand point.

The Splinter

We posit that the splinter firm will initially be optimistic with respect to the quantity which it can sell at low prices. That is, the initial slope (absolute value) of its demand curve will be somewhat less than that of the actual market demand curve. Secondly, we assume that initially the splinter firm perceives demand as increasing over time. Thus, until demand shows a down turn, the splinter firm estimates its demand to be 5 per cent greater than that found by repositioning its perceived demand through the last point observed in the marketplace.

Estimating Costs

In the process for forecasting and realizing costs, we do not make the assumption that the firm has achieved optimum costs. We assume, rather, that the firm has a simplified estimate of its average cost curve, that is, the curve expressing cost as a function of output. It is horizontal over most of the range of possible outputs; at high and low outputs (relative to capacity) costs are perceived to be somewhat higher.

Further, we make the assumption that these cost estimates are 'self-confirming', i.e., the estimated costs will, in fact, become the actual per-unit cost (Cyert and March, 1956). The concept of organizational slack as it affects costs is introduced at this point. Average unit cost for the present period is estimated to be the same as last period, but if the profit goal of the firm has been achieved for two consecutive time periods, then costs are estimated to be 5 per cent higher than 'last time'.

The specific values for costs are arbitrary. The general shape of the cost curves has been discussed in detail in the literature and studied empirically (Dean, 1951). The concept of organization slack has some important implications for the theory of the firm and has been defined earlier.

The Ex-monopolist

The monopolist's initial average unit cost is assumed to be $800 per unit in the range of outputs from 10 per cent to 90 per cent of capacity. Below 10 per cent and above 90 per cent the initial average unit cost is assumed to be $900.

The Splinter

It is assumed that the competitor will have somewhat lower initial costs. This is because its plant and equipment will tend to be newer and its production methods more modern. Specifically, initial average costs are $760 in the range of outputs from 10 per cent to 90 per cent of capacity. Below 10 per cent and above 90 per cent costs are assumed to average $870 per unit produced.

Specifying Objectives

The multiplicity of organizational objectives is a fact with which we hope to deal in later revisions of the present models. For the present, however, we have limited ourselves to a single objective defined in terms of profit. In this model the function of the profit objective is to restrict or encourage search as well as to determine the decision. If given the estimates of competitors, demand, and cost, there exists a production level that will provide a profit that is satisfactory, we assume the firm will adopt such a course. If there is more than one satisfactory alternative, the firm will adopt that quantity level that maximizes profit. Whether even such a restricted maximization procedure is appropriate is a subject for further research.

The Ex-monopolist

We assume that the monopolist, because of its size, its substantial computational ability, and its established procedures for dealing with a stable rather than a highly unstable environment, will tend to maintain a relatively stable profit objective. We assume that the objective will be the moving average of the realized profit over the last ten time periods.

Initially, of course, the monopolist will seek to maintain the profit level achieved during its monopoly.

The Splinter

The splinter firm will presumably be (for reasons indicated earlier) inclined to consider a somewhat shorter period of past experience. We assume that the profit objective of the splinter will be the average of experienced profit over the past five time periods and that the initial profit objective will be linked to the experience of the monopolist and the relative capacities of the two. Thus, we specify that the initial profit objectives of the two firms will be proportional to their initial capacities.

Re-examination of Costs

We assume that when the original forecasts define a satisfactory plan there will be no further examination of them. If, however, such a plan is not obtained, we assume an effort to achieve a satisfactory plan in the first instance by reviewing estimates and finally by revising objectives. We assume that cost estimates are reviewed before demand estimates and that the latter are only re-examined if a satisfactory plan cannot be developed by the revision of the former. The re-evaluation of costs is a search for methods of accomplishing objectives at lower cost than appeared possible under less pressure. We believe this ability to revise estimates when forced to do so is characteristic of organizational decision-making. It is, of course, closely related to the organizational slack concept previously introduced. In general, we have argued that an organization can ordinarily find possible cost reduction if forced to do so and that the amount of the reductions will be a function of the amount of slack in the organization.

It is assumed that the re-examination of costs under the pressure of trying to meet objectives enables each of the organizations to move in the direction of the 'real' minimum cost point. For purposes of this model it is assumed that both firms reduce costs 10 per cent of the difference between their estimated average unit costs and the 'real' minimum.

Re-examination of Demand

The re-evaluation of demand serves the same function as the re-evaluation of costs above. In the present models it occurs only if the re-evaluation of costs is not adequate to define an acceptable plan. It consists in revising upward the expectations of market demand. The reasoning is that some new alternative is selected which the firm believes will increase its demand.

The new approach may be changed advertising procedure, a scheme to work salesmen harder, or some other alternative which leads the firm to an increase in optimism. In any event, it is felt the more experienced firm will take a slightly less sanguine view of what is possible. As in the case of estimating demand, we assume that all firms persist in seeing a linear demand curve and that no changes are made in the perceived slope of that curve.

The Ex-monopolist

As a result of the re-examination of demand estimates, it is assumed that this firm revises its estimates of demand upward by 10 per cent.

The Splinter

The assumption here is that the upward revision of demand is 15 per cent.

Re-examination of Objectives

Because our decision-rule is one that maximizes among the available alternatives and our rule for specifying objectives depends only on outcomes, the re-evaluation of objectives does not, in fact, enter into our present models in a way that influences behavior. The procedure can be interpreted as adjusting aspirations to the 'best possible under the circumstances'. If our decision-rule were different or if we made (as we might prefer in future revisions) objectives at one time period a function of both outcomes and previous objectives, the re-evaluation of objectives would become important to the decision process.

Decision

We have specified that the organization will follow traditional economic rules for maximization with respect to its perception of costs, demand, and competitor's behavior. The specific alternatives selected, of course, depend on the point at which this step is invoked (i.e., how many re-evaluation steps are used before an acceptable plan is identified). The output decision is constrained in two ways: (1) a firm cannot produce, in any time period, beyond its present capacity. Both models allow for change in plant capacity over time. The process by which capacity changes is the same for both firms. If profit goals have been met for two successive periods and production is above 90 per cent of capacity, then capacity

Table 2.2 Initial and structural conditions for models exhibited in table 2.3

Initial market demand (unknown to firms)	$p = 2000 - q$
Initial perception of demand schedule by ex-monopolist	$p = 2200 - 3q$
Initial perception of demand schedule by splinter	$p = 1800 = q$
Ex-monopolist's average unit cost $\begin{cases} 0.1q_{MAX,M} < q_M < 0.9q_{MAX,M} \\ q_M > 0.9, q_M < 0.1 \end{cases}$	800 900
Splinter average unit cost $\begin{cases} 0.1q_{MAX,S} < q_S < 0.9q_{MAX,S} \\ q_S > 0.9, q_S < 0.1 \end{cases}$	760 870
'Real' minimum average unit cost	700
Ex-monopolist's capacity	400
Splinter's capacity	50
Market quantity	223
Market price	1500
Ex-monopolist's profit goal	163,100
Splinter's profit goal	20,387
Conjectural variations ($V'_{m,t}$ and $V'_{s,t}$)	All zero initially
Splinter's over-optimism of demand in forecast phase	5%
% Splinter raises demand forecast upon re-examination	15%
% Ex-monopolist raises demand forecast upon re-examination	10%
Cost reduction achieved in M's and S's search for lower costs	10% of costs above 'real' min. av. unit cost
% Cost rise attributable to increase in 'internal slack'	5%
% Actual demand schedule shifts to right each time period	8%
Constraint on changing output from that of the last period	±25%
% of capacity at which firm must be producing before it may expand (subject to other conditions)	90%
% change in capacity, when expansion occurs	20%

Table 2.3 Values of selected variables at two-period intervals

	I	III	V	VII	IX	XI	XIII	XV
Market								
Price	1,420	1,710	2,196	2,763	3,283	3,927	4,430	4,942
Output	290	311	262	205	209	195	303	466
Ex-Monopolist								
Aspiration level	163,100	165,671	169,631	176,800	173,221	178,385	203,693	246,746
Conjectural variations	0	0	0.74	−22.4	1.09	0.74	0.26	0.35
Costs (AUC)	826	813	881	994	1,041	1,106	1,219	1,344
Output	240	251	206	153	161	150	233	363
Number of re-examination steps	2	0	0	3	0	0	0	0
Competitor								
Aspiration level	20,387	27,107	31,448	39,763	46,218	39,684	54,245	79,060
Conjectural variations	0	0	9.2	−1.78	−6.58	8.72	3.39	3.96
Costs (AUC)	760	798	865	954	1,023	1,057	1,166	1,285
Output	50	60	56	52	48	45	70	103
Number of re-examination steps	0	0	0	3	3	0	0	0
Profit Ratio								
Competitors' profits ÷ monopolists' profits	0.19	0.21	0.26	0.34	0.30	0.30	0.30	0.28
Share of Market								
Competitors' output ÷ total output	0.17	0.19	0.21	0.25	0.23	0.23	0.23	0.22

Table 2.3 *(continued)*

	XVII	XIX	XXI	XXIII	XXV	XXVII	XXIX	XXXI
Market								
Price	5,425	3,722	2,785	2,573	2,229	1,719	2,286	2,970
Output	713	914	855	534	360	335	250	140
Ex-Monopolist								
Aspiration level	319,561	348,006	247,445	182,580	157,664	148,648	154,010	158,120
Conjectural variations	0.28	0.30	−0.38	0.05	0.64	−1.07	28.4	−1.40
Costs (AUC)	1,482	1,634	1,801	1,986	2,085	1,710	1,609	1,436
Output	566	703	658	369	207	193	143	80
Number of re-examination steps	0	0	0	0	1	3	0	3
Competitor								
Aspiration level	113,595	121,973	86,083	60,742	37,977	19,272	28,402	37,123
Conjectural variations	4.76	3.91	6.3	−17.1	2.21	−0.32	2.43	50.7
Costs (AUC)	1,417	1,562	1,623	1,790	1,853	1,821	1,608	1,669
Output	147	211	197	165	153	142	107	60
Number of re-examination steps	0	0	0	3	0	1	0	0
Profit Ratio								
Competitor's profit ÷ monopolist's profit	0.26	0.30	0.34	0.68	0.98	0.74	0.75	0.64
Share of Market								
Competitor's output ÷ total output	0.21	0.23	0.23	0.31	0.43	0.42	0.43	0.43

Table 2.3 (continued)

	XXXIII	XXXV	XXXVII	XXXIX	XLI	XLIII	XLV
Market							
Price	3,355	3,742	4,099	4,546	5,463	6,730	7,294
Output	218	340	529	735	777	727	1,126
Ex-monopolist							
Aspiration level	159,060	179,859	203,892	239,045	280,940	260,051	340,745
Conjectural variations	0.85	0.95	0.96	0.65	3.77	1.91	1.35
Costs (AUC)	1,363	1,502	1,656	1,826	2,013	2,071	2,283
Output	125	195	303	432	342	320	500
Number of re-examination steps	0	0	0	0	0	0	0
Competitor							
Aspiration level	38,627	53,005	77,001	109,136	164,566	266,512	396,911
Conjectural variations	1.32	1.31	1.32	2.3	−0.8	3.16	0.79
Costs (AUC)	1,840	2,029	2,237	2,466	2,719	2,771	3,055
Output	93	145	226	303	435	407	626
Number of re-examination steps	0	0	0	0	0	0	0
Profit Ratio							
Competitor's profit ÷ monopolist's profit	0.49	0.49	0.49	0.47	0.90	0.97	0.95
Share of market							
Competitor's output ÷ total output	0.43	0.43	0.43	0.41	0.56	0.56	0.56

increases 20 per cent; (2) a firm cannot change its output from one time period to the next more than ± 25 per cent. The rationale behind the latter assumption is that neither large cutbacks nor large advances in production are possible in the very short run, there being large organization problems connected with either.

The various initial conditions specified above are summarized in table 2.2, along with the other initial conditions required to program the models.

Results of the Duopoly Model

We have now described a decision-making model of a large ex-monopolist and a splinter competitor. In order to present some detail of the behavior that is generated by the interacting models, we have reproduced in table 2.3 the values of the critical variables on each of the major decision and output factors.[5] By following this chart over time, one can determine the time path of such variables as cost, conjectural variation, and output for both of the firms. More than any one thing, a careful study of this table will give a feeling for the major characteristics of the behavioral theory we have described.

In addition, we have compared the share of market and profit ratio results with actual data generated from the competition between American Can Company and its splinter competitor, Continental Can Company, over the period from 1913 to 1956. These comparisons are indicated in figures 2.1 and 2.2.[6] In general, we feel that the fit of the behavioral model to the data is rather surprisingly good, although we do not regard this fit as validating the approach.[7]

5 Market demand was varied in the following way: (1) The slope of the demand curve was held constant. (2) At each time period the intercept, I_t, was set equal to aI_{t-1}. The value of 'a' was 1.08 for periods 1–16, 0.90 for periods 17–20, 1.00 for periods 21–26, and 1.08 for periods 27–43.

6 One of the parameters in the model is the length of time involved in a single cycle. In comparing the output of the model with the American–Continental data, this parameter was set at 12 months.

7 It should be clear that the validity of the approach presented in this paper is not conclusively demonstrated by the goodness of fit to the can industry data. We have indicated that under the appropriate assumptions, models of firm decision processes can be specified that yield predictions approximating some observed results. However, the situation is one in which there are ample degrees of freedom in the specification of parameters to enable a number of time series to be approximated. Although in this case we have reduced the number of free parameters substantially by specifying most of them *a priori*, the problems of identification faced by any complex model are faced by this one and will have to be solved. The general methodology for testing models that take the form of computer programs remains to be developed.

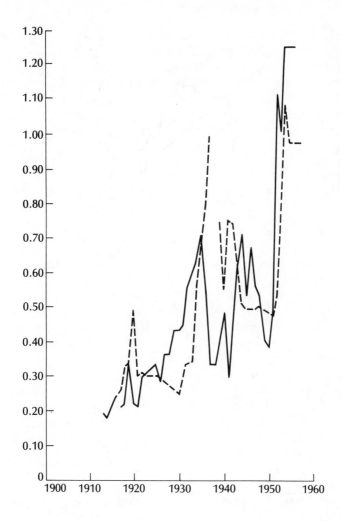

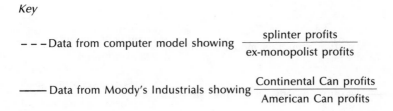

Key

– – –Data from computer model showing $\dfrac{\text{splinter profits}}{\text{ex-monopolist profits}}$

——Data from Moody's Industrials showing $\dfrac{\text{Continental Can profits}}{\text{American Can profits}}$

Fig. 2.1 Comparison of share of market data

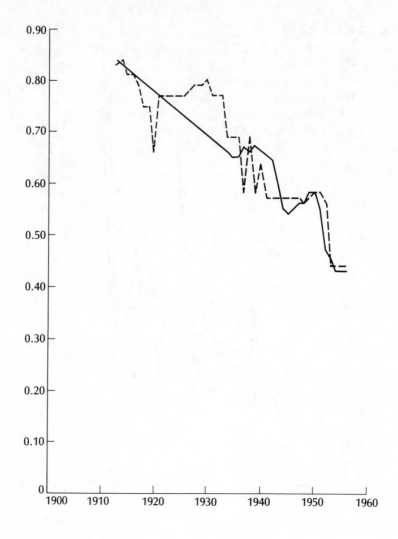

Key

– – –Data from computer model showing $\dfrac{\text{ex-monopolist output}}{\text{market output}}$

——Data from Moody's Industrials showing $\dfrac{\text{Continental Can sales}}{\text{Continental + American sales}}$

Fig. 2.2 Comparison of profit–ratio data

It should be noted that the results in period XLV do not necessarily represent an equilibrium position. By allowing the firms to continue to make decisions, changes in output as well as changes in share of market would result. One of the reasons for the expected change is the demand curve is shifting upward. Another, and more interesting reason, is that no changes have been made within the organizations. In particular, the splinter firm by period XLV is a mature firm, but the model has it behaving as a new, young firm. One of our future aims is to build in the effect on organization, and hence on decision-making, of growth and maturity of the organization.

An examination of table 2.3 indicates that the re-examination phase of the decision-making process was not used frequently by either firm. This characteristic is the result of a demand function that is increasing over most of the periods.

Whether this stems also from an inadequacy in the model's description of organizational goal-setting or is a characteristic of the real world of business decision-making is a question that can be answered only by empirical research.

Discussion

One of the primary points that has been stressed here is the importance of the decision-making process for the theory of the firm. The implication of this position is that the decisions studied by conventional theory can be better understood when variables relating to the internal operation of a business firm are added to the theory. Accordingly, we would hope that such a theory would not only lead to improved prediction on the usual questions but would also facilitate the investigation of other important problems, e.g., allocation of resources within the firm.

The theory we have used differs from conventional theory in six important respects:

1 The models are built on a description of the decision-making process. That is, they specify organizations that evaluate competitors, costs, and demand in the light of their own objectives and (if necessary) re-examine each of these to arrive at a decision.
2 The models depend on a theory of search as well as a theory of choice. They specify under what conditions search will be intensified (e.g., when a satisfactory alternative is not available). They also specify the direction in which search is undertaken. In general, we predict that a firm will look first for new alternatives or new information in the area it views as

most under its control. Thus, in the present models we have made the specific prediction that cost estimates will be re-examined first, demand estimates second, and organizational objectives third.

3 The models describe organizations in which objectives change over time as a result of experience. Goals are not taken as given initially and fixed thereafter. They change as the organization observes its success (or lack of it) in the market. In these models the profit objective at a given time is an average of achieved profit over a number of past periods. The number of past periods considered by the firm varies from firm to firm.

4 Similarly, the models describe organizations that adjust forecasts on the basis of experience. Organizational learning occurs as a result of observations of actual competitors' behavior, actual market demand, and actual costs. Each of the organizations we have used readjusts its perceptions on the basis of such learning. The learning rules used are quite simple. This is both because simple rules are easier to handle than complex rules and because we expect the true rules to be susceptible to close approximation by simple ones.

5 The models introduce organizational biases in making estimates. For a variety of reasons we expect some organizations to be more conservative with respect to cost estimates than other organizations, some organizations to be more optimistic with respect to demand than others, some organizations to be more attentive to and perceptive of changes in competitors' plans than others. As we develop more detailed submodels of the estimation process, these factors will be increasingly obvious. In the present models we have not attempted to develop such submodels but have simply predicted the outcome of the estimation process in different firms.

6 The models all introduce features of 'organizational slack'. That is, we expect that over a period of time during which an organization is achieving its goals a certain amount of the resources of the organization are funneled into the satisfaction of individual and subgroup objectives. This slack then becomes a reservoir of potential economies when satisfactory plans are more difficult to develop.

In order to deal with these revisions, the models have been written explicitly as computer programs. Such treatment has two major values. First, simulation permits the introduction of process variables. The language of the computer is such that many of the phenomena of business behavior that do not fit into classical models can be considered without excessive artificiality. Entering naturally into the model are cost and demand perceptions within the firm in relation to such factors as age of firm, organizational structure, background of executives, and phase of the business cycle; information handling within the firm and its relation to the communication structure, training, and reward system in the organization; and the effects of organizational success and failure on organizational goals and organizational slack.

Secondly, simulation easily generates data on the time path of outputs, prices, etc. For that large class of economic problems in which equilibrium theory is either irrelevant or relatively uninteresting, computer methodology provides a major alternative to the mathematics of comparative statics.

At the same time the models highlight our need for more empirical observations of organizational decision-making. Each of the major steps outlined in the program defines an area for research on business behavior. How do organizations predict the behavior of competitors? How do they estimate demand and costs? What determines organizational planning objectives? In the models we have specified we have introduced empirical assumptions for such things as organizational learning and changes in organizational aspiration levels. We have ignored several factors we consider quite important (e.g., informational biases stemming from variations in the communication structure). In the final development of the model these relationships must be defined from observable characteristics of business organizations.

We see three major directions for further research. First, we would hope that further attempts will be made to compare the results of the models with observable data. In these studies it will be possible to change such variables as have been indicated above and others that appear to be important in the model. Second, we need a great deal of work in actual organizations identifying the decision procedures used in such things as output decisions. Field research on organizations has frequently been extremely time-consuming and costly relative to the results it has produced, but we believe that research focused on the questions raised by the model is both necessary and feasible. Third, there is room for substantial basic research in the laboratory on human decision-making under the conditions found in business organizations. Many of the major propositions in organization theory depend on evidence generated by studies in the laboratory and many of the mechanisms with which we have dealt can be profitably introduced into controlled experiments.

References

Alt, R. M. (1949) The internal organization of the firm and price formation: An illustrative case. *Quarterly Journal Economics*, 58: 92–110.

Bushaw, D. W., and Clower, R. W. (1957) *Introduction to mathematical economics*. Homewood, Illinois: R. D. Irwin, Inc., pp. 176–190.

Chamberlin, E. H. (1946) *The Theory of Monopolistic Competition*. Cambridge: Harvard University Press, 5th edn, pp. 30–55, 117–29, 165–71.

Cooper, W. W. (1951) A proposal for extending the theory of the firm. *Quarterly Journal Economics,* 65: 87–109.

Cyert, R. M., and March, J. G. (1955) Organizational structure and pricing behavior in an oligopolistic market. *American Economical Review,* 45: 129–139.

Cyert, R. M., and March, J. G. (1956) Organizational factors in the theory of oligopoly. *Quarterly Journal Economics,* 70: 44–64.

Cyert, R. M., Simon, H. A., and Trow, D. B. (1956) Observation of a business decision. *J. of Business,* 29: 237–248.

Dean, Joel. (1951) *Managerial Economics*. New York: Prentice-Hall, pp. 292–6.

Friedman, Milton. (1953) *Essays in Positive Economics*. Chicago: University of Chicago Press, pp. 14–15.

Gordon, R. A. (1948) Short-period price determination. *American Economic Review,* 38: 265–68.

Koopmans, T. C. (1957) *Three Essays on the State of Economic Science*. New York: McGraw-Hill, Inc., pp. 208–217.

Papandreou, A. G. (1952) Some basic problems in the theory of the firm. In B. F. Haley (ed.) *A survey of Contemporary Economics,* Homewood, Illinois: R. D. Irwin, Inc., vol. 2.

Simon, H. A. (1955) A behavioral model of rational choice. *Quarterly Journal Economics,* 69: 99–118.

Simon, H. A. (1957) *Models of Man*. New York: John Wiley Co., pp. 204–5.

Weintraub, S. (1942) Monopoly equilibrium and anticipated demand. *Journal Political Economy,* 50: 427–34.

3

Financial Adversity, Internal Competition, and Curriculum Change in a University

Curtis L. Manns and James G. March

Abstract

Records at Stanford University were used to explore the relation between changes in the curriculum and financial adversity. Two hypotheses were derived from a model of universities as adaptive organizations with departments competing for resources. To test the hypotheses, changes in eight attributes of the curriculum were studied. The data show that university curriculum responded to changes in financial conditions and that departments of stronger research reputation were less responsive than departments of weaker reputation.

Basic Ideas

This paper reports a study of curriculum change in an American university. We examine a set of hypotheses about institutional response to adversity, treating change in the curriculum as one of several ways in which a university might react to financial adversity. The hypotheses were derived from standard organizational treatments of adaptive organizations, and college organizations were seen as responding to environmental change in ways similar to business firms (Cyert and March, 1963; Bower, 1970;

This paper first appeared in *Administrative Science Quarterly*, vol. 23, December 1978. The authors owe particular debts to Sally Mahoney for making much of the raw data available to them, Mark Barnett for developing and executing the procedures by which the data were organized into a computer file, and to William F. Miller and Stephen S. Weiner for their comments on the study.

Carter, 1971; Williamson, 1975) or public bureacracies (Lindblom, 1959; Crecine, 1969; Allison, 1971; Steinbruner, 1975; Wildavsky, 1975).

Rising costs, declining resources, and disappearing clientele were key elements of American university environment in the early 1970s (Cheit, 1971; O'Neill, 1971; Rubin, 1977). The problems of dealing with this environment have formed a substantial part of the literature addressed to university administrators in recent years (Bowen and Douglass, 1971; Carnegie Commission, 1972; Cyert, 1975). Administrative efforts to reduce costs and improve efficiency have been notable at most universities. It is less obvious, however, that the curriculum at major universities will also respond to such adversity. Particularly at stronger institutions, curriculum is more the prerogative of individual faculty members and collective faculty institutions than the responsibility of administrative officers (Cohen and March, 1974). It is not clear that faculty groups can, or will, respond to the university's financial adversity. The ways students move through college and receive degrees, the nature of their instruction, the options they have, the credits they accrue, the grades they receive, the accessibility of faculty and courses are central to the university and seem resistant to coordinated change.

The basic theoretical ideas are simple and well-known (March and Simon, 1958; Cyert and March, 1963; Radner, 1975; Steinbruner, 1975). Organizations are assumed to have various independent, aspiration-level goals. For example, a business firm might have a profit goal, sales goal, share-of-market goal, stock price goal. Performance with respect to each goal is compared with the aspiration level. If performance exceeds the goal, the result is organizational slack and rising aspirations. Slack includes 'payments' to coalition members in excess of the payments needed to keep them in the coalition. It may take the form of expenditures for managerial comfort, lighter workloads or reduced supervision, or unexploited opportunities (Cyert and March, 1963). The organization relaxes and reduces the level of search; but, at the same time, aspirations rise. Conversely, if performance fails to meet aspirations, the organization responds by reducing slack, and aspirations fall.

Taken together, these phenomena tend to keep performance and goals together. Slack and changes in aspiration levels are smoothing devices by which relatively large variations in external conditions are transformed into relatively small variations in subjective success. Slack also serves to reduce conflict among subunits. As a result, fluctuations in the external environment produce predictable patterns of organizational responses. During periods of rising external resources and opportunities, slack and aspiration levels rise; internal competition declines. During periods of decreasing resources, slack and aspirations decline; internal competition increases (March and Simon, 1958).

These general ideas about organizational response to environmental change suggest some ideas about how university curriculum adjusts to financial adversity. University departments earn 'profit' (or departmental slack) by increasing the difference between their revenue, which is approximately the budget of the department, and faculty effort in research and teaching. The economizing problem of a department arises from the fact that there is often some positive connection between the amount of effort (for example, the number of students taught) and the amount of resources received.

Cohen and March (1974) proposed a basic model for operating budget allocation that can be adapted for our purposes. According to their analysis, a fundamental mechanism for matching external pressures on the university with internal allocations is the enrollment market. The university (and departments within it) must maintain demand for enrollment in order to secure resources to meet the demand. The mechanism sometimes operates directly through student charges, sometimes indirectly through taxes and legislative subsidies. The effects of the enrollment market may be dampened by strong student demand or by the availability of resources that are not dependent on enrollment. When the economic environment becomes more severe, departments need to increase effort or efficiency in order to maintain revenue. One way of doing this is to change the curriculum.

Competition for resources through the enrollment market invites curriculum competition among departments. The salience of the invitation, however, depends on the extent to which resources are scarce and on the vulnerability of the department to the market. A department will be more likely to seek curriculum attractiveness in hard times; and a department that is able to use a strong research reputation to secure outside funds, student interest, and administrative favor is less dependent on maintaining an attractive curriculum in order to compete for resources (Salancik and Pfeffer, 1974).

Such ideas appear to be consistent with previous research on organizations generally and to make a certain amount of sense. It is possible, however, that the loose coupling and ordinary bureaucratic complexities of education make such fluctuations in slack and search irrelevant for the curriculum (Weick, 1976; Meyer and Rowan, 1977a, 1977b; March, 1978). It is possible that the political character of the decision process or the social structure of universities may make such adaptation imperceptible (March and Olsen, 1976). It is possible that academic organizations absorb variations in environmental conditions without modifying teaching and research activities.

Reactions of universities to financial adversity have emphasized efforts to find ways of reducing costs without making significant changes in the education offered. For example, universities have attempted to increase the number of contact hours for faculty, reduce staff costs, and eliminate or curtail services that are marginal to teaching and research activities. The possibility that adversity would also produce modifications in the curriculum that are less directly connected to the costs of education is clear in the Cohen and March (1974) argument. They describe some modifications of the curriculum intended to stimulate demand as well as some intended to reduce costs; but, as they point out, the procedures for changing the curriculum to stimulate demand are more decentralized in most universities than are those for reducing costs. This is particularly true in institutions with strong traditions of excellence and faculty control over the curriculum.

As a result, it may be useful to ask whether a detailed examination of curriculum drift in a major university shows movement that is consistent with the idea of organizational adaptation. The present paper reports an attempt to look at archival data on small shifts in the apparent attractiveness of the curriculum. The study emphasized those attributes of the curriculum that affected primarily the demand for courses rather than their costs. The question was whether such changes were connected systematically to changes in the severity of the financial environment. The study focused on two hypotheses:

Hypothesis 1: Departmental efforts to increase the attractiveness of the curriculum will be greater in times of financial adversity than in times of prosperity.

Hypothesis 2: Efforts to increase the attractiveness of the curriculum in time of adversity will be less in departments with strong research reputations than in departments with weaker reputations.

The hypotheses can be used to compare three alternative ideas about the response of a university to financial adversity. The first idea assumes that the curriculum changes as a function of educational processes that are not affected systematically by variations in the economic conditions facing the university. The second idea assumes that the curriculum changes as a university-wide response to environmental scarcity; variations in curriculum reflect variations in the environment, but they are not systematically related to departmental characteristics. The third idea assumes that the curriculum changes as a consequence of departmental competition for resources; some departments are more dependent on the enrollment market than others, and thus are more likely to make curriculum changes in times of adversity. If the first idea were correct, both of the hypotheses should be disconfirmed; if the second idea were correct, the first hypothesis should be confirmed, but not the second; if the third idea were correct, both hypotheses should be confirmed.

Data and Analysis

The study was made at Stanford University. Stanford provided a reasonable setting for examining the hypotheses. It had experienced a perceptible increase in financial stress; it had a relatively large number of departments varying in research reputation; it had unusually good records and administrative officers sympathetic to analytical explorations in those records. Nevertheless, the study ran some risk of failing to confirm the hypotheses even though they might be supported by data from other universities. Stanford, by comparison with the general population of American colleges and universities, is likely to be relatively less sensitive to the enrollment market because of student demand for admission; and Stanford faculty maintain considerable collective and individual control over the curriculum.

The data used in the study were secured from official records and publications of the university. These included grading sheets submitted to the registrar of the university by the faculty, computer tape records of the registrar, files and tapes maintained by the academic planning office, and university catalogues. Four academic years were considered. The first two (1964 and 1966) represent a period of relative plenty in the university, the second two (1971 and 1973) a period of relative stringency. Values on each of eight variables were recorded for each of the four years for 30 departments (table 3.1) that existed from 1964 to 1973 in the School of Humanities and Sciences and the School of Engineering. Graduate professional schools of business, education, law, and medicine were excluded, as well as a few departments that were eliminated or created in the interim between 1964 and 1973, and a few small departments having only graduate programs. The basic question asked about each department with respect to each variable was whether departmental responsiveness (i.e., change in the curriculum in the predicted direction) was greater between 1971 and 1973 than it was between 1964 and 1966.

It was easy to establish that several elements of the curriculum closely linked to the cost of instruction changed systematically over this period. For example, in 24 of the 30 departments the number of undergraduate courses offered per faculty member increased more between 1971 and 1973 than it did between 1964 and 1966. Similar results can be obtained for other cost-related measures of curriculum responsiveness. The interest here, however, was in exploring whether a similar trend could be detected in curriculum attributes having only minor and indirect cost effects. The attributes chosen were related to the amount of variety offered in the curriculum, the attractiveness of course packaging or advertising, the accessibility of courses to students, and direct course benefits to students.

Attributes measuring curriculum content would have been useful additions, but good records on course content were not available.

Variables

In selecting the variables, four criteria were used:

1 They should have only modest cost effects.
2 They should be plausibly connected to responsiveness; that is, it should be possible to make a prediction about the direction of change in the variables under the assumption that the basic hypotheses of the study were correct.
3 They should be independent; that is, the specific indices should involve different numbers and should not be constrained by the measurement procedures to correlate with each other.
4 The direction of movement for most departments should be unambiguous; that is, it should be true for each variable that at least 90 per cent of the departments were either more or less responsive between 1971 and 1973 (not tied).

On the basis of these criteria, eight variables were identified. Variables 1 and 2 measured some aspects of variety in course offerings; variables 3 and 4 measured some aspects of course packaging or advertising; variables 5 and 6 measured some aspects of course accessibility to students; and variables 7 and 8 measured some aspects of course benefits provided to students.

1 *Variance in course enrollment*. The enrollment recorded on the official grade sheets of the university was determined for each course in the university. Course enrollment was not identical with class size, though it was much closer to that than would be true at a larger university. Some courses had lecture/section or lecture/ laboratory formats, but instances in which the same course was divided into several lecture classes were very few. The variance across course enrollment was computed for each department each year and was treated as an index of one form of variety in course opportunities for students.

2 *Variance in average units earned in courses*. Students receive units (credits) toward graduation in each course successfully completed. The number of units earned by each student in each course was taken from the official grade sheets. The mean number of units for each course was computed, and the variance of those means was computed for each department each year. This variance was treated as an index of a second kind of variety in course opportunities for students.

3 *Length of course descriptions in the catalogue*. Each course is described in the university catalogue. Although university rules and tradition impose some restrictions on length, descriptions vary in length.

The number of print characters used by each department to describe its courses each year was estimated by counting lines of print and converting to characters (to correct for changes in type characteristics from one year to another). The mean length of a catalogue description was computed by dividing the total departmental characters by the number of courses listed. It was assumed that an increase in the average length of description increased the average market attractiveness of courses.

4 Proportion of undergraduate courses taught by full professors. The instructor for each undergraduate course was determined from the official grade sheets. The instructor's rank was determined from university catalogues and rosters maintained by the university planning office. The proportion of undergraduate courses taught by full professors was computed for each department each year. It was assumed that an increase in this proportion increased the market attractiveness of departmental course offerings.

5 Proportion of courses given at non-competitive times. Courses tend to be concentrated in the mornings (nine to twelve) of Monday, Wednesday, and Friday. Each course listed in the catalogue as being offered at times that included at least two of those nine busiest hours was classified as being given at a competitive time. The proportion of courses given at non-competitive times was calculated for each department each year. It was assumed that an increase in the proportion of courses scheduled at non-competitive times increased the average accessibility of a department's courses.

6 Proportion of courses not requiring a prerequisite. Admission to some courses is restricted to students meeting certain prerequisites (usually in the form of prior courses). Each course listed in the catalogue as having prerequisites was classified as being restricted. The proportion of courses without restrictions was computed for each department each year. It was assumed that an increase in the proportion of unrestricted courses increased the average accessibility of a department's courses.

7 Average number of units earned in courses. The number of units earned by each student in each course was taken from official grade sheets (see variable 2). It was assumed that an increase in the average unit value earned in courses increased the benefits provided to students by a department.

8 Average grade earned in courses. The grade received by each student in each course was taken from official grade sheets. A 13-point scale (including minuses and pluses) was used; pass/fail grades were excluded. The mean grade for each course was computed. From this the average of the mean course grade was computed for each department each year. It was assumed that an increase in the average grade earned in a course increased the benefits provided to students by a department.

Implicit in the analysis is the expectation that a department that is more responsive will be more likely to increase variety in course size, variety in units earned in courses, average length of course descriptions, and so on. These actions were seen as eight independent, equally likely alternative responses. We assumed that observed variations in the use of the eight responses were random fluctuations in a process in which the probability of a positive response was the same on each variable for any given department, but varied from one department to the other. In the absence of either any prior basis for predicting differences or any clear posterior pattern, we assume variations across variables are random fluctuations. Although such an assumption cannot be rejected at the 10 per cent level of significance on the basis of the present results, it might nonetheless be viewed as problematic. Elaboration of possible explanations for possible (real) variation is foregone here.

The specific predictions made here with respect to the direction of movement in the eight variables seem plausible, but they are not uniquely so. For example, it seems reasonable to treat increasing variety in courses as a way of improving competitive position, but the variance is not necessarily the only measure of that variety. Although longer course descriptions and more full professors teaching classes seem sensibly to reflect marketing improvements, it is possible that they do not. Scheduling courses at non-competitve times may seem a reasonable strategy, but it is possible that times are competitive precisely because that is when students want to take classes. Moreover, if some departments lengthen course descriptions in an effort to improve their attractiveness and other departments for the same reason shorten course descriptions, neither prediction will be supported strongly, even though the theory correctly specifies the true underlying mechanism. Although these problems are notable, they should not be exaggerated. The eight variables meet the criteria established, and the predictions about the direction of movement were made *a priori*.

Results

Table 3.1 shows for each department and each variable whether that department showed greater responsiveness under conditions of adversity (1971 and 1973) than under conditions of relative prosperity (1964 and 1966).

If a department was more responsive on a variable between 1971 and 1973 than between 1964 and 1966, the entry in the table is '1'; if it was less responsive on a variable between 1971 and 1973 than between 1964 and 1966, the entry in the table is '0'; if there was no difference, the entry in the table is '1/2'.

The data were reduced to table 3.1 through the following procedures. The raw data were tabulated and computed for each variable, each department, and each year, and recorded in a $30 \times 8 \times 4$ array, V. An entry in the array, $v_{i,j,k}$, showed a value for the ith department, jth curriculum variable, and kth year ($i = 1,30$; $j = 1,8$; $k = 1964, 1966, 1971, 1973$). From the V-array a $30 \times 8 \times 2$ change array, C was constructed. This array showed the difference between the values in the second and first years (i.e., 1964 and 1966, 1971 and 1973). Thus, an entry, $c_{i,j,k}$, in this array showed the changes that took place in the ith department and the jth variable during the kth time period. Since the different variables have quite different dimensions, $c_{i,j,k}$ was expressed as relative change ranging from $+ 1$ to $- 1$ by dividing the algebraic difference between the second and first years by their sum. A relative change array, D, was obtained by subtracting the change in the 1960s from the change in the 1970s, and was a 30×8 array that expressed the difference between the change in the 1970s and the change in the 1960s as a number that could vary from $+ 2$ to $- 2$. A 30×8 sign array, S (reproduced in table 3.1), was constructed from D by attending only to the signs of the differences.

These procedures reduced the information content of the data. The reduction is intended. The focus is on simple measures of the direction of change and low-power, non-parametric tests. The arguments for using such procedures are uncomplicated. The basic statistic computed for each department and each curricular variable is a reasonable measure of the extent to which a department modified its curriculum in the predicted direction more in the 1970s than it did in the 1960s; but the statistic has no known sampling characteristics. Moreover, it seems reasonable to reflect in the analysis no more precision than is reflected in the theory. The theory predicts the sign of the differences and some rough variations in their magnitude. The analysis focuses on the same level of precision. The simplicity of the scores and the analysis, however, should not conceal the large data base on which table 3.1 is based.

The row totals in table 3.1 are scores of departments. High scores indicate a department that was relatively responsive to adversity in the predicted direction; low scores indicate a department that was less responsive. Similarly, column totals are the scores of curriculum variables. High scores indicate a specific response that was used by relatively many departments; low scores indicate a response that was used by relatively few. All of these measures are measures of relative change. They gauge whether responses between 1971 and 1973 were more in the direction of making curriculum attractive than they were between 1964 and 1966. For example, the results with respect to mean course grade may seem surprising in the light of the widely-reported 'grade inflation' in American colleges and universities. In fact, 25 of the 30 departments showed an increase in

Table 3.1 Responsiveness of 30 academic departments in eight curriculum variables in times of financial adversity (1971 and 1973), compared with times of prosperity (1964 and 1966)[a]

Department		1	2	3	4	5	6	7	8	Departmental scores
					Responsiveness variable					
1	Aeronautics and astronautics	0	0	0	1	1	0	0	0	2
2	Chemical engineering	1	1	1	0	1	1	1	1	7
3	Civil engineering	0	0	0	1	1	1	0	1	4
4	Electrical engineering	0	0	0	0	1	1	0	0	2
5	Industrial engineering	1	1	0	1	1	0	1	1	6
6	Materials science and engineering	0	0	0	0	1	1	0	0	2
7	Mechanical engineering	1	1	0	1	0	1	1	1	6
8	Applied physics	1	1	1	1	0	0	1	½	5.5
9	Anthropology	1	1	1	1	0	1	1	0	6
10	Art	0	1	1	0	½	0	1	0	3.5
11	Asian studies	1	1	0	1	1	1	1	1	7
12	Biology	1	0	0	1	1	0	0	1	4
13	Chemistry	1	1	1	1	1	1	1	1	8
14	Classics	1	1	0	0	1	0	1	1	5
15	Communication	1	1	0	0	1	1	0	1	5
16	Economics	1	1	1	1	0	0	1	0	5
17	English	0	0	1	1	1	0	1	0	4
18	History	1	1	1	0	½	0	0	0	3.5
19	Humanities specials	1	1	0	0	1	0	0	1	4
20	Mathematics	1	0	1	1	0	0	1	0	4
21	French and Italian	0	1	0	1	1	1	1	0	5
22	Music	1	1	1	1	½	0	0	1	5.5
23	Philosophy	1	1	0	1	1	0	1	0	5
24	Physics	0	0	0	1	1	0	0	1	3
25	Political science	1	1	1	0	1	1	0	1	6
26	Psychology	0	0	0	1	0	1	0	1	3
27	Sociology	0	0	1	1	1	0	0	1	4
28	Drama	1	1	1	1	0	0	0	0	4
29	Statistics	1	1	0	1	1	1	0	1	6
30	Computer science	1	1	0	1	0	0	1	0	4
Variable scores		20	20	13	21	20.5	13	15	16.5	139

[a]0 = department less responsive to variable between 1971 and 1973 than between 1964 and 1966; 1 = department more responsive; ½ = no difference.

average grades between 1971 and 1973. Those increases were, however, often less than the increases in the same departments between 1964 and 1966. Departments and professors who wanted to raise the average grade in course during the 1970s period could not easily match the magnitude of the earlier increases. Only those departments for which grade inflation was greater in the 1970s were recorded positively on this variable.

These data can be used to test the two hypotheses. Changes in the curriculum in the direction predicted by Hypothesis 1 are indicated by '1's in table 3.1. If adversity did not affect changes in curriculum in these departments, we would expect that the cell entries in the table would sum to about 120. The observed number is 139, significantly greater than would be expected by chance ($p < .01$). Departments at Stanford responded to adversity as predicted by Hypothesis 1.

For Hypothesis 2, departments were ranked using two standard rankings, Carter (1966) and Roose and Andersen (1970). Eighteen departments were ranked on one or both of these rankings, and 16 were ranked on both. The other 12 departments were in fields that were not ranked, that is, none of them were unranked departments in a field for which there were rankings. As a result, 18 departments could be used for this part of the analysis. Departments were ordered on the basis of the mean of their reputational rankings. Ties were resolved by weighting the more recent (1970) ranking slightly more than the earlier one. Such a procedure treats a national ranking in one field as equivalent to the same rank position in another field, but this appears to be approximately what is done when a university or a student evaluates the relative distinction of its departments. Similarly, departments were ordered in terms of their responsiveness scores. The hypothesis was that the two orderings were not independent, but that departments that were relatively high in national reputation would be relatively low in curriculum responsiveness. Figure 3.1 shows the results. Although there are two clear outliers (departments 7 and 13), the null hypothesis that the two rankings are either independent or related in the opposite way can be rejected at the 0.05 level of significance. The test of significance is based on the sample distribution function and was developed by Blum, Kiefer, and Rosenblatt (1961). The value of B is 6176/1889568. Departments with stronger academic reputations made significantly fewer curriculum responses to adversity than departments with weaker reputations.

Discussion

Three alternative ideas about collegiate curriculum change were suggested. The present data reveal that under conditions of relative adversity Stanford

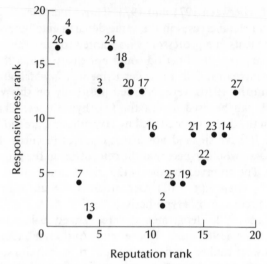

Fig. 3.1 Relation between responsiveness (rank) and reputation (rank)[a] for 18
academic departments (see table 3.1 for number code)
[a]Both ranks run from 1 (high) to 18 (low)

departments tended to increase variety in course offerings, provide more
attractive packaging, make courses more accessible, and increase course
benefits to a greater extent than the same department did during conditions
of relative financial plenty. Departments with strong academic reputations
were less likely to change than those with weaker reputations. The data
support the third idea better than they do the first two. Undoubtedly, the
faculty tried to develop a good curriculum that was responsive to the needs
of students and the society, but those efforts appeared to be affected
significantly by economic conditions and departmental reputation.

The effects were not dramatic. Without the relatively large data base
on which the study was built, they might not have been easily detected.
Stanford curricula were not determined completely by the problems of
adjusting to adversity. The impact of competition for resources may indeed
have been less than what was believed by some students, faculty, and
administrators, but the impact apparently was real. Since the data are based
on the fine structure of the curriculum as revealed by archival records,
they may represent more persuasive evidence than the observations of
participants in the process.

It might be speculated that observed differences in reputations among
departments mask some other underlying variable more directly connected
with departmental subject matter. Attitudes toward administrators,
students, or change might vary from one discipline to another. These
differences would then be reflected in different responsiveness in financial

adversity. Or it might be speculated that disciplines with certain kinds of students (e.g., males) would be systematically both more highly rated and less responsive because of their clientele. At least in this case, the data do not support any obvious hypothesis related to subject matter. There are almost no differences in mean and median responsiveness scores when departments were grouped into four broad categories: engineering, science, social science, humanities. In general, inspection of the data suggests considerable difficulty in formulating a simple counter-hypothesis that depends on subject matter. The eight most responsive departments included: chemical engineering, industrial engineering, mechanical engineering, anthropology, Asian studies, chemistry, political science, and statistics. The seven least responsive departments included: aeronautics and astronautics, electrical engineering, materials science and engineering, art, history, physics, and psychology. It is not easy to propose a way of sorting those 15 departments into those two groups on the basis of their subject matter.

The fact that departments change curriculum under conditions of adversity and that departments with stronger reputations respond less supports the Cohen and March model, but the support should not be exaggerated. We have suggested that reputation made a difference because it provided alternative financial opportunities, alternative bases for attracting students, and alternative sources of power for bargaining with administrators. Departments with strong reputations were seen as less dependent on curriculum responses to economic adversity. Such an interpretation is reasonable, and the data seem to support it. But there are alternative interpretations of the same result. For example, it is possible that strong departments already have unusually attractive programs and are unable to make significant improvements, while there is more room for improvement in weaker departments. More generally, it seems likely that variations in responsiveness are not entirely the semirational consequences of departmental competition for resources suggested by the model. Academia has traditions about change. Although one can control somewhat for variations in such traditions by considering relative change within departments, one cannot entirely control for them. There may be structural features of departments that encourage, or inhibit, responsiveness (Fox, Pate and Pondy, 1976). The curriculum and the various practices that it summarizes are also symbols of different importance in different departments, protected with varying degrees of internal cohesiveness.

Nevertheless, at a highly prestigious university that is relatively strong financially, with a tradition of decentralized faculty control over the curriculum, changes in the curriculum were influenced by changes in economic adversity in a subtle, but detectable way. However diffuse the procedures by which a university increased the variety in course offerings, improved the packaging and advertising for courses, made courses more accessible, and increased direct student benefits from courses, those procedures, at least in this case, seemed to move more in the direction of trying to stimulate demand during the 1970s than they did during the 1960s. However intricate and delicate the ways in which different departments compete with each other for scarce resources, strong departments generally exhibited fewer efforts to increase curriculum attractiveness in response to declining university resources than weaker departments. The results are neither surprising nor extraordinary, but the collection of small decisions and actions involved drifted in a way that conformed to ideas drawn from theories of organizations.

References

Allison, Graham T. (1971) *Essence of Decision: Explaining the Cuban Missile Crisis.* Boston: Little, Brown.

Blum, J. R., Kiefer, J., and Rosenblatt, M. (1961) Distribution free tests of independence based on the sample distribution function. *Annals of Mathematical Statistics*, 32: 485–98.

Bosen, Howard R., and Douglass, Gordon K. (1971) *Efficiency in Liberal Education: a Study of Comparative Instructional Costs for Different Ways of Organizing Teaching–Learning in a Liberal Arts College.* New York: McGraw-Hill.

Bower, Joseph L. (1970) *Managing the Resource Allocation Process: a Study of Corporate Planning and Investment*, Boston: Harvard Graduate School of Business Administration.

Carnegie Commission on Higher Education (1972) *The More Effective Use of Resources: an Imperative for Higher Education.* Berkeley, CA: Carnegie Commission.

Carter, E. Eugene (1971) The behavioral theory of the firm and top-level corporate decisions. *Administrative Science Quarterly*, 16: 413–29.

Cheit, Earl F. (1971) *The New Depression in Higher Education: a Study of 41 Colleges and Universities.* New York: McGraw-Hill.

Cohen, Michael D., and March, James G. (1974) *Leadership and Ambiguity. The American College President.* New York: McGraw-Hill.

Crecine, John P. (1969) *Governmental Problem Solving: a Computer Simulation of Municipal Budgeting.* Chicago: Rand McNally.

Cyert, Richard M. (1975) *The Management of Non-profit Organizations.* Lexington, MA: Heath.

Cyert, Richard M., and March, James G. (1963) *A Behavioral Theory of the Firm.* Englewood Cliffs, NJ: Prentice-Hall.

Fox, Frederick, V., Pate, Larry E. and Pondy, Louis R. (1976) Designing organizations to be responsive to their clients. In Ralph Kilmann, Louis R. Pondy, and Dennis Slevin (eds), *The Management of Organization Design*, vol. 1: 53–72. New York: Elsevier North-Holland.

Lindblom, Charles E. (1959) The science of muddling through. *Public Administration Review*, 19: 79–88.

March, James G. (1978) American public school administration: a short analysis. *School Review*, 86: 217–250.

March, James G., and Olsen, Johan P. (1976) *Ambiguity and Choice in Organizations*. Bergen, Norway: Universitetsforlaget.

March, James G., and Simon, Herbert A. (1958) *Organizations*. New York: Wiley.

Meyer, John W., and Rowan, Brian (1977a) Notes on the structure of educational organizations. In Marshall W. Meyer and associates, *Environments and Organizations: Theoretical and Empirical Perspectives*, San Francisco: Jossey-Bass, pp. 78–109.

Meyer, John W. and Rowan, Brian (1977b) Institutionalized organizations: formal structure as myth and ceremony. *American Journal of Sociology*, 83: 340–63.

O'Neill, June A. (1971) *Resource Use in Higher Education: Trends in Outputs and Inputs, 1930–1967*. Berkeley, CA: Carnegie Commission.

Radner, Roy (1975) A behavioral model of cost reduction. *Bell Journal of Economics*, 6: 196–215.

Roose, Kenneth D., and Anderson, Charles J. (1970) *A Rating of Graduate Programs*. Washington: American Council on Education.

Rubin, Irene (1977) Universities in stress: decision-making under conditions of reduced resources. *Social Science Quarterly*, 58: 242–54.

Salancik, Gerald R., and Pfeffer, Jeffrey (1974) The bases and use of power in organizational decision-making: the case of a university. *Administrative Science Quarterly*, 19: 453–473.

Steinbruner, John D. (1975) *The Cybernetic Theory of Decision: New Dimensions of Political Analysis*. Princeton, NJ: Princeton University Press.

Weick, Karl E. (1976) Educational organizations as loosely coupled systems. *Administrative Science Quarterly*, 21: 1–18.

Wildavsky, Aaron (1975) *Budgeting: a Comparative Theory of Budgetary Processes*. Boston: Little, Brown.

Williamson, Oliver, E. (1975) *Markets and Hierarchies, Analysis and Anti-trust implications: a Study in the Economics of Interest Organization*. New York: Free Press.

4

Managerial Perspectives on Risk and Risk-taking

James G. March and Zur Shapira

Abstract

This paper explores the relation between decision theoretic conceptions of risk and the conceptions held by executives. It considers recent studies of attitudes and behavior among managers against the background of conceptions of risk derived from theories of choice. We conclude that managers take risks and exhibit risk-preferences, but the processes that generate those observables are somewhat removed from the classical processes of choosing from among alternative actions in terms of the mean (expected value) and variance (risk) of the probability distributions over possible outcomes. We identify three major ways in which the conceptions of risk and risk-taking held by these managers lead to orientations to risk that are different from what might be expected from a decision theory perspective: Managers are quite insensitive to estimates of the probabilities of possible outcomes; their decisions are particularly affected by the way their attention is focused on critical performance targets; and they make a sharp distinction between taking risks and gambling. These differences, along with closely related observations drawn from other studies of individual and organizational choice, indicate that the behavioral phenomenon of risk-taking in organizational settings will be imperfectly understood within a classical conception of risk.

This paper was first published in *Management Science*, vol. 33 (1987). The research was supported by grants from the Recanati Foundation, the Russell Sage Foundation, the Spencer Foundation, and the Stanford Graduate School of Business. The authors are especially grateful for the support of Marshall Robinson, as well as for the assistance of Julia Ball and the comments of Elaine Draper and Dan Galai.

Risk as a Factor in Decision-Making

The importance of risk to decision-making is attested by its position in decision theory (Allais, 1953; Arrow, 1965), by its standing in managerial ideology (Peters and Waterman, 1982), and by the burgeoning interest in risk assessment and management (Crouch and Wilson, 1982). However, empirical investigations of decision-making in organizations have not generally focused directly on the conceptions of risk and risk-taking held by managers (March, 1981a); and empirical investigations of risk in decision-making have not generally focused on managerial behavior (Vlek and Stallen, 1980; Schoemaker, 1980; 1982; Slovic, Fischhoff, and Lichtenstein, 1982). As a result, the relation between decision theoretic conceptions of risk and conceptions of risk held by managers remains relatively murky.

The Definition of Risk

In classical decision theory, risk is most commonly conceived as reflecting variation in the distribution of possible outcomes, their likelihoods, and their subjective values. Risk is measured either by non-linearities in the revealed utility for money or by the variance of the probability distribution of possible gains and losses associated with a particular alternative (Pratt, 1964; Arrow, 1965). In the latter formulation, a risky alternative is one for which the variance is large; and risk is one of the attributes which, along with the expected value of the alternative, are used in evaluating alternative gambles. The idea of risk is embedded, of course, in the larger idea of choice as affected by the expected return of an alternative. Virtually all theories of choice assume that decision-makers prefer larger expected returns to smaller ones, provided all other factors (e.g., risk) are constant (Lindley, 1971). In general, they also assume that decision-makers prefer smaller risks to larger ones, provided other factors (e.g., expected value) are constant (Arrow, 1965). Thus, expected value is assumed to be positively associated, and risk is assumed to be negatively associated, with the attractiveness of an alternative.

Finding a satisfactory empirical definition of risk within this rudimentary framework has proven difficult. Simple measures of mean and variance lead to empirical observations that can be interpreted as being off the mean-variance frontier. This has led to efforts to develop modified conceptions of risk, particularly in studies of financial markets. Early criticisms of variance definitions of risk (Markowitz, 1952) as confounding downside risk with upside opportunities led to a number of efforts to develop models based on the semi-variance (Fishburn, 1977; Coombs, 1983). Both variance and semi-variance ideas of risk, however, have been shown to be inconsistent with von Neumann axioms except under rather narrow conditions (Levy and Markowitz, 1979; Levy and Sarnat, 1984); and this result has stimulated efforts to estimate risk and risk-preference from observed prices. This procedure is essentially the approach of much of the contemporary literature on risk in financial markets. One example is the capital asset pricing model that has become one standard approach to financial analysis (Sharpe, 1964; 1977). It defines the degree to which a given portfolio covaries with the market portfolio as the systematic risk. The residual (in a regression sense) is defined as non-systematic or specific risk. These elaborations have contributed substantially to the understanding of financial markets, but the risk-return implications of the model have not always found empirical support (Gibbons, 1982).

There are numerous additional complications with decision theoretic conceptions of risk when they are taken as descriptions of the actual processes underlying choice behavior. There are suggestions, for example, that individuals tend to ignore possible events that are very unlikely or very remote, regardless of their consequences (Kunreuther, 1976). There are suggestions that individuals look at only a few possible outcomes rather than the whole distribution, and measure variation with respect to those few points (Boussard and Petit, 1967; Alderfer and Bierman, 1970); and that they are more comfortable with verbal characterizations of risk than with numerical characterizations even though the translation of verbal expressions of risk into numerical form shows high variability and context dependence (Kahneman and Tversky, 1982). There are suggestions that the likelihoods of outcomes and their values enter into calculations of risk independently, rather than as their products (Slovic, Fischhoff and Lichtenstein, 1977). Such ideas seem to indicate that the ways in which human decision-makers define risk may differ significantly from the definitions of risk in the theoretical literature, and that different individuals will see the same situation in quite different ways (Budescu and Wallsten, 1985).

Attitudes toward Risk

Early treatments by Pratt (1964), Arrow (1965) and others, as well as more recent work (Ross, 1981), assumed that individual human decision-makers are risk-averse, that is, that when faced with one alternative having a given outcome with certainty, and a second alternative which is a gamble but has the same expected value as the first, an individual will choose the certain outcome rather than the gamble. Thus, it follows that decision-makers would normally have to be compensated for variability in possible outcomes; and the greater the return on investment that is observed in a situation, the greater should be the variance involved. Levy and Sarnat

(1984) studied 25 years of investments in mutual funds and discovered that investors were averse to the variance of returns. It is not certain, however, that managers believe that risk and return are positively correlated. Some studies of mergers (Brenner and Shapira, 1983; Mueller, 1969) suggest that this is not the case. Moreover, the aggregate data yield ambiguous results. Bowman (1980) has shown a negative relation between traditional risk (i.e., simple variance) and average return across industries.

Attitudes toward risk are usually pictured as stable properties of individuals, perhaps related to aspects of personality development or culture (Douglas and Wildavsky, 1982); and efforts have been made to associate risk-preference with dimensions of personality, such as achievement motivation (McClelland, 1961; Atkinson, 1964; Kogan and Wallach, 1964). Global differences between presumed risk-takers and others within a culture or job have, however, remained relatively elusive. For example, Brockhaus (1980) attempted to study the risk-taking propensities of entrepreneurs. The individuals who quit their managerial jobs and became owners of business or managers of business ventures were compared to regular managers. Using the choice dilemma questionnaire of Kogan and Wallach (1964), he found no differences in risk-propensity among the different groups.

It is possible that risk-preference is partly a stable feature of individual personality, but a number of variable factors such as mood (Hastorf and Isen, 1982), feelings (Johnson and Tversky, 1983), and the way in which problems are framed (Tversky and Kahneman, 1974) also appear to affect perception of and attitudes toward risk. In particular, Kahneman and Tversky (1979) have observed that when dealing with a risky alternative whose possible outcomes are generally good (e.g., positive monetary outcomes), human subjects appear to be risk-averse; but if they are dealing with a risky alternative whose possible outcomes are generally poor, human subjects tend to be risk-seeking. This pattern of context dependence is familiar to students of risk-taking by animals (Kamil and Roitblat, 1985), individuals (Griffith, 1949; Snyder, 1978; Laughhunn, Payne and Crum, 1980; Payne, Laughhunn and Crum, 1981) and organizations (Mayhew, 1979; Bowman, 1982). It forms the basis for several modern treatments of context-dependent risk-taking (Maynard Smith, 1978; Kahneman and Tversky, 1979; Lopes, 1986; March, 1988).

There are unresolved problems, however. The idea of risk-taking in the face of adversity certainly finds support, but the idea that major innovations and change are produced by misery is not well supported by history. For example, Hamilton (1978) analyzed the structural sources of adventurism using demographic data from the days of the gold rush in California. He found that gold rush 'entrepreneurs' were primarily professionals, upper class and young. They were not from marginal social groups. More inclusive studies of innovation (Mansfield, 1968) and revolution (Brinton, 1938) similarly suggest that risk-taking is not connected to adversity in a simple way.

Dealing with Risk

In conventional decision theory formulations, choice involves a trade-off between risk and expected return. Risk-averse decision-makers prefer relatively low risks and are willing to sacrifice some expected return in order to reduce the variation in possible outcomes. Risk-seeking decision-makers prefer relatively high risks and are willing to sacrifice some expected return in order to increase the variation. The theory assumes that decision-makers deal with risks by first calculating and then choosing among the alternative risk-return combinations that are available.

It is not clear that actual decision-makers treat risk in such a way. For example, Israeli defense decision-makers seem to have dealt with the subject of shelter construction in a way that ignored a decision theory definition of risk (Lanir and Shapira, 1984). There are indications that decision-makers sometimes deny risk, saying that there is no risk or that it is so small that it can be ignored. A common form of denial involves acceptance of the actuarial reality of the risk combined with a refusal to associate that reality with one's self (Weinstein, 1980). The word 'denial' suggests a psychological pathology; it may, of course, be a more philosophical rejection of the relevance of probabilistic reasoning for a single case, or a belief in the causal basis of events. The tendency for individuals to perceive chance events to be causal and under control has been documented in various experiments (Langer, 1975), as has the tendency to develop causal theories of events even when the relations between events are known to be only incidental (Tversky and Kahneman, 1982).

Managerial Perspectives

Two recent studies of managerial perceptions of risk (MacCrimmon and Wehrung, 1986; Shapira, 1986) can be used to consider managerial perspectives on these issues.[1] The study by MacCrimmon and Wehrung is based on questionnaire responses from 509 high-level executives in Canadian and American firms and interviews with 128 of those executives (all from Canadian firms). The study by Shapira is based on interviews with 50 American and Israeli executives. The MacCrimmon and Wehrung

---

1   A more complete description of the Shapira study, its methodology, and its results is available on request from the TIMS office in Providence, Rhode Island.

studies were conducted in 1973–1974. The Shapira study was conducted in 1984–1985. Taken together, these studies provide some rather consistent observations on how managers define risk, their attitudes toward risk, and how they deal with risk.

The Definition of Risk

The managers see risk in ways that are both less precise and different from risk as it appears in decision theory. In particular, there is little inclination to equate the risk of an alternative with the variance of the probability distribution of possible outcomes that might follow the choice of the alternative. Three differences from decision theory are obvious: First, most managers do not treat uncertainty about positive incomes as an important aspect of risk. Possibilities for gain are of primary significance in assessing the attractiveness of alternatives (MacCrimmon and Wehrung, 1986), but 'risk' is seen as associated with the negative outcomes. Shapira (1986) asked respondents: 'Do you think of risk in terms of distribution of all possible outcomes? Just the negative ones? Or just the positive ones?' Eighty per cent of the executives said they considered the negative ones only. There is, therefore, a persistent tension between 'risk' as a measure (e.g., the variance) on the distribution of possible outcomes from a choice and 'risk' as a danger or hazard. From the former perspective, a risky choice is one with a wide range of possible outcomes. From the latter perspective, a risky choice is one that contains a threat of a very poor outcome.

Secondly, for these managers, risk is not primarily a probability concept. About half (54 per cent) of the managers interviewed by Shapira (1986) saw uncertainty as a factor in risk, but the magnitudes of possible bad outcomes seemed more salient to them. A majority felt that risk could better be defined in terms of amount to lose (or expected to be lost) than in terms of moments of the outcome distribution. This led the vice-president of a venture capital firm to say, 'I take large risks regarding the probability but not the amounts.' And a vice-president for finance reported, 'I don't look at the probability of success or failure but at the volume of risk.' In describing the difference between risk-taking and gambling one manager said, 'A gamble of one million dollars in terms of success in a project is risk; however, a gamble of half a dollar is not a risk.' This tendency to ignore or downplay the probability of loss compared to the amount is probably better defined as loss-aversion (Kahneman and Tversky, 1982) or as regret-aversion (Bell, 1983) than as risk-aversion in conventional terms. It is also reflected in the tendency found by MacCrimmon and Wehrung (1986) for less risk-taking when greater stakes were involved. In evaluating uncertain prospects, 80 per cent of Shapira's executives asked for estimates of the 'worst outcome' or the 'maximum loss'. From such responses, it is difficult to assess the extent to which there are considerations of 'plausibility' introduced in determining the possible exposure involved in the alternative. Nevertheless, it is clear that these managers are much more likely to use a few key values to describe their exposure than they are to compute or use standard summary statistics grounded in ideas of probability.

Thirdly, although quantities are used in discussing risk, and managers seek precision in estimating risk, most show little desire to reduce risk to a single quantifiable construct. When MacCrimmon and Wehrung (1986) asked executives to rank nine investment alternatives, the ranks matched an ordering based on expected value in only 11 per cent of the respondents. Even fewer executives ranked the alternatives strictly in terms of maximizing major gain, breaking even, minimizing major loss, or minimizing variation. A vice-president for finance reported (Shapira, 1986) that 'No one is interested in getting quantified measures'; and a senior vice-president observed, 'You don't quantify the risk, but you have to be able to feel it'. Recognizing that there are financial, technical, marketing, production and other aspects of risk, a majority of the interviewees in the Shapira study felt that risk could not be captured by a single number or a distribution, that quantification of risks was not an easy task; and 42 per cent argued that there was no way to translate a multi-dimensional phenomenon into one number. On the other hand, 24 per cent of the same managers felt it could be done and with additional probing said that actually it should be. As one project manager said, 'Everything should be expressed in terms of the profit (or loss) at the end of the project, shouldn't it?' Several felt that one should average the different dimensions and get an overall weighted index of risk, but even among those who thought such a number should be produced, most reported that they didn't do it that way.

Attitudes towards Risk

Managerial risk-taking propensities vary across individuals and across contexts. Among the managers interviewed by Shapira (1986), the variation across individuals is seen as resulting from incentives and experience. In keeping with much of the literature, they think some people are more risk-averse than others, that there are intrinsic motivational factors associated with risk and encoded as a part of an individual personality (McClelland, 1961; Atkinson, 1964; Deci, 1975). They see these differences, however, as less significant than differences produced by incentives and normative definitions of proper managerial behavior. They feel that a manager who fails to take risks should not be in the business of managing. When asked if they could identify risk-prone and risk-averse managers, middle level managers were inclined to say that risk-prone individuals disappear as you move up the hierarchy. Higher level managers, on the other hand, feel there is a definite need to educate new managers into the importance of risk-taking. In the Shapira study, the inclination to encourage others to take risks increased as one moved up the hierarchy, and MacCrimmon and Wehrung (1986) found that higher level executives scored higher on their risk-taking measures than did lower level executives.

Managers recognize both the necessity and the excitement of risk-taking in management, but they report that risk-taking in organizations is sustained more by personal than by organizational incentives. Shapira (1986) found that managers at all levels generally picture organizational life as inhibiting risk-taking on the part of managers. As a result, and in contrast to their normative enthusiasm for risk-taking, these respondents were mostly conservative when asked what practical advice they would give to a new manager. They did not encourage risk-taking. Rather, they said things like: 'Let other managers participate in your decisions.' 'Don't gamble.' 'Arrange for a blanket.' This negative attitude toward individual risk-taking is particularly characteristic of managers who see risk as unconnected to uncertainty, that is as being defined in terms of the magnitude of a projected loss or gain rather than that magnitude weighted by its likelihood.

Despite this pessimism about organizational incentives for risk-taking, or perhaps because of it, most of the managers interviewed by Shapira (1986) portrayed themselves as judicious risk-takers and as less risk-averse than their colleagues. Similarly, MacCrimmon and Wehrung (1986) found that managers tended to believe they were greater risk-takers than they were. The executives studied by Shapira explained their willingness to take calculated risks in terms of three powerful motivations. First, they said that risk-taking is essential to success in decision-making. Eighty-seven per cent of the executives felt that risk and return were related, though they added 'ifs', 'buts' and 'it depends' to qualify this relation. In general, the managers studied by Shapira (1986) expect the choice of an alternative to be justified if large potential losses are balanced by similarly large potential gains, but they do not seem to think that they would require the expected value of a riskier alternative to be greater than that of the less risky in order to justify choice.

Secondly, these managers associate risk-taking more with the expectations of their jobs than with a personal predilection. They believe that risk-taking is an essential component of the managerial role. In the words of a senior vice-president of one firm, 'If you are not willing to assume risks, go deal with another business.' This link between risk-taking and management is less a statement of the measurable usefulness of risk-taking to a manager than an affirmation of a role. As the president of an electronic firm said, 'risk-taking is synonymous with decision-making under uncertainty.' In keeping with contemporary managerial ideology, he might have added that management is synonymous with decision-making. Consistent with such a spirit, both MacCrimmon and Wehrung (1986) and Shapira (1986) found that managers are inclined to show greater propensity toward risk-taking when questions are framed as business decisions than when they are framed as personal decisions.

Thirdly, these managers recognize the emotional pleasures and pains of risk-taking, the affective delights and thrills of danger. Risk-taking involves emotions of anxiety, fear, stimulation and joy. Many of the Shapira (1986) respondents seemed to believe that the pleasures of success were augmented by the threat of failure. One president said, 'Satisfaction from success is directly related to the degree of risk taken.' As we shall note below, this excitement with danger is confounded by a concomitant anticipation of mastery, the expectation that danger will be overcome.

These three motivational factors are background for a greater variation in risk-taking attributable to contextual factors. The managers interviewed by Shapira (1986) saw themselves and other managers as exhibiting different risk-preferences under different conditions, and the MacCrimmon and Wehrung (1986) measures of managerial risk-propensity were poorly correlated across decision situations. Some of this variation appears to be idiosyncratic to the details of particular situations, but there is one consistent theme. Both the managers interviewed by Shapira and those interviewed by MacCrimmon and Wehrung believe that fewer risks should, and would, be taken when things are going well. They expect riskier choices to be made when an organization is 'failing'. In short, risk-taking is affected by the relation between current position and some critical reference points (Kahneman and Tversky, 1979).

Two comparisons organize managerial thinking about how things are going. The first of these is a comparison between some performance or position (e.g., profit, liquidity, sales) and an aspiration level or 'target' for it. Most managers seem to feel that risk-taking is more warranted when faced with failure to meet targets than when targets were secure. In 'bad' situations risks would be taken. Some also feel that attention to the survival of an individual as a manager is involved, that executives will take riskier actions when their own positions or jobs are threatened than when they are safe. A second comparison is between the current position of an organization and its demise. There is strong sentiment that survival should not be risked. Over 90 per cent of the executives interviewed by Shapira said they would not take risks where a failure could jeopardize the survival of the firm, although one executive commented that 'in situations where a competitor threatens the market position of the firm, you have to take one of two risks: not surviving on the one hand and risking new strategies on the other.'

There is some obvious ambiguity in the ideas. Generally, the argument is that a strong position leads to conservative behavior with respect to risk, that the danger of falling below a target is minimized. At the same time, however, the greater the asset position relative to the target, the less the danger from any particular amount of risk (Arrow, 1965). As one vice-president said (Shapira, 1986), 'Logically and personally I'm willing to take more risks the more assets I have.' Conversely, performance below a target is argued to lead to greater willingness to take risks, in order to increase the chance of reaching the target; but the poorer the position, the greater the danger reflected in the downside risk. This would suggest that the value attached to alternatives differing in risk may depend not only on whether they are 'framed' as gains or losses but also on which of two targets (the 'success' target or the 'survival' target) is evoked (Lopes, 1986).

Dealing with Risk

Early studies of managers (Cyert and March, 1963) concluded that business managers avoid risk rather than accept it. They avoid risk by using short-run reaction to short-run feedback rather than anticipation of future events. They avoid the risk of an uncertain environment by negotiating uncertainty-absorbing contracts. In a similar way, MacCrimmon and Wehrung (1986) found managers avoiding risks in a simulated in-basket task. They delay decisions and delegate them to others.

Other studies suggest that managers avoid accepting risk by seeing it as subject to control. They do not accept the idea that the risks they face are inherent in their situation (Strickland, Lewicki, and Katz, 1966). Rather, they believe that risks can be reduced by using skills to control the dangers. Keyes (1985) pictured entrepreneurs and other risk-takers as seeking mastery over the odds of fate, rather than simply accepting long shots. Adler (1980) distinguished managers who were risk-avoiders, risk-takers and risk-makers. The latter are those who not only take risks but try to manage and modify them. The managers interviewed by MacCrimmon and Wehrung (1986) and by Shapira (1986) are similar. They believe that risk is manageable. Seventy-five per cent of the Shapira respondents saw risk as controllable. As a result, they make a sharp distinction between gambling (where the odds are exogenously determined and uncontrollable) and risk-taking (where skill or information can reduce the uncertainty). The situations they face seem to them to involve risk-taking, but not gambling. They report seeking to modify risks, rather than simply accepting them; and they assume that normally such a modification will be possible. As the president of a successful high technology company told Shapira, 'In starting my company I didn't gamble; I was confident we were going to succeed.'

In cases in which a given alternative promises a good enough return but presents an unacceptable danger, managers focus on ways to reduce the danger while retaining the gain. One simple action is to reject the estimates. Thus, only two of the 50 executives interviewed by Shapira (1986) said they accept estimates of risk as given to them. In most cases, rejection is supplemented by efforts to revise estimates. Seventy-four per cent of the managers said they tried to modify the descriptions of risk, partly by securing new information, partly by attacking the problem with different perspectives. More importantly, however, they try to change the odds. Managers see themselves as taking risks, but only after modifying and working on the dangers so that they can be confident of success. Prior to a decision, they look for risk-controlling strategies. Most managers believe that they can do better than is expected, even after the estimates have been revised. This tactic, called 'adjustment' by MacCrimmon and Wehrung (1986), is reported as a standard executive reponse to risk. In the Shapira interviews, managers spoke of 'eliminating the unknowns' and 'controlling the risk'. Managerial confidence in the possibilities for post-decision reduction in risk comes from an interpretation of managerial experience. Most executives feel that they have been able to better the odds in their previous decisions. Thus, managers accept risks, in part, because they do not expect that they will have to bear them.

Implications for Understanding Risk-Taking by Managers

These empirical observations call attention to three pervasive features of managerial treatment of risk that deviate from simple conceptions of risk and are important for understanding managerial decision-making.

Insensitivity of Risk-Taking to Probability Estimates

There are strong indications in these studies, as well as in others (Slovic, 1967; Kunreuther, 1976; Fischhoff, Lichtenstein, Slovic, Derby and Keeney, 1981), that individuals do not trust, do not understand, or simply do not much use precise probability estimates. Crude characterizations of likelihoods are used to exclude certain possibilities from entering the decision calculus. Possible outcomes with very low probabilities seem to be ignored, regardless of their potential significance. Where low prior probability is combined with high consequence, as in the case of unexpected major disasters or unanticipated major discoveries, the practice of excluding very low probability events from consideration makes a difference. In a world containing a very large number of very low probability, very high consequence possible events, it is hard to see how an organization can reasonably consider all of them. But if, as seems likely, *some* particular very low probability, high consequence events are certain to occur, the organization is placed in the position of preparing for a world that is certain not to be realized (i.e., a world in which *no* low probability, high consequence events occur). It is, of course, not necessarily given that there is an attractive solution to this dilemma, regardless of the treatment of probability estimates; but the practice of ignoring very low probability events has the effect of leaving organizations persistently surprised by, and unprepared for, realized events that had, *a priori*, very low probabilities.

The insenstivity to probability estimates extend beyond the case of very low probability events, however. Within a wide range of plausibility, it appears to be the magnitude of the value of the outcome that defines risk for managers, rather than some weighting of that magnitude by its likelihood. This is reflected in the use of terms such as 'maximum exposure', 'opportunity', or 'worst or best (plausible) case'. The behavior has consequences. It leads to a propensity to accept greater risk (in the sense of variance) when the probability distribution of possible outcomes is relatively rectangular than where there are relatively long tails.

Although it is arguable that this behavior is less intelligent than taking a fuller account of variations in likelihood, it may be useful to observe that the 'confusions' of managers about risk are echoes of ambiguity in the choice engineering literature. In decision theory terms, risk refers to the probabilistic uncertainty of outcomes stemming from a choice. In recent treatises on risk-assessment and risk-management, on the other hand, risk has become increasingly a term referring not to the *unpredictability* of outcomes but to their *costs*, particularly their costs in terms of mortality and morbidity (Fischhoff, Watson and Hope, 1984). Within the latter terminology, the main focus of concern has been not on variability but on defining trade-offs between a specific 'risk' and other costs, for example, between the frequency and severity of injury and the monetary costs of safety measures. The typical style is to deal with the expected value of the probability distribution over adverse outcomes, rather than any higher moments. Thus, 'risk' becomes 'hazard', the expected value of an outcome rather than its variability; and the central insight of theories of decision-making under risk, the importance of considering the whole distribution of possible outcomes, tends to become obscured in considerations of 'risk'.

Managerial insensitivity to probability estimates may, in part, reflect such terminological elasticity among writers on risk- and decision-engineers. It may also be attributable to some realities of decision-making that are not habitually noted by students of rational choice. Typically, the guesses of choice are not easy ones. Estimating the probabilities of outcomes is difficult, as is estimating the returns to be realized and the subjective value that might be associated with such returns when they are realized is unclear. Information is compromised by conflict of interest between the source of the information and the recipient. Since these difficulties are particularly acute in the estimation of probabilities, it is entirely sensible for a manager to conclude that the credibility of probability estimates is systematically less than is the credibility of estimates of the value of an outcome; and it is certainly arguable that the relative credibility of estimates should affect the relative attention paid to them.

The Importance of Attention Factors for Risk-Taking

Empirical studies of risk-taking, including the ones discussed here, indicate that risk-preference varies with context. Specifically, the acceptability of a risky alternative depends on the relation between the dangers and opportunities reflected in the risk and some critical aspiration levels for the decision-maker. From a behavioral point of view, this contextual variation in risk-taking seems to stem less from the revision of a coherent preference for risk (March, 1988) than from a change in focus among a set of inconsistent and ambiguous preferences (March, 1978). As a result of changing fortunes or aspirations, focus is shifted away from the dangers involved in a particular alternative and toward its opportunities (Lopes, 1986).

The tendency for managerial evaluations of alternatives to focus on a few key aspects of a problem at a time is a recurrent theme in the study of human problem solving. Consider, for example, the discussion of 'elimination by aspects' by individual decision-makers (Tversky, 1972), analyses of attention in human problem solving (Nisbett and Ross, 1980), the 'sequential attention to goals' by organizational decision-makers (Cyert and March, 1963), or 'garbage-can models of choice' (March and Olsen, 1976). These observations suggest that choice behavior normally interpreted as being driven primarily by preferences and changes in them is susceptible to an alternative interpretation in terms of attention. Theories that emphasize the sequential consideration of a relatively small number of alternatives (Simon, 1955; March and Simon, 1958), that treat slack and search as stimulated or reduced by a comparison of performance with aspirations (Cyert and March, 1963; Levinthal and March, 1981; Singh, 1986), or that highlight the significance of order of presentation and agenda effects (Cohen, March and Olsen, 1972; Kingdon, 1984) are all reminders that understanding action in the face of incomplete information may depend more on ideas about attention than on ideas about decision.

In several of these theories, there is a single critical focal value for attention, for example, the aspiration level that divides subjective success from subjective failure. The present observations with respect to the shifting focus of attention in risk seem to confirm the importance of two focal values rather than a single one (Lopes, 1986; March, 1988). The most frequently mentioned values are a target level for performance (e.g., breakeven) and a survival level. These two reference points partition possible states into three: success, failure and extinction. The addition of a focus value associated with extinction changes somewhat the predictions about attention (or risk-preference) as a function of success.

In general, if one is above a performance target, the primary focus is on avoiding actions that might place one below it. The dangers of falling below the target dominate attention; the opportunities for gain are less salient. This leads to relative risk-aversion on the part of successful managers, particularly those who are barely above the target. As long as the distribution of outcomes is symmetrical, the dangers and the opportunities covary; but since it is the dangers that are noticed, the opportunities are less important to the choice. For successful managers, attention to opportunities and thus risk-taking is stimulated only when performance exceeds the target by a substantial amount.

For decision-makers who are, or expect to be, below the performance target, the desire to reach the target focuses attention in a way that leads generally to risk-taking. In this case, the opportunities for gain receive attention, rather than the dangers, except when nearness to the survival point evokes attention to that level. If performance is well above the survival point, the focus of attention results in a predilection for relatively high variance alternatives, thus risk-prone behavior. If performance is close to the survival point, the emphasis on high variance alternatives is moderated by a heightened awareness of their dangers.

Risk-Taking, Gambling and Managerial Conceit

Managers have a strong normative reaction to risk and risk-taking. They care about their reputations for risk-taking and are eager to expound on their sentiments about the deficiencies of others and on the inadequacy of organizational incentives for making risky decisions intelligently. The rhetoric of these values is, however, decidedly two-pronged. On the one hand, risk-taking is valued, treated as essential to innovation and success. At the same time, however, risk-taking is differentiated from 'playing the odds'. A good manager is seen as 'taking risks' but not as 'gambling'. To a student of statistical decision theory, the distinction may be obscure since the idea of decision-making under risk in that tradition is paradigmatically captured by a vision of betting, either against nature or against other strategic actors. From that perspective, the choice of a particular business strategy depends on the same general considerations as the choice of a betting strategy in a game of poker. The significance of this parallel has been recognized by decision-engineers who have tried, with only modest success, to champion a criterion for evaluating managers that rewards 'good decisions' rather than 'good outcomes', arguing that the determination of a proper choice should not be confounded with the chance realizations of a risky situation.

We believe that managers distinguish risk-taking from gambling primarily because the society that evaluates them does, and because their experience teaches them that they can control fate. Society values risk-taking but not gambling, and what is meant by gambling is risk-taking that turns out badly. From the point of view of managers and a society dedicated to good management, the problem is to develop and maintain managerial reputations for taking 'good' (i.e., ultimately successful) risks and avoiding 'bad' (i.e., ultimately unsuccessful) risks, in the face of (possibly inherent) uncertainties about which are which. The situation was described rather precisely to Shapira (1986) by one senior vice-president. He said, 'You have to be a risk-taker, but you have to win more than you lose.'

Managers can engage in relatively conscious strategies designed to inflate the perceived riskiness of successful actions, but deliberate efforts on the part of managers to portray themselves as risk-takers are only a minor part of the story. Managerial reputations for risk-taking rather than gambling are sustained by the ordinary social processes for interpreting life and getting ahead. In historical perspective, we have no difficulty distinguishing those who have been brilliant risk-takers from those who have been foolish gamblers, however obscure the difference may have been at the time they were making their decisions. *Post hoc* reconstruction permits history to be told in such a way that 'chance', either in the sense of genuinely probabilistic phenomena or in the sense of unexplained variation, is minimized as an explanation (Fischhoff, 1975; Fischhoff and Beyth, 1975). Thus, risky choices that turn out badly are seen, after the fact, to have been mistakes. The warning signs that were ignored seem clearer than they were; the courses that were followed seem unambiguously misguided.

History not only sorts decision-makers into winners and losers but also interprets those differences as reflecting differences in judgment and ability. The experience of successful managers teaches them that the probabilities of life do not apply to them. Neither a society nor a manager has any particular reason to doubt the validity of the assessment that successful managers have the skill to choose good risks and reject bad risks, thus that they can solve the apparent inconsistency of social norms that demand both risk-taking and assured success. Managers believe, and their experience appears to have told them, that they can change the odds, that what appears to be a probabilistic process can usually be controlled. The result is to make managers somewhat more prone to accept risks than they might otherwise be.

Such risk-taking also fits into social definitions of managerial roles. Managers are expected to make things happen, to take (good) risks. Managerial ideology pictures managers as making changes, thus leading to a tendency for managers to be biased in the direction of making organizational changes and for others to be biased in expecting them to do so (March, 1981b). In a similar fashion, managerial ideology also portrays a good manager as being a risk-taker. Managerial conceits include beliefs that it is possible at the time of a decision to tell the difference between risks with good outcomes and risks with bad outcomes, and that it is possible to manage risks so as to improve on the apparent odds. And such conceits make risk-taking seem entirely consistent with the normative expectation that decisions will also reliably turn out well (Keyes, 1985).

Conclusion

In the tradition of behavioral studies of organizational decision-making (March and Simon, 1958; March and Shapira, 1982), behavioral decision research (Edwards, 1954; 1961; Nisbett and Ross, 1980; Kahneman, Slovic and Tversky, 1982), and the behavioral assessment of risk-perception (Slovic, Fischhoff, and Lichtenstein, 1985; Englander, Farago, Slovic, and Fischhoff, 1985), we have examined how executives actually define and react to risk, rather than how they ought to do so. We conclude not only that managers fail to follow the canons of decision theory, but also that the ways they think about risk are not easily fitted into classical theoretical conceptions of risk.

Standard conceptions of risk, with their emphasis on trait differences among individual decision-makers, are problematic as bases for talking about managerial risk-taking behavior. To a substantial extent, probability estimates are treated as unreliable and subject to post-decision control, and considerations of trade-offs are framed by attention factors that considerably affect action. Managers look for alternatives that can be managed to meet targets, rather than assess or accept risks. Although they undoubtedly vary in their individual propensities to take risks, those variations are obscured by processes of selection that reduce the heterogeneity among managers and encourage them to believe in their ability to control the odds, by systems of organizational controls and incentives that dictate risk-taking behavior in significant ways, and by variations in the demand for risk-taking produced by the context within which choice takes place. These factors are embedded in a managerial belief system that emphasizes the importance of risk and risk-taking for being a manager.

These features of managerial approaches to risk have implications not only for understanding decision-making in organizations, but also for the engineering of risk-taking and risk-management. It is conventional in modern discussions of management to deplore the pattern of risk-taking observed in management. Individual managers are often criticized for taking too many (or too few) risks, as is management as a whole. Proposals for changing the incentives for risk-taking are common. The present observations suggest that some of the policies proposed to change risk-taking may not match the situation as it is seen by managers. In the short run, if we wish to encourage, or inhibit, risk-taking on the part of managers, we probably need to shape our interventions to meet the ways in which managers think. For example, it may be more efficacious to try to modify managerial attention patterns and conceits than to try to change beliefs about the likelihood of events or to try to induce preferences for high variance alternatives.

In the longer run, there are possible implications for the education of managers. The managers who participated in these studies do not follow decision theory very closely. They do not reject the theory in an informed, reasoned way, but rather act according to some rules and procedures that are implicitly at variance with the theory, even while acknowledging it as decision dogma. This suggests that there might be solid prospects for changing managerial perspectives through direct training in decision-theoretic approaches to risk and risk-management. As we have recorded above, however, the perspectives that managers have are not simply matters of individual taste but are embedded in social norms and expectations. History and common sense both suggest that changes may be relatively slow, responding more to broad shifts in beliefs and formulations than to simple changes in the selection or training of managers.

Before we leap too enthusiastically into a program of comprehensive managerial education and social reform, moreover, we may wish to recognize the elements of intelligence in these managerial perspectives. Although there is ample evidence that the risk-taking behavior of managers is often far from optimal, we may want to examine the extent to which the managerial beliefs and behaviors we observe are accommodations of human organizations and their managers to the subtle practical problems of sustaining appropriate risk-taking in an imperfectly comprehended world. It is not hard to show that contextually varying risk-preferences, insensitivity to probabilities, and managerial illusions are intelligent under plausible conditions (Ibsen, 1884; Einhorn, 1986; March, 1988). Perhaps the most troubling feature of decision theory in this context is the invitation it provides to managerial passivity. By emphasizing the calculation of expectations as a response to risk, the theory poses the problem of choice in terms appropriate to decision-making in an uncontrollable world, rather than in a world that is subject to control. It is not intrinsic to that frame that decision-makers become passive with respect to modifying the probabilities they face, but that danger is real. We may prefer to have managers imagine (sometimes falsely) that they can control their fates, rather than suffer the consequences of their imagining (sometimes falsely) that they cannot. What are harder to specify are the details of the ways in which such impulses for discovering methods to improve the odds can be meshed with standard 'rational' calculations to induce more sensible managerial behavior.

References

Adler, Stanley (1980) Risk-making management, *Business Horizons*, 23(2): 11–14.
Alderfer, Clayton, P., and Harold Bierman, Jr. (1970) Choices with risk: beyond the mean and variance, *Journal of Business*, 43: 341–53.
Allais, Maurice (1953) Le comportement de l'homme rationnel devant le risque: critique des postulats et axiomes de l'école americaine, *Econometrica*, 21: 503–46.
Allison, Graham T. (1971) *Essence of Decision*. Boston, MA: Little, Brown.
Arrow, Kenneth J. (1965) *Aspects of the Theory of Risk Bearing*. Helsinki: Yrjö Jahnssonis Säätio.
Atkinson, John W. (1964) *An Introduction to Motivation*. New York, NY: Van Nostrand.
Bell, David E. (1983) Risk premiums for decision regret, *Management Science*, 29: 1156–66.
Boussard, Jean-Marc, and Michel Petit (1967) Representation of farmers behavior under uncertainty with a focus-loss constraint, *Journal of Farm Economics*, 49: 869–80.
Bowman, Edward H. (1980) A risk-return paradox for strategic management, *Sloan Management Review*, 21: 17–31.
Bowman, Edward H. (1982) Risk seeking by troubled firms, *Sloan Management Review*, 23: 33–42.
Brenner, Menachem and Zur Shapira (1983) Environmental uncertainty as determining merger activity, in Walter Goldberg (ed.), *Mergers: Motives, Modes, Methods*. New York, NY: Nichols, pp. 51–65.
Brinton, Crane (1938) *Anatomy of Revolution*. New York, NY: Norton.
Brockhaus, Robert H., Sr. (1980) Risk-taking propensity of entrepreneurs, *Academy of Management Journal*, 23: 509–20.
Budescu, David V., and Thomas S. Wallsten, (1985) Consistency in interpretation of probabilistic phrases, *Organizational Behavior and Human Decision Processes*, 36: 391–405.
Cohen, Michael D., James G. March, and Johan P. Olsen, (1972) A garbage can model of organizational choice, *Administrative Science Quarterly*, 17: 1–25.

Coombs, Clyde H. (1983) *Psychology and Mathematics*. Ann Arbor, MI: University of Michigan Press.

Crouch, Edmund A. C., and Richard Wilson (1982) *Risk/Benefit Analysis*. Cambridge, MA: Ballinger.

Cyert, Richard M., and James G. March (1963) *A Behavioral Theory of the Firm*. Englewood Cliffs, NJ: Prentice Hall.

Deci, Edward L. (1975) *Intrinsic Motivation*, New York: Plenum.

Douglas, Mary and Aaron Wildavsky (1982) *Risk and Culture*. Berkeley: University of California Press.

Edwards, Ward (1954) The theory of decision-making, *Psychological Bulletin*, 51: 380-417.

Edwards, Ward (1961) Behavioral decision theory, *Annual Review of Psychology*, 12: 473-98.

Einhorn, Hillel (1986) Accepting errors to make less error, *Journal of Personality Assessment*, 50: 387-95.

Englander, Tibor, Klara Farago, Paul Slovic, and Baruch Fischhoff (1985) A comparative analysis of risk perception in Hungary and the United States, unpublished ms.

Fischhoff, Baruch (1975) Hindsight ≠ foresight: The effect of outcome knowledge on judgement under uncertainty, *Journal of Experimental Psychology: Human Perception and Performance*, 1: 288-99.

Fischhoff, Baruch, and Ruth L. Beyth (1975) I knew it would happen – remembered probabilities of once-future things, *Organizational Behavior and Human performance*, 3: 552-64.

Fischhoff, Baruch, Sarah Lichtenstein, Paul Slovic, Stephen L. Derby, and Ralph Keeney (1981) *Acceptable Risk*. New York, NY: Cambridge University Press.

Fischhoff, Baruch, Stephen R. Watson, and Chris Hope (1984) Defining risk, *Policy Sciences*, 17: 123-39.

Fishburn, Peter C. (1977) Mean-risk analysis with risk associated with below-target returns, *American Economic Review*, 67: 116-26.

Gibbons, Michael R. (1982) Multivariate tests of financial models: A new approach, *Journal of Financial Economics*, 10: 3-27.

Griffith, R. M. (1949) Odds adjustments by American horse race bettors, *American Journal of Psychology*, 62: 290-94.

Hamilton, Gary G. (1978) The structural sources of adventurism: the case of the California gold rush, *American Journal of Sociology*, 83: 1466-90.

Hastorf, Albert, and Alice M. Isen, (eds) (1982) *Cognitive Social Psychology*. New York, NY: Elsevier.

Ibsen, Henrik (1884) *The Wild Duck*. Norton Critical Edition (1968), Dounia B. Christiani (trans.). New York, NY: W. W. Norton.

Johnson, Eric J., and Amos Tversky, (1983) Affect, generalization and the perception of risk, *Journal of Personality and Social Psychology*, 45: 20-31.

Kahneman, Daniel, Paul Slovik, and Amos Tversky (1982) *Judgment under Uncertainty: Heuristics and Biases.* Cambridge: Cambridge University Press.

Kahneman, Daniel, and Amos Tversky (1979) Prospect theory: an analysis of decision under risk, *Econometrica*, 47: 263-91.

Kahneman, Daniel, and Amos Tversky (1982) Variants of uncertainty, *Cognition*, 11: 143–57.

Kamil, Alan C., and Herbert L. Roitblat (1985) The ecology of foraging behavior: implications for animal learning and memory, *Annual Review of Psychology*, 36: 141–69.

Keyes, Ralph (1985) *Chancing it*. Boston, MA: Little, Brown.

Kingdon, John (1984) *Agendas, Alternatives, and Public Policies*. Boston, MA: Little, Brown.

Kogan, Nathan, and Michael A. Wallach (1964) *Risk-taking*. New York, NY: Holt, Rhinehart and Winston.

Kunreuther, Howard (1976) Limited knowledge and insurance protection, *Public Policy*, 24: 227–61.

Langer, Ellen J. (1975) The illusion of control, *Journal of Personality and Social Psychology*, 32: 311–28.

Lanir, Zvi, and Zur Shapira (1984) Analysis of decisions concerning the defense of rear areas in Israel: a case study in defense decision-making, in Zvi Lanir (ed.), *Israel's Security Planning in the 1980s*. New York, NY: Praeger.

Laughhunn, Dan J., John W. Payne, and Roy L. Crum (1980) Managerial risk-preferences for below target returns, *Management Science*, 26: 1238–49.

Levinthal, Daniel, and James G. March (1981) A model of adaptive organizational search, *Journal of Economic Behavior and Organization*, 2: 307–333.

Levy, Haim, and Harry M. Markowitz (1979) Approximating expected utility by a function of mean and variance, *American Economic Review*, 69: 308–17.

Levy, Haim and Marshall Sarnat (1984) *Portfolio and Investment Selection*. Englewood Cliffs, NJ: Prentice Hall.

Lindley, D. V. (1973) *Making Decisions*. London: John Wiley.

Lopes, Lola L. (1987) Between hope and fear: the psychology of risk, *Advances in Experimental Social Psychology*, 20: 255–95.

MacCrimmon, Kenneth R., and Donald A. Wehrung (1986) *Taking Risks: The Management of Uncertainty*. New York, NY: Free Press.

Mansfield, Edwin (1968) *The Economics of Technological Change*. New York, NY: Norton.

March, James G. (1978) Bounded rationality, ambiguity, and the engineering of choice, *Bell Journal of Economics*, 9: 587–608.

March, James G. (1981a) Decisions in organizations and theories of choice, in Andrew Van de Van, and William Joyce (eds), *Assessing Organizational Design and Performance*. New York: Wiley Interscience, pp. 205–244.

March, James G. (1981b) Footnotes to organizational change, *Administrative Science Quarterly*, 26: 563–77.

March, James G. (1988) Variable risk preferences and adaptive aspirations, *Journal of Economic Behavior and Organizations*, in press.

March, James G., and Johan P. Olsen (1976) *Ambiguity and Choice in Organizations*. Bergen, Norway: Universitetsforlaget.

March, James G., and Zur Shapira (1982) Behavioral decision theory and organizational decision theory, in Gerardo R. Ungson and Daniel N. Braunstein (eds), *Decision Making: An Interdisciplinary Inquiry*. Boston, MA: Kent, pp. 92–115.

March, James G., and Herbert A. Simon (1958) *Organizations*. New York, NY: Wiley.

Markowitz, Harry M. (1952) The utility of wealth, *Journal of Political Economy*, 60: 151–58.

Mayhew, Lewis B. (1979) *Surviving the Eighties*. San Francisco, CA: Jossey-Bass.

Maynard Smith, J. (1978) Optimization theory in evolution, *Annual Review of Ecology and Systematics*, 9: 31–56.

McClelland, David (1961) *The Achieving Society*. New York, NY: Van Nostrand.

Mueller, Dennis C. (1969) A theory of conglomerate mergers, *Quarterly Journal of Economics*, 83: 643–59.

Nisbett, Richard, and Lee Ross (1980) *Human Inference: Strategies and Shortcomings of Social Judgment*. Englewood Cliffs, NJ: Prentice-Hall.

Olsen, Johan P. (1983) *Organized Democracy*. Oslo: Universitetsforlaget.

Payne, John W., Dan J. Laughhunn, and Roy L. Crum (1981) Further tests of aspiration level effects in risky choice behavior, *Management Science*, 27: 953–8.

Peters, Tom, and Robert Waterman (1982) *In Search of Excellence*. New York, NY: Harper and Row.

Pratt, John W. (1964) Risk-aversion in the small and in the large, *Econometrica*, 32: 122–36.

Ross, Stephen A. (1981) Some stronger measures of risk-aversion in the small and in the large with applications, *Econometrica*, 49: 621–38.

Schoemaker, Paul J. H. (1980) *Experiments on Decisions under Risk: The Expected Utility Hypothesis*. Boston, MA: Nijhoff.

Schoemaker, Paul J. H. (1982) The expected utility model: its variants, purposes, evidence and limitations, *Journal of Economic Literature*, 20: 529–63.

Shapira, Zur (1986) Risk in managerial decision-making. Unpublished ms.

Sharpe, William F. (1964) Capital asset prices: a theory of market equilibrium under conditions of risk, *Journal of Finance*, 19: 425–42.

Sharpe, William F. (1977) The capital asset pricing model: a multi-beta interpretation, in Haim Levy and Marshall Sarnat (eds), *Financial Decision Making under Uncertainty*. New York, NY: Academic Press, pp. 127–136.

Simon, Herbert A. (1955) A behavioral model of rational choice, *Quarterly Journal of Economics*, 69: 99–118.

Singh, Jitendra V. (1986) Performance, slack, and risk-taking in strategic decisions, *Academy of Management Journal*, 29: 562–85.

Slovic, Paul (1967) The relative influence of probabilities and payoffs upon perceived risk of a gamble, *Psychonomic Science*, 9: 223–4.

Slovic, Paul, Baruch Fischhoff, and Sarah Lichtenstein (1977) Behavioral decision theory, *Annual Review of Psychology*, 28: 1–39.

Slovic, Paul, Baruch Fischhoff, and Sarah Lichtenstein (1982) Facts versus fears: understanding perceived risk, in Daniel Kahneman, Paul Slovic and Amos Tversky (eds), *Judgement under Uncertainty: Heuristics and Biases*. Cambridge: Cambridge University Press, pp. 463–492.

Slovic, Paul, Baruch Fischhoff, and Sarah Lichtenstein (1985) Characterizing perceived risk, in Robert W. Kates and Christoph Hohenemser (eds), *Perilous Progress: Managing the Hazards of Technology*. Boulder, CO: Westview Press, pp. 91–125.

Snyder, Wayne W. (1978) Horse racing: Testing the efficient markets model, *Journal of Finance*, 33: 1109-18.

Strickland, Lloyd, Roy J. Lewici, and Arnold M. Katz (1966) Temporal orientation and perceived control as determinants of risk taking, *Journal of Experimental Social Psychology*, 2: 143-51.

Tversky, Amos (1972) Elimination by aspects: a theory of choice, *Psychological Review*, 79: 281-99.

Tversky, Amos, and Daniel Kahneman (1974) The framing of decisions and the psychology of choice, *Science*, 185: 1124-31.

Tversky, Amos, and Daniel Kahneman (1982) Causal schemas in judgment under uncertainty, in Daniel Kahneman, Paul Slovic and Amos Tversky (eds), *Judgment under Uncertainty: Heuristics and Biases*. New York, NY: Cambridge University Press, pp. 117-28.

Ungson, Gerardo, R., and Daniel N. Braunstein (1982) *Decision Making: an Interdisciplinary Inquiry*. Boston, MA: Kent.

Vlek, Charles, and Pieter-Jan Stallen (1980) Rational and personal aspects of risk, *Acta Psychologica*, 44: 273-300.

Weinstein, N. D. (1980) Unrealistic optimism about future life events, *Journal of Personality and Social Psychology*, 39: 806-20.

Part II
Conflict in Organizations

5

The Business Firm as a Political Coalition

James G. March

The modern business firm is an organization for making and implementing decisions within a market economy. In most major industries of well-developed economies, most firms are large, complex organizations. These organizations render a set of key decisions for the economy. They establish prices, determine outputs, make investments, and allocate resources. These decisions and the consequences ensuing from them are the focus for the economic study of the firm. The economic theory of the firm attempts (1) to specify the decisions that business firms will make (as a basis for more aggregate predictions of the economy); and (2) to prescribe appropriate decision-rules for a rational firm operating in a market economy.

Except as it enters as a participant in the general political arena, the business firm has not been a focus of study for political scientists. Political scientists have generally defined their field in a relatively modest way, limiting their attention to phenomena that occur in, or in close conjunction with, explicitly governmental institutions. Except for a few attempts to define the field in terms of the study of power (or its variants), the major criterion for delimiting the field has been descriptive rather than analytic. By any reasonable descriptive definition of political science, the business firm is outside the domain. Similarly, economists have largely ignored political systems except as they impinge on the market. Although it is conventional for economists to identify their field in terms of an analytic

This paper was first published in *Journal of Politics* 24 (1962) 662–678. It is based on a paper presented at the annual meetings of the American Political Science Association in St Louis, 7 September, 1961. The research underlying it was conducted jointly with R. M. Cyert under a grant from the Ford Foundation for the study of organizational behavior. I wish to acknowledge the major contribution of Professor Cyert to the ideas expressed here.

definition (e.g., the study of the allocation of scarce resources), the vast bulk of economic research is linked to a descriptive definition of the field. For practical purposes, economics is the study of markets. The main attention to politics comes as a side issue in the area of economic policy.

At the risk of offending both economists and political scientists, I will assert that this division of labor is dysfunctional. It contributes to our inability as students to understand and predict the firm; it contributes to our inability as public-policy-makers to control and direct the firm. More specifically, I will argue that the business organization is properly viewed as a political system and that viewing the firm as such a system both clarifies conventional economic theories of the firm and (in conjunction with recent developments in theoretical languages) suggests some ways of dealing with classical problems in the theory of political systems generally. The argument depends on a general statement of the theoretical problem involved in decision models of complex systems, an evaluation of two major alternative approaches to that problem, and an examination of the implications of some recent attempts to develop a revised theory of the firm on the basis of a few key political concepts.

Conflict Systems

Consider a general class of purposive systems characterized by two attributes:

1 *There are consistent basic units.* Each elementary unit in the system can be described as having a consistent preference ordering defined over the possible states of the system. By a consistent preference ordering is meant an ordering such that for any realizable subset of possible states of the system there exists at least one state as good as any other state in the subset. Thus we require that the elementary units be able to make a choice among alternative states of the system (allowing for a chance decision-rule for the special case in which there is more than one state at least as good as all other states).

2 *There is conflict.* The preference orderings of the elementary units are mutually inconsistent relative to the resources of the system. Conflict, in this sense, arises when the most preferred states of all elementary units cannot be simultaneously realized. In order for conflict (in this sense) to exist it must be true that there is no allocative decision such that no one of the elementary units would prefer an alternative state of the system.

These two simple postulated attributes underlie a wide variety of theories about conflict resolution, choice, or the allocation of scarce resources.

Whether we are talking about the behavior of individuals in a simple learning experiment, the internal dynamics of a small group solving a problem, the interaction of parties and pressure groups in a legislative setting, or the pricing of commodities in a market system, we frequently make these two postulates. For convenience, let us call them the postulates of conflict. Any system satisfying the postulates we can call a conflict system.

One feature of studies of conflict systems that is puzzling from the point of view of the postulates of conflict is the extent to which the elementary units in one study are the conflict systems of another. The individual is treated as the system in some cases (e.g., in learning) and as the elementary unit in other (e.g., studies of small groups). Similarly, small groups are treated both as systems and as elementary units (e.g., in studies of organizations). Since the first postulate of conflict is essentially that the basic units themselves not be conflict systems, it seems awkward to be able to view a single system as either an elementary unit or a conflict system depending on the level of aggregation involved. In fact, most systems studied in the social sciences are apparently conflict systems of conflict systems.

The assumption of consistent basic units is justified by asserting either of two other characteristics of the macro-system involved. We may assert that the preference ordering of the subsystem (which we wish to identify as the elementary unit) is causally antecedent, and independent of, the decisions of the larger system. In such a case, we treat the preference ordering of the subsystem as given without considering the way in which that ordering is derived. Alternatively, we may assert that variation in system behavior due to conflict within the subsystem is trivial because of scale differences between the conflict within the subsystem on the one hand and conflict among subsystems on the other. In such a case, we take the preference ordering of the subsystem as subject to some minor error without attempting to eliminate the error entirely.

Such assertions are not simple technicalities. Consider, for example, either labor–management bargaining or bargaining among nations. Most of the literature and models of these phenomena accept the postulates of conflict. Since it is clear that (at the least) labor unions and nation states are themselves conflict systems, the theories are required to make some assertions that will allow the postulates of conflict to be made. A casual reading of this literature would suggest that either the assumption of causal antecedence or the assumption of scale difference is typically made. A casual reading of the literature also suggests, however, that the assumptions are suspect. In fact, one of the major recent developments in the study of these particular conflict systems has been a consideration of the complexities of interaction between the resolution of conflict within the subsystems and the resolution of conflict within the larger systems.

Despite such observations on the difficulties of satisfying the first postulate of conflict, most theories of conflict resolution essentially accept it as a reasonable approximation. If we restrict our attention to more or less well-defined theories susceptible to technical manipulation, virtually all theories use the postulate.

Political theory deals primarily with conflict systems as thus defined; and a rather large proportion of studies of the political process are concerned with discovering how conflict is resolved within a system revolving around some explicitly political institutions. Similarly, economic theory and economic studies focus to a large extent on conflict systems identified with explicitly economic institutions. In recent years a modest resurgence of political economy as a field of study has led to some important applications of economic concepts to the analysis of political conflict systems. This is particularly conspicuous in the work of Downs,[2] Davis and Whinston,[3] and Buchanan and Tullock.[4] In these attempts, allocation problems in politics have been studied from the point of view of concepts developed for economic systems. In some cases (e.g., Downs), this has meant the translation of a standard form of economic analysis into political terms. In other cases (e.g., Davis and Whinston), the general approach is clearly economic but the detailed form of analysis is relatively new for economics as well as politics. At the same time, some recent work in organization theory seems to indicate the utility of applying political concepts to the study of economic systems, particularly to the study of economic organizations. In many respects, March and Simon,[5] Thompson,[6] and Cyert and March[7] view the business organization as a socio-political conflict system subject to economic constraints.

Theories of Conflict Resolution

Given that we wish to describe a system as satisfying the postulates of conflict, and given that we wish to describe this system as 'acting', 'behaving', 'choosing', or 'deciding', we are required to introduce some mode of conflict resolution. By saying that the system does in fact 'act',

2 A. Downs, *An Economic Theory of Democracy* (New York, 1957).

3 O. A. Davis and A. B. Whinston, The Economics of Urban Renewal, *Law and Contemporary Problems*, 26, 1961, 105–17.

4 J. M. Buchanan and G. Tullock, *The Calculus of Consent* (Ann Arbor, 1962).

5 J. G. March and H. A. Simon, *Organizations* (New York, 1958).

6 V. A. Thompson, *Modern Organization* (New York, 1961).

7 R. M. Cyert and J. G. March, *A Behavioral Theory of the Firm* (New York, forthcoming).

we accept the proposition that the system in *some sense* prefers some state of the world to other possible states of the world. By describing the system as a conflict system, we assert that the system does not have a preference ordering in the usual sense of that term. The devices used to move from conflict to conflict resolution comprise the core of a theory of a conflict system. In general, extant theories take one of two directions for resolving conflict. Either they impute a superordinate goal in terms of which the conflict can be mediated, or they describe a process by which decisions are reached without explicit comparison of utilities. The latter approach is typical of theories of political coalitions; the former is typical of theories of business firms.

The Imputation of a Superordinate Goal

Any conflict system that can be observed and that can be described as 'behaving' is susceptible to description in terms of a superordinate goal. Given a sequence of behaviors, we impute a superordinate goal by accepting two simple assumptions: First, we assume there exists a joint preference ordering for the system at any particular point in time. Second, we assume the system always chooses the alternative behavior that is most preferred. Consider, for example, the familiar example of a conspicuous conflict system – a tree.[8] Is it reasonable to say that a tree seeks to maximize its total exposure to the sun subject to certain behavior limitations on the species, nutrients available, and environmental conditions? If, in fact, the behavior of the tree is such as to resolve conflict over a scarce resource (sunlight) so as to maximize total exposure, there is no reason why we cannot impute such a goal to a tree. Moreover, there may be many reasons why we would want to do so.

The usual objection to the imputation of a superordinate goal to conflict systems other than the human organism (or perhaps animals generally) is a curious one. Any such effort bears the onus of anthropomorphism. Yet in so far as a goal is simply an inferred rule for allocating resources, it is no more unique to anthropoids that is change of state. In the tree example, in fact, it can be argued that the concept of a goal is (under the assumed conditions) a more powerful tool for studying trees than it is for studying human beings. It permits us to make predictions about a variety of important phenomena (e.g., the location and movement of leaves and branches).

The tree example suggests two necessary conditions for effective use of an imputed superordinate goal in the construction of a theory. First,

8   M. Friedman, *Essays in Positive Economics* (Chicago, 1953), pp. 3–43; E. Rotwein, On the 'Methodology of Positive Economics', *Quarterly Journal of Economics,* 73, 1959, 554–78.

the goal must be stable (or at least change in a predictable way). Second, the goal must be meaningful. If the goal is not meaningful, it cannot be used for predictive purposes and simply becomes a restatement of the axiom that the system always chooses the most preferred alternative. A goal of maximizing subjective utility can, for example, be imputed to any system; but the imputation is largely useless unless operational meaning that is independent of the choices studied can be given to subjective utility. If the goal is not stable, the axioms underlying the importance of a superordinate goal are largely futile since the theory can only be applied *a posteriori*.

The Description of a Conflict Resolution Process

Just as any system that 'behaves' can be described as having a superordinate goal, it can also be described as having a conflict resolving process. If we adopt the process approach to a conflict system, we do not attempt to identify a joint preference ordering with respect to the ultimate decision. We replace the axioms of superordinate goals with two different assumptions. First, we assume that the ultimate decision results from a series of elementary decisions. Second, we assume that some sort of joint preference ordering exists for the elementary decisions.

If we consider the case of the tree again, it is clear that we can describe the tree in terms of a conflict resolution process. In fact, this is apparently the more common theoretical tool. We might, for example, stipulate a series of elementary decisions by individual leaves that, taken together, allocate sunshine to the various parts of the tree. Furthermore, we might be able to demonstrate the consistency of the process and a particular superordinate goal. This would be true, for example, if we could demonstrate that the elementary leaf decisions necessarily resulted in an ultimate allocation that maximized total exposure for the tree. The botanical invisible hand as it were.

The usual objection to a process description of a conflict system is its tendency to become analytically grotesque. A large elm tree has more than a million leaves on it. Even if we had a theory of leaf decision-making and could (conceptually) link leaf decisions to an aggregate exposure allocation, it is not easy to see how we analyze such a system.

Thus, two necessary conditions for effective use of a process description in the development of a theory for conflict systems are: (1) that the elementary decision processes be susceptible to treatment as consistent basic units; and (2) that analytic procedures be available with which to explore the properties of the model. The first is required to make the theory well-defined; the second is required to permit the theory to make meaningful predictions.

Studies of the Firm as an Economic Conflict System

Economic treatment of the firm as a conflict system is heavily influenced by the fact that the firm in economic theory is more commonly treated as the basic unit of a larger conflict system (industry, market, economic system) than as a conflict system itself. As a result, the economic theory of the firm is almost invariably constructed by explicitly imputing a super-ordinate goal to the conflict system represented by a business firm. In its classic form the theory asserts that the objective of the firm is to maximize long-run expected profits. The objective is accomplished by determining an output to be produced given a production function, a cost function, and a price. Given a set of factor prices, the firm determines the minimum cost-factor mix and the optimum output. Theories of imperfect competition are primarily modifications of this basic structure and do not change the basic approach. In the main, they modify the market structure faced by the firm or introduce new decision variables (e.g., price).

Thus, the economic theory of the firm assumes a joint preference ordering for the firm. In the standard form, that joint preference ordering is defined by profit-maximization. Such a characterization of business firm objectives has been subject to more or less continuous minority attack. Part of that attack we can ignore for present purposes. It stems from some misgivings about the social welfare implications of profit-maximization as a goal. The other source of the attack is more critical, however. It suggests that a theory assuming a profit-maximization goal is a poor predictive theory. Consequently, in some attempts at revision, profit-maximization is replaced by a more general utility function[9] or by an alternative goal (e.g., revenue-maximization).[10] In some revisions the preference ordering is a partial rather than complete ordering.[11] For the most part, the theory suppresses as outside its domain the process by which an organization composed of a rather complex mixture of people with considerable heterogeneity of individual goals generates a single preference ordering. It is assumed that conflict is resolved by the employment contract, or – more generally – by the factor prices and that the result is a joint preference ordering of some sort or other.

This implicit assumption that the firm represents a conflict system susceptible to useful description in terms of a superordinate goal (whether profit maximization or some other) is shared by most economists. It is apparently convenient for the construction of theories of macroeconomic

9 A. Papandreau, Some Basic Problems in the Theory of the Firm, in B. F. Haley (ed.) *A Survey of Contemporary Economics*, vol. 2 (Homewood, Illinois, 1952).

10 W. J. Baumol, *Business Behavior, Value and Growth* (New York, 1959).

11 H. A. Simon, *The New Science of Management Decision* (New York, 1961).

systems. Most economic theories build upon it (although not all necessarily depend upon it). It is relatively amenable to theoretical manipulation. It lends itself to the geometry and calculus familiar to economic thought.

Nevertheless, the assumption is almost certainly wrong as a micro-description of a business firm. It is extremely difficult to define a superordinate goal for a business firm that meets the two technical requirements of stability and meaningfulness as well as the empirical requirement of validity. Generally speaking, profit-maximization can be made perfectly meaningful (with some qualifications); but when made meaningful, it usually turns out to be invalid as a description of firm behavior. To achieve validity, we can substitute utility maximization; but this turns out to be either not stable or not meaningful. Thus, Machlup, who set out to save the profit-maximization assumption by generalizing it to utility-maximization, ended by reducing it largely to a definition[12] in so far as a micro-theory is concerned. With few exceptions, modern observers of actual firm behavior report persistent and significant contradictions between firm behavior and the classical assumptions.[13]

Despite their inadequacies, the assumptions have persisted. They have persisted for a simple but compelling reason. The alternative mode of theory – the process description of a conflict system – also has generally failed to satisfy its technical requirements. Until quite recently, case descriptions of the decision process in a business firm had approximately the same impact on a theorist of economic behavior as experiments on ESP had on a theorist of human perception. They were horror stories. They tended to demonstrate that there existed some unexplained variance in received theories. They did not provide us devices for reducing the variance. No matter how much we might think we knew about the decision process without the firm, we had no analytical apparatus for dealing with a process model. Such a disability means that few of the implications of the process could be determined except by direct observation and that a revised theory of the firm could not satisfactorily be grafted to existing economic theory. For most economists, such difficulties have seemed of decisive importance.

Studies of Political Conflict Systems

Whatever the reason may be, analytical disabilities appear to have had less impact on the development of political science than on economics.

12　F. Machlup, Marginal Analysis and Empirical Research, *American Economic Review*, 36, 1946, 519–54; F. Machlup, Rejoinder to an Anti-marginalist, *American Economic Review*, 37, 1947, 148–54.

13　For example, R. L. Hall and C. J. Hitch, Price Theory and Business Behavior, in T. Wilson (ed.) *Oxford Studies in Price Mechanisms* (Oxford, 1951); B. Fog, *Industrial Pricing Policies* (Amsterdam, 1960); Cyert and March, *A Behavioral Theory of the Firm*.

There is no political theory in the sense in which there is economic theory; and with only a few exceptions, little effort has been made to develop analytically tractable theories of political conflict systems. Generally speaking, there has been little pressure for simplification comparable to the pressure for simplification in the theory of the firm imposed by the needs of aggregation. The major exception (and only a partial one) is the study of international relations. In some treatments of bargaining among nation states, attempts have been made to characterize the behavior of the individual states in terms of simple models analogous in a loose way to the marginalist assumptions of economic theory.[14]

Most conspicuous by its absence in most of the modern literature on political conflict resolution is the imputation of a superordinate goal to political organizations. Except for some students of international relations, most modern observers have viewed concepts of the 'general will', 'national interest', or the 'common interest' as unsatisfactory concepts in the development of a theory of how political systems behave. 'Public interest' as a theoretical tool suffers from the standard problems of superordinate goals. It is almost impossible to make it simultaneously meaningful, stable, and valid. Because of such difficulties and because the existence of unresolved conflict is conspicuous in political systems, students of such systems have moved heavily toward process descriptive case studies of specific political organizations or decisions. By and large, these case studies have not yielded a set of theoretical propositions on which there is general agreement. The richness of specific case detail has tended to emphasize the uniqueness of the cases rather than contribute to theoretical model building.

Nevertheless, the basic outline of a process-oriented political theory of conflict resolution can be detected.[15] The theory assumes that there exist various interest groups in the system and that these groups make various demands. It further assumes that decisions within the system on the allocation of resources (i.e., in response to demands) are made by coalitions of interest groups and that each potential coalition has made a certain potential control over the system. The process postulated is one in which a broker – the politician – attempts to organize a coalition of interests that is viable (that is, one in which the demands are less than or equal to the resources available on the coalition). The theory ordinarily highlights phenomena such as bargaining, compromise, negotiation, inconsistency, and more or less continual conflict. In the descriptions of political systems

14   A. Rapport, Lewis Richard's Mathematical Theory of War, *Journal of Conflict Resolution*, 1, 1957, 249–99.

15   For example, see D. B. Truman, *The Governmental Process* (New York, 1951); R. A. Dahl and C. E. Lindblom, *Politics, Economics, and Welfare* (New York, 1953).

there is an emphasis of power, internal struggle, and expediency; a de-emphasis of order, cooperation, and problem-solving.

In so far as the interest group theory of political decision-making is a theory, it is a theory with modest analytic pretensions but rather impressive generality as a framework for observation. Most recent students of political organizations accept it in one form or another despite the obvious fact that the theory neither is particularly well-defined nor has a particularly powerful language. Thus, where the economic theory of the firm has moved to the imputation of a superordinate goal in order to gain analytic simplicity, the political theory of decision-making has moved to process description in order to gain empirical validity.

The Firm as a Political Coalition

The choice between an analytically elegant but empirically sterile theory on the one hand and an empirically fecund but analytically crude theory on the other is hardly a happy choice. Nor, I think, any longer a necessary one. To illustrate, let me outline a revised theory of the business firm and particularly a revised theory of the goals of a business firm. It is a theory that in some respects is more pristinely classic than many currently conventional economic conceptions of the firm, but it also bears a rather close relationship to current conceptions of political conflict systems. It is a theory that R. M. Cyert and I have used in developing some behavioral models of business firm decision-making.[16]

Basically, we assume that a business firm is a political coalition and that the executive in the firm is a political broker. The composition of the firm is not given; it is negotiated. The goals of the firm are not given; they are bargained.

We assume that there is a set of potential participants in the firm. At least initially, we think of such classes of potential participants as investors (stockholders), suppliers, customers, governmental agents and various types of employees. More realistically, we might supplement such a list with such actual or potential participants as investment analysts, trade associations, political parties and labor unions. Each potential participant makes demands on the system. These demands are essentially the price required for participation in the coalition. The demands are partly in the form of payments commonly assumed in economic theories (e.g., money) but they also are partly in the form of demands for policy commitments, personal treatment, etc. Thus, each set of demands can be characterized as having some degree of consistency with each combination of other demands. Some pairs of demands may be strictly inconsistent (under no

16 Cyert and March, *A Behavioral Theory of the Firm.*

circumstances can they both be satisfied). Some pairs of demands may be more or less consistent depending on external conditions (e.g., so long as the resources available to the coalition are substantial they may be consistent). Some pairs of demands may be completely complementary (e.g., if one demand is satisfied so also is the other one necessarily and without additional resource expenditure). As a result of this complementarity, we can describe the marginal 'cost' of any participant to any given coalition.

At the same time, we assume that the demands of the potential participants are subject to two important dynamic properties. First, the level of demand shifts in response to experience (both actual and vicarious). Second, attention to demands – the extent to which they are seen as relevant to action – shifts in response to the perception of problems.

We also assume that each possible coalition of participants has a certain 'value' with respect to the environment involved. It can gain a certain return from that environment. Thus, an over-simple model of a governmental coalition in a parliamentary democracy might assume that any coalition including more than 50 per cent of the voters would be able to do anything permissible within the system (thus would have maximum power) and that any coalition including less than 50 per cent of the voters would be able to do nothing (thus would have minimum power). In a similar way, alternative business coalitions can gain different returns from the economic system in which they operate; and we can (at least approximately) specify the marginal value of a particular given participant to a particular given coalition.

One way (not the only one) of describing the theory is from the point of view of the executive. Assume that the executive wishes to use the organization to maximize his own utility. His problem then is (in so far as he is able) to select a coalition so as to maximize the difference between the demands of his coalition members and the potential return from the environment of the coalition. The executive-political broker problem is twofold. On the one hand, he must select a coalition that has relatively low 'costs' of maintenance and relatively high returns from the environment. On the other hand, he must so structure the payments made to coalition members as to make the shifts in demands conducive to increasing the difference between total demands and total resources. The theory to this point becomes well-defined when we can specify the dimensions of participant demands, some measure of their complementarity, the functions by which they change over time, and the short-run internal constraints on the bargaining process by which goals are formed.

The terms 'marginal cost' and 'marginal value' suggest the sense in which this theory of business coalitions is close to classic economic views. Why do we describe the coalition involved as a political coalition? There are four critical ways in which the theory deviates from conventional economic views in the direction of a more 'political' treatment.

First, the focus of attention shifts from the owners (and their objectives) to the actual, operating organizers of the coalition – whoever they may be. In general, we view stockholders much as a theory of political systems might view citizens. Their demands form loose constraints on the more active members of the coalition. Their initiative in policy formation and in determining the nature of the coalitions is small.

Second, the theory emphasizes the non-uniqueness of short-run solutions to the coalition problem. At any point in time, there are a number of possible coalitions that are viable (that is, their total value exceeds their total cost of maintenance). As in the case of most political theories, some of the more interesting features of the theory depend on short-run deviations from a long-run position of equilibrium.

Third, the theory does not solve the problem of conflict by simple payments to participants and agreement on a superordinate goal. Rather it emphasizes the importance of policy demands and payments and of sequential rather than simultaneous mediation of demands.

Fourth, the theory emphasizes the importance of institutional constraints on the solution of the coalition problem. Most conspicuously there are constraints imposed: (1) by the institutionalization of commitments through the organizational structure, precedents, and budgetary agreements; (2) by the reification of attachments through identification and indoctrination; and (3) by the limitations in coordination and control imposed on an executive.

A theory of the business firm as a political coalition has both face validity and a certain amount of empirical support. In particular, such a theory seems more consistent than other available theories with the following widely observed attributes of business decision-making:

1 Organization goals seem to be a series of more or less independent constraints.
2 Business firms seem to tolerate a rather large amount of apparent inconsistency in goals and decisions, both over time and from one part of the organization to another.
3 Goals and decisions tend to be paired and decentralized with loose cross connections.
4 The extent to which decisions within the firm involve extensive conflict and 'marginal' decisions varies with the munificence of the environment.
5 The goals and commitments of business firms shift slowly over time in response to shifts in the coalition represented in the firm.

The fact (if it is one) that a description of a business firm as a political coalition is a more valid description than the classic economic description of the firm as an entrepreneur does not, however, solve the theoretical dilemma posed by the classic problems of analysis. For many years, economists as well as others have belabored the point that firms are organizations rather than entrepreneurs; only in the last few years have such strictures had any impact on the theory of the firm. Those students who were prepared to accept the evidence had no choice but to abandon not only the theory but also the field, since few of them were sympathetic intellectually with the journalist role implicit in the proliferation of case studies.

In recent years, the introduction of the computer and the computer program model to the repertoire of the theorist has changed dramatically the theoretical potential of process description models of conflict systems. Complex process description models of organizational behavior permit the development of a microeconomic theory of the firm. To illustrate, let me mention briefly three specific models:

First, a model of discretionary pricing and ordering decisions in a large departmental store. Cyert, March, and Moore have been able to simulate quite well three kinds of pricing decisions: regular pricing, scheduled sale pricing, and markdown pricing. In addition, they have been able to predict the amount and timing of orders (both original orders and reorders) with (as nearly as can be determined) reasonable accuracy.[17]

Second, a model of output determination in a duopoly, the American Can industry. On the basis of a few theoretical assumptions about differences between American and Continental Can Companies, Cyert, Feigenbaum, and March have been able to develop a model of decision-making within the industry. This model predicts quite well both the profit ratio of the two firms and their share of market over the 1913–56 period.[18]

Third, a general model of price and output determination. As a framework for other specific models and as a basis for investigation of the macroeconomic implications of a behavioral theory of the firm (including the assumption that the firm is a political coalition), Cohen, Cyert, March, and Soelberg have developed a general model of price and output determination in a modern oligopoly. The model has not been fully analyzed, but preliminary results seem to indicate a general correspondence between the output of the model and empirical data.[19]

Each of these models is written in the language of a computer program. All of them are process description models. Other comparable models of organizational behavior built on assumptions that differ in detail but are

17 Ibid.
18 Ibid.
19 Ibid.

generally process descriptive, are in various stages of development. Balderston and Hoggatt have developed a model of the wholesale lumber market.[20] Howard has developed a model of another wholesale market.[21] Clarkson has developed a model of the investment decisions of a trust bank.[22] Haines has developed a model of decision-making by an experimental group playing a complex business game.[23]

Not all of these models assume that the best characterization of a business firm is as a political coalition; however, they all illustrate the point that we are now in a position to explore the implications of viewing the firm as such a coalition. Process-descriptive, computer models are a natural form of theory in this area. As a result, theoretically-oriented students of the firm can afford to take seriously the detailed case studies of conflict systems both economic and political. For example, the recent work on a behavioral theory of the firm described briefly above has drawn rather heavily on political concepts. Within these models, it has been possible to introduce such 'political' features as unmediated conflict, multidimensional goals, and sequential attention to subunit pressures.

Implications for the Study of Political Conflict Systems

With a few exceptions, studies of political conflict systems have been largely atheoretical or quasi-theoretical in the past. Lacking an adequate theoretical language, we have had to work within the confines of simple verbal formulations. Nevertheless, some of these formulations seem to contribute to an understanding of the operation of the business firm, particularly when they are introduced into computer models of organizational decision-making. In the context of such models, I think it is quite likely that we will be able to expose both the theory of the firm as a coalition and the theory of political coalitions in general to new analytic attention.

Thus, we can identify three major implications for political science of recent research on the business firm as a decision-making coalition:

1 Recent experience indicates that the business firm can plausibly be conceived as a political conflict system; indeed the firm provides a useful test of the extent to which political phenomena are modified by a nongovernmental setting.

---

20   F. E. Balderston and A. C. Hoggatt, *The Simulation of Market Processes* (Berkeley, 1960).

21   J. A. Howard, *Marketing: Executive and Buyer Behavior* (New York, forthcoming), chapter 2.

22   G. P. E. Clarkson, *Portfolio Selection: A Simulation of Trust Investment* (New York, 1962).

23   G. H. Haines, Jr, The Rote Marketer *Behavioral Science*, 6, 1961, 357–65.

2 Successes with computer program models in the analysis of political systems within business firms support the view that computer programs provide a powerful language for treatment of political conflict systems generally.
3 The apparent theoretical similarity between the political coalition in business and the political coalition in governmental organizations suggests that the substantive features of recent behavioral models of the firm may be useful as a basis for comparable models of governmental decision-making.

Finally, we should identify the major theoretical job that remains to be done. Although they are adaptive in many respects, the models of firm decision-making discussed above have not gone beyond the static implications of the fact that firms are political coalitions. Essentially they assert that certain phenomena occur in the firm because of its character as a coalition. They do not attempt to reflect shifts in coalitions *per se*. The latter task – leading to a more general theory of coalition development – has hardly been touched except conceptually. The significance of such a theory to a theory of the business firm and its growth is obvious. Even more obvious, however, is the significance of such a theory to the development of a theory of politics.

6

The Power of Power

James G. March

Introduction

Power is a major explanatory concept in the study of social choice. It is used in studies of relations among nations, of community decision-making, of business behavior, and of small-group discussion. Partly because it conveys simultaneously overtones of the cynicism of *Realpolitik*, the glories of classical mechanics, the realism of elite sociology, and the comforts of anthropocentric theology, *power* provides a prime focus for disputation and exhortation in several social sciences.

Within this galaxy of nuances, I propose to consider a narrowly technical question: To what extent is one specific concept of power useful in the empirical analysis of mechanisms for social choice? The narrowness of the question is threefold. First, only theories that focus on mechanisms of choice are considered. Second, only considerations of utility for the development or testing of empirically verifiable theories are allowed. Third, only one concept of power – or one class of concepts – is treated. The question is technical in the sense that it has primary relevance for the drudgery of constructing a predictive theory; the immediate implications for general theories of society, for the layman confronted with his own

This paper first appeared in David Easton (ed.) *Varieties of Political Theory* (New York, Prentice-Hall, 1966). It received the American Political Science Association Pi Sigma Alpha Award for the best paper presented at the Association's annual meetings in 1963.

The author has profited considerably from the comments of John C. Harsanyi, Herbert Kaufman, Norton E. Long, Duncan MacRae, Jr, Dale T. Mortensen, and Raymond E. Wolfinger, and by a pre-publication reading of Robert A. Dahl's forthcoming article: 'The Power Analysis Approach to the Study of Politics', in the *International Encyclopedia of the Social Sciences*.

complex environment, or for the casual student, are probably meager. They certainly are not developed here.

By a mechanism for social choice, I mean nothing more mysterious than a committee, jury, legislature, commission, bureaucracy, court, market, firm, family, gang, mob, and various combinations of these into economic, political, and social systems. Despite their great variety, each of these institutions can be interpreted as a mechanism for amalgamating the behavior (preferences, actions, decisions) of subunits into the behavior of the larger institution; thus, each acts as a mechanism for social choice. The considerations involved in evaluating the usefulness of power as a concept are the same for all of the mechanisms cited above, although it is patently not necessarily true that the conclusions need be the same.

By an empirically verifiable theory, I mean a theory covered by the standard dicta about prediction and confirmation. We will ask under what circumstances the use of *power* contributes to the predictive power of the theory.

The specific concept of power I have in mind is the concept used in theories having the following general assumptions:

1 The choice mechanism involves certain basic components (individuals, groups, roles, behaviors, labels, etc.).
2 Some amount of power is associated with each of these components.
3 The responsiveness (as measured by some direct empirical observation) of the mechanism to each individual component is monotone increasing with the power associated with the individual component.

There are a number of variations on this general theme, each with idiosyncratic problems; but within a well-defined (and relatively large) class of uses of the concept of power, power plays the same basic role. It is a major intervening variable between an initial condition, defined largely in terms of the individual components of the system, and a terminal state, defined largely in terms of the system as a whole.

In order to explore the power of power in empirical theories of social choice, I propose to do two things: First, I wish to identify three different variations in this basic approach to power as an intervening variable to suggest the kinds of uses of *power* with which we will be concerned. Second, I wish to examine six different classes of models of social choice that are generally consistent with what at least one substantial group of students means by *social power*. In this examination, I will ask what empirical and technical problems there are in the use of the concept of power and in the use of alternative concepts, and under what circumstances the concept of power does, or can, contribute to the effective prediction of social choice.

Three Approaches to the Study of Power

The Experimental Study

The great variety of types of studies of power in the experimental literature is clear from a perusal of recent compendia and review articles.[1] Since many of these studies are only marginally relevant to the concerns of this paper, I will assume general awareness of the experimental literature rather than attempt to review it. This brief introduction is intended simply to provide a relatively coherent characterization of a class of approaches to the study of power. Although these approaches are predominantly used in experimental studies, the experimental setting is neither a necessary nor a sufficient condition for the approaches; the label 'experimental studies' is simply shorthand for the general approach.

Conceptual basis. The experimental studies of power are generally Newtonian. Many of them are directly indebted to Lewin, who defined the power of b over a 'as the quotient of the maximum force which b can induce on a, and the maximum resistance which a can offer'.[2] In general, the experimental studies assume that the greater the power of the individual, the greater the changes induced (with given resistance) and the more successful the resistance to changes (with given pressure to change).

The experimental studies tend to be reductionist. Although they are ultimately (and sometimes immediately) interested in the power of one individual over another, they usually seek to reduce that relationship to more basic components. Thus, we distinguish between the power of behavior and the power of roles, and characterize specific individuals as a combination of behavior and roles.[3] Or, we distinguish factors affecting the agent of influence, the methods of influence, and the agent subjected to influence.[4]

The experimental studies of interest here are generally synthetic. They attempt to predict the result of the interaction of known (experimentally manipulated) forces rather than to determine the forces by analysis of

1   See Dorwin Cartwright, (ed.) *Studies in Social Power* (Ann Arbor: University of Michigan Press, 1959): Dorwin Cartwright and A. F. Zander, (eds), *Group Dynamics* (New York: Harper & row, Publishers, 1959); and Dorwin Cartwright, Influence, Leadership, Control, in *Handbook of Organizations*, ed. J. G. March (Chicago: Rand McNally & Co., 1965).

2   Kurt Lewin, *Field Theory in Social Science* (New York: Harper & Row, Publishers, 1951), p. 336.

3   See J. G. March, Measurement Concepts in the Theory of Influence, *Journal of Politics*, XIX, 1957, 202–26.

4   See Cartwright, Influence, Leadership, Control.

known (or hypothetical) results. The problem is generally not to determine the power distribution, but to test the consequences of various power distributions.

Procedures.   The procedures used in this class of experimental studies are the classic ones. We determine power by some *a priori* measure or experimental manipulation, use a relatively simple force model to generate hypotheses concerning differences in outcomes from different treatments, and compare the observed outcomes with the predicted outcomes.

One of the better known variations on the basic Lewinian model is the one by French as further developed by Harary.[5] In this model, we predict shifts in opinion as a result of communication among subjects characterized by initial positions. Power exerted in a given direction is a function of the distribution of underlying power and the distances between the initial positions. In the two-person version of the model, change in opinion is inversely proportional to power. If we view an *n*-person group as being connected by a communication structure defining who can (or does) talk to whom, the model predicts the time series of opinion changes and the equilibrium opinions for various power distributions and communication structures. Theorems for the equal-power case are presented by French and Harary. Few theorems have been adduced for the unequal-power case in general, but the model can easily be used to generate specific predictions in specific cases.

Although few other models approach the specificity of the graph-theory version, the inverse relation between opinion- or behavior-change and power is normally used to derive hypotheses about differences among treatments.

Results.   There are several studies of social power that are substantially irrelevant for the present discussion. Studies of the consequences of apparent power for non-task or non-opinion behavior are potentially relevant, but they have rarely been interpreted in a way that fits this framework. For example, the responses to power are classified nominally, rather than along a continuum. Similarly, many of the studies of factors in differential influence (e.g., content of the communication) are only marginally relevant here.

For present purposes, two general results are particularly germane:

1 It is possible to vary power of a specific subject systematically and (within limits) arbitrarily in an experimental setting. This can be done

---

5 See J. R. P. French, Jr, A Formal Theory of Social Power, *Psychological Review,* LXIII, 1956, 181–94; and Cartwright, *Studies in Social Power.*

by manipulating some elements of his reputation[6] or by manipulating some elements of his power experience.[7] This apparently innocuous – and certainly minimal – result is in fact not so unimportant. It permits us to reject certain kinds of social-choice models for certain kinds of situations.

2 The effectiveness of *a priori* power (i.e., manipulated, or *a priori* measured power) in producing behavior change is highly variable. Although there are indications that some kinds of leadership behavior are exhibited by some people in several different groups,[8] most studies indicate that the effectiveness of specific individuals, specific social positions, and specific behaviors in producing behavior change varies with respect to the content and relevancy of subject matter,[9] group identifications,[10] and power base.[11] In fact, much of the literature is devoted to identifying these factors.

The Community Study

A second major approach to the study of power can be called *the community power approach*; it is typical of, but not limited to, community studies.[12] This paper is limited to the base problems of power and consequently does not do justice to the variety of substantive concerns represented in the research. As in the case of the experimental literature, it also exaggerates the conceptual homogeneity of the studies; I think, though, that there is general homogeneity with respect to the questions of interest here.

Conceptual basis.   The conceptual definition of power implicit (and often explicit) in the community studies is clearly Newtonian. The first two 'laws' of social choice form a simple definition:

6   See C. I. Hovland, I. L. Janis, and H. H. Kelley, *Communication and Persuasion* (New Haven: Yale University Press, 1953).

7   See B. Mausner, The Effect of Prior Reinforcement on the Interaction of Observer Pairs *Journal of Abnormal and Social Psychology,* XLIX, 1954, 65–8, and The Effect of One Partner's Success or Failure in a Relevant Task on the Interaction of Observer Pairs *Journal of Abnormal and Social Psychology*, XLIX, 1954, 577–60.

8   See E. F. Borgatta, A. S. Couch, and R. F. Bales, Some Findings Relevant to the Great Man Theory of Leadership, *American Sociological Review*, XIX, 1954, 755–59.

9   J. G. March, Influence Measurement in Experimental and Semi-Experimental Groups *Sociometry*, XIX, 1956, 260–71

10   Cartwright, *Studies in Social Power*.

11   Cartwright, *Studies in Social Power*.

12   For reviews of the literature, see P. H. Rossi, Community Decision Making, *Administrative Science Quarterly*, I, 1957, 415–43; and L. J. R. Herson, In the Footsteps of Community Power, *American Political Science Review*, LV, 1961, 817–30.

1 Social choice will be a predictable extension of past choices unless power is exerted on the choice.
2 When power is exerted, the modification of the choice will be proportional to the power.

The laws may lack some of the operational precision of Newton; in fact, it is not clear that they are any more Newton than Aristotle. But the community power studies generally assume that the decisions made by the community are a function of the power exerted on the community by various power holders. They assume some kind of 'power field' in which individual powers are summed to produce the final outcome.

The community studies are analytic in the sense that they attempt to infer the power of individuals within the community by observing (either directly or indirectly) their net effects on community choice. That is, they assume that a decision is some function of individual powers and the individual preferences. Hence, they observe the decision outcome and the preferences, and estimate the powers.

The community studies are personal in the sense that power is associated with specific individuals. The estimation procedures are designed to determine the power of an individual. This power, in turn, is viewed as some function of the resources (economic, social, etc.), position (office, role, etc.), and skill (choice of behavior, choice of allies, etc.); but the study and the analysis assume that it is meaningful to aggregate resource power, position power, and skill power into a single variable associated with the individual.

Procedures.   The controversy over the procedures used in community studies is well known.[13] Since that controversy forms part of the background to the more general discussion below, I will simply lay the descriptive groundwork here. The procedure most generally used involves some variation of asking individuals within the community to assess the relative power of other individuals in the community. Essentially the panel is given the following task: On the basis of past experience (both your

13   See W. V. D'Antonio and H. J. Ehrlich, *Power and Democracy in America* (South Bend, Ind.: Notre Dame University Press, 1961); W. V. D'Antonio and E. C. Erickson, The Reputational Technique as a Measure of Community Power: An Evaluation Based on Comparative and Longitudinal Studies *American Sociological Review*, XXVII, 1962, 362–76; N. W. Polsby, Three Problems in the Analysis of Community Power *American Sociological Review*, XXIV, 1959, 796–803; N. W. Polsby, Community Power: Some Reflections on the Recent Literature *American Sociological Review*, XXVII, 1962, 838–41; and R. E. Wolfinger, Reputations and Reality in the Study of Community Power *American Sociological Review*, XXV, 1960, 636–44.

own and that of other people with whom you have communicated), estimate the power of the following individuals.[14] In some cases the domain of power is specified only broadly (e.g., political decisions); in some cases it is specified relatively narrowly (e.g., urban renewal decisions).

A second procedure involves the direct observation of decision outcomes and prior preferences over a series of decisions.[15] Essentially, we define a model relating power to decisions, draw a sample of observations, and estimate the power of individuals on the basis of that model and those observations.

It seems rather clear that neither the direct nor the indirect method of estimation is necessarily better. As we will note below, there are many 'reasonable' models of power; and the estimation problems are somewhat different for the different models.

Results.   At a general level, the results of the community studies can be described in terms of three broad types of interests. First, we ask how power is distributed in the community. Second, we ask what relation exists between power and the possession of certain other socio-economic attributes. Third, we ask how power is exerted.

With respect to the distribution of power, most studies indicate that most people in most communities are essentially powerless. They neither participate in the making of decisions directly nor accumulate reputations for power. Whatever latent control they may have, it is rarely exercised. As a result, such control cannot be demonstrated by the power-measurement procedures of the community studies. Beyond the simple statement that only a minority of the population appears to exercise power, the studies are not really designed to elaborate the description of the power distribution. Some general statements of comparative variances can be made, but nothing approximating a systematic measure of power variance has been reported.

With respect to the relation between power and other individual characteristics, rather sharp differences among communities have been observed. Two results are conspicuous. First, in every study reported, the business and economic elite is overrepresented (in terms of chance expectations) among the high power-holders. By any of these measures, the economic notable is more powerful in the community than the average man. Second, the main influences on the extent to which non-economic characteristics are found to be important seem to be the procedures used

14   See F. Hunter, *Community Power Structures* (Chapel Hill: University of North Carolina Press, 1953).
15   See R. A. Dahl, *Who Governs?* (New Haven: Yale University Press, 1961).

in the investigation and the academic license of the investigator.[16] On the whole, studies using the general reputational technique seem to show business–economic characteristics[17] as more important than do studies using the direct-observation technique or a more narrowly defined reputation.[18] And studies by sociologists usually show business–economic characteristics as more important than do studies by political scientists. The two factors are hopelessly cross-contaminated, of course; and there are exceptions. If we assume that the correlation between results and technique (or discipline) is spurious, it may be possible to argue that the results are consistent with the hypothesis that power in somewhat older communities (e.g., English City, New Haven) is less linked to economic factors than is power in somewhat newer communities (e.g., Regional City, Pacific City).

With respect to the exercise of power, the studies have focused on specialization, activation, and unity of power-holders. Most studies have identified significant specialization in power: Different individuals are powerful with respect to different things. But most studies also have shown 'general leaders': Some individuals have significant power in several areas. Some studies have reported a significant problem associated with power activation: the more powerful members of the community are not necessarily activated to use their power, while less powerful members may be hyperactivated. The activation factor may be long-run[19] or short-run.[20] Although few systematic observations have been used to explore unity among the powerful, there has been some controversy on the extent to which the group of more powerful individuals represents a cohesive group with respect to community decisions. Some studies indicate a network of associations, consultations and agreements among the more powerful; other studies indicate rather extensive disagreement among the more powerful.[21]

The Institutional Study

The third alternative approach to the study of power is in one sense the most common of all. It is the analysis of the structure of institutions to

16   See N. W. Polsby, The Sociology of Community Power: A Reassessment Social Forces, XXXVII, 1959, 232–36; and P. Bachrach and M. S. Baratz, Two Faces of Power, American Political Science Review, LVI, 1962, 947–52.

17   See, for example, Hunter, Community Power Structures.

18   See, for example, Dahl, Who Governs?

19   See Dahl, Who Governs?

20   See R. C. Hanson, Predicting a Community Decision: A Test of the Miller-Form Theory American Sociological Review, XXIV, 1959, 662–71.

21   See W. H. Form and W. V. D'Antonio, Integration and Cleavage among Community Influentials in Two Border Cities American Sociological Review, XXIV, 1959, 804–14; and H. Scoble, Leadership Hierarchies and Political Issues in a New England Town in Community Political Systems, Morris Janowitz (ed.) New York: Free Press of Glencoe, Inc., 1961).

determine the power structure within them. Such studies are the basis of much of descriptive political science. Systematic attempts to derive quantitative indices of power from an analysis of institutional structure are limited, however. The approach will be characterized here in terms of the game-theory version, but other alternative *a priori* institutional interpretations of power would fall in the same class.[22]

The possibility of using the Shapley value for an *n*-person game as the basis for a power index has intrigued a number of students of bargaining and social-decision systems.[23] The present discussion will assume a general knowledge of game theory, the Shapley value,[24] and the original Shapley and Shubik article.[25]

Conceptual basis.   The Shapley value is Neumannian. We assume the General von Neumann concept of a game: There are *n* players, each with a well-defined set of alternative strategies. Given the choice of strategies by the player (including the mutual choice of coalitions), there is a well-defined set of rules for determining the outcome of the game. The outcomes are evaluated by the individual players in terms of the individual orderings of preference. The Shapley value for the game to an individual player (or coalition of players) has several alternative intuitive explanations. It can be viewed as how much a rational person would be willing to pay in order to occupy a particular position in the game rather than some other position. It can be viewed as the expected marginal contribution of a particular position to a coalition if all coalitions are considered equally likely and the order in which positions are added to the coalition is random. It can be viewed as how much a rational player would expect to receive from a second rational player in return for his always selecting the strategy dictated by the second player. Or, it can be viewed simply as a computational scheme with certain desirable properties of uniqueness.

The Shapley value is impersonal. It is associated not with a specific player but rather with a specific position in the game. It is not conceived to measure the power of President Kennedy or President Eisenhower; it is conceived to measure the power of the presidency.

22   See, for example, Karl Marx, *Capital* (New York, 1906).

23   Dahl, *Who Governs?* and H. A. Simon, *Models of Man* (New York: John Wiley & Sons, Inc., 1957), both of whom are conceptually much closer to the other approaches outlined here, seem to have been supportive. W. H. Riker, A Test of the Adequacy of the Power Index *Behavioral Science*, IV, 1959, 276–90, applies the value in an empirical study: and J. C. Harsanyi, Measurement of Social Power, Opportunity Costs, and the Theory of Two-Person Bargaining Games, *Behavioral Science*, VII, 1962, 67–80, extends the value.

24   L. S. Shapley, A Value for *n*-Person Games, in *Contributions to the Theory of Games*, H. W. Huhn and A. W. Tucker (eds), (Princeton: Princeton University Press, 1953), II.

25   L. S. Shapley and M. Shubik, A Method for Evaluating the Distribution of Power in a Committee System *American Political Science Review*, XLVIII, 1954, 787–92.

The value is analytic in the sense that it is derived from the rules of the game (e.g., the legislative scheme) rather than vice versa. The value is *a priori* in the sense that it does not depend on empirical observations and has no necessary empirical implications.

How do we move from such a conception of value to a conception of power? One way is to restrict ourselves to a parsimonious definition: 'When we use the word *power* in the rest of this paper, it shall mean only the numerical representation of rewards accruing to coalitions as evaluated by the members of these coalitions.' [26] Although such a procedure is defensible, it will not help us significantly in the present discussion. We need to relate the Shapley–Shubik measure to the Newtonian approaches previously described. In the standard Newtonian versions of power, power is that which induces a modification of choice by the system. Quite commonly, we measure the power by the extent to which the individual is able to induce the system to provide resources of value to him. We are aware that power, in this sense, is a function of many variables; we suspect that informal alliances and allegiances influence behavior; and we commonly allege that power is dependent on information and intelligence as well as formal position.

Suppose that we want to assess the contribution to power of formal position alone. One way to do so would be an empirical study in which we would consider simultaneously all of the various contributing factors, apply some variant of a multiple regression technique, and determine the appropriate coefficients for the position variables. A second way would be an experimental study in which non-position factors are systematically randomized. A third way would be the one taken by Shapley and Shubik. We can imagine a game involving position variables only (e.g., the formal legislative scheme), and we can assume rationality on the part of the participants and ask for the value of each position under that assumption. Since this value is a direct measure of the resources the individual can obtain from the system by virtue of his position in the game alone, it is a reasonable measure of the power of that position. Alternatively, we can view the resources themselves as power.[27]

Procedures.   There are two main ways in which we can use the Shapley–Shubik index in an empirical study: (1) We can construct some sort of empirical index of power, make some assumptions about the relation between the empirical and *a priori* measures, and test the consistency of the empirical results with the *a priori* measures. Thus, we might assume that

26   R. D. Luce and A. A. Rogow, A Game Theoretic Analysis of Congressional Power Distributions for a Stable Two-Party System, *Behavioral Science*, I, 1956, 85.

27   See R. D. Luce, 'Further Comments on Power Distributions for a Stable Two-Party Congress', Paper read at American Political Science Association meetings (1956): and Riker, 'A Test of the Adequacy of the Power Index'.

the empirical measure consists of the *a priori* measure plus an error term representing various other (non-position) factors. If we can make some assumptions about the nature of the 'error', we can test the consistency. Or, (2), we can deduce some additional propositions from the model underlying the index and test those propositions.

The first of these alternatives was suggested by Shapley and Shubik and considered by Riker. But neither they nor others have seen a way around the major obstacles in the way. The second alternative was the basis for a series of papers by Luce, Rogow, and Riker.[28]

Results. The main results in the application of the Shapley value have had only casual testing. Luce and Rogow have used the basic Shapley–Shubik approach in conjunction with Luce's conception of $\emptyset$-stability to generate some power distributions consistent with a stable two-party system. In this approach, one first assumes a two-party legislature and a President belonging to one of the two parties. Within each party, there is a subset that always votes with the party, a subset that is willing to defect to the other party, and a subset that is willing to form a coalition with a defecting subset from the other party. The President may be constrained always to vote with his party or to defect only to the coalition of defectors. Alternatively, he may be completely free to defect. This legislature operates under some voting rules which define (along with the size of parties, the permissible defections, and the size of defecting subsets) a set of coalitions that are able to pass a bill. The analysis produces a series of observations on the stability and other properties of power distributions found under various combinations of restrictions on the President and the size of the party subsets. These detailed results lead then to more general statements of the form: 'The richer the defection possibilities . . . the greater the localization of power'.[29] Although some of the results obtained seem intuitively sensible, only a footnoted bit of data has been adduced in support of them. In fact, most of the propositions are stated in a form that would require an empirical measure of power – and that would drive us back to the difficulty previously observed.

Riker has applied the basic Shapley–Shubik measure to the French Assembly to derive changes in power indices for the various parties in the French Assembly during the period 1953–4, as 34 migrations from one party to another produced 61 individual changes in affiliation.[30] On the assumption that party power is equally distributed among individual members, Riker tested the proposition that shifts in party affiliation tended

28   Luce and Rogow, 'A Game Theoretic Analysis'; Luce, 'Further Comments on Power Distributions'; and Riker, 'A Test of the Adequacy of the Power Index'.
29   Luce, 'Further Comments on Power Distributions', p. 10.
30   Riker, 'A Test of the Adequacy of the Power Index'.

to result in increases in individual power. The data did not support the hypothesis. In subsequent work, Riker has almost entirely abandoned the Shapley–Shubik approach.[31]

Six Models of Social Choice and the Concept of Power

The three general approaches described above illustrate the range of possible uses of the concept of power, and include most of the recent efforts to use the concept in empirical research or in empirically-oriented theory. I wish to use these three examples as a basis for exploring the utility of the concept of power in the analysis of systems for social choice. The utility depends first, on the true characteristics of the system under investigation. The concept of power must be embedded in a model and the validity of the model is a prerequisite to the utility of the concept. Second, the utility depends on the technical problems of observation, estimation, and validation in using the concept in an empirically reasonable model.

I shall now consider six types of models of social choice, evaluate their consistency with available data, and consider the problems of the concept of power associated with them. By a *model* I mean a set of statements about the way in which individual choices (or behavior) are transformed into social choices, and a procedure for using those statements to derive some empirically meaningful predictions. The six types of models are:

1 Chance models, in which we assume that choice is a chance event, quite independent of power.
2 Basic force models, in which we assume that the components of the system exert all their power on the system with choice being a direct resultant of those powers.
3 Force-activation models, in which we assume that not all the power of every component is exerted at all times.
4 Force-conditioning models, in which we assume that the power of the components is modified as a result of the outcome of past choices.
5 Force-depletion models, in which we assume that the power of the components is modified as a result of the exertion of power on past choices.
6 Process models, in which we assume that choice is substantially independent of power but not a chance event.

---

31   W. H. Riker, *The Theory of Political Coalitions* (New Haven: Yale University Press, 1962).

The list is reasonably complete in so far as we are interested in empirically oriented models of social choice. The approaches to the study of social power previously discussed and a fair number of other theories of social choice can be fitted into the framework.

Chance Models

Let us assume that there are no attributes of human beings affecting the output of a social-choice mechanism. Further, let us assume that the only factors influencing the output are chance factors, constrained perhaps by some initial conditions. There are a rather large number of such models, but it will be enough here to describe three in skeleton form.

The unconstrained model.   We assume a set of choice alternatives given to the system. These might be all possible bargaining agreements in bilateral bargaining, all possible appropriations in a legislative scheme, or all experimentally defined alternatives in an experimental setting. Together with this set of alternatives, we have a probability function. Perhaps the simplest form of the function would be one that made the alternatives discrete, finite, and equally probable; but we can allow any form of function so long as the probabilities do not depend on the behavior, attitudes, or initial position of the individual components in the system.

The equal-power model.   We assume a set of initial positions for the components of the system and some well-defined procedures for defining a social choice consistent with the assumption of equal power. For example, the initial positions might be arranged on some simple continuum. We might observe the initial positions with respect to wage rates in collective bargaining, with respect to legislative appropriations for space exploration, or with respect to the number of peas in a jar in an experimental group. A simple arithmetic mean of such positions is a social choice consistent with the assumption of equal power. In this chance model, we assume that the social choice is the equal-power choice plus some error term. In the simplest case, we assume that the error around the equal-power choice is random and normally distributed with mean zero and a variance that is some function of the variance of initial positions.

The encounter model.   We assume only two possible choice outcomes: We can win or lose; the bill can pass or fail; we will take the left or right branch in the maze. At each encounter (social choice) there are two opposing teams. The probability of choosing a given alternative if the teams have an equal number of members is 0.5. If the teams are unequal in size, we have three broad alternatives:

1 We can make the probability of choosing the first alternative a continuous monotone increasing function of the disparity between the sizes of the two teams.

2 We can assume that the larger teams always win.

3 We can assume that the probability is 0.5 regardless of the relative size of the teams, thus making the model a special case of the unconstrained model.

What are the implications of such models? Consider the encounter model. Suppose we imagine that each power encounter occurs between just two people chosen at random from the total population of the choice system. Further, assume that at each encounter we will decide who prevails by flipping a coin.[32] If the total number of encounters per person is relatively small and the total number of persons relatively large, such a process will yield a few people who are successful in their encounters virtually all the time, others who are successful most of the time, and so on. In a community of 4,000 adults and about a dozen encounters per adult, we would expect about 12 or 13 adults to have been unsuccessful no more than once. Similarly, if we assume that all encounters are between teams and that assignment to teams is random, the other encounter models above will yield identical results. A model of this general class has been used by Deutsch and Madow to generate a distribution of managerial performance and reputations.[33]

Similar kinds of results can be obtained from the unconstrained-chance model. If we assume that social choice is equi-probable among the alternatives and that individual initial positions are equi-probable among the alternatives, the only difference is that the number of alternatives is no longer necessarily two. In general, there will be more than two alternatives; as a result the probability of success will be less than 0.5 on every trial and the probability of a long-run record of spectacular success correspondingly less. For example, if we assume a dozen trials with ten alternatives, the probability of failing no more than once drops to about 10^{-10} (as compared with about 0.0032 in the two alternative cases).

Finally, generally similar results are obtained from the equal-power model. If we assume that the initial position is normally distributed with mean, M, and variance, V, and that the error is normally distributed around M with a variance that is some function of V, we obtain what amounts to variations in the continuous version of the discrete models.

32   See H. White, Uses of Mathematics in Sociology *Mathematics and the Social Sciences,* J. C. Charlesworth (ed.) (Philadelphia: American Academy of Political and Social Science, 1963).

33   K. W. Deutsch and W. G. Madow, A Note on the Appearance of Wisdom in Large Organizations *Behavioral Science,* VI, 1961, 72–8.

If we set the error variance equal to V, the relationship is obvious. Our measures of success now become not the number (or proportion) of successes but rather the mean deviation of social choices from individual positions; and we generate from the model a distribution of such distances for a given number of trials.[24]

All of the chance models generate power distributions. They are spurious distributions in the sense that power, as we usually mean it, had nothing to do with what happened. But we can still apply our measures of power to the systems involved. After observing such a system, one can make statements about the distribution of power in the system and describe how power was exercised. Despite these facts, I think that most students of power would agree that if a specific social-choice system is in fact a chance mechanism, the concept of power is not a valuable concept for that system.

To what extent is it possible to reject the chance models in studies of social choice? Although there are some serious problems in answering that question, I think we would probably reject a pure-chance model as a reasonable model. I say this with some trepidation because studies of power have generally not considered such alternative models, and many features of many studies are certainly consistent with a chance interpretation. The answer depends on an evaluation of four properties of the chance models that are potentially inconsistent with data either from field studies or from the laboratory.

First, we ask whether power is stable over time. With most of the chance models, knowing who won in the past or who had a reputation for winning in the past would not help us to predict who would win in the future. Hence, if we can predict the outcome of future social choices by weighting current positions with weights derived from past observations or from *a priori* considerations, we will have some justification for rejecting the chance model. Some efforts have been made in this direction, but with mixed results.[35] Even conceding the clarity of the tests and the purity of the procedures and assuming that the results were all in the predicted direction, the argument for the various power models against a chance model would be meager. The 'powerful' would win about half the time even under the chance hypothesis.

Second, we ask whether power is stable over subject matter. Under the chance models, persons who win in one subject-matter area would be no more likely to win in another area than would people who lost in the first area. Thus, if we find a greater-than-chance overlap from one area to another, we would be inclined to reject the chance model. The evidence on

34   See D. MacRae, Jr, and H. D. Price, Scale Positions and 'Power' in the Senate *Behavioral Science*, IV, 1959, 212–18.

35   See, for example, Hanson, 'Predicting a Community Decision'.

this point is conflicting. As was noted earlier, some studies suggest considerable specialization of power, while others do not. On balance, I find it difficult to reject the chance model on the basis of these results; although it is clear that there are a number of alternative explanations for the lack of stability, non-chance explanations are generally preferred by persons who have observed subject-matter instability.[36]

Third, we ask whether power is correlated with other personal attributes. Under the chance model, power is independent of other attributes. Although it might occasionally be correlated with a specific set of attributes by chance, a consistent correlation would cast doubt on the chance hypothesis. It would have to be saved by some assumption about the inadequacy (that is, irrelevance) of the power measure or by assuming that the covariation results from an effect of power on the correlated attribute. Without any exception of which I am aware, the studies do show a greater-than-chance relation between power and such personal attributes as economic status, political office, and ethnic group. We cannot account under the simple chance model for the consistent underrepresentation of the poor, the unelected, and the Negro.

And fourth, we ask whether power is *susceptible to experimental manipulation.* If the chance model were correct, we could not systematically produce variations in who wins by manipulating power. Here the experimental evidence is fairly clear. It is possible to manipulate the results of choice mechanisms by manipulating personal attributes or personal reputations. Although we may still want to argue that the motivational or institutional setting of real-world choice systems is conspicuously different from the standard experimental situation, we cannot sustain a strictly chance interpretation of the experimental results.

Chance models are extremely naïve; they are the weakest test we can imagine. Yet we have had some difficulty in rejecting them, and in some situations it is not clear that we can reject them. Possibly much of what happens in the world is by chance. If so, it will be a simple world to deal with. Possibly, however, our difficulty is not with the amount of order in the world, but with the concept of power. Before we can render any kind of judgment on that issue, we need to consider some models that might be considered more reasonable by people working in the field.

Basic Force Models

Suppose we assume that power is real and controlling, and start with a set of models that are closely linked with classical mechanics although

36   See, for example, N. W. Polsby, How to Study Community Power: The Pluralist Alternative *Journal of Politics,* XXII, 1960, 474–84.

the detailed form is somewhat different from mechanics. In purest form, the simple force models can be represented in terms of functions that make the resultant social choice a weighted average of the individual initial positions – the weights being the power attached to the various individuals. Let us identify three variations on this theme:

The continuous case. Let C_j be the outcome (social choice) on the jth issue and A_{ij} *be the initial position on the jth* issue of the ith individual power source. C_j and the A_{ij} may be vectors, but they have the same dimensions. Let m^*_{ij} be the total power resources available to the ith component at the jth issue, and let m_{ij} be the normalized form of this. Thus:

$$m_{ij} = m^*_{ij} / \sum_{i=1}^{n} m^*_{ij},$$

where n is the number of components.

The basic force model, in which we assume that m^*_{ij} is a constant over all j, is elegant in its simplicity:

$$C_j = \sum_{i=1}^{n} m_i A_{ij}.$$

Given a set of power indices and initial positions, we can predict the outcomes. Given a set of outcomes and the associated initial positions, we can determine the power indices.

The probabilistic binary case. Suppose C_j and A_{ij} can assume only two values (yes-no, pro-con, pass-fail, up-down, etc.). Associate the nominal values 1 and -1 with the two alternatives. Let P_j be the probability that $C_j = 1$. Then the basic force model assumes the form

$$P_j = \frac{1 + \sum_{i=1}^{n} m_i A_{ij}}{2}.$$

Alternative, we can define any function that maps $(-1, 1)$ onto $(0, 1)$, is monotone increasing, and is symmetric around the point $(0, 0.5)$. Most data suggest, in fact, that the function is not linear.[37]

Given the function, a set of power indices, and the initial positions, we can predict the outcomes subject to some chance error. Given the function, a set of outcomes, and the associated initial positions, we can determine the power indices subject to some errors in estimation.

37 F. M. Tonge, Models of Majority Influence in Unanimous Group Decision. Unpublished (1963).

The nearly determinate binary case.   In this special form of the binary case, we assume that the more powerful team carries the day unequivocally. Thus

$$P_j = \begin{Bmatrix} 1 \\ .5 \\ 0 \end{Bmatrix} \text{ if } \sum_{i=1}^{n} m_i A_{ij} \begin{Bmatrix} > \\ = \\ < \end{Bmatrix} 0.$$

As before, we can use the model to predict outcomes given the power and initial positions, or to estimate power given outcomes and initial positions. In the latter case, we would normally have a family of solutions rather than a single solution.

The only serious problem with the use of these models lies in potential difficulties in estimation. But it is clear that the estimation problems are relatively minor unless the required observations are difficult to obtain. Consider the continuous case. Since we know that

$$m_k = \frac{C_j - \sum_{i \neq k} m_i A_{ij}}{A_{kj}} \quad i = 1, \ldots, n$$

we need only $n-1$ distinct observations to determine the power (m_k) weights in a system having n distinct power sources. If the system involves only two individuals, we require only one observation to determine the weights. We get similar results in the case of the nearly determinate binary case, although if we deal in inequalities. If we ignore the possibility of a tie between the two sides, we know that

$$m_k < C_j \sum_{i \neq k} m_i A_{ij} \quad i = 1, \ldots, n.$$

Thus, given a set of observations we can define a family of values for the m_i that are consistent with the observations.

In the probabilistic case, the observations are the basis for estimating a set of weights that control the results (outcomes) only up to a probability value. If we have s observations, we know that

$$m_k = \frac{1 - 2\sum_{i=1}^{s} P_j - \sum_{i \neq k} \sum_{j=1}^{s} m_i A_{ij}}{\sum_{j=1}^{s} A_{kj}} \quad i = 1, \ldots, n.$$

However, we do not know $\sum_{j=1}^{s} P_j$, but have to estimate it from $\sum_{j=1}^{s} C_j$. As a result, our estimate of m_k is subject to sampling variation.

None of these estimation problems are severe. In fact, the first two models are determinate and trivial; the third involves the binomial distribution but is not overly complicated.

The force models, therefore, are reasonably well-defined and pose no great technical problems, and the estimation procedures are straightforward. The observations required are no more than the observations required by any model that assumes some sort of power. What are the implications of the models? First, unless combined with a set of constraints (such as the power-structure constraints of the French and Harary formulation), the models say nothing about the distribution of power in a choice system. Thus, there is no way to test their apparent plausibility by comparing actual power distributions with derived distributions.

Second, in all of the models, the distance between the initial position of the individual and the social choice (or expected social choice) is inversely proportional to the power when we deal with just two individuals. As we noted earlier, this is also a property of French's model. With more than two individuals, the relation between distance and power becomes more complex, depending on the direction and magnitude of the various forces applied to the system. Since the models are directly based on the ideas of center of mass, these results are not surprising. Given these results, we can evaluate the models if we have an independent measure of power, such as the Shapley–Shubik measure. Otherwise, they become, as they frequently have, simply a definition of power.

Third, we can evaluate the reasonableness of this class of models by a few general implications. Consider the basic characteristics of the simple force models:

1 There are a fixed number of known power sources.
2 At any point in time, each of these sources can be characterized as affecting the social choice by exerting force in terms of two dimensions, magnitude (power) and direction (initial position or behavior).
3 Any given source has a single, exogenously determined power. That is, power is constant (over a reasonable time period and subject-matter domain of observation) and always fully exercised.
4 The result (social choice) is some sum of the individual magnitudes and directions.

In so far as the determinate models are concerned, both experimental and field observations make it clear that the models are not accurate portrayals of social choice. In order for the models to be accepted, the m_i (as defined in the models) must be stable. As far as I know, no one has ever reported data suggesting that the m_i are stable in a determinate model. The closest thing to such stability occurs in some experimental groups where the choices consistently come close to the mean, and in some highly formal voting schemes. In such cases, the power indices are occasionally close to stable at a position of equal power. Nevertheless, few students of power have claimed stability of the power indices.

When we move to the probabilistic case – or if we add an error term to the determinate models – the situation becomes more ambiguous. Since it has already been observed that rejection of a purely chance model is not too easy with the available data, the argument can be extended to models that assume significant error terms, or to models in which the number of observations is small enough to introduce significant sampling variation in the estimate of underlying probabilities. However, most observers of power in field situations are inclined to reject even such variations on the theme, although no very complete test has been made.

The basis for rejecting the simple force models (aside from the necessity of making them untidy with error terms) is twofold:

1 There seems to be general consensus that either potential power is different from actually exerted power or that actually exerted power is variable. If, while potential power is stable, there are some unknown factors that affect the actual exercise of power, the simple force models will not fit; they assume power is stable, but they also assume that power exerted is equal to power. If actually exerted power is unstable, the simple force models will fit only if we can make some plausible assertions about the nature of the instability. For example, we can assume that there are known factors affecting the utilization of power and measure those factors. Or, we can assume that the variations are equivalent to observational errors with known distributions.

2 There appears to be ample evidence that power is not strictly exogenous to the exercise of power and the results of that exercise. Most observers would agree that present reputations for power are at least in part a function of the results of past encounters. Although the evidence for the proposition is largely experimental, most observers would probably also agree that power reputation, in turn, affects the results of encounters. If these assertions are true, the simple force model will fit in the case of power systems that are in equilibrium, but it will not fit in other systems.

These objections to the simple force model are general; we now need to turn to models that attempt to deal with endogenous shifts in power and with the problem of power activation or exercise. As we shall see, such models have been little tested and pose some serious problems for evaluation on the basis of existing data. We will consider three classes of models, all of which are elaborations of the simple force models. The first class can be viewed as *activation models*. They assume that power is a potential and that the exercise of power involves some mechanism of activation. The second class can be described as *conditioning models*. They assume that power is partly endogenous – specifically that apparent power leads to actual power. The third class can be classified as *depletion models*. They assume that power is a stock, and that exercise of power leads to a depletion of the stock.

Force-Activation Models

All of the models considered thus far accept the basic postulate that all power is exerted all of the time. In fact, few observers of social-choice systems believe this to be true, either for experimental groups or for natural social systems. With respect to the latter, Schulze argues that 'the Cibola study appears to document the absence of any neat, constant, and direct relationship between *power as a potential for determinative action, and power as determinative action itself*'.[38] Wolfinger criticizes the reputational method for attributing power on the grounds that it 'assumes an equation of potential for power with the realization of the potential'.[39] And Hanson suggests that predictions based on the Miller–Form theory will be less accurate 'when the issue does not arouse a high level of community interest and activity'.[40]

As before, let m_{ij}^* represent the total power resources of the ith component at the jth choice, and let x_{ij} be the share $(0 \le x_{ij} \le 1)$ of the total power resources that are exercised by the ith component at the jth choice. We associate the force activation models to the basic force models by means of the simple accounting expression

$$m_{ij} = \frac{x_{ij}m_{ij}^*}{\sum\limits_{i=1}^{n} x_{ij}m_{ij}^*} .$$

We can consider two general variations on this theme:

The partition model.   Suppose we let x_{ij} assume only two values, 1 and 0. That is, we assume that components in the system are either active or inactive on any particular choice. It is frequently suggested that power must be made relative to a specific set of actions or domain of joint decisions.[41]

38   R. O. Schulze, The Role of Economic Dominants in Community Power Structure *American Sociological Review*, XXXII, 1958, 9.

39   Wolfinger, 'Reputation and Reality'.

40   Hanson, 'Predicting a Community Decision'.

41   See H. A. Simon, Notes on the Observation and Measurement of Political Power *Journal of Politics*, XV, 1953, 500–16; J. G. March, An Introduction to the Theory and Measurement of Influence *American Political Science Review*, LIX, 1955, 431–51; March, Measurement Concepts; and R. A. Dahl, The Concept of Power *Behavioral Science*, II, 1957, 201–15.

The specialization hypothesis is one form of such a model. We assume that once we have made the basic partition, we can treat the activated group as the total system and apply the basic force model to it.

The continuous model. Suppose we let x_{ij} assume any value between 0 and 1. That is, we assume that the participants in the system can vary their exercised power from zero to the total of their power resource. Thus, a relatively weak person can sometimes exert more power than a relatively strong one simply by devoting more attention to the choice problems involved.

Consider the problem of relating the activation models to observations of reality. Let us assume initially that potential power (m_{ij}^*) is constant over all choices. We assume that there is something called *potential power* that is associated with a component of the choice system and that this power resource does not depend on the choice. In effect, this assumes that m_{ij}^* is also constant over time, for we will require a time series of observations in order to make our estimates. We will relax this assumption in subsequent classes of models, but the constancy assumption is characteristic of most activation models.

Given the assumption of fixed potential power, we have two major alternatives. First, we can attempt to determine the value of x_{ij} for each component and each choice and use that information to estimate the potential power for each component. If we can determine by direct observation either the level of power utilization or the distribution of power utilization (or if we can identify a procedure for fixing the extent of utilization), we can estimate the potential power by a simple modification of our basic force models.

Suppose, for example, that we have some measures of the activation of individual members of a modern community. One such measure might be the proportion of total time devoted by the individual to a specific issue of social choice. We could use such a measure, observations of initial positions and social choices, and one of the basic force models to assign power indices (potential power) to the various individuals in the community. Similarly, if we took a comparable measure in an experimental group (e.g., some function of the frequency of participation in group discussions), we could determine some power indices. Because direct observational measures of the degree of power utilization are not ordinarily the easiest of measurements to take, the partition version of the model has an important comparative advantage from the point of view of estimation problems. Since we assume that the x_{ij} must be either 1 or 0, we need only observe whether the individual involved did or did not participate in a choice, rather than the degree of his participation.

If we are unable or do not choose to observe the extent of utilization directly, we can, at least in principle, estimate it from other factors in the situation. For example, if we can determine the opportunity costs[42] to the individual of the exercise of power, we might be able to assume that the individual will exercise power only up to the point at which the marginal cost equals the marginal gain. If we can further assume something about the relation between the exercise of power and the return from that exercise, we can use the opportunity costs to estimate the power of utilization. The general idea of opportunity costs, or subjective importance,[43] as a dimension of power has considerable intuitive appeal. If procedures can be developed to make the concepts empirically meaningful, they will be of obvious utility in an activation model of the present type. This route, however, has not yet attracted most persons doing empirical studies.

The second major alternative, given the assumption of constant potential power, is also to assume a constant utilization of power over all choices. Under such circumstances, the product $x_{ij}m_{ij}^*$ is a constant over all j. If both utilization and potential power are constant, we are back to the simple force model and can estimate the product $x_i m_i$ in the same way we previously established the m_i. Under such circumstances, the introduction of the concepts of power utilization and power potential is unnecessary and we can deal directly with power exercised as the core variable.[44]

The force activation model has been compared with empirical data to a limited extent. Hanson and Miller undertook to determine independently the potential power and power utilization of community members and to predict from those measures the outcome of social choices.[45] Potential power was determined by *a priori* theory; utilization was determined by inviews and observation. The results, as previously noted, were consistent not only with the force activation model but also with a number of other models. The French and Harary graph theory models are essentially activation force models (with activation associated with a communication structure) and they have been compared generally with experimental data for the equal potential power case. The comparison suggests a general consistency of the data with several alternate models. Dahl used a force activation model as a definition of power in his study of New Haven.[46]

42   See Harsanyi, 'Measurement of Social Power, Opportunity Costs. . . .'

43   See R. Dubin, Power and Union-Management *Administrative Science Quarterly*, II (1957), 60–81; and A. S. Tannenbaum, An Event Structure Approach to Social Power and to the Problem of Power Comparability, *Behavioral Science,* VII, 1962, 315–31.

44   See Dahl, *Who Governs?* and Wolfinger, 'Reputation and Reality'.

45   Hanson, 'Predicting a Community Decision', D. C. Miller, The Prediction of Issue Outcome in Community Decision-Making, *Research Studies of the State College of Washington,* XXV, 1957, 137–47.

46   Dahl, *Who Governs?*

That is, he assumed the constancy of the x_{ij} and the m_{ij}^* within subject-matter partitions in order to estimate power. On the basis of other observations, Dahl, Polsby, and Wolfinger[47] seem to have concluded that it is meaningful to separate the two elements for certain special purposes (thus the classification as a force activation model rather than a simple force model). A New Haven test of the model, however, requires a subsequent observation of the stability of the indices.

It is clear from a consideration both of the formal properties of activation models and of the problems observers have had with such models that they suffer from their excessive *a posteriori* explanatory power. If we observe that power exists and is stable and if we observe that sometimes weak people seem to triumph over strong people, we are tempted to rely on an activation hypothesis to explain the discrepancy. But if we then try to use the activation hypothesis to predict the results of social-choice procedures, we discover that the data requirements of 'plausible' activation models are quite substantial. As a result, we retreat to what are essentially degenerate forms of the activation model – retaining some of the form but little of the substance. This puts us back where we started, looking for some device to explain our failures in prediction. Unfortunately, the next two types of models simply complicate life further rather than relieve it.

Force-conditioning Models

The conditioning models take as given either the basic force model or the activation model. The only modification is to replace a constant power resource with a variable power resource. The basic mechanisms are simple: (1) People have power because they are believed to have power. (2) People are believed to have power because they have been observed to have power. It is possible, of course, to have models in which one or the other of these mechanisms is not present. If we assume the first but not the second, we have a standard experimental paradigm. If we assume the second but not the first, we have an assortment of prestige learning models.[48]

Furthermore, it is clear that if power is accurately specified by observations and if social choices are precisely and uniquely specified by the power distribution, then the conditioning models are relatively uninteresting. They become interesting because of non-uniqueness in the results of the exercise of power or because of non-uniqueness in the attributions of power.

Let us assume that the C_js are ordered according to the time of their occurrence. C_1 occurs immediately before C_2, and so on. Then we can

47 Dahl, *Who Governs?* Polsby, How to Study Community Power; Wolfinger, Reputation and Reality.
48 White, Uses of Mathematics in Sociology.

view the general form of conditioning models as one of the basic force models as well as a procedure for modifying the m_{ij}^* as a consequence of the C_j. Consider, for example, the following model. We assume that the system re-evaluates the power of the individual components after each choice. At that time, it has information on the choice (C_j) and the previous power reputations, $R_{j-1} = (r_{1, j-1}, r_{2, j-1}, \ldots, r_{n, j-1})$. It must assign a new set of power attributions, R_j. In assigning the new attributions, we might reasonably assume that the system affects the classic compromise of adaptive systems between (1) making the new solutions as consistent as possible with the immediate past experience, and (2) making the new solutions as consistent as possible with the old solutions. In order to identify a dimension along which to affect this compromise, we define a minimum distance, $\overline{D}_j$, between the old attribution and the new choice: $\overline{D}_j\overline{Q}_j - \overline{R}_{j-1}$, where $\overline{Q}_j$ is chosen so as to minimize

$$\sum_{i=1}^{n} (r_{i,j=1} - q_{ij})^2,$$

subject to

$$\sum_{i=1}^{n} q_{ij}A_{ij} = C_j.$$

We can define an equivalent form for the other basic force models.

Now we can assume $\overline{R}_j = \overline{R}_{j-1} + a\overline{D}_j$, where $0 \leq a \leq 1$. If a is 0, we have a degenerate case of a system that does not adapt. If a is 1, we have a system that always adapts the power reputations to be completely consistent with the past observations. If actual power does not depend on the perceived power and is constant, this system simply solves the set of equations (that is, learns the correct answer) or (in the case of the error elements) improves the estimates of power. Under these latter circumstances, it seems reasonable to assume that reputational techniques for assessing power will be preferable to direct observational techniques.

Our interest here, however, is in combining this mechanism with a second one, making actual power a function of perceived power. Within one of our basic force models (or an activation force model) we can define a reputation error, $e_{ij} = r_{ij} - m_{ij}$, and a simple form of adaptation, $m_{ij} = m_{i,j-1} + be_{i,j-1}$ where $0 \leq b \geq 1$. If b is 0, we have our constant power model. If b is 1, we have a model that adjusts power immediately to reputation.

Models of this general class have not been explored in the power literature. Experimental studies have demonstrated the realism of each of the two mechanisms – success improves reputation, reputation improves success. As a result, conditioning models cannot be rejected out of hand. Moreover, they lead directly to some interesting and relevant predictions.

In most of the literature on the measurement of power, there are two nagging problems – the problem of the chameleon who frequently jumps in and agrees with an already decided issue and the satellite who, though he himself has little power, is highly correlated with a high-power person. Since these problems must be at least as compelling for the individual citizen as they are for the professional observer, they have served as a basis for a number of strong attacks on the reputational approach to the attribution of power. But the problem changes somewhat if we assume that reputations affect outcomes. Now the chameleon and the satellite are not measurement problems but important phenomena. The models will predict that an association with power will lead to power. Whether the association is by chance or by deliberate imitation, the results are substantially the same.

To the best of my knowledge, no formal efforts have been made to test either the satellite prediction in a real-world situation, or to test some of its corollaries, which include:

1 Informal power is unstable. Let the kingmaker beware of the king.
2 Unexercised power disappears. Peace is the enemy of victory.
3 Undifferentiated power diffuses. Beware of your allies lest they become your equals.

Moreover, it is really not possible to re-evaluate existing data to examine the plausibility of conditioning models. Virtually all of the studies are cross-sectional rather than longitudinal. The data requirements of the conditioning models are longitudinal. They are also substantially more severe than for the basic force models. Consider the minimally complex adaptive model outlined above. We have added two new parameters (a and b) and a changing m_{ij} to our earlier estimation problems. In order to have much chance of using the model (or variants on it), we will probably need to have data on variables in addition to simply social choice and individual attitudes or behavior. For example, we will probably need reputational data. We will need data that is subscripted with respect to time. We will probably have to make some additional simplifying assumptions, particularly if we want to allow for probabilistic elements in the model or introduce error terms. I do not think these are necessarily insuperable problems, but I think we should recognize that even simple conditioning models of this type will require more and different data than we have been accustomed to gather.

Force-Depletion Models

Within the conditioning models, success breeds success. But there is another class of plausible models in which success breeds failure. As in the conditioning models, we assume that power varies over time. As in the force-activation models, we assume that not all power is exercised at every point in time. Thus,

$$m_{ij} = x_{ij} m_{ij}^* / \sum_{i=1}^{n} x_{ij} m_{ij}^*.$$

The basic idea of the model is plausible. We consider power to be a resource. The exercise of power depletes that resource. Subject to additions to the power supply, the more power a particular component in the system exercises, the less power there is available for that component to use. In the simplest form we can assume

$$m_{ij}^* = m_{i,j-1}^* - x_{i,j-1} m_{i,j-1}^* = m_{i,j-1}^* (1 - x_{i,j-1}).$$

And, if we assume that there are no additions to the power resources,

$$m_{ij}^* = m_{i,0}^* (1 - x_{i,0}) \ldots (1 - x_{i,j-1}).$$

If the withdrawal rate is constant,

$$m_{ij}^* = m_{i,0}^* (1 - x_i)^j.$$

We can modify this to make the depletion proportional to utilization of power (rather than equal to it) without changing the basic structure of the model.

Under this scheme, it is quite possible for power to shift as a result of variations in the rates of power utilization. So long as additions to the power supply are independent of the exercise of power, the use of power today means that we will have less to use tomorrow. We can show various conditions for convergence and divergence of power resources or exercised power. We can also generate a set of aphorisms parallel to – but somewhat at variance with – the conditioning model aphorisms:

1 Formal power is unstable. Let the king beware of the kingmaker.
2 Exercised power is lost. Wars are won by neutrals.
3 Differentiation wastes power. Maintain the alliance as long as possible.

As far as I know, no one has attempted to apply such a model to power situations, although there are some suggestions of its reasonableness (at least as a partial model). Hollander has suggested a model of this class for a closely related phenomenon, the relation between the exercise of independence by a member of a group and the tolerance of independent behavior by the group; but his primary focus was on a system that involved, at the same time, systematic (but independent) effects on the resource (tolerance).[49] Some of the studies of interpersonal relations in organizations indicate that the exercise of power is often dysfunctional with regard to the effective exercise of power in the future. In those cases, the mechanism ordinarily postulated involves the impact of power on sentiments[50] rather than our simple resource notion. Nonetheless the grosser attributes of observed behavior in such studies are consistent with the gross predictions of models that view power as a stock.

Even if power resources are exogenous, the problems of testing a simple depletion model are more severe than the problems of testing the basic activation model. As in the case of the conditioning model, we require longitudinal data. Thus, if we can assume that power resources or increments to power resources are a function of social or economic status, skill in performing some task, or physical attributes (e.g., strength), the model probably can be made manageable if the simplifying assumptions made for force activation models are sensible. On the other hand, if we combine the depletion model with a conditioning model – I think we probably ought to – we will have complicated the basic force model to such a point that it will be difficult indeed to be sanguine about testing.

One way of moderating the test requirements is to use experimental manipulation to control some variables, and experimental observation to measure others. If we can control the resources available and directly measure the extent to which power is exercised, we can develop depletion and depletion-conditioning models to use in experimental situations.

If, however, we want to apply any of the more elaborate force models to a natural system, or if we want to develop natural-system predictions from our experimental studies, we will need far more data than recent research provides. Perhaps a model that includes considerations of activation, conditioning, and power depletion can be made empirically manageable, but such a model (and associated observations) would be a major technical achievement. We are not within shouting distance of it now.

Once we do get such a model, we may well find that it simply does not fit and that a new elaboration is necessary. From a simple concept of power in a simple force model, we have moved to a concept of power that is further and further removed from the basic intuitive notions captured by the simple model, and to models in which simple observations of power are less and less useful. It is only a short step from this point to a set of models that are conceptually remote from the original conception of a social-choice system.

49   E. P. Hollander, Conformity, Status, and Idiosyncrasy Credit *Psychological Review,* LXV, 1958, 117–27.

50   See W. G. Bennis, Effecting Organizational Change: A New Role for the Behavioral Sciences *Administrative Science Quarterly,* VIII, 1963.

Process Models

Suppose that the choice system we are studying is not random. Suppose further that power really is a significant phenomenon in the sense that it can be manipulated systematically in the laboratory and can be used to explain choice in certain social-choice systems. I think that both those suppositions are reasonable. But let us further suppose that there is a class of social-choice systems in which power is insignificant. Unless we treat *power* as true by definition, I think that suppression is reasonable. If we treat *power* as a definition, I think it is reasonable to suppose there is a class of social-choice systems in which power measurement will be unstable and useless.

Consider the following process models of social choice as representative of this class:

An exchange model.   We assume that the individual components in the system prefer certain of the alternative social choices, and that the system has a formal criterion for making the final choices (e.g., majority vote, unanimity, clearing the market). We also assume that there is some medium or exchange by which individual components seek to arrange agreements (e.g., exchanges of money or votes) that are of advantage to themselves. These agreements, plus the formal criterion for choice, determine the social decision. This general type of market system is familiar enough for economic systems and political systems.[51] It is also one way of viewing some modern theories of interpersonal influence[52] in which sentiments on one dimension ('I like you') are exchanged for sentiments on another ('You like my pots') in order to reach a social choice ('We like us and we like my pots').

A problem-solving model.   We assume that each of the individual components in the system has certain information and skills relevant to a problem of social choice, and that the system has a criterion for solution. We postulate some kind of process by which the system calls forth and organizes the information and skills so as systematically to reduce the difference between its present position and a solution. This

---

51   See, for example, Anthony Downs, *An Economic Theory of Democracy* (New York: Harper & Row, Publishers, 1957); J. M. Buchanan and Gordon Tullock, *The Calculus of Consent* (Ann Arbor: University of Michigan Press, 1962); and Riker, *The Theory of Political Coalitions*.

52   Dale Carnegie, *How to Win Friends and Influence People* (New York: Simon and Schuster, Inc., 1936); Leon Festinger, *A Theory of Cognitive Dissonance* (New York, Harper & Row, 1957).

general type of system is familiar to students of individual and group problem solving.[53]

A communication-diffusion model.   We assume that the components in the system are connected by some formal or informal communication system by which information is diffused through the system. We postulate some process by which the information is sent and behavior modified, one component at a time, until a social position is reached. This general type of system is familiar to many students of individual behavior in a social context.[54]

A decision-making model.   We assume that the components in the system have preferences with respect to social choices, and that the system has a procedure for rendering choices. The system and the components operate under two limitations:

1 Overload: they have more demands on their attention than they can meet in the time available.
2 Undercomprehension: the world they face is much more complicated than they can handle.

Thus, although we assume that each of the components modifies its behavior and its preferences over time in order to achieve a subjectively satisfactory combination of social choices, it is clear that different parts of the system contribute to different decisions in different ways at different times. This general type of system is a familiar model of complex organizations.[55]

In each of these process models, it is possible to attribute power to the individual components. We might want to say that a man owning a section of land in Iowa has more power in the economic system than a man owning a section of land in Alaska. We might want to say that, in a pot-selling competition, a man with great concern over his personal status has less power than a man with less concern. We might want to say that a man who knows Russian has more power than a man who does not in a group deciding

53   See, for example, A. Newell, J. C. Shaw, and H. A. Simon, Elements of a Theory of Human Problem Solving *Psychological Review*, LXV, 1958, 151–66; and D. W. Taylor, Decision Making and Problem Solving, in March (ed.) *Handbook of Organizations*.

54   See, for example, Elihu Katz and P. F. Lazarsfeld *Personal Influence* (New York: Free Press of Glencoe, Inc., 1955); and Angus Campbell, Philip Converse, W. E. Miller, and Donald Stokes, *The American Voter* (New York: John Wiley & Sons, Inc., 1960).

55   See C. E. Lindblom, The Science of Muddling Through *Public Administration Review*, XIX, 1959, 79–88; and R. M. Cyert and J. G. March, *A Behavioral Theory of the Firm* (Englewood Cliffs, NJ.: Prentice-Hall, Inc., 1963).

the relative frequency of adjectival phrases in Tolstoy and Dostoyevsky. Or, we might want to say that, within an organization, a subunit that has problems has more power than a subunit that does not have problems. But I think we would probably not want to say any of these things. The concept of power does not contribute much to our understanding of systems that can be represented in any of these ways.

I am impressed by the extent to which models of this class seem to be generally consistent with the reports of recent (and some not so recent)[56] students of political systems and other relatively large (in terms of number of people involved) systems of social choice. 'Observation of certain local communities makes it appear that inclusive over-all organization for many general purposes is weak or non-existent', Long writes. 'Much of what occurs seems to just happen with accidental trends becoming commulative over time and producing results intended by nobody. A great deal of the communities' activities consist of undirected cooperation of particular social structures, each seeking particular goals and, in doing so, meshing with the others'.[57]

Such descriptions of social choice have two general implications. On the one hand, if a system has the properties suggested by such students as Coleman, Long, Riesman, Lindblom, and Dahl, power will be a substantially useless concept. In such systems, the measurement of power is feasible, but it is not valuable in calculating predictions. The measurement of power is useful primarily in systems that conform to some variant of the force models. In some complex process systems we may be able to identify subsystems that conform to the force model, and thus be able to interpret the larger system in terms of a force-activation model for some purposes. But I think the flavor of the observations I have cited is that even such interpretations may be less common-sensible than we previously believed.[58]

On the other hand, the process models – and particularly the decision-making process models – look technically more difficult with regard to estimation and testing than the more complex modifications of the force model. We want to include many more discrete and nominal variables, many more discontinuous functions, and many more rare combinations of events. Although some progress has been made in dealing with the problems, and some predictive power has been obtained without involving the force model, the pitfalls of process models are still substantially uncharted.

---

56   For example, David Riesman, *The Lonely Crowd* (New Haven: Yale University Press, 1951).

57   N. E. Long, The Local Community as an Ecology of Games *American Journal of Sociology*, XLIV, 1958, 252.

58   See Bachrach and Baratz, Two Faces of Power.

The Power of Power

If I interpret recent research correctly, the class of social-choice situations in which power is a significantly useful concept is much smaller than I previously believed. As a result, I think it is quite misleading to assert that, 'Once decision-making is accepted as one of the focal points for empirical research in social science, the necessity for exploring the operational meaning and theoretical dimensions of influence is manifest.'[59] Although *power* and *influence* are useful concepts for many kinds of situations, they have not greatly helped us to understand many of the natural social-choice mechanisms to which they have traditionally been applied.

The extent to which we have used the concept of power fruitlessly is symptomatic of three unfortunate temptations associated with power:

Temptation No. 1: the obviousness of power.   To almost anyone living in contemporary society, power is patently real. We can scarcely talk about our daily life or major political and social phenomena without talking about power. Our discussions of political machinations consist largely of stories of negotiations among the influentials. Our analyses of social events are punctuated with calculations of power. Our interpretations of organizational life are built on evaluations of who does and who does not have power. Our debates of the grand issues of social, political, and economic systems are funneled into a consideration of whether i has too little power and j has too much.

Because of this ubiquity of power, we are inclined to assume that it is real and meaningful. There must be some fire behind the smoke. 'I take it for granted that in every human organization some individuals have more influence over key decisions than do others.'[60] Most of my biases in this regard are conservative, and I am inclined to give some credence to the utility of social conceptual validation. I think, however, that we run the risk of treating the social validation of power as more compelling than it is simply because the social conditioning to a simple force model is so pervasive.

Temptation No. 2: the importance of measurement.   The first corollary of the obviousness of power is the importance of the measurement problem. Given the obviousness of power, we rarely re-examine the basic model by which social choice is viewed as some combination of individual

---

59   March, 'An Introduction', p. 431.
60   R. A. Dahl, A Critique of the Ruling Elite Model *American Political Science Review,* LII, 1958.

choices, the combination being dependent on the power of the various individuals. Since we have a persistent problem discovering a measurement procedure that consistently yields results which are consistent with the model, we assert a measurement problem and a problem of the concept of power. We clarify and re-clarify the concept, and we define and redefine the measures.

The parallel between the role played by power in the theories under consideration here and the role played by subjective utility in theories of individual choice is striking. Just as recent work in power analysis has been strongly oriented toward conceptual and measurement problems, so recent work on utility theory has been strongly oriented toward conceptual and measurement problems.

Although I have some sympathy with these efforts, I think our perseveration may be extreme. At the least, we should consider whether subsuming all our problems under the rubric of conceptual and measurement problems may be too tempting. I think we too often ask *how* to measure power when we should ask *whether* to measure power. The measurement problem and the model problem have to be solved simultaneously.

Temptation No. 3: the residual variance.   The second corollary of the obviousness of power is the use of *power* as a residual category for explanation. We always have some unexplained variance in our data – results that simply cannot be explained within the theory. It is always tempting to give that residual variance some name. Some of us are inclined to talk about God's will; others talk about errors of observation; still others talk about some named variable (e.g., power, personality, extrasensory perception). Such naming can be harmless; we might just as well have some label for our failures. But where the unexplained variance is rather large, as it often is when we consider social-choice systems, we can easily fool ourselves into believing that we know something simply because we have a name for our errors. In general, I think we can roughly determine the index of the temptation to label errors by computing the ratio of uses of the variable for prediction to the uses for a posteriori explanation. On that calculation, I think power exhibits a rather low ratio, even lower than such other problem areas as personality and culture.

Having been trapped in each of these cul-de-sacs at one time or another, I am both embarrassed by the inelegance of the temptations involved and impressed by their strength. We persist in using the simple force model in a variety of situations in which it is quite inconsistent with observations. As a result, we bury the examination of alternative models of social choice under a barrage of measurement questions.

I have tried to suggest that the power depends on the extent to which a predictive model requires and can make effective use of such a concept.

Thus, it depends on the kind of system we are confronting, the amount and kinds of data we are willing or able to collect, and the kinds of estimation and validation procedures we have available to us. Given our present empirical and test technology, power is probably a useful concept for many short-run situations involving the direct confrontations of committed and activated participants. Such situations can be found in natural settings, but they are more frequent in the laboratory. Power is probably not a useful concept for many long-run situations involving the problems of component-overload and undercomprehension. Such situations can be found in the laboratory but are more common in natural settings. Power may become more useful as a concept if we can develop analytic and empirical procedures for coping with the more complicated forms of force models, involving activation, conditioning, and depletion of power.

Thus, the answer to the original question is tentative and mixed. Provided some rather restrictive assumptions are met, the concept of power and a simple force model represent a reasonable approach to the study of social choice. Provided some rather substantial estimation and analysis problems can be solved, the concept of power and more elaborate force models represent a reasonable approach. On the whole, however, power is a disappointing concept. It gives us surprisingly little purchase in reasonable models of complex systems of social choice.

7

Implementation and Ambiguity

Vicki Eaton Baier, James G. March and Harald Sætren

Abstract

Studies of implementation have established two conspicuous things: First, policies can make a difference. Bureaucracies often respond to policy changes by changing administrative actions. Second, policy as implemented often seems different from policy as adopted. Organizational actions are not completely predictable from policy-directives. Efforts to tighten the connection between policy and administration have, for the most part, emphasized ways of augmenting the competence and reliability of bureacracies, of making them more faithful executors of policy directives. Alternatively, they look for ways of making policy makers more sophisticated about bureaucratic limitations. Such recommendations, however, assume that policies either are clear or can be made so arbitrarily. By describing discrepancies between adopted policies and implemented policies as problems of implementation, students of policy-making obscure the extent to which ambiguity is important to policy-making and encourage misunderstanding of the processes of policy-formation and administration.

The 'Implementation Problem'

One of the oldest topics in the study of organizations is the relation between policy and practice, the way general directives and programs adopted by legislatures, boards of directors, or top managements are executed,

This paper was first published in the *Scandinavian Journal of Management Studies*, May 1986. The authors are grateful for the assistance of Julia Ball; for the comments of David Brereton, Anne Miner, Johan Olsen, and David Weckler, and for grants from the Spencer Foundation, the Hoover Institution, and the Stanford Graduate School of Business.

modified, and elaborated by administrative organizations. Contemporary forms of this interest are found in studies of program evaluation and policy implementation. Although there is no question that central policies affect organizational behavior (Attewell and Gerstein, 1979; Randall, 1979), students of implementation frequently report complications in moving from adoption of a policy to its execution (Marshall, 1974). They often describe a scenario in which the wishes of central offices and policy making bodies are frustrated by the realities of a decentralized administrative organization (Levine, 1972; Pressman and Wildavsky, 1973; Edwards and Sharkansky, 1978; Hanf and Scharpf, 1978).

Two interpretations of implementation problems are common. The first interpretation attributes difficulties in implementation to bureaucratic incompetence. Sometimes bureaucracies are unable to accomplish the tasks they are assigned. The technical difficulties of organizing for major programs are often substantial; the technical skills needed for a specific job may be unavailable (Allison and Halperin, 1971; Pressman and Wildavsky, 1973; Bardach, 1977). The second interpretation attributes difficulties in implementation to conflict of interest between policy makers and bureaucratic agents, and thus to deficiencies in organizational control. A bureaucracy responds to objectives and pressures from many persons within and outside the organization; bureaucrats are self-interested actors; they evade control (Tullock, 1965; Niskanen, 1971; Davis, 1972; Halperin, 1974).

The two interpretations are not mutually exclusive, and they are sensible. In the present article, however, we wish to suggest some limitations to such analyses and the importance of including an appreciation of the policy-making process in a discussion of implementation. At the limit, it has been observed that the details of a policy's execution can be systematically less important to policy makers than its proclamation (Christensen, 1976; Kreiner, 1976; Rein and White, 1977). Analyses of the United States Congress, for example, suggest that the act of voting for legislation with appropriate symbolic meaning can be more important to legislators than either its enactment or its implementation (Mayhew, 1974). This is not because legislators are unusually hypocritical. It comes from practical concerns with maintaining electoral support and the substantial symbolic significance of political actions. Voters seek symbolic affirmations as well as mundane personal or group advantage. An interest in the support of constituents, whether voters or stockholders or clients, leads policy makers to be vigorous in enacting policies and lax in enforcing them.

A desire to maintain the values, ideals, and commitments of an organization or society can easily lead to a similar course (March and Olsen, 1976). Political actors, citizens as well as legislators, workers as well as managers, symbolize their virtues and proclaim their values by seeking and securing policy changes. Policies are not simply guidelines for action. Often they are more significantly expressions of faith, acknowledgements of virtue, and instruments of education (Olsen, 1970; Christensen, 1976; Feldman and March, 1981; March and Sevon, 1984). Individuals and groups support (often with extraordinary vigor and at considerable cost) the adoption of policies that symbolize important affirmations, even where they are relatively unconcerned with the ultimate implementation of the policies. As Arnold (1935, p. 34) observed: 'It is part of the function of Law to give recognition to ideals representing the exact opposite of established conduct. Most of the complications arise from the necessity of pretending to do one thing, while actually doing another.'

Cases of such clear intentionality are, however, only a minor part of the story. They dramatize the limitations of talking about 'implementation problems', but they do not define those limitations. We will argue the more general point that an understanding of implementation cannot be divorced from an understanding of the processes that generate policies, and that some conspicuous features of policy-making contribute directly to the phenomena we have come to label as problems of implementation.

Bureaucracies as Instruments of Policy

Despite the pervasiveness and effectiveness of bureaucratic organization, there are ample grounds for doubting that a modern administrative agency will fulfill any policy directive that it might be assigned. For example, bureaucratic inability to cope with the size or scope of new responsibilities has been used to explain the difficulties of some business organizations implementing policies that lead them into foreign markets and of military organizations implementing policies that ask them to fight limited wars. One typical situation in the public sector involves the implementation of new national programs through local departments or bureaus seemingly ill-equipped to administer them.

Consider, for example, Sutherland's (1975, pp. 74–6) portrayal of problems in implementing the Elementary and Secondary Education Act of 1965 in the United States:

> Although some state agencies in 1965 were considered to be well managed, most were thought to lack sufficient personnel to supervise existing state programs or the capability to assume new responsibilities needed to meet future educational needs. Although all state departments of education had professionals capable of providing consultative and technical service to local educational agencies, the number of staff members available on a full-time basis was limited. Only one-fifth of the states had two or more supervisors of

teacher education and 15 did not have a part-time employee for this activity. One-third of the states provided no services or supervision of school libraries. Twenty-nine did not provide for the supervision of industrial arts programs and the remaining states had only a supervisor of vocational education. Four state agencies had no full-time staff members to consult with local school systems for special education and only 13 had one or more full-time consultants for the development of programs for the gifted. . . . Persons in possession of skills and the training to conduct research, evaluate findings and test and implement new instructional programs were also needed by state educational agencies. Although more than two-thirds of the state agencies had departments that included the word 'research' as a part of the title, only 108 persons were employed for research purposes, and nine state departments of education listed no research personnel.

Sutherland's description is specific to a particular mismatch between an educational policy and an educational bureaucracy, but it echoes a common concern in the implementation literature (Bardach, 1977). The idea that implementation is made difficult by the possibly unavoidable, and certainly ubiquitous, problems of bureaucratic and individual incompetence is found in many analyses of modern administrative agencies. Logistic complications are not solved in time. Coordination among agencies is not accomplished, even when there is no significant conflict among them (Pressman and Wildavsky, 1973). Materials, plans, and people are not available when needed (Bardach, 1977); personnel are not trained properly or are given inadequate instructions or supervision (Allison and Halperin, 1971).

Agencies are sometimes sloppy, disorganized, inadequately trained, poorly staffed and badly managed; but gross incompetence is not required to produce significant bureaucratic inadequacy. Some tasks are not feasible; some policies are ill-suited to administrative agencies. Moreover, it is possible to recognize the considerable individual and organizational skills represented in a bureaucracy and still observe a mismatch between a particular organization and a particular task. For example, the United States Forest Service has had difficulty playing the role of a narcotics police force in national forests.

These difficulties are frequently further complicated by a need to coordinate several different organizations in order to implement a single general policy (Elmore, 1975; Hanf and Scharf, 1978). Central policy may require coordination among organizations with sharply contrasting objectives, styles, or normal activities. Managing several relatively autonomous groups often demands capacities beyond those of elaborate bureaucratic structures, not to mention the largely ad hoc structures that are sometimes used. Policy-makers often ignore, or underestimate considerably, the administrative requirements of a policy, and thus make policies that assure administrative incapacity.

The problems of incompetence are paired with problems of control. Administrative organizations are neither reliably neutral nor easily controlled. They seem persistently to modify policies in the course of implementing them. Descriptions of such local adaptations tend to over-estimate the extent to which official policy, as interpreted by interested observers, can be equated either with the public interest or with the intentions of legislatures (Lynn, 1977). They are likely to picture national officials, top management, or major policy makers as defending general interests against the predations of local officials, subordinates, and special interest (Moynihan, 1969; Lowi, 1972; Murphy, 1974). The core idea, however, does not depend on that particular representation of a morality play. Whenever an agent is used to execute the policy of a principal, control problems arise. The problems are endemic to organization and have been extensively discussed in the literature on organizations (March and Simon, 1958; Crozier, 1964), as well as in treatises on optimal contracts, incentive schemes, and theories of agency (Hirschleifer and Riley, 1979).

Bureaucracies appear often to be thoroughly political, responding to claims made in the name of subunits, clients, and individual organizational actors. Political processes continue as policies filter through a bureaucracy to first-level administrative officials. Agencies adopt projects and implement programs in response to political pressure or financial incentives; they exercise discretion in order to improve their local position or address specific problems of interest to them (Berman and McLaughlin, 1976; Mayntz, 1976); they interpret policy directives in ways that transform their prior desires into the wishes of policy makers. For example, the Fort Lincoln project, seen by political leaders as a way to help poor people escape city slums, was converted into a program to build model communities and to try out the newest ideas in community planning (Derthick, 1972).

In dealing with organizational actors, policy makers find it hard to assure that incentives for following official policy are adequate to overcome incentives to deviate from it (Christie, 1964). Organizations, their clients, and their subunits pursue political tactics seeking renegotiation of policies and practices (Mayntz, 1977). Since from the point of view of most other groups and institutions, any new policy announced by policy makers is primarily an opportunity to pursue their own agenda (Bardach, 1977), those responsible for implementing policy have constituents who seek deviations from policy (Derthick, 1972; Pressman and Wildavsky, 1973; Nelson and Yates, 1978; Weiss, 1979). Some parts of any administrative organization will have incentives for pursuing objectives that deviate from any policy that might be adopted (Downs, 1967; Murphy, 1974).

The difficulties in coordinating the agendas of multiple actors are compounded by the way political and organizational actors move in and out of the arena in response to various claims on their attention (March and Olsen, 1976; Sproull, Weiner and Wolf, 1978). An organization is pressed to meet the inconsistent demands of a continually changing group of actors. Pressman and Wildavsky (1973) suggest some reasons for the inconstancy of attention: actors may find their commitments to a policy incompatible with other important commitments; they may have preferences for other programs; they may be dependent on others who lack the same sense of urgency; they may have differences of opinion on leadership or proper organizational roles; they may be constrained by legal or procedural questions or demands. In general, a shifting pattern of demands for attention made on the individuals involved in and around an organization tends to make the climate of implementation unstable in many small ways that cumulatively affect the course of events (Kaufman, 1981).

Programs for Reform of the Policy Process

Because it is part of classical administrative dogma, and because bureaucratic organizations do, in fact, have a rather impressive record for successfully coordinating large numbers of people in service of policies imposed from outside, it is persistently tempting to picture administrative agents as natural implements of prior policy. They are made innocent by an act of will or good management. In this spirit, problems of implementation lead to proposals to increase competence and control by hiring new personnel, developing new training or procedures, improving accountability, and providing new incentives. For example, foreign service organizations may respond to diagnoses of incompetence by increasing the length of service at a particular station for individual officers; they may respond to diagnoses of lack of control by requiring more frequent rotation of officers through stations. Implementation failures may lead to new organizational forms, for example, divisional management; to new investments, for example, in management information systems; to new routines, for example, evaluation studies; or to new personnel, for example, new top executives.

Such changes are intended to make an organization into a competent, reliable agent, executing a wide range of possible policies (Maass, 1951; Kaufman, 1960). They picture the problems of implementation as problems of securing neutral administrative compliance with prior, exogenous policies. This view of administration has, however, long been in disrepute among students of organizations (Herring, 1936; Leiserson, 1942; Truman, 1951). It suggests more clarity in the distinction between policy-making and administration than can usually be sustained; and it leads to a mechanistic perspective on the management of organizations that seems likely to be misleading. Trying to keep administrators innocent may, of course, simply reflect an instinct to use unachievable aspirations as a means of achieving less heroic, but admirable outcomes (March, 1978; 1979); but it tends to delusion. Consequently, many sophisticated observers of organizations take a more strategic posture with respect to designing administrative organizations.

Suppose we accept the proposition that bureaucracies are limited instrumentalities, that there are constraints on our abilities to make them more competent or to avoid the demands of self-interest. Then implementation problems are attributed not to characteristics of organizations – which are taken as essentially intractable – but to the *naïveté* of policy makers. In this view, policy makers do not specify objectives clearly enough (Løchen and Martinsen, 1962; Jacobsen, 1966; Lowi, 1969; Sabatier and Mazmanian, 1980), provide inadequate resources (Allison and Halperin, 1971; Bardach, 1977), fail to build a proper administrative organization (Williams, 1971; Derthick, 1972), fail to consult with affected groups (Bunkers, 1972; Derthick, 1972), or have too high expectations (Elmore, 1975; Bardach, 1977; Timpane, 1978). Such a strategic vision leads to recommendations to improve the policies, make them clearer and more consistent with the attitudes of the groups involved, and strengthen the incentives and capabilities for bureaucratic conformity to policy directives.

An example of such advice is found in Bardach's (1977, p. 253) discussion of policy design.

> . . . a management game is played against the entropic forces of social nature, and there is no permanent solution. Once this fact is recognized, the implication for policy designers is clear, design simple, straight-forward programs that require as little management as possible. To put it another way, if the management game is a losing proposition, the best strategy is to avoid playing. Programs predicated on continuing high levels of competence, on expeditious interorganizational coordination, or on sophisticated methods for accommodating diversity and heterogeneity are very vulnerable. They are not necessarily doomed to failure, but they are asking for trouble. . . . Other things equal, policy designers would prefer to operate through manipulating prices and markets rather than writing and enforcing regulations, through delivering cash rather than services, through communicating by means of smaller rather than larger units of social organizations, and through seeking clearances from fewer rather than more levels of consultation and review.

The advice seems well-taken. Many problems in implementation might be avoided if policy makers made less ambiguous policies and designed simple procedures that protected their intentions from the inadequacies and self-interest of administrative agencies. Rather than expecting to change the character of administrative organizations, we might design strategic policies, quasi-price systems, and incentive contracts that are likely to lead to desired ends even when executed by administrative organizations that are neither perfect nor neutral.

These efforts to increase the sophistication of policy makers in dealing with administrative agencies, like earlier attempts to improve the competence and reliability of the agencies, are vital to good administration. Without a struggle to link policy and action, any social system suffers. However, we want to argue that the problems of implementation are obscured by the terminology of implementation, even in its more sophisticated forms, that discussions of implementations assume a coherence in policy objectives that rarely exists. Understanding administrative implementation cannot be separated from understanding the ways in which policies are made and the implications of the policy-making process for administrative action.

Policy-Making and Policy Ambiguity

Proposals for implementations reform treat policy – or policy objectives – as given. They assume that policy goals and directives are (or can be) clear, that policy makers know what they want, and that what they want is consistent, stable, and unambiguous. The assumptions are similar to assumptions about preferences made in standard decision theory, and they have some of the same advantages (Raiffa, 1968). They made administration, like decision-making, a difficult technical job of optimization, subject to prior exogenous policies established by legitimate authority. They also have many of the same disadvantages (March, 1978; Elster, 1979; Cronbach et al., 1980).

In particular, the assumptions are often not true. They are frequently false in a way that makes the concept of implementation not only inaccurate as a portrayal of organizational reality, but often an inappropriate base for organizational reform. For example, the frequent advice that policies should be clear seems to assume that policy makers can arbitrarily choose the level of clarity of a policy, that policies are ambiguous because of some form of inadequacy in policy-making. Such a view ignores what we know about the making of policies. In fact, policies are negotiated in a way that makes the level of clarity no more accessible to arbitrary choice than other vital parts of the policy.

Forming a coalition in order to support a policy, whether in a legislature or a boardroom, involves standard techniques of horse-trading, persuasion, bribes, threats, and management of information. These are the conventional procedures of discussion, politics, and policy-formation. They are well-conceived to help participants form coalitions, explore support for alternative policies, and develop a viable policy. Much of the genius of modern organizational leadership lies in skills for producing policy from the conflicting and inchoate ideas, demands, preconceptions, and prejudices of the groups to which organizational leadership must attend. At the heart of several of these techniques for achieving policies, however, are features that make implementation problematic.

Adopted policies will, on average, be oversold. Even unbiased expectations about possible policies will lead to bias in the expectations with respect to those that are adopted. Since proposed programs for which expectations are erroneously pessimistic are rarely adopted, the sample of adopted programs is more likely to exhibit errors of over-optimism than of over-pessimism (Harrison and March, 1984). Inflated expectations about programs that are successful in gaining support from policy makers make subsequent disappointment likely. Thus, great hopes lead to action, but great hopes are invitations to disappointment. This, in turn, leads both to an erosion of support and to an awareness of 'failures of implementation'.

Such a structural consequence of intelligent decision-making under conditions of uncertainty is accentuated in situations of collective choice. Competition for policy support pushes advocates to imagine favorable outcomes and to inflate estimates of the desirability of those outcomes. Developing and communicating such expectations are a major part of policy discussions. Expectations become part of the official record, part of collective history, and part of individual beliefs. Others will, of course, try to deflate the estimates of advocates; but the advocates usually write the stories for their preferred policies and often come either to believe them or to be committed publicly to them. Tactical supporters of policies (i.e., those who support policies for reasons extraneous to their content) do not resist being misled. Extravagant claims justify their support and provide a basis, if one is ever needed, for claims that they are duped.

In addition, the centripetal processes of policy-making exaggerate the real level of support for policies that are adopted. Although commitment to a policy or program in its own right may be important for some coalition members, few major policies could be adopted without some supporters for whom the policy is relatively unimportant except as a political bargain. They may be persuaded to join a coalition by a belief the policy is sensible, by claims of loyalty or friendship, or by a logroll in which their support is offered in trade for needed support on other things in which they have a direct concern. There is no assurance that such groups and individuals will be equally supportive of its implementation. Except in so far as their continued active support is a part of the coalition agreement, and such extended coalition agreements are difficult to arrange and enforce, supporters will turn to other matters. Consequently, a winning coalition can easily be an illusion (Sætren, 1983).

Finally, one common method for securing policy support is to increase the ambiguity of a proposed policy (Page, 1976). It is a commonplace observation of the legislative process that difficult issues are often 'settled' by leaving them unresolved or specifying them in a form requiring subsequent interpretation. A similar observation can be made about policies in armies, hospitals, universities, and business firms. Particularly where an issue is closely contested, success in securing support for a program or policy is likely to be associated with increasing, rather than decreasing ambiguity. Policy ambiguity allows different groups and individuals to support the same policy for different reasons and with different expectations, including different expectations about the administrative consequences of the policy.

Thus, official policy is likely to be vague, contradictory, or adopted without generally shared expectations about its meaning or implementation. Aubert, in his study of the enactment of a Housemaid Law in Norway (Aubert, 1969, p. 125), discusses the apparent anomaly of legislation that paired a policy proclaiming the protection of household workers with a set of procedures for redress that were effectively inaccessible to victims:

> What is pretended in the penal clause of the Housemaid Law is that effective enforcement of the law is envisaged. And what the legislature is actually doing is to see to it that the privacy of the home and the interest of housewives are not ignored. . . . The ambivalence and the conflicting views of the legislators, as they can be gleaned from the penal clause, appear more clearly in the legislative debate. A curious dualism runs through the debates. It was claimed, on the one hand, that the law is essentially a codification of custom and established practice, rendering effective enforcement inessential. On the other hand, there was a tendency to claim that the Housemaid Law is an important new piece of labour legislation with a clearly reformatory purpose, attempting to change an unacceptable status quo. . . . The crucial point here is the remarkable ease with which such apparently contradictory claims were suffused in one and the same legislative action, which in the end received unanimous support from all political groups.

In this way, the ambiguity of a policy increases the chance of its adoption, but at the cost of creating administrative complications. For example, Øyen (1964) observed that the ambiguous text of a Norwegian welfare statute was simultaneously a necessary condition for the unanimity of its political support and a basis for considerable administrative discretion. As a policy unfolds into action, the different understandings of an ambiguous political agreement combine with the usual transformation of preferences over time to become bases for abandoning support, deploring administrative sabotage of the program, or embracing a special fantasy of what the policy means. As a result, many coalition members can easily feel betrayed; and observers can easily become confused.

In the long run, of course, political institutions learn from their experience. Administrative agencies seem likely to adapt to a history of ambiguous, contradictory, and grandiose policies by an administrative posture that tends to emphasize creative autonomy. They learn to establish independent political constituencies, to treat normal policies as problematic (or at least subject to interpretation), and to expect policy makers to be uncertain, or in conflict, about the expected consequences of a policy, or its importance. They come to realize that they cannot escape criticism by arguing that they were following policy but must develop an independent political basis for their actions.

Similarly, policy makers learn from their experiences with administrative agencies. As administrative practices become flexible, it becomes easier to use policy ambiguity as a basis for forming coalitions. It becomes plausible to attribute failures in programs to failures in implementation and thus to avoid possible criticism for mistakes. Policy ambiguity encourages administrative autonomy, which in turn encourages more policy ambiguity. Thus, it is not hard to see why we might observe organizations functioning with only a loose coupling between policies and actions, between plans and behavior, and between policy makers and administrators (March and Olsen, 1976; Weick, 1976).

The Concept of Implementation

The terminology of implementation conjures up a picture of clear, consistent, and stable policy directives waiting to be executed. It encourages us to think that a reasonable and responsible person can easily measure the discrepancy between policy and bureaucratic action, that the discrepancy can be attributed to some properties of the organization (e.g., its competence and reliability) or to some properties of the policy (e.g., its clarity and consistency), and that the properties of the organization and the properties of the policy can be chosen arbitrarily and independently in order to reduce the discrepancy.

As we have noted, studies of policy-making cast doubt on such a characterization. The implementation of policies is frequently problematic; but the difficulties cannot be treated as independent of the confusions in the policy. Those confusions, in turn, cannot be treated as independent of the ways in which winning policy coalitions are built. Policies are frequently ambiguous; but their ambiguities are less a result of deficiencies in policy makers than a natural consequence of gaining necessary support for the policies, and of changing preferences over time. Conflict of interest is not just a property of the relations between policy makers on the one hand and administrators on the other; it is a general feature of policy negotiation and bureaucratic life. As a result, policies reflect contradictory intentions and expectations and considerable uncertainty.

It may be tempting to deplore a policy process that sometimes seems to restrict us to a choice between inaction and ambiguity, and to wish for some alternative system in which policy agreements would be clear and their execution unproblematic. But that concern should be paired with an awareness of the complications. The problems involved in establishing and maintaining an effective policy-making and an administrative system that provides responsiveness, coherence, and symbolic affirmation of social values have occupied philosophers and managers for long enough to suggest that they are not trivial. Certainly, contemporary theories of policy-making and administration have not solved them. Nor have we. As a preface to such an effort, however, we have argued that the terms of discourse for discussing policy-making and implementation are misleading. Any simple concept of implementation, with its implicit assumption of clear and stable policy intent, is likely to lead to a fundamental misunderstanding of the policy process and to disappointment with efforts to reform it.

References

Allison, Graham T., and Morton H. Halperin (1971) Bureaucratic politics: A paradigm and some policy implications. *World Politics*, 24: 40–79.

Arnold, Thurman (1935) *The Symbols of Government* New Haven, CT: Yale University Press.

Attewell, Paul, and Dean R. Gerstein (1979) Government policy and local practice. *American Sociological Review*, 44: 311–27.

Aubert, Wilhelm (1969) Some social functions of legislation. In Vilhelm Aubert (ed.), *Sociology of Law,* London: Penguin.

Bardach, Eugene (1977) *The Implementation Game*, Cambridge, MA: MIT Press.

Berman, Paul, and Milbrey McLaughlin (1976) *Implementation Problems: Patterns and Parameters – Implications for Macro Policy*. Santa Monica, CA: Rand Corporation.

Bunker, Douglas R. (1972) Policy sciences perspectives on implementation processes. *Policy Sciences*, 3: 71–80.

Christensen, Søren (1976) Decision-making and socialization. In James G. March and Johan P. Olsen, *Ambiguity and Choice in Organizations*, pp. 351–85. Bergen: Universitetsforlaget.

Christie, Nils (1964) Edruelighetsnemnder: Analyse av en velferdslov. (Temperance committees: Analysis of a welfare statute), *Nordisk Tidskrift for Kriminalvitenskap*, 52: 89–118.

Cronbach, Lee J., et al. (1980) *Toward Reform of Program Evaluation*. San Francisco: Jossey-Bass.

Crozier, Michel (1964) *The Bureaucratic Phenomenon*. Chicago: University of Chicago Press.

Davis, David H. (1972) *How the Bureaucracy Makes Foreign Policy*. Lexington, MA: Lexington Books.

Derthick, Martha (1972) *New Towns – In Town*. Washington, DC: Urban Institute.

Downs, Anthony (1967) *Inside Bureaucracy*. Boston: Little, Brown.

Edwards, George C., and Ira Sharkansky (1978) *The Policy Predicament*, San Francisco: W. H. Freeman.

Elmore, Richard F. (1975) Lessons from follow through. *Policy Analysis,* 1: 459–67.

Elster, Jon (1979) *Ulysses and the Sirens*. Cambridge: Cambridge University Press.

Feldman, Martha S., and James G. March (1981) Information in organizations as signal and symbol. *Administrative Science Quarterly,* 26: 171–86.

Halperin, Morton H. (1974) *Bureaucratic Politics and Foreign Policy*. Washington DC: Brookings.

Hanf, Kenneth, and Fritz W. Scharpf (1978) *Interorganizational Policy Making: Limits to Coordination and Central Control*. London: Sage.

Harrison, J. Richard, and James G. March (1984) Decision-making and post-decision surprises. *Administrative Science Quarterly* 29: 26–42.

Herring, E. Pendleton (1936) *Public Administration and the Public Interest*. New York: McGraw-Hill.

Hirschleifer, J., and John C. Riley (1979) The analytics of uncertainty and information – An expository survey. *Journal of Economic Literature,* 17: 1375–421.

Jacobsen, Knut D, (1966) Public administration under pressure: the role of the expert in the modernization of traditional agriculture. *Scandinavian Political Studies,* 1: 69–93.

Kaufman, Herbert (1960) *The Front Ranger*, Baltimore: Johns Hopkins University Press.

Kaufman, Herbert (1981) *The Administrative Behavior of Federal Bureau Chiefs*. Washington, DC: Brookings Institution.

Kreiner, Kristian (1976) Ideology and management in a garbage can situation. In James G. March and John P. Olsen, *Ambiguity and Choice in Organizations,* pp. 156–73. Bergen: Universitetsforlaget.

Leiserson, Avery (1942) *Administrative Regulation: A Study in Representation of Interests*. Chicago: University of Chicago Press.

Levine, Robert A. (1972) *Public Planning: Failure and Redirection*. New York: Basic Books.

Løchen, Yngvar, and Arne Martinsen (1962) Samarbeidsproblemer ved gjennomføringen av lovene om attføringshjelp og unføretrygd. (Cooperation problems in the implementation of laws dealing with aid to the handicapped and disability insurance), *Tidsskrift for Samfunnsforskning,* 3: 133–68.

Lowi, Theodore J. (1969) *The End of Liberalism*. New York: W. W. Norton.

Lowi, Theodore J. (1972) Four systems of policy, politics and choice. *Public Administration Review*, 32: 298–310.

Lynn, Laurence E. (1977) Implementation: Will the hedgehogs be outfoxed? *Policy Analysis*, 3: 277–80.

Maass, Arthur A. (1951) *Muddy Waters: The Army Engineers and the Nation's Rivers*. Cambridge, MA: Harvard University Press.

March, James G. (1978) Bounded rationality, ambiguity, and the engineering of choice. *Bell Journal of Economics*, 9: 587–608.

March, James G. (1979) *Science, Politics, and Mrs. Gruenberg* Washington, DC: National Academy of Sciences.

March, James G., and Johan P. Olsen (1976) *Ambiguity and Choice in Organizations*: Bergen: Universitetsforlaget.

March, James G., and Guje Sevón (1984) Gossip, information and decision making. In Lee S. Sproull and Patrick D. Larkey (eds), *Advances in Information Processing in Organizations*, pp. 95–107. Greenwich, CT: JAI Press.

March, James G., and Herbert A. Simon (1958) *Organizations*. New York: Wiley.

Marshall, Dale Rogers (1974) Implementation of federal poverty and welfare policy: A review essay. *Policy Studies Journal*, 2: 152–7.

Mayhew, David R. (1974) *Congress: The Electoral Connection*. New Haven, CT: Yale University Press.

Mayntz, Renate (1976) Environmental policy conflicts: The case of the German Federal Republic. *Policy Analysis*, 2: 577–88.

Mayntz, Renate (1977) Die Implementation Politischer Programme: Theoretische Uberlegungen zu einem neuen Forschungsgebiet. (Implementation of political programs: Theoretical considerations for a new research area), *Die Verwaltung*, 10: 51–66.

Moynihan, Daniel P. (1969) *Maximum Feasible Misunderstanding*. New York: Free Press.

Murphy, Jerome T. (1974) *State Education Agencies and Discretionary Funds*. Lexington, MA: Lexington Books.

Nelson, Richard, and Douglas Yates (1978) *Innovation and Implementation in Public Organizations*. Lexington, MA: Lexington Books.

Niskanen, William A. (1971) *Bureaucracy and Representative Government*. Chicago: Aldine.

Olsen, Johan P. (1970) Local budgeting – Decision-making or ritual act. *Scandinavian Political Studies*, 5: 85–118.

Øyen, Else (1964) *Sosialomsorgen og dens Forvaltere* (Social care and its managers), Bergen: Universitetsforlaget.

Page, Benjamin I. (1976) The theory of political ambiguity. *American Political Science Review*, 70: 742–52.

Pressman, Jeffrey L., and Aaron B. Wildavsky (1973) *Implementation*. Berkeley, CA: University of California Press.

Raiffa, Howard (1968) *Decision Analysis*. Reading, MA: Addison Wesley.

Randall, Ronald (1979) Presidential power versus bureaucratic intransigence: The influence of the Nixon administration on welfare policy. *American Political Science Review*, 73: 795–810.

Rein, Martin, and Sheldon H. White (1977) Policy research: Belief and doubt. *Policy Analysis*, 3: 239–71.

Sabatier, Paul, and Daniel Mazmanian (1980) The implementation of public policy: A framework of analysis. *Policy Studies Journal*, 8: 538–60.

Sætren, Harald (1983) *Iverksetting av offentlig politikk*. (Implementation of public policy). Bergen: Universitetsforlaget.

Sproull, Lee S. Stephen Weiner, and David Wolf (1978) *Organizing an Anarchy*. Chicago: University of Chicago Press.

Sutherland, B. H. (1975) *Federal Grants to State Departments of Education for the Administration of the Elementary and Secondary Education Act of 1965*. Ann Arbor, MI: University of Michigan Press.

Timpane, Michael P. (1978) *The Federal Interest in Financing Schooling*. Cambridge, MA: Ballinger.

Truman, David (1951) *The Governmental Process*. New York: Knopf.

Tullock, Gordon (1965) *The Politics of Bureaucracy*. Washington, DC.: Public Affairs Press.

Weick, Karl (1976) Educational organizations as loosely coupled systems. *Administrative Science Quarterly*, 21: 1–19.

Weiss, Carol (1979) Many meanings of research utilization *Public Administration Review*, 39: 426–31.

William, Walter (1971) *Social Policy Research and Analysis*. New York: Elsevier.

Part III
Adaptive Rules

Part III
Adaptive Rules

8

Footnotes to Organizational Change

James G. March

Abstract

Five footnotes to change in organizations are suggested. They emphasize the relation between change and adaptive behavior more generally, the prosaic nature of change, the way in which ordinary processes combine with a confusing world to produce some surprises, and the implicit altruism of organizational foolishness.

Introduction

Organizations change. Although they often appear resistant to change, they are frequently transformed into forms remarkably different from the original. This paper explores five footnotes to research on organizational change, possible comments on what we know. The intention is not to review the research results but to identify a few speculations stimulated by previous work.

Footnote 1. Organizations are continually changing, routinely, easily, and responsively, but change within them cannot ordinarily be arbitrarily controlled. Organizations rarely do exactly what they are told to do.

This paper was first published in *Administrative Science Quarterly*, 26, in 1981: 563–77. The author would like to acknowledge the assistance of Julia Ball; the comments and collaboration of David Anderson, Vicki Eaton, Martha Feldman, Daniel Levinthal, Anne Miner, J. Rounds, Philip Salin and Jo Zettler; and support by the Spencer Foundation, the National Institute of Education, the Hoover Institution, and the National Center for Higher Education Management Systems.

Footnote 2. Changes in organizations depend on a few stable processes. Theories of change emphasize either the stability of the processes or the changes they produce, but a serious understanding of organizations requires attention to both.

Footnote 3. Theories of change in organizations are primarily different ways of describing theories of action in organizations, not different theories. Most changes in organizations reflect simple responses to demographic, economic, social, and political forces.

Footnote 4. Although organizational response to environmental events is broadly adaptive and mostly routine, the response takes place in a confusing world. As a result, prosaic processes sometimes have surprising outcomes.

Footnote 5. Adaptation to a changing environment involves an interplay of rationality and foolishness. Organizational foolishness is not maintained as a conscious strategy, but is embedded in such familiar organizational anomalies as slack, managerial incentives, symbolic action, ambiguity, and loose coupling.

Stable Processes of Change

A common theme in recent literature, particularly in studies of the implementation of public policy, is that of attempts at change frustrated by organizational resistance. There are well-documented occasions on which organizations have failed to respond to change initiatives or have changed in ways that were, in the view of some, inappropriate (Gross, Giaquinta, and Bernstein, 1971; Nelson and Yates, 1978).

What most reports on implementation indicate, however, is not that organizations are rigid and inflexible, but that they are impressively imaginative (Pressman and Wildavsky, 1973; Bardach, 1977). Organizations change in response to their environments, but they rarely change in a way that fulfills the intentions of a particular group of actors (Attewell and Gerstein, 1979; Crozier, 1979). Sometimes organizations ignore clear instructions; sometimes they pursue them more forcefully than was intended; sometimes they protect policy makers from folly; sometimes they do not. The ability to frustrate arbitrary intention, however, should not be confused with rigidity; nor should flexibility be confused with organizational effectiveness. Most organizational failures occur early in life when organizations are small and flexible, not later (Aldrich, 1979). There is considerable stability in organizations, but the changes we observe are substantial enough to suggest that organizations are remarkably adaptive, enduring institutions, responding to volatile environments routinely and easily, though not always optimally.

Because of the magnitude of some changes in organizations, we are inclined to look for comparably dramatic explanations for change, but the search for drama may often be a mistake. Most change in organizations results neither from extraordinary organizational processes or forces, nor from uncommon imagination, persistence or skill, but from relatively stable, routine processes that relate organizations to their environments. Change takes place because most of the time most people in an organization do about what they are supposed to do; that is, they are intelligently attentive to their environments and their jobs. Bureaucratic organizations can be exceptionally ineffective, but most of the organizations we study are characterized by ordinary competence and minor initiative (Hedberg, Nystrom, and Starbuck, 1976). Many of the most stable procedures in an organization are procedures for responding to economic, social, and political contexts. What we call organizational change is an ecology of concurrent responses in various parts of an organization to various interconnected parts of the environment. If the environment changes rapidly, so will the responses of stable organizations; change driven by such shifts will be dramatic if shifts in the environment are large.

The routine processes of organizational adaptation are subject to some complications, and a theory of change must take into account how those processes can produce unusual patterns of action. Yet, in its fundamental structure a theory of organizational change should not be remarkably different from a theory of ordinary action. Recent research on organizations as routine adaptive systems emphasizes six basic perspectives for interpreting organizational action:

1 *Rule following*. Action can be seen as the application of standard operating procedures or other rules to appropriate situations. The underlying process is one of matching a set of rules to a situation by criteria of appropriateness. Duties, obligations, roles, rules, and criteria evolve through competition and survival, and those followed by organizations that survive, grow, and multiply come to dominate the pool of procedures. The model is essentially a model of selection (Nelson and Winter, 1974).

2 *Problem solving*. Action can be seen as problem solving. The underlying process involves choosing among alternatives by using some decision-rule that compares alternatives in terms of their expected consequences for antecedent goals. The model is one of intendedly rational choice under conditions of risk and is familiar in statistical decision theory, as well as microeconomic and behavioral theories of choice (Lindblom, 1958; Cyert and March, 1963).

3 *Learning*. Action can be seen as stemming from past learning. The underlying process is one in which an organization is conditioned through

trial and error to repeat behavior that has been successful in the past and to avoid behavior that has been unsuccessful. The model is one of experiential learning (Day and Groves, 1975).

4 *Conflict.* Action can be seen as resulting from conflict among individuals or groups representing diverse interests. The underlying process is one of confrontation, bargaining, and coalition, in which outcomes depend on the initial preferences of actors weighted by their power. Changes result from shifts in the mobilization of participants or in the resources they control. The model is one of politics (March, 1962; Gamson, 1968; Pfeffer, 1981).

5 *Contagion.* Action can be seen as spreading from one organization to another. The underlying process is one in which variations in contact among organizations and in the attractiveness of the behaviors or beliefs being imitated affect the rate and pattern of spread. The model is one of contagion and borrows from studies of epidemiology (Rogers, 1962; Walker, 1969; Rogers and Shoemaker, 1971).

6 *Regeneration.* Action can be seen as resulting from the intentions and competencies of organizational actors. Turnover in organizations introduces new members with different attitudes, abilities, and goals. The underlying process is one in which conditions in the organization (e.g., growth, decline, changing requirements for skills) or deliberate strategies (e.g., cooptation, raiding of competitors) affect organizational action by changing the mix of participants. The model is one of regeneration (Stinchcombe, McDill, and Walker, 1968; White, 1970; McNeil and Thompson, 1971).

These six perceptives are neither esoteric, complicated, nor mutually exclusive. Although we may sometimes try to assess the extent to which one perspective or another fits a particular situation, it is quite possible for all six to be pertinent or for any particular history to involve them all. An organization uses rules, problem-solving, learning, conflict, contagion, and regeneration to cope with its environment, actively adapt to it, avoid it, seek to understand, change, and contain it. The processes are conservative. That is, they tend to maintain stable relations, sustain existing rules, and reduce differences among organizations. The fundamental logic, however, is not one of stability in behavior; it is one of responsiveness. The processes are stable; the resulting actions are not.

Some Complexities of Change

Organizations change in mundane ways, but elementary processes sometimes produce surprises in a complex world. As illustrations of such complexities, consider five examples: the unanticipated consequences of ordinary action, solution-driven problems, the tendency for innovations and organizations to be transformed during the process of innovation, the endogenous nature of created environments, and the interactions among the system requirements of individuals, organizations, and environments.

Unanticipated Consequences of Ordinary Action

Each of the six perspectives on action described above portrays organizations as changing sensibly; that is, solving problems, learning from experience, imitating others, and regenerating their capabilities through turnover of personnel. These processes, however, may be applied under conditions which, though difficult to distinguish from usual conditions, are sufficiently different to lead to unanticipated outcomes. In particular we can identify three such conditions.

First, the rate of adaptation may be inconsistent with the rate of change of the environment to which the organization is adapting. Unless an environment is perfectly stable, of course, there will always be some error arising from a history-dependent process (e.g., learning, selection); but where an environment changes quickly relative to the rate at which an organization adapts, a process can easily lose its claim to being sensible. It is also possible for an anticipatory process (e.g., problem-solving) to result in changes that outrun the environment and thereby become unintelligent. Second, the causal structure may be different from that implicit in the process. If causal links are ignored, either because they are new, or because their effects in the past have been benign, or because the world is inherently too complex, then changes that seem locally adaptive may produce unanticipated or confusing consequences. Such outcomes are particularly likely in situations in which belief in a false or incomplete model of causality can be reinforced by confounded experience. Third, concurrent, parallel processes of *prima facie* sensibility may combine to produce joint outcomes that are not intended by anyone and are directly counter to the interests motivating the individual actions (Schelling, 1978).

Most of the time, these unanticipated outcomes are avoided, but they are common. Consider the following illustrations:

Learning from the response of clients.   Clients and customers send signals to organizations, the most conspicuous one being the withdrawal of their patronage. We expect organizations to respond to such signals. For example, although customer withdrawal is a major device used by market organizations to maintain product quality, it is not always effective. As Hirschman (1970) observed, it is likely that the first customers to abandon a product of declining quality will be those customers with the highest quality standards. If it is assumed that new customers are a random sample from the market, a firm is left with customers whose standards are, on the average, lower and who complain less about the reduced quality. This leads to further decay of quality, and the cycle continues until the quality consciousness of new customers equals that of lost customers; i.e., until the firm's most quality-conscious customers are no more concerned about quality than the average customers in the market. This cycle of regeneration can lead to a fairly rapid degradation in product or service.

Rewarding friends and coopting enemies.   Employees of governmental regulatory agencies sometimes subsequently become employees of the organizations they regulate. The flow of people presumably affects the relations between the organizations. In particular, the usual presumption is that expectations of future employment will lead current governmental officials to treat the organizations involved more favorably than they would otherwise. However, if the regulated organizations provide possible employment as an incentive for favorable treatment, they risk producing a pattern of turnover in the regulatory agency in which friends leave the agency, and only those unfriendly to the organization remain. Alternatively, some organizations attempt to coopt difficult people (e.g., rebels), on the assumption that cooptation leads to controlled change, since opponents are socialized and provided with modest success. However, in so far as the basic strategy of cooptation is to strip leadership from opposition groups by inducing opposition leaders to accept more legitimate roles, a conspicuous complication is the extent to which cooptation provides an incentive for being difficult, and thereby increases, rather than reduces opposition.

Competency multipliers.   Organizations frequently have procedures to involve potentially relevant people in decision-making, planning, budgeting, or the like. The individuals vary in status, knowledge about a problem, and interest in it. Initial participation rates reflect these variations; however, individuals who participate slightly more than others become slightly more competent at discussing the problems of the group than others. This induces them to participate even more, which makes them even more competent. Before long, the *de facto* composition of the group can change dramatically (Weiner, 1976). More generally organizations learn from experience, repeating actions that are successful. As a result, they gain greater experience in areas of success than in areas of failure. This increases their capabilities in successful areas, thus increasing their chances of being successful there. The sensibleness of such specialization depends on the relation between the learning rates and the rate of change in the environment.

The process can easily lead to misplaced specialization if there are infrequent, major shifts in the environment.

Satisficing. It has been suggested that organizations satisfice, that is, that they seek alternatives that will satisfy a target goal rather than look for the alternative with the highest possible expected value (March and Simon, 1958; Cyert and March, 1963). Satisficing organizations can be viewed as organizations that maximize the probability of achieving their targets, but it is not necessary to assume quite such a precise formulation to suggest that organizations that satisfice will follow decision-rules that are risk-avoiding in good times, when the best alternatives have expected values greater than the target, and risk-seeking in bad times, when the best alternatives have expected values less than the target (Tversky and Kahneman, 1974). As is noted below, the association of risk-seeking behavior with adversity requires some qualification; but in so far as such a pattern is common, it has at least two important consequences. First, organizations that are facing bad times will follow riskier and riskier strategies, thus simultaneously increasing their chances of survival through the present crisis and reducing their life expectancy. Choices that seek to reverse a decline, for example, may not maximize expected value. As a result, for those organizations that do not survive, efforts to survive will have speeded the process of failure (Hermann, 1963; Mayhew, 1979). Second, if organizational goals vary with organizational performance and the performance of other comparable organizations, most organizations will face situations that are reasonably good most of the time. Consequently, the pool of organizations existing at any time will generally include a disproportionate number that are risk-avoiding.

Performance criteria. Organizations measure the performance of participants. For example, business firms reward managers on the basis of calculations of profits earned by different parts of the organization. The importance of making such links precise and visible is a familiar theme of discussions of organizational control, as is the problem of providing similar performance measures in non-business organizations. However, in an organization with a typical mobility pattern among managers, these practices probably lead to a relative lack of concern about long-term consequences of present action. Performance measurement also leads to exaggerated concern with accounts, relative to product and technology. Measured performance can be improved either by changing performance or by changing the accounts of performance. Since it is often more efficient, in the short run, to devote effort to the accounts rather than to performance (March, 1978a), a bottom-line ideology may over-stimulate the cleverness of organizational participants in manipulating accounts.

Superstitious learning. Organizations learn from their experience, repeating actions that have been associated with good outcomes, avoiding actions that have been associated with bad ones. If the world makes simple sense, and is stable, then repeating actions associated with good outcomes is intelligent. Yet relative to the rate of our experience in it, the world is sometimes neither stable enough nor simple enough to make experience a good teacher (March and Olsen, 1976). The use of associational, experiential learning in complex worlds can result in superstitious learning (Lave and March, 1975). Consider, for example, the report by Tversky and Kahneman (1974) of the lessons learned by pilot trainers who experimented with rewarding pilots who make good landings and punishing pilots who make bad ones. They observe that pilots who are punished generally improve on subsequent landings, while pilots who are praised generally do worse. Thus, they learn that negative reinforcement works; positive reinforcement does not. The learning is natural, but the experience, like all experience, is confounded, in this case by ordinary regression to the mean.

These six examples of unanticipated consequences are illustrative of the variation in behavior that can be generated by elementary adaptive processes functioning under special conditions. They suggest some ways in which undramatic features of organizational life can lead to surprising organizational change.

Solution-Driven Problems

There seems to be ample evidence that when performance fails to meet aspirations, organizations search for new solutions (Cyert and March, 1963), that is, for new people, new ways of doing things, new alliances. However, changes often seem to be driven less by problems than by solutions. Daft and Becker (1978) have argued the case for educational organizations and Kay (1979) for industrial organizations; but the idea is an established one, typical of diffusion theories of change.

We can identify at least three different explanations for solution (or opportunity) driven change. In the first, organizations face a large number of problems of about equal importance, but only a few solutions. Thus, the chance of finding a solution to a particular problem is small; if one begins with a solution, however, there is a good chance that the solution will match some problem facing the organization. Consequently, an organization scans for solutions rather than problems, and matches any solution found with some relevant problem. A second explanation is that the linkage between individual solutions and individual problems is often difficult to make unambiguously. Then, almost any solution can be linked to almost any problem, provided they arise at approximately the same time (Cohen, March, and Olsen, 1972; March and Olsen, 1975). When causality and technology are ambiguous, the motivation to have particular solutions adopted is likely to be as powerful as the motivation to have particular problems solved, and many of the changes we observe will be better predicted by a knowledge of solutions than by a knowledge of problems. A third interpretation is that change is stimulated not by adversity but by success, less by a sense of problems than by a sense of competence and a belief that change is possible, natural, and appropriate (Daft and Becker, 1978). Professionals change their procedures and introduce new technologies because that is what professionals do and know how to do. An organization that is modern adopts new things because that is what being modern means. When a major stimulus for change comes from a sense of competence, problems are created in order to solve them, and solutions and opportunities stimulate awareness of previously unsalient or unnoticed problems or preferences.

Transformation of Innovations and Organizations

Students of innovation in organizations have persistently observed that both innovations and organizations tend to be transformed during the process of innovation (Browning, 1968; Brewer, 1973; Hyman, 1973). This is sometimes treated as a measurement problem. In that guise, the problem is to decide whether a change in one organization is equivalent to a change in another, or to determine when a change has been implemented sufficiently to be considered a change, or to disentangle the labeling of a change from the change itself. To treat such problems as measurement problems, however, is probably misleading. Seeing innovations as spreading unchanged through organizations helps link studies of innovation to models drawn from epidemiology; but where a fundamental feature of a change is the way it is transformed as it moves from invention to adoption to implementation to contagion, such a linkage is not helpful.

   Organizational change develops meaning through the process by which it occurs. Some parts of that process tend to standardize the multiple meanings of a change, but standardization can be very slow, in some cases so slow as to be almost undetectable. When a business firm adopts a new policy (Cyert, Dill, and March, 1958), or a university a new program (March and Romelaer, 1976), specifying what the change means can be difficult, not because of poor information or inadequate analysis, but because of the fundamental ways in which changes are transformed by the processes of change. The developing character of change makes it difficult to use standard ideas of decision, problem-solving, diffusion, and the like, because it is difficult to describe a decision, problem solution, or innovation with precision, to say when it was adopted, and to treat the process as having an ending.

Organizations are also transformed in the process. Organizations develop and redefine goals while making decisions and adapting to environmental pressures; minor changes can lead to larger ones, and initial intent can be entirely lost. For example, an organization of evangelists becomes a gym with services attached (Zald and Denton, 1963); a social movement becomes a commercial establishment (Messinger, 1955; Sills, 1957); a radical rock radio station becomes an almost respectable part of a large corporation (Krieger, 1979); and a new governmental agency becomes an old one (Selznick, 1949; Sproull, Weiner and Wolf, 1978).

These transformations seem often to reflect occasions on which actions taken by an organization (for whatever reasons) become the source of a new definition of objectives. The possibility that preferences and goals may change in response to behavior is a serious complication for rational theories of choice (March, 1972, 1978a). Organizations' goals, as well as the goals of individuals in them, change in the course of introducing deliberate innovations, or in the course of normal organizational drift. As a result, actions affect the preferences in the name of which they are taken; and the discovery of new intentions is a common consequence of intentional behavior.

Created Environments

In simple models of organizational change, it is usually assumed that action is taken in response to the environment but that the environment is not affected by organizational action. The assumptions are convenient, but organizations create their environments in part, and the resulting complications are significant. For example, organizations are frequently combined into an ecology of competition, in which the actions of one competitor become the environment of another. Each competitor, therefore, partly determines its own environment as the competitors react to each other, a situation familiar to studies of prey-predator relations and markets (Mayr, 1963; Kamien and Schwartz, 1975). Also, if we think of adaptation as learning about a fixed environment, the model is somewhat different from one in which the environment is simultaneously adapting to the organization. The situation is a common one. Parents adapt to children at the same time that children adapt to parents, and customers and suppliers adapt to each other. The outcomes are different from those observed in the case of adaptation to a stable environment, with equilibria that depend on whether the process is one of hunting or mating and on the relative rates of adaptation of the organization and the environment (Lave and March, 1975). Finally, organizations create their own environments by the way they interpret and act in a confusing world. It is not just that the world is incompletely or inaccurately perceived (Slovic, Fischhoff, and Lichtenstein, 1977; Nisbet and Ross, 1980), but also that actions taken as a result of beliefs about the environment do, in fact, construct the environment, as, for example, in self-fulfilling prophecies and the construction of limits through avoidance of them (Meyer and Rowan, 1977; Weick, 1977, 1979).

It is possible, of course, for organizations to act strategically in an environment they help create, but created environments are not ordinarily experienced in a way different from other environments. For example, the experience of learning in a situation in which the environment is simultaneously adapting to the organization is not remarkably different from the experience of learning in simpler situations. The outcomes are, however, distinctive. When environments are created, the actions taken by an organization in adapting to an environment are partly responses to previous actions by the same organization; reflected through the environment. A common result is that small signals are amplified into large ones, and the general implication is that routine adaptive processes have consequences that cannot be understood without linking them to an environment that is simultaneously, and endogenously, changing.

Individuals, Organizations, and Environments

Although it is an heroic simplification out of which theoretical mischief can come, it is possible to see an organization as the intermeshing of three systems: the individual, the organization, and the collection of organizations that can be called the environment. Many of the complications in the study of organizational change are related to the way those three systems intermesh, as is reflected in the large number of studies that discuss managing change in terms of the relations between organizations and the individuals who inhabit them (Coch and French, 1948; Burns and Stalker, 1961; Argyris, 1965), between organizations and their environment (Starbuck, 1976; Aldrich, 1979), and among organizations (Evan, 1966; Benson, 1975).

Much of classical organization theory addresses the problems of making the demands of organizations and individuals consistent (Barnard, 1938; Simon, 1947; March and Simon, 1958); the same theme is frequent in modern treatments of information (Hirschleifer and Riley, 1979) and incentives (Downs, 1967). Although it is an old problem, it continues to be interesting for the analysis of organizational change. In particular, it seems very likely that both the individuals involved in organizations and systems of organizations have different requirements for organizational change than the organization itself. For example, individual participants in an organization view their positions in the organizations, e.g., their jobs, as an important part of their milieu. They try to arrange patterns of stability and variety within the organization to meet their own desires. However, there is no particular *a priori* reason for assuming that individual desires for change and stability will be mutually consistent or will match requirements for organizational survival. Moreover, the survival of an organization is a more compelling requirement for the organization than it is for a system of organizations. Survival of the system of organizations may require organizational changes that are inappropriate for the individual organization; it may require greater organizational flexibility or rigidity than makes sense for the individual organization. The organizational failure rates that are optimal for systems of organizations are somewhat different from those that are optimal for individual organizations. Complications such as these are common in any combination of autonomous systems. They form a focus for some standard issues in contemporary population genetics (Wright, 1978), as well as extensions of those ideas into social science in general (Wilson, 1975; Hannan and Freeman, 1977). That observed systems of individuals, organizations, and environments have evolved to an equilibrium is questionable, but it is possible that some of the features of organizations that seem particularly perverse make greater sense when considered from the point of view of the larger system of organizations.

Other illustrations of complications could easily be added, including problems introduced by the ways in which humans make inferences (Nisbet and Ross, 1980), and by the ways in which organizational demography affects regeneration (Reed, 1978). Each of the complications represents either a limitation in one of the standard models or a way in which a model of adaptation can be used to illuminate organizational change under complicated or confounding conditions. Familiar activities, rules, or procedures sometimes lead to unanticipated consequences.

Foolishness, Change and Altruism

Organizations need to maintain a balance (or dialectic) between explicitly sensible processes of change (problem-solving, learning, planning) and certain elements of foolishness that are difficult to justify locally but are important to the broader system (March, 1972, 1978a; Weick, 1979). Consider, for example, a classic complication of long-range planning. As we try to anticipate the future, we will often observe that there are many possible, but extremely unlikely, future events which would dramatically change the consequences of present actions and thus the appropriate choice to be made now. Because there are so many very unlikely future events that can be imagined, and each is so improbable, we ordinarily exclude them from our more careful forecasts, though we know that some very unlikely events will certainly occur. As a result, our plans are based on a future that we know, with certainty, will not be realized. More generally, if the most favorable outcomes of a particular choice alternative depend on the occurrence of very unlikely events, the expected value of that alternative will be low, and it would not be sensible to choose it. Thus, the best alternative after the fact is unlikely to be chosen before the fact by a rational process. For similar reasons, the prior expected value of any specific innovation is likely to be negative, and organizations are likely to resist proposals for such change. Indeed, we would expect that an institution eager to adopt innovative proposals will survive less luxuriantly and for shorter periods than others. Though some unknown change is almost certainly sensible, being the first to experiment with a new idea is not likely to be worth the risk.

The problem becomes one of introducing new ideas into organizations at a rate sufficient to sustain the larger system of organizations, when such action is not intelligent for any one organization. The conventional solution for such problems involves some kind of collaboration that pools the risk (Hirschleifer and Riley, 1979). Explicit risk-sharing agreements exist, but for the most part, organizational systems have evolved a culture of implicit altruism which introduces decentralized non-rational elements into rational choice procedures rather than relying on explicit contractual arrangements. These cultural elements of manifest foolishness have latent implications for innovation and change in organizations. New ideas are sustained in an organization by mechanisms that shield them, altruistically, from the operation of normal rationality, for example, by organizational slack, managerial incentives, symbolic action, ambiguity, and loose coupling.

Slack protects individuals and groups, who pursue change for personal or professional reasons, from normal organizational controls. As a result, it has been argued that one of the ways in which organizations search when successful is through slack (Cyert and March, 1963; Wilson, 1966). Several studies of change seem to lend support to this idea (Mansfield, 1968; Staw and Szwajkowski, 1975; Manns and March, 1978); but Kay (1979) concludes that it is hard to see consistent evidence for slack search in the data on research and development expenditures. Daft and Becker (1978) suggest that slack is associated not with excess resources but with high salaries and a consequent high level of professionalism.

Since managers and other leaders are selected by a process that is generally conservative (Cohen and March, 1974), it is probably unreasonable to see them as sources of intentional foolishness. Managerial incentives seem unlikely to stimulate managerial playfulness; incentive schemes try to tie individual rewards to organizational outcomes, so that managers help themselves by helping the organization. The ideology of good management, however, associates managers with the introduction of new ideas, new organizational forms, new technologies, new products, new slogans, or new moods. Consequently, some fraction of organizational resources is dedicated to running unlikely experiments in changes as unwitting altruistic contributions to the larger world.

Choice and decision-making touch some of the more important values of modern developed cultures, and thereby become major symbolic domains in contemporary organizations. Symbolic values, including those associated with change, are important enough and pervasive enough to dominate other factors in a decision situation (Christensen, 1976; Kreiner, 1976; Feldman and March, 1981). Symbolism shades into personal motivations easily for professionals (e.g., engineers, doctors) or managers, since they express their competence and authority by the introduction of changes or symbols of changes (Daft and Becker, 1978) in a more general way, the symbolic elaboration of processes of choice becomes more important than the outcomes, and the outcomes thus reflect more foolishness than would otherwise be expected.

Organizations do not always have a well-defined set of objectives; their preferences are frequently ambiguous, imprecise, inconsistent, unstable, and affected by their choices (March, 1978a; Elster, 1979). As a result, problem-solving and decision-making assume some of the features of a garbage can process (Cohen, March, and Olsen, 1972), learning becomes confounded by the ambiguity of experience (Cohen and March, 1974; March and Olsen, 1976), and actions become particularly sensitive to the participation and attention patterns of organizational actors (Olsen, 1976). Moreover, the uncertainties associated with trying to guess future preferences increase considerably the variance in any estimates that might be made of the expected utility of present action and thus decrease the reliability of the process.

Finally, organizations are complex combinations of activities, purposes, and meanings; they accomplish coordinated tasks that would be inconceivable without them, and without which it is difficult to imagine a modern developed society. This impressive integration of formal organizations should not, however, obscure the many ways in which organizations are loosely coupled. Behavior is loosely coupled to intentions; actions in one part of the organization are loosely coupled to actions in another part; decisions today are loosely coupled to decisions tomorrow (Cohen and March, 1974; March and Olsen, 1976; Weick, 1976, 1979). Such loose coupling does not appear to be avoidable. Rather, limits on coordination, attention, and control are inherent restrictions on the implementation of rationality in organizational action.

These organizational phenomena ensure that some level of foolishness will occur within an organization, no matter how dedicated to rational coordination and control it may be. Although it is easy to argue that foolishness is a form of altruism by which systematic needs for change are met, it is much harder to assess whether the mixture of rationality and foolishness that we observe in organizations is optimal. The ideology underlying the development of decision-engineering probably under-estimates the importance of foolishness, and the ideology underlying enthusiasm for some versions of undisciplined creativity probably under-estimates the importance of systematic analysis. What is much more difficult is to determine whether a particular real system errs on the side of excessive reason or excessive foolishness. We can solve the problem of appropriate foolishness within a specific model by assuming some characteristics of the environment over the future; solving the problem in a real situation, however, is not ordinarily within our ability.

Nor is it easy to devise realistic insurance, information, or contractual schemes that will reliably ensure reaching an optimum. Not only are the difficulties in analysis substantial, but, quite aside from those problems, there is also a difficulty posed by the cultural character of the existing solution. The mix of organizational foolishness and rationality is deeply embedded in the rules, incentives, and beliefs of the society and organization. It is possible to imagine changing the mix of rules, thereby changing the level of foolishness; but it is hard to imagine being able to modify broad cultural and organizational attributes with much precision or control.

Discussion

The five footnotes to organizational change suggested at the outset are comments on change, not a theory of change. Nevertheless, they may have some implications for organizational leadership and for research on adaptation in organizations. The general perspective depends on the proposition that the basic processes by which organizations act, respond to their environments, and learn are quite stable, and possibly comprehensible. These stable processes of change, however, produce a great variety of action and their outcomes are sometimes surprisingly sensitive to the details of the context in which they occur.

A view of change as resulting from stable processes realized in a highly contextual and sometimes confusing world emphasizes the idea that things happen in organizations because most of the time organizational participants respond in elementary ways to the environment, including that part of the environment that might be called management or leadership. Managers and leaders propose changes, including foolish ones; they try to cope with the environment and to control it; they respond to other members of the organization; they issue orders and manipulate incentives. Since they play conventional roles, organizational leaders are not likely to behave in strikingly unusual ways. And if a leader tries to march toward strange destinations, an organization is likely to deflect the effort. Simply to describe leadership as conventional and constrained by organizational realities, however, is to risk misunderstanding its importance. Neither success nor change requires dramatic action. The conventional, routine activities that produce most organizational change require ordinary people to do ordinary things in a competent way (March, 1978b). Moreover, within some broad constraints, the adaptiveness of organizations can be managed. Typically, it is not possible to lead an organization in any arbitrary direction that might be desired, but it is possible to influence the course of events by managing the process of change, and particularly by stimulating or inhibiting predictable complications and anomalous dynamics.

Such a view of managing organizations assumes that the effectiveness of leadership often depends on being able to time small interventions so that the force of natural organizational processes amplifies the interventions. It is possible to identify a few minor rules for such actions (Cohen and March, 1974), but a comprehensive development of managerial strategies (as well as of effective strategies for frustrating managers) requires a more thorough understanding of change in organizations, not a theory of how to introduce any arbitrary change, but a theory of how to direct somewhat the conventional ways in which an organization responds to its environment, experiences, and anticipations. The footnotes to change elaborated in this paper are much too fragmentary for such a task, but they indicate a possible way of understanding change. They argue for considering the fundamental adaptive processes by which change occurs, in terms of broader theoretical ideas about organizational action. They direct attention particularly to how substantial changes occur, as the routine consequence of standard procedures or as the unintended consequence of ordinary adaptation. And they suggest that understanding organizational change requires discovering the connections between the apparently prosaic and the apparently poetic in organizational life.

References

Aldrich, Howard E. (1979) *Organizations and Environments*. Englewood Cliffs, NJ: Prentice-Hall.
Argyris, Chris (1965) *Organization and Innovation*. Homewood, IL: Irwin-Dorsey.
Attewell, Paul, and Dean R. Gerstein (1979) Government policy and local practice. *American Sociological Review*, 44: 311–27.

Bardach, Eugene (1977) *The Implementation Game.* Cambridge, MA: MIT Press.

Barnard, Chester I. (1938) *Functions of the Executive.* Cambridge, MA: Harvard University Press.

Benson, J. Kenneth (1975) The interorganizational network as political economy. *Administrative Science Quarterly* 20: 229-49.

Brewer, Garry D. (1973) *Politicians, Bureaucrats and the Consultant: A Critique of Urban Problem Solving.* New York: Basic Books.

Browning, Rufus P. (1968) Innovation and non-innovation decision processes in governmental budgeting. In Robert T. Golembiewski (ed.), *Public Budgeting and Finance*, pp. 128-45. Itasca, IL: F. E. Peacock.

Burns, Tom, and G. M. Stalker (1961) *The Management of Innovation.* London: Tavistock.

Christensen, Søren (1976) Decision making and socialization. In James G. March and Johan P. Olsen (eds), *Ambiguity and Choice in Organizations*, pp. 351-85. Bergen, Norway: Universitetsforlaget.

Coch, Lester, and John R. P. French, Jr (1948) Overcoming resistance to change. *Human Relations*, 1: 512-32.

Cohen, Michael D., and James G. March (1974) *Leadership and Ambiguity: The American College President.* New York: McGraw-Hill.

Cohen, Michael D., James G. March, and Johan P. Olsen (1972) A garbage can model of organizational choice. *Administrative Science Quarterly*, 17: 1-25.

Crozier, Michel (1979) *On ne Change pas la Société par Décret.* Paris: Grasset.

Cyert, Richard M., William Dill, and James G. March (1958) The role of expectations in business decision making. *Administrative Science Quarterly*, 3: 307-40.

Cyert, Richard M., and James G. March (1963) *A Behavioral Theory of the Firm.* Englewood Cliffs, NJ: Prentice-Hall.

Daft, Richard L., and Selwyn W. Becker, (1978) *The Innovative Organization.* New York: Elsevier.

Day, R. H., and T. Groves (eds) (1975) *Adaptive Economic Models.* New York: Academic Press.

Downs, Anthony (1967) *Inside Bureaucracy*, Boston: Little, Brown.

Elster, Jon (1979) *Ulysses and the Sirens.* Cambridge: Cambridge University Press.

Evan, William M. (1966) The organization set: Toward a theory of interorganizational relations. In James D. Thompson (ed.), *Approaches to Organizational Design*, pp. 173-91. Pittsburgh: University of Pittsburgh Press.

Feldman, Martha S., and James G. March (1981) Information in organizations as signal and symbol. *Administrative Science Quarterly*, 26: 171-86.

Gamson, William A. (1968) *Power and Discontent.* Homewood, IL: Dorsey.

Gross, Neal, Joseph B. Giaquinta, and Marilyn Bernstein (1971) *Implementing Organizational Innovations: A Sociological Analysis of Planned Educational Change.* New York: Basic Books.

Hannan, Michael T., and John Freeman (1977) The population ecology of organizations. *American Journal of Sociology*, 82: 929-66.

Hedberg, Bo L. T., Paul C. Nystrom, and William H. Starbuck (1976) Camping on seesaws: Prescriptions for a self-designing organization. *Administrative Science Quarterly*, 21: 41-65.

Hermann, Charles F. (1963) Some consequences of crisis which limit the viability of organizations. *Administrative Science Quarterly* 8: 61–82.

Hirschleifer, J., and John G. Riley (1979) The analytics of uncertainty and information – An expository survey. *Journal of Economic Literature*. 17: 1375–421.

Hirschman, Albert O. (1979) *Exit, Voice, and Loyalty*. Cambridge, MA: Harvard University Press.

Hyman, Herbert H. (ed.) (1973) *The Politics of Health Care: Nine Case Studies of Innovative Planning in New York City*. New York: Praeger.

Kamien, Morton I., and Nancy L. Schwartz (1975) Market structure and innovation: A survey. *Journal of Economic Literature*. 13: 1–37.

Kay, Neil M. (1979) *The Innovating Firm: A Behavioral Theory of Corporate R & D*. New York: St Martin's.

Kreiner, Kristian (1976) Ideology and management in a garbage can situation. In James G. March and Johan P. Olsen (eds), *Ambiguity and Choice in Organizations:* 156–73. Bergen, Norway: Universitetsforlaget.

Krieger, Susan (1979) *Hip Capitalism*. Beverly Hills, CA: Sage.

Lave, Charles A., and James G. March (1975) *An Introduction to Models in the Social Sciences*. New York: Harper and Row.

Lindblom, Charles E. (1958) The science of muddling through. *Public Administration Review*, 19: 79–88.

Manns, Curtis L., and James G. March (1978) Financial adversity, internal competition, and curriculum change in a university. *Administrative Science Quarterly*, 23: 541–52.

Mansfield, Edwin (1968) *The Economics of Technological Change*. New York: Norton.

March, James G. (1962) The business firm as a political coalition. *Journal of Politics*, 24: 662–78.

March, James G. (1972) Model bias in social action. *Review of Educational Research*. 42: 413–29.

March, James G. (1978a) Bounded rationality, ambiguity, and the engineering of choice. *Bell Journal of Economics*, 9: 587–608.

March, James G. (1978b) American public school administration: A short analysis. *School Review*, 86: 217–50.

March, James G., and Johan P. Olsen (1975) The uncertainty of the past: Organizational learning under ambiguity. *European Journal of Political Research*. 3: 147–71.

March, James G., and Johan P. Olsen (1976) *Ambiguity and Choice in Organizations*. Bergen, Norway: Universitetsforlaget.

March, James G., and Pierre J. Romelaer (1976) Position and presence in the drift of decisions. In James G. March and Johan P. Olsen (eds), *Ambiguity and Choice in Organizations*, pp. 251–76. Bergen, Norway: Universitetsforlaget.

March, James G., and Herbert A. Simon (1958) *Organizations*. New York: Wiley.

Mayhew, Lewis B. (1979) *Surviving the Eighties*. San Francisco: Jossey-Bass.

Mayr, Ernst (1963) *Population, Species, and Evolution*. Cambridge, MA: Harvard University Press.

McNeil, Kenneth, and James D. Thompson (1971) The regeneration of social organizations. *American Sociological Review*, 36: 624-37.

Messinger, Sheldon L. (1955) Organizational transformation: A case study of a declining social movement. *American Sociological Review*, 20: 3-10.

Meyer, John W., and Brian Rowan (1977) Institutionalized organizations: Formal structure as myth and ceremony. *American Journal of Sociology*, 83: 340-60.

Nelson, Richard R., and Sidney G. Winter (1974) Neoclassical vs. evolutionary theories of economic growth: Critique and prospectus. *Economic Journal*, 84: 886-905.

Nelson, Richard R., and Douglas Yates, (eds) (1978) *Innovation and Implementation in Public Organizations*. Lexington, MA: D. C. Heath.

Nisbet, Richard, and Lee Ross (1980) *Human Inference: Strategies and Shortcomings of Social Judgment*. Englewood Cliffs, NJ: Prentice-Hall.

Olsen, Johan P. (1976) Reorganization as a garbage can. In James G. March and Johan P. Olsen (eds), *Ambiguity and Choice in Organizations*, pp. 314-37. Bergen, Norway: Universitetsforlaget.

Pfeffer, Jeffrey (1981) *Power in Organizations*. Marshfield, MA: Pitman.

Pressman, Jeffrey, and Aaron Wildavsky (1973) *Implementation*. Berkeley, CA: University of California Press.

Reed, Theodore L. (1978) Organizational change in the American foreign service, 1925-1965: The utility of cohort analysis. *American Sociological Review*, 43: 404-21.

Rogers, Everett M. (1962) *Diffusion of Innovations*. New York: Free Press.

Rogers, Everett M., and F. Floyd Shoemaker (1971) *Communication of Innovations*. New York: Free Press.

Schelling, Thomas C. (1978) *Micromotives and Macrobehavior*. New York: Norton.

Selznick, Philip (1949) *TVA and the Grass Roots*. Berkeley, CA: University of California Press.

Sills, David L. (1957) *The Volunteers*. New York: Free Press.

Simon, Herbert A. (1947) *Administrative Behavior*. New York: Macmillan.

Slovic, Paul, Bernard Fischhoff, and Sarah Lichtenstein (1977) Behavioral decision theory. *Annual Review of Psychology*, 28: 1-39.

Sproull, Lee S., Stephen S. Weiner, and David Wolf (1978) *Organizing an Anarchy*. Chicago: University of Chicago Press.

Starbuck, William H. (1976) Organizations and their environments. In Marvin D. Dunnette (ed.), *Handbook of Industrial and Organizational Psychology*: 1069-124. Chicago: Rand McNally.

Staw, Barry M., and Eugene Szwajkowski (1975) The scarcity–munificence component of organizational environments and the commission of illegal acts. *Administrative Science Quarterly*, 20: 345-54.

Stinchcombe, Arthur L., Mary Sexton McDill, and Dollie R. Walker (1968) Demography of organizations. *American Journal of Sociology*, 74: 221-29.

Tversky, Amos, and Daniel Kahneman (1974) Judgment under uncertainty: Heuristics and biases. *Science*. 185: 1124-131.

Walker, Jack L. (1969) The diffusion of innovations among the American states. *American Political Science Review*, 63: 880-99.

Weick, Karl E. (1976) Educational organizations as loosely-coupled systems. *Administrative Science Quarterly*, 21: 1–19.

Weick, Karl E. (1977) Enactment processes in organizations. In Barry M. Staw and Gerald R. Salancik (eds), *New Directions in Organizational Behavior*. 267–300. Chicago: St Clair.

Weick, Karl E. (1979) *The Social psychology of Organizing*, 2nd edn, Reading, MA: Addison-Wesley.

Weiner, Stephen S. (1976) Participation, deadlines and choice. In James G. March and Johan P. Olsen (eds). *Ambiguity and Choice in Organizations*; pp. 225–50. Bergen, Norway: Universitetsforlaget.

White, Harison C. (1970) *Chains of Opportunity: System Models of Mobility in Organizations*. Cambridge, MA: Harvard University Press.

Wilson, Edward O. (1975) *Sociobiology: The New Synthesis*. Cambridge, MA: Harvard University Press.

Wilson, James Q. (1966) Innovation in organizations: Notes toward a theory. In James D. Thompson (ed.) *Approaches to Organizational Design*; 193–218. Pittsburgh: University of Pittsburgh Press.

Wright, Sewall (1978) *Evolution and Genetics of Populations*, vol. 4. Chicago: University of Chicago Press.

Zald, Mayer N., and Patricia Denton (1963) From evangelism to general service: The transformation of the YMCA. *Administrative Science Quarterly*, 8: 214–234.

9

A Model of Adaptive Organizational Search

Daniel Levinthal and James G. March

Abstract

A model of organizational change through adaptive search for new technologies is developed and explored. The model is in the tradition of behavioral models of organizational choice and learning associated with work by Winter, Nelson, and Radner. It permits the exploration of simultaneous organizational adaptation in search strategies, competences, and aspirations under conditions of environmental instability and ambiguity. The model exhibits the extent to which variation in organizational behavior and performance reflect the distributional consequences of simple adaptation in ambiguous environments, as well as some adverse consequences of rapid learning.

Adaptive Search and Technological Change

In this paper, we present a model of adaptive search and technological change. By technology we mean any semi-stable specification of the way in which an organization deals with its environment, functions and prospers. Thus, it may be a production function, as in theories of the firm; it may be a normative structure, as in some theories of professional service organizations; it may be a constituency structure, as in some theories of political organizations. Our analysis is in the tradition of previous work

This paper was first published in the Journal of Economic Behavior and Organization 2 (1981), pp. 307–33. The research has been supported by grants from the Spencer Foundation, the National Institute of Education, the Hoover Institution, and the Stanford Graduate School of Business. The authors are grateful for comments by Julia Ball, Michael D. Cohen, Scott Herriott, John F. Padgett, Allyn Romanow, Harrison White, and Sidney Winter.

by Winter (1971), Radner (1975), and Nelson and Winter (1978). It is intended as an elaboration of their ideas, with some variations on the theme.

The model focuses on the search for new technologies through refinement and innovation, on the uncertain outcomes of that search, and on organizational learning as a result of experience in developing and implementing new technologies. It does not consider the effects of competition, imitation, or other interaction among organizations. It explores some ways simple adaptation might lead to organizational change, and how that process might be complicated by the confusions of a changing and autonomous environment and by the interrelation of different adaptive processes. The basic speculation (quite possibly wrong) is that significant elements of variation in organizational histories reflect the distributional characteristics of simple adaptation in ambiguous environments, rather than the results of fundamentally different processes or even significantly different environmental conditions. The model considers effects due primarily to interactions among five features of organizational life that have been observed in behavioral studies of decision-making.

1 The inclination of organizations to distinguish between success and failure, thus between slack times and harsh times, in allocating resources to innovation and refinement.
2 The tendency for organizations to modify search strategies on the basis of apparent experience with them.
3 The increase of organizational competence through experience, thus the effect of experience on the relative efficiency of alternative search strategies.
4 The adaptation of aspirations to performance and the consequent change in definitions of subjective success and failure.
5 The tendency for experience to be confounded by random fluctuations, systematic exogenous effects, and uncontrolled environmental change.

We assume the success of an organization depends partly on its technology. The connection may be partly obscured by many other factors, and causal inferences about the relation between technological change and improvement in performance may be difficult to make with assurance; but technology affects success. We treat research and development or other forms of search as equivalent to drawing from a distribution of search outcomes (in the form of possible technological opportunities). The number of draws is a function of the size of the expenditure on search and its efficiency; the expected result of a draw is a function of the distribution of technological opportunities associated with a particular mode of search and a particular technology. In the absence of learning, the optimization problem is straightforward as long as information is available on costs, the distribution of opportunities, and the way in which opportunities are sampled through search. The interest here, however, is not in solving the optimization problem. Though we examine the efficacy of learning in finding optimal solutions in simple situations, our primary intention is to model the behavior of organizations as they make decisions and learn about their search expenditures. We describe decision-making as a result of experiential learning, that is, as a consequence of an organization's successes and failures in meeting performance targets, of search expenditures made and their outcomes, and of the (sometimes mistaken) inferences made from experience.

Organizational experience leads to three distinct kinds of learning in such a situation. The first is adaptation of search *strategies*. Organizations attempt to modify their propensities to search for new technologies, as well as propensities to direct that search toward refinement or innovation, on the basis of experience. Second, organizations improve their search *competences*. The greater the experience in looking for refinement (or innovation) in a technology, the greater the efficiency in discovering them. Finally, organizations adapt their *aspirations*. They learn what to hope for. Discussions of organizational learning with respect to strategies (March and Olsen, 1976), competences (Alchian, 1959; Preston and Keachie, 1964), and aspirations (Cyert and March, 1963) are familiar. The present model extends those efforts to a consideration of some consequences of their interrelations.

In the spirit of behavioral studies of decision-making, we assume organizations both react to their environments in terms of existing rules and, at the same time, modify the rules. The first-order responses to experience are what Cyert and March (1963) called 'problemistic search' and what Steinbruner (1974) characterized as 'cybernetic'. The ideas are usually associated with Simon (1957) and others (March and Simon, 1958; Lindblom, 1959; Cyert and March, 1963; Allison, 1971; Kay, 1979). The organization is assumed to have a performance target (goal) against which it compares actual achievement. If the target exceeds performance, an organization searches for solutions to the problem. That search emphasizes relatively immediate refinements in the existing technology, greater efficiency, and discoveries in the near neighborhood of the present activities. Depending on the pool of opportunities for small changes in present behavior, search for technological refinements generates new actions that reduce, or eliminate, the discrepancy between target and performance.

If, on the other hand, performance exceeds the target, organizational slack accumulates. Slack is the difference between the potential performance of an organization and the performance actually achieved.

It represents various ways in which resources and energy that might have been devoted to pursuing organizational goals have been channeled into other things. It includes such manifest inefficiencies as over-designed equipment, over-qualified personnel, undiscovered improvements in current technology, and relaxed managerial control procedures. Although it is not ordinarily justified in such terms, organizational slack contributes to organizational adaptation in two similar ways. First, it conserves the pool of unexploited refinements in a technology. By failing to discover a refinement today, an organization maintains an inventory of possible refinements as a buffer against future uncontrolled exogenous adversity. Second, it allows 'irresponsible' search (slack search). By relaxing organizational controls, slack encourages search activities that cannot be justified in terms of their expected return for the organization. They are initiated because of their attractiveness to some individuals or subunits, and tolerated because of the organization's current success in achieving targets.

Some fraction of these slack search activities results (essentially for-tuitously) in discoveries of value to parts of the organization other than the original subunit involved. The prototypes are the pet projects of playful engineers, but the phenomenon extends to a wide variety of substantially foolish investments and activities with negative expected values from the point of view of the organization. Organizational slack may, therefore, be sensible under some circumstances (Knight, 1967; Keen, 1977). It is certainly possible that organizational procedures leading to slack have evolved in a mix of environments that encourages their endurance (Winter, 1975; Hannan and Freeman, 1977). For our purposes, however, slack exists simply as a characteristic of organizational behavior that has been widely observed.

First-order responses are rapid and match standard operating procedures to environmental signals. Second-order responses are slower. They involve changes in performance targets, technological opportunities, search behavior, and knowledge about opportunities. These changes occur in response to organizational actions taken and (possibly misleading) information received on their consequences. Aspirations adapt to actual performance. Organizations learn what is reasonable to expect by observing what they achieve. Typically, however, such adaptation takes time (and, of course, performance also changes simultaneously). Opportunities adapt to search and discoveries. A technological pool can become depleted by ordinary refinements; alternatively, it can be enriched by new innovations. Search behavior adapts through trial and error. Behavior that is associated with success tends to be repeated; behavior that is associated with failure tends not to be repeated. At the same time, the values of alternatives are clarified by implementing them and experiencing their consequences.

These elementary forms of learning occur in a world in which it is possible for experience to be misleading. If a stable environment associates particular performance outcomes with particular organizational actions, experiential learning can be an efficient mechanism for discovering intelligent rules for behavior. However, organizations often appear to be trying to learn in somewhat more confusing environments (March and Olsen, 1976). We wish to examine the consequences of adaptive search behavior in situations in which outcomes are affected by both random fluctuations and systematic exogenous effects, and where the rate of change in environmental conditions exceeds the adaptation rate. It is easy to show that basically sensible learning can lead to superstitious belief under such conditions (Cohen and March, 1974; Lave and March, 1975). Thus, we consider the impacts of systematic exogenous changes and environmental uncertainty on organizational learning when search strategies, search competences, and aspirations for performance outcomes are all simultaneously adapting to experience.

A Model

We assume that an organization sets a performance target, G_t, for each time period and modifies that target on the basis of performance experience. If P_t is an organization's performance in period t:

$$G_t = b_1 P_{t-1} + (1 - b_1) G_{t-1}. \tag{1}$$

As a result, the target is an exponentially weighted moving average of past performance.

Organizational learning is driven by the relationship between G_t and P_t, and thus by variations in both. We assume that the organization's performance in period t depends on the state of its technology at time t, $T_{*,t}$, the costs of search that it has undertaken, and an exogenous and randomly varying environmental variable, a_t. Specifically,

$$P_t = (1 + a_t) T_{*,t} - R_t - I_t, \tag{2}$$

where R_t and I_t are the levels of expenditure on the two types of search processes considered, refinement search and innovation search. By refinement we mean the fine-tuning and economizing designed to improve the efficiency of an existing technology. The second kind of search is technological innovation, finding a new improved technology. The distinctions are taken from Radner (1975) and are similar to those made by Knight (1967) and Nelson and Winter (1978).

The technology in period t, $T_{*,t}$, depends on the technology of the previous period and the realized outcomes of search. If we ignore the complications in forecasting the consequences of technologies before they are implemented, $T_{*,t}$ is the maximum of the technological outcomes from two search processes (the search for refinement and the search for innovation), and the (possibly changed) technology of the previous period. That is, it is assumed that existing technology changes by a constant factor, b_2. It is possible for technology to decay (i.e., $b_2 < 1$), remain constant (i.e., $b_2 = 1$), or improve (i.e., $b_2 > 1$) in the absence of search. Thus,

$$T_{*,t} = \max\ (T_{r,t}, T_{i,t}, b_2 T_{*,t-1}), \tag{3}$$

where $T_{r,t}$ is the value of the best technology discovered through refinement search during period t, and $T_{i,t}$ is the value of the best technology discovered through innovation search during period t. If the consequences of technological changes are subject to error, $T_{*,t}$ is the true value of the technology that appeared best, according to estimates at the time of decision.

Organizations are assumed to search by sampling some number of opportunities and to implement the best of those, provided it is believed to be better than the existing technology. The outcomes from search are a joint consequence of the sample size, the current technology, and the distributions of possible technologies. Assuming errors of estimation are unbiased, the technology expected as a result of search is better than the expected value of the pool of opportunities; and an increase in the variance of the distribution in the pool increases the expected improvement in technology to be realized from search (Kohn and Shavell, 1974).

The distributions of technological opportunities are assumed to be different for the two kinds of search. In the case of refinement, it is assumed that the distribution of opportunities is a normal distribution of changes from $b_2 T_{*,t-1}$ with a mean $= 0$, and a standard deviation, $V_{r,t}$, which declines with search until a new technology is invented and adopted (at time y). The initial standard deviation for a newly innovated technology is proportional to the value of the technology when adopted. Thus,

$$V_{r,y} = c_1 T_{*,y}, \text{ and} \tag{4}$$

$$V_{r,t+1} = c_2 V_{r,t} \text{ (if a refinement draw was made in period } t). \tag{5}$$

In the case of search for innovation, it is assumed that opportunities are distributed as a log normal distribution of changes from $b_2 T_{*,t-1}$ with a mean $= 0$, and a fixed standard deviation V_t, proportional to the value of the current (unrefined) technology. Thus,

$$V_t = c_3 T_{*,y}, \tag{6}$$

The value of a refinement or innovation discovered by search is assumed to be known with certainty once it is implemented. However, the values of unimplemented technological modifications may be known only up to some error. As a result, it is possible for search to result in technological decline rather than improvement even though choices of the best apparent technology are made; and it is possible for an organization to learn not to search because of estimation errors and thereby reduce the experience in search that would make search more useful. We assume that estimation errors are distributed normally with mean zero and a standard deviation that is initially greater in the case of innovation ($V_{e,i,t}$) than in the case of refinement ($V_{e,r,t}$). The standard deviation for errors for each kind of search declines with experience in implementing new technological change. Note that even though errors of estimation are assumed to be unbiased, the errors observed with respect to implemented technologies will more commonly be overestimates than underestimates, and that increasing the variance of (unbiased) errors decreases the expected real improvements to be realized from search.

We assume an organization affects its performance by changing search expenditures. Returns to search are assumed to depend on the size of current expenditures, current efficiencies in search, and current technological opportunities. We imagine that search consists of sampling opportunities from the pool of technological possibilities associated with either refinement or innovation. Each draw results in the 'discovery' of some opportunity. Many of these will be less attractive than the present technology; some may be more attractive. Thus the likelihood of discovering technological improvements depends on the sample size. We assume the sample size for each of the two kinds of search is proportional to the product of the current expenditure on search and current search efficiency. Thus, if we let $E_{r,t}$ be the efficiency in refinement search at time t and $E_{i,t}$ be the efficiency in innovation search, the sample sizes for refinement, $K_{r,t}$, and innovation, $K_{i,t}$, are given by the integer values of

$$K_{r,t} = k_r R_t E_{r,t}, \tag{7}$$

and

$$K_{i,t} = k_i I_t E_{i,t}, \tag{8}$$

We assume that efficiency in search increases with increasing search within a given technology, but at a decreasing rate. The carry-over of efficiency from the previous technology is proportional to the difference between the two technologies. Let

$$F_{d,t} = F_{d,y-1}(T_{*,y-1}/T_{*,y}) + \sum_{j=y}^{t-1} K_{d,j} \text{ if } T_{*,y-1} \leq T_{*,y}, \qquad (9)$$

and

$$F_{d,t} = F_{d,y-1}(T_{*,y}/T_{*,y-1}) + \sum_{j=y}^{t-1} K_{d,j} \text{ if } T_{*,y-1} > T_{*,y},$$

where y is the time period of the last adopted innovation, and d represents the particular mode of search (refinement or innovation). Then

$$E_{d,t} = (F_{d,t})^{1/wd}. \qquad (10)$$

Note that the efficiency of search is not affected by b_2, the exogenous change in technology, and that the cost of a sample declines with experience in the standard learning curve way (log linear in total sampling to date), except that each innovation of a new technology discounts prior experience.

We assume that the pools of resources available to the two kinds of search are different. The organization is assumed to have a (changing) propensity to search, $S_{s,t}$. This propensity establishes the fraction of apparent organizational resources that are available for search activities at times $t, U_{s,t}$. Thus,

$$\begin{aligned} U_{s,t} &= S_{s,t}(P_{t-1} + R_{t-1} + I_{t-1}) \\ &= S_{s,t}[(1 + a_{t-1}) T_{*,t-1}]. \end{aligned} \qquad (11)$$

The pool of resources available to innovation search and refinement search depends on, but does not equal, $U_{s,t}$. This partial decoupling of the investment budget and the allocation of resources to specific projects has been noted by several authors (Allen, 1970; Reeves, 1958). We assume that the primary source of resources for innovation, $U_{i,t}$, is organizational slack. That is, the model reflects a tendency for organizations to support search for innovation from 'excess' resources and to contract such search when resources are apparently short, and for successful firms to make more radical product and process innovations than unsuccessful firms (Mansfield, 1963). If the organization has been successful in meeting its performance goal in the previous time period, a relatively large pool of organizational resources is potentially available. If the goal has not been reached, the pool of resources potentially available is curtailed. Conversely, resources available for refinement, $U_{r,t}$, are greater after a failure to reach the performance goal than they are after success. Thus, if the performance goal was achieved:

$$U_{i,t} = U_{s,t}, \text{ and} \tag{12}$$

$$U_{r,t} = (U_{s,t})^{1/h_r}, \text{ where } h_r \geq 1. \tag{13}$$

If the performance goal was not achieved:

$$U_{r,t} = U_{s,t}, \text{ and} \tag{14}$$

$$U_{i,t} = (U_{s,t})^{1/h_i}, \text{ where } h_i \geq 1. \tag{15}$$

These resources are available for allocation in each time period. We assume that organizations adapt their actual search expenditures to their (possibly confusing) experiences in the following way. First, they observe the apparent relation between changes in search expenditures and changes in performance. Then they adjust their search propensity, an index of intention to allocate resources to search, in a direction that appears to be suggested by a simple consideration of the results. Thus, if search increased and targets subsequently were achieved, then search propensity increases; if search increased and targets subsequently were not achieved, then search propensity decreases; if search decreased and targets subsequently were achieved, then search propensity decreases; if search decreased and targets subsequently were not achieved, then search propensity increases.

The general propensity to devote resources to search of either type, $S_{s,t}$, the search propensity for refinement, $S_{r,t}$, and the search propensity for innovation, $S_{i,t}$, are numbers between 0 and 1. They are determined in the following way:

$$S_{r,t} = Q_{r,t}b_3 + S_{r,t-1}(1 - b_3), \tag{16}$$

$$S_{i,t} = Q_{i,t}b_4 + S_{i,t-1}(1 - b_4), \tag{17}$$

$$S_{s,t} = Q_{s,t}b_5 + S_{s,t-1}(1 - b_5). \tag{18}$$

Each Q is assigned a value of one or zero that reflects previous changes in search and subsequent experience (see above). For example, if refinement search increased in the previous period and the performance target was subsequently achieved, or if refinement search decreased and the target was not achieved, then $Q_{r,t}$ is assigned a value of one. The learning rates, b_3, b_4, b_5, are here treated as constants.

By applying the propensities to the resources available, we can specify the amount of search expenditure in period t. The effect of the general propensity to search $S_{s,t}$, has already been specified in defining $U_{s,t}$ above. Thus,

$$R_t = S_{r,t} U_{r,t},\tag{19}$$

$$I_t = S_{i,t} U_{i,t}.\tag{20}$$

These expenditures determine, stochastically, the outcomes and subsequent adaptation of the organization to its experience.

Some Results

The model generates a time series of decisions, results, and goals, the details of which depend on a number of initial conditions and parameters, as well as on stochastic variation. Table 9.1 displays one particular time series based on one specific set of parameters.[1] Repeated replication with any particular set of parameters produces a distribution of organizational histories. Although significant variation across replications with identical parameters is a distinctive feature of the model, the history in table 9.1 is typical in the sense that it is not conspicuously distinguishable from many others. In the remainder of this section we identify four general characteristics of the model derived from inspecting such histories.

Sensibility

We speculate that some interesting features of organizational learning result from an interaction between a sensible learning process and a confusing world. The present model exhibits both some properties of sensibility and some limitations imposed on sensibility by ambiguity and uncertainty. An elementary indication of sensibility in the model is the tendency for organizations to improve their performance over time. We observe a pattern of modest improvement with small oscillations for most organizations, and spectacular improvement for some. Figure 9.1 displays a 20-period record of the average performance of the model.

Since it is possible that improvement in performance is due more to properties of the search environment than to the learning process, we explore the sensibility of the process further by comparing learned propensities to invest, refine, and innovate with apparent optima for those propensities. By apparent optima we mean values for the three propensities that would result in maximum return if they were held fixed. The definition of maximum return is, however, ambiguous. In general, if we wish to

---

1 The initial conditions and parameter values are given in the program listing in the Appendix (lines 1140–570). Unless otherwise noted, these values are used in all results reported here.

Table 9.1 A 20-period sample of output from the model

Period	Propensities			Expenditures		Outcome	Technology	Performance	Success
	r	i	s	ref	inn				
1	0.45	0.45	0.45	7	10	innovate	51	33	failure
2	0.40	0.40	0.50	10	7	innovate	59	41	success
3	0.46	0.36	0.55	11	11	refine	60	39	success
4	0.51	0.42	0.59	13	16	refine	60	33	failure
5	0.46	0.38	0.53	15	9	refine	61	34	failure
6	0.41	0.44	0.58	14	11	refine	63	37	failure
7	0.47	0.40	0.52	15	9	refine	63	35	failure
8	0.42	0.46	0.57	15	11	refine	64	40	success
9	0.38	0.51	0.61	11	21	refine	65	34	failure
10	0.44	0.46	0.55	16	12	refine	65	35	failure
11	0.40	0.51	0.59	15	14	refine	65	37	failure
12	0.46	0.46	0.53	16	12	refine	66	36	failure
13	0.41	0.51	0.58	15	14	refine	67	38	success
14	0.37	0.56	0.62	11	24	refine	67	28	failure
15	0.43	0.51	0.56	15	13	refine	67	39	success
16	0.49	0.45	0.50	12	16	refine	68	37	success
17	0.44	0.51	0.45	9	15	refine	69	41	success
18	0.39	0.46	0.41	8	12	refine	69	50	success
19	0.35	0.41	0.37	7	11	refine	69	49	success
20	0.32	0.37	0.33	5	8	refine	69	55	success

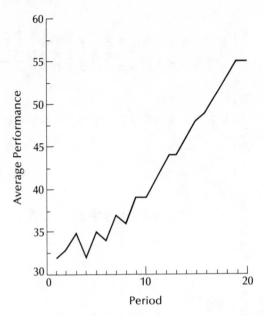

Figure 9.1. Average performance over time, 100 organizations

maximize expected value over the next n periods, the optimal value for the search propensities is either 0 or 1, depending on the value of n. For relatively short time horizons, it is best not to spend any resources on search; for relatively long time horizons it is best to spend as much as possible. Figure 9.2 shows average nth-period performance for various fixed propensities to invest and various time horizons for a particular set of parameters. Other parameters would change the specific results but not the general picture.

The model does not, in general, result in the extreme values for search propensities indicated by the previous analysis. Search propensitites near 1 are quite unusual. Propensities near zero are adopted frequently by organizations with very rapid propensity learning rates, but not by others. There is a tendency for most organizations to learn to set search propensities at a fairly low level, in the range of 0.1 to 0.4. This might be interpreted as an implicit setting of a short planning horizon, but the behavior stems from the learning process rather than any explicit calculation and suggests that the learning environment may not guarantee the development of optimal search propensities when the optimum propensity is 1. At the same time, it should be noted that large search propensities are associated with large variation in performance across runs of the model. The results for the propensity to search are shown in figure 9.3. Thus, if the criterion for maximum performance were to involve considerations of risk, the optimal propensity for large values of n might differ from 1.

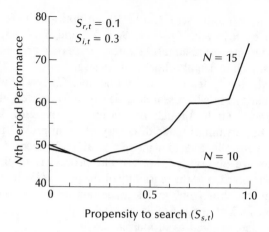

Figure 9.2. *N*th-period average performance as a function of propensity to search, 100 organizations

In order to examine the outcome of the model in a situation having a relatively clear optimum other than 0 or 1, the reward for refinement and innovation search can be set at some fixed number with no variance. Even under these circumstances, determination of the optimum propensities is a non-trivial problem. The mean of the reward from refinement search decays with refinement draws, thereby mitigating the desirability of refinement search; but the efficiency of search declines with each new innovation, so complete reliance on innovation search is not optimal. However, by searching the propensity space in increments of 0.1, we can approximate an optimum. If the mean reward for refinement and the mean

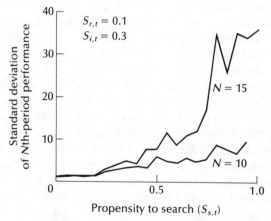

Figure 9.3. Standard deviation of *n*th-period performance as a function of propensity to search, 100 organizations

reward for innovation are set equal to 10, an optimum is found in the neighborhood of $S_{r,t}=0.2$, $S_{i,t}=0.3$, $S_{s,t}=0.3$ and $S_{r,t}=0.3$, $S_{i,t}=0.4$, $S_{s,t}=0.2$. Under modest adaptation rates for search propensities, the model reaches such a neighborhood, on average.

In general, the model learns in a way that does fairly well with strong signals. In situations in which search is clearly unwarranted, it generally learns to reduce search, though ordinarily not to zero. Where the technological opportunities make discovery of an improved technology likely, learning generally leads to higher propensities. Numerous exceptions to such results are observed, however. The process is sensitive to the learning rates involved, and the sensibility of the process is often obscured, particularly in the short run, by the uncertainties of evaluating technologies, by the limited number of draws, and by the fact that expenditure is affected by slack as well as propensities.

Success

The model leads to subjectively successful organizations. Despite the way goals adjust to performance as it improves, thus discounting past levels of performance in assessing current success, most organizations in stable environments are successful in their own terms most of the time. Table 9.2 shows the percentage of the time periods that the model achieves subjective success as a function of environmental uncertainty and exogenous changes in the technology. In cases where there is no uncertainty, and no exogenous change in the technology, goals are achieved about 93 per cent of the time. The precise fraction for any particular run depends, of course, on stochastic variation within the model and as we note below, on learning rates.

The tendency of the model to produce successful organizations under conditions of steady or improving environments has consequences for expenditures and learning. Period to period variations in resources allocated to innovation and refinement are generally due more to the amount of resources available and whether they are seen as slack resources (i.e, whether the organization has been successful in its own terms) than to the search propensities associated with the two. Short-run changes in resource allocation are, that is, less responsive to learning than to organizational success and failure. Thus, they both obscure the significance of adaptive propensities and provide the perturbations of decisions on which learning depends. The magnitude of the slack effect depends on the values of h_r and h_i. When $h_r=h_i=1$, there is no effect of success or failure on allocations. As h_r and h_i increase above 1, subjective feelings of success and failure have an increasing effect on the allocation of expenditures. Total expenditures on search are also affected by the slack

Table 9.2 Per cent successes, 100 organizations, periods 11–20, varying environmental uncertainty (*a*) and exogenous changes in technology (*b₂*)

Environmental uncertainty	Exogenous changes in technology				
	$b_2=0.975$	$b_2=0.990$	$b_2=1.000$	$b_2=1.010$	$b_2=1.025$
$a=0$	23	77	93	99	99
$a=0.05$	35	86	94	97	97
$a=0.10$	35	71	78	83	84
$a=0.15$	36	64	69	70	79
$a=0.20$	38	58	64	67	75
$a=0.25$	40	56	63	65	71
$a=0.50$	47	53	54	57	60

components. Increase in h_r and h_i will, other things being equal, decrease the allocation of resources to search.

The general pattern of success in steady or improving environments means that the model shows, under those conditions, a tendency for organizations to spend relatively more on innovation than refinement, and to become relatively more efficient at it. Conversely, any tendency to failure produces relatively more spending on refinement than innovation, and leads to an organization becoming relatively more efficient at it. Thus, the extent to which the propensity to refine and the propensity to innovate diverge depends in large measure on the relative frequency of successes and failures. An inspection of table 9.2 suggests that organizational differentiation in the propensity to engage in refinement and innovation search will depend, therefore, on the level of environmental uncertainty and the exogenous changes in technology as much as on differences in the efficacy of the two types of search. An exogenously declining technology will, by increasing the frequency of failure, increase relative efficiency in refinement search and result in relatively high propensities to engage in such search. On the other hand, an improving technology will, by increasing the frequency of success, produce refinement propensities that are relatively low. Environmental uncertainty tends to vitiate such effects. That is, high uncertainty reduces the frequency of subjective success when the technology is improving or declining slightly; it reduces the frequency of failure when the technology is declining significantly (i.e., when b_2 is less than 0.98).

Path Dependence

Two common properties of stochastic processes are conspicuous in the model. First, draws from the technological distributions occasionally yield extreme values. For the most part, low extreme values are irrelevant; but high extreme values (major innovations) affect the position of the organization significantly and, in most cases, permanently. Second, the consequence of one (random) step is often to change the probabilities associated with the next step. This is most obvious in the way in which the good fortune of discovering a major innovation not only makes substantial changes in technology, but also in the allocation of resources to search, in aspirations, and in efficiencies at search. These adaptations, in turn, lead to different sequences of events than would have been experienced in the absence of such discoveries. Organizational histories are produced through a combination of chance events and adaptations to those events that, in some cases, considerably amplify the effects of chance.

Path dependence is particularly notable in the case of extreme draws from the distribution of possible technologies, but it is also exhibited by the more prosaic tendency for a subjective success to lead to a subsequent success and a subjective failure to lead to a subsequent failure. The model produces fewer period-to-period changes from success to failure or failure to success than would be expected merely from their relative frequencies. This serial correlation is sensitive to the rate at which an organization adapts its goal to performance, the degree of environmental uncertainty, and the size of exogenous changes in the technology. The basic results are shown in table 9.3, where we record the number of organizations (out of ten) for which period-to-period changes from success to failure, or failure to success, exceeded the number that would have been expected simply from chance and the overall proportions of the two outcomes for that organization. Cases in which the number of changes precisely equaled the expected number are treated as being one-half above and one-half below expectations. If there were no serial correlation in results, the numbers in the table should vary around 5. Over most of the situations examined, the numbers are less than that (positive serial correlation), but high levels of environmental uncertainty in combination with rapid goal adaptation lead to more frequent changes than would be expected (negative serial correlation).

A positive serial correlation of successes and failures accentuates the effects of success and failure on the development of efficiencies in search and the propensities to search. Organizational slack tends to remain high, or low, for several periods, and the organization builds efficiency in one or the other of the types of search. At the same time, a series of successes has the effect (on average) of increasing expenditures on innovations and thus of increasing the propensity to invest in a search for innovations. When there is a shift from failure to success, the level of expenditure on innovation rises, due primarily to the slack condition. Subsequently, the propensity to search for innovation rises as a result of success (which is

Table 9.3 Number of organizations (out of 10) showing more than expected changes from success to failure or failure to success, 20 periods, varying environmental uncertainty (a), exogenous changes (b_2), and goal learning rate (b_1)

	Environmental uncertainty		
	$a = 0$	$a = 0.05$	$a = 0.10$
Exogenous decline ($b_2 = 0.99$)			
$b_1 = 0.1$	0	0	2
$= 0.3$	0	0	2
$= 0.5$	0	0	5
$= 0.7$	0	3	8
$= 0.9$	0	7	9
No exogenous change ($b_2 = 1$)			
$b_1 = 0.1$	0	0	1
$= 0.3$	0	0	3
$= 0.5$	0	0	6
$= 0.7$	0	2	9
$= 0.9$	0	5	7.5
Exogenous increase ($b_2 = 1.005$)			
$b_1 = 0.1$	0	0	1
$= 0.3$	0	0	4
$= 0.5$	0	2	4
$= 0.7$	0	1	8
$= 0.9$	0	5	10

likely because of the serial correlation of successes). The two effects combine to produce a further increase in expenditure, followed by further success, and so on. This result occurs even under conditions in which no actual innovation takes place, and does not depend on the relative desirability of innovation and refinement.

Sensitivity to Learning Rates

As is clear from the earlier discussion of the model's sensibility, one basic decision problem in the model is the following: given an indefinitely long planning horizon, the best search strategy is to set search propensities as high as possible and keep them there. Such a strategy will maximize the long-run potential of the technology and thus maximize performance in the long run. However, the return on that investment is highly chancy, and a discovery may take many time periods. Until a discovery is made, high search expenditures reduce the performance of the organization. As a result, the net advantage (or disadvantage) of high search propensities relative to low search propensities depends on the performance horizon (see figure 9.2).

A possible inference from such observations would be that, given indefinitely long experience, all organizations should learn to have relatively high search propensities, that average search propensity should increase over time and its variance decline, and that the main effect of learning rates would be on the time it took an organization to adopt high search propensities. The speculation is not quite correct. In an indefinitely long period all organizations will, in fact, ultimately make discoveries that put them into new technologies and dramatically improved performance. This result, however, does not depend on learning to have a large propensity to search, but comes simply from the stochastic features of the search assumptions. Each organization has, at each time period, a non-zero probability (however small) of discovering a spectacular technology and embarking on a long string of successes.

The expected length of time that it takes different organizations to make new discoveries depends, however, on variations that are produced in their search propensities by their learning experiences and the adaptation rates for propensities, efficiencies, and goals. Thus, an organization's performance expectations are a function of its learning rates. It is not, in general, true that fast learning is best. Fast learners adapt quickly to correct signals; they also adapt quickly to false signals. If the false signals lead them to take actions that reduce the experience on which they might correct the error, rapid adaptation can lead to persistent mistakes. In particular, fast learners may fairly easily learn to reduce expenditures on search to a low level and thus reduce the probability of technological improvement. Conversely, slow learners are not confused as much by false signals, but neither do they respond as quickly to correct signals. If their slow response leads them to continue erroneous policies, slow adaptation can also lead to persistent mistakes.

Within the present model, long-run performance is, on average, improved by relatively slow, relatively imprecise learning. Search propensities tend to be less than 0.5, and average propensities for different sets of parameters normally vary between about 0.1 and 0.4. In the long run, performance will be highest if an organization can learn to set relatively high search propensities in the face of short-run experience that indicates, most of the time, that expenditures on search are unwarranted, and in a situation in which the average quality of outcomes increases with experience. Quick, precise learning of propensities will do well in the short run, but not in the long run unless there is a lucky early discovery of a new technology or very rapid goal adaptation. Learning is slowed by having a relatively low rate of propensity adaptation. It is made imprecise by having a relatively high rate of goal adaptation (and relatively high environmental uncertainty).

Figure 9.4 shows, for horizons varying from one period to 100 periods, the average cumulative performance as a function of the propensity learning rate, where $b_3 = b_4 = b_5$. Differences in the outcomes produced by values from 0.2 to 0.9 are modest, but if the rate of learning is reduced to 0.1, the effect on performance is substantial. There appear to be two major reasons for such a result. First, organizations that adapt propensities rapidly to experience rather quickly reduce the propensities to relatively low levels. This, in turn, reduces expenditures and reduces the chances of making a major discovery. Second, low expenditures on search reduce the accumulation of efficiency at search, and thus make discoveries even more difficult. A comparable analysis with respect to the rate of goal adaptation shows a quite different picture. As figure 9.5 shows, the goal learning rate has no appreciable effect for planning horizons up to about 30 periods, but after that fast goal learners do systematically better than slow learners. Rapidly adjusting goals make the success experience of the organization problematic, make learning linked to success and failure difficult, and tend to keep an organization from learning the false lesson that search expenditures are undesirable.

The relation between learning rates and performance is complicated not only by the length of time considered but also by interactions among the learning rates. For example, figure 9.6 shows the cumulative average performance for various planning horizons and four different values for the propensity learning rates for the extreme case in which the goal learning rate is 1.0. This is the case in which the organization, in effect, compares performance at period t with performance at period $t-1$ in deciding

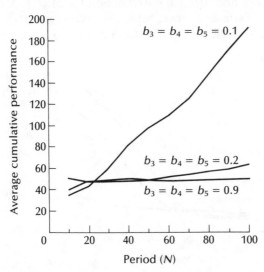

Figure 9.4. Average cumulative performance up to period n, as a function of propensity adaptation rate, 100 organizations

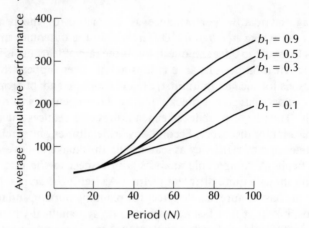

Figure 9.5. Average cumulative performance up to period *n*, as a function of goal adaptation rate, 100 organizations

whether to consider the new performance a success or failure. In this specific situation, the best propensity learning rate is 0.2 with a planning horizon less than 20 periods; it is 0.1 with a planning horizon between 20 and 80 periods; but it is 1.0 with a planning horizon between 80 and 100 periods. The details of these results, as well as the specific numbers involved, are, of course, a function of the other parameters and initial conditions in the model; but they illustrate the possibilities for significant interactions.

Learning rates also affect the likelihood of subjective success. As is clear from the discussion above, subjective success and performance are loosely coupled within the model. Most organizations are successful but

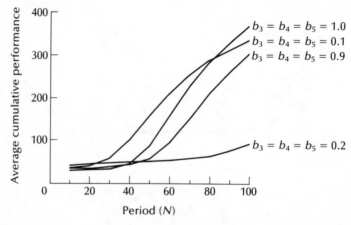

Figure 9.6. Average cumulative performance up to period *n*, as a function of propensity learning rate, with goal learning rate=1,100 organizations

organizations with the lowest proportion of successes (about 50 per cent) can show some of the highest performances. Indeed, low success rates and rapid alternation in success and failure are ways that false learning is avoided. Figure 9.7 shows the percentage of successes achieved over the first 50 periods for different rates of propensity and goal adaptation. Since the model is one in which organizations normally improve performance under conditions of no exogenous changes in technology, slowly adapting goals make it fairly easy to keep performance above the goal; thus, regardless of the propensity learning rate, success is associated with slowly adjusting goals. On the other hand, the propensity learning rate that is best for subjective success depends on the goal learning rate. For slowly adapting goals, rapid propensity learning leads to maximizing the proportion of periods in which subjective success is achieved; for rapidly adjusting goals, slow propensity learning maximizes the proportion of successes.

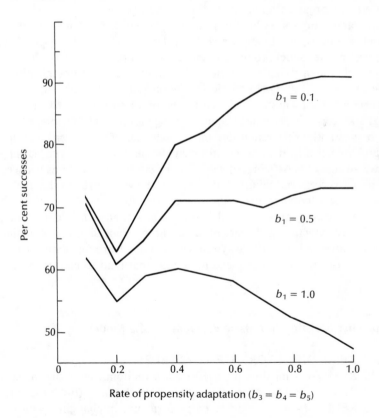

Figure 9.7. Per cent of success over 50 periods as a function of propensity and goal learning rates, 100 organizations.

Summary

The model is obviously incomplete. It does not consider the effects of competition and imitation among competitors; it ignores the problems produced by conflict of interest within a learning organization; it does not introduce any significant elements of cognition into a basically behavioral learning process; it assumes a very simple goal structure and a very simple conception of search. Despite this, or perhaps because of it, the model may tell us something about learning in organizations as a form of behavior and intelligence. The major assumptions we have used are drawn from the organizational literature. The four clusters of results are neither surprising nor inconsistent with what we think we know about organizations. The main claim for the model is that it may provide some link between speculations about organizational learning and observed patterns of organizational adaptation to experience.

By elaborating somewhat our potrayal of the relations among learning search strategies, developing search competences, and forming aspirations for search, the model provides an interpretation for some difficulties we have had in identifying consistent factors associated with organizational change (March, 1981). In particular, it suggests how experiences with exogenously or stochastically driven success or failure can lead to relatively large and relatively permanent changes in organizational behaviors, as well as to substantial differentiation among identical organizations learning in probabilistically identical environments. It shows some of the learning consequences of satisficing, of sharp organizational distinctions between subjective success and failure. It describes a behavioral process that makes successes serially correlated. And it identifies some situations in which sensible learning processes will lead to less than sensible learning, specifically, how the intelligence of rapid learning depends on the planning horizon involved and the ways in which false learning about search strategies or aspirations can lead to actions that tend to compound the error.

Appendix: A Listing of a Basic Program for the Model

```
00100 REM: DIRECTORY OF VARIABLES
00110 REM: A— maximum variation of a random factor that affects
00120 REM:     performance achieved from a technology (0< =a< =1).
00130 REM: B1—the weight given performance in changing goals.
00140 REM: B2—the period-to-period constant change in technology.
00150 REM: B3—controls rate of change of refinement search
```

00160 REM: propensity.
00170 REM: B4—controls rate of change in innovation search
00180 REM: propensity.
00190 REM: B5—controls rate of change of investment propensity.
00200 REM:
00210 REM:
00220 REM: C1—relates variance in refinement to new technology
00230 REM: C2—reduces variance in refinement draws with experience
00240 REM: C3—relates variance in innovation to new technology
00250 REM: C4—changes mean of refinement with experience
00260 REM: C5—reduces variance in innovation errors with innovation
00270 REM: C6—reduces variance in refinement errors with refinement
00280 REM: C7—changes mean of innovation with experience
00290 REM:
00300 REM:
00310 REM: E(r,t)—efficiency of refinement
00320 REM: E(i,t)—efficiency of innovation
00330 REM:
00340 REM: G(t)—the goal in the current time period.
00350 REM: G(t − 1)—the goal in the previous period.
00360 REM:
00370 REM: h(r)—refinement slack investment exponent
00380 REM: h(i)—innovation non-slack investment exponent
00390 REM:
00400 REM: I(t)—innovation investment in the current period.
00410 REM: I(t − 1)—innovation investment in the previous period.
00420 REM: I(t − 2)—innovation investment in period (t − 2).
00430 REM:
00440 REM: K(r,t)—number of refinement draws this period.
00450 REM: K(i,t)—number of innovation draws this period.
00460 REM:
00470 REM: Kr—constant for converting to refinement draws
00480 REM: Ki—constant for converting to innovation draws
00490 REM:
00500 REM: M—the total resources of the firm.
00510 REM:
00520 REM: N—the total number of time periods.
00530 REM: N1—the number of the current time period.
00540 REM:
00550 REM: P(t)—performance in the current time period.
00560 REM: P(t − 1)—performance in the previous time period.
00570 REM:
00580 REM: Q. . Q9 the Q-variables are all used to make internal

00590 REM: calculations.
00600 REM:
00610 REM: R(t)—refinement investment in the current period.
00620 REM: R(t − 1)—refinement investment in the previous period.
00630 REM: R(t − 2)—refinement investment in period (t − 2)
00640 REM:
00650 REM: S(r,t)—refinement search propensity this period.
00660 REM: S(r,t − 1)—refinement search propensity last period.
00670 REM: S(i,t)—innovation search propensity this period.
00680 REM: S(i,t − 1)—innovation search propensity last period.
00690 REM: S(s,t)—propensity to invest this period
00700 REM: S(s,t − 1)—propensity to invest last period
00710 REM:
00720 REM:
00730 REM: S9   used for calculating only (standard deviation)
00740 REM:
00750 REM: T1   T(*,t)—technology at start of period
00760 REM: T2   b1T(*,t − 1)—the current technology
00770 REM: T3   the initial value of the current technology
00780 REM: T4   b1T3(t − 1)—unrefined changed value of current
              technology.
00790 REM:
00800 REM: U(t)   U(s,t)—the resources available for investment
00810 REM: U(t − 1)   U(s,t − 1)—resources available for investment last
              period
00820 REM: U(t − 2)   U(s,t − 2)—the resources available for investment
              at (t − 2)
00830 REM:
00840 REM: V(r,t)—the standard deviation of the distribution
00850 REM: of refinement opportunities (this period)
00860 REM: V(i,t)—the standard deviation of the distribution
00870 REM: of innovation opportunities (this period)
00880 REM: Ve(r,t)—standard deviation of refinement estimation error
00890 REM: Ve(i,t)—standard deviation of innovation estimation error
00900 REM:
00910 REM:
00920 REM: w(r)—refinement efficiency exponent
00930 REM: w(i)—innovation efficiency exponent
00940 REM:
00950 REM: X5   current mean of distribution of refinement opportunities
00960 REM: X6   current mean of distribution of innovation opportunities
00970 REM: X7   mean of refinement estimation errors
00980 REM: X8   mean of innovation estimation errors

```
00990 REM: X9   used for calculating only (mean)
01000 REM:
01010 REM: Z      used for calculating only (random normal generator)
01020 REM:
01030 !
01040 !
01050 !
01060 REM: ESTABLISHING RANDOM NORMAL NUMBER
            FUNCTION
01070 RANDOMIZE
01080 DEF FNN(X9,S9) = X9 + SGR( - 2*LOG(RND))*COS
            (RND*6.28)*S9
01090 !
01100 !
01110 GOTO 3470 !MAIN PROGRAM LOOP
01120 !
01130 !
01140 REM: SETTING INITIAL VALUES
01150 r = 0 \ i = 1 \ s = 2 \ t = 3 !setting values for indexes
01160 A = 05
01170 B1 = .1
01180 B2 = 1
01190 B3 = 1
01200 B4 = 1
01210 B5 = 1
01220 C1 = .01
01230 C2 = .98
01240 C3 = .0135
01250 C4 = .9
01260 C5 = .98
01270 C6 = .98
01280 C7 = .9
01290 E(r,t) = 0
01300 E(i,t) = 0
01310 Q(t) = 40
01320 h(r) = 1.1
01330 h(i) = 1.1
01340 I(t) = 5
01350 I(t - 1) = 5
01360 K(r,t) = 3
01370 K(i,t) = 3
01380 kr = .2
01390 ki = .2
```

```
01400  N = 20
01410  P(t) = 40
01420  R(t) = 5
01430  R(t − 1) = 5
01440  S(r,t) = .5
01450  S(i,t) = .5
01460  S(s,t) = .5
01470  T1 = 50
01480  Ve(r,t) = .5
01490  Ve(i,t) = .75
01500  w(r) = 3.5
01510  w(i) = 3.5
01520  X5 = 0
01530  X6 = 0
01540  X7 = 0
01550  X8 = 0
01560  U(t) = 50
01570  U(t − 1) = 50
01580  REM: INITIAL VALUES (NEW TECHNOLOGY)
01590  T3 = T1
01600  V(r,t) = c1*T3
01610  V(i,t) = c3*T3
01620  RETURN
01630  !
01640  !
01650  REM: UPDATING VALUES
01660  G(t − 1) = G(t)
01670  I(t − 2) = I(t − 1)
01680  I(t − 1) = I(t)
01690  P(t − 1) = P(t)
01700  R(t − 2) = R(t − 1)
01710  R(t − 1) = R(t)
01720  S(r,t − 1) = S(r,t)
01730  S(i,t − 1) = S(i,t)
01740  S(s,t − 1) = S(s,t)
01750  T2 = T1*B2
01760  T4 = T3*B2
01770  U(t − 1) = U(t)
01780  U(t − 1) = U(t)
01790  !
01800  !
01810  !
01820  REM: DETERMINING SEARCH PROPENSITIES
```

```
01830 G = 0
01840 IF G(t - 1) > P(t - 1) THEN G = 1
01850   G3 = 0
01860   IF R(t - 1) > R(t - 2) THEN G3 = 1
01870     G4 = 0
01880     IF I(t - 1) > I(t - 2) THEN G4 = 1
01890 G1 = 1
01900 IF G = G3 THEN G1 = 0
01910   G2 = 1
01920   IF G = G4 THEN G2 = 0
01930 G5 = 0
01940 IF U(t - 1) > U(t - 2) THEN G5 = 1
01950   G6 = 1
01960   G = G5 THEN G6 = 0
01970 S(r,t) = (G1*B3) + (S(r,t - 1)*(1 - B3))
01980 S(i,t) = (G2*B4) + (S(i,t - 1)*(1 - B4))
01990 S(s,t) = (G6*B5) + ((1 - B5)*S(s,t - 1))
02000 !
02010 !
02020 REM: DETERMINING SEARCH INVESTMENTS
02030 M = P(t - 1) + I(t - 1) + R(t - 1)
02040 U(t) = S(s,t)*M
02050 IF G = 1 THEN GOTO 2090
02060 R(t) = S(r,t)*(U(t)∧(1/h(r)))
02070 I(t) = S(i,t)*U(t)
02080 GOTO 2130
02090 R(t) = S(r,t)*U(t)
02100 I(t) = S(i,t)*(U∧(1/h(i)))
02110 !
02120 !
02130 REM: COMPUTING SEARCH EFFICIENCIES
02140 E(r,t) = E(r,t) + K(r,t)
02150 E(i,t) = E(i,t) + K(i,t)
02160   IF E(r,t) = 0 THEN G1 = 0
02170   G1 = E(r,t)∧(1/w(r))
02180   IF E(i,t) = 0 THEN G2 = 0
02190   G2 = E(i,t)∧(1/w(i))
02200 !
02210 !
02220 REM: FIXING SAMPLE SIZES
02230 K(r,t) = INT(Kr*R(t)*G1)
02240 K(i,t) = INT(Ki*I(t)*G2)
02250 !
```

```
02260  !
02270  REM: SEARCHING FOR THE BEST REFINEMENT
02280  G1 = T2
02290  G2 = T2
02300  IF K(r,t) < 1 THEN 2580
02310  G = 0
02320  G5 = − 100000000000
02330  V(r,t) = c2*V(r,t)
02340  X5 = c4*X5
02350  REM: FIRST, DRAW A REFINEMENT
02360  X9 = X5
02370  S9 = V(r,t)
02380  G7 = FNN(X9,S9)
02390  REM: SECOND, ADD THE ESTIMATION ERROR
02400  X9 = X7
02410  S9 = Ve(r,t)
02420  G8 = FNN(X9,S9)
02430  REM: THIRD, COMPARE WITH OTHERS IN THIS SAMPLE
02440  G9 = T2 + G7 + G8
02450  IF G9 < = G5 THEN GOTO 2480
02460  G5 = G9
02470  G2 = T2 + G7
02480  G = G + 1
02490  IF G = K(r,t) THEN GOTO 2520
02500  GOTO 2360
02510  REM: FOURTH, RECORD THE BEST REFINEMENT FOUND
02520  IF G5 > T2 THEN GOTO 2540
02530  GOTO 2570
02540  G1 = G5
02550  !
02560  !
02570  REM: SEARCHING FOR THE BEST INNOVATION
02580  G3 = T2
02590  G4 = T2
02600  IF K(i,t) < 1 THEN GOTO 2880
02610  G = 0
02620  G6 = 10000000000
02630  X6 = c7*X6
02640  REM: FIRST, DRAW AN INNOVATION
02650  X9 = X6
02660  S9 = V(i,t)
02670  G7 = EXP(FNN(X9,S9)) − EXP(X9 + ·5*(S9∧2))
02680  REM: SECOND, ADD THE ESTIMATION ERROR
```

```
02690  X9 = X8
02700  S9 = Ve(i,t)
02710  G8 = FNN(X9,S9)
02720  REM: THIRD, COMPARE WITH OTHERS IN THIS SAMPLE
02730  G9 = T4 + G7 + G8
02740  IF G9 < = G6 THEN GOTO 2770
02750  G6 = G9
02760  G4 = T4 + G7
02770  G = G + 1
02780  IF G = K(i,t) THEN GOTO 2810
02790  GOTO 2650
02800  REM: FOURTH, RECORD THE BEST INNOVATION
                FOUND
02810  IF G6 > T2 THEN GOTO 2830
02820  GOTO 2860
02830  G3 = G6
02840  !
02850  !
02860  REM: ESTABLISHING THE NEW TECHNOLOGY
02870  CH$ = "NONE"
02880  IF G3 > G1 THEN GOTO 2960
02890    IF G1 > T2 THEN GOTO 2920
02900      T1 = T2
02910    GOTO 3130
02920      T1 = G2
02930      Ve(r,t) = c6*Ve(r,t)
02940      CH$ = "REFINEMENT"
02950    GOTO 3130
02960  IF G3 > T2 THEN GOTO 2990
02970  T1 = T2
02980  GOTO 3130
02990    T1 = G4
03000    T3 = T1
03010  IF G4 < T2 THEN GOTO 3050
03020  E(r,t) = E(r,t)*(T2/G4)
03030  E(i,t) = E(i,t)*(T2/G4)
03040  GOTO 3070
03050    E(r,t) = E(r,t)*(G4/T2)
03060    E(i,t) = E(i,t)*(G4/T2)
03070  V(r,t) = c1*T3
03080  V(i,t) = c3*T3
03090  Ve(i,t) = c5*Ve(i,t)
03100  CH$ = "INNOVATION"
```

```
03110 !
03120 !
03130 REM: CALCULATING PERFORMANCE AND CHANGING
          GOALS
03140 G = RND
03150 G1 = RND
03160 IF G1 < .5 THEN G = G*(-1)
03170 G = G*A
03180 REM: FIRST, THE PERFORMANCE
03190 P(t) = ((1 + G)*T1) - R(t) - 1(t)
03200 REM: SECOND, THE GOALS
03210 G(t) = ((1 - B1)*G(t-1)) + (B1*P(t-1))
03220 SF$ = "SUCCESS"
03230 IF G(t) > P(t) THEN SF$ = "FAILURE"
03240 RETURN
03250 !
03260 !
03270 REM: PRINTING THE RESULTS
03280 !
03290 IF N1 > THEN GOTO 3320
03300 PRINT
03310 PRINT "TIME", " ", "REFINE", "INNOVATE", "INVEST",
          "TECH", "PERFORMANCE"
03320 PRINT
03330 PRINT N1.
03340 IF CH$ = "NONE" THEN GOTO 3370
03350 PRINT CH$, INT(T1)
03360 GOTO 3380
03370 PRINT " "
03380 PRINT " ", "PROPENSITY", INT(S(r,t)*100)/100, INT(S(i,t)*
          100)/100,
03390 PRINT INT(S(s,t)*100)(100,INT(T1),INT(P(t))
03400 PRINT " ", "INVESTMENT", INT(R(t)),INT(I(t))," "," ",SF$
03410 PRINT " ", "DRAWS", K(r,t),K(i,t)
03420 PRINT
03430 RETURN
03440 !
93459 !
03460 !
03470 REM: MAIN PROGRAM LOOP
03480 GOSUB 1140 !INITIAL VALUES
03490 FOR N1 = 1 TO N
03500 GOSUB 1650 !MAIN PROGRAM
```

```
03510  GOSUB 3270 !PRINT RESULTS
03520  NEXT N1
03530  !
03540  !
03550  !
03560  !
03570  END
```

References

Alchian, Armen (1959) Cost and output. In Moses Abramovitz et al. (eds), *The Allocation of Economic Resources: Essays in Honor of B. F. Haley.* CA: Stanford University Press, Stanford.

Allen, J. M. (1970) A survey into the R&D evaluation and control procedures currently used in industry. *Journal of Industrial Economics*, 18, 16–81.

Allison, Graham T. (1971) Essence of Decision. MA: Little Brown, Boston.

Cohen, Michael, and James G. March (1974) *Leadership and Ambiguity: The American College President.* New York: McGraw-Hill.

Cyert, Richard M., and James G. March (1963). *A Behavioral Theory of the Firm.* Englewood Cliffs, NJ: Prentice Hall.

Hannan, Michael, and John Freeman (1977) The population ecology of organizations. *American Journal of Sociology*, 82, 929–61.

Kay, Neil M. (1979) *The Innovating Firm: A Behavioral Theory of Corporate R&D.* New York: St Martin's.

Keen, Peter G. W. (1977) The evolving concept of optimality. *TIMS Studies in the Management Sciences*, 6, 31–57.

Knight, Kenneth E. (1967) A descriptive model of the intra-firm innovative process. *The Journal of Business*, 40, 478–96.

Kohn, Meir G., and Steven Shavell (1974) Optimal adaptive search. *Journal of Economic Theory*, 9(2), 93–124.

Lave, Charles A., and James G. March (1975) *An Introduction to Models in the Social Sciences.* New York: Harper and Row.

Lindblom, Charles E. (1959) The science of muddling through. *Public Administration Review,* 19, 79–88.

Mansfield, Edwin (1963) Size of firm, market structure, and innovation. *Journal of Political Economy*, 71, 556–76.

March, James G. (1981) Footnotes to organizational change. *Administrative Science Quarterly*, 26, 563–77.

March, James G., and Johan P. Olsen (1976) *Ambiguity and Choice in Organizations.* Bergen: University Press of Norway.

March, James G., and Herbert A. Simon (1958) *Organizations.* New York: Wiley.

Nelson, Richard R., and Sidney G. Winter (1978) Forces generating and limiting concentration under Schumpeterian competition. *Bell Journal of Economics*, 9, 524–48.

Preston, L. D., and E. C. Keachie (1964) Cost functions and progress functions: an integration. *American Economic Review*, 54, 100–08.

Radner, Roy (1975) A behavioral model of cost reduction. *Bell Journal of Economics*, 6, 196–215.

Reeves, E. D. (1958) Development of the research budget. *Research Management*, 1, 133–42.

Simon Herbert A. (1957) *Models of Man*. New York: Wiley.

Steinbruner, John D. (1974) *The Cybernetic Theory of Decision: New Dimensions of Political Analysis*. Princeton, NJ: Princeton University Press.

Winter, Sidney G. (1971) Satisficing, selection and the innovating remnant. *Quarterly Journal of Economics*, 85, 237–61.

Winter, Sidney G. (1975) Optimization and evolution in the theory of the firm. In Richard H. Day and Theodore Groves (eds), *Adaptive Economic Models*. New York: Academic Press.

10

Learning from Experience
in Organizations

Scott R. Herriott, Daniel Levinthal, and James G. March

Abstract

This paper sketches a class of difference equation models for examining incremental experiential learning by economic actors, particularly organizations. The models reflect features of adaptive behavior drawn from observations of decision-making in organizations. They picture choice as stemming from decision-rules that adjust cumulatively on the basis of trial-by-trial monitoring of the success or failure associated with past adjustments. Such models are in a broad tradition that includes previous work not only in organizational learning and adaptive economics, but also hill-climbing optimization techniques, control theory, and modeling of elementary learning by humans and other animals. Some modest complexities associated with learning are introduced, particularly ways in which learning occurs along several interacting dimensions and within an ecology of learning.

Models of Experiential Learning

We assume a simple choice situation in which a fixed budget is allocated among several alternative, independent activities. Each of the activities provides a return that is proportional to the allocation and the competence (efficiency) of the system at that activity. In the absence of competition, total performance is the potential (or capacity) of each activity weighted by the allocation to that activity and the competence at it, summed over

---

This paper first appeared in the *American Economic Review*, 75 (1985) pp. 298–302. The research has been supported by grants from the Spencer Foundation, the Mellon Foundation, the Stanford Graduate School of Business, and the Hoover Institution.

the activities. If $A_{i,t}$ is the fraction of the budget allocated to activity i at time t, $k_{i,t}(0 < k_{i,t} < 1)$ is the competence at activity i at time t, and $C_{i,t}$ is the potential return from activity i at time t, then, P_t, the performance at time t, is

$$P_t = \sum_i k_{i,t} A_{i,t} C_{i,t}. \tag{1}$$

Within this choice situation, simple trial-by-trial learning will commonly lead an actor to increase the allocation to activities for which $k_{i,t} C_{i,t}$ is relatively large, decrease it for those for which it is relatively small.

There are two sets of complications in discovering sensible allocations in this way. The first is that learning occurs along several simultaneous dimensions. Competences and goals adapt at the same time as allocations, and each affects the other. The second complication is that any one learner exists in an ecology of other learners whose actions, goals, and competences affect each other.

Dimensions of Learning

Adaptive allocations. We assume that decision-making consists in choosing an allocation $(A_{1,t}, A_{2,t}, ..., A_{n,t})$ to available alternatives that exhausts the budget. That choice is made by adjusting the previous allocation. The adjustment is made in two steps. At the first step, a proposed allocation to each activity, $A_{i,t}^*$, is determined:

$$A_{i,t}^* = A_{i,t-1} + b_1(L_{i,t} - A_{i,t-1}). \tag{2}$$

The learning limit $L_{i,t}$, for a proposed allocation to activity i at time t, assumes values of 0 or 1 (alternatively 0 and the total budget) with probability $1 - U_{i,t}$ and $U_{i,t}$. Thus, $U_{i,t}$ is the probability of proposing an increase in the fraction of the budget allocated to alternative i. The value of $U_{i,t}$ changes in response to experience, depending on the adjustment in allocation made on the previous trial and the outcome on that trial (P_{t-1}) relative to some goal (G_{t-1}). Specifically,

$$U_{i,t} = U_{i,t-1} + b_2(1 - U_{i,t-1}) \tag{3}$$

if $\qquad A_{i,t-1} > A_{i,t-2};\ P_{t-1} > G_{t-1}$

or if $\qquad A_{i,t-1} < A_{i,t-2};\ P_{t-1} < G_{t-1};$

$$= U_{i,t-1} - b_2 U_{i,t-1}$$

if $\qquad A_{i,t-1} > A_{i,t-2};\ P_{t-1} < G_{t-1}$

or if $\qquad A_{i,t-1} < A_{i,t-2};\ P_{t-1} > G_{t-1}.$

Equation (3) defines a variation on a standard stochastic learning model. Where $b_2 = 1$, the direction of the adaptations is determined without stochastic variation. The two learning parameters, b_1 and b_2, affect the rate at which adjustments in allocations are made. The adjustment of $A_{i,t-1}^*$ and $U_{i,t-1}$ from one trial to the next are proportional to the difference between the current values and the upper or lower limits of those variables. They can also be made proportional to the absolute difference between P_{t-1} and G_{t-1}, more specifically to $[\,|G_{t-1} - P_{t-1}|\,]/[\,G_{t-1} + P_{t-1}\,]$. In such a case, the adaptations are more finely tuned to the magnitude of success or failure. Another form of fine-tuning would disaggregate performance and goal, associating each with a specific activity rather than to their sum. Moving from $A_{i,t}^*$ to $A_{i,t}$ involves satisfying the constraint that the sum of allocation increases in individual activities must equal the sum of allocation decreases while maintaining the relative sizes of individual changes projected by $A_{i,t}^*$.

Adaptive competence.   Models of adaptive learning (for example, binary choice learning, two-armed bandits) commonly assume that the outcome from a current choice is independent of the history of choices. In many situations of economic allocation, however, it seems more reasonable to assume that competence at an activity decreases with the passage of time and increases with allocation to the activity. Thus,

$$k_{i,t} = (1 - b_3)k_{i,t-1} \qquad (4)$$

$$+ A_{i,t-1}b_4[1 - (1 - b_3)k_{i,t-1}]\,.$$

The coefficients of competence decay (b_3) and learning (b_4) control the rate at which efficiency at an activity responds to disuse and experience. Equation (4) is a variant of a standard learning-by-doing model.

Adaptive goals.   We assume that performance aspirations adapt to past performance so that the goal in any time period is a mix between the previous goal and the previous performance.

$$G_t = (1 - b_5)G_{t-1} + b_5 P_{t-1}\,. \qquad (5)$$

The result is to make the goal an exponentially weighted moving average of performance, with b_5 determining the relative weight attached to relatively recent performance results. If $b_5 = 1$, then $G_t = P_{t-1}$; and the adaptation responds simply to changes in performance. If $b_2 = 1 = b_5$, the model becomes a standard hill-climbing procedure.

The Ecology of Learning

Diffusion of Experience. In a social environment, learning from direct experience is supplemented by the diffusion of experience, that is, by copying others. From a rational perspective, copying can be seen as a way of increasing (on average) the amount of experience from which an individual draws while decreasing (on average) the linkage between that individual's situation and the experience base of action. From a behavioral perspective, it can be seen as a standard way by which adaptive systems deal with uncertainty and ambiguity.

If we let $A^*_{j,i,t}$ be the proposed allocation of individual j to activity i at time t, a natural extension of (2) yields

$$A^*_{j,i,t} = (1 - d_1) \tag{6}$$

$$\times [A_{j,i,t-1} + b_1(L_{i,t} - A_{j,i,t-1})]$$

$$+ d_1 \sum_{h \neq j} A_{h,i,t-1}/(n-1).$$

That is, allocations adapt to the mean allocation made by other actors, as well as to direct experience.

If we let $k_{j,i,t}$ be the competence of individual j at activity i at time t, a natural extension of (4) yields

$$k_{j,i,t} = (1 - d_2)\{(1 - b_3)k_{j,i,t-1} \tag{7}$$

$$+ A_{j,i,t-1}b_4[1 - (1 - b_3)k_{j,i,t-1}]\}$$

$$+ d_2 \max_h k_{h,i,t-1}.$$

That is, competences adapt to the highest level of competence exhibited within the population of actors.

If $G_{j,t}$ is the goal of individual j at time t, then a natural extension of (5) yields

$$G_{j,t} = (1 - b_4)G_{j,t-1} \tag{8}$$

$$+ b_4 \left\{ \left[d_3 \sum_{h \neq j} P_{h,i-1}/(n-1) \right] \right.$$

$$+ [(1 - d_3)P_{j,t-1}] \right\}.$$

That is, an actor's goals adapt to the mean performance of other actors, as well as to her own performance. The adaptation coefficients (d_1, d_2, d_3)

determine the rate at which allocations, competences, and goals spread from one learner to another.

Interdependence of experience.   Where experience is interdependent, the performance realized by any one actor depends not only on that actor's allocations and competences, but also on the actions of others. The interdependencies may involve 'mating', in which actor's rewards for a particular activity are augmented by having other actors engaged in the same activity. They may involve competition, in which each actor's rewards for a particular activity are decreased by having other actors engaged in the same activity. They may involve 'hunting', in which the rewards of some actors are increased by the presence of other actors engaged in the same activity who, themselves, have their rewards decreased by the joint presence. In the present paper, we consider only the competitive case. If more than one actor allocates effort to a particular activity, the allocation and competence of each reduces the return for the others. Specifically, in any time period where $\Sigma_j k_{j,i,t} A_{j,i,t} > 1$, the return from activity i for actor j is

$$P_{j,i,t} = \frac{(k_{j,i,t} A_{j,i,t})^w}{\underset{h \neq j}{\Sigma} (k_{h,i,t} A_{h,i,t})^w} C_{i,t}. \tag{9}$$

The power w determines the way in which an overexploited activity is shared among competitors.

Organizational subunits.   Many economic actors are organizations – firms, armies, public bureaucracies, schools, unions. Organizations have subunits whose actions affect outcomes and whose rewards are linked to local results, as well as to overall performance. We have modeled organizations consisting in subunits, similarly allocating among activities, while adapting allocation competences, and goals over time. Since allocations within subunits affect not only the performance of subunits but also the performance of the organization as a whole, organizational learning is heavily interactive. The details are omitted here. They parallel the earlier characterizations of learning but include some additional features to link the learning and performance of subunits with the overall organization.

Some Results

We report here some fragmentary results based on analysis of the determinate ($b_2 = 1$) case involving only two alternative activities with unchanging (but different) potentials. We address ourselves to four general questions relevant to assessing trial-by-trial learning as a form of intelligence:

1 To what extent does incremental learning of this type produce, after a suitably long period of time, sensible adaptations to environmental possibilities?
2 To what extent are long-run outcomes independent of initial allocations, competences, and goals?
3 To what extent is the long-run performance of learners improved by increasing the learning parameters?
4 To what extent is the long-run performance of learners improved by tuning the adjustment of allocations more finely to the magnitude of success or failure?

The Isolated Learner

If adjustment of allocations over time is roughly tuned (i.e., if b_1 is fixed), the isolated learner specializes. That is, an equilibrium is reached at which all resources are devoted to one alternative or the other, and where $k_i = b_4 A_i/(b_3 + b_4 A_i - b_3 b_4 A_i)$. Specialization is also characteristic of the stochastic version of the model (i.e., $b_2 < 1$). Specialization may not involve the superior alternative, however. The equilibrium outcome depends not only on the learning parameters but also on the initial allocation, competence, and goal. In general, as the initial conditions become more favorable to the inferior alternative, the set of learning values that result in specialization at the inferior value expands.

Given initial conditions in which competence in and allocation to an inferior alternative are high, specialization in that activity is likely. It can be avoided by slow adjustment of allocations and rapid adjustment of goals, or by learners whose absolute level of performance declines over time (thus producing failures). With fixed capacities for the two alternatives, the latter result requires that the competence decay rate (b_3) be high relative to the competence learning rate (b_4), that is, slow learning and fast forgetting.

In the 'finely tuned' case, where the adjustment of allocations is made proportional to the absolute disparity between performance and goal, the model also reaches a stable mixture of allocations, competences, goal, and performance; but the allocation does not, in general, reach 1 or 0. Rather, it locates an equilibrium combination at some interior, suboptimal point. Thus, fine-tuning yields higher performance in situations in which rough-tuning leads to specialization in the inferior alternative, but not in those cases where rough tuning leads to specialization in the superior alternative.

Diffusion of Experience

The effects of diffusion of experience among parallel (but non-interacting) learners depends on characteristics of the population of learners. The discussion here is limited to the case of a population heterogeneous with respect to the values of b_1 and b_5, but homogeneous with respect to the other learning rates (i.e., $b_2 = 1, b_3 = 0.1, b_4 = 0.5$). Diffusion of allocations decreases both the mean and the variance of performance within the population (relative to isolated learners), normally driving all actors to a common set of allocations, competences, and goals. Diffusion of competence, goals, or both normally increases average performance. In addition, the diffusion of competence changes the region of the parameter space that leads to specialization in the superior alternative, giving an advantage in that respect to learners who adjust allocations relatively quickly and adjust goals relatively slowly.

Goal diffusion, by making goals more homogeneous among learners than is performance, tends to divide a population of non-competing learners into one group with a history of subjective successes, another with a history of subjective failures. Since persistent success produces specialization and persistent failure produces non-specialization, goal diffusion partitions the population into three groups of actors. The first group allocates all its resources to the inferior alternative; the second allocates all its resources to the superior alternative; the allocation by the third group oscillates around an equal division between the two. The proportion in each group depends on the initial conditions and learning parameters. It also depends on whether the allocation adjustments are finely or roughly tuned, with fine-tuning tending to produce a large number of learners who fail consistently and thus divide their allocations equally among the alternatives.

Interdependence of Experience

The effects of competition depend on the number of competitors and the parameter w that controls the way in which the resources in an overexploited activity are divided among competitors, as well as the characteristics of the population of competitors. With small numbers of competitors ($n = 2, n = 3$), specialization is common. In the case of two competitors, this means each competitor specializes in a different activity. Under many, but not all, conditions, the slower learner becomes the specialist in the superior alternative, thus has higher performance. In the case of three competitors, a quite typical result is that one or two of the three specialize, while the other does not. Faster learners tend to become specialists, but whether that results in their also having higher performance depends on the alternative in which they specialize and the pattern of allocations by the others.

With larger numbers, both the analysis and the story become more complicated. In general, if $w > 1$, rapid adjustment of allocations leads to better performance than slow adjustment; if $w < 1$, the converse is true. If the adjustment of allocations is made proportional to the magnitude of success or failure (the fine-tuning option), the system reaches an apparent equilibrium which depends on the initial allocations and competences as well as the learning rates. In the fine-tuning case, moderate rates of goal adaptation often seem advantageous, but not always. There are also numerous situations with relatively idiosyncratic outcomes. In otherwise apparently smooth response surfaces mapping variations of performance onto variations in learning rates, substantial spikes appear.

Competition with Diffusion

If diffusion and competition are both present, we obtain many of the same basic results observed in the case of either alone. Goal diffusion, however, confounds the general observation that rapid, rough-tuned adjustment of allocations gives an advantage where $w > 1$. When goals diffuse, competitors who are persistently successful tend to become specialists in one activity or the other. Fast learners tend to specialize, but the fastest learners often specialize in the inferior alternative, leaving the superior alternative to the their somewhat slower cousins. In addition, variation in performance within the population of competitors tends to be decreased by allocation diffusion, but increased by competence or goal diffusion.

Organizational Subunits

Over a fair range of situations, the consequence of introducing learning subunits is to make both the intelligence of learning through trial-by-trial adaptation and its analysis somewhat problematic. The interactions make it less likely that organizations will specialize in inferior activities, but also less likely that they will specialize in superior activities. In this respect, the existence of subunits produces effects not unlike the presence of random error in performance. Although it seems likely that there are regular cycles in the resulting patterns of adaptations, we have not as yet discovered them.

Discussion

To provide a base for considering experiential learning as a form of adaptive intelligence, we have modeled a collection of behavioral observations about the forms of learning common in organizations. Since there is ample experimental and observational evidence for believing that simple experiential learning can be a powerful procedure for improving human performance and since the informational, computational, and coordinative requirements of adaptive intelligence seems to be closer to the capabilities of individual and organizational decision-makers than are the demands of anticipatory intelligence, we explore the conditions for sensibility of this kind of incremental adaptation.

Although analysis of the models is very incomplete and much of the structure remains unexplored, we can begin to answer the four questions with which the present discussion began.

1 Learning of the sort we have described leads reliably to optimal choices in some situations, but does not do so in others.
2 Allocations at equilibrium are not determined uniquely by activity potentials, but are extensively dependent on the rates at which adaptations take place and on initial allocations and competences.
3 Although fast learners often do better than slow learners, there are many plausible situations in which slow learners do better than fast learners.
4 Although fine-tuned adjustment of allocations facilitates locating an equilibrium, the equilibria achieved are not reliably better than the long-term results of a rougher-tuned adjustment, in fact, are often worse.

11

Decision-Making and Postdecision Surprises

J. Richard Harrison and James G. March

Abstract

Most ideas of intelligent choice assume that decision-making involves estimating the probable future values of currently available alternatives and choosing the best of them. Sometimes chosen alternatives turn out to be better than anticipated; sometimes they turn out to be worse. The difference between the predecision estimated value of a chosen alternative and its postdecision value, determined after some of its consequences have been experienced, can be defined as postdecision surprise. This paper examines a systematic bias in the distribution of postdecision surprises attributable to the structure of intelligent choice itself. It is shown that unbiased, random errors in estimation result in a structural tendency toward postdecision disappointment, which will be most characteristic of decision situations in which variation among the true values of alternatives is relatively small, the ambiguity or uncertainty in evaluation is relatively high, and the number of alternatives considered is relatively large. The decision dilemma is clear. Choosing apparently better alternatives will, on average, produce higher returns; however, in the absence of behavioral adjustments, higher expected benefits will be associated with greater expected disappointments. The effects are illustrated with results computed for the special case of normally distributed values and errors. Some implications are suggested for understanding postdecision surprise and the development of social norms of intelligent choice in individuals and organizations.

This paper was first published in *Administrative Science Quarterly*, 29, 1984, 26–42. The authors' research has been supported by grants from the Spencer Foundation, the Stanford Graduate School of Business, and the Hoover Institution. They are grateful for comments by Gerhard Arminger, Terry Connolly, Daniel Levinthal, John Meyer, Stephen Peters, and Allyn Romanow.

Postdecision Surprises

It is a canon of rationality that intelligent choices are based on beliefs about their consequences for personal or collective values. Although it is clear that actual human behavior frequently follows other kinds of logics with their own claims to intelligence (March, 1978), decisions made by individuals, organizations, and societies often are guided by an explicit calculation of the benefits and costs anticipated from alternative actions. These calculations reflect two kinds of guesses about the future, conditional on current action. The first guess is an estimate of probable future states of the world; the second is an estimate of probable future values, or tastes. Conventional decision procedures have a decision-maker combine the two guesses into estimates of the expected values of available alternatives and select the alternative with the highest expected value.

After a decision is made and its consequences experienced, additional information is available. This information normally clarifies the outcomes and values of the alternative that was selected; and it is, at least in principle, possible to examine the relation between expectations and realizations. We can ask whether forecasts of the net benefits to be achieved from a chosen alternative are unbiased estimates of those benefits; or whether there are features of pre- and postdecision processes that lead to systematic bias in the distribution of postdecision surprises, that is, realizations minus expectations.

Empirical studies of predecision expectations and postdecision evaluations in individuals and organizations are well known in the literature; but there is another, possibly prior, kind of question that can be raised about the relationship between intelligent choice and the distribution of surprises. We may be interested in whether there are structural features of decision-making that affect postdecision surprise. By structural features of decision-making, we mean consequences of the process that are implicit in the decision model itself, rather than a result of behavioral applications of the model. These structural characteristics are particularly important for understanding the inherent properties of intelligence, as it is reflected in calculated choice, and can be viewed both as defining a base-line distribution of surprises against which to compare the behavioral results and as a factor in the long-run adaptation of decision-making norms. In this paper we examine one such structural feature of intelligent choice, the way in which unbiased errors in making estimates about available alternatives produce biased distributions of postdecision surprises.

Calculated Choice with Unbiased Estimates

Consider standard problems of choice such as the following:

1 *The adoption of a new technology*: we evaluate alternative technologies and install the one we estimate to have the best ratio of efficiency to cost.
2 *The selection of a new manager*: we evaluate candidates for a job and choose the one whom we estimate to have the greatest ability.
3 *The passage of new legislation*: we evaluate alternative legislative programs in terms of their political consequences and support the one that seems to offer the greatest improvement in prospects for our reelection. Innumerable similar choices (e.g., choices of marital partners, occupations, products, investments, and foreign policies) are made by individuals, groups, and societies.

Such decisions can be viewed in the following general way: There is a pool of possible alternatives. These alternatives differ with respect to their values. These values are not known with certainty, but can be estimated. In order to make a choice, decision-makers evaluate some alternatives drawn from the pool and choose the alternative that they think will be best.

The process is conventional and general. It presumes a general process of choice, not a specific decision-rule. Thus, it includes the case in which decision-makers select the best option among a predetermined number of alternatives drawn from the pool, or one in which alternatives are considered sequentially and the first one that satisfies some predetermined aspiration level is selected, or one in which alternatives are considered sequentially and choice follows Bayesian rules. It does not require that all alternatives be considered, or that knowledge about them be complete or accurate.

Suppose estimates are unbiased, but subject to random error. Random error, or noise, in estimation can be seen as arising either from stochastic properties of the world or from problems of observation, measurement, communication, or inference. On the one hand, the underlying attributes of interest may be subject to random fluctuation in their realizations. For example, suppose good managers, on average, perform better than poor managers, but any level of talent produces a distribution of results. Fluctuations could arise from inherent stochastic properties of managerial ability, from random variation in the situations in which they are observed, or from random changes in the evaluation criteria. Similarly, the realizations of technologies or legislative programs may show random fluctuation around their average values. The history of such fluctuations will affect current estimations of the values, and future fluctuations will affect future realizations. On the other hand, random fluctuation may be introduced by the estimation or evaluation process. There may be random error in observations or measurements, or in the recording or transmittal of this information, or in forming inferences about the future. In the remainder of this paper we consider how the distribution of postdecision surprises is affected by random errors in estimation, without regard to whether that error is a property of the attributes of interest or their estimation. We restrict our discussion to the case in which alternatives are evaluated on a single criterion; the general results also hold for each attribute dimension of a multi-attribute decision problem.

Let X be the value of some attribute of an alternative. X is not precisely known to the decision-maker: it is a random variable. Let Y be the random error in the estimate of the attribute value. We assume that X and Y are stochastically independent, that Y has a mean of zero ($m_y = 0$), and that the estimated value for the alternative is $Z = X + Y$. Thus, Z is random also. The assumption that the error and underlying value combine additively to produce the estimate is not necessary to the general argument of the paper, but it is required for the detailed computations. Different quantitative results, but not a different basic conclusion, would be obtained if the errors entered multiplicatively (e.g., $Z = e^{(X+Y)}$). The distributions of attribute values, X, and of the errors, Y, depend on the particular choice situation involved. If X is distributed with mean m_x and standard deviation s_x, and Y is distributed with mean zero and standard deviation s_y, then Z has mean $m_z = m_x$, and standard deviation $s_z = (s_x^2 + s_y^2)^{1/2}$. If we think of X as a signal and Y as noise, then we can define $w = s_x^2/s_y^2$ as the signal-to-noise ratio (Marschak and Radner, 1972). In discussions of communication channels, $s_x^2/(s_x^2 + s_y^2)$ is known as the reliability, k, of a channel. In the present situation, k might be defined as the reliability of an estimation process. It is easy to see, from equation (2) below, that $k = w/(w+1) = r_{xz}^2$; and that $w = k/(1-k)$. We assume that all alternatives have the same signal-to-noise ratio, which is a structural property of the estimation process. Consequently, the variances of X and Y, given Z, do not depend on the particular value of Z.

Let x_c, y_c, and z_c be the value, error, and estimate respectively for a *chosen* alternative. The chosen alternative is determined so that $z_c \geq z_i$ for all $i \neq c$, where z_i is the estimated value of the ith of n alternatives considered. We wish to examine the distribution of y_c, given an estimate z_c, and to determine the probability that y_c will be positive. In the absence of postdecision behavioral adjustment, the distribution of y_c over a set of decisions is the distribution of postdecision surprises. A surprise-neutral decision process is one that implies a symmetric distribution around a mean of zero, thus one whose structure is equally likely to produce euphoria (positive surprise) or disappointment (negative surprise), and on average produces neither. We ask whether a standard rational decision process is surprise-neutral in such a sense. The answer is that it is not.

Regression to the Mean

A basic structural property of decision-making processes such as those we have described is that an alternative with a relatively high estimated value will have associated with it, on average, a relatively large positive error, so that choosing the alternative with the highest estimated value will tend to elicit postdecision disappointment. This property stems from the well-known (Pearson, 1897; Snedecor, 1946) fact that the covariance of Y and Z must be positive. In fact, the correlation between the two, r_{yz}, depends only on the value of w and the assumption that X and Y are independent random variables. Specifically:[1]

$$r_{yz} = 1/(w+1)^{1/2}. \tag{1}$$

On average, the greater the value of z_i, the greater the value of y_i. Thus, if we make a decision by estimating the value of several alternatives, the higher the estimated value of the chosen alternative, the more disappointed we are likely to be in it. As Capen, Clapp, and Campbell (1971) observed in studying oil-lease bidding, 'In competitive bidding, the winner tends to be the player who most overestimates true tract value'. The result has come to be called 'the winner's curse'.

These disappointments, i.e., $E(y_c) > 0$, generated by making decisions intelligently are a form of regression to the mean. The phenomenon occurs in situations in which the future value of a variable having some random components is estimated on the basis of previously observed values of that variable. As equation (1) suggests, relatively extreme observations will be associated with relatively extreme random components, and less extreme observations will be associated with less extreme random components. Thus, if an extreme value is observed, the next observation can be expected to be less extreme, i.e., closer to the mean. Regression to the mean has long been recognized and widely discussed by biologists, statisticians, and social scientists. It was discussed as early as 1877 by Galton (1879), who observed that large sweet peas produced offspring with slightly smaller seeds. Regression to the mean has been noted in IQ scores (Anastasi, 1958), as a characteristic of managerial evaluation (March and March, 1978),

---

1   The derivations for all equations are straightforward. Those that may not be immediately obvious are shown in the Appendix.

and as a problem in such empirical research as measuring attitude change (Hovland, Lumsdaine, and Sheffield, 1949), assessing the impact of communication (Campbell and Clayton, 1961), and studying consumer attitudes (Morrison, 1973). Most treatments have emphasized the specific complications associated with specific examples rather than the generality of the phenomenon in any estimation or choice situation. Perhaps as a result, many people, including those with knowledge of statistics, do not reliably take regression into consideration in making predictions or in making decisions or judgments in uncertain situations. They do not seem to expect regression in many situations in which it is bound to occur (in the absence of behavioral reevaluations); and they invent spurious causal explanations for regression when it is observed (Tversky and Kahneman, 1974; Ross, 1977; Kahneman and Tversky, 1979; Nisbett and Ross, 1980; Hogarth, 1980).

Although higher estimated values are associated with greater disappointment, they are also associated with greater underlying values. The correlation between X and Z is also positive:

$$r_{xz} = [\ w/(\ w+1)]^{1/2}. \tag{2}$$

Or:

$$r_{xz} = r_{yz}(\ w^{1/2}). \tag{3}$$

The decision dilemma is clear. Choosing apparently better alternatives will, on average, produce higher returns. Thus, it is sensible to choose alternatives that are estimated to be relatively good. However, such a procedure is not surprise neutral. In the absence of behavioral adjustments, higher expected benefits will be associated with greater expected disappointments.

The Signal-to-Noise Effect

Any choice based on noisy estimates can be expected to exhibit a structural tendency toward disappointment. As is obvious from the equations above, the magnitude of the expected disappointment is a function of the signal-to-noise ratio, w. Large values of w produce a high correlation between estimates (z_i) and realizations (x_i), and a low correlation between estimates (z_i) and errors (y_i). As a result, high signal-to-noise ratios result in smaller disappointments.

To illustrate the magnitude of the signal-to-noise effect for one general class of decision situations, we introduce the assumption that X and Y, and consequently Z, are normally distributed. We can then determine the expected values of x_i and y_i for any given z_i as a function of w. These expectations of x_i and y_i are valid for *any* noisy estimate z_i (assuming normality), including the z_i that is associated with the chosen alternative. The expectation of x_i, given an estimate z_i, is given by:

$$E(x_i|z_i) = m_x + r_{xz}(s_x/s_z)(z_i - m_z). \tag{4}$$

Using equation (2), we can rewrite equation (4) as:

$$E(x_i|z_i) = m_z + r_{xz}^2(z_i - m_z). \tag{5}$$

Or, as a function of w:

$$E(x_i|z_i) = m_z + [w/(w+1)](z_i - m_z). \tag{6}$$

Analogously, using equation (1), we can estimate the magnitude of the error, y_i, given the estimate, z_i, as:

$$E(y_i|z_i = r_{yz}^2(z_i - m_z). \tag{7}$$

Or, as a function of w:

$$E(y_i|z_i) = (z_i - m_z)/(w+1). \tag{8}$$

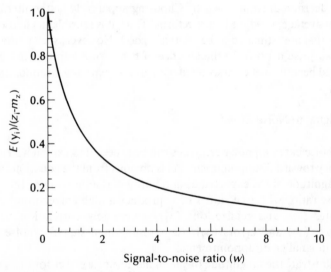

Figure 11.1. Expected fraction of deviation from the mean attributable to estimation error as a function of the signal-to-noise ratio (w)

In figure 11.1, we use these estimates to show, for any given deviation of z_i from $m_z = m_x$, the expected proportion of that deviation attributable to estimation error, as a function of w. The expected proportion attributable to the underlying value is one minus the value plotted in figure 11.1. As the figure confirms, the average contribution of estimation error to the apparent quality of an alternative is large when the signal-to-noise ratio is small.

Using equations (1) and (2) and the well-known (e.g., Mood and Graybill, 1963, p. 202) fact that if x_i and y_i are normally distributed, their conditional standard deviations are $s_{x_i|z_i} = s_x(1 - r_{xz}^2)^{1/2}$, and $s_{y_i|z_i} = s_y$ $(1 - r_{yz}^2)^{1/2}$, it is possible to specify the likelihood that structural post-decision disappointment will occur. The standard deviation of x_i given z_i, equals the standard deviation of y_i, given z_i, and is a function of the signal-to-noise ratio, w:

$$s_{x_i|z_i} = s_{y_i|z_i} = s_z[\, w^{1/2}/(w+1)\,]. \tag{9}$$

Note that $s_{x_i|z_i}$ and $s_{y_i|z_i}$ are equal, although in general s_x and s_y are not, because $x_i + y_i = z_i$.

With equation (9), it is possible to determine the probability, for a given estimate $z_i > m_z$, that the estimation error y_i is positive:

$$\Pr(y_i > 0 |_{z_i}) = 1 - \Pr\{V_N > [\,(z_i - m_z)/(w^{1/2}s_z)\,]\}. \tag{10}$$

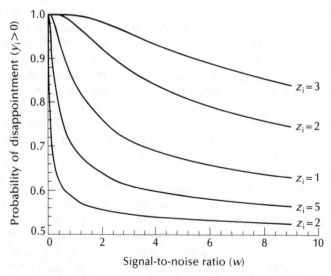

Figure 11.2. Probability of disappointment as a function of the signal-to-noise ratio (w) and the estimated value (z_i); $m_x = m_z = 0$; $s_z = 1$

where V_N is the standard normal variable. Figure 11.2 uses equation (10) to plot the probability that y_i is positive (i.e., the likelihood of disappointment) as a function of w, for various values of z_i, assuming $m_x = m_z = 0$ and $s_z = 1$. We have focused on y_i since it is the behavior of y_i that is associated with postdecision surprise. For a given z_i, a similar result could be obtained for the probability that $x_i > m_x$. Figure 11.2 quantifies the observation that the likelihood of postdecision disappointment decreases as the signal-to-noise ratio, w, increases. Specifically, the probability of positive expectation error approaches one as the signal-to-noise ratio approaches zero, and approaches $1/2$ as the signal-to-noise ratio becomes large. Figure 11.2 also shows the effect of the magnitude of z_i on the probability of disappointment. The higher the estimated value, z_i, of an alternative, the greater the chance of disappointment. Since choices are made by selecting that alternative that has the highest estimated value among the alternatives considered, z_c is likely to be relatively high – and so is disappointment.

The Number of Alternatives Effect

The expected level of disappointment is also affected by the number of alternatives considered. As is clear from the previous analysis, both the expected amount of postdecision surprise and the probability that disappointment will occur depend on the signal-to-noise ratio, w, and the estimated value, z_c, of the chosen alternative. If a decision is made by choosing the best of several alternatives, then it is clear that z_c will, on average, increase with the number of alternatives considered. Suppose a decision-maker considers precisely n alternatives and estimates the value, z_i, of each. If these alternatives are arranged in decreasing order of their estimated values, we can designate the alternative with the largest estimated value as a_1, the second largest as a_2, and so forth to a_n. These ordered estimates are normally called order statistics. In general, their expected values and distributions depend on the number of alternatives considered, n, and the distribution, A, of estimated values for the population of possible alternatives.

The properties of order statistics can be computed for any ordered alternative, a_i; but the primary interest here is in the particular case of a_1, the highest estimated value among n different, randomly chosen alternatives. Although there are no simple formulae to calculate expected values and distributions for extreme order statistics (e.g., a_1, a_n), the expected values for order statistics of many commonly used distributions have been approximated to a high degree of accuracy using numerical methods (e.g., Hastings et al., 1947; Harter, 1969). If a decision-maker estimates $z_i = x_i + y_i$ for each of n alternatives drawn at random, the expected estimated value of the highest ranking alternative depends on n and the standard deviation of the estimates, $s_z = (s_x^2 + s_y^2)^{1/2} = s_x[(w+1)/w]^{1/2}$. For example, figure 11.3 plots the expected value of the largest of n items drawn from a standard normal distribution. If alternatives are not drawn at random from the pool of possibilities, the specific quantitative results would be different, but not the general implications. If a decision-maker excludes some (bad) alternatives on the basis of prior knowledge, then alternatives can be seen as drawn at random from the subset of alternatives that are left. Such a procedure has the consequence of reducing the s_x and thus also reducing w.

Given w, n, and assumptions about the distributions of X and Y, we can find the expected estimated value for the highest ranked alternative. Then we can use the estimates of the signal-to-noise effect from the previous section to find its expected value and expected error. To illustrate, suppose X and Y, and therefore Z, are normally distributed. If $A_1(n)$ is the expected estimated value for the highest ranking alternative out of n drawn from a normal distribution, A, of estimated values for alternatives, and N denotes the standard normal distribution, then:

$$E(z_c) = A_1(n) = m_z + s_z N_1(n). \qquad (11)$$

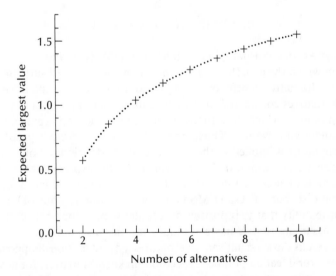

Figure 11.3. Expected value of largest alternative as a function of the number of alternatives (n), where alternatives are drawn from a standard normal distribution

Or:

$$E(z_c) = A_1(n) = m_x + s_x[(w+1)/w]^{1/2}N_1,(n),\qquad(12)$$

where z_c is the estimated value of the chosen alternative.

We wish to determine the expectations of x_c and y_c, the true value and error for the chosen alternative. Since we have assumed normality, we can use equations (6) and (8) to specify the expectations for x_i and y_i:

$$E(x_i) = m_z + [w/(w+1)][E(z_i) - m_z];\qquad(13)$$

$$E(y_i) = [E(z_i) - m_z]/(w+1).\qquad(14)$$

And from those and the expression for $E(z_c)$ in equation (11), we can derive the expectations for x_c and y_c:

$$E(x_c) = m_z + [w/(w+1)][s_z N_1(n)];\qquad(15)$$

$$E(y_c) = s_z N_1(n)/(w+1).\qquad(16)$$

Or, in terms of the distribution of X:

$$E(x_c) = m_x + [w/w+1)]^{1/2}[s_x N_1(n)]:\qquad(17)$$

$$E(y_c) = [s_x N_1(n)]/[w(w+1)]^{1/2}.\qquad(18)$$

If we assume normality, equations (15), (16), (17), and (18) show the way in which the expected underlying value and expected surprise of the chosen alternative depend on the signal-to-noise ratio, w, and the number of alternatives considered, n. In particular, equations (16) and (18) give the amount by which the estimated value of a choice, on average, inflates the underlying value. Thus, they show the expected postdecision disappointment implicit in the structure of the decision-making process, as a function of w and n. Figure 11.4 shows the expected value of y_c as a function of w for a range of values of n, assuming X has a standard normal distribution. Using Monte Carlo procedures, figure 11.5 shows the probability that y_c is positive as a function of w for a range of values of n, assuming that X has a standard normal distribution.

The results show a significant level of expected postdecision disappointment as a structural feature of rational decision-making. Moreover, for any given signal-to-noise ratio, the level of structural disappointment increases with the number of alternatives considered. Since the expected value of the chosen alternative also increases with the number of alternatives, the pains

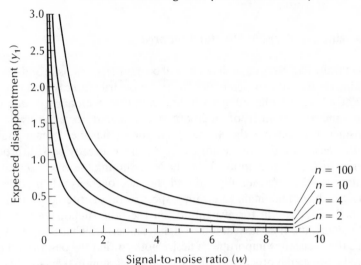

Figure 11.4. Expected disappointment as a function of the signal-to-noise ratio (w) and the number of alternatives (n), where x has a standard normal distribution

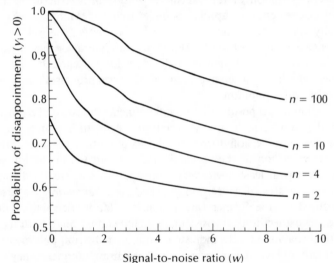

Figure 11.5. Probability of disappointment as a function of the signal-to-noise ratio (w) and the number of alternatives (n), where x has a standard normal distribution

of greater disappointment are presumably somewhat ameliorated by the pleasures of greater benefit. However, if neither prior corrections for the effect nor behavioral adjustments of expectations occur, each additional alternative evaluated before making a decision adds to the risk and expected magnitude of postdecision disappointment.

Managing Postdecision Structural Surprise

Structurally induced disappointment will be most characteristic of decision-making conditions in which variation among the true values of alternatives is relatively small, the ambiguity or uncertainty in evaluation is relatively high, and the number of alternatives considered is relatively large. Consider, for example, the choice of a top-level manager from a pool of senior executives. Eligible senior executives have already passed through a series of filters (promotions) that have, assuming the filters screen on similar criteria, substantially reduced the heterogeneity of the original cohort of beginning managers with respect to those criteria. That is, s_x^2 is small. The criteria for evaluation, on the other hand, are relatively ambiguous, and their use subject to significant error. That is, s_y^2 is large. Since the decision is important, a desire both to find the best person and to make the search process legitimate compel decision-makers to consider a relatively large number of candidates. That is, n is large. Consequently, the careful selection of top executives results in a structural tendency toward postselection disappointment (March and March, 1978). More generally, in any decision situation that is relatively novel, in which experience is modest, in which criteria are ambiguous or their estimation noisy, and that is important enough or prolonged enough to stimulate extended search for alternatives, sensible decision processes imply notable postdecision disappointment.

A recognition that postdecision disappointment is a structural characteristic of intelligent choice in many situations leads to attempts to avoid or manage postdecision surprises. An examination of such efforts is a natural extension of the previous analysis, but the discussion should be prefaced by at least one caveat. Our analysis has tried to distinguish *structural* features of a decision process from *behavioral* features and has focused on the former rather than the latter. Sensible advice on managing postdecision surprise should include attention to both features. Since the behavioral results indicate postdecision distributions of surprises that sometimes involve euphoria, sometimes disappointment, they cannot be understood as simple consequences of the properties of the decision process we have discussed. For example, although we have shown that the structural bias toward postdecision disappointment increases with the number of alternatives considered, there is some behavioral evidence that increasing the number of alternatives considered actually decreases the postdecision dissatisfaction of individuals (O'Reilly and Caldwell, 1981). Our analysis, by identifying a baseline of disappointment, makes such results even more striking than they might otherwise appear. At the same time, the behavioral results are cautions against basing managerial actions simply on structural features of the decision model (March, 1978)

The most obvious way to manage postdecision disappointment is to deflate expectations; assuming we wish to eliminate structural effects on postdecision surprise, deflating expectations seems sensible whenever it is feasible. If w is known and expectations can be arbitrarily adjusted, an appropriate correction will eliminate the structural bias. For the case of normally distributed errors, equation (8) defines the expected inflation of estimates as a function of w, and thus the necessary correction. Where w is not known with precision, it may be estimated. Alternatively, it is possible simply to introduce a less quantitative skepticism about expectations that varies with guesses about the signal-to-noise ratio and the number of alternatives. Murphy's Law for example. As Brown (1975) pointed out, such adjustments may be incorrectly interpreted by observers as 'risk aversion'.

In many situations, however, explicitly deflating expectations may not be feasible or desirable. When the decision process involves conflict, persuasion, discussion, and commitment, if one participant unilaterally deflates expectations, it simply makes that participant less persuasive, or makes that participant's commitment to a chosen alternative less than may be needed for its success. Consequently, we may want to consider an alternative form of surprise management. We can treat w and n as decision variables, chosen by allocating resources either to clarifying the values of known alternatives or to locating and evaluating new alternatives. If we ignore postdecision disappointment, any costless increase in either the signal-to-noise ratio, w, or the number of alternatives, n, is unambiguously advantageous in terms of increasing the expected returns from choice. The expected value of a chosen alternative will be increased if either w or n is increased. However, since increasing either w or n introduces costs of gathering and processing information, there is an optimization problem involved in allocating resources to them.

Given cost functions in terms of w and n, the expected net benefit of a choice conditional on w and n can be determined. By expected net benefit, we mean simply the expected value of the chosen alternative minus the expected information or search costs, $c(w,n)$, of achieving w and n. Relatively little is known about the cost of information (Marschak and Radner, 1972). Linear cost functions have been assumed for the cost of additional alternatives (Arrow, Blackwell, and Girschick, 1949; Wald, 1950; Savage, 1954), and it is possible to make similar linear assumptions about the cost of improving w. For example, it can be shown that increasing w by a strategy of multiple estimates of each alternative leads to a cost function linear in w if cost is linear in n. In figures 11.6 and 11.7 it is assumed that the cost of information is given by $c(n,w) = a + bnw$.

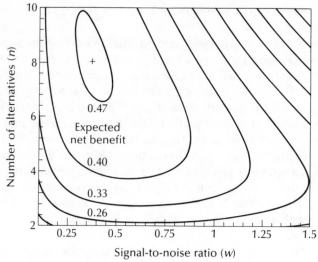

Figure 11.6. Expected net benefit as a function of the signal-to-noise ratio (w) and the number of alternatives (n)

It is also assumed that X has a standard normal distribution, and that Y is normally distributed with $m_y = 0$. Alternative cost and distribution assumptions would yield different quantitative results. Note also that figure 11.6 and 11.7 treat n as a continuous variable for illustrative purposes; only integer values of n are realizable.

Figure 11.6 shows a set of constant expected net benefit (indifference) curves conditional on w and n, and defines an optimum information policy for a decision-maker wanting to maximize expected net benefits. That is, it shows what level of w and n to choose, considering the costs of achieving those levels and the benefits accruing from them. Since increasing w or n offers improved expected performance, and each is costly, an optimal policy involves choosing between them. In the example displayed in figure 11.6, it would appear that major improvements in expected performance come less expensively from increases in n than from increases in w. Thus, at least in this particular case, there is some justification for devoting resources to expanding the number of alternatives rather than improving the precision of estimates about known alternatives.

Such an analysis, however, ignores the problems associated with post-decision disappointment. In general, if disappointment has negative utility, the above analysis will lead to overinvestment in n relative to w. Increasing the number of alternatives considered, n, increases expected realization, but it increases expected disappointment at the same time. Thus, each additional alternative considered increases the likelihood and expected magnitude of postdecision disappointment. On the other hand, increasing

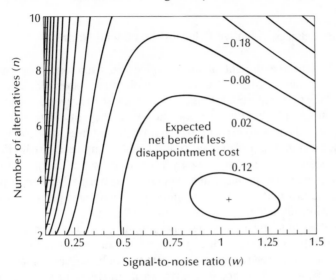

Figure 11.7. Expected net benefit minus disappointment cost $(d = 1/3)$ as a function of the signal-to-noise ratio (w) and the number of alternatives (n)

the signal-to-noise ratio, w, both improves the expected value of the chosen alternative and reduces expected disappointment.

If we consider postdecision disappointment as one of the potential costs of making decisions, however, we can then examine possible trade-offs between the gains of net realized benefits and the losses of disappointments. As in the case of the information-cost analysis, an analysis involving disappointment involves assumptions about information costs, as well as assumptions about the exchange rate between outcomes and disappointments. That is, although realizations and disappointments are measured in the same units within the model, the utility of one unit of net benefit and the disutility of one unit of disappointment may be different. If we assume a simple exchange rate, d, we can plot the net gains minus the costs of disappointment as a function of w and n. Figure 11.7 shows net benefits minus disappointments for $d = 1/3$, for various values of w and n. When $d = 1/3$, a decision-maker is indifferent between increasing net benefits by one unit or decreasing disappointment by three units. In other words, the 'penalty' for a unit of disappointment is relatively low compared to the 'reward' for a unit of benefit. A comparison of figures 11.6 and 11.7 suggests that under some circumstances decision-makers might prefer – for reasons of disappointment costs – to invest in increasing w rather than in increasing n.

Structural Biases, Adaptive Behavior, and Social Norms

According to the present analysis, individuals and organizations are exposed to the risk of postdecision disappointment relatively frequently, not because they make poor decisions, nor because their world is unusually cruel, but simply because the way in which they (intelligently) make decisions leads them to expect too much. Intelligent decision-making with unbiased estimation of future costs and benefits implies a distribution of postdecision surprises that is biased in the direction of disappointment. Thus, a society that defines intelligent choice as normatively appropriate for individuals and organizations imposes a structural pressure toward postdecision unhappiness.

This does not mean that disappointment with decisions will be a necessary characteristic of individuals or organizations within such a society, however. The relation between structural biases and actual human behavior in a culture is not straightforward. In trying to identify biases inherent in the logic of the rules of decision-making, the present analysis is similar in spirit to game-theoretic efforts to describe power relations implicit in structural properties of a political system (Shapley and Shubik, 1954). Speculations about the impact of such structural properties on human behavior include two quite different kinds of propositions. The first, implicit in the analysis above, generates predictions about variations in reported postdecision surprise as a function of variations in signal-to-noise ratios and numbers of alternatives. The second considers the ways in which individuals, social norms, and social institutions have adapted to the bias over a history of experience with it, and the ways in which norms of choice fit with other important norms of social organization.

The second kind of speculation is more important. It is also more difficult. Differences in the magnitude of the structural bias are fundamental to understanding postdecision surprise; but they will not account directly for observed differences in surprise. Observed postdecision subjective experiences of euphoria and disappointment reflect behavioral adjustments to the structural biases of choice, as well as to other structural constraints on social life. The adjustments include both deliberate strategic actions and long-term adaptation. As was suggested in the previous section, it is possible to anticipate and manage the bias in postdecision surprise. Individuals and organizations can be taught to anticipate the bias, make corrections, and operate in terms of the corrected expectations. More importantly in the present context, adjustments to implicit bias in surprises may be found in less deliberate attributes of ordinary individual and organizational behavior, rules of thumb, motives, and sentiments.

For example, empirical studies of decision-making in political institutions and organizations indicate that surprises are often negative, that realizations from decisions tend to be disappointing (Pressman and Wildavsky, 1973; Bardach, 1977; Sproull, Weiner, and Wolf, 1978). Most empirical research on individual decision-making, on the other hand, reports positive post-decision surprises (Festinger, 1957, 1964; Staw, 1974, 1976; Salancik, 1977). It seems possible that psychological and normative mechanisms have evolved to offset the disappointment bias in individual decision-making; but the same mechanisms are either less powerful or less pervasive in collective choice.

A number of studies (Staw, 1974, 1976; Salancik, 1977) suggest that a key feature of individual postdecision satisfaction is the acceptance of personal responsibility for personal action, thereby for the consequences of that action, and thereby for discomfort with postdecision disappointment. That is, postdecision disappointment conflicts with individual norms of personal autonomy, control, and competence. The conventional response in cultures committed to such norms is to accept responsibility for the decisions (at least in the short run), deny disappointment, and behave as though the disconfirmations of expectations either did not occur or were unimportant (Aronson, 1968).

Similar acceptance of responsibility for past decisions is less conventional in the kind of collectivities that have been studied (but see Hägg, 1977). Rather, the norms are norms of conflict, competition, ambition, and turnover, and the expectation is that successors will be appropriately disappointed with the results of actions by predecessors. The conventional response in cultures committed to norms of competition and turnover is to accept disappointment, deny responsibility, and find justification for turnover in the failure to realize expectation. Disappointments are sustained by the way deliberative or political processes of decision undermine the commitment that is essential both to implementing decisions and to postdecision euphoria (Brunsson, 1982) and by the way advocates of alternative actions inflate their estimates of net return (Allison, 1969; Halperin, 1974; Williamson, 1975).

Thus, we suggest that organizational norms of turnover and competition for control and individual norms of personal responsibility can be understood as different adaptations to a bias introduced by intelligent choice. The suggestion may be overly brave, but it has the appeal of introducing a bit of sociology into a statistical analysis of a psychological problem. It may also lead us to ask whether the normative glorification of intelligent choice is to be considered simply a given of modern life or can be understood in terms of the fit between rules of intelligence and other social imperatives. Norms of intelligent choice are undoubtedly encouraged in both individuals and organizations by the way such choices improve average returns from decision-making. The norms may also be reinforced, particularly in organizations, by the way intelligent choice produces normatively appropriate disappointments. Where a central normative feature of social organization is competition for promotion and control, as it is in democratic political systems and many bureaucratic organizations, postdecision disappointment helps sustain important social norms.

Appendix: Derivations of Equations

The derivations of the equations in the text are substantially trivial. Those that are not immediately obvious are provided here.

Equation 1 (and, analogously, 2):

$$
\begin{aligned}
r_{yz} &= \mathrm{Cov}(Y,Z)/s_y s_z \\
&= E\left[(Y-m_y)(Z-m_z)\right]/s_y s_z \\
&= E\left[(Y-m_y)(X+Y-m_x-m_y)\right]/s_y s_z \\
&= E\left[(Y-m_y)(X-m_x)+(Y-m_y)^2\right]/s_y s_z \\
&= \{E\left[(Y-m_y)(X-m_z)\right]+E\left[(Y-m_y)^2\right]\}(s_y s_t \\
&= \{\mathrm{Cov}(Y,X)+s_y^2\}/s_y s_z \\
&= s_y^2/s_y s_z \quad \text{(since } X \text{ and } Y \text{ are independent)} \\
&= s_y/s_z \\
&= s_y/(s_x^2+s_y^2)^{1/2} \\
&= 1/\left[(s_x^2/s_y^2)+1\right]^{1/2} \\
&= 1/(w+1)^{1/2}
\end{aligned}
$$

Equation 4:

The result in equation (4) is well known (e.g., Mood and Graybill, 1963, p. 202; Marschak and Radner, 1972; Nisbett and Ross, 1980).

Equation 5 (and, analogously, 7):

$$
\begin{aligned}
E(x_i|z_i) &= m_x + r_{xz}(s_x/s_z)(z_i-m_z) \\
&= m_z + r_{xz}\left[s_x/(s_z^2+s_y^2)^{1/2}\right](z_i-m_z) \\
&= m_z + r_{xz}\{\left[s_x/s_y\right]/\left[(s_x^2/s_y^2)+1\right]^{1/2}\}(z_i-m_z) \\
&= m_z + r_{xz}\left[w/(w+1))\right]^{1/2}(z_i-m_z) \\
&= m_z + r_{xz}^2(z_i-m_z) \quad \text{(using equation 2).}
\end{aligned}
$$

Equation 9:

$$
\begin{aligned}
s_{x_i|z_i} &= s_x(1-r_{xz}^2)^{1/2} \\
&= s_z(s_x^2/s_z^2)^{1/2}\left[1-(w/w+1)\right]^{1/2} \\
&= s_z\left[s_x^2/(s_x^2+s_y^2)\right]^{1/2}\left[1/(w+1)\right]^{1/2} \\
&= s_z\left[w/(w+1)\right]^{1/2}\left[1/(w+1)\right]^{1/2} \\
&= s_z\left[w^{1/2}/(w+1)\right].
\end{aligned}
$$

Similarly:

$$
\begin{aligned}
s_{y_i|z_i} &= s_y(1-r_{yz}^2)^{1/2} \\
&= \ldots \\
&= s_z\left[w^{1/2}/(w+1)\right].
\end{aligned}
$$

Equation 10:
$$\Pr(y_i > 0 | z_i) = \Pr\{ [\{ y_i - E(y_i | z_i) \} / s_{y_i | z_i}] > [\{ 0 - E(y_i | z_i) \} / s_{y_i | z_i}) \}$$
$$= \Pr\{ V_N > [- (z_i - m_z) / (w + 1) / [s_z w^{1/2} / (w + 1)]] \}$$
$$= \Pr\{ V_N > - [(z_i - m_z) / (w^{1/2} s_z)]] \}$$
$$= 1 - \Pr\{ V_N > [(z_i - m_z) / (w^{1/2} s_z)]] \}$$

Equation 13 (and, analogously, 14):
$$E(x_i) E [E(x_i | z_i)]$$
$$= E\{ m_z + [w / (w + 1)] (z_i - m_z) \}$$
$$= m_z + [w / (w + 1)] [E(z_i) - m_z].$$

References

Allison, Graham T. (1969) *Essense of Decision: Explaining the Cuban Missile Crisis*. Boston: Little Brown.

Anastasi, Anne (1958) *Differential Psychology*, 3rd edn New York: Macmillan.

Aronson, Elliot (1968) Disconfirmed expectancies and bad decisions – Discussion: Expectancy vs. other motives. In Robert P. Abelson, Elliot Aronson, William McGuire, Theodore Newcomb, Milton Rosenberg, and Percy H. Tannenbaum (eds), *Theories of Cognitive Consistency:* 491–3. Chicago: Rand McNally.

Arrow, Kenneth J., David Blackwell, and Meyer A. Girshick (1949) Bayes and minimax solutions of sequential decision problems. *Econometrica*, 17: 213–44.

Bardach, Eugene (1977) *The Implementation Game*. Cambridge, MA: MIT Press.

Brown, Keith C. (1975) A note on optimal fixed-price bidding with uncertain production cost. *Bell Journal of Economics*, 6: 695–97.

Brunsson, Nils (1982) The irrationality of action and action rationality: Decisions, ideologies and organizational actions. *Journal of Management Studies*, 19: 29–44.

Campbell, Donald T., and Keith T. Clayton (1961) Avoiding regression effects in panel studies of communication impact. *Studies in Public Communication*, 3: 99–118.

Capen, E. C., R. V. Clapp, and W. M. Campbell (1971) Competitive bidding in high-risk situations. *Journal of Petroleum Technology*, 23: 641–53.

Festinger, Leon (1957) *A Theory of Cognitive Dissonance*. Stanford, CA: Stanford University Press.

Festinger, Leon (ed.) (1964) *Conflict, Decision, and Dissonance*. Stanford, CA: Stanford University Press.

Galton, Francis (1879) Typical laws of heredity. *Proceedings of the Royal Institute of Great Britain (1875–8):* 282–301.

Hägg, Ingemund (1977) *Review of Capital Investments* Uppsala, Sweden: University of Uppsala, Department of Business Administration.

Halperin, Morton H. (1974) *Bureaucratic Politics and Foreign Policy*. Washington, DC: Brookings Institution.

Harter, Harmon L. (1969) *Order Statistics and Their Use in Testing and Estimation*, vol. 2. Wright-Patterson Air Force Base, OH: Aerospace Research Laboratories.

Hastings, Cecil, Jr., Frederick Mosteller, John W. Tukey, and Charles P. Winsor (1947) Low moments for small samples: A comparative study of order statistics. *Annals of Mathematical Statistics,* 18: 413–26.

Hogarth, Robin M. (1980) *Judgement and Choice. The Psychology of Decision.* New York: Wiley.

Hovland, Carl I., Arthur A. Lumsdaine, and Fred D. Sheffield (1949) *Experiments on Mass Communications.* Appendix D: 329–40. Princeton, NJ: Princeton University Press.

Kahneman, Daniel, and Amos Tversky (1979) Intuitive prediction: Biases and corrective procedures. *Management Science,* 12: 313–27.

March, James C., and James G. March (1978) Performance sampling in social matches. *Administrative Science Quarterly,* 23: 434–53.

March, James G. (1978) Bounded rationality, ambiguity, and the engineering of choice. *Bell Journal of Economics,* 9: 587–608.

Marschak, Jacob, and Roy Radner (1972) *Economic Theory of Teams.* New Haven, CT: Yale University Press.

Mood, Alexander M., and Franklin A. Graybill (1963) *Introduction to the Theory of Statistics.* New York: McGraw-Hill.

Morrison, Donald G. (1973) Reliability of tests: A technique using the 'regression to the mean' fallacy. *Journal of Marketing Research,* 10: 91–3.

Nisbett, Richard, and Lee Ross (1980) *Human Inference: Strategies and Shortcomings of Social Judgment.* Englewood Cliffs, NJ: Prentice-Hall.

O'Reilly, Charles A., and David F. Caldwell (1981) The commitment and job tenure of new employees: Some evidence of postdecisional justification. *Administrative Science Quarterly,* 26: 597–616.

Pearson, Karl (1897) Mathematical contributions to the theory of evolution. On: a form of spurious correlation which may arise when indices are used in the measurement of organs. *Proceedings of the Royal Society,* Series A, 60: 489–98.

Pressman, Jeffrey L., and Aaron B. Wildavsky (1973) *Implementation.* Berkeley, CA: University of California Press.

Ross, Lee (1977) The intuitive psychologist and his shortcomings: Distortion in the attribution process. In Leonard Berkowitz (ed.) *Advances in Experimental Psychology:* 173–220. New York: Academic Press.

Salancik, Gerald R. (1977) Commitment and the control of organizational behavior and belief. In Barry M. Staw and Gerald R. Salancik (eds), *New Directions in Organizational Behavior;* 1–54. Chicago: St. Clair.

Savage, Leonard J. (1954) *The Foundations of Statistics.* New York: Wiley.

Shapley, L. S., and Martin A. Shubik (1954) A method for evaluating the distribution of power in a committee system. *American Political Science Review,* 48: 787–92.

Snedecor, George W. (1946) *Statistical Methods,* 4th edn Ames, IO: Iowa State College Press.

Sproull, Lee S., Stephen Weiner, and David B. Wolf (1978) *Organizing an Anarchy.* Chicago: University of Chicago Press.

Staw, Barry M (1974) Attitudinal and behavioral consequences of changing a major organizational reward: A natural field experiment. *Journal of Personality and and Social Psychology,* 6: 742–51.

Staw, Barry M. (1976) Knee-deep in the Big Muddy: A study of escalating commitment to a chosen course of action. *Organizational Behavior and Human Performance*, 16: 27–44.

Tversky, Amos, and Daniel Kahneman (1974) Judgment under uncertainty: Heuristics and biases. *Science*, 185: 1124–31.

Wald, Abraham (1950) *Statistical Decision Functions*. New York: Wiley.

Williamson, Oliver E. (1975) *Markets and Hierarchies*. New York: Free Press.

Part IV
Decision-Making under Ambiguity

12

The Technology of Foolishness

James G. March

Choice and Rationality

The concept of choice as a focus for interpreting and guiding human behavior has rarely had an easy time in the realm of ideas. It is beset by theological disputations over free will, by the dilemmas of absurdism, by the doubts of psychological behaviorism, by the claims of historical, economic, social, and demographic determinism. Nevertheless, the idea that humans make choices has proven robust enough to become a major matter of faith in important segments of contemporary Western civilization. It is a faith that is professed by virtually all theories of social policy-making.

The major tenets of this faith run something like this:

> Human beings make choices. If done properly, choices are made by evaluating alternatives in terms of goals on the basis of information currently available. The alternative that is most attractive in terms of the goals is chosen. The process of making choices can be improved by using the technology of choice. Through the paraphernalia of modern techniques, we can improve the quality of the search for alternatives, the quality of information, and the quality of the analysis used to evaluate alternatives. Although actual choice may fall short of this ideal in various ways, it is an attractive model of how choices should be made by individuals, organizations, and social systems.

These articles of faith have been built upon, and have stimulated, some scripture. It is the scripture of theories of decision-making. The scripture is

This chapter is based on a paper first published in *Civiløkonomen* (Copenhagen) 18 (1971).

partly a codification of received doctrine and partly a source for that doctrine. As a result, our cultural ideas of intelligence and our theories of choice bear some substantial resemblance. In particular, they share three conspicuous interrelated ideas:

The first idea is the *pre-existence of purpose*. We find it natural to base an interpretation of human-choice behavior on a presumption of human purpose. We have, in fact, invented one of the most elaborate terminologies in the professional literature: 'values', 'needs', 'wants', 'goods', 'tastes', 'preferences', 'utility', 'objectives', 'goals', 'aspirations', 'drives'. All of these reflect a strong tendency to believe that a useful interpretation of human behavior involves defining a set of objectives that (a) are prior attributes of the system, and (b) make the observed behavior in some sense intelligent *vis-á-vis* those objectives.

Whether we are talking about individuals or about organizations, purpose is an obvious presumption of the discussion. An organization is often defined in terms of its purpose. It is seen by some as the largest collectivity directed by a purpose. Action within an organization is justified (or criticized) in terms of the purpose. Individuals explain their own behavior, as well as the behavior of others, in terms of a set of value premises that are presumed to be antecedent to the behavior. Normative theories of choice begin with an assumption of a pre-existent preference ordering defined over the possible outcomes of a choice.

The second idea is the *necessity of consistency*. We have come to recognize consistency both as an important property of human behavior and as a prerequisite for normative models of choice. Dissonance theory, balance theory, theories of congruency in attitudes, statuses, and performances have all served to remind us of the possibilities for interpreting human behavior in terms of the consistency requirements of a limited capacity information-processing system.

At the same time, consistency is a cultural and theoretical virtue. Action should be made consistent with belief. Actions taken by different parts of an organization should be consistent with each other. Individual and organizational activities are seen as connected with each other in terms of their consequences for some consistent set of purposes. In an organization, the structural manifestation of the dictum of consistency is the hierarchy with its obligations of coordination and control. In the individual, the structural manifestation is a set of values that generates a consistent preference ordering.

The third idea is the *primacy of rationality*. By rationality I mean a procedure for deciding what is correct behavior by relating consequences systematically to objectives. By placing primary emphasis on rational techniques, we implicitly have rejected – or seriously impaired – two other procedures for choice: (a) the processes of intuition, by means of which people may do things without fully understanding why; (b) the processes of tradition and faith, through which people do things because that is the way they are done.

Both within the theory and within the culture we insist on the ethic of rationality. We justify individual and organizational action in terms of an analysis of means and ends. Impulse, intuition, faith, and tradition are outside that system and viewed as antithetical to it. Faith may be seen as a possible source of values. Intuition may be seen as a possible source of ideas about alternatives. But the analysis and justification of action lie within the context of reason.

These ideas are obviously deeply imbedded in the culture. Their roots extend into ideas that have conditioned much of modern Western history and interpretations of that history. Their general acceptance is probably highly correlated with permeation of rationalism and individualism into the style of thinking within the culture. The ideas are even more obviously imbedded in modern theories of choice. It is fundamental to those theories that thinking should precede action; that action should serve a purpose; that purpose should be defined in terms of a consistent set of pre-existent goals; and that choice should be based on a consistent theory of the relation between action and its consequences.

Every tool of management decision that is currently a part of management science, operations research, or decision theory assumes the prior existence of a set of consistent goals. Almost the entire structure of microeconomic theory builds on the assumption that there exists a well-defined, stable, and consistent preference-ordering. Most theories of individual or organizational choice behavior accept the idea that goals exist and that (in some sense) an individual or organization acts on those goals, choosing from among some alternatives on the basis of available information. Discussions of educational policy, for example, with the emphasis on goal-setting, evaluation, and accountability, are directly in this tradition.

From the perspective of all of man's history, the ideas of purpose, consistency, and rationality are relatively new. Much of the technology currently available to implement them is extremely new. Over the past few centuries, and conspicuously over the past few decades, we have substantially improved man's capability for acting purposively, consistently, and rationally. We have substantially increased his propensity to think of himself as doing so. It is an impressive victory, won – where it has been won – by a happy combination of timing, performance, ideology, and persistence. It is a battle yet to be concluded, or even engaged, in many cultures of the world; but within most of the Western world, individuals and organizations see themselves as making choices.

The Problem of Goals

The tools of intelligence as they are fashioned in modern theories of choice are necessary to any reasonable behavior in contemporary society. It is difficult to see how we could, and inconceivable that we would, fail to continue their development, refinement, and extension. As might be expected, however, a theory and ideology of choice built on the ideas outlined above is deficient in some obvious, elementary ways, most conspicuously in the treatment of human goals.

Goals are thrust upon the intelligent man. We ask that he act in the name of goals. We ask that he keep his goals consistent. We ask that his actions be oriented to his goals. We ask that a social system amalgamate individual goals into a collective goal. But we do not concern ourselves with the origin of goals. Theories of individual organizational and social choice assume actors with pre-existent values.

Since it is obvious that goals change over time and that the character of those changes affects both the richness of personal and social development and the outcome of choice behavior, a theory of choice must somehow justify ignoring the phenomena. Although it is unreasonable to ask a theory of choice to solve all of the problems of man and his development, it is reasonable to ask how something as conspicuous as the fluidity and ambiguity of objectives can plausibly be ignored in a theory that is offered as a guide to human choice behavior.

There are three classic justifications. The first is that goal development and choice are independent processes, conceptually and behaviorally. The second is that the model of choice is never satisfied in fact that deviations from the model accommodate the problems of introducing change. The third is that the idea of changing goals is so intractable in a normative theory of choice that nothing can be said about it. Since I am unpersuaded of the first and second justifications, my optimism with respect to the third is somewhat greater than most of my fellows.

The argument that goal development and choice are independent behaviorally seems clearly false. It seems to me perfectly obvious that a description that assumes goals come first and action comes later is frequently radically wrong. Human choice behavior is at least as much a process for discovering goals as for acting on them. Although it is true enough that goals and decisions are 'conceptually' distinct, that is simply a statement of the theory. It is not defense of it. They are conceptually distinct if we choose to make them so.

The argument that the model is incomplete is more persuasive. There do appear to be some critical 'holes' in the system of intelligence as described by standard theories of choice. There is incomplete information, incomplete goal consistency, and a variety of external processes impinging on goal development – including tuition and tradition. What is somewhat disconcerting about the argument, however, is that it makes the efficacy of the concepts of intelligent choice dependent on their inadequacy. As we become more competent in the techniques of the model, and more committed to it, the 'holes' become smaller. As the model becomes more accepted, our obligation to modify it increases.

The final argument seems to me sensible as a general principle, but misleading here. Why are we more reluctant to ask how human beings might find 'good' goals than we are to ask how they might make 'good' decisions? The second question appears to be a relatively technical problem. The first seems more pretentious. It claims to say something about alternative virtues. The appearance of pretense, however, stems directly from the theory and the ideology associated with it.

In fact, the conscious introduction of goal discovery as a consideration in theories of human choice is not unknown to modern man. For example, we have two kinds of theories of choice behavior in human beings. One is a theory of children. The other is a theory of adults. In the theory of childhood, we emphasize choices as leading to experiences that develop the child's scope, his complexity, his awareness of the world. As parents, or psychologists, we try to lead the child to do things that are inconsistent with his present goals because we know (or believe) that he can only develop into an interesting person by coming to appreciate aspects of experience that he initially rejects.

In the theory of adulthood, we emphasize choices as a consequence of our intentions. As adults, or economists, we try to take actions that (within the limits of scarce resources) come as close as possible to achieving our goals. We try to find improved ways of making decisions consistent with our perceptions of what is valuable in the world.

The asymmetry in these models is conspicuous. Adults have constructed a model world in which adults know what is good for themselves, but children do not. It is hard to react positively to the conceit. The asymmetry has, in fact, stimulated a rather large number of ideologies and reforms designed to allow children the same moral prerogative granted to adults – the right to imagine that they know what they want. The efforts have cut deeply into traditional child-bearing, traditional educational policies, traditional politics, and traditional consumer economics.

In my judgment, the asymmetry between models of choice for adults and models of choice for children is awkward; but the solution we have adopted is precisely wrong-headed. Instead of trying to adapt the model of adults to children, we might better adapt the model of children to adults. For many purposes, our model of children is better. Of course, children know what they want. Everyone does. The critical question is whether they are encouraged to develop more interesting 'wants'. Values change. People become more interesting as those values and the interconnections made among them change.

One of the most obvious things in the world turns out to be hard for us to accommodate in our theory of choice: A child of two will almost always have a less interesting set of values (yes, indeed, a *worse* set of values) than a child of twelve. The same is true of adults. Values develop through experience. Although one of the main natural arenas for the modification of human values is the area of choice, our theories of adult and organizational decision-making ignore the phenomenon entirely.

Introducing ambiguity and fluidity to the interpretation of individual, organizational, and societal goals, obviously has implications for behavioral theories of decision-making. The main point here, however, is not to consider how we might describe the behavior of systems that are discovering goals as they act. Rather it is to examine how we might improve the quality of that behavior, how we might aid the development of interesting goals.

We know how to advise a society, an organization, or an individual if we are first given a consistent set of preferences. Under some conditions, we can suggest how to make decisions if the preferences are only consistent up to the point of specifying a series of independent constraints on the choice. But what about a normative theory of goal-finding behavior? What do we say when our client tells us that he is not sure his present set of values is the set of values in terms of which he wants to act?

It is a question familiar to many aspects of ordinary life. It is a question that friends, associates, students, college presidents, business managers, voters, and children ask at least as frequently as they ask how they should act within a set consistent and stable values.

Within the context of the normative theory of choice as it exists, the answer we give is: First determine the values, then act. The advice is frequently useful. Moreover, we have developed ways in which we can use conventional techniques for decision analysis to help discover value premises and to expose value inconsistencies. These techniques involve testing the decision implications of some successive approximations to a set of preferences. The object is to find a consistent set of preferences with implications that are acceptable to the person or organization making the decisions. Variations on such techniques are used routinely in operations research, as well as in personal counseling and analysis.

The utility of such techniques, however, apparently depends on the assumption that a primary problem is the amalgamation or excavation of pre-existent values. The metaphors – 'finding oneself', 'goal clarification', 'self-discovery', 'social welfare function', 'revealed pre-reference' – are metaphors of search. If our value premises are to be 'constructed' rather than 'discovered', our standard procedures may be useful; but we have no *a priori* reason for assuming they will.

Perhaps we should explore a somewhat different approach to the normative question of how we ought to behave when our value premises are not yet (and never will be) fully determined. Suppose we treat action as a way of creating interesting goals at the same time as we treat goals as a way of justifying action. It is an intuitively plausible and simple idea, but one that is not immediately within the domain of standard normative theories of intelligent choice.

Interesting people and interesting organizations construct complicated theories of themselves. In order to do this, they need to supplement the technology of reason with a technology of foolishness. Individuals and organizations need ways of doing things for which they have no good reason. Not always. Not usually. But sometimes. They need to act before they think.

Sensible Foolishness

In order to use the act of intelligent choice as a planned occasion for discovering new goals, we apparently require some idea of sensible foolishness. Which of the many foolish things that we might do now will lead to attractive value consequences? The question is almost inconceivable. Not only does it ask us to predict the value consequences of action, it asks us to evaluate them. In what terms can we talk about 'good' changes in goals?

In effect, we are asked either to specify a set of super-goals in terms of which alternative goals are evaluated, or to choose among alternatives *now* in terms of the unknown set of values we will have at some future time (or the distribution over time of that unknown set of future values). The former alternative moves us back to the original situation of a fixed set of values – now called 'super-goals' – and hardly seems an important step in the direction of inventing procedures for discovering new goals. The latter alternative seems fundamental enough, but it violates severely our sense of temporal order. To say that we make decisions now in terms of goals that will only be knowable later is nonsensical – as long as we accept the basic framework of the theory of choice and its presumptions of pre-existent goals.

I do not know in detail what is required, but I think it will be substantial. As we challenge the dogma of pre-existent goals, we will be forced to re-examine some of our most precious prejudices: the strictures against imitation, coercion, and rationalization. Each of those honorable prohibitions depends on the view of man and human choice imposed on us by conventional theories of choice.

Imitation is not necessarily a sign of moral weakness. It is a prediction. It is a prediction that if we duplicate the behavior or attitudes of someone else, the chances of our discovering attractive new goals for ourselves are relatively high. In order for imitation to be normatively attractive we need a better theory of who should be imitated. Such a theory seems to be eminently feasible. For example, what are the conditions for effectiveness of a rule that you should imitate another person whose values are in a close neighborhood of yours? How do the chances of discovering interesting goals through imitation change as the number of other people exhibiting the behavior to be imitated increases?

Coercion is not necessarily an assault on individual autonomy. It can be a device for stimulating individuality. We recognize this when we talk about parents and children (at least sometimes). What has always been difficult with coercion is the possibility for perversion that it involves, not its obvious capability for stimulating change. What we require is a theory of the circumstances under which entry into a coercive system produces behavior that leads to the discovery of interesting goals. We are all familiar with the tactic. We use it in imposing deadlines, entering contracts, making commitments. What are the conditions for its effective use? In particular, what are the conditions for coercion in social systems?

Rationalization is not necessarily a way of evading morality. It can be a test for the feasibility of a goal change. When deciding among alternative actions for which we have no good reason, it may be sensible to develop some definition of how 'near' to intelligence alternative 'unintelligent' actions lie. Effective rationalization permits this kind of incremental approach to changes in values. To use it effectively, however, we require a better idea of the kinds of metrics that might be possible in measuring value distances. At the same time, rationalization is the major procedure for integrating newly discovered goals into an existing structure of values. It provides the organization of complexity without which complexity itself becomes indistinguishable from randomness.

There are dangers in imitation, coercion, and rationalization. The risks are too familiar to elaborate. We should, indeed, be able to develop better techniques. Whatever those techniques may be, however, they will almost certainly undermine the superstructure of biases erected on purpose, consistency, and rationality. They will involve some way of thinking about action now as occurring in terms of a set of unknown future values.

Play and Reason

A second requirement for a technology of foolishness is some strategy for suspending rational imperatives toward consistency. Even if we know which of several foolish things we want to do, we still need a mechanism for allowing us to do it. How do we escape the logic of our reason?

Here, I think, we are closer to understanding what we need. It is playfulness. Playfulness is the deliberate, temporary relaxation of rules in order to explore the possibilities of alternative rules. When we are playful, we challenge the necessity of consistency. In effect, we announce – in advance – our rejection of the usual objections to behavior that does not fit the standard model of intelligence.

Playfulness allows experimentation. At the same time, it acknowledges reason. It accepts an obligation that at some point either the playful behavior will be stopped or it will be integrated into the structure of intelligence in some way that makes sense. The suspension of the rules is temporary.

The idea of play may suggest three things that are, in my mind, quite erroneous in the present context. First, play may be seen as a kind of Mardi Gras for reason, a release of emotional tensions of virtue. Although it is possible that play performs some such function, that is not the function with which I am concerned. Second, play may be seen as part of some mystical balance of spiritual principles: Fire and water, hot and cold, weak and strong. The intention here is much narrower than a general mystique of balance. Third, play may be seen as an antithesis of intelligence, so that the emphasis on the importance of play becomes a support for simple self-indulgence. My present intent is to propose play as an instrument of intelligence, not a substitute.

Playfulness is a natural outgrowth of our standard view of reason. A strict insistence on purpose, consistency, and rationality limits our ability to find new purposes. Play relaxes that insistence to allow us to act 'unintelligently' or 'irrationally', or 'foolishly' to explore alternative ideas of possible purposes and alternative concepts of behavioral consistency. And it does this while maintaining our basic commitment to the necessity of intelligence.

Although play and reason are in this way functional complements, they are often behavioral competitors. They are alternative styles and alternative orientations to the same situation. There is no guarantee that the styles will be equally well-developed. There is no guarantee that all individuals, all organizations, or all societies will be equally adept in both styles. There is no guarantee that all cultures will be equally encouraging to both.

Our design problem is either to specify the best mix of styles or, failing that, to assure that most people and most organizations most of the time use an alternation of strategies rather than perseverate in either one. It is a difficult problem. The optimization problem looks extremely difficult on the face of it, and the learning situations that will produce alternation in behavior appear to be somewhat less common than those that produce perseveration.

Consider, for example, the difficulty of sustaining playfulness as a style within contemporary American society. Individuals who are good at consistent rationality are rewarded early and heavily. We define it as intelligence, and the educational rewards of society are associated strongly with it. Social norms press in the same direction, particularly for men. Many of the demands of modern organizational life reinforce the same abilities and style preferences.

The result is that many of the most influential, best-educated, and best-placed citizens have experienced a powerful overlearning with respect to rationality. They are exceptionally good at maintaining consistent pictures of themselves, of relating action to purposes. They are exceptionally poor at a playful attitude toward their own beliefs, toward the logic of consistency, or toward the way they see things as being connected in the world. The dictates of manliness, forcefulness, independence, and intelligence are intolerant of playful urges if they arise. The playful urges that arise are weak ones.

The picture is probably overdrawn, but not, I believe, the implications. For societies, for organizations, and for individuals, reason and intelligence have had the unnecessary consequence of inhibiting the development of purpose into more complicated forms of consistency. In order to move away from that position, we need to find some ways of helping individuals and organizations to experiment with doing things for which they have no good reason, to be playful with their conception of themselves. It is a facility that requires more careful attention than I can give it, but I would suggest five things as a small beginning:

1 We can treat *goals as hypotheses.* Conventional decision theory allows us to entertain doubts about almost everything except the thing about which we frequently have the greatest doubt – our objectives. Suppose we define the decision process as a time for the sequential testing of hypotheses about goals. If we can experiment with alternative goals, we stand some chance of discovering complicated and interesting combinations of good values that none of us previously imagined.

2 We can treat *intuition as real.* I do not know what intuition is, or even if it is any one thing. Perhaps it is simply an excuse for doing something we cannot justify in terms of present values or for refusing to follow the logic of our own beliefs. Perhaps it is an inexplicable way of consulting that part of our intelligence that is not organized in a way anticipated by standard theories of choice. In either case, intuition permits us to see some possible actions that are outside our present scheme for justifying behavior.

3 We can treat *hypocrisy as a transition.* Hypocrisy is an inconsistency between expressed values and behavior. Negative attitudes

about hypocrisy stem from two major things. The first is a general onus against inconsistency. The second is a sentiment against combining the pleasures of vice with the appearance of virtue. Apparently, that is an unfair way of allowing evil to escape temporal punishment. Whatever the merits of such a position as ethics, it seems to me distinctly inhibiting toward change. A bad man with good intentions may be a man experimenting with the possibility of becoming good. Somehow it seems to me more sensible to encourage the experimentation than to insult it.

4 We can treat *memory as an enemy*. The rules of consistency and rationality require a technology of memory. For most purposes, good memories make good choices. But the ability to forget, or overlook, is also useful. If I do not know what I did yesterday or what other people in the organization are doing today, I can act within the system of reason and still do things that are foolish.

5 We can treat *experience as a theory*. Learning can be viewed as a series of conclusions based on concepts of action and consequences that we have invented. Experience can be changed retrospectively. By changing our interpretive concepts now, we modify what we learned earlier. Thus, we expose the possibility of experimenting with alternative histories. The usual strictures against 'self-deception' in experience need occasionally to be tempered with an awareness of the extent to which all experience is an interpretation subject to conscious revision. Personal histories, and national histories, need to be rewritten rather continuously as a base for the retrospective learning of new self-conceptions.

Each of these procedures represents a way in which we temporarily suspend the operation of the system of reasoned intelligence. They are playful. They make greatest sense in situations in which there has been an overlearning of virtues of conventional rationality. They are possibly dangerous applications of powerful devices more familiar to the study of behavioral pathology than to the investigation of human development. But they offer a few techniques for introducing change within current concepts of choice.

The argument extends easily to the problems of social organization. If we knew more about the normative theory of acting before you think, we could say more intelligent things about the functions of management and leadership when organizations or societies do not know what they are doing. Consider, for example, the following general implications.

First, we need to re-examine the functions of management decision. One of the primary ways in which the goals of an organization are developed is by interpreting the decisions it makes, and one feature of good managerial decisions is that they lead to the development of more interesting value-premises for the organization. As a result, decisions should not be seen as flowing directly or strictly from a pre-existent set of objectives. Managers who make decisions might well view that function somewhat less as a process of deduction or a process of political negotiation, and somewhat more as a process of gently upsetting preconceptions of what the organization is doing.

Second, we need a modified view of planning. Planning in organizations has many virtues, but a plan can often be more effective as an interpretation of past decisions than as a program for future ones. It can be used as a part of the efforts of the organization to develop a new consistent theory of itself that incorporates the mix of recent actions into a moderately comprehensive structure of goals. Procedures for interpreting the meaning of most past events are familiar to the memoirs of retired generals, prime ministers, business leaders, and movie stars. They suffer from the company they keep. In an organization that wants to continue to develop new objectives, a manager needs to be relatively tolerant of the idea that he will discover the meaning of yesterday's action in the experiences and interpretations of today.

Third, we need to reconsider evaluation. As nearly as I can determine, there is nothing in a formal theory of evaluation that requires that the criterion function for evaluation be specified in advance. In particular, the evaluation of social experiments need not be in terms of the degree to which they have fulfilled our *a priori* expectations. Rather we can examine what they did in terms of what we now believe to be important. The prior specification of criteria and the prior specification of evaluational procedures that depend on such criteria are common presumptions in contemporary social policy-making. They are presumptions that inhibit the serendipitous discovery of new criteria. Experience should be used explicitly as an occasion for evaluating our values as well as our actions.

Fourth, we need a reconsideration of social accountability. Individual preferences and social action need to be consistent in some way. But the process of pursuing consistency is one in which both the preferences and the actions change over time. Imagination in social policy formation involves systematically adapting to and influencing preferences. It would be unfortunate if our theories of social action encouraged leaders to ignore their responsibilities for anticipating public preferences through action and for providing social experiences that modify individual expectations.

Fifth, we need to accept playfulness in social organizations. The design of organizations should attend to the problems of maintaining both playfulness and reason as aspects of intelligent choice. Since much of the literature on social design is concerned with strengthening the rationality of decision, managers are likely to overlook the importance of play. This is partly a matter of making the individuals within an organization more playful by encouraging the attitudes and skills of inconsistency. It is also a a matter of making organizational structure and organizational procedure more playful. Organizations can be playful even when the participants in them are not. The managerial devices for maintaining consistency can be varied. We encourage organizational play by permitting (and insisting on) some temporary relief from control, coordination, and communication.

Intelligence and Foolishness

Contemporary theories of decision-making and the technology of reason have considerably strengthened our capabilities for effective social action. The conversion of the simple ideas of choice into an extensive technology is a major achievement. It is, however, an achievement that has reinforced some biases in the underlying models of choice in individuals and groups. In particular, it has reinforced the uncritical acceptance of a static interpretation of human goals.

There is little magic in the world, and foolishness in people and organizations is one of the many things that fail to produce miracles. Under certain conditions, it is one of several ways in which some of the problems of our current theories of intelligence can be overcome. It may be a good way. It preserves the virtues of consistency while stimulating change. If we had a good technology of foolishness, it might (in combination with the technology of reason) help in a small way to develop the unusual combinations of attitudes and behaviors that describe the interesting people, interesting organizations, and interesting societies of the world.

13

Bounded rationality, ambiguity, and the engineering of choice

James G. March

Abstract

Rational choice involves two guesses, a guess about uncertain future consequences and a guess about uncertain future preferences. Partly as a result of behavioral studies of choice over a 20-year period, modifications in the way the theory deals with the first guess have become organized into conceptions of bounded rationality. Recently, behavioral studies of choice have examined the second guess, the way preferences are processed in choice behavior. These studies suggest possible modifications in standard assumptions about tastes and their role in choice. This paper examines some of those modifications, some possible approaches to working on them, and some complications.

The Engineering of Choice and Ordinary Choice Behavior

Recently I gave a lecture on elementary decision theory, an introduction to rational theories of choice. After the lecture, a student asked whether it was conceivable that the practical procedures for decision-making implicit in theories of choice might make actual human decisions worse rather than

This paper was first published in *The Bell Journal of Economics*, Vol. 9, No. 2, Autumn 1978. Prior to that it was presented at a conference on the new industrial organization at Carnegie–Mellon University, 14–15 October 1977. The conference was organized to honor the contributions of Herbert A. Simon to economics, and his contribution to this paper is obvious. In addition, the author has profited from comments by Richard M. Cyert, Jon Elster, Alexander L. George, Elisabeth Hansot, Nannerl O. Keohane, Robert O. Keohane, Tjalling Koopmans, Mancur Olson, Louis R. Pondy, Roy Radner, Giovanni Sartori, and Oliver E. Williamson. The research was supported by a grant from the Spencer Foundation.

better. What is the empirical evidence, he asked, that human choice is improved by knowledge of decision theory or by application of the various engineering forms of rational choice? I answered, I think correctly, that the case for the usefulness of decision-engineering rested primarily not on the kind of direct empirical confirmation that he sought, but on two other things: on a set of theorems proving the superiority of particular procedures in particular situations if the situations are correctly specified and the procedures correctly applied, and on the willingness of clients to purchase the services of experts with skills in decision sciences.

The answer may not have been reasonable, but the question clearly was. It articulated a classical challenge to the practice of rational choice, the possibility that processes of rationality might combine with properties of human beings to produce decisions that are less sensible than the un-systematized actions of an intelligent person, or at least that the way in which we might use rational procedures intelligently is not self-evident. Camus (1951) argued, in effect, that man was not smart enough to be rational, a point made in a different way at about the same time by Herbert A. Simon (1957). Twenty years later, tales of horror have become contemporary cliches of studies of rational analysis in organizations (Wildavsky, 1971; Wildavsky and Pressman, 1973; Warwick, 1975).

I do not share the view of some of my colleagues that microeconomics, decision science, management science, operations analysis, and the other forms of rational decision-engineering are mostly manufacturers of massive mischief when they are put into practice. It seems to me likely that these modern technologies of reason have, on balance, done more good than harm, and that students of organizations, politics, and history have been overly gleeful in their compilation of disasters. But I think there is good sense in asking how the practical implementation of theories of choice combines with the ways people behave when they make decisions, and whether our ideas about the engineering of choice might be improved by greater attention to our descriptions of choice behavior.

At first blush, pure models of rational choice seem obviously appropriate as guides to intelligent action, but more problematic for predicting behavior. In practice, the converse seems closer to the truth for much of economics. So long as we use individual choice models to predict the behavior of relatively large numbers of individuals or organizations, some potential problems are avoided by the familiar advantages of aggregation. Even a small signal stands out in a noisy message. On the other hand, if we choose to predict small numbers of individuals or organizations or give advice to a single individual or organization, the saving graces of aggregation are mostly lost. The engineering of choice depends on a relatively close articulation between choice as it is comprehended in the assumptions of the model and choice as it is made comprehensible to individual actors.

This relation is reflected in the historical development of the field. According to conventional dogma, there are two kinds of theories of human behavior; descriptive (or behavioral) theories that purport to describe actual behavior of individuals or social institutions, and prescriptive (or normative) theories that purport to prescribe optimal behavior. In many ways, the distinction leads to an intelligent and fruitful division of labor in social science, reflecting differences in techniques, objectives, and professional cultures. For a variety of historical and intellectual reasons, however, such a division has not characterized the development of the theory of choice. Whether one considers ideas about choice in economics, psychology, political science, sociology, or philosophy, behavioral and normative theories have developed as a dialectic rather than as separate domains. Most modern behavioral theories of choice take as their starting point some simple ideas about rational human behavior. As a result, new developments in normative theories of choice have quickly affected behavioral theories. Contemplate, for example, the impact of game theory, statistical decision theory, and information theory on behavioral theories of human problem-solving, political decision-making, bargaining, and organizational behavior (Rapoport, 1960; Vroom, 1964; Binkley, Bronaugh, and Marras, 1971; Tversky and Kahneman, 1974; Mayhew, 1974). It is equally obvious that prescriptive theories of choice have been affected by efforts to understand actual choice behavior. Engineers of artificial intelligence have modified their perceptions of efficient problem-solving procedures by studying the actual behavior of human problem solvers (Simon, 1969; Newell and Simon, 1972). Engineers of organizational decision-making have modified their models of rationality on the basis of studies of actual organizational behavior (Charnes and Cooper, 1963; Keen, 1977).

Modern students of human choice frequently assume, at least implicitly, that actual human choice behavior in some way or other is likely to make sense. It can be understood as being the behavior of an intelligent being or a group of intelligent beings. Much theoretical work searches for the intelligence in apparently anomalous human behavior. This process of discovering sense in human behavior is conservative with respect to the concept of rational man and to behavioral change. It preserves the axiom of rationality; and it preserves the idea that human behavior is intelligent, even when it is not obviously so. But it is not conservative with respect to prescriptive models of choice. For if there is sense in the choice behavior of individuals acting contrary to standard engineering procedures for rationality, then it seems reasonable to suspect that there may be something inadequate about our normative theory of choice or the procedures by which it is implemented.

Rational choice involves two kinds of guesses: guesses about future consequences of current actions and guesses about future preferences for those consequences (Savage, 1954; Thompson, 1967). We try to imagine what will happen in the future as a result of our actions and we try to imagine how we shall evaluate what will happen. Neither guess is necessarily easy. Anticipating future consequences of present decisions is often subject to substantial error. Anticipating future preferences is often confusing. Theories of rational choice are primarily theories of these two guesses and how we deal with their complications. Theories of choice under uncertainty emphasize the complications of guessing future consequences. Theories of choice under conflict or ambiguity emphasize the complications of guessing future preferences.

Students of decision-making under uncertainty have identified a number of ways in which a classical model of how alternatives are assessed in terms of their consequences is neither descriptive of behavior nor a good guide in choice situations. As a result of these efforts, some of our ideas about how the first guess is made and how it ought to be made have changed. Since the early writings of Herbert A. Simon (1957), for example, bounded rationality has come to be recognized widely, though not universally, both as an accurate portrayal of much choice behavior and as a normatively sensible adjustment to the costs and character of information gathering and processing by human beings (Radner, 1975a, 1975b; Radner and Rothschild, 1975; Connolly, 1977).

The second guess has been less considered. For the most part, theories of choice have assumed that future preferences are exogenous, stable, and known with adequate precision to make decisions unambiguous. The assumptions are obviously subject to question. In the case of collective decision-making, there is the problem of conflicting objectives representing the values of different participants (March, 1962; Olson, 1965; M. Taylor, 1975; Pfeffer, 1977). In addition, individual preferences often appear to be fuzzy and inconsistent, and preferences appear to change over time, at least in part as a consequence of actions taken. Recently, some students of choice have been examining the ways individuals and organizations confront the second guess under conditions of ambiguity (i.e., where goals are vague, problematic, inconsistent, unstable) (Cohen and March, 1974; Weick, 1976; March and Olsen, 1976; Crozier and Friedberg, 1977). Those efforts are fragmentary, but they suggest that ignoring the ambiguities involved in guessing future preferences leads both to misinterpreting choice behavior and to misstating the normative problem facing a decision-maker. The doubts are not novel; John Stuart Mill (1838) expressed many of them in his essay on Bentham. They are not devastating; the theory of choice is probably robust enough to cope with them. They are not esoteric; Hegel is relevant, but may not be absolutely essential.

Bounded Rationality

There is a history. A little over 20 years ago, Simon published two papers that became a basis for two decades of development in the theory of choice (1955, 1956). The first of these examined the informational and computational limits on rationality by human beings. The paper suggested a focus on stepfunction utility functions and a process of information-gathering that began with a desired outcome and worked back to a set of antecedent actions sufficient to produce it. The second paper explored the consequences of simple payoff functions and search rules in an uncertain environment. The two papers argued explicitly that descriptions of decision-making in terms of such ideas conformed more to actual human behavior than did descriptions built upon classical rationality, that available evidence designed to test such models against classical ones tended to support the alternative ideas.

Because subsequent developments were extensive, it is well to recall that the original argument was a narrow one. It started from the proposition that all intendedly rational behavior is behavior within constraints. Simon added the idea that the list of technical constraints on choice should include some properties of human beings as processors of information and as problem-solvers. The limitations were limitations of computational capability, the organization and utilization of memory, and the like. He suggested that human beings develop decision procedures that are sensible, given the constraints, even though they might not be sensible if the constraints were removed. As a short-hand label for such procedures, he coined the term 'satisficing'.

Developments in the field over the past 20 years have expanded and distorted Simon's original formulation. But they have retained some considerable flavor of his original tone. He emphasized the theoretical difficulty posed by self-evident empirical truths. He obscured a distinction one might make between individual and organizational decision-making, proposing for the most part the same general ideas for both. He obscured a possible distinction between behavioral and normative theories of choice, preferring to view differences between perfect rationality and bounded rationality as explicable consequences of constraints. Few of the individual scholars who followed had precisely the same interests or commitments as Simon, but the field has generally maintained the same tone. Theoretical puzzlement with respect to the simplicity of decision behavior has been extended to puzzlement with respect to decision inconsistencies and instability, and the extent to which individuals and organizations do things without apparent reason (March and Olsen, 1976). Recent books on decision-making move freely from studies of organizations to studies of individuals (Janis and Mann, 1977). And recent books on normative decision-making accept many standard forms of organizational behavior as sensible (Keen, 1977).

Twenty years later, it is clear that we do not have a single, widely-accepted, precise behavioral theory of choice. But I think it can be argued that the empirical and theoretical efforts of the past 20 years have brought us closer to understanding decision processes. The understanding is organized in a set of conceptual vignettes rather than a single, coherent structure; and the connections among the vignettes are tenuous. In effect, the effort has identified major aspects of some key processes that appear to be reflected in decision-making; but the ecology of those processes is not well captured by any current theory. For much of this development. Simon bears substantial intellectual responsibility.

Simon's contributions have been honored by subsumption, extension, elaboration, and transformation. Some writers have felt it important to show that aspiration level goals and goal-directed search can be viewed as special cases of other ideas, most commonly classical notions about rational behavior (Riker and Ordeshook, 1974). Others have taken ideas about individual human behavior and extended them to organizations (both business firms and public bureaucracies) and to other institutions, for example, universities (Bower, 1968; Allison, 1969; Steinbruner, 1974; Williamson, 1975). Simon's original precise commentary on specific difficulties in rational models has been expanded to a more general consideration of problems in the assumptions of rationality, particularly the problems of subjective understanding, perception, and conflict of interest (Cyert and March, 1963; Porat and Haas, 1969; Carter, 1971; R. N. Taylor, 1975; Slovic, Fischhoff, and Lichtenstein, 1977). The original articles suggested small modifications in a theory of economic behavior, the substitution of bounded rationality for omniscient rationality. But the ideas ultimately have led to an examination of the extent to which theories of choice might subordinate the idea of rationality altogether to less intentional conceptions of the causal determinants of action (March and Olsen, 1976).

Alternative Rationalities

The search for intelligence in decision-making is an effort to rationalize apparent anomalies in behavior. In a general way, that effort imputes either calculated or systemic rationality to observed choice behavior. Action is presumed to follow either from explicit calculation of its consequences in terms of objectives, or from rules of behavior that have evolved through processes that are sensible but which obscure from present knowledge full information on the rational justification for any specific rule.

Most efforts to rationalize observed behavior have attempted to place that behavior within a framework of calculated rationality. The usual argument is that a naïve rational model is inadequate either because it focuses on the wrong unit of analysis, or because it uses an inaccurate characterization of the preferences involved. As a result, we have developed ideas of limited rationality, contextual rationality, game rationality, and process rationality.

Ideas of *limited rationality* emphasize the extent to which individuals and groups simplify a decision problem because of the difficulties of anticipating or considering all alternatives and all information (March and Simon, 1958; Lindblom, 1959, 1965; Radner, 1975a, 1975b). They introduce, as reasonable responses, such things as step-function tastes, simple search rules, working backward, organizational slack, incrementalism and muddling through, uncertainty avoidance, and the host of elaborations of such ideas that are familiar to students of organizational choice and human problem-solving.

Ideas of *contextual rationality* emphasize the extent to which choice behavior is embedded in a complex of other claims on the attention of actors and other structures of social and cognitive relations (Long, 1958; Schelling, 1971; Cohen, March, and Olsen, 1972; Weiner, 1976; Sproull, Weiner, and Wolf, 1978). They focus on the way in which choice behavior in a particular situation is affected by the opportunity costs of attending to that situation and by the apparent tendency for people, problems, solutions, and choices to be joined by the relatively arbitrary accidents of their simultaneity rather than by their *prima facie* relevance to each other.

Ideas of *game rationality* emphasize the extent to which organizations and other social institutions consist of individuals who act in relation to each other intelligently to pursue individual objectives by means of individual calculations of self-interest (Farquharson, 1969; Harsanyi and Selten, 1972; Brams, 1975). The decision outcomes of the collectivity in some sense amalgamate those calculations, but they do so without imputing a super-goal to the collectivity or invoking collective rationality. These theories find reason in the process of coalition formation, sequential attention to goals, information bias and interpersonal gaming, and the development of mutual incentives.

Ideas of *process rationality* emphasize the extent to which decisions find their sense in attributes of the decision process, rather than in attributes of decision outcomes (Edelman, 1960; Cohen and March, 1974; Kreiner, 1976; Christensen, 1976). They explore those significant human pleasures (and pains) found in the ways we act while making decisions, and in the symbolic content of the idea and procedures of choice. Explicit outcomes are viewed as secondary and decision-making becomes sensible through the intelligence of the way it is orchestrated.

All of these kinds of ideas are theories of intelligent individuals making calculations of the consequences of actions for objectives, and acting sensibly to achieve those objectives. Action is presumed to be consequential, to be connected consciously and meaningfully to knowledge about personal goals and future outcomes, to be controlled by personal intention.

Although models of calculated rationality continue to be a dominant style, students of choice have also shown considerable interest in a quite different kind of intelligence, systemic rather than calculated. Suppose we imagine that knowledge, in the form of precepts of behavior, evolves over time within a system and accumulates across time, people, and organizations without complete current consciousness of its history. Then sensible action is taken by actors without comprehension of its full justification. This characterizes models of adaptive rationality, selected rationality, and posterior rationality.

Ideas of *adaptive rationality* emphasize experiential learning by individuals or collectivities (Cyert and March, 1963; Day and Groves, 1975). Most adaptive models have the property that if the world and preferences are stable and the experience prolonged enough, behavior will approach the behavior that would be chosen rationally on the basis of perfect knowledge. Moreover, the postulated learning functions normally have properties that permit sensible adaptation to drifts in environmental or taste attributes. By storing information on past experiences in some simple behavioral predilections, adaptive rationality permits the efficient management of considerable experiential information; but it is in a form that is not explicitly retrievable – particularly across individuals or long periods of time. As a result, it is a form of intelligence that tends to separate current reasons from current actions.

Ideas of *selected rationality* emphasize the process of selection among individuals or organizations through survival or growth (Winter, 1964, 1971, 1975; Nelson and Winter, 1973). Rules of behavior achieve intelligence not by virtue of conscious calculation of their rationality by current role players but by virtue of the survival and growth of social institutions in which such rules are followed and such roles are performed. Selection theories focus on the extent to which choice is dominated by standard operating procedures and the social regulation of social roles.

Ideas of *posterior rationality* emphasize the discovery of intentions as an interpretation of action rather than as a prior position (Hirschman, 1967; Weick, 1969; March, 1973). Actions are seen as being exogenous and as producing experiences that are organized into an evaluation after the fact. The valuation is in terms of preferences generated by the action and its consequences, and choices are justified by virtue of their posterior consistency with goals that have themselves been developed through a critical interpretation of the choice. Posterior rationality models maintain the idea that action should be consistent with preferences. but they conceive action as being antecedent to goals.

These explorations into elements of systemic rationality have, of course, a strong base in economics and behavioral science (Wilson, 1975; Becker, 1976); but they pose special problems for decision-engineering. On the one hand, systemic rationality is not intentional. That is, behavior is not understood as following from a calculation of consequences in terms of prior objectives. If such a calculation is asserted, it is assumed to be an interpretation of the behavior but not a good predictor of it. On the other hand, these models claim, often explicitly, that there is intelligence in the suspension of calculation. Alternatively, they suggest that whatever sense there is in calculated rationality is attested not by its formal properties but by its survival as a social rule of behavior, or as an experientially verified personal propensity.

In a general way, these explications of ordinary behavior as forms of rationality have considerably clarified and extended our understanding of choice. It is now routine to explore aspects of limited, contextual, game, process, adaptive, selected, and posterior rationality in the behavioral theory of choice. We use such ideas to discover and celebrate the intelligence of human behavior. At the same time, however, this discovery of intelligence in the ordinary behavior of individuals and social institutions is an implicit pressure for reconstruction of normative theories of choice, for much of the argument is not only that observed behavior is understandable as a human phenomenon, but that it is, in some important sense, intelligent. If behavior that apparently deviates from standard procedures of calculated rationality can be shown to be intelligent, then it can plausibly be argued that models of calculated rationality are deficient not only as descriptors of human behavior but also as guides to intelligent choice.

The Treatment of Tastes

Engineers of intelligent choice sensibly resist the imputation of intelligence to all human behavior. Traditionally, deviations of choice behavior from the style anticipated in classical models were treated normatively as errors, or correctable faults, as indeed many of them doubtless were. The objective was to transform subjective rationality into objective rationality by removing the needless informational, procedural, and judgmental constraints that limited the effectiveness of persons proceeding intelligently from false or incomplete informational premises (Ackoff and Sasieni, 1968). One of Simon's contributions to the theory of choice was his challenge of the self-evident proposition that choice behavior necessarily would be improved if it were made more like the normative model of rational choice. By asserting that certain limits on rationality stemmed from properties of the human organism, he emphasized the possibility that actual human choice behavior was more intelligent than it appeared.

Normative theories of choice have responded to the idea. Substantial parts of the economics of information and the economics of attention (or time) are tributes to the proposition that information-gathering, information-processing, and decision-making impose demands on the scarce resources of a finite capacity human organism (Stigler, 1961; Becker, 1965; McGuire and Radner, 1972; Marschak and Radner, 1972; Rothschild and Stiglitz, 1976). Aspiration levels, signals, incrementalism, and satisficing rules for decision-making have been described as sensible under fairly general circumstances (Hirschman and Lindblom, 1962; Spence, 1974; Radner, 1975a, 1975b; Radner and Rothschild, 1975).

These developments in the theory of rational choice acknowledge important aspects of the behavioral critique of classical procedures for guessing the future consequences of present action. Normative response to behavioral discussions of the second guess, the estimation of future preferences, has been similarly conservative but perceptible. That standard theories of choice and the engineering procedures associated with them have a conception of preferences that differs from observations of preferences has long been noted (Johnson, 1968). As in the case of the informational constraints on rational choice, the first reaction within decision-engineering was to treat deviations from well-defined, consistent preference functions as correctable faults. If individuals had deficient (i.e., inconsistent, incomplete) preference functions, they were to be induced to generate proper ones, perhaps through revealed preference techniques and education. If groups or organizations exhibited conflict, they were to be induced to resolve that conflict through prior discussion, prior side payments (e.g., an employment contract), or prior bargaining. If individuals or organizations exhibited instability in preferences over time, they were to be induced to minimize that instability by recognizing a more general specification of the preferences so that apparent changes became explicable as reflecting a single, unchanging function under changing conditions or changing resources.

Since the specific values involved in decision-making are irrelevant to formal models of choice, both process rationality and contextual rationality are, from such a perspective, versions of simple calculated rationality. The criterion function is changed, but the theory treats the criterion function as any arbitrary set of well-ordered preferences. So long as the preferences associated with the process of choice or the preferences involved in the broader context are well-defined and well-behaved, there is no deep theoretical difficulty. But, in practice, such elements of human preference functions have not filtered significantly into the engineering of choice.

The record with respect to problems of goal conflict, multiple, lexicographic goals, and loosely coupled systems is similar. Students of bureaucracies have argued that a normative theory of choice within a modern bureaucratic structure must recognize explicitly the continuing conflict in preferences among various actors (Tullock, 1965; Downs, 1967; Allison and Halperin, 1972; Halperin, 1974). Within such systems 'decisions' are probably better seen as strategic first-move interventions in a dynamic internal system than as choices in a classical sense. Decisions are not expected to be implemented, and actions that would be optimal if implemented are suboptimal as first moves. This links theories of choice to game-theoretic conceptions of politics, bargaining, and strategic actions in a productive way. Although in this way ideas about strategic choice in collectivities involving conflict of interest are well established in part of the choice literature (Elster, 1977a), they have had little impact on such obvious applied domains as bureaucratic decision-making or the design of organizational control systems. The engineering of choice has been more explicitly concerned with multiple criteria decision procedures for dealing with multiple, lexicographic, or political goals (Lee, 1972; Pattanaik, 1973). In some cases these efforts have considerably changed the spirit of decision analysis, moving it toward a role of exploring the implications of constraints and away from a conception of solution.

Behavioral inquiry into preferences has, however, gone beyond the problems of interpersonal conflict of interest in recent years and into the complications of ambiguity. The problems of ambiguity are partly problems of disagreement about goals among individuals, but they are more conspicuously problems of the relevance, priority, clarity, coherence, and stability of goals in both individual and organizational choice. Several recent treatments of organizational choice behavior record some major ways in which explicit goals seem neither particularly powerful predictors of outcomes nor particularly well-represented as either stable, consistent preference orders or well-defined political constraints (Cohen and March, 1974; Weick, 1976; March and Olsen, 1976; Sproull, Weiner, and Wolf, 1978).

It is possible, of course, that such portrayals of behavior are perverse. They may be perverse because they systematically misrepresent the actual behavior of human beings or they may be perverse because the human beings they describe are, in so far as the description applies, stupid. But it is also possible that the description is accurate and the behavior is intelligent, that the ambiguous way human beings sometimes deal with tastes is, in fact, sensible. If such a thing can be imagined, then its corollary may also be imaginable: Perhaps we treat tastes inadequately in our engineering of choice. When we start to discover intelligence in decision-making where goals are unstable, ill-defined, or apparently irrelevant, we are led to ask some different kinds of questions about our normative conceptions of choice and walk closely not only to some issues in economics but also to some classical and modern questions in literature and ethics, particularly the role of clear prior purpose in the ordering of human affairs.

Consider the following properties of tastes as they appear in standard prescriptive theories of choice:

1. Tastes are *absolute*. Normative theories of choice assume a formal posture of moral relativism. The theories insist on morality of action in terms of tastes; but they recognize neither discriminations among alternative tastes, nor the possibility that a person reasonably might view his own preferences and actions based on them as morally distressing.

2. Tastes are *relevant*. Normative theories of choice require that action be taken in terms of tastes, that decisions be consistent with preferences in the light of information about the probable consequences of alternatives for valued outcomes. Action is willful.

3. Tastes are *stable*. With few exceptions, normative theories of choice require that tastes be stable. Current action is taken in terms of current tastes. The implicit assumption is that tastes will be unchanged when the outcomes of current actions are realized.

4. Tastes are *consistent*. Normative theories of choice allow mutually inconsistent tastes only in so far as they can be made irrelevant by the absence of scarcity or reconcilable by the specification of trade-offs.

5. Tastes are *precise*. Normative theories of choice eliminate ambiguity about the extent to which a particular outcome will satisfy tastes, at least in so far as possible resolutions of that ambiguity might affect the choice.

6. Tastes are *exogenous*. Normative theories of choice presume that tastes, by whatever process they may be created, are not themselves affected by the choices they control.

Each of these features of tastes seems inconsistent with observations of choice behavior among individuals and social institutions. Not always, but often enough to be troublesome. Individuals commonly find it possible to express both a taste for something and a recognition that the taste is something that is repugnant to moral standards they accept. Choices are often made without respect to tastes. Human decision-makers routinely ignore their own, fully conscious, preferences in making decisions. They follow rules, traditions, hunches, and the advice or actions of others. Tastes change over time in such a way that predicting future tastes is often difficult. Tastes are inconsistent. Individuals and organizations are aware of the extent to which some of their preferences conflict with other of their preferences; yet they do nothing to resolve those inconsistencies.

Many preferences are stated in forms that lack precision. It is difficult to make them reliably operational in evaluating possible outcomes. While tastes are used to choose among actions, it is often also true that actions and experience with their consequences affect tastes. Tastes are determined partly endogenously.

Such differences between tastes as they are portrayed by our models and tastes as they appear in our experience produce ordinary behavioral phenomena that are not always well accommodated within the structure of our prescriptions.

We manage our preferences. We select actions now partly in terms of expectations about the effect of those actions upon future preferences. We do things now to modify our future tastes. Thus, we know that if we engage in some particularly tasty, but immoral, activity, we are likely to come to like it more. We know that if we develop competence in a particular skill, we shall often come to favor it. So we choose to pursue the competence, or not, engage in an activity, or not, depending on whether we wish to increase or decrease our taste for the competence or activity.

We construct our preferences. We choose preferences and actions jointly, in part, to discover – or construct – new preferences that are currently unknown. We deliberately specify our objectives in vague terms to develop an understanding of what we might like to become. We elaborate our tastes as interpretations of our behavior.

We treat our preferences strategically. We specify goals that are different from the outcomes we wish to achieve. We adopt preferences and rules of actions that if followed literally would lead us to outcomes we do not wish, because we believe that the final outcome will only partly reflect our initial intentions. In effect, we consider the choice of preferences as part of an infinite game with ourselves in which we attempt to deal with our propensities for acting badly by anticipating them and outsmarting ourselves. We use deadlines and make commitments.

We confound our preferences. Our deepest preferences tend often to be paired. We find the same outcome both attractive and repulsive, not in the sense that the two sentiments cancel each other and we remain indifferent, but precisely that we simultaneously want and do not want an outcome, experience it as both pleasure and pain, love and hate it (Catullus, 58 BC, 1.1).

We avoid our preferences. Our actions and our preferences are only partly linked. We are prepared to say that we want something, yet should not want it, or wish we did not want it. We are prepared to act in ways that are inconsistent with our preferences, and to maintain that inconsistency in the face of having it demonstrated. We do not believe that what we do must necessarily result from a desire to achieve preferred outcomes.

We expect change in our preferences. As we contemplate making choices that have consequences in the future, we know that our attitudes about possible outcomes will change in ways that are substantial but not entirely predictable. The subjective probability distribution over possible future preferences (like the subjective probability distribution over possible future consequences) increases its variance as the horizon is stretched. As a result, we have a tendency to want to take actions now that maintain future options for acting when future preferences are clearer.

We suppress our preferences. Consequential argument, the explicit linking of actions to desires, is a form of argument in which some people are better than others. Individuals who are less competent at consequential rationalization try to avoid it with others who are more competent, particularly others who may have a stake in persuading them to act in a particular way. We resist an explicit formulation of consistent desires to avoid manipulation of our choices by persons cleverer than we at that special form of argument called consistent rationality.

It is possible, on considering this set of contrasts between decision-making as we think it ought to occur and decision-making as we think it does occur to trivialize the issue into a 'definitional problem'. By suitably manipulating the concept of tastes, one can save classical theories of choice as 'explanations' of behavior in a formal sense, but probably only at the cost of stretching a good idea into a doubtful ideology (Stigler and Becker, 1977). More importantly from the present point of view, such a redefinition pays the cost of destroying the practical relevance of normative prescriptions for choice. For prescriptions are useful only if we see a difference between observed procedures and desirable procedures.

Alternatively, one can record all of the deviations from normative specifications as stupidity, errors that should be corrected; and undertake to transform the style of existing humans into the styles anticipated by the theory. This has, for the most part, been the strategy of operations and management analysis for the past 20 years; and it has had its successes. But it has also had failures.

It is clear that the human behavior I have described may, in any individual case, be a symptom of ignorance, obtuseness, or deviousness. But the fact that such patterns of behavior are fairly common among individuals and institutions suggests that they might be sensible under some general kinds of conditions – that goal ambiguity, like limited rationality, is not necessarily a fault in human choice to be corrected but often a form of intelligence to be refined by the technology of choice rather than ignored by it.

Uncertainty about future consequences and human limitations in dealing with them are relatively easily seen as intrinsic in the decision situation and the nature of the human organism. It is much harder to see in what way ambiguous preferences are a necessary property of human behavior. It seems meaningful in ordinary terms to assert that human decision-makers are driven to techniques of limited rationality by the exigencies of the situation in which they find themselves. But what drives them to ambiguous and changing goals? Part of the answer is directly analogous to the formulations of limited rationality. Limitations of memory organization and retrieval and of information capacity affect information processing about preferences just as they affect information processing about consequences (March and Simon, 1958; Cyert and March, 1963; Simon, 1973; March and Romalaer, 1976). Human beings have unstable, inconsistent, incompletely evoked, and imprecise goals at least in part because human abilities limit preference orderliness. If it were possible to be different at reasonable cost, we probably would want to be.

But viewing ambiguity as a necessary cost imposed by the information processing attributes of individuals fails to capture the extent to which similar styles in preferences would be sensible, even if the human organism were a more powerful computational system. We probably need to ask the more general question: Why might a person or institution choose to have ambiguous tastes? The answer, I believe, lies in several things, some related to ideas of bounded rationality, others more familiar to human understanding as it is portrayed in literature and philosophy than to our theories of choice.

1 Human beings recognize in their behavior that there are limits to personal and institutional integration in tastes. They know that no matter how much they may be pressured both by their own prejudices for integration and by the demands of others, they will be left with contradictory and intermittent desires partially ordered but imperfectly reconciled. As a result, they engage in activities designed to manage preferences or game preferences. These activities make little sense from the point of view of a conception of human choice that assumes people know what they want and will want, or a conception that assumes wants are morally equivalent. But ordinary human actors sense that they might come to want something that they should not, or that they might make unwise or inappropriate choices under the influence of fleeting, but powerful, desires, if they do not act now either to control the development of tastes or to buffer action from tastes (Elster, 1977b).

2 Human beings recognize implicitly the limitations of acting rationally on current guesses. By insisting that action, to be justified, must follow preferences and be consistent both with those preferences and with estimates of future states, we considerably exaggerate the relative power of a choice based consistently upon two guesses compared to a choice that is itself a guess. Human beings are both proponents

for preferences and observers of the process by which their preferences are developed and acted upon. As observers of the process by which their beliefs have been formed and consulted, they recognize the good sense in perceptual and moral modesty (Williams, 1973; Elster, 1977c).

3 Human beings recognize the extent to which tastes are constructed, or developed, through a more or less constant confrontation between preferences and actions that are inconsistent with them, and among conflicting preferences. As a result, they appear to be comfortable with an extraordinary array of unreconciled sources of legitimate wants. They maintain a lack of coherence both within and among personal desires, social demands, and moral codes. Though they seek some consistency, they appear to see inconsistency as a normal, and necessary, aspect of the development and clarification of tastes (March, 1973).

4 Human beings are conscious of the importance of preferences as beliefs independent of their immediate action consequences. They appear to find it possible to say, in effect, that they believe something is more important to good action than they are able (or willing) to make it in a specific case. They act as though some aspects of their beliefs are important to life without necessarily being consistent with actions, and important to the long-run quality of choice behavior without controlling it completely in the short run. They accept a degree of personal and social wisdom in ordinary hypocrisy (Chomsky, 1968; March, 1973; Pondy and Olson, 1977).

5 Human beings know that some people are better at rational argument than others, and that those skills are not particularly well correlated with either morality or sympathy. As a result, they recognize the political nature of argumentation more clearly, and more personally, than the theory of choice does. They are unwilling to gamble that God made clever people uniquely virtuous. They protect themselves from cleverness by obscuring the nature of their preferences; they exploit cleverness by asking others to construct reasons for actions they wish to take (Shakespeare, 1623).

Tastes and the Engineering of Choice

These characteristics of preference processing by individual human beings and social institutions seem to me to make sense under rather general circumstances. As a result, it seems likely to me that our engineering of choice behavior does not make so much sense as we sometimes attribute to it. The view of human tastes and their proper role in action that we exhibit in our normative theory of choice is at least as limiting to the engineering applicability of that theory as the perfect knowledge assumptions were to the original formulations.

Since it has taken us over 20 years to introduce modest elements of bounded rationality and conflict of interest into prescriptions about decision-making, there is no particular reason to be sanguine about the speed with which our engineering of choice will accept and refine the intelligence of ambiguity. But there is hope. The reconstruction involved is not extraordinary, and in some respects has already begun. For the doubts I have expressed about engineering models of choice to be translated into significant changes, they will have to be formulated a bit more precisely in terms that are comprehensible within such theories, even though they may not be consistent with the present form of the theories or the questions the theories currently address. I cannot accomplish such a task in any kind of complete way, but I think it is possible to identify a few conceptual problems that might plausibly be addressed by choice theorists and a few optimization problems that might plausibly be addressed by choice engineers.

The conceptual problems involve discovering interesting ways to reformulate some assumptions about tastes, particularly about the stability of tastes, their exogenous character, their priority, and their internal consistency.

Consider the problem of *intertemporal comparison* of preferences (Strotz, 1956; Koopmans, 1964; Bailey and Olson, 1977; Shefrin and Thaler, 1977). Suppose we assume that the preferences that will be held at every relevant future point in time are known. Suppose further that those preferences change over time but are, at any given time, consistent. If action is to be taken now in terms of its consequences over a period of time during which preferences change, we are faced with having to make intertemporal comparisons. As long as the changes are exogenous, we can avoid the problem if we choose to do so. If we can imagine an individual making a complete and transitive ordering over possible outcomes over time, then intertemporal comparisons are implicit in the preference orderings and cause no particular difficulty beyond the heroic character of the assumption about human capabilities. If, on the other hand, we think of the individual as having a distinct, complete, and consistent preference relation defined over the outcomes realized in a particular time period, and we imagine that those preferences change over time, then the problem of intertemporal comparisons is more difficult. The problem is technically indistinguishable from the problem of interpersonal comparison of utilities. When we compare the changing preferences of a single person over time to make trade-offs across time, we are, in the identical position as when we attempt to make comparisons across different individuals at a point in time. The fact that the problems are identical has the advantage of immediately bringing to bear on the problems of intertemporal comparisons the apparatus developed to deal with interpersonal comparisons (Mueller, 1976). It has the disadvantage that that apparatus allows a much weaker conception of solution than is possible within a single, unchanging set of preferences. We are left with the weak theorems of social welfare economics, but perhaps with a clearer recognition that there is no easy and useful way to escape the problem of incomparable preference functions by limiting our attention to a single individual, as long as tastes change over time and we think of tastes as being defined at a point in time.

Consider the problem of *endogenous change* in preferences (Von Weiszäcker, 1971; Olson, 1976). Suppose we know that future tastes will change in a predictable way as a consequence of actions taken now and the consequences of those actions realized over time. Then we are in the position of choosing now the preferences we shall have later. If there is risk involved, we are choosing now a probability distribution over future preferences. If we can imagine some 'super goal', the problem becomes tractable. We evaluate alternative preferences in terms of their costs and benefits for the 'super goal'. Such a strategy preserves the main spirit of normal choice theory but allows only a modest extension into endogenous change. This is the essential strategy adopted in some of the engineering examples below. In such cases desirable preferences cannot always be deduced from the 'super goal', but alternative preferences can be evaluated. In somewhat the same spirit, we can imagine adaptive preferences as a possible decision procedure and examine whether rules for a sequence of adaptations in tastes can be specified that lead to choice outcomes better in some easily recognized sense than those obtained through explicit calculated rationality at the start of the process. One possible place is the search for cooperative solutions in games in which calculated rationality is likely to lead to outcomes desired by no one (Cyert and de Groot, 1973; 1975). Also in the same general spirit, we might accept the strict morality position and attempt to select a strategy for choice that will minimize change in values. Or we might try to select a strategy that maximizes value change. All of these are possible explorations, but they are not fully attentive to the normative management of adaptation in tastes. The problem exceeds our present concepts: How do we act sensibly now to manage the development of preferences in the future when we do not have a criterion for evaluating future tastes that will not itself be affected by our actions? There may be some kind of fixed-point theorem answer to such a problem, but I suspect that a real conceptual confrontation with endogenous preferences will involve some reintroduction of moral philosophy into our understanding of choice (Friedman, 1967; Williams, 1973; Beck, 1975).

Consider the problem of *posterior preferences* (Schutz, 1967; Hirschman, 1967; Weick, 1969; Elster, 1976). The theory of choice is built on the idea of prior intentions. Suppose we relax the requirement of priority, allow preferences to rationalize action after the fact in our theories as well as our behavior. How do we act in such a way that we conclude, after the fact, that the action was intelligent, and also are led to an elaboration of our preferences that we find fruitful? Such a formulation seems closer to a correct representation of choice problems in politics, for example, than is conventional social welfare theory. We find meaning and merit in our actions after they are taken and the consequences are observed and interpreted. Deliberate efforts to manage posterior constructions of preferences are familiar to us. They include many elements of child-rearing, psychotherapy, consciousness-raising, and product advertising. The terms are somewhat different. We talk of development of character in child-rearing, of insight in psychotherapy, of recognition of objective reality in political, ethnic, or sexual consciousness-raising, and of elaboration of personal needs in advertising. But the technologies are more similar than their ideologies. These techniques for the construction (or excavation) of tastes include both encouraging a reinterpretation of experience and attempting to induce current behavior that will facilitate posterior elaboration of a new understanding of personal preferences. I have tried elsewhere to indicate some of the possibilities this suggests for intelligent foolishness and the role of ambiguity in sensible action (March, 1973). The problem is in many ways indistinguishable from the problem of poetry and the criticism of poetry (or art and art criticism). The poet attempts to write a poem that has meanings intrinsic in the poem but not necessarily explicit at the moment of composition (Ciardi, 1960). In this sense, at least, decisions, like poems, are open; and good decisions are those that enrich our preferences and their meanings. But to talk in such a manner is to talk the language of criticism and aesthetics, and it will probably be necessary for choice theory to engage that literature in some way (Eliot, 1933; Cavell, 1969; Steinberg, 1972; Rosenberg, 1975).

Finally, consider the problem of *inconsistency* in preferences (Elster, 1977c). From the point of view of ordinary human ideas about choice, as well as many philosophical and behavioral conceptions of choice, the most surprising thing about formal theories of choice is the tendency to treat such terms as values, goals, preferences, tastes, wants, and the like, as either equivalent or as reducible to a single objective function with properties of completeness and consistency. Suppose that instead of making such an assumption, we viewed the decision-maker as confronted simultaneously with several orderings of outcomes. We could give them names, calling one a moral code, another a social role, another a personal taste, or whatever. From the present point of view what would be critical would be that the several orderings were independent and irreducible. That is, they could not be deduced from each other, and they could not be combined into a single order. Then instead of taking the conventional step of imputing a preference order across these incomparables by some kind of revealed preference procedure, we treat them as truly incomparable and examine solutions to internal inconsistency that are more in the spirit of our efforts to provide intelligent guidance to collectivities in which we accept the incomparability of preferences across individuals. Then we could give better advice to individuals who want to treat their own preferences strategically, and perhaps move to a clearer recognition of the role of contradiction and paradox in human choice (Farber, 1976; Elster, 1977c). The strategic problems are amenable to relatively straightforward modifications of our views of choice under conflict of interest; the other problems probably require a deeper understanding of contradiction as it appears in philosophy and literature (Elster, 1977c).

Formulating the conceptual problems in these ways is deliberately conservative *vis-à-vis* the theory of choice. It assumes that thinking about human behavior in terms of choice on the basis of some conception of intention is useful, and that the tradition of struggle between normative theories of choice and behavioral theories of choice is a fruitful one. There are alternative paradigms for understanding human behavior that are in many situations likely to be more illuminating. But it is probably unwise to think that every paper should suggest a dramatic paradigm shift, particularly when the alternative is seen only dimly.

Such strictures become even more important when we turn to the engineering of choice. Choice theorists have often discussed complications in the usual abstract representation of tastes. But those concerns have had little impact on ideas about the engineering of choice, because they pose the problems at a level of philosophic complexity that is remote from decision-engineering. Thus, although I think the challenges that ambiguity makes to our models of choice are rather fundamental, my engineering instincts are to sacrifice purity to secure tractability. I suspect we should ask the engineers of choice not initially to reconstruct a philosophy of tastes but to re-examine, within a familiar framework, some presumptions of our craft, and to try to make the use of ambiguity somewhat less of a mystery, somewhat more of a technology. Consider, for example, the following elementary problems in engineering.

The Optimal Ambition Problem

The level of personal ambition is not a decision variable in most theories of choice; but as a result of the work by Simon and others on satisficing, there has been interest in optimal levels of aspiration. These efforts consider an aspiration level as a trigger that either begins or ends the search for new alternatives. The optimization problem is one of balancing the expected costs of additional search with the expected improvements to be realized from the effort (March and Simon, 1958).

But there is another, rather different, way of looking at the optimum ambition problem. Individuals and organizations form aspirations, goals, targets, or ambitions for achievement. These ambitions are usually assumed to be connected to outcomes in at least two ways: they affect search (either directly or through some variable like motivation) and thereby performance; they affect (jointly with performance) satisfaction (March and Simon, 1958). Suppose we wish to maximize some function of satisfaction over time by selecting among alternative ambitions over time, alternative initial ambitions, or alternatives defined by some other decision variable that affects ambition. Examples of the latter might be division of income between consumption and savings, tax policies, or choice among alternative payment schemes. In effect, we wish to select a preference function for achievement that will, after the various behavioral consequences of that selection are accounted for, make us feel that we have selected the best ambition. It is a problem much more familiar to the real world of personal and institutional choice than it is to the normative theory of choice, but it is something about which some things could be said.

The Optimal Clarity Problem

Conventional notions about intelligent choice often begin with the presumption that good decisions require clear goals, and that improving the clarity of goals unambiguously improves the quality of decision-making. In fact, greater precision in the statement of objectives and the measurement of performance with respect to them is often a mixed blessing. There are arguments for moderating an unrestrained enthusiasm for precise performance measures: Where contradiction and confusion are essential elements of the values, precision misrepresents them. The more precise the measure of performance, the greater the motivation to find ways of scoring well on the measurement index without regard to the underlying goals. And precision in objectives does not allow creative interpretation of what the goal might mean (March, 1978). Thus, the introduction of precision into the evaluation of performance involves a tradeoff between the gains in outcomes attributable to closer articulation between action and performance on an index of performance and the losses in outcomes attributable to misrepresentation of goals, reduced motivation to development of goals, and concentration of effort on irrelevant ways of beating the index. Whether one is considering developing a performance evaluation scheme for managers, a testing procedure for students, or an understanding of personal preferences, there is a problem of determining the optimum clarity in goals.

The Optimal Sin Problem

Standard notions of intelligent choice are theories of strict morality. That is, they presume that a person should do what he believes right and believe that what he does is right. Values and actions are to be consistent. Contrast that perspective with a view, somewhat more consistent with our behavior (as well as some theology), that there is such a thing as sin, that individuals and institutions sometimes do things even while recognizing that what they do is not what they wish they did, and that saints are a luxury to be encouraged only in small numbers. Or contrast a theory of strict morality with a view drawn from Nietzsche (1918) or Freud (1927) (see also Jones, 1926) of the complicated contradiction between conscience and self-interest. Although the issues involved are too subtle for brief treatment, a reasonably strong case can be made against strict morality and in favor of at least some sin, and therefore hypocrisy. One of the most effective ways of maintaining morality is through the remorse exhibited and felt at immoral action. Even if we are confident that our moral codes are correct, we may want to recognize human complexities. There will be occasions on which humans will be tempted by desires that they recognize as evil. If we insist that they maintain consistency between ethics and actions, the ethics will often be more likely to change than the actions. Hypocrisy is a long-run investment in morality made at some cost (the chance that, in fact, action might otherwise adjust to morals). To encourage people always to take responsibility for their actions is to encourage them to deny that bad things are bad – to make evil acceptable. At the same time, sin is an experiment with an alternative morality. By recognizing sin, we make it easier for persons to experiment with the possibility of having different tastes. Moral systems need those experiments, and regularly grant licenses to experiment to drunks, lovers, students, or sinners. These gains from sin are purchased by its costs. Thus, the optimization problem.

The Optimal Rationality Problem

Calculated rationality is a technique for making decisions. In standard versions of theories of choice it is the only legitimate form of intelligence. But it is obvious that it is, in fact, only one of several alternative forms of intelligence, each with claims to legitimacy. Learned behavior, with its claim to summarize an irretrievable but relevant personal history, or conventional behavior and rules, with their claims to capture the intelligence of survival over long histories of experience more relevant than that susceptible to immediate calculation, are clear alternative contenders. There are others: Revelation or intuition, by which we substitute one guess for two; or imitation, or expertise, by which we substitute the guess of someone else for our own. Among all of these, only calculated rationality really uses conscious preferences of a current actor as a major consideration in making decisions. It is easy to show that there exist situations in which any one of these alternative techniques will make better decisions than the independent calculation of rational behavior by ordinary individuals or institutions. The superiority of learned or conventional behavior depends, in general, on the amount of experience it summarizes and the similarity between the world in which the experience was accumulated and the current world. The superiority of imitation depends, in general, on the relative competence of actor and expert and the extent to which intelligent action is reproducible but not comprehendible. At the same time, each form of intelligence exposes an actor to the risks of corruption. Imitation risks a false confidence in the neutrality of the process of diffusion; calculated rationality risks a false confidence in the neutrality of rational argument; and so on. It is not hard to guess that the relative size of these risks vary from individual to individual, or institution to institution. What is harder to specify in any very precise way is the extent and occasions on which a sensible person would rely on calculated rationality rather than the alternatives.

A Romantic Vision

Prescriptive theories of choice are dedicated to perfecting the intelligence of human action by imagining that action stems from reason and by improving the technology of decision. Descriptive theories of choice are dedicated to perfecting the understanding of human action by imagining that action makes sense. Not all behavior makes sense; some of it is unreasonable. Not all decision-technology is intelligent; some of it is foolish. Over the past 20 years, the contradiction between the search for sense in behavior and the search for improvement in behavior has focused on our interpretation of the way information about future consequences is gathered and processed. The effort built considerably on the idea of bounded rationality and a conception of human decision-making as limited by the cognitive capabilities of human beings. Over the next 20 years. I suspect the contradiction will be increasingly concerned with an interpretation of how beliefs about future preferences are generated and utilized. The earlier confrontation led theories of choice to a slightly clearer understanding of information-processing and to some modest links with the technologies of computing inference, and subjective probability. So perhaps the newer confrontation will lead theories of choice to a slightly clearer understanding of the complexities of preference processing and to some modest links with the technologies of ethics, criticism, and aesthetics. The history of theories of choice and their engineering applications suggests that we might appropriately be pessimistic about immediate, major progress. The intelligent engineering of tastes involves questions that encourage despair over their difficulty (Savage, 1954). But though hope for minor progress is a romantic vision, it may not be entirely inappropriate for a theory built on a romantic view of human destiny.

References

Ackoff, R. L., and Sasieni, M. W. (1968) *Fundamentals of Operations Research*. New York: Wiley.

Allison, G. T. (1969) *Essence of Decision: Explaining the Cuban Missile Crisis*. Boston: Little, Brown.

Allison, G. T., and Halperin, M. H. (1972) Bureaucratic Politics: Paradigm and Some Policy Implications, in R. Tanter and R. H. Ullman (eds), *Theory and Policy in International Relations*. Princeton: Princeton University Press.

Bailey, M. J., and Olson M. (1977) Pure Time Preference, Revealed Marginal Utility, and Friedman-Savage Gambles. Unpublished manuscript.

Beck, L. W. (1975) *The Actor and the Spectator*. New Haven: Yale University Press.

Becker, G. S. (1965) A Theory of the Allocation of Time. *Economic Journal*, Vol. 75, 493–517.

Becker, G. S. (1976) Altruism, Egoism, and Genetic Fitness: Economics and Socio-biology. *Journal of Economic Literature*, Vol. 14, 718–26.

Binkley, R., Bronaugh, R., and Marras, A., (eds) (1971) *Agent, Action, and Reason*. Toronto: University of Toronto Press.

Bower, J. L. (1968) Descriptive Decision Theory from the 'Administrative Viewpoint', in R. A. Bauer and K. J. Gergen (eds), *The Study of Policy Formation*, New York: Free Press.

Brams, S. J. (1975) *Game Theory and Politics*. New York: Free Press.

Camus, A. (1951) *L'Homme Révolte*. Paris: Gallimard. (Published in English as *The Rebel*.)

Carter, E. E. (1971) The Behavioral Theory of the Firm and Top-Level Corporate Decisions. *Administrative Science Quarterly,* Vol. 16, 413–29.

Catallus, G. V. (58 BC) *Carmina*, 85. Rome.

Cavell, S. (1969) *Must We Mean What We Say?* New York: Scribner.

Charnes, A., and Cooper, W. W. (1963) Deterministic Equivalents for Optimizing and Satisficing under Chance Constraints. *Operations Research*, Vol. 11, 18–39.

Christensen, S. (1976) Decision Making and Socialization, in J. G. March and J. P. Olsen (eds) *Ambiguity and Choice in Organizations*, Bergen: Universitetsforlaget.

Chomsky, N. (1968) *Language and Mind*. New York: Harcourt, Brace, & World.

Ciardi, J. (1960) *How Does a Poem Mean?* Cambridge: Houghton Mifflin.

Cohen, M. D., and March, J. G. (1974) *Leadership and Ambiguity: The American College President*. New York: McGraw-Hill.

Cohen, M. D., and Olsen, J. P. (1972) A Garbage Can Model of Organizational Choice. *Administrative Science Quarterly*, Vol. 17, 1–25.

Connolly, T. (1977) Information Processing and Decision Making in Organizations, in B. M. Staw and G. R Salancik (eds), *New Directions in Organizational Behavior*, Chicago: St. Clair.

Crozier, M., and Friedberg, E. (1977) *L'Acteur et le Système*. Paris: Seuil.

Cyert, R. M., and De Groot, M. H. (1973) An Analysis of Cooperation and Learning in a Duopoly Context. *The American Economic Review*, Vol. 63, No. 1, 24–37.

Cyert, R. M., and De Groot, M. H. (1975) Adaptive Utility in R. H. Day and T. Groves (eds), *Adaptive Economic Models*, New York: Academic Press.

Cyert, R. M., and March, J. G. (1963) *A Behavioral Theory of the Firm*. Englewood Cliffs, NJ: Prentice-Hall.

Day, R. H., and Groves, T. (eds) (1975) *Adaptive Economic Models*. New York: Academic Press.

Downs, A. (1967) *Inside Bureaucracy*. Boston: Little, Brown.

Edelman, M. (1960) *The Symbolic Uses of Politics*. Champaign, Ill.: University of Illinois Press.

Eliot, T. S. (1933)*The Use of Poetry and the Use of Criticism*. Cambridge: Harvard University Press.

Elster, J. (1976) A Note on Hysteresis in the Social Sciences. *Synthese*. Vol. 33, pp.371–91.

Elster, J. (1977a) *Logic and Society*. London: Wiley.

Elster, J. (1977b) Ulysses and the Sirens: A Theory of Imperfect Rationality. *Social Science Information,* Vol. 16, No. 5, 469–526.

Elster, J. (1977c) Some Unresolved Problems in the Theory of Rational Behavior. Unpublished manuscript.

Farber, L. (1976) *Lying, Despair, Jealousy, Envy, Sex, Suicide, Drugs, and the Good Life*. New York: Basic Books.

Farquharson, R. (1969) *Theory of Voting*. New Haven: Yale University Press.

Freud, S. (1927) *The Ego and the Id*. London: Hogarth.

Friedman, M. (1967) *To Deny Our Nothingness: Contemporary Images of Man*. New York: Delacorte.

Halperin, M. H. (1974) *Bureaucratic Politics and Foreign Policy*. Washington, DC: The Brookings Institution.

Harsanyi, J. C., and Selten, R. (1972) A Generalized Nash Solution for Two-Person Bargaining Games with Incomplete Information. *Management Science*, Vol. 18, 80–106.

Hegel, G. W. F. (1832) *G. W. F. Hegel's Werke*. Berlin: Duncker und Humblot.

Hirschman, A. O. (1967) *Development Projects Observed*. Washington, DC: The Brookings Instituion.

Hirschman, A. O., and Lindblom, C. E. (1962) Economic Development, Research and Development, Policy Making: Some Converging Views, *Behavioral Science*, Vol. 7, 211–22.

Janis, I. L., and Mann, L. (1977) *Decision Making*, New York: Free Press.

Johnson, E. (1968) *Studies in Multiobjective Decision Models.* Lund: Studentlitteratur.

Jones, E. (1926) The Origin and Structure of the Superego. *International Journal of Psychoanalysis.* Vol. 7, 303–11.

Keen, P. G. W. (1977) The Evolving Concept of Optimality. *TIMS Studies in the Management Sciences,* Vol. 6, 31–57.

Koopmans, T. C. (1964) On Flexibility of Future Preferences, in M. W. Shelly and G. L. Bryan (eds), *Human Judgments and Optimality*, New York: Wiley.

Kreiner, K. (1976) Ideology and Management in a Garbage Can Situation, in J. G. March and J. P. Olsen (eds), *Ambiguity and Choice in Organizations*, Bergen: Universitetsforlaget.

Lee, S. M. (1972) *Goal Programming for Decision Analysis.* Philadelphia: Auerbach.

Lindblom, C. E. (1959) The Science of Muddling Through. *Public Administration Review*, Vol. 19, 79–88.

Lindblom, C. E. (1965) *The Intelligence of Democracy.* New York: Macmillan.

Long, N. E. (1958) The Local Community as an Ecology of Games. *American Journal of Sociology*, Vol. 44, 251–61.

Mao, T. T. (1952) *On Contradiction.* Published in English by Foreign Language Press. Peking.

March, J. G. (1962) The Business Firm As a Political Coalition. *Journal of Politics*, Vol. 24, 662–78.

March, J. G. (1973) Model Bias in Social Action. *Review of Educational Research,* Vol. 42, 413–29.

March, J. G. (1978) American Public School Administration: A Short Analysis. *School Review*, Vol. 86, 217–50.

March, J. G., and Olsen, J. P. (eds) (1976) *Ambiguity and Choice in Organizations.* Bergen: Universitetsforlaget.

March, J. G., and Romelaer, P. J. (1976) Position and Presence in the Drift of Decisions, in J. G. March and J. P. Olsen (eds) *Ambiguity and Choice in Organizations*, Bergen: Universitetsforlaget.

March, J. G., and Simon, H. A. (1958) *Organizations.* New York: Wiley.

Marschak, J. and Radner, R. (1972) *Economic Theory of Teams.* New Haven: Yale University Press.

Mayhew, D. R. (1974) *Congress: The Electoral Connection.* New Haven: Yale University Press.

McGuire, C. B., and Radner, R. (eds) (1972) *Decision and Organization.* Amsterdam: North-Holland.

Mills, J. S. (1838). (1950) *Bentham.* Reprinted in *Mill on Bentham and Coleridge.* London: Chatto and Windus.

Mueller, D. C. (1976) Public Choice: A Survey. *Journal of Economic Literature*, Vol. 14, 395–433.

Nelson, R. R., and Winter, S. G. (1973) Towards an Evolutionary Theory of Economic Capabilities. *The American Economic Review*, Vol. 63, 440–9.

Newell, A., and Simon, H. A. (1972) *Human Problem Solving.* Englewood Cliffs, NJ: Prentice-Hall.

Nietzsche, F. (1918) *The Geneology of Morals.* New York: Boni and Liveright.

Olson, M. (1965) *The Logic of Collective Action*. New York: Schocken.

Olson, M. (1976) Exchange, Integration, and Grants, in M. Pfaff, ed., *Essays in Honor of Kenneth Boulding,* Amsterdam: North-Holland, 1976.

Pattanaik, P. K. (1973) Group Choice with Lexicographic Individual Orderings. *Behavioral Science,* Vol. 18, 118–23.

Pfeffer, J. (1977) Power and Resource Allocation in Organizations, in B. M. Staw and G. R. Salancik (eds), *New Directions in Organizational Behavior,* Chicago: St. Clair.

Pondy, L. R., and Olson, M. L. (1977) Organization and Performance. Unpublished manuscript.

Porat, A. M., and Haas, J. A. (1969) Information Effects on Decision Making. *Behavioral Science,* Vol. 14, 98–104.

Radner, R. (Spring 1975a) A Behavioral Model of Cost Reduction. *The Bell Journal of Economics,* Vol. 6, No. 1, 196–215.

Radner, R. (1975b) Satisficing. *Journal of Mathematical Economics,* Vol. 2, 253–62.

Radner, R., and Rothschild, M. (1975) On the Allocation of Effort. *Journal of Economic Theory,* Vol. 10, 358–76.

Rapoport, A. (1960) *Fights, Games, and Debates*. Ann Arbor: University of Michigan Press.

Riker, W., and Ordeshook, P. (1974) *An Introduction to Positive Political Theory.* Englewood Cliffs, NJ: Prentice-Hall.

Rosenberg, H. (1975) *Art on the Edge: Creators and Situations*. New York: Macmillan.

Rothschild, M., and Stiglitz, J. (1976) Equilibrium in Competitive Insurance Markets: An Essay on the Economics of Imperfect Information. *Quarterly Journal of Economics,* Vol. 90, 629–49.

Savage, L. J. (1954) *Foundations of Statistics*. New York: Wiley.

Schelling, T. (1971) On the Ecology of Micro-Motives. *Public Interest,* Vol. 25, 59–98.

Schutz, A. (1967) *The Phenomenology of the Social World*. Evanston, Ill.: Northwestern.

Shakespeare, W. (1623) *Hamlet, Prince of Denmark*. Stratford-upon-Avon.

Shefrin, H. M., and Thaler, R. (1977) An Economic Theory of Self-Control. Unpublished manuscript.

Simon, H. A. (1955) A Behavioral Model of Rational Choice. *Quarterly Journal of Economics,* Vol. 69, 99–118.

Simon, H. A. (1956) Rational Choice and the Structure of the Environment. *Psychological Review.* Vol. 63, 129–38.

Simon, H. A. (1957) *Models of Man*. New York: Wiley.

Simon, H. A. (1969) *The Science of the Artificial*. Cambridge: MIT Press.

Simon, H. A. (1973) The Structure of Ill-Structured Problems. *Artificial Intelligence,* Vol. 4, 181–201.

Slovic, P., Fischhoff, B., and Lichtenstein, S. (1977) Behavioral Decision Theory. *Annual Review of Psychology,* Vol. 28, 1–39.

Spence, A. M. (1974) *Market Signalling*. Cambridge: Harvard University Press.

Sproull, L. S. Weiner, S. S., and Wolf, D. B. (1978) *Organizing an Anarchy.* Chicago: University of Chicago Press.

Steinbruner, J. D. (1974) *The Cybernetic Theory of Decision*. Princeton: Princeton University Press.

Steinberg, L. (1972) *Other Criteria: Confrontations with Twentieth Century Art*. New York: Oxford University Press.

Stigler, G. J. (1961) The Economics of Information. *Journal of Political Economy*, Vol. 69, 213-25.

Stigler, G. J., and Becker, G. S. (1977) *De Gustibus Non Est Disputandum. The American Economic Review*, Vol. 67, 76-90.

Strotz, R. H. (1956) Myopia and Inconsistency in Dynamic Utility Maximization. *Review of Economic Studies*, Vol. 23.

Taylor, M. (1975) The Theory of Collective Choice in F. I. Greenstein and N. W. Polsby (eds), *Handbook of Political Science*, Vol. 3, Reading, Mass.: Addison-Wesley.

Taylor, R. N. (1975) Psychological Determinants of Bounded Rationality: Implications for Decision-making Strategies. *Decision Sciences*, Vol. 6, 409-29.

Thompson, J. (1967) *Organizations in Action*. New York: McGraw-Hill.

Tullock, G. (1965) *The Politics of Bureaucracy*. Washington, DC: Public Affairs.

Tversky, A., and Kahneman, D. (1974) Judgment under Uncertainty: Heuristics and Biases. *Science*, Vol. 185, 1124-31.

Von Weiszäcker, C. C. (1971) Notes on Endogenous Change of Taste. *Journal of Economic Theory*, Vol. 3, 345-72.

Vroom, V. H. (1964) *Work and Motivation*. New York: Wiley.

Warwick, D. P. ((1975) *A Theory of Public Bureaucracy: Politics, Personality, and Organization in the State Department*. Cambridge: Harvard University Press.

Weick, K. E. (1969) *The Social Psychology of Organizing*. Reading, Mass.: Addison-Wesley.

Weick, K. E. (1976) Educational Organizations as Loosely Coupled Systems. *Administrative Science Quarterly*, Vol. 21, 1-18.

Weiner, S. S. (1976) Participation, Deadlines, and Choice, in J. G. March and J. P. Olsen (eds), *Ambiguity and Choice in Organizations*, Bergen: Universitetsforlaget.

Wildavsky, A. (1971) *Revolt Against the Masses and Other Essays on Politics and Public Policy*. New York: Basic Books.

Wildavsky, A., and Pressman, H. (1973) *Implementation*. Berkeley: University of California Press.

Williams, B. A. O. (1973) *Problems of the Self*. Cambridge: Cambridge University Press.

Williamson, O. E. (1975) *Markets and Hierarchies*. New York: Free Press.

Wilson, E. O. (1975) *Sociobiology*. Cambridge: Harvard University Press.

Winter, S. G. (1964) Economic 'Natural Selection' and the Theory of the Firm. *Yale Economic Essays*, Vol. 4, 225-72.

Winter, S. G. (1971) Satisficing, Selection, and the Innovating Remnant. *Quarterly Journal of Economics*, Vol. 85, 237-61.

Winter, S. G. (1975) Optimization and Evolution in the Theory of the Firm, in R. H. Day and T. Groves (eds), *Adaptive Economic Models,* New York: Academic Press.

14

A Garbage Can Model of
Organizational Choice

Michael D. Cohen, James G. March, and Johan P. Olsen

Abstract

Organized anarchies are organizations characterized by problematic preferences, unclear technology, and fluid participation. Recent studies of universities, a familiar form of organized anarchy, suggest that such organizations can be viewed for some purposes as collections of choices looking for problems, issues and feelings looking for decision situations in which they might be aired, solutions looking for issues to which they might be an answer, and decision-makers looking for work. These ideas are translated into an explicit computer simulation model of a garbage can decision process. The general implications of such a model are described in terms of five major measures on the process. Possible applications of the model to more narrow predictions are illustrated by an examination of the model's predictions with respect to the effect of adversity on university decision-making.

Consider organized anarchies. These are organizations – or decision situations – characterized by three general properties.[1] The first is problematic preferences. In the organization it is difficult to impute a set of

---

1   This paper was first published in *Administrative Science Quarterly*, Vol. 17, No. 1, March 1972. The authors are indebted to Nancy Block, Hilary Cohen, and James Glenn for computational, editorial, and intellectual help; to the Institute of Sociology, University of Bergen, and the Institute of Organization and Industrial Sociology, Copenhagen School of Economics, for institutional hospitality and useful discussions of organizational behavior; and to the Ford Foundation for the financial support that made our collaboration feasible. We also wish to acknowledge the helpful comments and suggestions of Søren Christensen, James S. Coleman, Harald Enderud, Kåre Rommetveit, and William H. Starbuck.

preferences to the decision situation that satisfies the standard consistency requirements for a theory of choice. The organization operates on the basis of a variety of inconsistent and ill-defined preferences. It can be described better as a loose collection of ideas than as a coherent structure; it discovers preferences through action more than it acts on the basis of preferences.

The second property is unclear technology. Although the organization manages to survive and even produce, its own processes are not understood by its members. It operates on the basis of simple trial-and-error procedures, the residue of learning from the accidents of past experience, and pragmatic inventions of necessity. The third property is fluid participation. Participants vary in the amount of time and effort they devote to different domains; involvement varies from one time to another. As a result, the boundaries of the organization are uncertain and changing; the audiences and decision-makers for any particular kind of choice change capriciously.

These properties of organized anarchy have been identified often in studies of organizations. They are characteristic of any organization in part – part of the time. They are particularly conspicuous in public, educational, and illegitimate organizations. A theory of organized anarchy will describe a portion of almost any organization's activities, but will not describe all of them.

To build on current behavioral theories of organizations in order to accommodate the concept of organized anarchy, two major phenomena critical to an understanding of anarchy must be investigated. The first is the manner in which organizations make choices without consistent, shared goals. Situations of decision-making under goal ambiguity are common in complex organizations. Often problems are resolved without recourse to explicit bargaining or to an explicit price system market – two common processes for decision-making in the absence of consensus. The second phenomenon is the way members of an organization are activated. This entails the question of how occasional members become active and how attention is directed toward, or away from, a decision. It is important to understand the attention patterns within an organization, since not everyone is attending to everything all of the time.

Additional concepts are also needed in a normative theory of organizations dealing with organized anarchies. First, a normative theory of intelligent decision-making under ambiguous circumstances (namely, in situations in which goals are unclear or unknown) should be developed. Can we provide some meaning for intelligence which does not depend on relating current action to known goals? Second, a normative theory of attention is needed. Participants within an organization are constrained by the amount of time they can devote to the various things demanding attention. Since variations in behavior in organized anarchies are due largely to questions of who is attending to what, decisions concerning the allocation of attention are prime ones. Third, organized anarchies require a revised theory of management. Significant parts of contemporary theories of management introduce mechanisms for control and coordination which assume the existence of well-defined goals and a well-defined technology, as well as substantial participant involvement in the affairs of the organization. Where goals and technology are hazy and participation is fluid, many of the axioms and standard procedures of management collapse.

This article is directed to a behavioral theory of organized anarchy. On the basis of several recent studies, some elaborations and modifications of existing theories of choice are proposed. A model for describing decision-making within organized anarchies is developed and the impact of some aspects of organizational structure on the process of choice within such a model is examined.

The Basic Ideas

Decision opportunities are fundamentally ambiguous stimuli. This theme runs through several recent studies of organizational choice.[2] Although organizations can often be viewed conveniently as vehicles for solving well-defined problems or structures within which conflict is resolved through bargaining, they also provide sets of procedures through which participants arrive at an interpretation of what they are doing and what they have done while in the process of doing it. From this point of view, an organization is a collection of choices looking for problems, issues and feelings looking for decision situations in which they might be aired, solutions looking for issues to which they might be the answer, and decision-makers looking for work.

Such a view of organizational choice focuses attention on the way the meaning of a choice changes over time. It calls attention to the strategic effects of timing, through the introduction of choices and problems, the time pattern of available energy, and the impact of organizational structure.

To understand processes within organizations, one can view a choice opportunity as a garbage can into which various kinds of problems and solutions are dumped by participants as they are generated. The mix of garbage in a single can depends on the mix of cans available, on the labels

2   We have based the model heavily on seven recent studies of universities: Christensen (1971), Cohen and March (1974), Enderud (1971), Mood (1971), Olsen (1970, 1971), and Rommetveit (1971). The ideas, however, have a broader parentage. In particular, they obviously owe a debt to Allison (1969), Coleman (1957), Cyert and March (1963), Lindblom (1965), Long (1958), March and Simon (1958), Schilling (1968), Thompson (1967), and Vickers (1965)

attached to the alternative cans, on what garbage is currently being produced, and on the speed with which garbage is collected and removed from the scene.

Such a theory of organizational decision-making must concern itself with a relatively complicated interplay among the generation of problems in an organization, the deployment of personnel, the production of solutions, and the opportunities for choice. Although it may be convenient to imagine that choice opportunities lead first to the generation of decision alternatives, then to an examination of their consequences, then to an evaluation of those consequences in terms of objectives, and finally to a decision, this type of model is often a poor description of what actually happens. In the garbage can model, on the other hand, a decision is an outcome or interpretation of several relatively independent streams within an organization.

Attention is limited here to interrelations among four such streams.

Problems. Problems are the concern of people inside and outside the organization. They might arise over issues of lifestyle; family; frustrations of work; careers; group relations within the organization; distribution of status, jobs, and money; ideology; or current crises of mankind as interpreted by the mass media or the nextdoor neighbor. All of these require attention.

Solutions. A solution is somebody's product. A computer is not just a solution to a problem in payroll management, discovered when needed. It is an answer actively looking for a question. The creation of need is not a curiosity of the market in consumer products; it is a general phenomenon of processes of choice. Despite the dictum that you cannot find the answer until you have formulated the question well, you often do not know what the question is in organizational problem-solving until you know the answer.

Participants. Participants come and go. Since every entrance is an exit somewhere else, the distribution of 'entrances' depends on the attributes of the choice being left as much as it does on the attributes of the new choice. Substantial variation in participation stems from other demands on the participants' time (rather than from features of the decision under study).

Choice opportunities. These are occasions when an organization is expected to produce behavior that can be called a decision. Opportunities arise regularly and any organization has ways of declaring an occasion for choice. Contracts must be signed; people hired, promoted, or fired; money spent; and responsibilities allocated.

Although not completely independent of each other, each of the streams can be viewed as independent and exogenous to the system. Attention will be concentrated here on examining the consequences of different rates and patterns of flows in each of the streams and different procedures for relating them.

The Garbage Can

A simple simulation model can be specified in terms of the four streams and a set of garbage-processing assumptions. Four basic variables are considered; each is a function of time.

A stream of choices.   Some fixed number, m, of choices is assumed. Each choice is characterized by (1) an entry time, the calendar time at which that choice is activated for decision; and (2) a decision structure, a list of participants eligible to participate in making that choice.

A stream of problems.   Some number, w, of problems is assumed. Each problem is characterized by (1) an entry time, the calendar time at which the problem becomes visible, (2) an energy requirement, the energy required to resolve a choice to which the problem is attached (if the solution stream is as high as possible), and (3) an access structure, a list of choices to which the problem has access.

A rate of flow of solutions.   The verbal theory assumes a stream of solutions and a matching of specific solutions with specific problems and choices. A simpler set of assumptions is made and focus is on the rate at which solutions are flowing into the system. It is assumed that either because of variations in the stream of solutions or because of variations in the efficiency of search procedures within the organization, different energies are required to solve the same problem at different times. It is further assumed that these variations are consistent for different problems. Thus, a solution coefficient, ranging between 0 and 1, which operates on the potential decision energies to determine the problem-solving output (effective energy) actually realized during any given time period is specified.

A stream of energy from participants.   It is assumed that there is some number, v, of participants. Each participant is characterized by a time series of energy available for organizational decision-making. Thus, in each time period, each participant can provide some specified amount of potential energy to the organization.

Two varieties of organizational segmentation are reflected in the model. The first is the mapping of choices onto decision-makers, the decision structure. The decision structure of the organization is described by D, a v-by-m array in which d_{ij} is 1 if the ith participant is eligible to participate in the making of the jth choice. Otherwise, d_{ij} is 0. The second is the mapping of problems onto choices, the access structure. The access structure of the organization is described by A, a w-by-m array in which a_{ij} is 1 if the jth choice is accessible to the ith problem. Otherwise, a_{ij} is 0.

In order to connect these variables, three key behavioral assumptions are specified. The first is an assumption about the additivity of energy requirements, the second specifies the way in which energy is allocated to choices, and the third describes the way in which problems are attached to choices.

Energy additivity assumption.   In order to be made, each choice requires as much effective energy as the sum of all requirements of the several problems attached to it. The effective energy devoted to a choice is the sum of the energies of decision-makers attached to that choice, deflated, in each time period, by the solution coefficient. As soon as the total effective energy that has been expended on a choice equals or exceeds the requirements at a particular point in time, a decision is made.

Energy allocation assumption.   The energy of each participant is allocated to no more than one choice during each time period. Each participant allocates his energy among the choices for which he is eligible to the one closest to decision, that is the one with the smallest energy deficit at the end of the previous time period in terms of the energies contributed by other participants.

Problem allocation assumption.   Each problem is attached to no more than one choice each time period, choosing from among those accessible by calculating the apparent energy deficits (in terms of the energy requirements of other problems) at the end of the previous time period and selecting the choice closest to decision. Except to the extent that priorities enter in the organizational structure, there is no priority ranking of problems.

These assumptions capture key features of the processes observed. They might be modified in a number of ways without doing violence to the empirical observations on which they are based. The consequences of these modifications, however, are not pursued here. Rather, attention is focused on the implications of the simple version described. The interaction of organizational structure and a garbage can form of choice will be examined.

Organizational Structure

Elements of organizational structure influence outcomes of a garbage can decision process (1) by affecting the time pattern of the arrival of problems, choices, solutions, or decision-makers, (2) by determining the allocation of energy by potential participants in the decision, and (3) by establishing linkages among the various streams.

The organizational factors to be considered are some that have real-world interpretations and implications and are applicable to the theory of organized anarchy. They are familar features of organizations, resulting from a mixture of deliberate managerial planning, individual and collective learning, and imitation. Organizational structure changes as a response to such factors as market demand for personnel and the heterogeneity of values, which are external to the model presented here. Attention will be limited to the comparative statics of the model, rather than to the dynamics produced by organizational learning.

To exercise the model, the following are specified:

1 a set of fixed parameters which do not change from one variation to another;
2 the entry times for choices;
3 the entry times for problems;
4 the net energy load on the organization;
5 the access structure of the organization;
6 the decision structure of the organization;
7 the energy distribution among decision-makers in the organization.

Some relatively pure structural variations will be defined in each and examples of how variations in such structures might be related systematically to key exogenous variables will be given. It will then be shown how such factors of organizational structure affect important characteristics of the decisions in a garbage can decision process.

Fixed Parameters

Within the variations reported, the following are fixed:

1 number of time periods – twenty;
2 number of choice opportunities – ten;
3 number of decision-makers – ten;

4 number of problems – twenty; and
5 the solution coefficients for the 20 time periods – 0.6 for each period.[3]

Entry Times

Two different randomly generated sequences of entry times for choices are considered. It is assumed that one choice enters per time period over the first ten time periods in one of the following orders: (a) 10, 7, 9, 5, 2, 3, 4, 1, 6, 8, or (b) 6, 5, 2, 10, 8, 9, 7, 4, 1, 3.

Similarly, two different randomly generated sequences of entry times for problems are considered. It is assumed that two problems enter per time period over the first ten time periods in one of the following orders: (a) 8, 20, 14, 16, 6, 7, 15, 17, 2, 13, 11, 19, 4, 9, 3, 12, 1, 10, 5, 18, or (b) 4, 14, 11, 20, 3, 5, 2, 12, 1, 6, 8, 19, 7, 15, 16, 17, 10, 18, 9, 13.

Net Energy Load

The total energy available to the organization in each time period is 5.5 units. Thus, the total energy available over twenty time periods is $20 \times 5.5 = 110$. This is reduced by the solution coefficients to 66. These figures hold across all other variations of the model. The net energy load on the organization is defined as the difference between the total energy required to solve all problems and the total effective energy available to the organization over all time periods. When this is negative, there is, in principle, enough energy available. Since the total effective energy available is fixed at 66, the net load is varied by varying the total energy requirements for problems. It is assumed that each problem has the same energy requirement under a given load. Three different energy load situations are considered.

Net energy load 0: light load.   Under this condition the energy required to make a choice is 1.1 times the number of problems attached to that choice. That is, the energy required for each problem is 1.1. Thus, the minimum total effective energy required to resolve all problems is 22, and the net energy load is $22 - 66 = -44$.

Net energy load 1: moderate load.   Under this condition, the energy required for each problem is 2.2. Thus, the energy required to make a

---

3   The model has also been exercised under conditions of a set of solution coefficients that varies over the time periods. Specifically, the following series has been used: 1, 0.9, 0.7, 0.3, 0.1, 0.1, 0.3, 0.7, 0.9, 1, 0.6, 0.6, 0.6, 0.6, 0.6, 0.6, 0.6, 0.6, 0.6, 0.6. This simulation, using only one combination of choice and problem entry times, gives results consistent with all of the conclusions reported in the present article.

choice is 2.2 times the number of problems attached to that choice, and the minimum effective energy required to resolve all problems is 44. The net energy load is $44 - 66 = -22$.

Net energy load 2: heavy load.   Under this condition, each problem requires energy of 3.3. The energy required to make a choice is 3.3 times the number of problems attached to that choice. The minimum effective energy required to resolve all problems is 66, and the net energy load is $66 - 66 = 0$.

   Although it is possible from the total energy point of view for all problems to be resolved in any load condition, the difficulty of accomplishing that result where the net energy load is zero – a heavy load – is obviously substantial.

Access Structure

Three pure types of organizational arrangements are considered in the access structure (the relation between problems and choices).

Access structure 0: unsegmented access.   This structure is represented by an access array in which any active problem has access to any active choice.

$$
\begin{array}{l}
1111111111 \\
1111111111 \\
1111111111 \\
1111111111 \\
1111111111 \\
1111111111 \\
1111111111 \\
1111111111 \\
A_0 = 1111111111 \\
1111111111 \\
1111111111 \\
1111111111 \\
1111111111 \\
1111111111 \\
1111111111 \\
1111111111 \\
1111111111 \\
1111111111 \\
1111111111
\end{array}
$$

Access structure 1: hierarchical access. In this structure both choices and problems are arranged in a hierarchy such that important problems – those with relatively low numbers – have access to many choices, and important choices – those with relatively low numbers – are accessible only to important problems. The structure is represented by the following access array:

$$
A_1 =
\begin{matrix}
1111111111 \\
1111111111 \\
0111111111 \\
0111111111 \\
0011111111 \\
0011111111 \\
0001111111 \\
0001111111 \\
0000111111 \\
0000111111 \\
0000011111 \\
0000011111 \\
0000001111 \\
0000001111 \\
0000000111 \\
0000000111 \\
0000000011 \\
0000000011 \\
0000000001 \\
0000000001 \\
\end{matrix}
$$

Access structure 2: specialized access.   In this structure each problem has access to only one choice and each choice is accessible to only two problems, that is, choices specialize in the kinds of problems that can be associated to them. The structure is represented by the access array at the top of p. 304.

Actual organizations will exhibit a more complex mix of access rules. Any such combination could be represented by an appropriate access array. The three pure structures considered here represent three classic alternative approaches to the problem of organizing the legitimate access of problems to decision situations.

Decision Structure

Three similar pure types are considered in the decision structure (the relation between decision-makers and choices).

$$
A_2 = \begin{array}{l}
1000000000 \\
1000000000 \\
0100000000 \\
0100000000 \\
0010000000 \\
0010000000 \\
0001000000 \\
0001000000 \\
0000100000 \\
0000100000 \\
0000010000 \\
0000010000 \\
0000001000 \\
0000001000 \\
0000000100 \\
0000000100 \\
0000000010 \\
0000000010 \\
0000000001 \\
0000000001
\end{array}
$$

Decision structure 0: unsegmented decisions. In this structure any decision-maker can participate in any active choice opportunity. Thus, the structure is represented by the following array:

$$
D_0 = \begin{array}{l}
1111111111 \\
1111111111 \\
1111111111 \\
1111111111 \\
1111111111 \\
1111111111 \\
1111111111 \\
1111111111 \\
1111111111 \\
1111111111
\end{array}
$$

Decision structure 1: hierarchical decisions. In this structure both decision-makers and choices are arranged in a hierarchy such that important choices – low numbered choices – must be made by important decision-makers – low numbered decision-makers – and important decision-makers can participate in many choices. The structure is represented by the following array:

$$
D_1 =
\begin{matrix}
1111111111 \\
0111111111 \\
0011111111 \\
0001111111 \\
0000111111 \\
0000011111 \\
0000001111 \\
0000000111 \\
0000000011 \\
0000000001
\end{matrix}
$$

Decision structure 2: specialized decisions. In this structure each decision-maker is associated with a single choice and each choice has a single decision-maker. Decision-makers specialize in the choices to which they attend. Thus, we have the following array:

$$
D_2 =
\begin{matrix}
1000000000 \\
0100000000 \\
0010000000 \\
0001000000 \\
0000100000 \\
0000010000 \\
0000001000 \\
0000000100 \\
0000000010 \\
0000000001
\end{matrix}
$$

As in the case of the access structure, actual decision structures will require a more complicated array. Most organizations have a mix of rules for defining the legitimacy of participation in decisions. The three pure cases are, however, familiar models of such rules and can be used to understand some consequences of decision structure for decision processes.

Energy Distribution

The distribution of energy among decision-makers reflects possible variations in the amount of time spent on organizational problems by different decision-makers. The solution coefficients and variations in the energy requirement for problems affect the overall relation between energy available and energy required. Three different variations in the distribution of energy are considered.

Energy distribution 0: important people – less energy.   In this distribution important people, that is people defined as important in a hierarchial decision structure, have less energy. This might reflect variations in the combination of outside demands and motivation to participate within the organization. The specific energy distribution is indicated as follows:

Decision-maker	Energy	
1	0.1	
2	0.2	
3	0.3	
4	0.4	
5	0.5	$= E_0$
6	0.6	
7	0.7	
8	0.8	
9	0.9	
10	1.0	

The total energy available to the organization each time period (before deflation by the solution coefficients) is 5.5.

Energy distribution 1: equal energy.   In this distribution there is no internal differentiation among decision-makers with respect to energy. Each decision-maker has the same energy (0.55) each time period. Thus, there is the following distribution:

Decision-maker	Energy	
1	0.55	
2	0.55	
3	0.55	
4	0.55	
5	0.55	$= E_1$
6	0.55	
7	0.55	
8	0.55	
9	0.55	
10	0.55	

The total energy available to the organization each time period (before deflation by the solution coefficients) is 5.5.

Energy distribution 2: important people – more energy.   In this distribution energy is distributed unequally but in a direction opposite to that in E_0. Here the people defined as important by the hierarchical decision structure have more energy. The distribution is indicated by the following:

Decision-maker	Energy	
1	1.0	
2	0.9	
3	0.8	
4	0.7	
5	0.6	$= E_2$
6	0.5	
7	0.4	
8	0.3	
9	0.2	
10	0.1	

As in the previous organizations, the total energy available to the organization each time period (before deflation by the solution coefficients) is 5.5.

Where the organization has a hierarchical decision structure, the distinction between important and unimportant decision-makers is clear. Where the decision structure is unsegmented or specialized, the variations in energy distribution are defined in terms of the same numbered decision-makers (lower numbers are more important than higher numbers) to reflect possible status differences which are not necessarily captured by the decision structure.

Simulation Design

The simulation design is simple. A Fortran version of the garbage can model is given in the appendix, along with documentation and an explanation. The $3^4 = 81$ types of organizational situations obtained by taking the possible combinations of the values of the four dimensions of an organization (access structure, decision structure, energy distribution, and net energy load) are studied here under the four combinations of choice and problem entry times. The result is 324 simulation situations.

Summary Statistics

The garbage can model operates under each of the possible organizational structures to assign problems and decision-makers to choices, to determine the energy required and effective energy applied to choices, to make such choices and resolve such problems as the assignments and energies indicate are feasible. It does this for each of the twenty time periods in a 20-period simulation of organizational decision-making.

For each of the 324 situations, some set of simple summary statistics on the process is required. These are limited to five.

Decision Style

Within the kind of organization postulated, decisions are made in three different ways:

By resolution. Some choices resolve problems after some period of working on them. The length of time may vary, depending on the number of problems. This is the familiar case that is implicit in most discussions of choice within organizations.

By oversight. If a choice is activated when problems are attached to other choices and if there is energy available to make the new choice quickly, it will be made without any attention to existing problems and with a minimum of time and energy.

By flight. In some cases choices are associated with problems (unsuccessfully) for some time until a choice more attractive to the problems comes along. The problems leave the choice, and thus it is now possible to make the decision. The decision resolves no problems; they having now attached themselves to a new choice.

Some choices involve both flight and resolution – some problems leave, the remainder are solved. These have been defined as resolution, thus slightly exaggerating the importance of that style. As a result of that convention, the three styles are mutually exclusive and exhaustive with respect to any one choice. The same organization, however, may use any one of them in different choices. Thus, the decision style of any particular variation of the model can be described by specifying the proportion of completed choices which are made in each of these three ways.

Problem Activity

Any measure of the degree to which problems are active within the organization should reflect the degree of conflict within the organization or the degree of articulation problems. Three closely-related statistics of problem activity are considered. The first is the total number of problems not solved at the end of the 20 time periods; the second is the total number of times that any problem shifts from one choice to another, while the third is the total number of time periods that a problem is active and attached to some choice, summed over all problems. These measures are strongly correlated with each other. The third is used as the measure of problem activity primarily because it has a relatively large variance; essentially the same results would have been obtained with either of the two other measures.

Problem Latency

A problem may be active, but not attached to any choice. The situation is one in which a problem is recognized and accepted by some part of the organization, but is not considered germane to any available choice. Presumably, an organization with relatively high problem latency will exhibit somewhat different symptoms from one with low latency. Problem latency has been measured by the total number of periods a problem is active, but not attached to a choice, summed over all problems.

Decision-Maker Activity

To measure the degree of decision-maker activity in the system, some measure which reflects decision-maker energy expenditure, movement, and persistence is required. Four are considered:

1 the total number of time periods a decision-maker is attached to a choice, summed over all decision-makers;
2 the total number of times that any decision-maker shifts from one choice to another;
3 the total amount of effective energy available and used;
4 the total effective energy used on choices in excess of that required to make them at the time they are made. These four measures are highly intercorrelated. The second was used primarily because of its relatively large variance; any of the others would have served as well.

Decision Difficulty

Because of the way in which decisions can be made in the system, decision difficulty is not the same as the level of problem activity. Two alternative measures are considered: the total number of choices not made by the end of the 20 time periods and the total number of periods that a choice is active, summed over all choices. These are highly correlated. The second is used, primarily because of its higher variance; the conclusions would be unchanged if the first were used.

Implications of the Model

An analysis of the individual histories of the simulations shows eight major properties of garbage can decision processes.

First, resolution of problems as a style for making decisions is not the most common style, except under conditions where flight is severely restricted (for instance, specialized access) or a few conditions under light load. Decision-making by flight and oversight is a major feature of the process in general. In each of the simulation trials there were twenty problems and ten choices. Although the mean number of choices not made was 1.0, the mean number of problems not solved was 12.3. The results are detailed in table 14.1. The behavioral and normative implications of a decision process which appears to make choices in large part by flight or by oversight must be examined. A possible explanation of the behavior of organizations that seem to make decisions without apparently making progress in resolving the problems that appear to be related to the decisions may be emerging.

Table 14.1 Proportion of choices that resolve problems under four conditions of choice and problem entry times, by load and access structure

		Access structure			
		All	*Unsegmented*	*Hierarchical*	*Specialized*
	Light	0.55	0.38	0.61	0.65
Load	Moderate	0.30	0.04	0.27	0.60
	Heavy	0.36	0.35	0.23	0.50
	All	0.40	0.26	0.37	0.58

Second, the process is quite thoroughly and quite generally sensitive to variations in load. As table 14.2 shows, an increase in the net energy load on the system generally increases problem activity, decision-maker activity, decision difficulty, and the uses of flight and oversight. Problems are less likely to be solved, decision-makers are likely to shift from one problem to another more frequently, choices are likely to take longer to make and are less likely to resolve problems. Although it is possible to specify an organization that is relatively stable with changes in load, it is not possible to have an organization that is stable in behavior and also has other desirable attributes. As load changes, an organization that has an unsegmented access structure with a specialized decision structure stays quite stable. It exhibits relatively low decision difficulty and decision-maker activity, very low problem latency, and maximum problem activity. It makes virtually all decisions placed before it, uses little energy from decision-makers, and solves virtually no problems.

Table 14.2 Effects of variations in load under four conditions of choice and problem entry times

		Mean problem activity	Mean decision-maker activity	Mean decision difficulty	Proportion of choices by flight or oversight
	Light	114.9	60.9	19.5	0.45
Load	Moderate	204.3	63.8	32.9	0.70
	Heavy	211.1	76.6	46.1	0.64

Third, a typical feature of the model is the tendency of decision-makers and problems to track each other through choices. Subject to structural restrictions on the tracking, decision-makers work on active problems in connection with active choices; both decision-makers and problems tend to move together from choice to choice. Thus, one would expect decision-makers who have a feeling that they are always working on the same problems in somewhat different contexts, mostly without results. Problems, in a similar fashion, meet the same people wherever they go with the same result.

Fourth, there are some important interconnections among three key aspects of the efficiency of the decision processes specified. The first is problem activity, the amount of time unresolved problems are actively attached to choice situations. Problem activity is a rough measure of the potential for decision conflict in the organization. The second aspect is problem latency, the amount of time problems spend activated but not linked to choices. The third aspect is decision time, the persistence of choices. Presumably, a good organizational structure would keep both problem activity and problem latency low through rapid problem solution in its choices. In the garbage can process such a result was never observed. Segmentation of the access structure tends to reduce the number of unresolved problems active in the organization but at the cost of increasing the latency period of problems and, in most cases the time devoted to reaching decisions. On the other hand, segmentation of the decision structure tends to result in decreasing problem latency, but at the cost of increasing problem activity and decision time.

Fifth, the process is frequently sharply interactive. Although some phenomena associated with the garbage can are regular and flow through nearly all of the cases, for example, the effect of overall load, other phenomena are much more dependent on the particular combination of structures involved. Although high segmentation of access structure generally produces slow decision time, for instance, a specialized access structure, in combination with an unsegmented decision structure, produces quick decisions.

Sixth, important problems are more likely to be solved than unimportant ones. Problems which appear early are more likely to be resolved than later ones. Considering only those cases involving access hierarchy where importance is defined for problems, the relation between resolution, problem importance and order of arrival is shown in table 14.3. The system, in effect, produces a queue of problems in terms of their importance, to the disadvantage of late-arriving, relatively unimportant problems, and particularly so when load is heavy. This queue is the result of the operation of the model. It was not imposed as a direct assumption.

Table 14.3 Proportion of problems resolved under four conditions of choice and problem entry times, by importance of problem and order of arrival of problem (for hierarchical access)

| | | Time of arrival of problem | |
		Early, first 10	Late, last 10
Importance	High first 10	0.46	0.44
of problem	Low last 10	0.48	0.25

Seventh, important choices are less likely to resolve problems than unimportant choices. Important choices are made by oversight and flight. Unimportant choices are made by resolution. These differences are observed under both of the choice entry sequences but are sharpest where important choices enter relatively early. Table 14.4 show the results. This property of important choices in a garbage can decision process can be naturally and directly related to the phenomenon in complex organizations of important choices which often appear to just happen.

Eighth, although a large proportion of the choices are made, the choice failures that do occur are concentrated among the most important and least important choices. Choices of intermediate importance are virtually

Table 14.4 Proportion of choices that are made by flight or oversight under four conditions of choice and problem entry times, by time of arrival and importance of choice (for hierarchical access or decision structure)

| | | Time of arrival of choice | |
		Early, first 5	Late, last 5
Importance of	High first 5	0.86	0.65
of choice	Low last 5	0.54	0.60

always made. The proportion of choice failures, under conditions of hierarchical access or decision structures is as follows:

Three most important choices 0.14
Four middle choices   0.05
Three least important choices 0.12

In a broad sense, these features of the process provide some clues to how organizations survive when they do not know what they are doing. Much of the process violates standard notions of how decisions ought to be made. But most of those notions are built on assumptions which cannot be met under the conditions specified. When objectives and technologies are unclear, organizations are charged to discover some alternative decision procedures which permit them to proceed without doing extraordinary violence to the domains of participants or to their model of what an organization should be. It is a hard charge, to which the process described is a partial response.

At the same time, the details of the outcomes clearly depend on features of the organizational structure. The same garbage can operation results in different behavioral symptoms under different levels of load on the system or different designs of the structure of the organization. Such differences raise the possibility of predicting variations in decision behavior in different organizations. One possible example of such use remains to be considered.

Garbage Cans and Universities

One class of organization which faces decision situations involving unclear goals, unclear technology, and fluid participants is the modern college or university. If the implications of the model are applicable anywhere, they are applicable to a university. Although there is great variation among colleges and universities, both between countries and within any country, the model has general relevance to decision-making in higher education.

General Implications

University decision-making frequently does not resolve problems. Choices are often made by flight or oversight. University decision processes are sensitive to increases in load. Active decision-makers and problem track one another through a series of choices without appreciable progress in solving problems. Important choices are not likely to solve problems.

Decisions whose interpretations continually change during the process of resolution appear both in the model and in actual observations of universities. Problems, choices, and decision-makers arrange and rearrange themselves. In the course of these arrangements the meaning of a choice can change several times, if this meaning is understood as the mix of problems discussed in the context of that choice.

Problems are often solved, but rarely by the choice to which they are first attached. A choice that might, under some circumstances, be made with little effort becomes an arena for many problems. The choice becomes almost impossible to make, until the problems drift off to another arena. The matching of problems, choices, and decision-makers is partly controlled by attributes of content, relevance, and competence; but it is also quite sensitive to attributes of timing, the particular combinations of current garbage cans, and the overall load on the system.

Universities and Adversity

In establishing connections between the hypothetical attributes of organizational structure in the model and some features of contemporary universities, the more detailed implications of the model can be used to explore features of university decision-making. In particular, the model can examine the events associated with one kind of adversity within organizations, the reduction of organizational slack.

Slack is the difference between the resources of the organization and the combination of demands made on it. Thus, it is sensitive to two major factors: (1) money and other resources provided to the organization by the external environment; and (2) the internal consistency of the demands made on the organization by participants. It is commonly believed that organizational slack has been reduced substantially within American colleges and universities over the past few years. The consequences of slack reduction in a garbage can decision process can be shown by establishing possible relations between changes in organizational slack and the key structural variables within the model.

Net energy load.   The net energy load is the difference between the energy required within an organization and the effective energy available. It is affected by anything that alters either the amount of energy available to the organization or the amount required to find or generate problem solutions. The energy available to the organization is partly a function of the overall strength of exit opportunities for decision-makers. For example, when there is a shortage of faculty, administrators, or students in the market for participants, the net energy load on a university is heavier than it would be when there is no shortage. The energy required to find solutions depends on the flow of possible problem solutions. For example, when the environment of the organization is relatively rich, solutions are easier to find and the net energy is reduced. Finally, the comparative attractiveness and permeability of the organization to problems affects the energy demands on it. The more attractive, the more demands. The more permeable, the more demands. Universities with slack and with relatively easy access, compared to other alternative arenas for problem carriers, will attract a relatively large number of problems.

Access structure. The access structure in an organization would be expected to be affected by deliberate efforts to derive the advantages of delegation and specialization. Those efforts, in turn, depend on some general characteristics of the organizational situation, task, and personnel. For example, the access structure would be expected to be systematically related to two features of the organization: (1) the degree of technical and value heterogeneity; and (2) the amount of organizational slack. Slack, by providing resource buffers between parts of the organization, is essentially a substitute for technical and value homogeneity. As hetero- geneity increases, holding slack constant, the access structure shifts from an unsegmented to a specialized to a hierarchical structure. Similarly, as slack decreases, holding heterogeneity constant, the access structure shifts from an unsegmented to a specialized to a hierarchical structure. The combined picture is shown in figure 14.1.

Figure 14.1. Hypothesized relationship between slack, heterogeneity and the access structure of an organization.

Decision structure.   Like the access structure, the decision structure is partly a planned system for the organization and partly a result of learning and negotiation within the organization. It could be expected to be systematically related to the technology, to attributes of participants and problems, and to the external conditions under which the organization operates. For example, there are joint effects of two factors: (1) relative administrative power within the system, the extent to which the formal administrators are conceded substantial authority; and (2) the average degree of perceived interrelation among problems. It is assumed that high administrative power or high interrelation of problems will lead to hierarchical decision structure, that moderate power and low interrelation of problems leads to specialized decision structures, and that relatively low administrative power, combined with moderate problem interrelation, leads to unsegmented decision structures. The hypothetical relations are shown in figure 14.2.

Energy distribution.   Some of the key factors affecting the energy distribution within an organization are associated with the alternative opportunities decision-makers have for investing their time. The extent to which there is an active external demand for attention affects the extent to which decision-makers will have energy available for use within the organization. The stronger the relative outside demand on important people in the organization, the less time they will spend within the organization relative to others. Note that the energy distribution refers only to the relation between the energy available from important people and less important people. Thus, the energy distribution variable is a

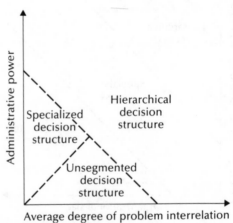

Figure 14.2. Hypothesized relationship between administrative power, interrelation of problems, and the decision structure of an organization

Figure 14.3. Hypothesized relationship between exit opportunities and the distribution of energy within an organization

function of the relative strength of the outside demand for different people, as shown in figure 14.3.

Within a university setting it is not hard to imagine circumstances in which exit opportunities are different for different decision-makers. Tenure, for example, strengthens the exit opportunities for older faculty members. Money strengthens the exit opportunities for students and faculty members, though more for the former than the latter. A rapidly changing technology tends to strengthen the exit opportunities for young faculty members.

Against this background four types of colleges and universities are considered:

1 large, rich universities;
2 large, poor universities;
3 small, rich colleges;
4 small, poor colleges.

Important variations in the organizational variables among these schools can be expected. Much of that variation is likely to be within-class variation. Assumptions about these variables, however, can be used to generate some assumptions about the predominant attributes of the four classes, under conditions of prosperity.

Under such conditions a relatively rich school would be expected to have a light energy load, a relatively poor school a moderate energy load. With respect to access structure, decision structure, and the internal distribution of energy, the appropriate position of each of the four types of schools is is marked with a circular symbol on figures 14.4, 14.5, and 14.6. The result is the pattern of variations indicated below:

	Load	Access structure	Decision structure	Energy distribution
Large, rich	Light	Specialized	Unsegmented	Less
	0	2	0	0
Large, poor	Moderate	Hierarchical	Hierarchical	More
	1	1	1	2
Small, rich	Light	Unsegmented	Unsegmented	More
	0	0	0	2
Small, poor	Moderate	Specialized	Specialized	Equal
	1	2	2	1

With this specification, the garbage can model can be used to predict the differences expected among the several types of school. The results are found in table 14.5. They suggest that under conditions of prosperity, overt conflict (problem activity) will be substantially higher in poor schools than in rich ones, and decision time will be substantially longer. Large, rich schools will be characterized by a high degree of problem latency. Most decisions will resolve some problems.

What happens to this group of schools under conditions of adversity – when slack is reduced? According to earlier arguments, slack could be expected to affect each of the organizational variables. It first increases net energy load, as resources become shorter and thus problems require a larger share of available energy to solve, but this effect is later compensated by the reduction in market demand for personnel and in the relative attractiveness of the school as an arena for problems. The market effects also reduce the differences in market demand for important and unimportant people. The expected results of these shifts are shown by the positions of the square symbols in figure 14.6.

At the same time, adversity affects both access structure and decision structure. Adversity can be expected to bring a reduction in slack and an increase in the average interrelation among problems. The resulting hypothesized shifts in access and decision structures are shown in figures 14.4 and 14.5.

Table 14.5 shows the effects of adversity on the four types of schools according to the previous assumptions and the garbage can model. By examining the first stage of adversity, some possible reasons for discontent among presidents of large, rich schools can be seen. In relation to other schools they are not seriously disadvantaged. The large, rich schools have a moderate level of problem activity, a moderate level of decision by

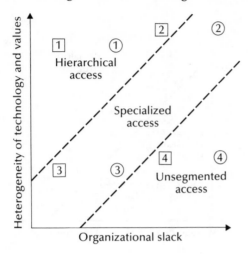

Figure 14.4. Hypothesized location of different schools in terms of slack and heterogeneity

resolution. In relation to their earlier state, however, large, rich schools are certainly deprived. Problem activity and decision time have increased greatly; the proportion of decisions which resolve problems has decreased from 68 per cent to 21 per cent; administrators are less able to move around from one decision to another. In all these terms, the relative deprivation of the presidents of large, rich schools is much greater, in the early stages of adversity, than that of administrators in other schools.

The large, poor schools are in the worst absolute position under adversity. They have a high level of problem activity, a substantial decision time, a low level of decision-maker mobility, and a low proportion of decisions being made by resolution. But along most of these dimensions, the change has been less for them.

The small rich schools experience a large increase in problem activity, an increase in decision time, and a decrease in the proportion of decisions by resolution as adversity begins. The small, poor schools seem to move

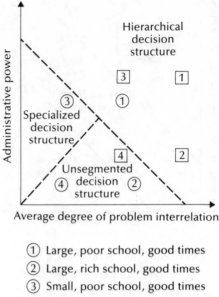

Figure 14.5. Hypothesized location of different schools in terms of administrative power and perceived interrelation of problems

in a direction counter to the trends in the other three groups. Decision style is little affected by the onset of slack reduction, problem activity, and decision time decline, and decision-maker mobility increases. Presidents of such organizations might feel a sense of success in their efforts to tighten up the organization in response to resource contraction.

The application of the model to this particular situation among American colleges and universities clearly depends upon a large number of assumptions. Other assumptions would lead to other interpretations of the impact of adversity within a garbage can decision process. Nevertheless, the derivations from the model have some face validity as a description of some aspects of recent life in American higher education.

The model also makes some predictions of future developments. As adversity continues, the model predicts that all schools, and particularly rich schools, will experience improvement in their position. Among large, rich schools decision by resolution triples, problem activity is cut by almost

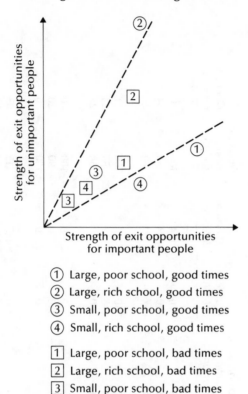

① Large, poor school, good times
② Large, rich school, good times
③ Small, poor school, good times
④ Small, rich school, good times

[1] Large, poor school, bad times
[2] Large, rich school, bad times
[3] Small, poor school, bad times
[4] Small, rich school, bad times

Figure 14.6. Hypothesized location of different schools in terms of text opportunties

three-quarters, and decision time is cut more than one-half. If the model has validity, a series of articles in the magazines of the next decade detailing how President X assumed the presidency of large, rich university Y and guided it to 'peace' and 'progress' (short decision time, decisions without problems, low problem activity) can be expected.

Conclusion

A set of observations made in the study of some university organizations has been translated into a model of decision-making in organized anarchies, that is, in situations which do not meet the conditions for more classical models of decision-making in some or all of three important ways: preferences are problematic, technology is unclear, or participation is fluid. The garbage can process is one in which problems, solutions, and

Table 14.5 Effect of adversity on four types of colleges and universities operating within a garbage can decision process

Type of school/ type of situation	Organizational type	Decision style proportion resolution	Outcome				
			Problem activity	Problem latency	Decision-maker activity	Decision time
Large, rich universities						
Good times	0200	0.68	0	154	100	0
Bad times, early	1110	0.21	210	23	58	34
Bad times, late	0111	0.65	57	60	66	14
Large, poor universities						
Good times	1112	0.38	210	25	66	31
Bad times, early	2112	0.24	248	32	55	38
Bad times, late	1111	0.31	200	30	58	28
Small, rich colleges						
Good times	0002	1.0	0	0	100	0
Bad times, early	1002	0	310	0	90	20
Bad times, late	0001	1.0	0	0	100	0
Small, poor colleges						
Good times	1221	0.54	158	127	15	83
Bad times, early	2211	0.61	101	148	73	52
Bad times, late	1211	0.62	78	151	76	39

participants move from one choice opportunity to another in such a way that the nature of the choice, the time it takes, and the problems it solves all depend on a relatively complicated intermeshing of elements. These include the mix of choices available at any one time, the mix of problems that have access to the organization, the mix of solutions looking for problems, and the outside demands on the decision-makers.

A major feature of the garbage can process is the partial uncoupling of problems and choices. Although decision-making is thought of as a process for solving problems, that is often not what happens. Problems are worked upon in the context of some choice, but choices are made only when the shifting combinations of problems, solutions, and decision-makers happen to make action possible. Quite commonly this is after problems have left a given choice arena or before they have discovered it (decisions by flight or oversight).

Four factors were specified which could be expected to have substantial effects on the operation of the garbage can process: the organization's net energy load and energy distribution, its decision structure, and problem access structure. Though the specifications are quite simple their interaction is extremely complex, so that investigation of the probable behavior of a system fully characterized by the garbage can process and previous specifications requires computer simulation. No real system can be fully characterized in this way. None the less, the simulated organization exhibits behaviors which can be observed some of the time in almost all organizations and frequently in some, such as universities. The garbage can model is a first step toward seeing the systematic interrelatedness of organizational phenomena which are familiar, even common, but which have previously been regarded as isolated and pathological. Measured against a conventional normative model of rational choice, the garbage can process does appear pathological, but such standards are not really appropriate. The process occurs precisely when the preconditions of more normal rational models are not met.

It is clear that the garbage can process does not resolve problems well. But it does enable choices to be made and problems resolved, even when the organization is plagued with goal ambiguity and conflict, with poorly-understood problems that wander in and out of the system, with a variable environment, and with decision-makers who may have other things on their minds.

There is a large class of significant situations in which the preconditions of the garbage can process cannot be eliminated. In some, such as pure research, or the family, they should not be eliminated. The great advantage of trying to model garbage can phenomena is the possibility that that process can be understood, that organizational design and decision-making can take account of its existence and that, to some extent, it can be managed.

Appendix

Version five of the Fortran program for the garbage can model reads in entry times for choices, solution coefficients, entry times for problems, and two control variables. *NA* and *IO*. *NA* controls various combinations of freedom of movement for decision-makers and problems. All results are based on runs in which *NA* is 1. Comment cards included in the program describe other possibilities. The latter variable, *IO*, controls output. At the value 1, only summary statistics are printed. At the value 2, full histories of the decision process are printed for each organizational variant.

The following are ten summary statistics:

1 (*KT*) Problem persistence, the total number of time periods a problem is activated and attached to a choice, summed over all problems.
2 (*KU*) Problem latency, the total number of time periods a problem is activated, but not attached to a choice, summed over all problems.
3 (*KV*)Problem velocity, the total number of times any problem shifts from one choice to another.
4 (*KW*) Problem failures, the total number of problems not solved at the end of the twenty time periods.
5 (*KX*) Decision-maker velocity, the total number of times any decision-maker shifts from one choice to another.
6 (*KS*) Decision-maker inactivity, the total number of time periods a decision-maker is not attached to a choice, summed over all decision makers.
7 (*KY*) Choice persistence, the total number of time periods a choice is activated, summed over all choices.
8 (*KZ*) Choice failures, the total number of choices not made by the end of the twenty time periods.
9 (*XR*) Energy reserve, the total amount of effective energy available to the system but not used because decision makers are not attached to any choice.
10 (*XS*) Energy wastage, the total effective energy used on choices in excess of that required to make them at the time they are made.

In its current form the program generates both the problem access structure and the decision structure internally. In order to examine the performance of the model under other structures, modification of the code or its elimination in favor of Read statements to take the structures from cards will be necessary.

Under *IO* = 2, total output will be about ninety pages. Running time is about two minutes under a Watfor compiler.

Appendix Table: Fortran Program for
Garbage Can Model; Version Five

```
C   THE GARBAGE CAN MODEL. VERSION 5
C   ***
C   IO IS 1 FOR SUMMARY STATISTICS ONLY
C   IO IS 2 FOR SUMMARY STATISTICS PLUS HISTORIES
C   ***
C   NA IS 1 WHEN PROBS AND DMKRS BOTH MOVE
C   NA IS 2 WHEN DMKRS ONLY MOVE
C   NA IS 3 WHEN PROBS ONLY MOVE
C   NA IS 4 WHEN NEITHER PROBS NOR DMKRS MOVE
C   ***
C   IL IS A FACTOR DETERMINING PROB ENERGY REQ
C   ***
C   VARIABLES
C   ***
C   NUMBERS
C   COUNTERS UPPER LIMITS NAME
C   ***
C   I           NCH           CHOICES
C   J           NPR           PROBLEM
C   K           NDM           DECMKRS
C   LT          NTP           TIME
C   ***
C   ARRAYS
C   CODE        DIMEN         NAME
C   * **
C   ICH         NCH           CHOICE ENTRY TIME
C   ICS         NCH           CHOICE STATUS
C   JET         NPR           PROB. ENTRY TIME
C   JF          NPR           PROB. ATT. CHOICE
C   JFF         NPR           WORKING COPY JF
C   JPS         NPR           PROB. STATUS
C   KDC         NDM           DMKR. ATT. CHOICE
C   KDCW        NDM           WORKING COPY KDC
C   XEF         MCH           ENERGY EXPENDED
C   XERC        NCH           CHOICE EN. REQT.
C   XERP        NPR           PROB. EN. REQT.
C   XSC         NTP           SOLUTION COEFFICIENT
C   ***
C   2-DIMENSIONAL ARRAYS
```

```
C  ***
C  CODE       DIMEN         NAME
C  ***
C  IKA        NCH,NDM       DECISION STRUCTURE
C  JIA        NPR,NCH       ACCESS STRUCTURE
C  XEA        NDM,NTP       ENERGY MATRIX
C  ***
C  ***
C  ***
C  ***
C  SUMMARY STATISTICS FOR EACH VARIANT
C     COL 1: KZ: TOTAL DECISIONS NOT MADE
C     COL 2: KY: TOTAL NUMBER ACTIVE CHOICE PERIODS
C     COL 3: KX: TOTAL NUMBER CHANGES BY DECISION
C     MAKERS
C     COL 4: KW: TOTAL PROBLEMS NOT SOLVED
C     COL 5: KV: TOTAL NUMBER CHANGES BY PROBLEMS
C     COL 6: KU: TOTAL NUMBER LATENT PROBLEM PERIODS
C     COL 7: KT: TOTAL NUMBER ATTACHED PROBLEM PERIODS
C     COL 8: KS: TOTAL NUMBER PERIODS DMKRS RESTING
C     COL 9: XR: TOTAL AMOUNT OF UNUSED ENERGY
C     COL 10:XS: TOTAL AMOUNT OF WASTED ENERGY
C  ***
C  INPUT BLOCK. READ-IN AND INITIALIZATIONS.
      DIMENSION ICH(20),JF(20),XERC(20),XEE(20),XSC(20),JFF(20),
     XERP(20),JET(20),JPS(20),ICS(20),KDC(20),KDCW(20),JIA(20,
     20),IKA(20,20),CXEA(20,20),KABC(20,20),KBBC(20,20),KCBC(20,20)
1001  FORMAT(5(I3,1X))
1002  FORMAT(10(I3,1X))
1003  FORMAT(25(I1,1X))
1004  FORMAT(10F4.2)
      NTP = 20
      NCH = 10
      NPR = 20
      NDM = 10
8   READ(5,1002)(ICH(I),I = 1,NCH)
      READ(5,1004)(XSC(LT),LT = 1,NTP)
      READ(5,1002)(JET(J),J = 1,NPR)
      READ(5,1003) NA,IO
      WRITE(6,1050) NA
1050  FORMAT('1   DEC.MAKER MOVEMENT CONDITION (NA)
      IS ',I1/)
      DO 998 IL = 1.3
```

```
        IB = IL − 1
        DO 997 JAB = 1,3
        JA = JAB − 1
        DO 996 JDB = 1,3
        JD = JDB − 1
        DO 995 JEB = 1,3
        JE = JEB − 1
        XR = 0.0
        XS = 0.0
        KS = 0
        DO 10 I = 1,NCH
        XERC(I) = 1.1
        XEE(I) = 0.0
10      ICS(I) = 0
        DO 20 K = 1,NDM
        KDC(K) = 0
20      KDCW(K) = KDC(K)
        DO 40 J = 1,NPR
        XERP(J) = IL*1.1
        JF(J) = 0
        JFF(J) = 0
40      JPS(J) = 0
C       SETTING UP THE DECISION MAKERS ACCESS TO CHOICES.
        DO 520 I = 1,NCH
        DO 510 J = 1,NDM
        IKA(I,J) = 1
        IF(JD.EQ.1) GO TO 502
        IF(JD.EQ.2) GO TO 504
        GO TO 510
502     IF(I.GE.J) GO TO 510
        IKA(I,J) = 0
        GO TO 510
504     IF(J.EQ.) GO TO 510
        IKA(I,J) = 0
510     CONTINUE
520     CONTINUE
C       SETTING UP THE PROBLEMS ACCESS TO CHOICES.
        DO 560 I = 1,NPR
        DO 550 J = 1,NCH
        JIA(I,J) = 0
        IF(JA.EQ.1) GO TO 532
        IF(JA.EQ.2) GO TO 534
        JIA(I,J) = 1
```

```
         GO TO 550
532      IF ((I – J).GT.(1/2)) GO TO 550
         JIA(I,J) = 1
         GO TO 550
534      IF(I.NE.(2*J)) GO TO 550
         JIA(I,J) = 1
         JIA(I – 1,J) = 1
550      CONTINUE
560      CONTINUE
         DO 590 I = 1,NDM
         DO 580 J = 1,NTP
         XEA(I,J) = 0.55
         IF(JF.EQ.1)GO TO 580
         XXA = I
         IF(JE.EQ.0)GO TO 570
         XEA(I,J) = (11.0 – XXA)/10.0
         GO TO 580
570      XEA(I,J) = XXA/10.0
580      CONTINUE
590      CONTINUE
C        *** FINISH READ INITIALIZATION
         DO 994 LT = 1,NTP
1006     FORMAT(2X.6HCHOICE,2X,I3,2X,6HACTIVE )
C        CHOICE ACTIVATION
         DO 101 I = 1,NCH
         IF(ICH(I).NE.LT)GO TO 101
         ICS(I) = 1
101      CONTINUE
C        PROB. ACTIVATION
         DO 110 J = 1,NPR
         IF(JET(J).NE.LT)GO TO 110
         JPS(J) = 1
110      CONTINUE
C        FIND MOST ATTRACTIVE CHOICE FOR PROBLEM J
         DO 120 J = 1,NPR
         IF (JPS(J).NE.1) GO TO 120
         IF(NA.EQ.2)GO TO 125
         IF(NA.EQ.4)GO TO 125
         GO TO 126
125      IF(JF(J).NE.0)GO TO 127
126      S = 1000000
         DO 121 I = 1,NCH
         IF (ICS(I).NE.1) GO TO 121
```

```
       IF(JIA(J.I).EQ.0)GO TO 121
       IF(JF(J).EQ.0)GO TO 122
       IF(JF(J).EQ.I)GO TO 122
       IF((XERP(J)+XERC(I)−XEE(I)).GE.S)GO TO 121
       GO TO 123
122    IF((XERC(I)−XEE(I)).GE.S)GO TO 121
       S=XERC(I)−XEE(I)
       GO TO 124
123    S=XERP(J)+XERC(I)−XEE(I)
124    JFF(J)=I
121    CONTINUE
       GO TO 120
127    JFF(J)=JF(J)
120    CONTINUE
       DO 130 J=1,NPR
131    JF(J)=JFF(J)
130    JFF(J)=0
       LTT=LT−1
       IF(LT.EQ.1)LTT=1
C      FIND MOST ATTRACTIVE CHOICE FOR DMKR K
       DO 140 K=1,NDM
       IF(NA.EQ.3)GO TO 145
       IF(NA.EQ.4) GO TO 145
       GO TO 146
145    IF(KDC(K).NE.0)GO TO 147
146    S=1000000
       DO 141 I=1,NCH
       IF (ICS(I).NE.1) GO TO 141
       IF(IKA(I.K).EQ.0)GO TO 141
       IF(KDC(K).EQ.0)GO TO 142
       IF(KDC(K).EQ.I)GO TO 142
148    IF((XFRC(I)−XEE(I)−(XEA(K,LTT)*XSC(LTT))).GE.S)GO
       TO 141
       GO TO 143
142    IF((XERC(I)−XEE(I)).GE.S)GO TO 141
       S=XERC(I)−XEE(I)
       GO TO 144
143    S=XERC(I)−XEE(I)−XEA(K,LTT)*XSC(LTT)
144    KDCW(K)=I
141    CONTINUE
       GO TO 140
147    KDCW(K)=KDC(K)
140    CONTINUE
```

```
         DO 150 K = 1,NDM
151      KDC(K) = KDCW(K)
         IF(KDC(K).NE.0)GO TO 150
         XR = XR + (XEA(K,LT)*XSC(LT))
         KS = KS + 1
150      KDCW(K) = 0
C        ESTABLISHING THE ENERGY REQUIRED TO MAKE EACH
         CHOICE.
         DO 199 I = 1,NCH
         IF(ICS(I).EQ.0)GO TO 199
         XERC(I) = 0.0
         DO 160 J = 1,NPR
         IF (JPS(J).NE.1) GO TO 160
         IF(JF(J).NE.I)GO TO 160
         XERC(I) = XERC(I) + XERP(J)
160      CONTINUE
         DO 170 K = 1,NDM
         IF(IKA(I.K).EQ.0)GO TO 170
         IF(KDC(K).NE.I)GO TO 170
         XEE(I) = XEE(I) + XSC(LT)*XEA(K,LT)
170      CONTINUE
199      CONTINUE
C        MAKING DECISIONS
         DO 299 I = 1,NCH
         IF (ICS(I).NE.1) GO TO 299
         IF(XERC(I).GT.XEE(I)GO TO 299
         XS = XS = XEE(I) − XERC(I)
         ICS(I) = 2
         DO 250 J = 1,NPR
         IF(JF(J).NE.I)GO TO 250
         JPS(J) = 2
250      CONTINUE
         IF(NA.EQ.3)GO TO 261
         IF(NA.EQ.4)go to 261
         GO TO 299
261      DO 262 K = 1,NDM
         IF(KDC(K).NE.1)GO TO 262
         KDCW(K) = 1
262      CONTINUE
299      CONTINUE
         DO 200 I = 1,NCH
200      KABC(LT.I) = ICS(I)
         DO 210 K = 1,NDM
```

```
        KBBC(LT,K) = KDC(K)
        IF(KDCW(K).EQ.0)GO TO 210
        KDC(K) = 0
210     KDCW(K) = 0
        DO 220 J = 1,NPR
        KCBC(LT,J) = JF(J)
        IF(JPS(J).EQ.0) GO TO 230
        IF(JPS(J).EQ.1) GO TO 220
        KCBC(LT,J) = 1000
        GO TO 220
230     KCBC(LT,J) = - 1
220     CONTINUE
992     CONTINUE
C       FINISH TIME PERIOD LOOP. BEGIN ACCUMULATION OF
        10 SUMMARY STATISTICS.
        KZ = 0
        KY = 0
        KX = 0
        KW = 0
        KV = 0
        KU = 0
        KT = 0
        DO 310 I = 1,NTP
        DO 320 J = 1,NCH
        IF(KABC(I,J).NE.1)GO TO 320
        KY = KY + 1
        IF(I.NE.NTP)GO TO 320
        KZ = KZ + 1
320     CONTINUE
310     CONTINUE
        DO 330 I = 2,NTP
        DO 340 J = 1,NDM
        IF(KBBC(I,J).EQ.KBBC(I - 1,J))GO TO 340
        KX = KX + 1
340     CONTINUE
330     CONTINUE
        DO 350 I = 1,NTP
        DO 360 J = 1,NPR
        IF(KCBC(I.J).EQ.0)GO TO 351
        IF(KCBC(I.J).EQ. - 1) GO TO 360
        IF(KCBC(I.J).EQ.1000) GO TO 352
        KT = KT + 1
        GO TO 360
```

```
351    KU = KU + 1
       GO TO 360
352    IF(I.NE.NTP)GO TO 360
       KW = KW + 1
360    CONTINUE
350    CONTINUE
       KW = NPR = KW
       DO 370 I = 2,NTP
       DO 380 J = 1,NPR
       IF(KCBC(I,J).EQ.KCBC(I – 1,J))GO TO 380
       KV = KV + 1
380    CONTINUE
370    CONTINUE
C      BEGIN WRITEOUT OF MATERIALS FOR THIS ORGANIZA-
       TIONAL VARIANT.
1000   FORMAT(1H1)
1019   FORMAT(2X,'LOAD = ',I1,'PR.ACC. = ',I1,'DEC.STR. = ',I1'.
       'EN.DIST. = '.BI1,2X,'STATS I – 10',3X,8I5,1X,2F6.2/)
       WRITE(6,1019)IB,JA,JD,JE,KZ,KY,KX,KW,KV,KY,KT,KS,ZR,
       XS
       IF(IO.EQ.1) GO TO 995
2000   FORMAT(' CHOICE ACTIVATION HISTORY',34X,'DEC.
       MAKER ACTIVITY HISTOR BY'/'20 TIME PERIODS,10
       CHOICES',33X,'20 TIME PERIODS,10 DEC. MAKE CRS
       '/' 0 = INACTIVE,1 = ACTIVE,2 = MADE',33X,'0 = INACTIVE,
       X = WORKING ON CHOICE X'//9X,' 1 2 3 4 5 6 7 8 9 10',
       30X,'1 2 3 4 5 6 7 8 9 10'/)
       WRITE(6,2000)
2001   FORMAT( 5X,I2,3X,10I2,25X,I2,3X,10I2)
       WRITE(6,2001)(LT,(KABC(LT,J),J = 1,NCH).LT.( KBBC(LT,J),
       J = 1,NDM), LT = 1,NTP )
2002   FORMAT(/' PROBLEM HISTORY:ROWS = TIME,COLS =
       PROBS., – 1 = NOT ENTERED,, O = UNATTACHED,X =
       ATT.TO CH.X,** = SOLVED'/10X.
       ' 1 2 3 4 5 6 7 8 9 10 11 12 13 14 15 16 17 18 19 20'/)
       WRITE(6,2002)
2003    FORMAT(20(5X,I2,3X,20(1X,I2)/))
       WRITE(6,2003)(LT,(KCBC(LT,J),J = 1,NPR),LT = 1,NTP)
       WRITE(6,1000)
995    CONTINUE
996    CONTINUE
997    CONTINUE
998    CONTINUE
```

STOP
END

******* DATA AS FOLLOWS (AFTER GUIDE CARDS) ***********

```
0         1         2         3         4
123456789012345678901234567890123456 7890
          5         6         7         8
12345678901234567890123456789012345 67890

008.005.006.007.004.009.002.010.003.001
1.000.900.700.300.100.100.300.700.901.00
0.600.600.600.600.600.600.600.600.600.60
009.005.008.007.010.003.003.001.007.009
006.008.005.002.004.002.004.010.006.001
1 2
```

References

Allison, Graham T. (1969) Conceptual models and the Cuban missile crises. *American Political Science Review,* 63, 689–718.

Christensen, Søren (1971) *Institut og laboratorieorganisation på Danmarks tekniske Højskole.* Copenhagen: Copenhagen School of Economics.

Cohen, Michael D., and James G. March (1974) *The American College President.* New York: McGraw-Hill, Carnegie Commission on the Future of Higher Education.

Coleman, James S. (1957) *Community Conflict.* Glencoe: Free Press.

Cyert, Richard M., and James G. March (1963) *Behavioral Theory of the Firm.* Englewood Cliffs: Prentice-Hall.

Enderud, Harald (1971) *Rektoratet og den centrale administration på Danmarks tekniske Højskole.* Copenhagen: Copenhagen School of Economics.

Lindblom, Charles E. (1965) *The Intelligence of Democracy.* New York: Macmillan.

Long, Norton (1958) The local community as an ecology of games. *American Journal of Sociology,* 44, 251–61.

March, James G., and Herbert A. Simon (1958) *Organizations.* New York: John Wiley.

Mood, Alexander (ed.) (1971) *More Scholars for the Dollar.* New York: McGraw-Hill, Carnegie Commission on the Future of Higher Education.

Olsen, Johan P. (1970) *A Study of Choice in an Academic Organization.* Bergen: University of Bergen.

Olsen, Johan P. (1971) *The Reorganization of Authority in an Academic Organization.* Bergen: University of Bergen.

Rommetveit, Kåre (1971) *Framveksten av det medisinske fakultet ved Universitet i Tromsø.* Bergen: University of Bergen.

Schilling, Warner R. (1968) The H-bomb decision: how to decide without actually choosing. In W. R. Nelson (ed.), *The Politics of Science*. London: Oxford University Press.

Thompson, James D. (1967) *Organizations in Action*. New York: McGraw-Hill.

Vickers, Geoffrey (1965) *The Art of Judgment*. New York: Basic Books.

15

The Uncertainty of the Past: Organizational Learning under Ambiguity

James G. March and Johan P. Olsen

Abstract

Classical theories of omniscient rationality in organizational decision-making have largely been replaced by a view of limited rationality, but no similar concern has been reflected in the analysis of organizational learning. There has been a tendency to model a simple complete cycle of learning from unambiguous experience and to ignore cognitive and evaluative limits on learning in organizations. This paper examines some theoretical possibilities for assuming that individuals in organizations modify their understanding in a way that is intendedly adaptive even though faced with ambiguity about what happened, and whether it is good. To develop a theory of learning under such conditions, we probably require ideas about information exposure, memory, and retrieval; learning incentives; belief structures; and the micro-development of belief in organizations. We exhibit one example by specifying a structural theory of the relations among liking, seeing, trusting, contact, and integration in an organization. The argument is made that some understanding of factors affecting learning from experience will not only be important to the improvement of policy-making in an organizational context, but also a necessary part of a theory of organizational choice.

This paper was first published in the *European Journal of Political Research*, 3, 1975, 147–71. It is a revised version of a paper read at the ECPR workshop on 'Models and Cases in Administrative Decision-Making', Strasbourg, 29 March – 2 April, 1974. The authors have profited considerably from their discussions with Søren Christensen, Michael D. Cohen, James R. Glenn, Kristian Kreiner, Kåre Rommetveit, Per Stava, Harald Sætren, and Stephen S. Weiner.

Organizational intelligence, like individual intelligence, is built on two fundamental processes. The first of these is rational calculation, by which expectations about future consequences are used to choose among current alternatives. Rationality in policy-making is typified by planning, analysis, forecasting and the paraphernalia of decision theory and management science; it is the logic of most recent efforts to improve the quality of decision-making in public policy (as well as in non-public organizations).

The second process is learning from experience. Through learning, feedback from previous experience is used to choose among present alternatives. Learning in policy-making is typified by experimentation, evaluation, assessment, and the paraphernalia of experimental design and control theory; it is the logic of an increasing number of efforts to improve policy-making, particularly in areas such as education, social welfare, and social organization.

In the last two decades there has been considerable examination of the cognitive and evaluative limitations on rationality. Although presumptions of rationality both as an objective and as a reality are still common, the literature is full of attempts to develop the major implications of limitations on the awareness of alternatives, on the precision of information about consequences, and on the clarity and consistency of goals (Simon, 1955; March and Simon, 1958; Cyert and March, 1963; Lindblom, 1965). There is no longer general acceptance of a model of superhuman organizational omniscience in the service of rationality. Instead, there is an inclination to accept the proposition that while organizations are intendedly rational, they frequently act on incomplete or incorrect information and without being aware of all of their alternatives. Similarly, there is no longer general acceptance of a simple view of a well-defined organizational preference function. Instead, there is an effort to accommodate in the theory the frequent observations of inconsistent and conflicting organizational objectives.

Little comparable effort has been devoted to assessing the cognitive and evaluative limitations on organizational learning. As a result, learning is ordinarily understood in terms of a model of simple rational adaptation.[1] Policy makers may have limited abilities to predict consequences or control events, but they are presumed to be able to see what happens and understand why. They can distinguish success from failure. If organizations

---

1   A recent exception is Axelrod (1973); Cohen and March (1974) discuss the relevance of superstitious learning as an organizational phenomenon; see also Weick (1969). Olsen (1970) shows that a decision-making process is a process of interpretation as well as a process of choice. Thompson (1967) has a very interesting discussion of how organizations keep score: 'Even if we concede that organizations sometimes maximize, the organizational question is whether the organization has any way of knowing that it has done so. And how does it assess itself on the ultimate question, its fitness for the future' (p. 84).

fail to improve, the explanation is found in various forms of organizational rigidities that inhibit the adoption of changes even though clearly indicated by experience, or in lack of motivation, or in some other inexplicable failure of the organization to learn.

We wish to examine some limitations on learning from experience. We will assume that organizations adapt their behavior in terms of their experience, but that experience requires interpretation. They learn under conditions in which goals (and therefore 'success' and 'failure') are ambiguous or in conflict, in which what happened is unclear, and in which the causality of events is difficult to untangle. People in organizations come to believe what happened, why it happened, and whether it was good; but the process by which those beliefs are established in the face of a quite problematic 'objective' world affects systematically what is learned.

Such a focus does not suggest that organizations are conspicuously foolish in their learning, any more than that idea of limited rationality suggests that they are conspicuously foolish in their rational calculations. Both notions recognize some constraints on human action and some utility in theories of organizational intelligence that consider those constraints.

The Complete Cycle of Choice

Consider what might be called the complete cycle of organizational choice. It is a familiar conception, and a useful one:

> At a certain point in time some participants see a discrepancy between what they think the world ought to be (given present possibilities and constraints) and what the world actually is. This discrepancy produces individual behavior, which is aggregated into collective (organizational) action or choices. The outside world then 'responds' to this choice in some way that affects individual assessments both of the state of the world and of the efficacy of the actions.

This conception of choice assumes a closed cycle of connections (figure 15.1):

1 The cognitions and preferences held by individuals affect their behavior.
2 The behavior (including participation) of individuals affects organizational choices.
3 Organizational choices affect environmental acts (responses).
4 Environmental acts affect individual cognitions and preferences.

These basic ideas are fundamental to much of our understanding of decisions in organizations. The ideas are implicit in most ordinary conversations about organizations and about important events of policy-making. They are the basis for many theoretical treatments, including our own. While we think this conception of choice illuminates choice situations significantly, we want to modify the details of that perspective and explore some specific limitations in a theory based on the closed sequence shown in figure 15.1. The limitations we will consider are of considerable significance under some situations, of little significance under others. The limitations are particularly important when the cycle is incomplete, when one or more of the connections are broken or confounded by exogenous factors.

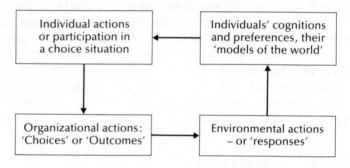

Figure 15.1. The complete cycle of choice

Limitations in the Complete Cycle

The complete cycle of organizational choice assumes four simple relations. Each of those relations is obviously more complex than the closed cycle represents it to be. More importantly, those relations are more complex in ways that lead to systematic limitations in the theory.

Individual Beliefs and Individual Action

Most organization theory is purposive. It assumes that behavior and attention[2] follow belief and attitude. Beliefs and attitudes, in turn, are stable enough so that attention is stable over the course of a choice; and differential levels of attention are predictable from the content of the decision. Decision-making activity thus stems from self-interest and is generally attractive so long as the resources being allocated are significant.

2   The concept of attention is deliberately broad. We will use it with reference to activities like searching information, discussing, proselytising, attending meetings, voting, making speeches, campaigning and competing for offices, with no references to the motivation for or the effect of the activities.

Our observations suggest a modification of this view.[3] Instead of a stable activity level we find that people move in and out of choice situations. There is considerable variation among individuals, and over time for the same individual, in terms of the degree and form of attention to decision problems. A step toward understanding this flow of attention, and its connection to individual beliefs and attitudes, is to note that time and energy are scarce resources.

Involvement in decisions is not attractive for everyone in all relevant choice situations, all the time. The capacity for beliefs, attitudes, and concerns is larger than the capacity for action. A choice situation may be perceived as relevant, but the individual may not have any time or energy for action. Under such circumstances, we will observe beliefs and values without behavioral implications. Even given the time and energy, there are alternative choice situations where an individual can present his concerns. The flow of attention will not depend on the content of a single choice alone, but upon the collection of choice situations available. We should not expect that a set of beliefs and preferences will have behavioral implications in any specific choice situation independent of the available claims on attention.

A theory that recognizes time as a scarce resource (Becker, 1965; Linder, 1970) makes attention contextual, subject to resource constraints and alternative 'consumption' possibilities. Such a conception assumes some hierarchy of beliefs and preferences, and some hierarchy of choice situations in terms of attractiveness. Individuals are seen to allocate available energy by attending to choice situations with the highest expected return. They do not act in one arena because they are acting in another. Although it clarifies some aspects of decision involvement, even this contextual version of the connection between values and action is problematic in an organization. It ignores the importance of roles, duties, and standard operating procedures for determining behavior; and it underestimates the ambiguity of self-interest.

3   Modifications have been suggested by a rather broad range of people. Weick (1969, p. 29) notes that the assumption in organization theory 'that once the perceptions or organization members are affected, action consistent with these perceptions will follow automatically' has not been affected by recent work by psychologists interested in how beliefs and values get translated into action. Both Weick (1969) and Bem (1970) argue for theories assuming that cognition follows action. The primacy of behavior or praxis over ideas or theory is a classical theme in Marxist theory. Often the point of departure is Marx's statement that life is not determined by consciousness, but consciousness by life (Marx, 1962). However, the debate between Marxists and non-Marxists has to some degree detracted attention from the debate among Marxists on the role of ideas as a driving force in history. Ibsen reflected some of the complexity when he had Peer Gynt state (on observing a man chopping off a finger to avoid being drafted): 'The thought, perhaps – the wish – the will. Those I could understand, but really to do the deed! Ah, no – that astounds me'.

Any complex social structure has considerable capability for weakening the connection between individual behavior and individual beliefs and preferences. The potential has produced some affective ambivalence. It has been celebrated as an important device in fighting personal favoritism and establishing equity and equality. It has been portrayed as a major source of organizational inertia preventing progress. Here we are not primarily concerned with a normative evaluation, but with the simple fact that roles, duties, and obligations are behaviorally important to involvement. People attend to decisions not only because they have an interest at stake, but because they are expected to or obliged to. They act according to rules.

Even when they act in self-interest terms, participants in organizations do not appear to act in a way fully anticipated by self-interest theories. They have an abundance of preferences and beliefs. The complexity increases as one moves from interest in immediate, substantive outcomes to long-term effects and to various side agendas (e.g., status) involved in a decision situation. The architecture of these values does not easily lend itself to description in terms of well-behaved preference functions. The behavior apparently stemming from the values proceeds without concern about those values. Not all values are attended to at the same time; attention focus, rather than utility, seems to explain much of the behavior (Cyert and March, 1963). At the same time, beliefs and preferences appear to be the results of behavior as much as they are the determinants of it. Motives and intentions are discovered *post factum* (March, 1972).

We require a theory that takes into consideration the possibility that there may be attitudes and beliefs without behavioral implications, that there may be behavior without any basis in individual preferences, and that there may be an interplay between behavior and the definition (and redefinition) of 'self-interest'.

Individual Action and Organizational Choice

Organizational choices are ordinarily viewed as derivative of individual actions. A decision process transforms the behavior of individuals into something that could be called organizational action. Explorations into the nature of this 'visible hand' comprise much of the literature; and most of the theoretical issues are questions of suitable metaphors for characterizing the process. It is sometimes captured by metaphors of deduction (organizational goals, sub-goals, efficiency); sometimes by metaphors of implicit conflict (markets, bureaucracy); sometimes by metaphors of explicit conflict (bargaining, political processes, power). Each of these metaphors accepts the basic notion that organizational choice is understandable as some consequence of individual action. They interpret organizations as instruments of individuals.

Our observations suggest that the connection between individual action and organizational action is sometimes quite loose. Sometimes we observe that the (internal) decision-making process is not strongly related to the organizational action, i.e., the policy selected, the price set, the man hired. Rather it is connected to the definition of truth and virtue in the organization, to the allocation of status, to the maintenance or change of friendship, goodwill, loyalty, and legitimacy; to the definition and redefinition of 'group interest'. In short, the formal decision-making process sometimes is directly connected to the maintenance or change of the organization as a social unit, as well as to the accomplishment of making collective decisions and producing substantive results. A theory of organizational choice probably should attend to the interplay between two aspects of the internal process.

Sometimes we observe a considerable impact on the process of the temporal flow of autonomous actions. We need a theory that considers the timing of different individual actions, and the changing context of each act. Most theories imply the importance of the context of an act. Typically, however, they have assumed that this context has stable properties that allow unconditional predictions. We observe a much more interactive, branching, and contextual set of connections among the participants, problems, and solutions in an organization.

Sometimes we observe an internal process swamped by external events or factors. Organizational action is conspicuously independent of internal process. The dramatic version – where some external actor intervenes directly, or where some external event completely changes the conditions under which the organization is operating – is well-known. In a similar way, macro-theorists of social process rarely feel required to consider the details of organizational phenomena. Theories of the market or long-run social movements have identified important characteristics of the deep structure in which organizational phenomena occur; and it would be foolish for a theory of organizational choice situations not to recognize the extent to which the decision process is part of a broader stream of events. We need a theory of choice that articulates the connections between the environmental context of organizations and their actions in such a way that neither is simply the residual unexplained variance for the other.

In general, we need a theory of organizational choice that considers the connection between individual actions and organizational actions as sometimes variable. Organizational action may be determined, or strongly constrained, by external forces. Internal process may be related to other phenomena than the organizational choice (i.e., allocating status, defining organizational truth and virtue). The structure of the internal process may be highly time-dependent; changing contexts of the individual acts may produce organizational actions not anticipated or desired by anyone.

Organizational Choice and Environmental Response

The complete cycle of choice assumes a connection between organizational actions and environmental actions. The latter are treated as *responses* to the choices made in the organization.[4] The notion is a simple one. We assume that there is an environment with a schedule of responses to alternative actions on the part of the organization. Voters respond to party platforms or candidate images. Consumers respond to produce quality and price. Competitors respond to challenges. Students respond to curricula. Citizens respond to social experiments. Out of such a paradigm come many of our ideas about organizational learning and natural selection (Cohen and March, 1974; Winter, 1964).

We need a theory of the environment which is less organization-centered, a theory where the actions and events in the environment sometimes may have little to do with what the organization does. Environmental acts frequently have to be understood in terms of relationships among events, actors, and structures in the environment, not as responses to what the organization does. As a result the same organizational action will have different responses at different times; different organizational actions will have the same response. The world of the absurd is sometimes more relevant for our understanding of organizational phenomena than is the idea of a tight connection between action and response.

The independence of action and response is accentuated by our tendency to attempt to explain fine gradations in both. Organizations act within environmentally constrained boundaries. On the rare occasions on which they violate those constraints, the environment is likely to react unambiguously. Most of the time, however, the range of behavior is relatively small; and within that range very little of the variation in response is attributable to variations in the action. In so far as we wish to explain variations in organizational behavior within the range in which we observe it, we will require a theory that recognizes only a modest connection between environmental response and organizational decision.[5]

---

4 There are two versions of the theory: The strong organization making the environment adapt to its decisions, and the weak organization being 'conditioned' by the environment.

5 Participants in an organization are likely, under a variety of circumstances, to see the connection between action and response as tighter than it is. As a result, one of the major phenomena that we will need to comprehend is superstitious learning within organizations; the way in which the subjective experience of learning can be compelling without any learning taking place.

Environmental Response and Individual Beliefs

Classical theory offers two alternative versions on how environmental actions and events are connected to individual cognition. In the first version, the problem is assumed away. Organizational decision-makers are equipped with perfect information about alternatives and consequences. Since the full cycle is well understood ahead of any individual action there is no learning in the system. In the second version, the connection is understood in terms of a model of individual, rational adaption. Beliefs and models of the world are tied to reality through experience. Events are observed; the individual changes his beliefs on the basis of his experience; he improves his behavior on the basis of this feedback.

Our observations suggest a modification of this view. There is a need for introducing ideas about the process by which beliefs are constructed in an organizational setting. In many contexts the interpretation of an organizational choice process is as important as the immediate, substantive action we commonly consider.[6] Individuals, as well as organizations or nations, develop myths, fictions, legends, and illusions. They develop conflicts over myths and ideology. We need models of the development of belief which do not assume necessary domination by events or 'objective reality'.

Environmental actions and events frequently are ambiguous. It is not clear what happened, or why it happened. Ambiguity may be inherent in the events, or be caused by the difficulties participants have in observing them. The complexity of, and change in, the environment often overpower our cognitive capacity. Furthermore, our interpretations are seldom based only on our own observations; they rely heavily on the interpretations offered by others. Our trust in the interpretations is clearly dependent on our trust in the interpreters. The degree of ambiguity will be strongly dependent upon the efficiency of the channels through which interpretations are transmitted.

The elaboration of such a theory is particularly germane to the study of organizations. Much of what we know, or believe we know, is based on our interpretation of reports from participants. When we ask a participant to report what happened, we solicit his model of events. When we ask a participant to assess the relative power of various individuals or groups, we ask him to carry out a complex theoretical analysis (March, 1966). It is often true that participants differ in significant ways among

---

6 Vickers (1965, p. 15) is interested in both these two outcomes of choices: 'events' and 'ideas'. He views the Royal Commissions as units which seldom are supposed to make direct choices, but to affect opinions and conceptions or 'the appreciative setting' of a certain phenomenon.

themselves or differ in significant ways from the interpretations that we, as outside observers, report. In order to sort out the complications of developing an understanding of participant reports, we need to understand the development of belief structures in an organization under conditions of ambiguity.

Implications for Theories of Choice Situations

We remain in the tradition of viewing organizational participants as problem solvers and decision-makers. However, we assume that individuals find themselves in a more complex, less stable, and less understood world than standard theories of organizational choice suppose; they are placed in a world over which they often have only modest control. Nevertheless, we assume organizational participants will try to understand what is going on, to activate themselves and their resources in order to solve their problems and move the world in desired directions. These attempts will have a less heroic character than assumed in the perfect cycle theories, but they will be real.

We have argued that any of the connections in the basic cycle of choice can be broken or changed so significantly as to modify the implications of the whole system. Intention does not control behavior precisely. Participation is not a stable consequence of properties of the choice situation or individual preferences. Outcomes are not a direct consequence of process. Environmental response is not always attributable to organizational action. Belief is not always a result of experience.

In addition, the cycle is frequently touched by exogenous factors outside the control of the internal process. The process is embedded in a larger system. Under relatively easily realized situations, any one of the connections may be overwhelmed by exogenous effects. External factors may dictate individual action without regard to individual learning, organizational action without regard to individual action, environmental action without regard to organizational action, or individual learning without regard to environmental action.

In order to respond to such concerns in a theory of organizations, we require three clusters of interrelated theoretical ideas:

First, we need a modified theory of organizational choice. Such a theory will need to be contextual in the sense that it reflects the ways in which the linkages in the complete cycle of choice are affected by exogenous events, by the timing of events, by the varieties of ways in which the participants wander onto and off the stage. It will need to be structural in the sense that it reflects ways in which stabilities can arise in a highly contextual system. We have tried to suggest the basis for such a theory elsewhere (Cohen, March and Olsen, 1972).

Second, we need a theory of organizational attention. Such a theory should treat the allocation of attention by potential participants as problematic. Where will they appear? What are the structural limits on their decision-activity? How do they allocate time within those limits? Such a theory must attend to the elements of rational choice in attention allocation, to the importance of learning to the modification of attention rules, and to the norms of obligation that affect individual attention to alternative organizational concerns. We have attempted to indicate an outline to such a theory elsewhere (March and Olsen, 1976).

Third, we need a theory of learning under conditions of organizational ambiguity. The complete cycle is implicitly a theory of learning. What happens when the cycle is incomplete? What is a possible perspective on the development and change of belief structures? The present paper is directed to an understanding of these issues of learning in the face of ambiguity.

Learning under Ambiguity

Choice situations provide occasions for argumentation and interpretation as well as decision-making. The ideas, beliefs and attitudes that participants come to hold are themselves important outcomes of the process. Interpretations of the ways in which meanings arise, the ways in which participants in an organization come to 'know' or 'believe', build on a set of simple theoretical ideas about rational adaptation. Beliefs are modified on the basis of experience. These ideas, however, seem inadequate for understanding some familiar phenomena. For example, we have been impressed by the regularities in the ways in which different individuals develop different interpretations of their common experience in a decison situation, with the ways in which organizations rewrite their histories and facilitate retrospective learning, with the ease with which participants come to have impressions of the power distribution within an organization, and with the importance for leadership in organizations of managing historical interpretation and the formation of belief. All these observations signal the significance and complexity of learning and the construction of belief to an understanding of organizational behavior.

Our general focus is on experimental learning within organizations. We ask how individuals and organizations make sense of their experience and modify behavior in terms of their interpretations of events. Our attempts are in the tradition of efforts to understand organizational behavior in terms of adaptive rationality. That tradition assumes a simple logic of experiential learning: an action is taken; there is some response from the environment; and then a new action is taken reflecting the impact of the sequence. A basic presumption in the literature is that as an organization gains experience, it learns more and more about coping with its environment and with its internal problems. Normally it is argued that organizations try to perpetuate the fruits of their learning by formalizing them (Starbuck, 1965, p.480). There is a belief that 'when the problem is solved, mass productions begins' (Perrow, 1970, p. 68).

The situation is familiar and has been portrayed in figure 15.1. It captures some important domains of behavior in organizations. There is a rather large family of models designed to interpret behavior within such a situation. The ideas of the complete cycle are made explicit in the following model by Cyert and March (1963, p. 99):

1 There exist a number of states of the system (organization). At any point in time, the system in some sense 'prefers' some of these states to others.
2 There exists an external source of disturbance or shock to the system. These shocks cannot be controlled.
3 There exist a number of decision variables internal to the system. These variables are manipulated according to some decision-rules.
4 Each combination of external shocks and decision variables in the system changes the state of the system. Thus, given an existing state, an external shock, and a decision, the next state is determined.
5 Any decision-rule that leads to a preferred state at one point is more likely to be used in the future than it was in the past.

We wish to examine what happens when the cycle is incomplete; in particular, to consider the development of belief under conditions of ambiguity.

Incomplete Learning Cycles

Some of the more interesting phenomena in organizations occur when the learning cycle is not complete, when one or more of the connections is attenuated. As we have indicated above, there are a number of ways in which the cycle may be broken. Although it is not necessarily true that the cycle is broken at only one place, we can illustrate the study of incomplete cycles by considering the four incomplete cycles involving only one missing link. The first situation is *role-constrained* experiential learning. In this situation, everything proceeds in the same manner as in the complete cycle except that individual learning has little or no effect on individual behavior. The circle is broken by constraints of role-definition and standard operating procedures (see figure 15.2).

The situation is one that reflects some important dynamics of organizational behavior. One of the conspicuous things about complex organizations

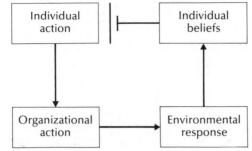

Figure 15.2. Role-constrained experiential learning

(or any complex social structure) is their ability to inhibit the modification of individual behavior on the basis of individual learning. The complication has formed the basis of a number of studies of organizations, most commonly in treatments of organizational inertia; but we do not have a systematic theory of the implications (for the time path of organizational behavior) of a separation of knowledge from action.

The second incomplete cycle is *superstitious* experiential learning. In this situation we assume that individuals within an organization take action, that action produces organizational behavior, that individuals learn from the apparent environmental response, and that subsequent action is modified in what appears to be an appropriate fashion. The critical feature is that the connection between organizational action and environmental response is severed. Learning proceeds. Inferences are made and action is changed. Organizational behavior is modified as a result of an interpretation of the consequences, but the behavior does not affect the consequences significantly. Although superstitious learning in organizations has not received as much attention as it deserves, some discussion of it can be found in Cohen and March (1974) and Lave and March (1975). As Hill (1971, p. 75) observes: 'Many of man's beliefs, not only in charms and magic, but also in medicine, mechanical skills, and administrative techniques probably depend on such superstitious learning' (see figure 15.3).

The third situation is *audience* experiential learning. In this situation the connection between individual action and organizational action becomes problematic. The individual no longer affects (at least in an unambiguous way) organizational action. What he learns cannot affect subsequent behavior by the organization. Learning occurs, but adaptation does not (necessarily). Much of our understanding of learning within politics or research falls within this situation, although it has not received much attention within modern organization theory, except in conjunction with the fourth situation below, when adaptation through interpretation becomes conspicuous as an alternative.

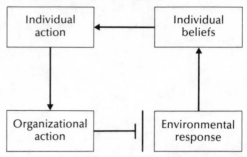

Figure 15.3. Superstitious experiential learning

Thus, the final incomplete cycle is one of experiential learning under *ambiguity*. In this situation it is not clear what happened or why it happened.[7] The individual tries to learn and to modify his behavior on the basis of his learning. In the simple situation, he affects organizational action and that action affects the environment; but subsequent events are seen only dimly, and causal connections among events have to be inferred (see figure 15.5). Learning takes place and behavior changes; but a model of the process requires some ideas about the imputation of meaning and structure to events. Such ideas have had little role in the organizational literature.

Information, Incentives, Cognitive Structures and Micro-Development

The problems of ambiguity in organizations are conspicuous. Nevertheless, the literature on organizational learning is rarely uncoupled from the idea that learning is adaptive. Experience is viewed as producing wisdom and

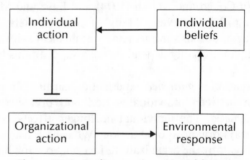

Figure 15.4. Audience experiential learning

7 Ambiguity here refers to an 'objective' assessment of the situation (in practice the assessment of the researcher). The individual participants may view the situation as quite unambiguous, though they disagree about the content of that interpretation

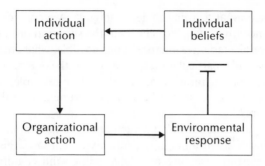

Figure 15.5. Experiential learning under ambiguity

improved behavior. For purposes of studying experiential learning under ambiguity it is necessary to relax such an assumption. Modern organizations develop myths, fictions, legends, folklore, and illusions. They develop conflict over myths. The connection between environmental response to organizational action and individual and organizational interpretation of that response is often weak.

We relax the presumption of improvement but not the presumption of a process of learning. We assume that individuals modify their understandings in a way that is intendedly adaptive. They are, however, operating under conditions in which (a) what happened is not immediately obvious; (b) why it happened is obscure; and (c) whether what happened is good is unclear.

A theory of adaptation under conditions of ambiguity might reasonably include four broad categories of ideas:

1 Some ideas of information exposure, memory, and retrieval. Organizations have communication structures through which individuals and parts of the organization 'see' different worlds. The occasions for seeking information, as well as where information is searched for, are presumably not random, but vary with both organizational and environmental factors. Organizations have records and other ways of recording history. These records are more or less accurate, more or less complete, more or less shared, and more or less retrievable at some future date. How organizational memory functions and how it functions differently at different times and for different parts of the organization are questions that considerably affect the pattern of organizational beliefs. The tendency to use or activate different parts of an organizational memory will vary across individuals as well as organizational subunits.

2 Some ideas about learning incentives. Incentives in learning are usually associated with 'motivation', some measure of factors that influence an inclination to accept information and modify behavior.

In organizational learning under ambiguity, we confront a different form of incentive. If lack of clarity in the situation or in the feedback makes several alternative interpretations possible, what are the incentives that might lead a particular person, or part of the organization, to select one interpretation rather than another. For example, what are the incentives for an evaluator of a social experiment to find it a success? Or a failure?

3 Some ideas about belief structures. The development of beliefs under conditions of ambiguity probably accentuates the significance of a pre-existing structure of related values and cognitions. Understandings of events are connected to previous understandings, to the understandings of other people, and to social linkages of friendship and trust. Learning is a form of attitude formation.

4 Some ideas about the micro-development of belief. It is reasonable to suspect that beliefs, like decisions, are sensitive to the fine detail of the timing, order, and context of information. Suppose, for example, that we think of one process that determines the current degrees of salience of various elements of organizational information and another process that relates new information to the structure of existing information. Then modifications in response to experience will depend importantly on the interleaving of the two processes. Similarly, suppose that the elaboration of the meaning of experience is a claim (for time or energy) on a limited capacity system. Then learning will be affected by the characteristics of the other demands on the system.

We do not propose here to specify a theory of audience learning under ambiguity that deals with all of these clusters of ideas. We can, however, illustrate the kinds of considerations that are important by elaborating one version of the ideas about structure – that associated with various notions of consistency or balance in belief and perception. The spirit of the effort is strongly in the tradition of Heider (1958), Newcomb (1959), and Abelson (1968).

An Example – Seeing, Liking and Trusting

We assume that organizational participants generally try to make sense of ongoing events and processes. They discover or impose order, attribute meanings, and provide explanations. We wish to identify a simple set of ideas about the ways in which persons in organizations come to learn from experience, how they come to believe what they believe. We are not primarily interested in the ultimate validity of different beliefs. Our focus is on the process by which conceptions of reality are affected by experience in an organizational setting. We do not attempt to specify all of the detail of that process.

For expository purposes, a distinction is made between beliefs about what a person 'sees' and beliefs about what a person 'likes'. The beliefs about what a person sees include the ways in which the individual defines actions and outcomes, the theories he has about the world, and his interpretations of those theories. The beliefs about what a person likes include the affective sentiments he has, his values, and his tastes. By making this distinction, we will be able to link our ideas to ordinary discourse about fact and value; but it should be clear as we proceed that we do not postulate a fundamentally different process for coming to believe that something exists or is true from a process for coming to believe that something is desirable.

The tightness of the connection between environmental response and individual learning hinges on the extent to which the interpretation of events is controlled by six presumptions of ordinary life in unambiguous systems:

He sees what is to be seen.
He likes what is to be liked.
He sees what he expects to see.
He likes what he expects to like.
He sees what he is expected to see.
He likes what he is expected to like.

The first two presumptions reflect the extent to which the processes of perception and preference are effectively self-evident. The second two reflect the intra-personal limitations on perceptions and preferences. The last reflect the role of social norms. By presenting the six as distinct, we mean to suggest some possible utility in avoiding the dictum that all knowledge is necessarily 'social'.

An organizational participant sees what is to be seen. There is an ordinary process of perceiving reality. The process is normatively well-defined. Through it, an individual establishes reliably what has happened in the phenomenal world. He is able to relate observed events to their future consequences, and to their more stable underlying causes. A correct link can be established between his past choices and subsequent states of the world (i.e., it is possible to disentangle the effects of own choices and the effects of external factors). There exist some criteria for determining what choice situations are similar. Although much of what we want to discuss relates to other factors, we wish to acknowledge the possibility, and frequent dominance, of what is usually called objective reality.

An organizational participant likes what is to be liked. There are objective interests in the sense that given an individual's position in society (or organization) it is possible to assert that some things are in his interest and others are not, even if that is not his own present awareness. Although such a conception of interest is uncommon in modern social science, we consider it a defensible assumption of a theory that intends to predict actual behavior over time. Indeed, it is the basis of much effective prediction in social behavior.

An organizational participant sees what he expects to see. We assume that an individual approaches any perceptual situation with expectations. Those expectations may come from experience; they may come from the structure of his beliefs about the world. In either case, the expectations help to control their own realization.

An organizational participant likes what he likes. Individuals come to any particular choice situation with a set of values, attitudes, and opinions. These values are substantially fixed. Changes that occur within a relatively brief time period must attend to problems of consistency with the pre-existing attitude structure. In some cases, the restrictions imposed by this presumption will dominate the behavior.

An organizational participant sees what he is expected to see and likes what he is expected to like. The role of social norms in facilitating the interpretation of events and attitudes is a familiar theme in the analyses of social behavior. Among the best-known examples of social provision of precision are the studies of strongly ideological, religious, and political messianistic movements (e.g., Festinger et al., 1956). The phenomenon extends well beyond such cases, however.

In many cases, seeing and liking are controlled by the elemental exogenous forces of objective reality, attitude structures, social reality, and social norms. In the rest of this paper, however, we wish to examine situations in which the six elementary presumptions of seeing and liking do not completely determine the interpretations of events, where there is some degree of contextual ambiguity. Under such conditions a different set of assumptions becomes important and some attributes of organizations have significant impact on the development of belief and the process of learning.

Situations of ambiguity are common. The patterns of exposure to events and the channels for diffusing observations and interpretations often obscure the events. In situations where interpretations and explanations are called forth some time after the events, the organizational 'memory' (e.g., files, budgets, statistics, etc.) and the retrieval-system will affect the degrees to which different participants can use past events, promises, goals, assumptions, behavior, etc. in different ways. Pluralism, decentralization, mobility and volatility in attention all tend to produce perceptual and attitudinal ambiguity in interpreting events.

Despite ambiguity and uncertainty, organizational participants interpret and try to make sense out of their lives. They try to find meaning in happenings and provide or invent explanations. These explanations and their development over time are our primary focus.

For the present purposes an organization is considered to consist of individuals characterized by:

1 Varying *patterns of interaction* with each other. The frequency and duration of contacts between any two people may vary. In part this may reflect choice; in part it may be a consequence of organizational structure.

2 Varying *degrees of trust* in each other. The belief in another person's ability and strength, together with the confidence in his motives, varies.

3 Varying *degrees of integration* into the organization. A person is integrated to the extent to which he accepts responsibility for the organization and feels that the actions of the organization are fundamentally his actions or the actions of those he trusts. The converse relation with the organization is alienation. We will view an individual as alienated from the organization to the extent to which he does not accept responsibility for it and feels that the actions of the organization are neither his actions nor the actions of others whom he trusts.

4 Varying *orientations to events* in the phenomenal world. These orientations have four key dimensions: (a) the extent to which the event is *seen*; (b) the extent to which the event is *liked*; (c) the extent to which the event is *relevant* to different interpersonal relations; (d) the extent to which an event is seen as *controlled* by different individuals.

We assume that the individuals in an organization develop their interpretations of events in a way broadly consistent with some hypotheses of cognitive consistency. In a general way, we assume that there are clear interdependencies between cognitive organization (i.e., perceiving someone as causing something, owning something, being close, etc.) and attitudinal organization (i.e., liking or disliking something or someone). The inter-dependencies with which we will concern ourselves reflect various tendencies toward consistency. We believe that such tendencies capture important aspects of the formation of beliefs in organizations. At the same time, however, it should be obvious that we do not anticipate that the attitude structures we will observe in organizations will exhibit a high degree of consistency on some absolute scale. Ambiguity in the environment, short attention spans, and considerable human tolerance for inconsistency (Bem, 1970) conspire to maintain a high level of incongruence at any one point of time even in a process in which there are substantial efforts toward cognitive structure.

To focus on a simple set of ideas about movement toward cognitive consistency, we make four propositions about seeing and liking:

Proposition 1:   An organizational participant will – to the extent to which he is integrated into the organization – see what he likes. To the extent to which he is alienated from the organization he will see what he dislikes.

Thus we assume that the elementary screening devices used by the individual in looking at the world tend to obscure those elements of reality that are not consonant with his attitudes. To the extent possible, the individual sees what he wants to see. The result of such wishful thinking is highly dependent upon his integration into the organization. If he is alienated from the organization, he will see evidence confirming his alienation.

Proposition 2:   An organizational participant will – to the degree he is integrated into the organization – like what he sees. To the extent to which he is alienated from the organization he will dislike what he sees.

Not only does the individual modify his perceptions to accommodate his attitudes, he also modifies his attitudes to accommodate his perceptions. We assume that individuals discover pleasures in the outcomes arising from worlds into which they are integrated relatively independent of what those outcomes are; and displeasures from worlds from which they are alienated.

Proposition 3:   An organizational participant will – to the extent to which he trusts others with whom he has contact – like what they like. To the extent to which he distrusts others with whom he has contact, he will dislike what they like.

Most organizational participants most of the time will not be eye-witnesses to most relevant events. Both what they 'see' and what they 'like' will be dependent upon available sources of information, which of the sources available they are exposed to, which of those they are exposed to they trust. Learning under such conditions becomes dependent both upon processes like discussions and persuasion, and upon relationships like trust and antagonism. We assume that sentiments diffuse through the contact network characterized by variations in trust. They spread positively across trust relationships, negatively across distrust relationships.

The frequency of interaction will be especially important when different trusted people hold different likes. We assume that an organizational participant under such conditions will tend to like what those whom he most frequently interacts with, like.

Proposition 4:   An organizational participant will – to the degree he trusts others with whom he has contact – see what they see. To the extent to which he distrusts others with whom he has contact, he will not see what they see.

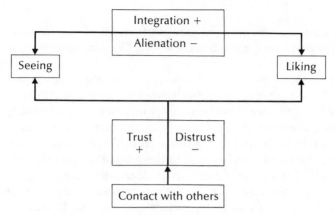

Figure 15.6. Seeing, liking, and trusting

Perceptions also diffuse through the contact network, mediated by the trust structure. Individuals (most of the time) have difficulties in seeing things different from what a unanimous group of trusted people see.

This elementary set of propositions results in a simple system for coming to believe what one believes, as portrayed in figure 15.6.

Finally we need to complete the basic system by adding six propositions that reflect the dynamics of balancing within the organizations of life for each participant:

Proposition 5:   An organizational participant will come to trust others whom he sees as producing relevant events that he likes and preventing relevant events that he dislikes.

Proposition 6:   An organizational participant will come to believe that people he trusts cause events he likes and that people he distrusts cause events he dislikes.

Proposition 7:   An organizational participant will come to believe that events are relevant if he agrees about them with people he trusts and disagrees about them with people he distrusts.

Proposition 8:   An organizational participant will be active to the extent to which his seeing, liking, and trusting are unambiguous.

Proposition 9:   An organizational participant will – to the extent to which the organizational structure and his activity level permit – seek contact with people he trusts and avoid contact with people he distrusts.

Proposition 10:   An organizational participant will feel integrated into an organization to the extent to which he likes the relevant events that he sees.

Taken together these propositions suggest a view of reality forming that emphasizes the impact of interpersonal connections within the organization and the affective connection between the organization and the participant on the development of belief, as well as the interaction between seeing and liking. In keeping with the balance ideas, the propositions emphasize the organization of belief as vital to the substance of belief, and accept a particular form of consistency as an organizing device.

The propositions appear to fit the observations in some case studies. They also seem to fit some more casual observations of organizational life. Their ultimate utility, however, hinges heavily on the extent to which the dynamics they postulate can be used to interpret more subtle aspects of changes in beliefs over time.

Conclusion

Organizations, and the people in them, learn from their experience. They act, observe the consequences of their action, make inferences about those consequences, and draw implications for future action. The process is adaptively rational. If the information is accurate, the goals clear and unchanging, the inferences correct, the behavior modification appropriate, and the environment stable, the process will result in improvement over time.

As we have come to recognize the limitations on rational calculation, planning, and forecasting as bases for intelligence in many organizations, interest in the potential for organizational learning has increased. That interest, however, tends to underestimate the extent to which adaptive rationality is limited by characteristics of human actors and organizations. The problems are similar to, and probably as profound as, the limits on calculated rationality. We have tried to suggest a few of the complications involved in assuming that organizations 'improve' through learning, particularly under conditions of ambiguity.

Despite the difficulties, it is important to study the process of learning in organizations. Individuals try to make sense of their experience, even when that experience is ambiguous or misleading and even when that learning does not affect organizational actions. They impose order, attribute meaning, and provide explanations. We have outlined an application of one set of ideas about cognitive consistency to the question of how ambiguous events in organizations are interpreted, and thus how people in an organization come to believe what they believe.

Some significant understanding of the factors affecting learning from experience will not only be important to the improvement of policy-making in an organizational context. It will also be a necessary part of a theory of the full cycle of organizational choice and of the consequences that accrue from breaking the cycle in different ways under different circumstances. Policy analysts interested in designing organizations that can learn intelligently and organization theorists interested in understanding the dynamics of organizational choice share the need for an effective model of organizational learning under conditions of uncertainty about what events happened, why they happened, and whether they were good or bad. Such situations are common in a wide variety of organizations; they are conspicuous in most public organizations, somewhat more concealed in business organizations.

References

Abelson, R., et al (1968) *Theories of Cognitive Consistency: A Sourcebook.* Chicago: Rand McNally.

Axelrod, R. (1973) Schema Theory: An Information Processing Model of Perception and Cognition. *The American Political Science Review,* Vol. 57, 1248–66.

Becker, G. S. (1965) A Theory of the Allocation of Time. *Economic Journal,* Vol. 75, 493–517.

Bem, D. J. (1970) *Beliefs, Attitudes and Human Affairs.* Belmont: Brooks/Cole.

Cohen, R. M., and March, J. G. (1974) *Leadership and Ambiguity.* New York: McGraw-Hill.

Cohen, M. D., March, J. G., and Olsen, J. P. (1972) A Garbage Can Model of Organizational Choice. *Administrative Science Quarterly,* Vol. 17, 1–25.

Cyert, R. M., and March, J. G. (1963) *A Behavioral Theory of the Firm.* Englewood Cliffs: Prentice Hall.

Festinger, L. et al. (1956) *When Prophecy Fails.* Minneapolis: University of Minnesota Press.

Heider, F. (1958) *The Psychology of Interpersonal Relations.* New York: John Wiley.

Hill, W. F. (1971) *Learning* (revised edn). Scranton: Chandler.

Lave, C. A., and March, J. G. (1975) *Introduction to Models in the Social Sciences.* New York: Harper and Row.

Lindblom, C. E. (1965) *The Intelligence of Democracy.* New York: The Free Press.

Linder, S. (1970) *The Harried Leisure Class.* New York: Columbia University Press.

March, J. G. (1966) The Power of Power, in D. Easton, *Varieties of Political Theories.* Englewood Cliffs: Prentice Hall.

March, J. G. (1972) Model Bias in Social Action. *Review of Educational Research,* Vol. 42, 413–29.

March, J. G., and Olsen, J. P. (1976) *Ambiguity and Choice in Organizations.* Bergen: Universitetsforlaget.

March, J. G., and Simon, H. A. (1958) *Organizations*. New York: John Wiley & Sons.

Marx, K., and Engels, F. (1962) *Die Deutsche Ideologie*. Marx Engels Werk Band 3, Berlin: Dietz Verlag.

Olsen, J. P. (1970) 'A Study of Choice in an Academic Organization', Bergen (mimeo).

Newcomb, T. M. (1959) Individual Systems of Orientation in Koch, *Psychology: A Study of Science*. New York: McGraw Hill.

Perrow, C. (1970) *Organizational Analysis: A Sociological View*. London: Tavistock Publications.

Simon, H. A. (1955) A Behavioral Model of Rational Choice *Quarterly Journal of Economics,* Vol. 69. Reprinted in H. A. Simon (1957), *Models of Man*. New York: John Wiley.

Starbuck, W. H. (1967) Organizational Growth and Development, in March, *Handbook of Organizations*. Chicago: Rand McNally.

Thompson, J. D. (1967) *Organizations in Action*. New York: McGraw Hill.

Vickers, G. (1965) *The Art of Judgement*. London: Chapman and Hall.

Weick, K. (1969) *The Social Psychology of Organizing*. Reading: Addison, Wesley.

16

Performance Sampling
in Social Matches

James C. March and James G. March

Abstract

Many social structures can be viewed as collections of interconnected voluntary social pairings, for example, matches between jobholders and jobs, husbands and wives, or residents and neighborhoods. A general performance sampling model is suggested as a framework for exploring how mutual evaluation within such matches affects their continuation, and thus the structure of matches involved. The model treats continuation in a pairing as a decision made under conditions of imperfect information. It emphasizes the sampling errors involved in using small samples of observations to form judgments about matches. There are indications that the sampling characteristics of the process will often be robust enough to obscure other effects. The specific implications of one version of the model are shown to agree well with general observations from social mobility studies and more specific data from Wisconsin school superintendents. The implications of performance sampling for understanding careers in organizations and social pairings more generally are discussed. In contrast to an earlier paper, which explored major features of the gross structure of matches between superintendencies and superintendents, the present paper looks at the fine structure of the ways in which individuals leave jobs. The attempt is both to illuminate how a particular system of careers might arise from a series of elementary decisions with respect to job exits, and to connect a theory of organizational careers more explicitly with theories of other social pairings.

This paper was first published in the *Administrative Science Quarterly*, Vol. 25, no. 3, September 1978. The research was supported by grants from the Ford Foundation and the Spencer Foundation. The Ford Foundation grant was made through the National Academy of Education. The paper has profited from comments by Louis R. Pondy, Aage Sørensen, and Nancy B. Tuma.

Many social linkages can be viewed as voluntary pairings. The relation between husband and wife, resident and residence, job and jobholder, teacher and student, product and buyer are all examples of social matches that are voluntary in the sense that we imagine them to require some form of mutual consent.[1] Interconnected changes in pairings produce social structures of marriages, residences, careers, consumption patterns , and other matches. Associated with such structures are theoretical ideas about social mobility, specifically market theories of pairings (Stigler, 1961; Edwards, 1969; Becker, 1973) and Markovian and semi-Markovian models of movement (Blumen, Kogan, and McCarthy, 1955; White, 1970; Singer and Spilerman, 1974; Tuma, 1975). Although there are manifest differences between a social structure of careers and structures of marriages, residences, consumption, or other matches, there are broad similarities in mobility data taken from these apparently different domains. As a result, there is some reason to look for simple explanations of matching processes that are general enough to apply to different kinds of social pairings.

An earlier paper on Wisconsin school superintendents (March and March, 1977) showed how major features of the structure of matches between high-level management jobs and managers (Wisconsin school super-intendents) could be approximated by assuming random matches between indistinguishable individuals and indistinguishable jobs. Such an approximation seems adequate for many ordinary forecasting and decision purposes and suggests some important features of careers in top management positions. In particular, it was argued that a nearly random career structure was produced by the increasing difficulty of making reliable discriminations among individuals and jobs for the higher positions in a career structure. Such an explanation, however, does not tie the gross structure of movement within a career system tightly to the fine structure of how individuals leave jobs. Nor does it link the process of job matching to a broader conception of social matches. The present paper is an effort in both directions. We elaborate a simple, baseline model of performance assessment in social matches. The model describes how important features of data on social mobility, including the key deviations from randomness observed in the data on Wisconsin school superintendents (March and March, 1977) may be attributed to statistical consequences of forming estimates of attributes

---

1   A more conservative listing might have pairings between resident and neighbors, employer and employee, and seller and buyer; and we will occasionally use such language. We believe, however, that it is a mistake to limit the metaphor of choice to individuals, and wish to question our conventional theological and linguistic preferences for such a limitation. Similarly, in using terms like 'voluntary' and 'consent' to describe behavior, we do not intend to suggest that the behavior is unconstrained, that the relation is without coercion, or that consent is necessarily informed consent. The terms are used as a plain language interpretation of social pairings that are terminated by withdrawal of either party.

on the basis of samples of performances. The main focus for much of the paper is on top managerial careers, but the intention is to describe a general framework for looking at any kind of voluntary pairing.

Imperfect Information and Performance Sampling

The most common theoretical notions about formation and dissolution of pairings treat them as a result of some kind of rational calculation. A pairing is formed when, for each partner, there is no other available partnership that would be better. It is terminated when that condition does not hold. The formation and continuation of a match depend on its attractiveness relative to alternatives. Matches are assumed to be stable if, for each partner, the advantages of the existing pairing over alternative pairings continue or are augmented over time. For example, for marriage formation the world is viewed as consisting of a pool of men and a pool of women. Each man and each woman has certain attributes that are valued by potential partners. Men and women marry, divorce, and remarry until no one can do better through voluntary pairing. Similarly, the world of work is viewed as consisting of a pool of workers and a pool of jobs. Each worker and each job has certain attributes that are valued by potential partners. The pairings of jobs and workers are such that neither workers nor jobs can do better through voluntary pairing.

Assumptions of rationality in the formation of social pairings, like assumptions of rationality in other domains of human behavior, seem to require substantial qualification to fit observed patterns of pairing. For example, there are legal and social constraints on the formation and dissolution of social pairings. At most, the rationality of pair-formation is rationality subject to constraints.

In addition, two familiar complications in rationality affect rational theories of social pairings:

Imperfect Information.   In order to make rational pairings, potential partners must assess all relevant attributes of all possible partners, or at least gather as much of that information as is justified by the costs of obtaining it. The information available for some kinds of pairings in which we are interested (e.g., marriage, jobs) is generally incomplete. As a result, it may be necessary to make assumptions about how information is obtained, inferences are formed, and decisons made without complete information.

Endogenous changes.   In simple theories of rationality it is assumed that attributes of goods and the preference functions of actors for them are exogenous to decisions based on them. Similarly, stationary Markov models assume exogenous rates of movement. But there is considerable indication that both attributes and preferences change as a result of actions. It may be necessary to make some assumptions about how attributes of partners or values associated with attributes change as a consequence of a match (Scitovsky, 1976; March, 1978).

Such limitations of simple rational models have generated theories of imperfect information, of the economics of information, and of the impact of decisions on cognitions, and mutual learning. In this paper we describe an imperfect information model as a possible interpretation of the process of forming and breaking voluntary matches.

Most studies seem to indicate that duration of a match increases the likelihood of its future continuation (Bartholomew, 1973). A frequent explanation is to view the outcome as the consequence of differential retention within a heterogenous population. If each pairing has some chance of persisting from one year to the next, and this chance is constant over time for each pair but varies among pairs, the collection of enduring pairs will include a smaller and smaller representation of low persistence pairs as time passes. As a result of this social sorting, the average chance of continuation will increase with length of match, even though no pair changes.

Alternative explanations relate increases in the likelihood of continuation with duration of a match to changes in the probabilities associated with individual pairs. For the most part, these explanations emphasize the transformation of the strength of the pairing through mutual adaptation of the partners. It is possible to imagine that experience in a pairing will lead partners to become more strongly attached to each other. That is, husbands and wives, or workers and jobs, increase their competence for dealing with each other, or the rewards they provide each other, at the cost of more generalized competences or rewards relevant to the whole pool of pairings (March and Simon, 1958; Tuma, 1976; Hannan, Tuma, and Groeneveld, 1977). Alternatively, the changes can be seen as changes in preferences. Husbands and wives, or workers and jobs, modify their preferences for attributes so as to increase their mutual attractiveness relative to the attraction each has for outsiders. This bilateral specialization of competences, rewards, or affections will generally reduce the chance that either partner will want to end the pairing.

Social sorting and adaptation theories posit similar effects on the propensities of both partners. Some other theories of change over time predict that the propensities should move in opposite directions. An unanticipated decrease in the wealth of a husband should, according to some theories, increase his interest in maintaining his present marriage, but reduce his wife's interest. An increase in general competence of a worker should (according to some theories) decrease the attractiveness of the current job to the worker, but increase the worker's attractiveness to the job. According to such theories, the rates of voluntary and involuntary departures from a job will move in opposite directions over time. Since many forms of mobility data do not permit disaggregation of voluntary and involuntary exits, it has not always been easy to use empirical data to test the alternative theoretical ideas unambiguously.

The model in this paper also considers the effect of duration of a match on future continuation of the match. Like models of social sorting and adaptation, the present model treats the attributes of partners as controlling the process. However, it emphasizes the informational consequences of performance sampling. The core idea is that matches are formed on the basis of imperfect information. Additional information is provided by experience in the match. As information is accumulated, estimates of partner attributes change in a way that is (on average) predictable. Longer duration of a match leads (on average) to better information about the partners. Although the model is a social sorting model, it emphasizes the sampling errors involved in sorting on the basis of small samples of performances (Deutsch and Madow, 1961; White, 1963; Tversky and Kahneman, 1971).

As students of the economics of information have noted, consumers secure information about products through various forms of prior signals (e.g., price) and through consumption (Nelson, 1970; Spence, 1974; Rosener, 1976). Similar comments can be made about information used in other social pairings. Workers use signals such as wages; employers use signals such as education; and both supplement such signals with experience in the employment relation. Men and women use premarital signals to assess the attractiveness of a potential marriage, and they supplement that information with actual experience in a marriage.

Performance sampling is the experiential observation of partners in a match. Two partners observe each other and themselves to gain information about their attributes, capabilities, and feelings. The information gained through experience affects subsequent assessments of the attractiveness of the match. Although it would be possible to imagine the deliberate design of a performance sample by one or both partners, the emphasis here is on the natural experiments that life provides.

Information gathering through performance sampling is complicated by the ways individuals observe and assess events in significant social relations. It seems obvious that inference and belief are subject to predictable systematic biases that would affect the duration of pairs. It seems likely that information on attributes often induces efforts (perhaps successful) to change those attributes. No attempt to include such complications is made here. The present intent is to describe a simple model structure that shows the central ideas of performance sampling in the hope that others will elaborate those ideas in ways that more adequately reflect the subtlety of our knowledge about how individuals form estimates of each other on the basis of observations. For purposes of the present discussion, it is assumed that observation is made without error, that attributes do not change as a result of information about them, and that only very simple beliefs are formed.

In this elementary version of performance sampling, performance of one of the partners provides information about some attribute of that partner to both members of the pair. The information may support each partner's intentions to remain in the match; it may encourage one or the other (or possibly both) to look elsewhere. For example, information on the capabilities of a husband as a lover may lead either husband or wife to revise prior estimates of the attractiveness of the match. As those observations continue over time, the relevant estimates may reach a point at which withdrawal by one of the partners is precipitated.

Performance Sampling in Managerial Careers

Although performance sampling is relevant to any form of social pairing, both the data and the specific models to be used here are specific to the process by which individual managers and specific managerial positions are joined. The focus allows both the models and their implications to be made more specific, and to be related to some empirical data. It has the usual costs of limiting generality.

The structure of a performance sampling career system is built into the procedures of most formal organizations and forms the basis for the model of the process. In a general way, it is assumed that individuals enter an organization with some performance capabilities. These capabilities may reflect factors that do not change (e.g., ability, prior training), factors that change as a career develops (e.g., job experience, reputation), or factors related to the difficulty of the job. Jobs provide opportunities for exhibiting the capabilities of an individual. As a result of being observed exercising capabilities when given opportunities, an individual accumulates a record of performance. That record is a history of the outcomes attributed to an individual's behavior. The record is translated into the reputation of an individual by memory and recall. Careers are produced by vacancies and reputations. When vacancies occur, workers with good reputations progress in their careers, workers with moderate reputations do not progress, and workers with poor reputations are fired, and thus create new vacancies.

In such a description, careers are produced by organizations making distinctions among individuals (as indeed they appear to try to do). At the same time, individuals make distinctions among jobs and organizations. Jobs have capabilities for satisfying demands of jobholders and accumulate records and reputations based on those capabilities. Better jobs have lower turnover than poorer jobs, and careers are produced by the sequential selection of jobs. The duality of matches, the fact that they involve mutual choice, is easily obscured by a metaphor of careers.

The mutuality of choice may be particularly important in considering careers in top managerial positions. At least in some cases (March and March, 1977), social sorting in executive careers appears to be characterized by more enduring differentiation among jobs than among jobholders. Because individuals are ordinarily more likely to disappear from a top management career system than are jobs (positions), a system of dual social sorting on jobs and jobholders leaves greater heterogeneity among jobs than among jobholders. As a result, it is easier to distinguish among jobs than among executives.

This description of the process has the virtue of conforming to the apparent procedures of most formal organizations and to conventional terminology of careers. The one-sidedness of the description can be moderated by viewing promotion as an occasion on which a match is broken by the individual and exit as an occasion on which it is broken by the job, by considering performance to be a joint consequence of individual and job capabilities, and by remembering that both individuals and jobs develop reputations over a series of matches.

Performance-based sorting systems are a standard feature not only of organizations but of social life more generally. Such systems have been subject to numerous critiques in recent years, questioning many aspects of the meaning, measurement, and moral significance of merit as exhibited through performance sampling. Our interest is much narrower. It emphasizes how important features of career systems can be understood as arising from the problems of imperfect information in the evaluation of performance and the use of experience as a source of information.

Careers, of course, are both produced by vacancies and produce vacancies (White, 1970). Net aggregate rates of movement are connected by some simple accounting equations. In a relatively large, relatively stable system of jobs, however, fluctuations in vacancies are small enough that they can probably be ignored; and the movement of individuals through careers can be considered as a process in which vacancies will exist for individuals who qualify for promotion and the rates of movement will be in balance. In such a system of jobs, it is possible to treat the world as evaluating administrators and trying to promote good ones and remove bad ones, subject to limitations of information.

Such a description of the process conforms to most casual efforts to understand how managers get ahead, or don't, in executive careers. It assumes that things are, in some sense, what they appear to be. It remains to ask whether, if things are what they appear to be, the process would produce the pattern of careers that we observe.

Data and Results

Data from a career system in educational administration were used to explore the model. A career in educational administration can be seen as consisting of a period of experience before becoming a school superintendent, a series of appointments to superintendencies, and a period after leaving the last superintendency. It may also include interruptions of various lengths between appointments to superintendencies. The present study considers careers as superintendents for all persons who held at least one school superintendency in Wisconsin during the period 1940–72 (March and March, 1977). The data were gathered from the records of the Wisconsin State Department of Public Instruction, standard biographies, records of the University of Wisconsin School of Education, and personal interviews.[2] A record of Wisconsin superintendency careers that was essentially complete for the 33-year period was constructed. The restriction to a single state introduces some error produced by individuals whose careers as superintendents involved crossing state boundaries. Previous studies have indicated that the error is small (Knezevich, 1971), since almost all careers in educational administration are limited to a single state. The data involved 1,528 individuals and 454 school districts.[3] Appointments of individuals to superintendencies generated 2,516 pairings. Data on superintendency matches formed during the period are complete. Data on attributes of individuals are less complete. For example, we know the ages of individuals in 60 per cent of all cases, and 95 per cent of the cases of individuals beginning careers after 1949.

The main interest is in understanding variations in the age-and-tenure-specific promotion and exit rates. The promotion rate is the rate at which superintendents of given age, length of service in their present superintendency, and number of previous superintendencies go to new superintendencies. The exit rate is the rate at which they go to other jobs or retirement.

---

2   Special acknowledgment is due H. Thomas James, who initiated the collection of the data while he was Assistant State Superintendent of Public Instruction in Wisconsin and who supervised its completion for this study; and Mary E. James and Louise Morrisey for their work in filling the holes in the data.

3   Separate elementary districts are excluded from the data. The number of such districts varies over time but consisted of 54 districts in 1972.

The data on Wisconsin superintendents from 1940 through 1972 were used to determine the promotion and exit rates specific to a particular age, tenure, and number of previous superintendencies.[4] In an earlier paper (March and March, 1977) we discussed the extent to which the careers of these superintendents could be approximated by the simplest of random models in which the chance of going to another superintendency and the chance of leaving the ranks of superintendents in any year was the same for all years and all superintendents. A strict random model assumes only chance variations from constant rates of promotion or exit. The observed surfaces show some systematic deviations from such expectations.[5]

1 As superintendents approach retirement age (i.e., from about age fifty-eight onward), the promotion rate declines to a value very close to zero, and the exit rate rises very rapidly.
2 Before age fifty-eight, both the promotion rate and the exit rate show a similar pattern as a function of tenure (controlling for age and number of superintendencies). The rates are relatively low the first year, rise to a peak about the second, third, or fourth year, and decline thereafter. The exit rate appears to peak a year or two later than the promotion rate.
2 Before age fifty-eight, the relative magnitudes of the promotion rate and the exit rate change as a function of the number of superintendencies served. Promotion rate becomes relatively larger with each additional superintendency.
4 Before age fifty-eight, promotion rate decreases as age increases (controlling for length of tenure and number of superintendencies). This effect is small and subject to relatively large fluctuations.

The retirement effect seems largely irrelevant to other processes that lead to dissolution of a match, and is used only to justify limiting our attention to data on superintendents younger than fifty-eight. The other features of the deviations from strictly constant departures are generally consistent with previous studies of the duration of jobs (Lane and Andrew, 1955; Bartholomew, 1973; Tuma, 1976). Duration of matches in employment can often be approximated by distributions (e.g., the lognormal) characterized by a long right-side tail and a mode near, but not at, the left extreme point.

4 For a discussion of such career surfaces and an examination of them for the American college presidency, see Cohen and March (1974).
5 In the present paper only those deviations that are associated with duration of the match, number of matches, and age of superintendents are considered. Another source of deviation from the career patterns predicted by a pure chance model is heterogeneity among school districts (jobs) in their attractiveness. Jobs are graded by the size and location of the districts. This heterogeneity among jobs is clearer than is any grading among individual superintendents by their individual characteristics.

Performance Sampling Models

In a career system in which managerial performance is sampled, individual managers are sorted (i.e., fired, retained, or promoted) on the basis of estimates about their capabilities formed from observations of their performances. Such a system is describable in terms of the attributes of individuals that affect their performances (individual capabilities), sampling procedures by which performances are observed (observation rules), the inferences that transform a specific history of observations into a reputation (estimation rules), and the procedures by which a reputation is converted into a career through personal mobility (decision-rules).

In the models to be explored, the following assumptions are made:

Capabilities.   Individual capabilities are assumed to be summarized by the probability that a particular individual will execute a successful performance at a particular time.

Observation.   Opportunities for performances are assumed to occur at a fixed rate over time and a random sample of those performances is assumed to be observed. The observations are assumed to be without error. The history of observations of a particular individual is a record of successes and failures, each with a time subscript.

Estimation.   Once a minimum number of observations is recorded, reputation is assumed to be a moving average of the proportion of observed performances that are successes. The relative importance of past performances declines with distance from the present, where distance is measured in terms of both time and job changes.[6]

Decision.   Decisions are assumed to be dictated by a retention band defined on the range of possible reputations. Reputations higher than the band lead to promotion; reputations lower than the band lead to exit.

Thus, managers are assumed to bring some skills to their jobs. They and the world form estimates of those skills by sampling outcomes

---

6   A moving average accommodates reasonably well some standard observations about the greater impact of recent observations, i.e., recency effects; it does not accommodate observations about the differential impact of early observations, i.e., primacy effects. Adding primacy effects would have two modest consequences: (1) it would accentuate sampling error; and (2) it would reduce slightly the exit rate from a job after the first few performances. Neither of these affects the general implications drawn, though such a modification might be useful in a specific case. A more fundamental modification, in which the outcome of one performance affects the probability of success on a subsequent performance, is more complicated and has not been investigated.

determined (probabilistically) by the skills. On the basis of these estimates, managers are promoted, retained, or removed. A career is produced by a sequence of observed performances, their outcomes, and the resultant promotions or exits. Except for sampling error, variations in managerial careers will reflect variations in managerial skill. Better managers will be promoted faster and to better jobs than poorer managers.

Performance sampling models are essentially acceptance inspection schemes, in which a manager's performances over time are seen as a sample drawn from the universe of all possible performances. Decisions are made to accept (i.e., promote), reject (i.e., fire), or continue sampling (i.e., retain) a manager on the basis of the number of observations and the number of those observations in which the performances are judged to be failures.

Acceptance inspection plans usually seek a minimal cost procedure ensuring both that the probability of rejecting a lot does not exceed some fixed level, α, whenever the true proportion of failures is less than some number, p_0; and that the probability of accepting a lot does not exceed another fixed level, β, whenever the true proportion of failures is greater than another number, p_1. This leads to a continuation band defined by two parallel lines on an inspection chart, and is the basis for an extensive literature (Wald, 1947; Shiriaev, 1973).

The focus is reversed when performance sampling is considered as an organizational phenomenon. Instead of deriving decision-rules from prior objectives, we examine consequences arising from given decision-rules.

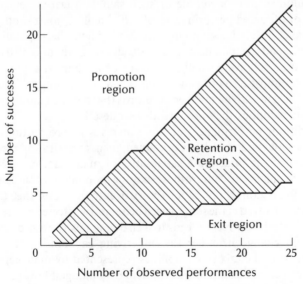

Figure 16.1. Acceptance graph for performance sample ($S = 0.90, F = 0.25$)

Decision-rules are assumed to be specified in terms of a fixed proportion of successes for promotion and some other fixed proportion of successes for exit. The resulting retention region is defined by two diverging lines on an inspection chart, as shown in figure 16.1. A manager's record of successes and failures can be plotted on this chart. Each observed performance leads to movement of one unit on the horizontal axis. If that performance is a success, it leads to movement of one unit on the vertical axis. The objective here is not to design a better performance sampling procedure but to understand the implications for careers of following such procedures.

The record of an individual is a sequential sample of successes and failures determined probabilistically by the rate of performances, the chance of success, and the chance of observation. Part of the variation in records will be due to differences in individual capabilities. Highly capable individuals will have, on average, better records than less capable individuals. Part of the variation in records, however, will be due to probabilistic variation in success and observation. Even if the chance of success in any particular performance were the same for all managers, there would be variation among managers in the proportion of successes. Even if the sampling proportion of observations were the same for all managers, there would be variation among managers in the actual number of observations taken, per unit time. In combination, these sources of random variation will produce differences in records of managerial performance that are not due to underlying differences in capabilities.

The number and magnitude of such sampling errors depend on the number of observed performances of individuals (a joint product of the performance rate, the sampling rate, and time), the capability of the individuals, and the total number of individuals on whom records are kept. If there are a relatively small number of observations, capabilities that are neither almost zero nor almost one, and a large number of individuals, there will be a nontrivial number of records that deviate considerably from the true capabilities they are intended to describe.

In addition, performance sampling involves record sorting. That is, managers with good records are promoted; managers with bad records exit. Regardless of the underlying capabilities of managers, records held by managers remaining in a job are those showing proportions of successes within the retention region. If reputations carry over to new jobs, then the mix of reputations involved at the start of each better job is affected by the decision-rules. This sorting of record leads to a changing mix of records even when there is no change in either the underlying capabilities of individual managers or in the mix of capabilities represented by managers in jobs.

These effects are explored initially here by looking at how performance sampling yields a distribution of records and thus a distribution of promotions and exits under conditions in which all individuals have the same capabilities. That is, variations in careers are due to chance fluctuations in a probabilistic process of gathering performance information about managers. First, a simplified form of performance sampling is considered, in which the relevance of past performance does not decay with time or change of job.

If it is assumed that each individual has the same, unchanging capability and that estimation procedures treat every observation as equally valid (i.e., there is no loss of memory or relevance for observed performance over time), exit and promotion rates per performance depend on:

P = the probability that a performance will be successful,
R = the probability that a performance will be observed,
F = the minimum acceptable proportion of observed performances that are successes (the exit level),
S = the maximum acceptable proportion of observed performances that are successes (the promotion level), and
L = the minimum number of observations required before decision.

Exit and promotion rates per unit time depend, in addition, on the performance rate over time.

The procedures described make promotion and exit a compound result of two stochastic processes: sampling and performance. The performance process generates a distribution of successes and failures. The sampling process selects a sample of those performances. If sampling and success rates are fixed and independent, they yield a fixed probability of an observed success for each period. These processes are, however, further affected by the delay in first judgment and the sequential decision process. Delay in the first judgment generates a distribution of first judgment times (from the sampling rate). The decision process sequentially chops the tails off the distribution of successes and failures and fills the next jobs with individuals who have records in the successful tail of the distribution.

Performance sampling generates a record of performance outcomes. A record has as its numerator the number of observed successes, K, and as its denominator the number of observations, J. Exit and promotion rates depend on the relation between this record and the retention region, (F,S), at a series of decision points beginning at $J = L$ and continuing through $J = L + 1$, $J = L + 2$, and so on.

If we ignore the optional stopping produced by the decision-rules, it is clear that K/J approaches P as J becomes indefinitely large, and that the variance of K/J around P is approximately $P(1 - P)/J$. Thus, exit or promotion 'errors' at the first decision point will become smaller as L becomes larger. If P lies within the retention region, exit and promotion rates at the first decision point will decline monotonically with L.

First decision points will be distributed across individuals. The performance, H, at which the Lth observation will be made is distributed as the negative binomial:

$$\text{Probability } (H = h) = \binom{h-1}{L-1} R^L (1-R)^{h-L}, \tag{1}$$

where $h \geq L$. For any number of observations, J, it is possible to determine U_J, the highest integer value for K that makes $K/J < S$; and W_J, the lowest integer value for K that makes $K/J > F$. U_J and W_J correspond to the acceptance and rejection numbers of acceptance sampling, a_m and r_m, in Wald's notation. At the first decision point, $J = L$, the probability that a record will lie within the retention region is given by

$$\text{Probability } (U_L \geq K \geq W_L) = \sum_{i=W_L}^{U_L} \left[\binom{L}{i} P^i (1-P)^{L-i} \right]; \tag{2}$$

therefore, D_1, the performance immediately preceding a first decision departure is distributed according to

$$\text{Probability } (D_1 = h) = \binom{h-1}{L-1} R^L (1-R)^{h-L}$$

$$\left\{ 1 - \sum_{i=W_L}^{U_L} \left[\binom{L}{i} P^i (1-P)^{L-i} \right] \right\} \tag{3}$$

Although this fairly simple expression for first decision departures over time can be generated, nth decision departures are more complicated. In particular, the probability that K/J will be in the retention region for $J = T$ is not independent of the value of K/J at $T - 1$, and thus the effect of the decision truncation of the distribution when $T > L$ cannot be ignored. For any particular set of values for the parameters, calculating the result is frequently not overly complicated, but a general analytical expression for the distribution of all departures over time is relatively cumbersome to write and involves a cascade of conditional probabilities. However, it is possible to show the results for selected cases. This is done for promotion probabilities in figure 16.2.

The distributions shown in figure 16.2 are plotted across performances in the first job. Converting a performance axis to a time axis requires specifying the rate of performance over time. Extending the analysis to subsequent jobs is not so simple, but the general character of the outcomes can be derived. Individuals entering their first jobs are assumed in the model to have no records. In second and subsequent jobs, they bring with them a record in which $K/J \geq S$. As a result, it is clear that departures in the

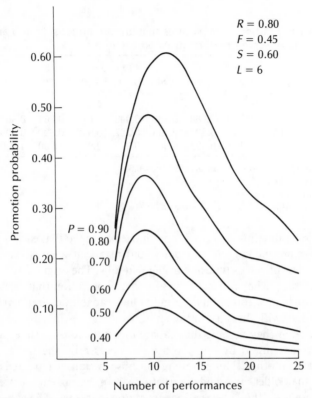

Figure 16.2. Promotion probability as a function of number of performances for various capabilities (*P*)

second job will have a higher proportion of promotions (rather than exits) than will departures in the first job. This assumes that the only individuals who have a second job are promoted directly from a first. Among the Wisconsin superintendents, the analysis is complicated by some people exiting from a first job and subsequently (after an interruption of one or more years) returning to a second. This moderates, but does not change the effect, as long as the numbers of such people are fairly small. It is also possible, of course, that the record accumulated during the interruption brings such superintendents back with starting records in which $K/J \geq S$. In the third and subsequent jobs, starting values for K/J are not systematically different from those on entering the previous job (if the retention region is the same for all jobs), but J becomes systematically larger from one job to the next. As a result, it is also clear that each subsequent job will have a higher proportion of all departures that are promotions. Some results for selected values are shown in table 16.1

Table 16.1 Proportion of departures that are promotions, by job and value of P, first 12 observed performances on each job[a]

	Value of P								
	0.10	0.20	0.30	0.40	0.50	0.60	0.70	0.80	0.90
Job									
1	0.001	0.020	0.088	0.230	0.442	0.674	0.861	0.964	0.997
2	0.004	0.047	0.201	0.495	0.787	0.940	0.990	0.999	1.000
3	0.015	0.131	0.493	0.849	0.972	0.996	1.000	1.000	1.000

[a] R-probability of observing a performance = 0.80
F-exit level = 0.45
S-promotion level = 0.60
L-minimum number of observations = 6

In the discussion thus far not only has it been assumed that each individual has the same unchanging capability, but also that all observations are equally relevant across time and changes in jobs. The original assumptions were different. They reflected the ordinary expectation that relevance of past performance for estimating individual capabilities in a current job would decay with distance in time and with changes in jobs. Estimators act as though they assume that capabilities change over time, and that capabilities required by one job are not necessarily the same as those required by another. Thus, more recent observations are treated as more relevant than older ones, and observations from the current job are treated as more relevant than observations from previous ones. The consequence of this is to increase sampling error and thus (if P lies within the retention region) to reduce the rate of change in departure rates as a function of tenure in a match and number of previous matches. The weighting of recent experiences more heavily than distant ones increases sampling error, if P is constant across individuals and time. It reflects the fact that such weighting schemes surrender some precision in estimating P, if it is constant, in order to protect against the possibility that it is not. Departure rates will decline over duration of a match and across a sequence of matches, but the decline will be slower than would be observed if all outcomes were counted without regard to their recency. The magnitude of the difference depends on the specific estimation function assumed, but the data from Wisconsin suggest a relatively high discount rate on the relevance of past successes to current reputation.

Performance sampling models predict the basic qualitative features of data on the length of Wisconsin superintendencies, as well as other data on job duration. For reasonable parameters, they will produce promotion and exit rates that rise briefly at the beginning of a match and then decline with duration, and they predict that the ratio of promotion rates to exit rates will increase over a sequence of jobs. These qualitative characteristics are not unique properties of performance sampling models. Theories of social sorting and mutual adaptation in social matches both predict that promotion and exit rates will decline with increased duration of a match. Although neither theory predicts the relatively low level of departure rates in the early years of a match, it is not hard to graft a distribution of first decision times onto either in such a way as to produce a 'honeymoon'. The changing ratio of promotions to exits is easily accommodated within a social sorting theory, less easily within a mutual adaptation theory.

A potential advantage of a performance sampling model is that it conforms to ordinary descriptions of performance evaluation and does not require either that there be heterogeneity in the capabilities of individuals or that their capabilities be changing over time. If the population of managers varies in fit to a match, either across individuals or across duration of the match, performance sampling will (under fairly general conditions) produce the same basic results. But even if they do not vary, or if they improve not their fit to the match but their capabilities for promotion, performance sampling will still yield the same pattern. This last property of performance sampling can be exhibited by considering three variations of the models and comparing them to the observed pattern of promotions and exits from Wisconsin superintendencies.[7] The three versions posit different basic ideas about superintendents:

---

7   When the models were compared with the Wisconsin data, the same parameters were used for all three cases, except for the assumptions about individual capabilities. Some effort was made to find a set of parameters that fit Wisconsin data reasonably well, but the search was not exhaustive through the parameter space. The acceptance region was set at (0.25, 0.95) for all jobs, the sampling rate at 0.30, and the first decision point after two observations. In addition, it was necessary to specify the rate at which performances occurred over time (4 per year) and the reputation function that made the relative importance of past successes and failures decline with the passage of time and change of jobs, an exponentially weighted moving average. After n observations, of which m were successes, the reputation of an individual manager was given by:

$$\sum_{k=1}^{m} 1.1^{D(k)} \Big/ \sum_{j=1}^{n} 1.1^{D(j)}$$

where $D(k)$ is the distance from the start of a career to the kth success, and $D(j)$ is the distance from the start of a career to the jth observation, and where distance is simply the number of performances observed thus far in a career plus eight times the number of job changes. Thus, a job change is treated as reducing the relevance of past successes and failures by the same amount as the instantaneous passage of the time required for eight observations. Since only superintendents who were less than 58 years old were considered, some assumptions were required about the entering ages of individuals. Superintendents were assumed to begin their last pre-superintendency job at ages uniformly distributed from age twenty-six to forty. Finally some superintendents were assumed to have had interruptions in their careers. That is, they left a superintendency to go to some other job and subsequently returned to a superintendency. This accounts for a minority of the cases; but in the model, superintendents

Version 1: Heterogeneity. The pool of potential superintendents has a distribution of individual capabilities.[8] Those capabilities remain constant for any one individual, but the average capability of the group of remaining superintendents can change over time.

Version 2: Learning. The pool consists of individuals who initially have the same capabilities. However, an individual's capability improves with each observed performance. Learning rates are the same for each individual, but the history of experiences may differ.[9]

Version 3: Homogeneity. The pool consists of individuals, each of whom has the same capability. Those capabilities remain constant throughout their experience.[10]

The three versions are different. In the first, individuals differ but do not change over time (although the mix does); in the second, individuals are initially the same but change over time as a result of their experiences; in the third, individuals are indistinguishable in capabilities and do not change with experience. Superimposed on these differences is a performances sampling process. In each case, individuals accumulate records on the basis of experience and are promoted or exit on the basis of their reputations.

Each version of a performance sampling model predicts annual rates of promotion, exit, and arrival at age fifty-eight across complete histories of three (or fewer) consecutive appointments to superintendencies, including the effects of interruptions in careers between jobs. More precisely, each version predicts a distribution of such histories.[11] The

---

who exited returned to a new superintendency after some number of years (during which they aged and changed the relevance of past reputation by the equivalent of one additional job change) at a rate determined by parameters estimated in an earlier paper (March and March, 1977).

8   The initial pool of potential superintendents is assumed to include individuals with a uniform distribution of capabilities ranging from $P = 0.30$ to $P = 0.60$.

9   The initial capability is the same for all potential superintendents ($P_0 = 0.45$). Whenever a performance is observed, the individual manager involved learns. If P_J is the probability of success on the Jth observed performances, the probability of success on the next performance will be $P_J + 0.003(1 - P_J)$.

10   The capability is fixed at $P = 0.50$.

11   The results discussed are based on monte carlo simulations of the models. The models take individuals from the start of their final pre-superintendency jobs and follow them through their careers until they become fifty-eight, or leave the ranks of superintendents permanently. The predictions from the models are compared with the observed data through 1972 for Wisconsin superintendents who began their careers between 1940 and 1972. From either the data or the models we can obtain the age-and-tenure-specific rates of promotion to another superintendency and exit for first, second, and subsequent superintendencies. The analyses reported are based on comparing these outcomes. In some cases, the report is in terms of the departure rate (the sum of promotion and exit rates) or the continuation rate (1-departure rate).

versions can be compared with each other and with the data in a number of ways, but the interpretation must be cautious. The number of parameters is relatively large, and the observed data on age-and-tenure-specific departure rates are, in many cases, based on only a few observations. No attempt was made to find the best-fitting estimates for the parameters of the models, and the comments that follow are limited to those that are relatively insensitive to changes in parameters.

Three things can be said with modest confidence about these three versions of a performance sampling model. First, performance sampling generates the same basic pattern of predictions under any of the versions specified. The correlations across the predicted career surfaces of pairs in the versions are 0.47, 0.36, and 0.33;[12] and the general character of the surfaces is the same in each case.

The specific quantitative predictions are not, of course, independent of the specific assumptions, about the magnitudes and character of distributions of capabilities (as well as other parameters). In particular, it should be noted that the version in which variation among individuals is assumed yields a different pattern of departures during the (early) pre-superintendency phase of careers. Specifically, exit rates are higher than in the other models. These exits reduce skill heterogeneity among individuals who are promoted to a first superintendency. Since performance sampling will obscure moderate variations among individuals, but not large ones, the closer you come to the top of a career chain, the less the variation, and the more version 1 and version 3 become indistinguishable. Similarly, version 2 in which learning is assumed, will not produce the same qualitative results as the others under all conditions. If learning is rapid or the learning experience prolonged, there should be a tendency for promotion rates to rise while exit rates decline. What is significant here is that such a clear long-run implication of a model is not seen in the short run.

The similarities among results under a wide range of assumptions about the attributes of individuals suggest that sampling phenomena associated with performance evaluation can become significant enough to mask variations in the underlying attributes of individuals, even in cases in which those underlying attributes are known to affect job performance. If the world were a performance sampling world of the kind described, it would

12   All of the correlations across career surfaces reported in this section consider the 170 points in the first two superintendencies of careers for which an estimate of the age-and-tenure-specific departure rate was based on at least 12 cases in the observed data. 104 of the points involve the first superintendency, and 66 involve the second. The correlations compared estimates of departure rates generated by the model with estimates obtained from the data. Because of the relatively high attrition rate, most of the points are concentrated in the early tenures and ages between thirty and forty-nine.

be difficult, on the basis of observing the structure of careers, to tell whether managers differed considerably or were truly indistinguishable.

Second, all of the versions improve on simple Markov models of the process, but none of them is a very precise predictor of observed rates. When observed continuation rates associated with duration of match and age of superintendent are correlated with the predicted rates of each version of the model, the correlations are consistently greater than zero. The correlations are not high, ranging from 0.26 to 0.17.

The process shows significant sampling variation in the estimates of age-and-tenure-specific departure rates when the cohort size is the same as is found in the Wisconsin data. When several probabilistically identical Monte Carlo simulations of the same version of the model are correlated with each other, using cohorts of the same approximate size as the data cohort, correlations across replications of the same model are only slightly higher than those found in comparing such simulations with the data. This indicates that the models would be unlikely to fit the data much better than they do, even if the theory precisely captured reality; but one should perhaps be conservative about using such a result as a basis for confidence in a theory.

Third, each of the models captures the qualitative features already noted as characteristics of the data. In the models, as in the data, both promotion rate and exit rate show a similar pattern as a function of tenure, controlling for age and number of superintendencies. The rates are relatively low the first year, rise to a peak about the second, third, or fourth year, and decline irregularly thereafter. The exit rate appears to peak a little later than the promotion rate. Before age fifty-eight, the relative magnitudes of promotion rate and exit rate change as a function of the number of superintendencies served. Promotion rates become relatively larger from one superintendency to the next. Before age fifty-eight, promotion rates decrease as age increases, controlling for length of match and number of superintendencies. This effect is small and subject to relatively large fluctuations. In all these respects, the models match the data.

The consistency of the models with the data suggests performance sampling explanations for some phenomena that have more commonly been interpreted otherwise. In addition, it is possible to suggest some reasons why promotion rates decline with age and why exit rates peak later than promotion rates. Since age does not enter explicitly into the models, any predicted age effect is spurious. Within the models, promotion rate decreases as age increases, controlling for length of match and number of superintendencies, apparently because age is related to differences in the past records of superintendents that are not controlled by length of match and number of earlier superintendencies, specifically such things as whether arrival at the present superintendency has followed directly upon departure from a previous one and the length of the record in earlier jobs.

Similarly, the fact that exit rates in the model (as in the data) peak slightly later in the duration of a match than promotion rates has a natural performance sampling interpretation. Exit rates peak later because of record sorting. Individuals beginning a job tend to have good records. That is how they were promoted to the job. Over time, some of them will accumulate enough new performance failures to reach the exit point, but on the average it will take longer to reach that point than the promotion point, given that they begin with a successful record.

Within the limitations of the data and the character of the models, these specific performance sampling models predict patterns of movement through careers that are consistent with the Wisconsin data. Personnel evaluation and promotion procedures having the basic characteristics of performance sampling can be expected to produce outcomes similar to those observed in Wisconsin even under circumstances that deviate considerably (as in the case of version 3) from the rationale of those procedures and common interpretations of those outcomes. If managers get ahead because they do well, and the procedures by which they are evaluated involve performance sampling, about the same pattern of careers should be expected regardless of moderate heterogeneity among them in their abilities to perform successfully on the job, or to learn over the course of the job.

Discussion

The formation of a match between an individual and a job in an administrative or career hierarchy is based on imperfect information gathered partly through the observation of performances. On the basis of such observations, organizations sort individual managers into reputational categories. People come to be viewed as incompetent, and are fired; as exceptionally qualified, and are promoted; or as adequate, and are retained. Similarly, managers sort organizations into reputational categories. Organizations come to be viewed as unmanageable, and are avoided; as outstanding, and are sought; or as adequate, and are neither avoided nor pursued.

Since performance sampling is subject to sampling variation, at least some of the sorting among individuals and organizations and the variations in careers and turnover they produce could be due to sampling error, rather than to individual differences in administrative competence or organizational differences in manageability. This seems particularly likely near the top levels in an administrative career hierarchy, where the samples of performance are comparatively small, their evaluation comparatively difficult, and the variation among individuals at the end of a series of evaluations comparatively small.

Performance sampling processes show properties that are independent of their details and are of some importance for appreciating how careers can yield subjectively compelling impressions of causal determinacy, as in the following specific examples.

1 *False record effect*. A group of managers of identical (moderate) ability will show considerable variation in their performance records in the short run. Some will be found at one end of the distribution and will be viewed as ineffective. The longer a manager stays in a job, the less the probable difference between the observed record of performance and actual ability. Time on the job increases the expected sample of observations, reduces expected sampling error, and thus reduces the chance that the manager (of moderate ability) will either be promoted or exit.

2 *Hero effect*. Within a group of managers of varying abilities, the faster the rate of promotion, the less likely it is to be justified. Performance records are produced by a combination of underlying ability and sampling variation. Managers who have good records are more likely to have high ability than managers who have poor records, but the reliability of the differentiation is small when records are short.

3 *Disappointment effect*. On the average, new managers will be a disappointment. The performance records by which managers are evaluated are subject to sampling error. Since a manager is promoted to a new job on the basis of a good previous record, the proportion of promoted managers whose past records are better than their abilities will be greater than the proportion whose past records are poorer. As a result, on the average, managers will do less well in their new jobs than they did in their old ones, and observers will come to believe that higher level jobs are more difficult than lower level ones, even if they are not.

The generality of such characteristics of performance sampling is supported by the present examination of three alternative variants of a performance sampling model. Although the three variants are quite different and make different assumptions about individual managers, they all yield results similar to each other, and they all capture the major features of data on a 33-year record of careers in educational administration in Wisconsin. Apparently, the general behavior of these models is due less to assumptions about managers than to assumptions about the process of evaluating success and failure in management. Specifically, if managers are evaluated on the basis of critical incidents that are infrequent (but not rare) and accumulate reputations based on those evaluations, aggregate career results will be dominated by chance variations in sample observations, and patterns in top administrative careers will not be much affected either by variations in initial skill among entrants into the pool of administrators or by learning on the job.

There are reasons for anticipating nearly random careers among top administrators in educational organizations (March and March, 1977). The social sorting that takes place on the way to the career and during it, the ambiguity of judgment within educational organizations, and the stability of educational activities often seem to operate to make superintendents indistinguishable. The present results reinforce the idea that indistinguishability among managers is a joint property of the individuals being evaluated and the process by which they are evaluated. Performance sampling models show how careers may be the consequence of erroneous interpretations of varitions in performances produced by equivalent managers. But they also indicate that the same pattern of careers could be the consequence of unreliable evaluation of managers who do, in fact, differ, or of managers who do, in fact, learn over the course of their experience.

The role of performance sampling in other organizations or matches is unclear, but there is reason to suspect that the model may be applicable in other settings. For example, a key assumption of the performance sampling model is that promotion and retention decisions depend only on the proportion of successes observed and not on the total number of observations on which that proportion is based, once the first decision point is reached. Since such an assumption ignores the unreliability of estimates based on small samples, it might be questioned as improbable, or perhaps listed as unique to educational organizations. In fact, the assumption is consistent with experimental studies of individual decision behavior. Tversky and Kahneman, as well as others (Tversky and Kahneman, 1971; Kahneman and Tversky, 1972; Tversky and Kahneman, 1974; Slovic, Fischhoff, and Lichtenstein, 1977), have cited considerable evidence that individuals confronted with problems requiring the estimation of proportions act as though sample size were substantially irrelevant to the reliability of their estimates. The present analysis can be viewed as an extension of those studies as well as some indirect confirmation of the generality of their results.

The plausibility of the process suggests that other social pairings should be expected to show patterns attributable to the ways in which performance sampling generates reputations not necessarily identical to the underlying distribution of qualities. Husbands and wives, buyers and sellers, landlords and tenants, students and teachers all resolve some elements of uncertainty about their choices through the sampling of performance in a match. Where the variation in qualities is modest, as it often is in a socially-controlled system of matches, the opportunities for evaluation infrequent, and the memory (or presumed relevance) of previous experience declines over time, many of the details of a system of matches among those individuals, institutions, or goods permitted to enter the pool of eligibles will be explicable in terms of sampling variation in performance evaluation. If there are differences in individual attributes, these differences will not translate reliably into differences in reputations. If there are no differences in attributes, there will nevertheless appear to be some; and those appearances will be nearly as compelling as they would be if the true differences were substantial.

References

Bartholomew, David J. (1973) *Stochastic Models for Social Processes*, 2nd edn London: Wiley.

Becker, Gary S. (1973) A theory of marriage: part I. *Journal of Political Economy*, 81: 813–46.

Blumen, Isadore, Marvin Kogan, and Philip J. McCarthy (1955) *The Industrial Mobility of Labor as a Probability Process*. Ithaca, NY: Cornell University Press.

Deutsch, Karl W., and William G. Madow (1961) A note on the appearance of wisdom in large bureacratic organizations. *Behavioral Science*, 6: 72–8.

Edwards, John N. (1969) Familial behavior as social exchange. *Journal of Marriage and the Family*, 31: 518–26.

Hannan, Michael T., Nancy B. Tuma, and Lyle P. Groenveld (1977) Income and marital events: evidence from an income maintenance experiment. *American Journal of Sociology*, 82: 1186–211.

Kahneman, Daniel, and Amos Tversky (1972) Subjective probability: a judgment of representativeness. *Cognitive Psychology*, 3: 430–54.

Knezevich, Steven (ed.), (1971) *The American School Superintendent*. Washington: American Association of School Administrators.

Lane, K. F., and J. E. Andrew (1955) A method of labour turnover analysis. *Journal of the Royal Statistical Society*, A118: 296–323.

March, James C., and James G. March (1977) Almost random careers: the Wisconsin school superintendency, 1940–1972. *Administrative Science Quarterly*, 22: 377–409.

March, James G. (1978) Bounded rationality, ambiguity, and the engineering of choice. *Bell Journal of Economics* 9: 587–608.

March, James G., and Herbert A. Simon (1958) *Organizations*. New York: Wiley.

Nelson, Phillip (1970) Information and consumer behavior. *Journal of Political Economy*, 78: 311–29.

Rosener, Lynn (1975) 'Identification of problems associated with household pre- and post-purchase information behavior'. Unpublished honors thesis, Department of Economics, Stanford University.

Scitovsky, Tibor (1976) *The Joyless Economy*. New York: Oxford University Press.

Shiriaev, Albert N. (1973) *Statistical Sequential Analysis: Optimal Stopping Rules.* Lisa and Judah Rosenblatt (trans.), Providence, RI: American Mathematical Society.

Singer, Burton, and Seymour Spilerman (1974) Social mobility models for heterogeneous populations. In Herbert L. Costner (ed.), *Sociological Methodology* 1973-4: 356-401. San Francisco: Jossey-Bass.

Slovic, Paul, Baruch Fischhoff, and Sarah Lichtenstein (1977) Behavioral decision theory. *Annual Review of Psychology*, 28: 1-39.

Spence, A. Michael (1974) *Market Signalling*. Cambridge, MA: Harvard University Press.

Stigler, George (1961) The economics of information. *Journal of Political Economy*, 69: 213-25.

Tuma, Nancy B. (1976) Rewards, resources, and the rate of mobility: a nonstationary multivariate stochastic model. *American Sociological Review*, 41: 338-60.

Tversky, Amos, and Daniel Kahneman (1971) The belief in the law of small numbers. *Psychological Bulletin,* 76: 105-10.

Tversky, Amos, and Daniel Kahneman (1974) Judgment under uncertainty: heuristics and biases. *Science*, 185: 1124-31.

White, Harrison C. (1963) Uses of mathematics in sociology. In James C. Charlesworth (ed.), *Mathematics and the Social Sciences:* Philadelphia: American Academy of Political and Social Science, pp. 77-94.

White, Harrison C. (1970) *Chains of Opportunity: System Models of Mobility in Organizations*. Cambridge, MA: Harvard University Press.

Wald, Abraham (1947) *Sequential Analysis*. New York: Wiley.

17

Ambiguity and Accounting:
The Elusive Link between Information
and Decision-Making

James G. March

Abstract

This paper argues that theories of choice, as reflected in microeconomics, n-person game theory, or statistical decision theory, are incomplete and potentially misleading bases for thinking about and modifying the design of information systems, including accounting systems. The argument stems from recent behavioral research on the ambiguities surrounding individual and organizational decision-making. It is developed around four simple assertions:

1 Contemporary ideas about information engineering tie strategies for seeking, organizing, and utilizing information to ideas of anticipatory, consequential choice as pictured in decision theory.
2 Behavioral studies of decision-making in organizations indicate that the portrayal of decision-making and information found in decision theory ignores or significantly underestimates the ambiguities of choice.
3 Analysis of discrepancies between the actual behavior of decision-makers and the recommendations of decision theory shows that the behavior often

This paper was first published in *Àccounting, Organizations and Society* 12 (1987) 153–168. It is an extension and elaboration of an address given at the annual meetings of the American Accounting Association, New York, 22 August 1986. It is based on research supported by grants from the Spencer Foundation, the Stanford Graduate School of Business, and the Hoover Institution. The author is grateful for the comments of Robert H. Aston, Gary C. Biddle, Robert A. Burgelman, George Foster, Anthony G. Hopwood, Charles T. Horngren, Maureen F. McNichols, Johan P. Olsen, James M. Patell, Jeffrey Pfeffer, Allyn Romanow, Robert J. Swieringa, Eugene J. Webb and Mark A. Wolfson.

introduces elements of good sense not routinely recognized within the theory, so an information system that is closely articulated with choices in the way anticipated by decision theory is often incomplete.

4 As a result, the engineering of information might profit from conceptions of decision-making and information that blend the traditions of theories of choice with an understanding of the traditions of history, culture and literature.

Introduction

The history of information engineering can be written as a story of the search for a theory, a conception of information that might, in principle, be used to justify or improve the information processing instruments and procedures used in accounting and other information systems (Horngren, 1981; Tinker, Merino and Neimark, 1982; Davis, Menon and Morgan, 1982). The intention in this paper is not to write such a history but to examine contemporary information doctrine. The argument is that efforts to embed information engineering in theories of choice, as reflected in microeconomics, n-person game theory, or statistical decision theory, are clearly useful; but they are incomplete and potentially misleading for thinking about and modifying the design of information systems.

The argument stems, in part, from recent behavioral research on individual and organizational decison-making. It is developed around four simple assertions:

1 Contemporary ideas about information engineering tie strategies for seeking, organizing, and utilizing information to ideas of anticipatory, consequential choice as pictured in decision theory.

2 Behavioral studies of decision-making in organizations indicate that the portrayal of decision-making and information found in decision theory ignores or significantly underestimates the ambiguities of choice.

3 Analysis of discrepancies between the actual behavior of decision-makers and the recommendations of decision theory shows that the behavior often introduces elements of good sense not routinely recognized within the theory, so an information system that is closely articulated with choices in the way anticipated by decision theory is often incomplete.

4 As a result, the engineering of information might profit from conceptions of decision-making and information that blend the traditions of theories of choice with the traditions of history, culture, and literature.

Information and Decision-Making

Most recent writing on information in organizations links it to decision-making. Information systems, such as accounting, are seen as part of a decision-support system for managers, financial analysts, stockholders, or others with a stake in the organization (Keen and Scott Morton, 1978; Demski, 1980; Sprague and Carlson, 1982). The axiomatic foundations are found in statistical decision theory, n-person game theory, and microeconomics. The main uncertainty in decision-making is portrayed as ignorance about future consequences of possible current actions, including ignorance about the knowledge possessed by others and their probable actions, and the main rationale for information is its role in reducing that uncertainty.

Rather early in the development of information engineering, these connections to choice led to concern with problems of estimation and inference (Trueblood and Cyert, 1957; Morgenstern, 1963). It is not trivial for an organization to assure that the events observed are representative of the universe, that they are observed accurately and consistently, and that models for analysis of data are specified so as to lead to valid estimates and inferences. For example, in classical sampling theory, where observations are assumed to be independent, the accuracy (i.e., the standard error) of an estimate depends on the variability in the universe and the number of observations (sample size). This leads to an emphasis on increasing accuracy through increasing sample size. In organizational life, however, the independence of observations cannot be assumed, so sample size declines in (relative) importance, and some of the more powerful strategies for improving the accuracy of information involve increasing the independence of observations rather than simply increasing their numbers.

Contemporary theories of decision-making, however, are less inclined to highlight biases in estimation and inference, and more inclined to focus on two additional complications in the use of information for making decisions in organizations: those of limited rationality and conflict of interest. The fundamental idea of *limited rationality* is that not everything can be known, that decision-making is based on incomplete information about alternatives and their consequences. There are costs associated with gathering, organizing, and retrieving information (Simon, 1955; March and Simon, 1958). From the point of view of rational choice, therefore, expected costs of information must be justified by expected benefits. The expected benefits from an information source are well specified in single-person, single-period decision theory. They are equal to the expected value of a choice situation if the information were available (taking into account its expectation) minus the expected value of the situation without the information (Lindley, 1971). The formulation yields some precise calculations in well-defined specific cases. It also yields some familiar caveats of information: Don't pay good money for bad data; don't ask a question if you already know the answer. Extensions to multi-person, multi-period decisions are more complicated, less completely understood, and a major focus of contemporary work (Hilton, 1981).

The fundamental idea of *conflict of interest* is that an organization is a coalition of individuals and groups pursuing different objectives (March, 1962; Cyert and March, 1963). As a result, information in organizations is not innocent. Accounting and accounting standards are arenas of power politics (Horngren, 1984). Information providers try to shape decisions through judicious management of the information under their control (Akerlof, 1970; Rothschild, 1973). Unless an organization can ensure that information providers will not lie or withhold information that should be valuable to a decision-maker, classical statistics loses some of its force. Interest in designing cost-effective incentives that induce rational, self-interested agents to be honest in their reports is a major theme of contemporary theories of agency (Ross, 1973; Hirshleifer and Riley, 1979; Fama, 1980; Milgrom, 1981; Levinthal, 1984).

To a student of organizations, the flowering of information economics and agency theory as bases for microeconomics and information engineering is a gratifying reminder that empirical research can affect theoretical conceptions. Twenty to thirty years ago, behavioral students of organizations criticized theories of the firm for ignoring limited rationality and conflict of interest in decision-making (March and Simon, 1958; Cyert and March, 1963). Although one may question whether contemporary information economics attends to these problems with all the delicacy and grace that they deserve, they have certainly captured the attention of many economists, including applied economists concerned with accounting (Demski, 1980; Verrecchia, 1982).

Ambiguities in the Link between Information and Decision-Making

Without denying the importance of contributions made from a perspective build around limited rationality and conflict of interest, more recent research on decision-making in organizations indicates that such a frame may provide an incomplete representation of the problems of decision-making, thus possibly also of information engineering. These additional qualifications can be summarized in terms of four observations about the ambiguities of organizational decision-making:

Observation 1: the ambiguities of preferences. The preferences of organizations, their owners, and their managers are frequently less clear than is assumed in theories of rational choice. Preferences are often vague or contradictory. The develop over time, changing as a result of experience and the decision process.

The conception of choice enshrined in the axioms of contemporary decision theory and microeconomics assumes optimization over given alternatives on the basis of two guesses: The first guess is about the uncertain future consequences that will follow from alternative actions that might be taken. The second guess is about the uncertain future preferences the decision-maker will have with respect to those consequences when they are realized.

The first guess has received most of the attention from students of decision-making. Much of modern management science, micro-economics, and operations research is devoted either to improving the optimization calculations involved in complex choices, or to improving the procedures for estimating the probability distribution over future consequences conditional on an action. No comparable effort has been devoted to understanding or improving either the generation of alternatives or the guess about future preferences (Von Weizsacker, 1971; Winston, 1980). For the most part, both alternatives and preferences are taken as given. In practice, of course, management science and decision theoretic techniques are often used by skillful decision-makers to help discover alternatives and clarify objectives (Lindley, 1971); but decision theory yields little assistance in that effort. It treats the preferences as controlling choice but excludes their development from consideration.

The usual justification for exempting preferences from engineering is a commitment to value neutrality. Whereas one can claim that a particular optimization technique has certain unambiguously admirable qualities, or that a particular treatment of data has certain attractive properties of statistical efficiency, no comparable claim is thought to be possible with respect to procedures for preference engineering. The argument can be faulted both for ignoring the ways in which any decision calculus favors preferences measurable within that calculus over preferences that are not, and for failing to recall that the classic trinity is one of truth, beauty, and justice, rather than truth alone. But it is not the intent here to doubt the virtues of decision-engineering that is, as nearly as possible, independent of the specific value premises that a decision-maker may wish to entertain.

The argument being made is narrower and more technical than that. It is that the preferences assumed in decision theory differ in important ways from the preferences of human decision-makers.[1] Within the theory, preferences are assumed either to be consistent, stable, and exogenous, or to be beneficially convertible to preferences that are. Such assumptions are clearly deficient as a description of actual human preferences. Both individuals and organizations regularly have inconsistent preferences, wanting things that are conflicting, yet doing little to resolve the inconsistency. Preferences change over time, and predicting future preferences is not easy.[2] And while preferences are expected to control actions and often do, experience with actions and their consequences affects preferences at the same time. That is, preferences are endogenous to a decision process.

Each of these features of preferences complicates decision theory (March, 1978; Elster, 1979; 1983). The theory deals awkwardly with inconsistent preferences that cannot be reconciled through utility trade-offs. Since preferences change over time and the preferences relevant to a decision are the uncertain future preferences that will be held when the consequences of current action are realized, the usefulness of a theory that assumes stable preferences is in doubt. And when preferences are endogenous, decision-making cannot be decomposed into separable problems of defining prior preferences and taking subsequent actions, thereby compromising the basic framework of conventional expected utility decision theory. Although it is possible that the theory may be suitably robust against such difficulties, the assumptions of consistency, stability, and exogeneity are *prima facie* suspect.

It might be imagined that the problems posed by ambiguous preferences could be avoided by training human decision-makers to have the desired consistent, stable and exogenous preferences; but such an approach requires more confidence in the virtues of unambiguous preferences than our experience supports. It is not hard to specify conditions under which poorer decisions will be made by specifying explicit trade-offs than by struggling with inconsistent desires. For example, Camus (1951) argues that simple rules against killing, though they clearly cannot be sustained as absolute against the claims of other values, consistently lead to more moral action than do efforts to place an explicit value on life and calculate net benefits (March, 1979). It is not hard to specify conditions under which an intelligent decision-maker would prefer to have or anticipate changing preferences (Kreps, 1979). For example, it is not clear why we should want to value jogging or eating the same at all times (Winston, 1980; 1985).

---

1   Throughout this paper, a conception of preferences is assumed in which preferences are taken to exist independent of choices. The same problems exist, but in slightly different form, in a 'revealed preference' theory.

2   For a contrary opinion, see Stigler and Becker (1977).

And it is not hard to specify conditions under which the construction of preferences in the course of making choices is more appropriately encouraged than avoided. For example, parents routinely require children to attend cultural events they would otherwise not attend in order to help them develop a taste for fine music or art (March, 1971). In short, the ambiguous preferences observed in actual human decision-makers often are more intelligent than are the kinds of preferences normally specified in decision theory (March, 1978).

These complications in preferences have led to suggestions that decision-engineers might well spend more time understanding the implications of intertemporal comparisons of preferences, endogenous changes in preferences, and the problem of optimal inconsistency among preferences and between preferences and actions – sometimes called the optimal sin problem. A similar set of conclusions could be extended to information engineering in the service of decision-making. Information systems contribute to the construction of preferences as well as to their implementation, to their complication as well as to their simplification (Follett, 1930).

> Observation 2: The ambiguities of relevance. Organizational decision-making often has less coherence than decision theory attributes to it. Problems, solutions, and actions are frequently only loosely coupled, or connected by their simultaneity rather than their consequentiality. Information strategies are relatively independent of specific anticipated decisions.

In decision-theoretic treatments, information strategies are consciously designed to resolve uncertainties about future states of the world that are relevant to choice. Actual information behavior in organizations in general and more specifically in decision-making often does not fit such a characterization very well. Information seems to be gathered and processed with scant regard for its relevance to specific decisions. In general, empirical studies of organizational decision-making indicate that most theories of choice overestimate the coherence of decision processes (Cohen, March and Olsen, 1972; Cohen and March, 1986). Organizations seem to be loosely coupled systems in which the connections between problems and solutions are obscure, as are the connections between means and ends, between action today and action yesterday, and between action in one part of the organization and action in another part (March and Olsen, 1976; Weick, 1976). People, problems, solutions, and choice opportunities seem to be combined in confusing ways that make predicting agenda and outcomes difficult (Kingdon, 1984; March and Olsen, 1986).

Observations such as these have led some people to describe decision processes in organizations as completely without order. Others, however, have tried to specify alternative conceptions of order that might be used to understand the process. One example of the latter is the garbage can model of organizational choice (Cohen, March and Olsen, 1972). Garbage can models substitute a temporal order for a consequential order among solutions, problems and decision-makers. In a garbage can decision process, the explicit intentions of actors and the consequential coherence of choices are often lost in context dependent flows of problems, solutions, people, and choices. Solutions are linked to problems, and decision-makers to choices, primarily by their simultaneity (March and Olsen, 1986).

Studies of the uses of information in policy-making suggest a similar disconnection of information strategies from decision strategies. Policy-analysis offices are disconnected from policy makers, yet continue to produce policy papers (Feldman, 1986). Research reports produce diffuse changes in world-views, rather than direct effects on decisions (Weiss, 1977). The generation and elaboration of information about problems and solutions is sustained more by professional and sub-culture norms than by anticipation of a direct contribution to decisions.

There are a number of possible rationalizations for the divorce of an information structure from the decision structure in organizations. It is probably true, for example, that tight linkages between information and its uses increase the vulnerability of decision-makers to manipulation by information providers (Feldman and March, 1981). It is also probably true that future decision options are sufficiently obscure as to make the possible benefits from different information strategies almost indistinguishable. In such circumstances, cost/benefit calculations over alternative information strategies are sensitive primarily to relative costs, and choice of an information strategy does not depend significantly on the decision structure that it serves (March and Sevón, 1984). The rationalizations are, however, less significant here than the facts they seek to rationalize. The structure of relevance in an organization is more complicated and less articulated to decisions than decision theory anticipates. An information system designed to link information with a set of well-defined decisions will not necessarily be useful in decision-making where attention and consequential connections between problems and solutions are ambiguous.

Observation 3: The ambiguities of intelligence in complex ecologies. Although individual actors within organizations often try to act intelligently by calculating the expected consequences of possible actions, such a basis for action is typically supplemented by, or subordinated to, the following of rules that encode historical lessons learned within a complex ecology of nested organizations.

Modern theories of interactive decision-making and competition are theories of calculated cleverness in the interest of self. We imagine a world of self-interested decision-makers nested within organizations that are, in turn, nested within markets, communities and political institutions. Each of the actors within this world attempts to make and influence decisions in a way that advances his or her self-interest as he or she calculates it by considering alternatives in terms of their expected consequences. These considerations pervade the decision process and the production of information involved in decisions.

Consider, for example, the production of income statements. There are ample signs that managers, investors, and workers attend to income statements. Because income statements matter, many clever people try to make the statements say what they would like them to say (Greenhouse, 1986). Clever managers try to outwit clever accountants and clever analysts, who are at the same time trying to outwit them. Clever investors and clever public officials try to interpret the information provided through this culture of cleverness. And clever economists try to develop theories specifying the equilibria of clever processes, that is processes involving multiple interacting clever people and the pervasive cleverness of calculation.

The literature on clever processes describes a kind of morality play in three acts:

In the beginning　God created innocents and sophisticates. Sophisticates are clever; innocents are not. Cleverness pursues self-interest with as much guile and imagination as possible. Information is an instrument in the service of the clever, and competition rewards people in proportion to their relative cleverness with information instruments. This is the creed of numerous articles on how to exploit information to further self-interest. If reports in the *Wall Street Journal* or *New York Times* are to be given credence, much of modern management and finance is based on a belief that it is frequently easier and more rewarding to manage the accounts of organizations than it is to manage the activities and processes of which they are accounts.

Before long:　Competition destroys innocence. Less clever people are eliminated from the competition, either by losing their innocence or by losing their livelihood. Once the innocent are gone, variations in cleverness are small and the effects of cleverness on the distribution of winnings is nil. Everyone in the game is clever (or can hire someone who is). This is the argument of numerous theories of competition in politics, ecology, and economics, the most prominent recent reincarnations being ideas of rational expectations and efficient markets in economics. The assumptions that adaptation is relatively fast, that there is no exogenous replenishment of innocents, and that adequate supplies of cleverness are readily available are, of course, questionable, but they may perhaps be glossed over in a simple story. The key conclusion is that the cleverness of competitors makes cleverness necessary but insignificant in affecting distributional outcomes. Since only very clever people survive, no one outwits anyone else – though everyone tries.

But ultimately: Sophistication loses both victims and competitive advantage. The elimination of innocents reduces the competitive value of the kinds of cleverness that eliminated them. However, it is in the interest of each surviving participant to continue being clever as long as the others do, even though the effect of clever behavior on the relative competitve strength of survivors is nil when all engage in it. The energy devoted to cleverness is not devoted to other things, thereby making all of the clever participants vulnerable to new kinds of predation from outside. Thus, a clever system of account management is likely to be destroyed by the depletion of innocents to exploit and the specialization of managerial competence to skills that are irrelevant to new threats.

This story is an old one, hardly unique to information engineering. It calls attention to, but underestimates the complexity of, the problems in understanding the evolution of ecologies of competition (Aldrich, 1979; Gould, 1982; Axelrod, 1984; Arthur, 1985). When competition takes place over long periods of time, at several nested levels of organization, and in a changing world, exclusive reliance on cleverness – the conscious calculation of guileful strategies by self-interested individuals – is by no means guaranteed to evolve as a dominant style of behavior.

The ecological difficulty with calculated self-interest and cleverness is not that they are immoral in the usual sense, but that they are forms of incompetence. Recent efforts to improve cleverness are instructive in this regard. It is not an accident that modern students of competition have discovered the significance of trust relations, reputations, and conventions of behavior for success in games played repetitively over long periods of time (Kreps and Wilson, 1982; Milgrom and Roberts, 1982; Wilson, 1983; Wolfson, 1985). Nor is it surprising that behavioral students of decision have discovered that the rules individuals follow in forming inferences from data and making decisions often (though not always) seem to be wiser than the decision theory and statistical canons they violate (March and Shapira, 1982; 1987; Einhorn, 1986).

The recognition of intelligence in rules encourages hope that ultimately we may be able to rationalize the information content of rules by solving analytically the complicated problem of fitness that is addressed (imperfectly) by historical processes. For example, rules of thumb for dealing with moral hazard or adverse selection have been assessed and probably improved. In general, however, such efforts reflect a hope, not a guarantee. The history is one of repeated revelations of inadequate analyses. The intelligence of rules is found not in their ability to solve problems that are recognized and understood correctly, but in their treatment of the many problems that are incompletely understood, misunderstood, or not seen at all. Recognition of such implicit capabilities in rules might suggest more effort to understand and improve history-dependent processes, rather than assume they can be replaced.

In information engineering, the primary manifestations of history-dependent rules are the professional standards of accountants, statisticians, and other dealers in information. These rules of appropriate behavior have evolved from experience. They are codified through discussion and debate, and sanctified through the creation of a profession with attendant educational institutions. Clearly, such professional standards interfere with the free competition of cleverness and are unwarranted if it is possible to claim the unlimited efficacy of such competition, just as restrictions on physical assault are unwarranted if the unlimited efficacy of physical competition can be demonstrated. The standards of information engineering are, from this point of view, cultural standards of decency. They encompass experience with limitations (and advantages) of calculated intelligence that cannot be retrieved explicitly by an individual actor operating within a framework of cleverness. As a result, their claims to intelligence are real.

In the contemporary competition between reason and tradition, as has been true since Aristotle, there are victories for each; but the difficult questions associated with specifying the likely conditions for each remain largely unanswered. The evolution of tradition is affected by several complications of ecological complexity: the environment is an endogenously changing one; maximizing the likelihood of the survival of an ecology of rules and institutions is different from maximizing the survival of its components; a system may have multiple stable equilibria, and the optimality of any particular one is not assured; history can branch dramatically thus making outcomes sensitive to near random events at critical times; and the adaptive processes involved are typically too slow to reach an equilibrium before conditions change.

Because of these complexities, history-dependent processes of experiential learning and evolution, like processes of rational calculation, have traps that no theory of intelligence can ignore. These include tendencies toward superstitious and self-serving learning (March and Olsen, 1975); but perhaps the most significant restrictions on learning or evolution as devices for intelligence are connected to their dependence on experimentation (Herriott, Levinthal and March, 1985; Lounamaa and March, 1987). Without experimentation, history-dependent adaptation tends to become obsolescent (Kaplan, 1984). Nevertheless, as we study the standard rules and roles of organizational life, we discover elements of intelligence in them (Axelrod, 1984). Those artifacts of history store lessons of experience that appear to be unattractive or inaccessible to individual actors, thus supplement and caution conscious self-interested calculation (March, 1981a; 1981b).

Observation 4: The ambiguities of meaning. Most information in organizations is collected and recorded not primarily to aid decision-making directly, but as a basis for interpretations that allow coherent histories to be told. As a structure of meaning evolves from information and from the process of decision-making, specific decisions are fitted into it.

Theories of rational choice obscure the extent to which information handling and decision-making contribute, largely independently, to the development of meaning. Decisions are not so much made in organizations as they develop within a context of meaning. Organizational information processing seems to be driven less by uncertainty about the consequences of specific decision alternatives than by lack of clarity about how to talk about the world – what alternatives there are and how they related to stories we think we understand, how we describe history and how we interpret it (March and Feldman, 1981; March and Sevón, 1984). Information shapes the meaning of a decision situation, thus normally changes both the structure of alternatives and the preferences being pursued. Through the processing of information and the unfolding of decisions, the meanings of shared experience are elaborated and modified: foolish recklessness is redefined as creative independence (or vice versa), and elegant argument is redefined as sophistry (or vice versa).

Standard accounts are part of the social language by which organizations comprehend what they are doing, why they are doing it, and how they might do it better. New accounting instruments stimulate interest in new dimensions of organizational description and redefine decision alternatives (Burchell, Clubb and Hopwood, 1986; Hopwood, 1986). And information that is generated for decision-irrelevant reasons becomes a topic of conversation, and ultimately contributes to redefining the way we think about decision strategies. As a result, a good information strategy is not so much one that removes uncertainty from a prestructured array of decision alternatives connected to a predetermined array of preferences, as it is one that moves the whole apparatus of information, desires, and options in a productive direction, simultaneously developing ideas of what is 'productive' and instruments for achieving it.

Similarly, decision processes are not simply ways to choose among alternatives. Indeed, they seem to be only imperfectly understood as being concerned with substantive decisions at all. As March and Olsen (1986, pp. 16–17) report:

It has been observed that individuals fight for the right to participate in decision-making, then do not exercise that right with any vigor (Olsen, 1976); that organizations ignore formation they have, ask for more information, then ignore the new information when it is available (Feldman and March, 1981; March and Sevón, 1984); that organizations buffer processes of thought from processes of action (Brunsson, 1982; 1985); that managers spend substantial amounts of time in activities that appear to have few consequences beyond acknowledging the importance of others, as well as themselves (Cohen and March, 1986); that minor issues create a governmental crisis and unexpected patterns of political activation, then drift away again (Olsen, 1983: chapter 3); that organizational participants contend acrimoniously over adoption of a policy, but once the policy is adopted, the same contenders appear to be largely indifferent to its implementation, or lack of it (Christensen, 1976; Sætren, 1983; Baier, March and Sætren, 1986).

In short, decision-making is a sacred ritual involving highly symbolic activities. It celebrates central values of a society, in particular the ideas that life is under intentional human control and that control is exercised through individual and collective choices based on an explicit anticipation of alternatives and their probable consequences (Feldman and March, 1981; March and Olsen, 1984). It reinforces the legitimacy of existing authorities, and at the same time provides a basis for interpreting their downfall as appropriate. These sacred values are interpreted and reinforced through the information systems and decision processes of organizations. Individuals establish their reputations for virtue; an interpretation of history is developed, shared, and enforced; dissent is nurtured and contained; new ideas are grafted to old ones or disassociated from them; alliances are developed, tested, and displayed; the young are socialized.

The processes of choice in organization are also processes through which participants become committed to action (Hedberg, Nystrom and Starbuck, 1976; Swieringa and Weick, 1986). They organize arguments and information to create and sustain a belief in the wisdom of the action chosen, thus in the enthusiasm required to implement it. Where the process fails to do this, implementation is compromised (Brunsson, 1982; 1985; Baier, March and Sætren, 1986). Where it does this too well, decisions are ill-considered and their consequences poorly evaluated (Janis and Manns, 1977; George, 1980). The extensive postdecision elaboration of the reasons for action already chosen, including the development of information to support it (Feldman and March, 1981), and the avoidance of postdecision evaluation (Meyer and Rowan, 1977; Harrison and March, 1984), can be seen as part of this process of commitment. Postdecision justification of choices already made reflects an awareness that, as Salancik has observed (Pfeffer, 1986), we spend more time living with our decisions than we do in anticipating or making them.

These ritual, symbolic, and affirmative components of decisions and decision processes are not unfortunate manifestations of an irrational culture. They are important aspects of the way organizations develop the common culture and vision that become primary mechanisms for effective action, control and innovation. As a result, information strategies are as much strategies for managing interpretations and creating visions as they are strategies for clarifying decisions. And if this sometimes seems perverse, it may be well to remind ourselves that human life is, in many ways, less a collection of choices than a mosaic of interpretations. It involves both discovering reality and constructing it.

Implications for Information-Engineering

These observations about the ambiguities surrounding decision-making in organizations are persistent themes of recent behavioral research. If they are true, or partly true, they have implications for thinking about information systems. The implications stem in part from the fact that an information system that is to be used by humans in an organization must be attentive to properties of individuals and organizations, even when those properties are disconcerting. And they stem in part from the fact that, even if there were no individuals or organizations involved, the model of choice that is used in current thinking about information would be incomplete.

Attending to Problems with Human Decision-Makers

There are three classical engineering approaches to dealing with apparent deficiencies in human beings. The first is to adapt the system to observed characteristics of human beings (George, 1980; Newman, 1980). Rather than having a decision-support system that is unconnected to the world as seen by decision-makers and that they do not use, the system can be designed to provide information in a form familiar and useful to decision-makers. For example, if decision-makers feel more comfortable with multiple financial ratios, even though the information contained in them is redundant, the ratios should be provided. If the main information of interest is information on the conventions of behavior observed by others, the system should provide that. If corporate directors can deal with pie charts but not with regression equations or confidence intervals, they should have pie charts.

Under this approach to engineering, the major problem is understanding the decision questions of particular users and shaping the system to their wishes. Such an approach is not as easy as it appears. Although it is frequently observed that the language of organizational discourse seems only partly consonant with the language of accounts, or rudely forced into that language, careful information about the ways in which decision-makers use information and make decisions is scarce. There are remarkably few analyses of what managers actually do with their time, or what information they use or might use. Moreover, a system of accounts and reports that is useful for one decision-maker is not guaranteed to be useful for another. For example, an information system designed to help solve the decision problems of stock speculators will be of interest and concern to a corporate manager and will stimulate efforts to control the reports generated within it; but such a system will not necessarily be of much use to management of the productive or service activities in a firm (Johnson and Kaplan, 1987). Conversely, a system of accounts useful to a manager will not necessarily be of much use to the person to whom the manager is accountable (Ijiri, 1975).

The second engineering strategy for coping with human characteristics is to change the ways in which human decision-makers make decisions and think about information. In over 30 years of education and consultation, the technology of management science and operations research has made important changes in decision-making in modern organizations. More recently, research on decision behavior of human beings has been associated with strategies for improving the capabilities of human information processors to deal with human biases (Fischhoff, 1982; Nisbett, et al., 1982). Decades of trying to make human decision-makers behave more in keeping with the precepts of decision theory indicate, however, that the task is not trivial, that the biases, prejudices, and wisdom of decision-makers are resistant to profound corruption in the name of decision theory and modern statistics (Nisbett and Ross, 1980; Kahneman, Slovik and Tversky, 1982).

The third strategy is to replace human beings with machines, in this case primarily with computers and the software associated with them. The substitution of electronic information processing for human information processing is now commonplace, as are phrases such as 'artificial intelligence', 'knowledge-engineering', and 'expert systems'. Although the rate at which machines will replace humans in complex decision-making has been persistently and spectacularly exaggerated, progress has been made in situations where problems are decomposable into hierarchical structures (Simon, 1969; Cohen, 1986), and where the availability of patently relevant information exceeds the retrieval capabilities of human memory. The prospects for improving human decision-making through some form of computer-based program appear to be substantial where a decision involves storing and retrieving large amounts of data, or modeling complex processes, and where the organizational structure is conducive to the effort (Kunreuther and Schoemaker, 1981). Information retrieval systems with large data bases have been shown to be useful in coping with such things as historical financial data, medical diagnosis where the main difficulty in diagnosis is the organization and recovery of available information, estimating future personnel flows or loan losses, and the details of internal audit review.

It should also be observed that the capabilities of computer-based information systems for storing and retrieving data would appear to have reduced substantially the classical advantages of carefully conceived data collection. Contemporary work in data-handling seems to suggest that the trade-offs between careful prior formulation of information needs and the exploratory analysis of data collected without much anticipation of possible uses may be shifting considerably in the favor of the latter. This would appear to lend some credence to an argument that the computer-based information system of the future will not draw its model from ideas that emphasize a close linkage between information gathering and anticipations of information use.

Attending to Problems in the Theory of Decision-Making

Research on decision-making not only describes individuals and organizations as making decisions in a way that violates the recommendations of decision theory; it also suggests that the differences between the ways humans use information and make decisions, and the ways our theories say they should do so, are partly attributable to limitations in the theories, rather than limitations in the behavior. In particular, a close articulation of decisions and information is of little use in ambiguous situations where preferences, causal structures and meanings are unclear and changing. As has been observed above, those situations are not unusual (March, 1984; March and Olsen, 1986). Thus, although many decision problems in contemporary organizations will fall comfortably within the domain of decision theory and yield gracefully to its dictates, many of the more interesting ones will not.

The complications introduced by the ambiguities of preferences, relevance, intelligence and meaning can be illustrated by considering some common theoretical aphorisms about information and decision-making:

Look before you leap! As long as you operate within the framework of anticipatory, consequential rationality, it is important to know what you want before you act. But it is clear that intelligent decision-makers frequently act as though they do not believe in absolute conformity to such a dictum. They recognize action as a way of discovering and developing preferences, as well as acting on them.

Don't act if you don't understand! It is an axiom of ideas of rational choice that actions are justified by understanding and anticipating their consequences. Although less than complete understanding of consequences is often recommended, the magnitude of optimal ignorance is calibrated by its expected consequences. But it is clear that it is possible to act intelligently without an explicit comprehension of the consequential reasons for the actions. By following intuitions, rules, duties, and the advice of others, intelligent decision-makers act without conscious understanding.

Don't ask a question if the answer can't affect a decision! Within decision theory conceptions, the value of information lies in its ability to reduce uncertainties that affect choices. Yet, most of the information gathered, purchased, or communicated has no such direct decision relevance. It develops a context of knowledge and meaning for unknown possible actions and for talking about experience. Human actors understand the significance of information gathering as an investment in an inventory of knowledge and as an aid to defining preferences and alternatives as well as choosing among them.

Know what you want to say before you speak! Some treatments of communication assume that a message must be fully comprehended by a sender and then transmitted as precisely as possible to a receiver. But much of the most effective communication in organizations, as in the rest of life, is quite different, using ambiguous formulations to evoke responses that interpret and elaborate possible meanings.

The conclusion is simple: one can design an information system around a precise, static decision structure, and for many elementary decision problems in organizations that is a good idea. But the more difficult and more important task for information engineering involves the design of a system for an imprecise, changing decision structure. The relevant question is: How do you construct an account when you do not know when that account is going to be used, or by whom, or for what purpose, or in what context (Marshall, 1972; Hedberg and Jönsson, 1978; Mitroff and Mason, 1983)? The problem is fundamentally different in spirit from that of specifying an optimal set of accounts within a well-defined decision structure. In some cases, it can be reduced to a variant of the standard problem by assuming that the probability distribution over possible future uses and users is known or can be estimated; but such a contrivance is ordinarily of limited use. Quite aside from the fact that an explicit solution to the expanded problem is several orders of magnitude more difficult than the standard one, it does not really address the deeper problems of ambiguity.

These more general issues have been discussed, but not really solved, in institutions associated with knowledge systems of an educated culture. At least in principle, it is possible to imagine designing a system for knowledge generation and dissemination that explicitly identifies the probable decisions to be made, prior knowledge about them, and the marginal expected return from various alternative knowledge instruments, given that structure. Such an approach has been proposed from time to time for making allocation decisions within such familiar knowledge systems as those of science, journalism, and education. In each of these cases, however, it is clear that the *ex ante* linkages among the expected uses of information in making decisions, its generation and its actual uses are rather loose.

This is not simply because the people involved in science, journalism, and education have been powerful enough to resist intrusions into their fiefdoms. Within limits and with sporadic doubts, the rest of society seems to accept the propostion that such independence makes sense. Scientific research institutions, particularly the best of them, are traditionally buffered from anticipation of their uses. Funding arrangements, security of tenure, and an ideology of serendipity conspire to make those information systems remarkably independent of the decision systems they presumably serve. Journalism generates accounts of daily events intended to be sold to readers, ostensibly because they find the accounts worthy of their attention. From a decision point of view, however, most of the information generated by journalism is gossip as far as most readers are concerned (March and Sevón, 1984). It resolves no immediate decision problems (save perhaps what TV shows are available). And this feature is particularly true of those newspapers that cost the most and have the highest reputations. Educational curricula are sometimes designed around a specification of the particular uses, ordinarily employment uses, that will be made of the knowledge learned. But such curricula seem to be systematically less characteristic of educational programs that command a higher price and greater demand.

Suppose we see the relation between organizational accounts and the users of those accounts as similar to the relation between science and the users of science, or journalism and the readers of journalism, or education and the users of education. From this perspective, the structure of accounts should be rather independent of the *ex ante* intentions or desires of its users or the existing decision structure. The organizational implications of seeing information in this way are not novel, but they are somewhat different from proposals to link information and decision-making closely. They call for the relative autonomy of information gatherers, a loose articulation of information activities and decision activities, rather than a close articulation. Buffers to articulation are provided by professional standards and the development of legitimacy in sub-cultures that create their own conceptions of relevant and interesting information.

More generally, we note that preferences are developed in the course of solving problems and constructing interpretations (March, 1978). We ask whether that development can be made more intelligent (March, 1971; Cohen and Axelrod, 1984). We note that rules store the implications of otherwise irretrievable historical experience (March and Olsen, 1987). We ask how we can assess or augment the probable information value of specific inexplicable rules (Lounamaa and March, 1987). We note that ambiguous problems are often best approached through less structured, exploratory problem-solving (Lindblom, 1959; 1979). We ask how that can be implemented within modern information technology (Vancil, 1979; Sheil, 1983). We note that meaning evolves through the evocative exploration of the deep structure of language. We ask how information engineering can contribute to that evolution (Weick, 1979).

Many of these considerations can be folded into conventional theoretic models with suitable will and ingenuity. The paradigm is impressively flexible. The perspective outlined here also suggests, however, that information engineering – like research, journalism, and education – might well find part of its character grounded in theories of history, language, culture, art, and criticism. The writing of good history is the exploration of possible histories. It is also the exploration of the efficiencies and inefficiencies of the accumulation of history in tradition and belief. Theories of language engage questions of the way in which the use of properly chosen language exploits the structure of language to capture and impart meaning that is not fully comprehended. Theories of culture explore the ways cultural development reflects adaptation to, and enactment of, a changing environment. Theories of art and criticism permit us to see good information engineering not as a passive or manipulative activity in a decision scheme, but as an instrument of interpretation (March, 1976; Broms, 1985).

Thus, a system of accounts can be judged in terms of its evocativeness, its power to provide not just confirmation of familiar orders but also suggestions of alternative orders, not just communication of what is known but the transformation of what is knowable. Portraying information engineers as poets is a form of romanticism that glorifies each unconscionably. Yet, it is not without a certain charm. When he was a young man, T. S. Eliot wrote a tribute to the complexities of aging, called 'The Love Song of J. Alfred Prufrock'. Later, on reading the comments of a critic (Joseph Margolis) about 'Prufrock', Eliot wrote (1961, pp. 125–6) that the analysis of 'Prufrock': 'was an attempt to find out what the poem really meant – whether that was what I had meant it to mean or not. And for that I was grateful'. To Eliot, apparently, the essence of poetry lay in providing stimuli to the elaboration of meaning, rather than in providing unequivocal texts. Toward that end, he created ambiguous, textured accounts and invited others to find greater meaning in them than he had consciously created.

It is, perhaps, a strange vision of information engineering to say that an accounting report should be a form of poetry, using the language of numbers, ledgers, and ratios to extend our horizons and expand our comprehensions, rather than simply fill in the unknowns on a decision tree. But it is not an entirely unworthy vision of professionals to say that their accounts and reports can be richer in meaning than they are aware or intend, and that they can enrich our senses of purpose and enlarge our interpretations of our lives. And it may not be entirely ludicrous to imagine a day when professional students of accounting will discuss the aesthetics and evocative power of ambiguity in a proposed accounting procedure with as much fervor as they exhibit in debating its impact on tax liability.

References

Akerlof, George (1970) The market for 'lemons': qualitative uncertainty and the market mechanism, *Quarterly Journal of Economics*, 89, 488–500.

Aldrich, Howard E. (1979) *Organizations and Environments*. Englewood Cliffs, NJ: Prentice-Hall.

Arthur, W. Brian (1985) Competing technologies and lock-in by historical small events: The dynamics of allocation under increasing returns. Unpublished ms., Stanford University.

Axelrod, Robert (1984) *The Evolution of Cooperation*. New York, NJ: Basic Books.

Baier, Vicki Eaton, James G. March, and Harald Sætren (1986) Implementation and ambiguity, *Scandinavian Journal of Management Studies*, forthcoming.

Broms, Henri (1985) Mantras that look like plans, *Scandinavian Journal of Management Studies*, 1, 257–70.

Brunsson, Nils (1982) The irrationality of action and action rationality: decisions, ideologies and organizational actions, *Journal of Management Studies*, 19, 29–44.

Brunsson, Nils (1985) *The Irrational Organization: Irrationality as a Basis for Organizational Action and Change*. Chichester, UK: Wiley.

Burchell, Stuart, Colin Clubb, and Anthony G. Hopwood (1985) Accounting in its social context: towards a history of value added in the United Kingdom. *Accounting, Organizations, and Society*, 11.

Camus, Albert (1951) *L'Homme Révolté*. Paris: Gallimard.

Christensen, Søren (1976) Decision making and socialization. In James G. March and Johan P. Olsen, *Ambiguity and Choice in Organizations*, 351–85. Bergen, Norway: Universitetsforlaget.

Cohen, Michael D. (1986) Artificial intelligence and the dynamic performance of organizational design. In James G. March and Roger Weissinger-Baylon (eds), *Ambiguity and Command: Organizational Perspectives on Military Decision Making*, 53–71. Cambridge, MA: Ballinger.

Cohen, Michael D., and Robert Axelrod (1984) Coping with complexity: the adaptive value of changing utility. *American Economic Review*, 74, 30–42.

Cohen, Michael D., and James G. March (1986) *Leadership and Ambiguity*, 2nd ed. Boston, MA: Harvard Business School Press.

Cohen, Michael D., James G. March, and Johan P. Olsen (1972) A garbage can model of organizational choice, *Administrative Science Quarterly*, 17, 1–25.

Cyert, Richard M., and James G. March (1983) *A Behavioral Theory of the Firm*. New York, NY: Prentice-Hall.

Davis, Stanley W., Krishnagopal Menon, and Gareth Morgan (1982) The images that have shaped accounting theory, *Accounting, Organizations and Society*, 7, 307–18.

Demski, Joel (1980) *Information Analysis*, Reading, MA: Addison Wesley.

Einhorn, Hillel (1986) Accepting error to make less error, *Journal of Personality Assessment*, in press.

Eliot, T. S. (1961) *On Poetry and Poets*. New York, NY: Noonday Press.

Elster, Jon (1979) *Ulysses and the Sirens*. Cambridge: Cambridge University Press.

Elster, Jon (1983) *Sour Grapes: Studies in the Subversion of Rationality*. Cambridge, UK: Cambridge University Press.

Fama, Eugene F. (1980) Agency problems and the theory of the firm, *Journal of Political Economy*, 88, 288–307.

Feldman, Martha S. (1986) The invisible mind: order without design. Unpublished ms., University of Michigan.

Feldman, Martha S., and James G. March (1981) Information as signal and symbol, *Administrative Science Quarterly*, 26, 171–86.

Fischhoff, Baruch (1982) Debiasing. In Daniel Kahneman, Paul Slovic, and Amos Tversky (eds), *Judgment under Uncertainty: Heuristics and Biases*. Cambridge: Cambridge University Press, pp. 422–44.

Follett, Mary Parker (1930) *Creative Experience*. New York, NY: Longman, Green and Co.

George, Alexander L. (1980) *Presidential Decision making in Foreign Policy: The Effective Use of Information and Advice*. Boulder, CO: Westview Press.

Gould, Stephen Jay (1982) Darwinism and the expansion of evolutionary theory, *Science*, 216, 380–7.

Greenhouse, Steven (1986) The folly of inflating quarterly profits, *New York Times*, 2 March.

Harrison, J. Richard, and James G. March (1984) Decision making and postdecision surprises, *Administrative Science Quarterly*, 25, 26–42.

Hedberg, Bo L. T., and Sten Jönsson (1978) Designing semi-confusing information systems for organizations in changing environments, *Accounting Organizations, and Society*, 3, 47–64.

Hedberg, Bo L. T., Paul C. Nystrom, and William H. Starbuck (1976) Camping on seesaws: prescriptions for a self-designing organization, *Administrative Science Quarterly*, 21, 41–65.

Herriott, Scott R., Daniel Levinthal, and James G. March (1985) Learning from experience in organizations, *American Economic Review*, 75, 298–302.

Hilton, Ronald W. (1981) The determinants of information value: synthesizing some general results, *Management Science*, 27, 57–64.

Hirshleifer, J., and John G. Riley (1979) The analytics of uncertainty and information – an expository survey, *Journal of Economic Literature*, 17, 1375–421.

Hopwood, Anthony G. (1986) The archaeology of accounting systems, *Accounting, Organizations, and Society*, 11, in press.

Horngren, Charles T. (1981) Uses and limitations of a conceptual framework, *Journal of Accountancy*, 151, 88–95.

Horngren, Charles T. (1984) Institutional alternatives for regulating financial reporting. Unpublished ms., Stanford University.

Ijiri, Yuji (1975) *Theory of Accounting Measurement*. Sarasota, FL: American Accounting Association.

Janis, Irving L., and L. Mann (1977) *Decision-Making: A Psychological Analysis of Conflict, Choice and Commitment*. New York, NY: Free Press.

Johnson, H. Thomas, and Robert S. Kaplan (1987) *Relevance Lost: The Rise and Fall of Management Accounting*. Boston, MA: Harvard Business School Press.

Kahneman, Daniel, Paul Slovik, and Amos Tversky (1982) *Judgment under Uncertainty: Heuristics and Biases*. Cambridge: Cambridge University Press.

Kaplan, Robert S. (1984) The evolution of management accounting, *Accounting Review*, 59, 390–418.

Keen, Peter G. W., and Michael S. Scott Morton (1978) *Decision Support Systems: An Organizational Perspective*. Reading, MA: Addison-Wesley.

Kingdon, John W. (1984) *Agendas, Alternatives, and Public Policies*. Boston, MA: Little, Brown.

Kreps, David M. (1979) A representation theorem for 'preference for flexibility', *Econometrica*, 47, 565–77.

Kreps, David M., and Robert Wilson (1982) Reputation and imperfect information, *Journal of Economic Theory*, 27, 253–79.

Kunreuther, Howard C., and Paul J. H. Schoemaker (1981) Decision analysis for complex systems: integrating descriptive and prescriptive components, *Knowledge*, 3, 389–412.

Levinthal, Daniel (1984) A survey of agency models of organizations. Technical Report Number 443, Institute for Mathematical Studies in the Social Sciences, Stanford University.

Lindblom, Charles E. (1959) The science of 'muddling through', *Public Administration Review*, 19, 79–88.

Lindblom, Charles E. (1979) Still muddling, not yet through, *Public Administration Review*, 39, 517–26.

Lindley, D. V. (1970) *Making Decisions*. London: Wiley.

Lounamaa, Pertti, and James G. March (1987) Adaptive coordination of a learning team. *Management Science*, 33, 107–123.

March, James G. (1962) The business firm as a political coalition, *Journal of Politics*, 24, 662–78.

March, James G. (1971) The technology of foolishness, *Civiløkonomen*, 18(4), 4–12.

March, James G. (1976) Susan Sontag and heteroscedasticity. Unpublished address to the American Education Research Association.

March, James G. (1975) Bounded rationality, ambiguity, and the engineering of choice, *Bell Journal of Economics*, 9, 587–608.

March, James G. (1979) Science, politics and Mrs Gruenberg. In *The National Research Council in 1979*, 27–36. Washington, DC: National Academy of Science.

March, James G. (1981a) Decisions in organizations and theories of choice. In Andrew Van de Ven and William Joyce (eds), *Assessing Organizational Design and Performance*. New York: Wiley, 205–44.

March, James G. (1981b) Footnotes to organizational change, *Administrative Science Quarterly*, 26, 563–77.

March, James G. (1984) How we talk and how we act: administrative theory and administrative life. In Thomas J. Sergiovanni and John E. Corbally (eds), *Leadership and Organizational Culture*. Urbana, IL: University of Illinois Press, 18–35.

March, James G., and Johan P. Olsen (1975) The uncertainty of the past: organizational learning under ambiguity, *European Journal of Political Research*, 3, 147–71.

March, James G., and Johan P. Olsen (1976) *Ambiguity and Choice in Organizations*. Bergen, Norway: Universitetsforlaget.

March, James G., and Johan P. Olsen (1984) The new institutionalism: organizational factors in political life, *American Political Science Review*, 78, 734–49.

March, James G., and Johan P. Olsen (1986) Garbage can models of decision making in organizations. In James G. March and Roger Weissinger-Baylon (eds), *Ambiguity and Command: Organizational Perspectives on Military Decision Making*. Cambridge, MA: Ballinger, 11–35.

March, James G., and Johan P. Olsen (1987) Popular sovereignty and the search for appropriate institutions, *Journal of Public Policy*, in press.

March, James G., and Guje Sevón (1984) Gossip, information, and decision making. In Lee S. Sproull and J. Patrick Crecine (eds), *Advances in Information Processing in Organizations*, Vol. I, 95–107. Greenwich, CT: JAI Press.

March, James G., and Zur Shapira (1982) Behavioral decision theory and organizational decision theory. In Gerardo R. Ungson and Daniel N. Braunstein (eds), *Decision Making: An Interdisciplinary Inquiry*, 92–115. Boston, MA: Kent Publishing.

March, James G., and Zur Shapira (1987) Managerial perspectives on risk and risk taking, *Management Science*, in press.

March, James G., and Herbert A. Simon (1958) *Organizations*. New York, NY: Wiley.

Marshall, Ronald M. (1972) Determining an optimal accounting system for an unidentified user, *Journal of Accounting Research*, 10, 286–307.

Meyer, John W., and Brian Rowan (1977) Institutionalized organizations: formal structure as myth and ceremony, *American Journal of Sociology*, 83, 340–60.

Milgrom, Paul (1981) Good news and bad news: representation theorems and applications, *Bell Journal of Economics*, 12, 380–91.

Milgrom, Paul, and John Roberts (1982) Predation, reputation, and entry deterrence, *Journal of Economic Theory*, 27, 280–312.

Mitroff, Ian, and R. O. Mason (1983) Can we design systems for managing messes? Why so many management information systems are uninformative, *Accounting, Organizations, and Society*, 8, 195–203.

Morgenstern, Oskar (1963) *On the Accuracy of Economic Observations*, 2nd edn, Princeton, NJ: Princeton University Press.

Newman, D. Paul (1980) Prospect theory: implications for information evaluation, *Accounting, Organizations, and Society*, 5, 217–30.

Nisbett, Richard E., David H. Krantz, Christopher Jepson, and Geoffrey T. Fong (1982) Improving inductive inference. In Daniel Kahneman, Paul Slovic, and Amos Tversky (eds), *Judgment under Uncertainty: Heuristics and Biases*. Cambridge: Cambridge University Press, pp. 445–59.

Nisbett, Richard, and Lee Ross (1980) *Human Inference: Strategies and Shortcomings in Social Judgment*. Englewood Cliffs, NJ: Prentice-Hall.

Olsen, Johan P. (1976) University governance: non-participation as exclusion or choice. In James G. March and Johan P. Olsen, *Ambiguity and Choice in Organizations*, 277–313. Bergen, Norway: Universitetsforlaget.

Olsen, Johan P. (1983) *Organized Democracy*. Bergen, Norway: Universitetsforlaget.

Pfeffer, Jeffrey (1986) Personal communication.

Ross, Stephen A. (1973) The economic theory of agency: the principal's problem, *American Economic Review*, 63, 134–9.

Rothschild, M. (1973) Models of market organization with imperfect information: a survey, *Journal of Political Economy*, 81, 1283–308.

Sætren, Harald (1983) *Iverksetting av Offentlig Politikk: Utflytting av Statsinstitusjoner fra Oslo*. Bergen, Norway: Universitetsforlaget.

Sheil, Beau (1983) Power tools for programmers, *Datamation*, February, 131–43.

Simon, Herbert A. (1955) A behavioral model of rational choice, *Quarterly Journal of Economics*, 69, 99–118.

Simon, Herbert A. (1969) *The Sciences of the Artificial*. Cambridge, MA: MIT Press.

Sprague, Ralph H., Jr, and Eric Carlson (1982) *Building Effective Decision Support Systems*. Englewood Cliffs, NJ: Prentice-Hall.

Stigler, George J., and Gary S. Becker (1977) De gustibus non est disputandum, *American Economic Review*, 67, 76–90.

Swieringa, Robert J., and Karl E. Weick (1986) Action rationality in managerial accounting, *Accounting, Organizations, and Society*, 11.

Tinker, Anthony M., Barbara D. Merino, and Marilyn Dale Neimark (1982) The normative origins of positive theories: ideology and accounting thought, *Accounting, Organizations and Society*, 7, 167–200.

Trueblood, Robert M., and Richard M. Cyert (1957) *Sampling Techniques in Accounting*. Englewood Cliffs, NJ: Prentice-Hall.

Vancil, Richard F. (1979) *Decentralization: Managerial Ambiguity by Design*. Homewood, IL: Dow-Jones-Irwin.

Verrecchia, Robert E. (1982) Use of mathematical models in financial accounting, *Journal of Accounting Research*, 20, supplement 1–42.

von Weizsacker, C. C. (1971) Notes on endogenous changes of tastes, *Journal of Economic Theory*, 3, 345–72.

Weick, Karl E. (1976) Educational organizations as loosely coupled systems, *Administrative Science Quarterly*, 21, 1–19.

Weick, Karl E. (1979) *The Social Psychology of Organizing*, 2nd edn. Reading, MA: Addison-Wesley.

Weiss, Carol H. (1977) Research for policy's sake: the enlightenment function of social science research, *Policy Analysis*, 3, 531–45.

Wilson, Robert (1983) Auditing: perspectives from multiperson decision theory, *Accounting Review*, 58, 305–18.

Winston, Gordon C. (1980) Addiction and backsliding: a theory of compulsive consumption, *Journal of Economic Behavior and Organization*, 1, 295–324.

Winston, Gordon C. (1985) The reasons for being of two minds: a comment on Shelling's 'Enforcing rules on oneself', *Journal of Law, Economics, and Organization*, 1, 375–9.

Wolfson, Mark A. (1985) Empirical evidence of incentive problems and their mitigation in oil and gas tax shelter programs. In John W. Pratt and Richard J. Zeckhauser (eds), *Principals and Agents: The Structure of Business*. Cambridge, MA: Harvard Business School Press.

18

Information in Organizations as Signal and Symbol

Martha S. Feldman and James G. March

Abstract

Formal theories of rational choice suggest that information about the possible consequences of alternative actions will be sought and used only if the precision, relevance, and reliability of the information are compatible with its cost. Empirical studies of information in organizations portray a pattern that is hard to rationalize in such terms. In particular, organizations systematically gather more information than they use, yet continue to ask for more. We suggest that this behavior is a consequence of some ways in which organizational settings for information use differ from those anticipated in a simple decision-theory vision. In particular, the use of information is embedded in social norms that make it highly symbolic. Some of the implications of such a pattern of information use are discussed.

Introduction

Organizations are consumers, managers, and purveyors of information. Rules for gathering, storing, communicating, and using information are essential elements of organizational operating procedures. The technologies associated with using and managing information are the bases for several major growth industries, most notably computing and consulting.

This paper was first published in the *Administrative Science Quarterly*, 26, 1981, 171–86. The authors are grateful for the comments of Kenneth Arrow, Kennette Benedict, Robert Biller, David Brereton, Louise Comfort, Jerry Feldman, Victor Fuchs, Anne Miner, J. Rounds, Alan Saltzstein, Guje Sevón, and J. Serge Taylor; for the assistance of Julia Ball; and for grants from the Spencer Foundation, Brookings Institution, Hoover Institution, and National Institute of Education.

Reputations for organizational intelligence are built on capabilities for securing, analyzing, and retrieving information in a timely and intelligent manner. This practical consciousness of the importance of information is mirrored by research intended to understand and improve the uses of information by human beings. Information-processing interpretations of cognition, economic theories of information, and cybernetic perspectives on adaptation all build on the idea that the processing of information is a vital aspect of human behavior.

The study of information in organizations, like the study of choice with which it is often closely allied, involves a dialectic between students of information behavior on one hand and information engineers (or economists) on the other. Information engineers hope to design information systems with some clear elements of sensibility in them, or, in the best of all worlds, to design optimal systems (Kanter, 1972; Keen, 1977; Henderson and Nutt, 1978). For students of behavior, the problem is to understand actual human encounters with information. They focus on such things as the ways in which individuals and organizations deal with information on environmental uncertainty and risk (Tversky and Kahneman, 1974; Janis and Mann, 1977; Slovic, Fischhoff, and Lichtenstein, 1977; Nisbett and Ross, 1980), the ways in which individuals and organizations initiate and discontinue search activities (March and Simon, 1958; Cyert and March, 1963; Staw and Szwajkowski, 1975; Sabatier, 1978), and the ways in which organizational biases are reflected in information processing (Cyert, March and Starbuck, 1961; Wilensky, 1967; Allen, 1969; Adelman, Stewart and Hammond, 1975).

The dialogue between information engineers and students of information processing is most direct when differences between actual human behavior and apparently optimal information behavior are observed. Engineers characteristically seek to improve behavior, to instruct human actors in techniques for making better use of information. Students of information behavior characteristically suspect that some strange human behavior may contain a coding of intelligence that is not adequately reflected in engineering models. This paper follows the latter tradition. It recounts some familiar observations about information in organizations that are difficult to make consistent with simple notions of the value of information in making decisions; and it attempts to identify ways in which the behavior might make sense if placed in a somewhat broader frame.

Information and Organizational Choice

The classic representation of organizational choice is a simple extension of decision theory visions of individual choice. In particular, decisions are seen as derived from an estimate of uncertain consequences of possible actions and an estimate of uncertain future preferences for those consequences (Luce and Raiffa, 1957; Taylor, 1975). Both estimates are problematic. They depend on information that is imperfect in a number of obvious ways. Organizations make explicit and implicit decisions about seeking and using information that might improve estimates of future consequences and future preferences. These decisions are, of course, also presumed to be based on estimates of the expected benefits and costs of particular information, information strategies, or information structures.

Within this basic framework, search behavior, investments in information, and the management of information are driven by the desire to improve decisions. The value of information depends in a well-defined way on the information's relevance to the decision to be made, and on its precision, cost, and reliability. Information has value if it can be expected to affect choice. It is a good investment if its marginal expected return in improving decisions exceeds its marginal cost. The calculation of information value in a particular case is likely to be quite difficult. The framework, however, is simple and the idea is appealing (Raiffa, 1968; Marschak and Radner, 1972). This perspective on decision-making leads to some simple expectations for information utilization. For example, relevant information will be gathered and analyzed prior to decision-making; information gathered for use in a decision will be used in making that decision; available information will be examined before more information is requested or gathered; needs for information will be determined prior to requesting information; information that is irrelevant to a decision will not be gathered.

Studies of the uses of information in organizations, however, reveal a somewhat different picture. Organizations seem to deal with information in a different way from that anticipated from a simple reading of decision theory. The following three stories of decision-making in organizations illustrate the contrasts. These stories provide a contextual description of the relation between information and decision-making. The three episodes are not exceptional. They are taken from studies by Merewitz and Sosnick (1971), Bower (1970), and Hägg (1977). Others could easily have been used. They include examples taken from private and public, profit and non-profit, American and foreign, and large and small organizations. None of the studies was primarily concerned with the information focus of the present paper. Rather, each study portrays a typical, minor example of the process of problem-solving and decision-making in an undramatic situation. The descriptions here are brief and incomplete, but we have tried to retain the flavor of the use of information reported in the original studies.

Illustration 1: Supersonic Transport

Consider decision-making within the American national government regarding governmental support for the development of a commercial supersonic aircraft (Merewitz and Sosnick, 1971). In 1961, Congress appropriated funds for exploratory research on supersonic transports. Earlier studies had been commissioned by both the air force and the Federal Aviation Agency. These studies indicated that aircraft manufacturers were unlikely to undertake construction of a supersonic aircraft without government support. The FAA feasibility study commissioned in 1960 was available in 1963. It found 'no economic justification for the SST' (Merewitz and Sosnick, 1971, p. 252). In 1963, after Pan American Airways took options on six Concordes (the British–French SST), President Kennedy committed the United States to developing a supersonic transport in partnership with private industry. By 1966, construction of a prototype was underway. In 1967, the FAA found the supersonic transport to be 'viable as a public investment' (Merewitz and Sosnick, 1971, p. 254). The same year, Congress voted to continue prototype construction. In 1970, Congress rejected a $290 million appropriation for the project, finally approving (in 1971) only $85 million. This meant an end to the development, at least for the near future.

Illustration 2: A New Manufacturing Facility

Consider this standard example of corporate planning and capital investment (Bower, 1970). The case involved a project that originally developed as a sideline at one plant of a manufacturing company. As the project expanded, it outgrew existing facilities, and proposals were made either to expand the plant or to build a new facility for the project. Between February 1966 and April 1967, repeated analyses and forecasts about the project were made. In April 1966, the project was losing more than had been forecast. The loss was attributed to low sales and high development costs. By October 1966 the project was showing increasingly poor operating results, lower than predicted by the forecasts. This was interpreted as having been caused by marketing problems; no change in the project was considered. Initial proposals to modify an existing plant by building a new warehouse were expanded to include building a whole new facility as well. As the plans for capital investment went forward, estimates of the projected performance were adjusted downward several times to make the proposal more believable.

Illustration 3: New Equipment

Consider the *post hoc* review of a project involving buying and installing packaging equipment in the manufacturing department of a Swedish firm (Hägg, 1977). The project was seen as a way to reduce personnel and thereby avoid production delays attributable to absenteeism. The investment proposal was submitted and approved in September 1973. By mid-1974, the equipment had been bought and installed and was in operation. In December 1974, a review report was written. The review showed that the project had, in fact, reduced the number of personnel by two. However, it also showed that the resetting times had been longer than expected and that installation problems had delayed the achievement of normal working conditions beyond the projected date. These problems produced the types of delays that the reduction in the number of personnel was supposed to eliminate. No action was taken as a result of the review. Installation problems were attributed to 'the supplier who had given wrong information and who had not supplied the needed expert service' (Hägg, 1977, p. 81), and the longer resetting times were seen as a result of inadequately trained mechanics. The review was seen as a good idea, nevertheless.

These case studies show a relation between information and decision-making that is rather distant from the one anticipated by classical conceptions drawn from decision theory. Considerable information was gathered by the organizations involved in the decisions. Considerable information was sometimes volunteered by other organizations. There was little systematic relation between the time of receiving the results of a study and the time of making a decision. There was no obvious consistent relation between the findings of studies and the decision made. Information was gathered. More information was sought. Information was considered. But the link between decisions and information was weak.

Similar stories are told repeatedly in the research literature. Their number could be increased almost at will.[1] The literature reports phenomena that can be summarized by six observations about the gathering and use of information in organizations. The observations are consistent with the research literature yet close enough to personal experience to be almost self-evident:

1 For example, Lindblom (1959); Wohlstetter (1962, 1965); Cyert and March (1963); Wilensky (1967); Olsen (1970); Allison (1971); Beneviste (1972); Cohen and March (1974); Eliasson (1974); Halperin (1974); Lucas and Dawson (1974); Steinbruner (1974); Lynch (1975); Graham (1976); Kreiner (1976); March and Olsen (1976); Meltsner (1976); Tietenberg and Toureille (1976); Weiss (1977); Estler (1978); Sabatier (1978); Sproull, Weiner, and Wolf (1978); Clark and Shrode (1979); Krieger (1979).

1 Much of the information that is gathered and communicated by individuals and organizations has little decision relevance.
2 Much of the information that is used to justify a decision is collected and interpreted after the decision has been made, or substantially made.
3 Much of the information gathered in response to requests for information is not considered in the making of decisions for which it was requested.
4 Regardless of the information available at the time a decision is first considered, more information is requested.
5 Complaints that an organization does not have enough information to make a decision occur while available information is ignored.
6 The relevance of the information provided in the decision-making process to the decision being made is less conspicuous than is the insistence on information. In short, most organizations and individuals often collect more information than they use or can reasonably expect to use in the making of decisions. At the same time, they appear to be constantly needing or requesting more information, or complaining about inadequacies in information.

It is possible, on considering these phenomena, to conclude that organizations are systematically stupid. There is no question that organizational processes are sometimes misguided and that organizational procedures are sometimes incomprehensibly inattentive to relevant information. Nevertheless, it is possible to try to discover why reasonably successful and reasonably adaptive organizations might exhibit the kinds of information behaviors that have been reported. Perhaps the stories of information perversity tell us less about the weaknesses of organizations than about the limitations of our ideas about information.

Information Incentives, Gossip, and Misrepresentation

There are several elementary instrumental reasons why information use in organizations deviates from a standard decision theory vision. At the outset two relatively conventional explanations should be noted. First, organizations may be unable, because of organizational or human limitations, to process the information they have. They experience an information glut as a shortage. Indeed, it is possible that the overload contributes to the breakdown in processing capabilities (Wohlstetter, 1962; Miller, 1977). The second explanation is that the information available to organizations is sytematically the wrong kind of information. Limitations of analytical skill or coordination lead decision-makers to collect information that cannot be used. Thus, although there is a great deal of information, there is not enough relevant information (Janis and Mann, 1977). These interpretations certainly have bases in what we know about the uses of information in organizations, but they seem to be limited by their implicit acceptance of the standard formulation of the decision problem in an organization.

There are three other conspicuous features affecting the instrumental use of information in organizations. First, ordinary organizational procedures provide positive incentives for underestimating the costs of information relative to its benefits. Second, much of the information in an organization is gathered in a surveillance mode rather than in a decision mode. Third, much of the information used in organizational life is subject to strategic misrepresentation.

Information Incentives

Organizations provide incentives for gathering more information than is optimal from a strict decision perspective (Bobrow, 1973; Handel, 1977; Chan, 1979). Consider, for example, two simple speculations about systematic bias in estimating the benefits and costs of information. First, the costs and benefits of information are not all incurred at the same place in the organization. Decisions about information are often made in parts of the organization that can transfer the costs to other parts of the organization while retaining the benefits. Suppose having too much information (i.e., having an information overload) increases the risk of being unable either to comprehend the information or to use it effectively in a decision. Since the information-gathering functions are typically separated from the information-using functions of organizations, incentives are modest for gatherers to avoid overloading users. The user of information invites a bias by accepting responsibility for the utilization of information while delegating responsibility for its availability.

Second, *post hoc* accountability is often required of both individual decision-makers and organizations. An intelligent decision-maker knows that a decision made in the face of uncertainty will almost always be different from the choice that would have been made if the future had been precisely and accurately predicted. As a consequence, a decision-maker must anticipate two *post hoc* criticisms of information-gathering behavior: (1) that the likelihoods of events that in fact subsequently occurred were, on the average, underestimated, and thus that less information about these events was secured than should have been; and (2) that the likelihoods of events that in fact subsequently did not occur were, on average, overestimated, and thus that *more* information about them was secured than should have been. If, as seems very likely, the first criticism is more likely to be voiced than the second, it is better from the decision-maker's point of view to have information that is not needed than not to have information that might be needed. The asymmetry in *post hoc* assessment leads directly to an incentive for gathering too much information.

Information as Surveillance

Organizations, as well as individuals, collect gossip (Aguilar, 1967; Mintzberg, 1972). They gather information that has no apparent immediate decision consequences. As a result, the information seems substantially worthless within a decision theory perspective. The perspective is misleading. Instead of seeing an organization as seeking information in order to choose among given alternatives in terms of prior preferences, we can see an organization as monitoring its environment for surprises (or for reassurances that there are none). The surprises may be new alternatives, new possible preferences, or new significant changes in the world. The processes are more inductive than deductive. The analysis is more exploratory data analysis than estimation of unknown parameters or hypothesis-testing.

The surveillance metaphor suggests either a prior calculation of needed information or a kind of thermostatic linkage between observations and actions. In this metaphor, systems for surveillance are justified in terms of the expected decisions and environments to be faced. Systems for surveillance are connected to decision-rules in such a way that the relatively long lead times required for information-gathering can be linked to relatively short decision times. This vision, however, can easily become overly heroic if it presumes explicit calculations by the organization. Such calculations are made in organizations, but they do not seem to account for much of what we observe. Organizations gather gossip – news that might contain something relevant but usually does not – in situations in which relevance cannot be specified precisely in advance.

Strategic Information

Many studies of human information-processing involve situations in which experimental subjects are asked to respond to information known by the experimenter to be reasonable, neutral information. Very few situations in the real world of organizations are of that sort. Most information that is generated and processed in an organization is subject to misrepresentation. Information is gathered and communicated in a context of conflict of interest and with consciousness of potential decision consequences. Often information is produced in order to persuade someone to do something. It is obvious that information can be an instrument of power, and substantial recent efforts to refine the economics of information and the economics of agency focus on managing the problems of strategic unreliability in information (Crozier, 1964; Rothschild and Stiglitz, 1976; Hirshleifer and Riley, 1979).

When strategic misrepresentation is common, the value of information to a decision-maker is compromised. Strategic misrepresentation also stimulates the oversupply of information. Competition among contending liars turns persuasion into a contest in (mostly unreliable) information. If most received information is confounded by unknown misrepresentations reflecting a complicated game played under conditions of conflicting interests, a decision-maker would be curiously unwise to consider information as though it were innocent. The modest analyses of simplified versions of this problem suggest the difficulty of devising incentive schemes that yield unambiguously usable information (Mirrlees, 1976; Demski and Feltham, 1978). Yet organizations somehow survive and even succeed. Individuals develop rules for dealing with information under conditions of conflict. Decision-makers discount much of the information that is generated. Not all information is ignored, however, and inferences are made. Decision-makers learn not to trust overly clever people, and smart people learn not to be overly clever (March, 1979).

The significant organizational incentives for gathering information, the gathering of information in a surveillance mode rather than a decision mode, and the strategic misrepresentation of information in organizations all contribute to the information phenomena that have been noted in organizations and provide reasons for decoupling information from decisions. Rational, sensible individuals in organizations, pursuing intelligent behavior, will often gather more information than would be expected in the absence of such considerations and will attend to information less. Such instrumental complications affecting information behavior in organizations are, however, not the only explanations for the anomalies we observe. In fact, they are probably less important than a more profound linkage between decision behavior and the normative context within which it occurs. Information is a symbol and a signal.

Information as Symbol and Signal

Information as Symbol

Organizational decisions allocate scarce resources and are thereby of considerable social and individual importance. But decision-making in organizations is more important than the outcomes it produces. It is an arena for exercising social values, for displaying authority, and for exhibiting proper behavior and attitudes with respect to a central ideological construct of modern Western civilization: the concept of intelligent choice.[2] Bureaucratic organizations are edifices built on ideas of rationality. The cornerstones of rationality are values regarding decision-making (Weber, 1947). There are no values closer to the core of Western ideology than these ideas of intelligent choice, and there is no institution more proto-typically committed to the systematic application of information to decisions than the modern bureaucratic organization.

The gathering of information provides a ritualistic assurance that appropriate attitudes about decision-making exist. Within such a scenario of performance, information is not simply a basis for action. It is a representation of competence and a reaffirmation of social virtue. Command of information and information sources enhances perceived competence and inspires confidence. The belief that more information characterizes better decisions engenders a belief that having information, in itself, is good and that a person or organization with more information is better than a person or organization with less. Thus the gathering and use of information in an organization is part of the performance of a decision-maker or an organization trying to make decisions intelligently in a situation in which the verification of intelligence is heavily procedural and normative. A good decision-maker is one who makes decisions in the way a good decision-maker does, and decision-makers and organizations establish their legitimacy by their use of information.

Observable features of information use become particularly important in this scenario. When there is no reliable alternative for assessing a decision-maker's knowledge, visible aspects of information gathering and storage are used as implicit measures of the quality of information possessed and used. For example, being the first to have information and having more and different information indicate the proximity of an individual or organization to important information sources. Similarly, the resources expended on gathering, processing, and displaying information indicate the quantity and quality of information an individual or organization is likely to have. Displaying information and being able to explain decisions or ideas in terms of information indicate an ability to use information easily and appropriately.

These symbols of competence are simultaneously symbols of social efficacy, and they secure part of their justification there. Belief in the appropriateness of decisions, the process by which they are made, and the roles played by the various actors involved is a key part of a social structure. It is important not only to decision-makers that they be viewed as legitimate; it is also vital to society. Ritual acknowledgement of important

---

2   For more general discussion of the role of symbols in decision-making, see Edelman (1964, 1977); March and Olsen (1976); Pfeffer (1980).

values celebrates a shared interpretation of reality (Berger and Luckman, 1966). Thus, requesting information and assembling it are ways of making social life meaningful and acceptable.

Standard decision theory views of choice seem to underestimate these symbolic importances of information and the use of information in decision-making. Because the acts of seeking and using information in decisions have important symbolic value to the actors and to the society, individuals and organizations will consistently gather more information that can be justified in conventional decision theory terms. Decisions are orchestrated so as to ensure that decision-makers and observers come to believe that the decisions are reasonable – or even intelligent. Using information, asking for information, and justifying decisions in terms of information have all come to be significant ways in which we symbolize that the process is legitimate, that we are good decision-makers, and that our organizations are well managed.

Information as Signal

When legitimacy is a necessary property of effective decisions, conspicuous consumption of information is a sensible strategy for decision-makers. The strategy need not be chosen deliberately. It will accompany processes that work. Decisions that are viewed as legitimate will tend to be information-intensive. Decision-makers who are persuasive in securing acceptance of decisions will request information, gather information, and cite information. The behavior is a representation of appropriate decision-making.

From this point of view, we can examine information-gathering and requesting as the kind of signal familiar to the economics of information (Spence, 1974; Nelson, 1974; Meyer, 1979). It is possible that the signal is a valid one. This would be true if organizations that generally produce better decisions are also able to gather and exhibit information at lower cost than those who produce poorer decisions. Even if information contributes nothing directly to the quality of decisions, better decision-makers would invest more in information, and decision-maker quality could be estimated accurately by monitoring information practice.

A strategy of legitimation through the use of information cannot, however, be chosen at will. The arbitrary symbolic use of information is subject to limits imposed by competition for legitimacy and variations in the costs of exhibiting information consumption. Since organizations compete for legitimacy, no single organization can control its own relative reputation by its own actions, and the comparative positions of different organizations depend critically on differences in the costs to organizations of maintaining an information posture.

The price of securing information is the value of foregone opportunities. The cost calculation depends not only on the usual considerations of efficiency but also on the kinds of alternative investments that are available. If, for example, the quality of decisions is automatically reflected in costless performance measures, the net returns from further signaling would be negatively correlated with decision quality. As a result, the signal would not be a valid one. By this analysis, information use is more likely to be a valid signal when performance criteria are obscure than when they are clear. Indeed, when the intrinsic quality of decisions is exceptionally difficult to assess, the signaling process may itself affect quality. Suppose, for example, that belief in the legitimacy of a decision is encouraged by the conspicuous utilization of information, and that the legitimacy of a decision, in turn, affects its implementation (an element of quality). Then those organizations that have relatively low signaling costs (or that for other reasons invest in information) will ultimately become better decision-makers. The signal will, by this mechanism, become a valid one.

When benefits from information use are approximately equal among organizations, and costs of maintaining an information system are less for good decision-makers than for others, conspicuous consumption of information is neither organizationally nor socially foolish. The behavior is an effective signal. It is, of course, possible that an alternative signaling system might be devised that would be less costly for organizations and for society and would still provide equally reliable information. In particular, a system that dampened the competition for legitimacy homogeneously across organizations might be preferred. But the signal that exists appears to have some of the properties associated with signaling validity and cannot be casually discarded.

The information economics perspective is instructive, particularly in its focus on conditions for signal validity and stability in a signaling system. But that perspective is not essential to an appreciation of the symbolic significance of information posturing. Reason, rationality, and intelligence are central values in modern industrial societies. Within such societies, life is choice; choice is appropriately informed when the best available information about possible future consequences of present actions is sought. In a society committed to intelligent choice, requests for information and the gathering of information will generally be rewarded by observers; less systematic procedures are common, but they tend to be less reliably rewarded. Whether we think of simple learning, of some ideas about role-taking, or of socialization into basic values, we develop a similar conclusion. The pattern of information-gathering and utilization that characterizes such a society must be as much a part of ordinary experience as the most elementary social values of honesty, autonomy, and self-reliance.

The Dynamics of Symbols

This paper has presented some possible reasons for certain apparently peculiar information behavior in organizations. The reasons suggested above emphasize the strategic and symbolic incentives for gathering information. Such reasons are, however, only an introduction to understanding the process. In particular, there is no reason to assume that organizational behavior with respect to information is stable, that the process is in equilibrium. Consider, for example, the classic dynamics of symbolic life: I learn French to symbolize my commitment to a cultured life, but having learned French I discover ways in which it is useful; I buy a car to symbolize my affluence, but having the car leads me to discover the pleasures of automobile travel; I work for a political candidate to symbolize civic duty and solidarity, but in the process I discover opportunities for political power. When organizations establish information systems, however symbolic or strategic the initial reasons may be, they create a dynamic that reveals new justifications as the organizational process unfolds.

The analytical problem is similar to the problem of understanding hypocrisy in individual behavior. The hypocrite presumably adopts the assertion of a value as a symbolic substitute for action. In the short run, hypocrisy is both a social acknowledgement of the importance of a value and an evasion of the value. In the long run, however, proclamation of social values, particularly when associated with opportunities for social approbation, changes the action. The changes are not necessarily intentional. It is not easy to be a stable hypocrite. Similarly, it is hard to find stable symbols or tactics in organizations. Each creates a dynamic by which it is transformed.

At the individual level, symbols produce belief and belief stimulates the discovery of new realities. For example, suppose that individuals in organizations are inclined to attribute successes, but not failures, to factors they control (Davis and Davis, 1972; Miller and Ross, 1975) and suppose that information-gathering decisions are something that successful decision-makers feel they control. Then successful decision-makers would come to believe that the information rituals they control are, in fact, important to decision-making. If they then act to make information important to decision-making, and discover new ways of making these tools indispensable, the circle is complete. Tactical uses of information are transformed into belief, and thence into functional necessity.

The process at the organizational level is similar, though the mechanisms are slightly different. An example is the creation of a special office symbolizing a newly important value (e.g., environmental protection, affirmative action). The office may have been established as a symbolic alternative to more substantial action (Edelman, 1964, 1977). New offices, however, are not passive. They affect their own functions. Consider the dynamics of flak-catching (Wolfe, 1970). Organizations create flak-catching offices – special offices to display their concern for outside complaints, pressures, and the like. But flak-catchers, who are commissioned to protect an organization from flak and to symbolize a commitment to deal appropriately with flak, quickly learn to enhance the importance of flak. The mechanisms are familiar. Partly, flak-catchers are chosen because of some willingness to deal with outsiders, perhaps because of prior affinity to them. Partly, they learn from their association with outsiders to identify with them. Partly, they discover that their importance in the organizations depends on the existence of flak (Taylor, 1980).

These dynamics apply to almost any specialized function in an organization. Individuals and organizations gathering, storing, and analyzing information are likely to behave in this way. Organizational departments assigned information-processing responsibilities are unlikely to remain neutral with respect to the uses of information. Partly, people who gather and use information will tend to be people who believe that information gathering is important. Individuals who discover they are good at solving problems using information will discover more ways for making it sensible to do so. Partly, people who gather and use information will associate with other information gatherers and users and will come to identify with them. As a class, they will generate belief in their importance. Partly, people who gather and use information will try to convince others of its importance as a natural way of ensuring their own importance. People who prepare reports are likely to try to persuade others to read them. Individuals who use information because it serves a particular purpose are likely to come to believe information is useful in a more general way. Individuals who request information are likely occasionally to find it useful, even to come to believe in the general utility of information-gathering.

Although it is easy to observe that arbitrary actions induce instrumental interpretations and become effective practical instruments under fairly general conditions, it is clear that the process does not always proceed rapidly and rarely goes to the limit. Exploring such dynamics significantly is beyond the scope of the present paper. These dynamics are, however, important to its spirit. We have tried to describe some ways in which apparently anomalous behavior is sensible and have explored particularly the symbolic significance of information use. In the process, we have suggested that simple decision theory visions of information and its value do not match the ways in which information is used in organizations as we observe them. The argument has been made in a form that might suggest a stable separation of symbolic and instrumental action. But organizations as we observe them are not stable. They change, and they change in a way that weaves the symbolic and instrumental aspects of life together, not in the sense that everything is both (though that is true enough) but in the sense that interpretations of life affect life. If there is substantial decision value in information, the present pattern of investment in information may be a good strategy for discovering that value. Symbolic investments in information are likely to convert to more instrumental investments.

A strategy of using symbolic investments in information as an instrument of change is dependent on a corresponding ideology. The symbolic value of information is a function of the social norms of a society and of a belief in rational decision processes of a particular kind. It is not hard to imagine a society in which requests for information, and insistence on reports and analyses, would be signs of indecisiveness or lack of faith. Even within the rational traditions of the enlightenment, decision theory perspectives on intelligence have competitors. Suppose that interpretations of decision-making that emphasize loose coupling rather than organizational structure, ambiguity rather than precision, and limited rather than complete rationality succeed in changing the normal conception of organizational life. Then the symbolic value of information will be compromised. Organizations will be less inclined to treat information gathering as a precious manifestation of their virtue. Information will be a less effective signal of their competence.

Conclusion

From a classical decision theory point of view, information is gathered and used because it helps make a choice. Investments in information are made up to the point at which marginal expected cost equals marginal expected return. Observations of organizations are not easy to reconcile with such a picture. Individuals and organizations invest in information and information systems, but their investments do not seem to make decision theory sense. Organizational participants seem to find value in information that has no great decision relevance. They gather information and do not use it. They ask for reports and do not read them. They act first and receive requested information later.

It is possible, on considering these phenomena, to conclude that organizations and the people in them lack intelligence. We prefer to be somewhat more cautious. We have argued that the information behavior observed in organizations is not, in general, perverse. We have suggested four broad explanations for the conspicuous over-consumption of information. First, organizations provide incentives for gathering extra information. These incentives are buried in conventional rules for organizing (e.g., the division of labor between information gathering and information using) and for evaluating decisions. Second, much of the information in organizations is gathered and treated in a surveillance mode rather than a decision mode. Organizations scan the environment for surprises as much as they try to clarify uncertainties. Third, much of the information in organizations is subject to strategic misrepresentation. It is collected and used in a context that makes the innocence of information problematic. Fourth, information use symbolizes a commitment to rational choice. Displaying the symbol reaffirms the importance of this social value and signals personal and organizational competence.

These factors seem important enough to a affect organizational information behavior significantly. They can influence organizational behavior through any of the usual mechanisms of adaptation. To some extent, individuals and organizations calculate the alternatives and decide to buy information (or use information). Such conscious decisions, if taken sensibly with knowledge of the factors we have discussed, will lead to an information strategy that is more like what is observed than what is expected from a simple model of information investment. Even without conscious calculation, organizations will learn from experience to follow strategies that generate information without using it. Strategies developed from calculation or learning could spread through a population of organizations by imitation. Alternatively, some process of natural selection among procedural rules can be seen as selecting rules that encourage considerable investment in information. In such cases, the intelligence of the behavior is buried in the rules and is not easily retrieved (or expressed) by individuals within the organization. Learning, imitation, and selection tend to hide the intelligence of behavior within rules and rule-following. Understanding fully the ways in which particular kinds of experience are coded into particular kinds of rules requires a precise specification of the adaptive mechanisms. For present purposes, however, all that is needed is to note that the factors identified here need not necessarily affect behavior by inducing incentives, conscious calculation, and intentionally strategic action. The mechanisms may be considerably more indirect than that, yet retain the same essential effect.

These general ideas have some obvious research implications. The factors we have identified are not homogeneously relevant across organizations, decision situations, and time. We should observe some systematic variation in the information behavior of organizations and the individuals in them. That is not to say that the phenomena are limited to a small number of organizations. On the contrary, they are very general. Nevertheless, we might expect investment in information to be particularly sensitive to variations in the symbolic requirements and signaling opportunities of the organization.

The kinds of information behavior noted here should be more common in situations in which decision criteria are ambiguous than in situations in which they are clear, more common where performance measures are vague than where they are precise, more common when decision quality requires a long period to establish than when there is quick feedback, more common where the success of a decision depends on other decisions that cannot be predicted or controlled than where a decision can be evaluated autonomously, more common where other legitimating myths (e.g., tradition or faith) are not important than where they are, more common in institutions and occasions closely linked to rational ideologies than in those that are distant from such ideologies. Thus, we might reasonably predict that the phenomena are more conspicuous in policy-making than in engineering, more conspicuous in the public sector than in the private, more conspicuous at the top of an organization than at the bottom, more conspicuous in business than in the church or family, more conspicuous in universities than in football teams. To list such speculations is not to claim their correctness. Indeed, casual evidence seems unsupportive of one or two of them. Nor is the present paper a good occasion for attempting to assess the ideas empirically. Such pleasures are left, in the grand tradition of such things, to the reader.

A static analysis of information use, however, is likely to be misleading. The symbolic significance of any activity depends on the social norms within which it is undertaken. Information is significant symbolically because of a particular set of beliefs in a particular set of cultures. These beliefs include broad commitments to reason and to rational discourse, as well as to the modern variants that are more specifically linked to decision theory perspectives on the nature of life. As social norms change, the relevance of information as a symbol, or signal, changes with them. At the same time, symbolic actions reveal more instrumental consequences. Like other behavior, symbolic behavior explores possible alternative interpretations of itself and creates its own necessity. Thus, it is possible that norms that are changing will be simultaneously losing symbolic significance and gaining instrumental importance. An elegant manifestation of the process would occur should values shift enough to leave information and information-based analysis as the true basis of organizational action that is legitimized by symbols of ambiguity and intuition.

References

Adelman, Leonard, Thomas R. Stewart, and Kenneth R. Hammond (1975) A case history of the application of social judgment to policy information, *Policy Sciences*, 6: 137–59.

Aguilar, Francis Joseph (1967) *Scanning the Business Environment*. New York: Macmillan.

Allen, Thomas J. (1969) The differential performance of information channels in the transfer of technology. In W. H. Gruber and D. G. Marquis (eds), *Factors in the Transfer of Technology*. Cambridge, MA: MIT Press.

Allison, Graham T. (1971) *Essence of Decision: Explaining the Cuban Missile Crisis*. Boston: Little, Brown.

Beneviste, Guy (1972) *The Politics of Expertise*. Berkeley, CA: Glendessary Press.

Berger, Peter L., and Thomas Luckman (1966) *The Social Construction of Reality: A Treatise in the Sociology of Knowledge*. New York: Doubleday.

Bobrow, David B. (1973) Analysis and foreign policy choice, *Policy Sciences*, 4: 437-51.

Bower, Joseph L. (1970) *Managing the Resource Allocation Process: A Study of Corporate Planning and Investment*. Boston: Harvard School of Business Administration.

Chan, Steve (1979) The intelligence of stupidity: Understanding failures in strategic warning, *American Political Science Review*, 73: 171-80.

Clark, Thomas D., Jr, and William A. Shrode (1979) Public sector decision structures: An empirically based description, *Public Administration Review*, 39: 343-54.

Cohen, Michael D., and James G. March (1974) *Leadership and Ambiguity: The American College President*. New York: McGraw-Hill.

Crozier, Michel (1964) *The Bureaucratic Phenomenon*. Chicago: University of Chicago Press.

Cyert, Richard M., and James G. March (1963) *A Behavioral Theory of the Firm*. Englewood Cliffs, NJ: Prentice-Hall.

Cyert, Richard M., James G. March, and William H. Starbuck (1961) Two experiments on bias and conflict in organizational estimation. *Management Science*, 8: 254-64.

Davis, William L., and D. Elaine Davis (1972) Internal-external control and attribution of responsibility for success and failure. *Journal of Personality*, 40: 123-36.

Demski, Joel S., and Gerald A. Feltham (1978) Economic incentives in budgetary control systems. *The Accounting Review*, 53: 336-59.

Edelman, Murray (1964) *The Symbolic Uses of Politics*. Urbana: University of Illinois Press.

Edelman, Murray (1977) *Political Language: Words that Succeed and Policies that Fail*. New York: Academic Press.

Eliasson, Gunnar (1974) *Corporate Planning - Theory, Practice, Comparison*. Stockholm: Federation of Swedish Industries.

Estler, Suzanne (1978) Rationality, Politics and Values: Systematic Analysis and the Management of Sexual Equity in the University. Unpublished PhD dissertation, Stanford University.

Graham, Otis L. Jr (1976) *Toward a Planned Society: From Roosevelt to Nixon*. New York: Oxford University Press.

Hägg, Ingemund (1977) *Review of Capital Investments*. Uppsala, Sweden: University of Uppsala, Department of Business Administration.

Halperin, Morton H. (1974) *Bureaucratic Politics and Foreign Policy*. Washington, DC: Brookings Institution.

Handel, Michael I. (1977) The Yom Kippur War and the inevitability of surprise. *International Studies Quarterly*. 21: 461–502.

Henderson, John D., and Paul C. Nutt (1978) On the design of planning information systems, *Academy of Management Review*, 3: 774–85.

Hirshleifer, J., and John C. Riley (1979) The analytics of uncertainty and information – an expository survey, *Journal of Economic Literature*, 17: 1375–421.

Janis, Irving L., and Leon Mann (1977) *Decision Making*. New York: Free Press.

Kanter, Jerome (1972) *Management-Oriented Management Information Systems*. Englewood Cliffs, NJ: Prentice-Hall.

Keen, Peter G. W. (1977) The evolving concept of optimality. TIMS *Studies in the Management Sciences*, 6: 31–57.

Kreiner, Kristian (1976) *The Site Organization*. Copenhagen: Technical University of Denmark.

Krieger, Susan (1979) *Hip Capitalism*. Beverly Hills, CA: Sage Publications.

Lindblom, Charles E. (1959) The science of muddling through, *Public Administration Review*, 19: 79–88.

Lucas, William A., and R. H. Dawson (1974) *The Organizational Politics of Defense*. Washington, DC: The International Studies Association.

Luce, R. Duncan, and Howard Raiffa (1957) *Games and Decisions*. New York: Wiley.

Lynch, Thomas D. (1975) *Policy Analysis in Public Policymaking*. Lexington, MA: Lexington Books, D. C. Heath.

March, James G. (1979) Science, politics, and Mrs. Gruenberg. In the *National Research Council in 1979*. Washington, DC: National Academy of Sciences.

March, James G., and Johan P. Olsen (1976) *Ambiguity and Choice in Organizations*. Bergen, Norway: Universitetsforlaget.

March, James G., and Herbert A. Simon (1958) *Organizations*. New York: Wiley.

Marschak, Jacob, and Roy Radner (1972) *Economic Theory of Teams*. New Haven: Yale University Press.

Meltsner, Arnold J. (1976) *Policy Analysis in the Bureaucracy*. Berkeley, CA: University of California Press.

Merewitz, Leonard, and Stephen H. Sosnick (1971) *The Budget's New Clothes*. Chicago: Rand McNally.

Meyer, Marshall W. (1979) Organizational structure as signaling. *Pacific Sociological Review*, 22: 481–500.

Miller, Dale T., and Michael Ross (1975) Self-serving biases in the attribution of causality. *Psychological Bulletin*, 82: 213–25.

Miller, James G. (1977) *Living Systems*. New York: McGraw-Hill.

Mintzberg, Henry (1972) The myth of MIS. *California Management Review*, 15: 92–7.

Mirrlees, James A. (1976) The optimal structure of incentives and authority within an organization, *Bell Journal of Economics*, 7: 105–31.

Nelson, Phillip (1974) Advertising as information *Journal of Political Economy*. 82: 729–54.

Nisbett, Richard, and Lee Ross (1980) *Human Inference: Strategies and Shortcomings of Social Judgment*. Englewood Cliffs, NJ: Prentice-Hall.

Olsen, Johan (1970) *A Study of Choice in an Academic Organization*. Bergen, Norway: Institute of Sociology, University of Bergen.

Pfeffer, Jeffrey (1980) Management as symbolic action: The creation and maintenance of organizational paradigms. Unpublished manuscript, Graduate School of Business Administration, Stanford University.

Raiffa, Howard (1968) *Decision Analysis: Introductory Lectures on Choices under Uncertainty*. Reading, MA: Addison-Wesley.

Rothschild, Michael, and Joseph Stiglitz (1976) Equilibrium in competitive insurance markets: An essay on the economics of imperfect information, *Quarterly Journal of Economics*, 90: 629-49.

Sabatier, Paul (1978) The acquisition and utilization of technical information by administrative agencies, *Administrative Science Quarterly*, 23: 396-417.

Slovic, Paul, Baruch Fischhoff, and Sarah Lichtenstein (1977) Behavioral decision theory, *Annual Review of Psychology*. 23: 1-39.

Spence, Michael (1974) *Market Signaling*. Cambridge, MA: Harvard University Press.

Sproull, Lee S., Stephen Weiner, and David Wolf (1978) *Organizing an Anarchy*. Chicago: University of Chicago Press.

Staw, Barry M., and Eugene Szwajkowski (1975) The scarcity-munificence component of organizational environments and the commission of illegal acts, *Administrative Science Quarterly*, 20: 345-54.

Steinbruner, John D. (1974) *The Cybernetic Theory of Decision*. Princeton: Princeton University Press.

Taylor, J. Serge (1980) Environmentalists in the bureaucracy. Unpublished manuscript, Graduate School of Business Administration, Stanford University.

Taylor, Michael (1975) The theory of collective choice. In Fred L. Greenstein and Nelson W. Polsby (eds), *Handbook of Political Science*, 3: 413-81. Reading, MA: Addison-Wesley.

Tietenberg, Thomas H., with Pierre Toureille (1976) *Energy Planning and Policy: The Political Economy of Project Independence*. Lexington, MA: Lexington Books, D. C. Heath.

Tversky, Amos, and Daniel Kahneman (1974) Judgment under uncertainty: Heuristics and biases, *Science*, 185: 1124-31.

Weber, Max (1947) *The Theory of Social and Economic Organization*. A. M. Henderson and T. Parsons (trans.) Oxford: Oxford University Press.

Weiss, Carol H. (ed.) (1977) *Using Social Research in Public Policy Making*. Lexington, MA: Lexington Books, D. C. Heath.

Wilensky, Harold L. (1967) *Organizational Intelligence*. New York: Basic Books.

Wohlstetter, Roberta (1962) *Pearl Habor: Warning and Decision*. Stanford, CA: Stanford University Press.

Wohlstetter, Roberta (1965) Cuba and Pearl Harbor: Hindsight and foresight. *Foreign Affairs*, 43: 691-707.

Wolfe, Tom (1970) *Radical Chic and Mau-Mauing the Flak Catchers*. New York: Farrar, Straus and Giroux.

19

Gossip, Information and Decision-Making

James G. March and Guje Sevón

Abstract

This paper examines the relation between information and decision-making, particularly in organizations. We observe that much of the information that human beings seek and receive is gossip, that is, information without decision relevance. We ask two general questions: Why do we observe so much idle talk in life? And what are the implications for understanding organizational decison-making and the design of management information systems? We conclude that the prevalence of idle talk stems from some systematic ways in which ordinary life, including ordinary managerial life, differs from the life anticipated by a focus on decision-making, and that information engineering may, as a result, be somewhat less informed by decision theory than we sometimes expect and somewhat more informed by literary criticism and the philosophy of education.

Introduction

In discussions of the design of information systems in organizations, the value of information is ordinarily linked to management in a simple way. We imagine that management is primarily a matter of making decisions and that a decision-maker chooses among several alternatives on the basis of information about consequences and preferences that are conditional on

---

This paper was first published in Lee S. Sproull and J. Patrick Crecine (eds), *Advances in Information Processing in Organizations*, Vol. 1, 1984, pp. 95–107. It was prepared for a symposium on information in organizations, at Carnegie–Mellon University, 16–17 October 1981. The authors are grateful for the comments of Nelly de Camargo, Omar El Sawy and Johan Olsen.

a choice. Additional information has value to the extent to which it can be expected to affect the choice. Thus, a prediction of snow in Helsinki has no value to a road maintenance crew in New York, as does a prediction of snow in New York in July. In the first case, the information is irrelevant to any decision; in the second it is redundant with prior information.

Within a decision theory frame, investments in information sources are made up to the point at which the marginal expected cost of the source equals the marginal expected improvement in decisions; and information systems are designed to assure that scarce resources of money and attention are allocated efficiently from such a point of view. The value of information depends on the decisions to be made, the precision and reliability of the information, and the availability of alternative sources (Marschak and Radner, 1972; Hirschleifer and Riley, 1979). Although calculating the relevant expected costs and returns is rarely trivial, the framework suggests some very useful rules of thumb: Don't pay for information that cannot affect choices you are making. Don't pay for information if the same information will be freely available anyway before you have to make a decision for which it is relevant. Don't pay for information that confirms something you already know. In general, we are led to an entirely plausible stress on the proposition that allocation of resources to information gathering or to information systems should depend on a clear idea of how potential information might affect decisions. Who needs the information and how is it relevant?

Actual investments in information and information sources appear to deviate considerably from these conventional canons of information management. Consider, for example, the daily newspaper. Significant numbers of individuals and institutions, including many located a considerable distance from New York, purchase and read the *New York Times*. The newspaper provides some information that is potentially relevant to some decisions faced by its readers: schedules of events, advertisements, reviews of books and various performances, market information, betting odds, etc. But what is the likely decision relevance of the information on sporting events? Or of the news from Washington, London, and Tokyo? Much of the political news we devour, like much of the news from Hollywood, is essentially gossip. It may have relevance to some decisions made by major political actors, but it is hard to see any analysis of the decision situations of professors in Palo Alto that would lead to an investment in the political or sports news of the *New York Times*, or indeed to much of the other content if the primary reason for such an investment were information value in standard decision terms (Simon, 1967).

The daily newspaper is only a mundane illustration of a more general phenomenon. Even in job situations with a good deal of task specificity, we devote substantial time to gathering and transmitting information that has no obvious connection to the immediate decisions we contemplate. Individual and organizational consumers of information invest in decision-support systems and patronize reports and conversations with little apparent attention to their decision relevance. Studies of the use of research in the public sector identify little connection between the research information that agencies seek and the decisions they make (Rich, 1977; Weiss, 1977; Deshpande, 1981). Business firms, armies, hospitals, and other organizations we observe systematically, gather, store, and display information that they do not, indeed could not, use; they invest in large information systems and in irrelevant forecasts (Swanson, 1978; Feldman and March, 1981). Although there is no question that individuals and organizations invest in decision-relevant information under many circumstances, much of the information that is gathered and reported makes little direct contribution to resolving choices. In that sense at least, it is essentially idle talk.

Understanding Idle Talk

The persistence and pervasiveness of idle talk makes it relevant not only to understanding everyday life but also to improving managerial behavior and to designing management information systems. Gossip cannot easily be ignored. It is either an inefficiency in information or a symptom of inadequacy in our ways of thinking about information. Without denying the former possibility, we wish to explore the latter. The information investments of individuals and organizations seem to suggest that the connection between information and action is more subtle than we have made it, or that our focus on choice as the central metaphor of life is misleading. We want to argue that both things are true and that they have implications for understanding and improving the uses of information in organizations.

Research on gossip is primarily concerned with information, with or without a known basis in fact, about the personal affairs of individuals (Hannertz, 1967; Rosnow and Fine, 1976). Gossip is sometimes seen as a simple source of entertainment (Rosnow and Fine, 1976). However, much of the research portrays gossip as contributing to system maintenance more than to decision-making. It is seen as a way to communicate rules, values, and morals – usually by pointing at failures to satisfy them. It facilitates the diffusion of community traditions and history (Lumley, 1925; Gluckman, 1968; Haviland, 1977), and the maintenance of exclusivity (Gluckman, 1963). Gossip is a way of making friends (Rosnow and Fine, 1976), a way of protecting personal interests (Paine, 1976; 1970), and a way of legitimizing collective action, such as a riot (Mitchell, 1956). Though it often reinforces existing beliefs by providing an interpretation of ambiguous experience that is consistent with them (Allport and Postman, 1965), and offering a guide to existing social structure (Hannertz, 1967), gossip is also a vehicle for social change. It is a mechanism for a collective reconstruction of reality in which existing explanations of the nature of things are modified and new sensibilities and ideas emerge and are elaborated (Shibutani, 1966).

It is clear that such research on gossip can hope to provide only indirect clues to the analysis of idle talk in organizations, but it suggests that there may be somewhat more intelligence in the social processing of decision-irrelevant information than a decision theoretic analysis would indicate. Although our search for reasons for idle talk will extend beyond the relatively narrow focus of gossip research, it is in the same general spirit. We will argue that an exclusive focus on the role of information in well-defined decisions is likely to lead to an inadequate characterization of the information investment problem and thus to inadequacies in the design of management information systems. In particular, we will argue that:

1 Information systems need to be exercised in slack times in order to be useful when needed. Information is processed, in part, to maintain the system rather than to use it.
2 Human action is often less a matter of choice than a matter of imitating the actions of others, learning from experience, and matching rules and situations on the basis of appropriateness.
3 Decisions are often made in situations that are quite distant from the situations implicit in ideas of rational choice. Neither the precise decisions, the alternatives, the objectives, nor the causal structures are clear.
4 Information is often as much dedicated to developing interpretations, explanations, understandings, and enjoyments of the events of life as it is to resolving specific choices.

Gossip as System Maintenance

Idle talk is a way an information system is kept effective. On the one hand, it smooths interpersonal and inter-group strains introduced by organizational life. People engage in idle talk in order to exhibit their reasonability and legitimacy, to exchange sentiments of solidarity, to reduce the risks of misunderstanding, and to make it easier to arrange the minor flexibilities that allow an organization to function (Frankenberg, 1957; Gluckman, 1963; Rosnow and Fine, 1976). Arguments that Finnish business organizations need the sauna in order to thrive, or that American businesses need the three-martini lunch, may be as fatuous as they appear; but coordination in families, neighborhoods, societies, and organizations is facilitated by the gossip that fills such institutions. This integrating and catalytic consequence of talk is hard to link concretely to specific actions or specific consequences, but it appears to almost all observers of social systems to be relatively fundamental.

Moreover, a communication system may need irrelevant exercise to maintain effectiveness. Individuals, organizations, and species risk developing specializations that reflect optimal short-run allocations of effort and ignore long-run investments in capabilities for dealing with infrequent or unlikely situations of importance. From this perspective, the specific content of talk is largely irrelevant. Gossip maintains links among people, for example in a neighborhood or between organizations, during those long periods when communication is unneeded, so that the communication links will be easily available should they be needed. Similarly, an organization may find that idle talk has the consequence of maintaining connections among parts of the organization that require few regular connections. Idle talk of this sort is an inexpensive substitute for emergency drills. From such a point of view, the justification for idle talk comes not from some subtle relevance but directly from its irrelevance. If it is desirable to maintain links among parts of an organization that are, under normal conditions, quite sensibly not connected, the decision irrelevance of gossip has the admirable property of producing contact between parts of an organization having no current need for coordination.

Information and Alternative Concepts of Action

The idea of choice and the idea of expected value maximization with which it is joined in contemporary decision theory are possible metaphors for thinking about action in organizations, but they are not the only possible metaphors. The idea of decision-making implies an anticipatory, consequential logic. That is, it assumes that action results from two guesses about the future: a guess about the uncertain future consequences of taking one action or another, and a guess about the uncertain future feelings a decision-maker will have about those consequences when they are realized. Such a vision seems often to be a useful one for understanding some parts of organizational action, but students of organizations generally note several other ways in which organizational actions might be interpreted (March, 1981).

It is possible to see action as reflecting *experiential learning* in which propensities for doing one thing or another change as a result of simple behavioral reinforcement. In such a view, action is history dependent rather than expectational; the relevant information is information on contemporaneous events or past experiences rather than forecasts of the future. It is possible to see action as reflecting *contagion*, as spreading through a population of actors like measles through a population of children. In such a view, action diffuses on the basis of exposure and susceptibility; the relevant information is information on what other people are doing. It is possible to see action as *rule-following*, as the matching of rules, procedures and routines to appropriate situations. The routines may be seen as having evolved or been learned. Experiential history is stored in the rules and cannot easily be retrieved in encoded form. As a consequence, the logic of routine action is classificatory rather than consequential or anticipatory. It is filled with calculations of appropriateness and the relevant information is information that maps a set of rules for action onto a situation.

These alternative metaphors for action have been used extensively in interpreting individual and organizational behavior. They imply a different conception of relevant information than that based on a conception of anticipatory choice. In general, the information requirements for learning, diffusion, and for rule, procedure, and routine following place a greater emphasis on knowing what has been happening in the past, or is happening now, than do the requirements for decision-making, and a lesser emphasis on forecasting the future. The cognitive questions they ask involve description and classification more than they do chains of conditional consequences. The dominant vision is one that sees an organization as monitoring the environment for surprises (threats or opportunities) rather than assessing alternatives. Some information that looks like idle talk within the frame of intentional, anticipatory choice is more relevant to action when it is seen within these other metaphors.

The Decision Context of Information

Some decisions in organizations are readily amenable to a tight linkage between flows of specific information and the making of specific decisions. The chatter between an aircraft pilot and an air traffic controller, for example, normally contains very little idle talk. Information is precoded in decision-relevant form. Similar situations are common throughout modern organizations, as are successful efforts to design and maintain sensible information inventories. An optimal information inventory can be determined as long as it is possible to make reliable and precise predictions of future decision deadlines and information requirements. In a stable, uncomplicated environment, such forecasts will often be accurate enough to connect the collection of specific information to specific future decisions. We would expect an optimal decision-support system to develop an inventory of information that has, relative to its cost, a reasonable chance of being useful in future decisions.

There are, however, other kinds of decision contexts and it seems at least possible that the pervasiveness of gossip is due, in part, to the ways some decision contexts lead to loose linkages between specific current decisions and specific current information. First, there is no necessary reason to expect that decision deadlines will be consistent with the timing of information. One reason for an organization to gather information that is irrelevant to immediate choices is the disparity between the time (or other resources) required to obtain the information and the time that will be available when a decision using the information has to be made. If it takes a relatively long time to assemble and interpret information, it may be necessary to invest in information inventories in anticipation of the future stream of decisions. Decisions in modern warfare are an obvious example of a situation in which the real time demand for decisions in battle may easily overload an army's information gathering capabilities unless substantial information inventories are developed in advance. Planning for emergencies in general involves building inventories of information and routines whose relevance depends on a possibly unlikely contingency. Similarly, the work of collecting and organizing information about customers, competitors, friends, and enemies often cannot reasonably be postponed until the specific decisions involved are immediate.

Under such circumstances, it is possible that the 'irrelevance' of many investments in information is a *post hoc* illusion. Normally, we commit ourselves to attending to a source with only an estimate of what will be said; we invest in a spy system with only an estimate of what it will produce; we buy an econometric forecasting service with only an estimate of what information it will generate. If only a few possible signals are important to decision, but they are very important and very unlikely, most of the information actually received from a decision-relevant source will appear to be decision-irrelevant.

Second, where the future stream of decisions is unclear and future preferences are ambiguous, the selection of an information inventory is likely to be difficult. Returns in terms of improved future decisions are hard to assess when the long-run decision stream is not well specified. We do not know what we might need to know. This ambiguity tends to make the collection of information more dependent on properties of the information available than on predictions of possible future decision contexts and leads to the accumulation of knowledge of unknown decision relevance. Since estimates of the costs of gathering and storing information are less affected by decision uncertainties than are estimates of the benefits, calculations of the net return from alternative information strategies are likely to be primarily sensitive to variations in costs. For example, organizations are likely to gather considerable information of dubious benefit to decision-makers when it is possible to transfer the costs of gathering it to another budget, as in the case of government agencies that require others to collect data for them or the case of central office functionaries in dealing with district offices. If information inventory decisions are primarily a function of the costs of information gathering and processing, idle talk is likely to be an attractive information system for many organizations and many individuals. It provides information in a timely and inexpensive way. The information may or may not turn out to be relevant in the long run, but future decisions are sufficiently unclear as to make such uncertainties characteristic of almost any information that is available.

Third, a loose link between decisions and information can be strategic. It is common in talking about the design of information systems to disregard conflicts of interest between information sources and decision-makers, or to assume such conflicts are managed through explicit principal-agent contracts that assure jointly consistent behavior. In this way, strategic manipulation of information can be ignored. Where such contracts are difficult to specify or conclude, however, innocent information sources cannot be assumed. A request by a decision-maker for information is a signal of decision relevance and thereby an invitation for information sources to try to manipulate the content or increase the implicit price of information. Consequently, it may be useful for a decision-maker to obscure information relevance, to encourage the free flow of mostly irrelevant information in order to reduce the precision with which decision consequences can be anticipated by information sources. Such a strategy does not reduce the incentive toward lying by information sources, but it limits the potential for lying effectively and increases the innocence of the unwittingly relevant information that is provided.

Information and Interpretation

At most, the *New York Times* is relevant to only a few decisions most of us can expect to make in the foreseeable future. It is filled with gossip about politics, sports, art and finance that is distant from choices that we face. Yet, we think it possible that the *New York Times* is, nonetheless, useful to our lives. It provides the storyline for our pretenses and the content of our conversations. To see life or management as decision-making is to see it inadequately; and one of the reasons that much of the information that is communicated in organizations, as in life, is not obviously relevant to decision-making is that choice is not as compelling a metaphor for managers or other individuals as it is for students for choice. From many points of view, individual and organizational life is better seen as dedicated to developing interpretations of events and understandings of history than as making choices.

Intelligent choice often presumes understanding, of course, and it is possible to see the interpretation of history as instrumental to the action (choices) by which we seek to control our fate. It can, however, be seen as more fundamental than that. Perhaps interpretation is more a primary feature of human behavior than a servant of choice. From such a perspective, information is sought and considered because it contributes to understanding what is going on in life; and understanding what is going on is important independent of any purpose to which the knowledge might be put. Perhaps we can better understand the uses of information in organizations if we see information, and decision-making, as part of an effort to comprehend and appreciate human existence, as driven by elementary curiosity as much as by a hope for instrumental advantage. Information is not gathered in preparation for life. Gathering information *is* life. Moreover, this process of appreciation, of discovering, elaborating, and communicating inter- pretations of events, is a pleasure. Individuals and organizations are entertained by exchanging information and constructing what might be imagined to be true or just imagined. Fantasy is a part of understanding and idle talk is fun.

Such a viewpoint is not novel. It is familiar to literature, as well as anthropology and sociology, less familiar to economics. We can see organizations as having been designed (or evolved) around some problems of developing, enjoying, and sharing interpretations of reality; communic- ation in organizations as tied to the discovery, clarification, and elaboration of meaning, and the process of decision-making in organizations as a performance within which individuals and groups construct an inter- pretation of experience that can be shared meaningfully and enjoyably.

Because understanding what is going on is important, people who understand what is going on are viewed as people of importance. People who know what is going on are eager to exhibit that fact and the exchange of information is the exchange of signals about power, position and competence. Note that from this perspective what makes information a source of power is not any added capabilities for effective action that knowledge provides, but rather the simple possession of a scarce and valued resource and the capability for signaling individual and organizational significance. Information is exchanged for other information (or other goods); it is exhibited as testimony to worth, much the way a plutocrat exhibits wealth.

If we see decisions as being somewhat less central to life than they are to decision theory, it should not be surprising that a theory of information *for decision-making* finds parts of information life irrelevant, and if the purpose of a formal information system is to strengthen the information base of current decision-making, it may not be necessary to be overly concerned with these 'irrelevant' considerations. If management can be seen as decision-making in a decision theory mode, then there is no substantial difference between the idea of a good management information system and the idea of a good decision-support system. Designing the former consists in designing the latter.

However, if we take a more general perspective on management, the design implications of these other factors may not be trivial. If we relax the presumption that the primary interpretive theme of management is choice and, thus, that the quality of management is determined primarily by the intelligence of the managerial decision-making, we may conclude that we have been excluding some important things in thinking about information in organizations. If management is seen as involving discovering new objectives, developing myths and interpretations of life, and modifying the diffuse beliefs and cultural understandings that make organizational events comprehensible and life enjoyable (March, 1973; 1978; 1984; Jönsson and Lundin, 1977; Feldman and March, 1981), then it is not obvious that the best management information system is a decision-support system. Intelligent managers might pay more for, and attend more to, something different.

Management Information Systems and Education

If the arguments made in the preceding section have merit, then it is not hard to see why the gathering and the processing of information in organizations would involve a significant amount of idle talk. At the same time, there seems little reason to assume that the chorus of idle talk that we hear in organizations is optimal. We require some way of approaching the design of information systems that is sensitive to the sensibility of idle talk, yet seeks to improve the quality of information available. We have tried to argue that a decision-oriented view of information, however valuable within the context of decision-making, may sometimes be misleading as a more general base for understanding and improving a management information system. If the innocence of information cannot be assumed, or if the future stream of decisions cannot be anticipated well, or if action is based on matching behavioral rules to appropriate situations, or if the point of information is the elaboration of a system of meaning, organizational engineers need a somewhat different set of models for designing information systems.

As always, it is easier to see the limitations of a decision perspective on information than to develop a clear alternative. One major problem, of course, is that the several complications we have identified do not immediately suggest a common remedy. If we focus on the complexities of the information context of decision-making while still retaining a general decision theory frame, we can generate a set of suggestions that emphasize exploiting reductions in the costs (or improvements in the speed) of gathering, storing, and retrieving information, working on reducing response time and retrieval time rather than anticipating specific needs. If we focus on alternative ideas for examining action, we generate a set of suggestions that emphasize monitoring the environment for critical signals and surprises, working on our capabilities for timely notice of environmental events rather than analytical or expectational capabilities. If we focus on the uses of information in the construction of meaning, we generate a set of suggestions that emphasize the ways in which meaningful stories are constructed and shared and the understanding of experience, working on the flexibility and imagination of the system for creating and articulating interpretations.

These different ideas lead to different implications, not obviously mutually consistent and not trivial to accomplish. It would appear that we require some notion of the value of alternative information sources that is less tied to a prior specification of a decision (or class of decisions) than to a wide spectrum of possible decisions impossible to anticipate in the absence of the information; less likely to show the consequences of known alternatives for existing goals than to suggest new alternatives and new objectives; less likely to test old ideas than to provoke new ones; less pointed toward anticipating uncertain futures than toward interpreting ambiguous pasts. The requirements considerably exceed our capabilities. We neither understand idle talk well enough nor are rash enough to propose a precise alternative model for the design of information systems in organizations. Our objective is more timid, to propose some caution in treating the problems of organizational information as problems in improving decision-making and to suggest that alternative perspectives are not completely alien to our intellectual traditions.

In fact, a view of information and life not far from the one we have sketched is a quite traditional one, associated classically with literature, art and education; and if there are appropriate models for a management information system of this sort, perhaps they lie in discussions of the nature and design of education rather than in modern theories of decision. Perhaps management information designers could profit from some attention to the ancient and modern discussions of the linkage between education and life, the arguments over the relevance of 'relevance' in thinking about a curriculum, and the efforts of art and literary criticism to explicate the expression of meaning.

To be sure, there are differences between an organization and a society and between managers and educators or artists. Many of those differences involve the relative specificity of activities and objectives in organizations, compared with the relative diffuseness of broader social relations. The differences make the leap from the analysis of education to the analysis of organizational information a large and possibly treacherous one, but not entirely foolish. As we discover the elements of loose coupling and ambiguity in organizations, the role of symbols in decision-making and information processing, the place of myths, stories and rituals in management and the significance of beliefs in the transformation of organizations (March and Olsen, 1976; Sproull, 1981), some of the distances between the properties of organizations and the properties of other social systems seem to grow smaller.

Proposing education as a possible alternative model for the design of information systems is undoubtedly disquieting. It seems possible that we know less about designing an education than we know about almost anything. At least, our confidence about it is gone. Discussions of curriculum cycle endlessly through questions of relevance without apparent resolution and educational philosophers seem hardly less confused than we. Indeed, some recent proposals for educational reform seem to be dedicated to thinking of education as a decision-support system and to tying educational activities and information rather tightly to their relevance for individual actions. It has become common to justify elements of a curriculum in terms of the improvement they provide in some specifiable activities that students will face in the future; some choices they will make.

That is not the philosophy of education – or of life – that we have in mind. We recall another long tradition in education and literature, one that views both education and poetry as linked loosely to a variety of ill-perceived possible future worlds and to understanding the confusions of life (Eliot, 1961; Freire, 1973). Such a vision sees education and literature as elegant forms of idle talk, as ways in which we gain appreciation of our existence and develop our sensitivity. To describe organizational management in such terms is, of course, to glorify it. It suggests that office memoranda might be viewed as forms of poetry and staff meetings as forms of theater and we may perhaps wonder whether it would be better to admit a distinction between a divisional sales chart and a Picasso painting – if only to assure that each may achieve its unique qualities. The dangers are real, but to a glorified view of idle talk and memoranda, we will add a romantic view of the possibilities for artistry in organizational engineering. Perhaps, with a little imagination here and there, educational philosophy and literary criticism could be used to point management information systems in the direction of a useful quality of irrelevance.

References

Allport, G. W., and L. Postman (1965) *The Psychology of Rumor*. New York: Henry Holt.

Deshpande, R. (1981) Action and enlightenment functions of research: comparing private- and public-sector perspectives. *Knowledge: Creation, Diffusion, Utilization,* 2: 317–30.

Eliot, T. S. (1961) *On Poetry and Poets.* New York: Noonday.

Feldman, M. S., and J. G. March (1981) Information in organizations as signal and symbol, *Administrative Science Quarterly,* 26: 171–86.

Frankenberg, R. (1957) *Village on the Border.* London: Cohen and West.

Freire, P. (1973) *Education for Critical Consciousness.* New York: Seabury.

Gluckman, M. (1963) Gossip and scandal. *Current Anthropology,* 4: 307–16.

Gluckman, M. (1968) Psychological, sociological and anthropological explanations of witchcraft and gossip: a clarification, *Man* 3, (n.s.), 20–34.

Hannertz, U. (1967), Gossip, networks and culture in a black American ghetto, *Ethnos,* 32: 35–60.

Haviland, J. B. (1977) *Gossip, Reputation, and Knowledge in Zinacantan.* Chicago: University of Chicago Press.

Hirshleifer, J., and J. G. Riley (1979) The analytics of uncertainty and information: an expository survey, *Journal of Economic Literature,* 17: 1375–417.

Jönsson, S. A., and R. A. Lundin (1977) Myths and wishful thinking as management tools. In Paul C. Nystrom and William H. Starbuck (eds), *Prescriptive Models of Organizations.* Amsterdam: North-Holland, pp. 151–70.

Lumley, F. E. (1925) *Means of Social Control.* New York: Century.

March, J. G. (1973) Model bias in social action, *Review of Educational Research,* 42, 413–29.

March, J. G. (1978) American public school administration: a short analysis, *School Review,* 82: 217–50.

March, J. G. (1984) How we talk and how we act: administrative theory and administrative life. In T. J. Sergiovanni and J. E. Corbally (eds), *Leadership and Organizational Culture,* Urbana, Ill: University of Illinois Press, pp. 18–35.

March, J. G. (1981) Footnotes to organizational change, *Administrative Science Quarterly,* 26: 563–77.

March, J. G., and J. P. Olsen (1976) *Ambiguity and Choice in Organizations.* Bergen: Universitetsforlaget.

Marschak, J., and R. Radner (1972) *Economic Theory of Teams.* New Haven: Yale.

Mitchell, J. C. (1956) *The Yao Village.* Manchester: Manchester University Press.

Paine, R. (1967) What is gossip about: an alternative hypothesis, *Man* 2 (n.s.), 278–85.

Paine, R. (1970) Information communication and information management, *The Canadian Review of Sociology and Anthropology,* 7: 172–88.

Rich, P. F. (1977) Uses of social science information by federal bureaucrats: knowledge for action versus knowledge for understanding. In Carol H. Weiss (ed.), *Using Social Research in Public Policy Making.* Lexington: Heath.

Rosnow, R. L., and G. A. Fine (1976) *Rumor and Gossip: The Social Psychology of Hearsay.* New York: Elsevier.

Shibutani, T. (1966) *Improvised News: A Sociological Study of Rumor.* Indianapolis: Bobbs-Merrill.

Simon, H. A. (1967) Information can be managed, *Think,* December, 7–11.

Sproull, L. S. (1981) Beliefs in organizations. In Paul C. Nystrom and William H. Starbuck (eds), *Handbook of Organizational Design*. New York: Oxford, pp. 203–24.

Swanson, E. B. (1978) The two faces of organizational information, *Accounting, Organizations and Society*, 3: 237–46.

Weiss, C. H. (1977) Research for policy's sake: the enlightenment function of social research, *Policy Analysis*, 3: 531–46.

Index